P9-CEF-245

Praise for Kathryn Lynn Davis's New York Times Bestseller *Too Deep for Tears*

"Stunning.... It will remind you of *The Far Pavilions* or *The Thorn Birds*.... Davis's story is as richly textured as a fine old tapestry.... The emotions and conflicts are ageless."

—*Chicago Tribune*

"Populated with unforgettable characters, *Too Deep for Tears* sweeps the reader around the world and back.... [a] compelling story of loss, betrayal, love, and discovery."

—*Affaire de Coeur*

"Complex, beautiful and sensitive.... lyrical and lovely."

—*Roanoke Times and World News*

"Elegant.... lovely.... Davis has done an enormous amount of research and easily captures the flavor of each disparate setting.... Her characters are richly drawn, and the relationships between lovers, friends, parents, and children are beautifully portrayed."

—*Inside Books*

"What happens when the strong-willed women meet their father and [one another] for the first time makes a great ending to three powerful stories.... a definite winner."

—*Oklahoma City Oklahoman*

"Engrossing ... moving ... every woman will find a part of herself in *Too Deep for Tears.*"

—*Rave Reviews*

"Get out your handkerchiefs...."

—*Dallas News*

"Captivating.... a major novel."

—*San Bernardino Sun*

"A compelling story.... You won't want to miss this richly detailed saga."

—*Midwest Review of Books*

Praise for Kathryn Lynn Davis's
Sing to Me of Dreams

"Kathryn Lynn Davis does for the Salish Indians of British Columbia what Tony Hillerman does for the Navajo of the southwestern United States. . . . Her new novel, *Sing to Me of Dreams* . . . will establish her once and for all as a major novelist."
—*San Bernardino County Sun*

"*Sing to Me of Dreams* is a graceful . . . lushly romantic portrait of a woman's odyssey."
—*Publishers Weekly*

"A story to be read slowly and thoughtfully. Soothing warmth fills each page . . . *Sing to Me of Dreams* is a very special book!"
—*Rendezvous*

"Deep, richly eloquent. . . . Readers may never look at life in quite the same way after reading *Sing to Me of Dreams,* and that can only be for the better."
—*Rave Reviews*

Books by Kathryn Lynn Davis

All We Hold Dear
Too Deep for Tears
Child of Awe
Sing to Me of Dreams

Published by POCKET BOOKS

For orders other than by individual consumers, Pocket Books grants a discount on the purchase of **10 or more** copies of single titles for special markets or premium use. For further details, please write to the Vice-President of Special Markets, Pocket Books, 1633 Broadway, New York, NY 10019-6785, 8th Floor.

For information on how individual consumers can place orders, please write to Mail Order Department, Simon & Schuster Inc., 200 Old Tappan Road, Old Tappan, NJ 07675.

KATHRYN LYNN DAVIS

ALL WE HOLD DEAR

POCKET BOOKS

New York   London   Toronto   Sydney   Tokyo   Singapore

The sale of this book without its cover is unauthorized. If you purchased this book without a cover, you should be aware that it was reported to the publisher as "unsold and destroyed." Neither the author nor the publisher has received payment for the sale of this "stripped book."

This book is a work of fiction. Names, characters, places and incidents are products of the author's imagination or are used fictitiously. Any resemblance to actual events or locales or persons, living or dead, is entirely coincidental.

POCKET BOOKS, a division of Simon & Schuster Inc.
1230 Avenue of the Americas, New York, NY 10020

Copyright © 1995 by Kathryn Lynn Davis

All rights reserved, including the right to reproduce this book or portions thereof in any form whatsoever. For information address Pocket Books, 1230 Avenue of the Americas, New York, NY 10020

Library of Congress Cataloging-in-Publication Data

Davis, Kathryn Lynn.
    All we hold dear / by Kathryn Lynn Davis.
        p.   cm.
    ISBN: 0-671-73604-3
    1. Women—Scotland—Hebrides—Fiction. 2. Women—Scotland—Highlands—Fiction. 3. Women—Scotland—Glasgow—Fiction.
    I. Title.
    PS3554.A934924A79   1995
    813'.54—dc20   94-33241
                                                                    CIP

First Pocket Books paperback printing August 1996

10 9 8 7 6 5 4 3 2 1

POCKET and colophon are registered trademarks of Simon & Schuster Inc.

Stepback illustration by Robert Berran

Printed in the U.S.A.

To Virginia Magnuson Odien
  Who, one night in a smoke-filled bar,
  asked a casual question out of which
  grew Eva Crawford—
  fully formed and searching.

And to Valerie Englin
  Who allowed me to glimpse vivid fragments
  of the myriad stories in her hands,
  in her pockets, and in her dreams.

Acknowledgments

I know now, as I did not when I began, that nothing could have kept me from writing this book: The story insisted on being told, and my own obstinance did the rest. No matter my personal doubts and traumas, the characters called out importunately, the story ran through my head like a song, gathering momentum until it was a roaring in my ears that I could not ignore.

But without these people to sustain and badger and stimulate me, the writing of this book would have been an arduous task, rather than a journey of discovery which restored my faith in instinct, spontaneity, and the exhilaration of letting the rushing tide of inspiration take me where it will. Fervently, I thank you all. I am especially grateful for your honesty. Soothing lies, while momentarily comforting, are of no use in the long run.

—As always, my husband Michael, an extraordinary man with an extraordinary ability to believe, to listen and envision my words as clearly as he does his photographic images. I can always trust him to tell me the truth, to see what I'm saying and help me hear my own voice through his, even when I'd rather not know.

—Jillian Gardner/Hunter, whose excitement over the nature of Eva's search was irresistible, and who pointed out that what I once thought was a weakness might well be a strength.

—My mother Anna Davis and my sister Annie James, who wept in all the right places, offered encouragement and sensitivity when I despaired, and enthusiasm when I exulted.

—My friend and assistant, Cheri Jones, who, with her quick tongue and astute observations, has, over the past turbulent years, made me understand myself better and take myself far less seriously.

—Nora Roberts, who wisely pointed out that perhaps my particular kind of peace is really a kind of turmoil.

—Catherine Coulter, who helped keep my feet on the ground, and almost managed to conceal her uncommon compassion beneath her sharp wit and forceful advice (offered in her inimitably delicate manner).

—My editor, Linda Marrow, who employed exceptional tact, diplomacy and perception, and who seemed to know intuitively when admiration was most needed.

—Finally, my agent, Andrea Cirillo, who refused to worry or lose faith, and who, in her exuberance over this book, reminded me (as she'd pointed out six years ago when we began) that the things most hard-won are often the most rewarding.

Part One

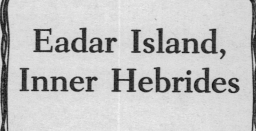

Eadar Island, Inner Hebrides

SCOTLAND

1988

1

THE SEA SANG AND SNARLED AND WEPT IN A VOICE THAT echoed the ancient cry of mermaids in their shimmering isolation. It echoed, as well, the confusion in Eva's aching spirit.

She saw the harsh beauty in the explosions of foam against towering pitted stone, felt it in the sodden, salty weight of her tennis shoes and blue jeans and the mist upon her skin, heard it in the endless thunder of the waves against the rugged island shore. She knew it in her soul, where a sense of betrayal flourished.

Eva felt at one with the waves that battered the tall cliffs, destroying themselves, making luminescent splendor of their own destruction. Yet again and again, the fragmented drops fell back into the water, where the cerulean sea was replenished and reborn.

In much the same way, her nightmare was reborn over and over in the dark of early morning. Her other dreams shifted in pace and vivid color, transformed themselves according to her mood and imagination. But the nightmare never changed. Invariably she dreamed she was short and slight, caught at the edge of the cliff, afraid to look down, afraid of falling into water that would drag her to its cold blue heart and suffocate her.

She tried to hide in cave or crevice, but the sea was always there before her, blocking her way. She saw her reflection in a pool of tide water, her pallid skin and long white-blond hair, gray eyes and softly molded cheekbones, her lips pressed tight in fear. It was the face of a stranger, yet in the dream it was her own.

She never saw the wave coming, only cried out as she stumbled and lost her footing in the swirling foam. She fell from the steep cliff, clawing as she gasped and choked, confused and without hope. Drowning.

Earlier this very day, Eva had awakened from the nightmare to her eighteenth birthday with the darkness upon her, as it often was after dreams of the wraith who was and was not herself. She awoke depressed, disgusted with her own weakness. She did not know why the nightmare affected her this way, lingering long after the sun had risen. She only knew she felt helpless and out of control, and the feeling terrified her.

Glancing around her bright, airy room, she felt the terror fade. The walls were clean, white and familiar; one large window looked out over the sea, while the dormer window revealed the lush green woods nearby, giving the room a liberating sense of space and light. The oak bedstead was large and comfortable, draped in a pale green duvet that echoed the green leafy swirls in the thick warm rug beside the bed.

Longing for the company of her parents, Eva had dressed quickly in blue jeans and a loose wool jersey, stopping to glance into the antique mirror on the simple vanity. She saw with relief that she looked the same; her hair was short, chestnut colored, thick and curly on top, cut close to her head so the wind would not blow it into her eyes as she walked the island. Her cheekbones were high and distinct, her eyes green ringed in gray. She was always afraid, after the nightmare, that she would see that woman in the glass, that pitiful stranger struggling in despair.

Eva stretched to reassure herself that she was not short and slight but tall, and, though her bones were small, she was muscular from climbing and swimming, her skin warm and brown from the sun.

"I should look a *little* different today," she told the mirror in disappointment. She was eighteen, after all. Surely her age should show in her eyes. But no new knowledge or sophistication was visible on her familiar face. With a sigh, she turned away.

As she came downstairs, the smell of peat seemed to fill the spacious rooms, to rise toward the high-beamed ceiling in invisible swirls of pungent air. Eva stopped to sniff appreciatively. Though her parents were lucky and could afford to burn wood and coal to keep their stone and timbered house warm, Eva preferred the smell of peat; it reminded her vividly of the lush, dangerous earth of the island.

She had moved through the sitting room, which was dominated by a fine stone fireplace and the carved beams overhead, scuffing her feet against the worn Aubusson carpet that covered the shiny hardwood floors. Affectionately, she'd brushed the back of one of the three brocaded wing-backed chairs where she often spent the evenings with her parents. The dining room, with its formal dark wainscoting, long lace curtains, and antique rosewood table and chairs, was rarely used, though the curtains had been drawn back to let in the fitful morning light.

Finally, Eva had reached the kitchen, huge and bright with its wide sparkling windows, gleaming modern cooker, sink and worktop. Most often, the family chose to gather at the scrubbed pine table, with the blue-checked curtains open and the island spread below them.

Samuel and Agnes Crawford had been strangely silent this morning, though it was an important birthday for Eva. She had looked forward to it for months, perhaps even years. She thought becoming a woman might fill the hole inside her, ease her restlessness, and give her answers to questions she did not know.

As always, her mother had prepared Eva's favorite breakfast, tattie scones and bannocks with homemade black currant jam, porridge and kippers, as well as strong tea. There were flowers on the table and linen napkins. The fire, along with the heat from the huge old stove in the kitchen, had long since burned away the biting chill of dawn. But her parents' faces had been grim, though they tried to pretend everything was normal. Usually, on any day, let alone her birthday, they were laughing before the first bite was taken, hands wrapped securely around hot, sweetened, milky tea. Eva had watched and listened to the strained silence, the murmured but meaningless comments, until she could stand it no more. Putting down her tea, she'd asked, "What is it? You're frightening me."

Samuel had waved his hand and answered gruffly, " 'Tis naught that can't wait till the sun has a chance to burn away the clouds, or the wind comes." But he did not smile.

Eva had insisted. So, in the soft light of the comfortable kitchen, which should have bound them together in its warmth and safety, they had told her. The light had splintered like ice at the edge of a shallow loch. Eva had listened numbly, cried out hoarsely, pushed back her chair and left them, passing near the always hot Aga stove to grab her anorak and toss it around her shoulders.

In shock, too stunned to think, she had gone, as she often did, to the cliffs where the sea surged in and out of caves and caverns of tortured stone. She had walked the narrow ledges, climbed and clamored upward, lunged down again to where the water thrashed at her jeans and inadequate shoes. She had been numb with disbelief, moving without awareness. She'd pushed her body until her breath rasped painfully, her legs ached and the sea spray mingled with the sweat of her skin.

The wrens dipped past, singing sweetly, while the curlews hovered and disappeared, their melancholy cry drifting on the air, a haunting echo after they had gone. Eva had walked inside that mournful song for many hours. She had let the water take her, oblivious of sodden clothes or throbbing muscles.

She'd climbed until the numbness was pierced by sharp, darting thoughts. Everything she had believed was a lie. She was a stranger from herself, her parents, everyone. She was no longer Eva Crawford. She was no one. She was more a part of the ballet of seabirds above the water, more one of the shadows dancing beneath the elegant wingspans of fulmar and gannet, than she was of the people among whom she had grown.

Once or twice she had thought of throwing herself into the sea, whose seething waves seemed friendlier than her own muddled feelings. But something always stopped her. Perhaps the thought of the bewildered grief of her family and friends. Eva was certain they had never known the darkness, that they would not understand her desire to leave it behind, to find a moment of peace and the end of turmoil.

She wanted to jump but did not really wish to die—just to let go, to be free, to let the sea cradle her, subsume her. In some fundamental way, she sensed that her spirit belonged there.

Usually, as she walked the cliffs, the ferocity of the ocean ate away at the darkness, a wave at a time, until her thoughts stopped spinning, questioning, wondering. But today was not like other days.

Today the thunder of the sea and the exertion of scaling the dangerous cliffs had not eased her. She stared at the horizon, mesmerized by the waves that hurled themselves against the scarred black stone. In that violence there was so much beauty. The paradox intrigued her; she ached with it. There was a promise of something evanescent and enchanting in that transformation from seething blue-gray waves to fleeting white lace foam.

Today that promise was not enough. The darkness did not lift nor the morning brighten. Because today Agnes and Samuel Crawford had given the darkness a name—Celia Ward. Eva's birth mother.

2

EVA DREW HER LEGS IN TIGHT AGAINST HER BODY, ROCKING slowly, her eyes dry with shock. She sat on her favorite promontory, high above the surging water, isolated from Eadar Island and those who peopled it. *"Eilean Eadar,"* she whispered in Gaelic. The Island Between. She was intrigued by the ambiguity of the name, the bizarre legends that explained how Eadar Island had come into existence. Eva herself had imagined many different accounts of the Gael from the ancient Kingdom of Dalriada who might have chosen such a name. Now she found in it a bitter irony.

Eva was alone with the fulmars, the gannets, the kittiwakes that dipped and glided, tracing the sky with graceful arcs of flight, setting down to fill the cliff hollows with the sound of their voices. She ended up here more often than not, where she could think without being disturbed. Here she could lose herself in blustering clouds and azure sky, in wind and sea and the light on the water. Here she could forget the nagging feeling that she did not belong among these people, or anywhere at all, that somehow, despite her family and friends, she was alone, different, adrift. In between.

Eva smiled crookedly. *Eilean Eadar.*

Nearby was an ancient stone broch—a tower built by people long dead, whose spirits remained in the crevices of weathered stone. This crumbling circular tower had once guarded the island. High among clouds and swooping birds, reigning over the sea, it still held the power of those who had built it. Eva felt that power in the island's Celtic legends, songs and poetry. They were fanciful, dancing at the edge of magic, weaving a pattern that revealed a people

8

bound to nature, ruled by it, beloved by it and it by them. The rhythms of nature shaped their lives and deaths, to it they clung when the crops failed and the sheep died, when the crofts fell empty and the wind blew landlords and strangers here to despoil and degrade.

The puffins who made their nest at the base of the broch did not seem impressed by the age and mystery of the stones. They waddled about, undisturbed by Eva's presence, even seeking it, as the fulmars did and the starlings and peewits. She had made herself part of their landscape and was, to them, no stranger.

Agnes and Samuel Crawford were religious people who attended the New Church every Sunday. Eva went with them, though she sensed from the beginning that she did not belong there. She worshiped here, beside the broch, with the wide sky above, the restless sea and jagged rocks below, the lush moors and woods behind her. Eva loved this beauty, this freedom, this power. And envied it.

Often, she brought her flute or her guitar and played her own music, inspired by the songs of wind and sea. The tunes, ancient and newly created moment by moment as her fingers moved over strings and keys, came easily, naturally, with a sense of elation she had never tried to put in words. This rare communion made her more a part of this place, yet lifted her beyond it in her mind, her imagination.

Sometimes she saw herself as a mermaid or a kelpie—mischievous, magic, with an instinct that was its own kind of power. Here, in her private, eccentric worship, there had been no liars, no deceivers. Until now.

She started, heart pounding irrationally at an unexpected sound, and glanced back to see the distant figure of Agnes Crawford coming toward her.

The woman had reached the edge of the bog that grew out of the hill sloping away from the cliff top. Eva froze. She opened her mouth to call out to the woman she had always believed, naively and completely, to be her mother.

The compact, muscular figure began to move forward, picking her way among hummocks of turf and wild grass, treacherous bogbean with its beautiful white flowers,

9

through yellow water lilies scattered among thick moss and bog myrtle. Agnes Crawford was afraid of the bog with a bone-deep fear that had kept her from approaching the cliff top all these years. One misstep and she would slide into the lush greenness and be sucked into the slime—trapped and helpless. As Eva watched her mother's dogged determination, she fought back tears. She could not cry. She did not dare. Her throat ached at the despair she saw in Agnes's bent head and hunched shoulders. Even Eva's anger at her parents' betrayal could not obliterate her compassion for the woman toiling toward her.

Eva had to turn away, gripping her legs so tightly that her arms ached. She had never doubted, despite her dreams, her restlessness, her fear, that she was deeply loved. To discover that she had no blood tie to these people who had made her safe and warm and happy, was a thought too terrible to contemplate. She could turn away from the sight of Agnes trying desperately to overcome her greatest fear, but Eva could not turn from her own deep sense of loss.

The sound of pebbles crunching under heavy footsteps, the ragged puff of labored breath made Eva wince. No one had ever followed her here before. Eva suspected they feared this side of her, this depression laced with longing, with power and intensity, but without shape or color. She had sensed more than once that the uncertainty, the darkness, even her free, uninhibited laughter, frightened her parents.

She could see the fear now in Agnes Crawford's eyes as her head appeared above gray stone. Agnes, who was not her mother.

"Eva, come home, please," Agnes pleaded in her rough but oddly pleasant voice. She was shaking and uncertain for the first time Eva could remember, and it broke the girl's heart.

That morning, Samuel had said, "You're not our daughter by blood, though by all else, you are. It's just that someone else bore you long ago. Not of our blood, but of our hearts."

Eva had heard, but could make no sense of the words. She had stared blankly at her parents' brown eyes and light brown hair. Their coloring was alike, and both were a little shorter than normal, though Samuel's body was square and solid, while Agnes's was more shapely, more compact beneath her bulky aprons. Dependable. She knew that from one look into their kind, weathered faces.

Not of our blood.

They had said other things, kind things, desperate things, but Eva had blinked, uncomprehending. The meanings were obscure and threatening. She did not want to know.

"You were a wee baby when we adopted you," Samuel had said.

"Adopted," Eva repeated, her voice hollow and strange.

"Your mother was ill. She was too weak to care for you."

"My mother." Words and phrases began to take on meaning, to penetrate the fog of incredulity. Agnes was not her mother. Some stranger was. Samuel was not her father. Eva stood abruptly. "You're lying!" She knew the accusation was ridiculous. She trusted them implicitly, as they trusted her. But if they were telling the truth, she could not comprehend the enormity of this revelation.

Before they could respond, Eva cried, "Where's my mother been all these years then, through all these lies? Where?" She was hoping they would have no answer, that this was a mistake, a cruel test she did not understand. With each moment that passed, she felt the ground shifting beneath her. She was drifting in air too thin to breathe, with nothing to hold on to.

Samuel and Agnes exchanged wary glances before Samuel cleared his throat and said softly, "Your mother is dead now."

"Dead." Eva could not think, did not know what she said or where she was or why. She hugged herself, but there was no one there. "My mother," she repeated. "And what about my father? Is he dead too?"

Agnes stared down at the rough skin of her hands. "I'm not certain she knew who your father was. She said things that made us think ..." She stumbled over the words. "When Samuel asked, she got distraught and cried so high and queer like, 'Eva's *my* child. Mine alone.' She would say no more than that."

Eva glanced around the house that had been her home. All the years of her life she'd believed the Crawfords were her only family, though she'd resembled them so little. In the midst of her odd dreams and exaltations and inexplicable longings, they had been her comfort, her security. The normalcy of their slow, structured lives had sustained her and made her strong. She had clung to it, and in clinging, had survived.

Eva refocused now on Agnes's face full of agony and felt a pang of guilt and anger both. Agnes had been baking. A smudge of flour merged with a smudge of soil beside her strong nose. She always baked—meat pies and scones and bannocks and black buns—when she was upset. She was wearing the bright apron Eva had made to replace the dun-colored one she used to wear. It was brilliant orange, with the sun, moon, stars and fire embroidered on it in gold. It waved in the breeze like a warning flag.

Agnes's long sandy brown hair, her finest feature, had been braided and pinned, but the wind had torn many strands loose, and her cheeks were flushed from the dangerous climb. Her eyes were red and swollen; she had been crying, a thing Agnes rarely did. Her hands, raw from water and flour and heat, trembled as she tried to push her hair back into place.

She had been married to Samuel for many years, and the couple was far better off than most of the Islanders. Agnes could well afford to pay a girl to come in to clean and cook. But Agnes enjoyed those tasks, seemed to need little else besides her family's affection to make her happy. She was comfortable in her life and felt no need to struggle to make it better or richer. In Agnes's heart, she was already rich beyond measure. Eva envied her that certainty, that peace.

The girl sobbed once and turned to bury her head in the floury orange apron. She wrapped her arms around her mother's thighs and held on tightly. She wanted to turn time back to last evening, when they'd sat companionably around the fire, she'd strummed her guitar and sung the song she'd been working on, and they'd eaten spiced fruit dumplings, licking their fingers shamelessly, and laughed. "I want to go back!" she gasped into her mother's skirts. The flapping fabric muffled the sound.

Agnes hesitated, unused to violent displays of emotion, but torn with such desolation that she almost understood. She cupped her daughter's head and pulled Eva close. This might be her last chance to hold the girl, a woman now. Agnes inhaled sharply, and the wet wind stung her throat. She was losing her daughter, and there was nothing she could do.

This feeling of helplessness was new to her. Agnes did not know what to say. They clung together, mother and daughter, strangers who had once loved each other wholly, without fear or doubt. The waves thundered against the rocks below, roaring with the force of the wild north wind.

Samuel Crawford trudged down the narrow path through moor and tumbled stones, around bog and vibrant clumps of spring flowers. He had decided to go to the tweed factory he'd owned for years, though he'd meant to stay home for Eva. He'd trained his men well and knew they could get along without him for one day. Once Eva had left, he could not forget the disbelief on her face, the outrage and disappointment. He had known better than to follow; she needed to be alone. He'd often worried that her walks along the cliffs increased her isolation from himself and Agnes and the close-knit community on Eadar Island. It reminded him too much of the fragile, lost woman who had left Eva in his care.

But he'd learned early that his daughter was beyond his reach at those times when her lively, lovely voice fell silent and her face was full of shadows.

He felt he might be ill, remembering the scene that morning. He paused to catch his breath, but the weight in his chest did not ease.

"Why didn't you tell me before?" She did not believe them, and did not wish to; he could see that.

Agnes had answered softly, "Because we promised Celia

Ward we'd wait till you were eighteen." She could not say the words *your mother,* even now. "She was verra ill, and—"

"What difference does it make? You told me she's *dead.* I'm alive. She wouldn't know the difference," Eva cried.

Samuel was appalled. " 'Tis not like you to say such a thing," he rebuked his daughter gently. "A promise is a promise. We gave Celia our word, and she believed us." He paused, running his fingers through his short, graying beard. "And how do you know what happens after death? You, who talk so freely of spirits and lingering souls?"

Eva had looked away, stricken. Samuel suspected she knew he was right, but was too angry, too hurt to say so. She would not meet their eyes.

Agnes touched Eva's knee and the girl flinched. "We told Celia we would do this thing for her, though we didn't understand her reasons. Eva, she gave us the child of her body when we could have none of our own. The least we could do for Celia Ward was keep our promise. No matter how much we wanted to tell you."

Eva looked up sharply. "Did you want to? Did you really?" She raised her chin and her green eyes glittered with a challenge, a demand, a doubt.

Now Samuel and Agnes could not meet their daughter's eyes. "Perhaps we didn't want you to know. Perhaps 'twas easier to keep silent," Samuel admitted with regret.

Eva must have heard the misery in his voice; she looked ashamed. "I hadn't thought of your distress," she murmured. "Only my own." She'd bowed her head, hands pressed to her ears. "It's too hard. I can't—I have to go, to walk." She stood unsteadily. Samuel knew his daughter well enough to see that she hurt so much each breath was painful. And it was his fault. His and Agnes's and Celia Ward's. Miserably, he'd watched Eva go, knowing there was nothing he could say, debilitated and ashamed by that knowledge.

Many hours had passed, but his apprehension had not faded. Against his will, Samuel glanced up at the cliff top where the broch stood—a giant watchtower, guarding nothing but Eva and her private sorrow. Samuel frowned when he saw the flapping bit of orange that must be Agnes's apron and saw a slim figure uncurl itself from the sheltering earth and grasp that apron tight.

"Damned fool!" he said to himself with uncharacteristic harshness and unfamiliar profanity. "What made you think you could leave her to herself while you added up columns?" If Agnes had braved the bog, then Samuel could brave his guilt. He turned resolutely toward his daughter's aerie, her refuge.

The two figures did not move as he approached, though he knew Eva was aware that he came. She was aware of too much; her intuition was strong, and her sensitivity. He saw it in the way she clung to her mother, in the expression on her face when she looked up to meet Samuel's gaze.

She reached out to him blindly and he knelt beside her, drawing Agnes with him. They closed themselves into a tight circle, while the fulmars swooped around them, and the starlings warbled into the relentless wind.

"I don't understand," Eva said at last.

Samuel raised his head to look into his daughter's tear-streaked face. Her eyes were veiled with a look that told him she was seeing more than his bearded, weathered face; she was looking beyond, searching, always searching. "I know you don't. We made a promise, 'tis all, to give you the happiest childhood we could, and when you became a woman, to tell you the truth."

Eva looked toward the sea and the green-gray islands in the distance. She shifted, leaning toward the expanse of sky that reflected the water, the water that reflected the sky.

"I wish you'd never told me," she said at last in a muffled voice. "I didn't want to know."

Samuel grimaced, but Agnes squared her shoulders and forced Eva to meet her eyes. "Is it sure of that you are, *mo-run?* You've not always been happy here, and you've wondered why. Mayhap now you know."

Eva blinked, surprised by the flicker of response within her. She *had* always felt isolated, not bound by the same ideas and values that steadied her parents and friends. Sometimes she felt more confident here, among the seabirds nesting in the cliffs, with the water and mist on her hair, than in her home.

She shook her head to push the thought away. "I told you, I don't *want* to know."

Samuel ruffled her short hair, damp from the spray and tangled by the wind. He could not decide what was best, to have kept her in ignorance, safe and secure, or to tell her the truth. "I'm sorry if that's true," he said.

Eva looked at him hopefully, as if he might say more, but her expression struck him dumb. He feared for his daughter. She was too fanciful, too full of illusions and dreams, too young to face a truth so cold and hard. He was afraid it would break her spirit, which soared far beyond where his own leaden soul could reach. He *knew* it would break him.

He had not meant to love Eva quite so fiercely, but the very things he feared in her, the things he had tried to discourage in order to protect her from her mother's fate—her wild, untrammeled imagination, her uneasy, vivid dreams, her dramatic changes of mood, her fragile but volatile emotions, even her lovely, ephemeral music—those were the things that had *made* him love her, demanded that he do so. She needed his protection, his unswerving faith, his strength.

Samuel Crawford did not recognize Eva's own strength, though Agnes did. To her father, the girl was a butterfly, vibrant, frail and beautiful. He did not want to see her vivid color disappear altogether. It was too precious to him, too extraordinary in his otherwise ordinary life.

While Eva waited, the weight of her parents holding her in place, she remembered that Agnes and Samuel had tried to give her a note from Celia Ward, but she had ignored it. She had been too overcome for curiosity to flicker to life. Now vague questions like ribbons of fine mist curled coldly through her.

"You lied to me." She spoke with dangerous calm. "I trusted you, and you lied to me."

Agnes gasped, contracted inward as if from a hard blow, while Samuel remained rigid. "We had no choice," he said.

Chestnut hair caught in the wind, Eva glared in disbelief.

She could feel herself losing control. She did not know how to hold on any longer.

"All right." Samuel sat, despite the damp turf, his wool trousers barely protected by his overcoat. "We *did* have a choice. But we didn't choose without a great deal o' thinking. Eva"—he touched her shoulder—"we did what we thought was best."

Her eyes blazed with doubt, but before she could voice her new question, he answered it. "Best for you, for all of us."

"Best," Eva cried in a plea as much as an accusation, "or easiest?"

Samuel sighed and answered, "In a way, I suppose 'twas easier to let you think you belonged to us completely, maybe to begin to believe it ourselves. But we love you, Eva. You trusted us. Do you know how hard it was to meet your eyes every day, knowing that in keeping silent, we were lying with every breath, that one day we might destroy not only your faith in us, but in everyone else, as well? We wanted to tell you and go on, to give the wound time to heal."

Eva locked her arms around her knees, shuddering violently.

Her father opened his greatcoat and drew her near, closing her within its generous warmth. "We really did think it was best, more comfortable, when you were young, just to let you believe." He paused to clear his throat; his voice had gone raspy. "A happy childhood was what we all wanted for you. Didn't we give you that, at least?"

In spite of herself, Eva was comforted by the warmth of Samuel's body, his coat that kept the wind away, the uncertainty in his tone. He was always so sure of things. But not today. He waited, not breathing, for her answer. She thought back over the days of her childhood, the moments of darkness that had plagued her, then disappeared with the wind. She thought of the flute and piano tutors, the instruments generously given, which had allowed her to lose herself in music. She thought of the island that had been her domain, the freedom she had been given to come to know land and sea, to fly in her mind with the graceful seabirds; certain her parents would be there when she returned, waiting and eager to hear of her discoveries, with a mug of chocolate and biscuits and a roaring fire. Her family and her home, always open to her, welcoming, warm and safe. "Yes," she said softly, "you did give me that."

3

THEY WERE STILL CROUCHED TOGETHER WHEN A FOURTH figure appeared, making his careful way around the flower-strewn but deadly bog. Eva saw his brown hair and knew it was Daniel Macauly, her fiancé. He was comfortably medium in height and build, comfortably attractive as well, with his hazel eyes and slow smile. When he reached the final hill, he looked up, saw the rigid figures on the cliff top, and stopped still. Though he was too far away to see his features, Eva felt him draw in his breath sharply, as if it were her own gasp of distress. With trepidation, she watched him move upward.

"He's a good, stable young man," her mother had said a month earlier when Daniel asked Eva to marry him. "Soon he'll be a partner in his father's bank. He can make you comfortable and happy. I know you're young to be getting engaged, but Daniel's a fine man, and he's loved you so long and so tenderly." It was one of the longest speeches her mother had ever made. Eva had wondered at the time why Agnes felt the need to speak so fervently on Daniel's behalf.

She had been surprised at how quickly her parents had given their consent, though she was not quite eighteen. In fact, she had been surprised by her own acceptance of Daniel's proposal. It was not that she did not love him; she had loved him for years, for his kindness, his quick intelligence, his sense of humor, but most of all because he accepted her, was not afraid to look directly in her eyes.

Yet, having passed all her school exams, she had been thinking seriously about going to university, not only for the knowledge she would gain there, but for the experience of a world beyond Eadar Island. Her restless spirit yearned for that freedom. Why then bind herself to a man, a marriage, a life shaped by the geography of an island held separate by the sea from ideas, change, and possibilities?

She suspected she had agreed to marry Daniel because she thought he could obliterate her fear of the future, a specter that haunted her, because she could not imagine what the future would be. She had always felt she was different, in some indefinable but fundamental way, from the people on the island. Somehow she did not belong among them. That terrified her, because it left a dark nothingness where tomorrow should have been. But Daniel would change that. With him she would be safe.

She wondered if her parents thought the same. Perhaps Samuel and Agnes hoped that Eva's feelings for Daniel would act as a lure stronger than the mystery of Celia Ward, stronger even than the call of the stranger's blood that flowed in Eva's veins.

Daniel approached warily, reluctant to face the three stone figures, caught a glimpse of Eva's expression and released his breath in a rush. He turned to Samuel and Agnes, frightened into indiscretion. "You told her, didn't you?"

Before they could answer, Eva gasped, cold and frightened, "You *knew?*" She glanced accusingly at her parents.

Daniel tried to intercept that accusation with his unsteady reply. "I found out from my father long ago. Bankers handle lots of legal documents, you know."

Agnes clutched her arms in a painful grip. "I wasn't wanting anyone to know. 'Tis too dangerous. They could have hurt our Eva." She stared at Eva but did not try to touch her.

Sighing in resignation, Samuel said, " 'Tis a small island we live on, *mo-cridhe*. We tried to keep it quiet, but 'twasn't possible to keep a secret in such a community. They've long and sharp memories, the islanders. We can but thank God that they know how to keep such knowledge close."

Eva bit her lip, though she did not taste the blood in her mouth. They had kept silent for her, because they loved her, were afraid for her. She tugged at the damp turf, digging her fingernails into the thin soil beneath.

That did not change the fact that Daniel had known. He had known while she was kept in ignorance. That explained, in part, her sense of isolation, the dreams that haunted her. She had always thought of Eadar as *her* island, partly because her father owned the largest factory as well as acres of land, partly because she knew and understood the earth and sea so well.

But now her father was not her father, her island was not her island. It never really had been. Just as Daniel never had. He was part of a world she could not understand, a world that belonged to the gods who had imbued it with a terrible beauty she could not resist. The island belonged to the gods, and Eva had thought she belonged, after Agnes and Samuel, with Daniel. But did she? Did she belong anywhere, now that she knew?

She did not look up when her fiancé sat beside her and placed his hand carefully next to hers, barely brushing the edge of her palm with his own. "You knew," she said in a whisper, "and you didn't tell me. I thought we had no secrets."

Daniel stared at the wind-tossed water. " 'Twas not my place. It was your parents' decision and their right. Besides, I promised my father, and myself."

Another promise that had kept her in darkness, kept her apart and alone. Another betrayal out of kindness. Eva knew she could not hold back tears much longer.

She looked at the three people she had trusted, and felt their sorrow and concern. She was devastated by that concern. It undermined her rage. She needed to clutch that fury, or she feared she would fragment, implode. Yet at the same time, their distress *fed* her rage. If they cared so much, why had they lied for so long?

Daniel swallowed dryly. "I'm sorry," he said inadequately.

"When my father realized ... how I felt about you, he thought I ought to know." He groped for words that would soothe her. "It helped, in a way. I understood better why you are the person you are." For Daniel, the knowledge of her adoption had added to her mystery and allure, but it had frightened him too. She was not of the island, and that widened the gap between them further.

Eva shook her head blindly, hopelessly.

Samuel stood still for a moment, considering. He was relieved that Daniel knew the truth. Now Eva would not have to tell him. More important, he had known for some time and had not shut their daughter out. Perhaps, after all, Daniel could accept Eva just as she was. Samuel nodded to Agnes. "We'd best leave her be for a time."

With tears in her eyes, his wife rose stiffly. She wanted to touch Eva, but was afraid.

Samuel rested his hand on Daniel's shoulder. "Will you stay with her? See her home safely?"

"I'll do what I can," the young man replied. His hazel eyes were full of doubt.

" 'Tis all you *can* do, as I've learned this day to my grief," Samuel answered. "We'll be waiting for you, Eva, whenever you choose to come home. I know you doubt what I say just now, but that you must believe. We will be there." He took his wife's arm to help her down the hill and they disappeared in silence.

In silence, Daniel and Eva sat, while the evening turned to gloaming. Daniel sensed that to speak now would only make her desolation greater. Her anguished silence broke his heart.

When the fading light and the awkward hush began to weigh him down, he took the risk of grasping Eva's hand. To her surprise, she welcomed the contact, the warmth of Daniel's hands, which had been buried in his pockets while hers were exposed to wind and sea. She held on tight, transferring her pain from her chest into her fingers, and then into his.

Shocked by the icy stiffness of her hand, Daniel opened his overcoat and drew it around her, as Samuel had done before him. Eva pressed close, and he flinched at the damp chill of her body. "You're so cold," he muttered, his own teeth chattering.

"Yes," Eva said bleakly. She let him put his arm around her and begin to rub gently to restore the flow of blood, which seemed to have ceased without her noticing.

"You'll be ill if you don't get warm soon."

Eyes glazed, she answered absently, "Perhaps."

He did not know what she meant, but that was not unusual. Eva's thoughts had always followed their own paths, clear to her but invisible to others. Daniel put his other arm around her, drawing her near enough to feel her shallow breath on his throat. She was slipping away from him, just when he should be binding her closer by offering comfort and warmth and affection. But he did not know how to reach her.

Once, quite recently, Eva had regarded him long and quizzically, before she said, "We're so different, Daniel, you and I." There was a question in her voice.

"I like ye the more for it," he'd told her. "I see enough of my own face in the mirror. It's nice to see yours instead, now and then."

"But I'm not normal." She did not sound chagrined. In fact, she could not quite disguise a flicker of pride.

Daniel grinned. "Normal is so uninteresting. I couldn't bear to be bored for the rest of my life."

Eva's eyes widened.

"You look surprised. Do you really think me so dull?"

"No," she said, touching his hand shyly. "I enjoy being with ye too much. But ye know how my moods come over me. Sometimes I think I'm haunted. It's no' easy to be around me then."

"I know that," he told her. "You're human after all. It's the only reason I thought I might someday have you. It's part of my luck that others are dismayed by your differences from them. Because I'm not afraid."

She had hugged him then, tightly, and he'd caught a glimmer of tears in her arresting eyes.

Now, as he held her close on the cliff top, he felt the

remembered weight of her gratitude as well as her current despair. "I know you can't yet forgive the way your parents deceived you, but it doesn't change how they feel about you. You're more than just their daughter, Eva. You're their hope and their joy. Don't doubt that, not even today."

Eva knew he was right. As Samuel had said, her parents' devotion was in some ways more intense because she had not simply been born to them, a child they had no choice but to accept. "I know it shouldn't matter that a lost and mysterious stranger is my real mother," she whispered. "It shouldn't, but it does." She looked up at him, face shadowed by his overcoat. "Can you understand that? It's not the same. It'll never be the same."

He drew her head into the hollow of his throat and rested his chin on her windblown hair. He felt so helpless he wanted to howl. "I know. I understand."

Eva shuddered with relief. She was so lucky he had found her, for she had not been looking when first he took her hand. Now she depended on his imperturbability, his determination, his direction. He was never confused or bewildered. She felt his fingers stroking her hair, calming her, as he had so often. Yet as many times as he brought her back to earth, to sanity, he never tried to stop her when she needed to fly free.

A wave crashed against the face of the cliff, and, despite Daniel's soothing touch, realization pulsed through her with debilitating suddenness. She closed her eyes against the bright anguish. "I need to walk," she murmured.

She did not have to add *alone;* Daniel heard the word more clearly than those she had said aloud. "I'll be waiting here for you, to walk you home," he said.

Eva turned, eyes damp with tears she would not weep. "Thank you." She leaned forward to kiss his cheek, but the brush of her lips was little more than a breath released— fleeting and insubstantial. Then she rose to scramble away.

Daniel shook his brown hair out of his eyes, watching with trepidation as Eva disappeared and reappeared, making her nimble way down the face of the cliff. It terrified him, the way she climbed steep pitted rock, searching out handholds he could not see, hollows where her feet caught momentarily to balance her weight. Sometimes she seemed to hang suspended by one hand and the toe of one foot. He had the odd sense that she was about to let go, to fly out to join the soaring fulmars and fade forever into overlapping shades of blue that did not end.

Daniel started when he saw Eva's agitation as she gained a level stretch of path. She was walking too quickly, moving without her usual grace. He watched, holding his breath, letting it out in sharp bursts each time he caught sight of her, while the gloaming drifted over him, deepening the shadow of his apprehension.

Eva approached the jagged rocks at the water's edge and slipped from view. Just when Daniel was about to go after her, when he had begun to conquer his fear of those unfriendly cliffs, she reappeared far out in the water. He was certain he saw a dolphin too as Eva dove deep, bare feet pointed gracefully, body undulating in the sleek golden light. She emerged in a froth of effervescent bubbles, just as the sinking sun touched the water, setting Eva afire with copper radiance.

She glided fluidly, naked in the cold sea water. Daniel watched, mesmerized, with no sense of surprise that his fiancée had so carelessly discarded her clothes to go swimming at sunset. She belonged in the water without encumbrance, free, lithe and natural. Clothes would have been an intrusion. Even Daniel, who believed in the safety of proper behavior, could see that.

The dolphin appeared again, with a mate this time, and Eva clung to their fins, moving like a mermaid, floating, as if born of water and sun and the sky that had darkened from bronze to deep violet. He strained, but could not see her face as her sleek head broke the water. She was too far away. But Daniel knew then, in his stomach, where the knowledge burned, that if she found an instant of comfort in this long, dark night, it would not be in his words or his arms. Not even in the solid, loving presence of her parents.

If Eva found any comfort at all, it had been in that moment when the water took her, when the dolphins rose beside her, heads sleek as her own, and all three moved with the breath of the sea. Eva had become part of the rhythm of those mingled breaths, and that rhythm would ease her, for a while. She was at one with these things, at peace.

He remembered with sudden clarity the day he had first noticed her, when she was only six. He had watched skeptically as she said to a visiting bird-watcher, "If you'll be a gentleman and lend me your pocket for a minute, I'll give you back a story." The surprised man had bent down so she could reach his shirt pocket, and Eva had slid her hand inside and told a story Daniel could not remember. But he remembered the look on the man's face, for the little fable Eva told had touched too closely on the stranger's hidden feelings and fears.

Seeing Daniel nearby, Eva had confided in her little girl's voice, "Sometimes people don't like it when I tell my pocket stories. I guess I hit a bad memory or something. I don't mean to. The story just comes out."

Daniel had been touched by the way she confided in him, engaged by her clear green eyes rimmed in gray, her concern over the stranger's distress. But he had been uncomfortable as well. He remembered that sharply now.

Years later, he could not help but notice when Eva's body changed, when she grew slim and tall and gently rounded. He noticed too that she sought the water more urgently, that her eyes more often had a cast of sorrow on them. He saw that she was different from everyone else he knew. She had about her an air of expectancy, of waiting for miracles, in which she fully believed, despite her dark mood swings. That belief gave him hope, while her otherness tantalized. He'd decided when he was seventeen that one day he would marry her, if she would have him.

He did not want only Eva's attractive face or supple body. He wanted the spark in her that made her soul a visible, palpable thing, a light to penetrate the gray enigma that was his own soul. She could make him complete.

"Why do you love me?" Eva had asked, head tilted, eyes intent. "I'm so confused and moody, and you're so certain, so determined. You know which way you're going, and I haven't the first idea." She could not seem to let go of that question.

"You know you want to make music," Daniel had reminded her, "to tell your pocket stories in poems and songs." He'd paused, surprised at the thought that came to his lips. "Besides, maybe I want you to help me get lost once in a while. I suspect there's a part of me deep down that can't grow without someone like you. It might never find its way to the light."

Daniel felt an odd fulfillment watching Eva swim as she did now, melding with the water, making patterns on the surface, then submerging and melding again, only to float slowly upward, hair a nimbus on the shining sea. She touched him in a way that frightened him, as her honesty and prescience had frightened him when she was six. He could not feel or be those things, but he wanted to know them through her. Wherever she was going, though she didn't know where that was, he wanted to be there.

Daniel ground his fingers into the soil, grasping handfuls of turf to distract himself from the pain in his chest. He was a fool, he and Samuel both, to think Eva needed his protection against the night or the angry sea or her own sorrow. She could find her way home barefoot on a moonless night. The wind would whisper, guiding her; the earth would echo her footsteps, warning her; the burn would lead her, filling her ears with the sound of home. Earth, water and air would cocoon and protect her; she knew how to listen to those voices he had never heard.

Daniel could not find his way around the bog in the dark. He had never tried to do so. But Eva knew the way. She would have to lead *him* through the hummocks of turf and peat, the clinging wet moss and deceptive blossoms of butterwort and sundew. He stood on this cliff top, helpless without her. The thought made him more than a little desperate. He understood in a flash of illumination how superfluous, even ridiculous was his promise to walk her home.

But he had said he would wait, and wait he would, as gloaming became darkness and the mist settled like tears on his cold cheeks.

4

EVA BEGAN TO SHIVER WHEN SHE TOUCHED THE IRON LATCH and felt it give beneath her hand. Inside, Agnes and Samuel were waiting.

She had not known until that moment how cold she was—outside and in. Her teeth chattered and she struggled to stop her hands from shaking. She had not felt the cold of the water; her senses had been filled with the setting sun and the sea and the fluid motion of the dolphins' bodies. The sensations had filled her, stopping all thought, bringing an exultation that made her drunk with joy. It was worth every moment of darkness that had come before.

As soon as her bare feet had touched the sand, the wind whined about her, chilling her with its icy touch. She had stood, arms crossed over her naked body, staring at her jumbled clothes, damp from the mist, while water dripped from her hair and skin. She could not think what to do next. Then she had discovered Daniel's flannel shirt nearby, still warm from his body. He had left it for her, knowing she would need its heat to dry herself.

Eva glanced around, flushed with embarrassment and fighting back tears. Although she had had no thought of modesty as she swam, now she was shy of her nakedness, protective of her privacy, unbearably touched by Daniel's gesture. She did not want him to see her this way, stripped and vulnerable. Not tonight.

But he was not nearby. He had left his shirt and gone. Once again, he had understood. Eva bit her lip to hold in her feelings while she dried her painfully tingling skin as best she could with the quickly cooling flannel, then dressed in her own damp clothes.

When she reappeared at the top of the cliff, Daniel regarded her in concern. "I don't want you to make yourself ill."

"I won't." She had no other reassurance to offer. Eva had huddled close to him as they went toward home, unspeaking. When they approached the house, she'd offered to dry his shirt by the fire, but he'd shaken his head. "My coat is buttoned tight, and I'm warm enough to make it home to the electric fire. You can return the shirt tomorrow." Beneath the casual words, Eva sensed his sadness, his unwillingness to leave her. She simply had no strength to try to ease his sorrow tonight.

She knew her parents were waiting for her. She did not know what they would say, or what she felt or if she would answer. She knew only that they were there—inevitable, solid, unchanging.

"Daniel!" At the last moment she called him back, reaching out blindly with voice and hand. He turned to grip her cold fingers, in which his sodden shirt hung chilled and heavy. Eva felt the warmth of his touch, and her eyes pleaded silently, though she did not know for what. Reassurance perhaps. Honesty.

Daniel was profoundly moved by the desperation in her eyes and grasp. For an instant he could not find his voice, then he said softly, firmly, "It'll be all right. You're strong, Eva. Strong enough."

Frowning, Eva thought of the woman in her oft-repeated dream, the woman who stumbled, was afraid, and fell. When Daniel had turned and could not hear her, she whispered, "I don't believe you," as she opened the heavy oak door.

After she had changed and eaten, Eva sat with her parents around the glowing embers of the fire, her birthday gifts in the center. The warm Burberry Agnes had chosen to replace her tattered overcoat, the stout boots for climbing her beloved cliffs, which Samuel had ordered from London, and, surprisingly, a blown-glass butterfly to hang in her window. Lifeless but lovely, it would fragment the light into rainbows of color that would sway with the motion of frozen wings.

She was intensely aware of the cozy warmth of the room, the beautiful stone fireplace, the brocaded chairs, the carved beams in the ceiling that gave a sense of history to a stone house barely thirty years old. Tonight she did not play or sing or conjure a song out of the shimmering firelight. Instead, she dug her toes into the thick carpet and glanced from Agnes to Samuel with a new kind of curiosity.

The differences between them were accentuated, either by the flickering light, or their worry, or Eva's own freshly opened eyes.

Samuel leaned toward the fire, tugging on his sandy-gray beard, brown eyes thoughtful and full of curiosity. He had always been curious and intelligent, could never know enough about any topic. Samuel liked a mental challenge, which was how he'd viewed the tweed factory when he purchased it. He had an eye for practical improvements and a knack for making money, though he was not greedy. He only wanted his family to be comfortable and his workers contented. His quick mind led to his quick temper, which usually disappeared as abruptly as it flared.

Agnes shared none of that tendency to anger. She did not question things the way Eva and Samuel did. Numbers and profits and losses were a mystery to her, one she did not wish to solve. She cared more deeply about the human mysteries in her own home, about smoothing over distress and unpleasantness. She wanted life to be simple and straightforward, and had tried to make it so, at least within these walls. She was not pretty, though her features were pleasant, her cheeks full, her nose distinctive and her eyes large, her lips curiously well shaped. Tonight she had brushed out her long hair and left it loose as she rarely did. It made her look younger somehow, and vulnerable. The sight gave Eva a pang of sadness.

She sat with an envelope in her hand, which rested palm up on her knee. The letter had come from a small wooden box that held no photographs, no keepsakes, just this small note, Eva's birth certificate from a hospital in Glasgow, with no name in the place where her father's should be, and the adoption papers. It was not much. Just all that Celia Ward had left behind.

For a long time Eva did not open the letter. Her curiosity battled with anger and confusion, and she wondered more than once, as she looked from Agnes's to Samuel's stricken face, if she really wanted to know what words that fragile envelope concealed. Her mother's last, perhaps her only, message to her daughter.

Eva contemplated the low flames flickering at the edges of peat and birch, aware that her parents watched anxiously, until their anxiety made her put aside her own. Besides, in her heart, she needed to understand where she had come from eighteen years ago. She had shouted at Samuel this morning for telling her the truth, but she had been wrong. If she was not part of these people, if she had always felt a little lost and alone, perhaps this woman could change that. This woman of whom Eva *was* part, this illusive stranger.

Eva tore the envelope open and slipped the single sheet of paper into her lap.

Eva,

That is the name I've chosen for you, which Agnes and Samuel Crawford have promised to retain. Know that they wanted to tell you the truth as soon as you were old enough to understand, but I asked for their silence. Another promise extracted, and, I pray, kept.

When you have read this letter, I would have you go to my friend Eilidh Stanley at the address below in Glasgow, if you are curious about your past. If you are not, then I am glad for you. It means you feel complete as you are, that your life will follow the path Agnes and Samuel have cleared for you. Questions and wondering are troublesome, and often the answers are painful. I hope you have no questions, and so no doubts or pain. I hope you find happiness.

> *Your mother,*
> *Celia Ward*

Eva blinked, stared at the sparse, cryptic note, blinked again. "Why?" she asked. "I don't understand."

Samuel leaned back in his chair, watching his daughter gravely. He frowned, fingering his beard as he considered Eva's question. "To tell ye the God's truth, neither do we. We could no' figure the woman out, Agnes and I. She was a bittie fey mayhap. I just don't know."

Eva sensed that she too was fey, at least in the Crawfords' eyes, and Daniel's, and her best friend Alexina's. The townspeople all thought her odd. "I've read about that in William Sinclair's books. He said the ancient Celts called it the fatal gift of the imagination. Did Celia Ward have it?"

Samuel gazed at his daughter long and hard. You have it, he wanted to say, and it frightens me. But sometimes I wonder what it would be like to see the things you see, to see through your eyes for a moment only. He shook his head sadly. "I'd not be able to say for certain. She'd not let us close, you see. But she must have had some kind of imagination, for she had fear, was consumed by it. That much she could not hide."

Eva blinked peat green eyes and pulled her knees up to her chin, wrapping her arms tight about her shins to hide the emotion that shook her. Shock, disappointment, and the gnawing edges of the darkness. She found she could look at neither father nor mother and rested her forehead on the worn knees of her trousers.

Agnes Crawford reached out to touch her cropped, curly hair gently, more like a breath than a touch. "That's why we're worried about you now, Eva. Your mother"—the word did not come naturally to her, any more than did the meaning of Eva's dreams—"was running from something. The knowledge and the weight of it never left her. Not for a moment." Agnes put her hand awkwardly in her pocket. "We'd not want you running that way, afraid and crippled by your fear."

Eva glanced up, fingers locked together. "What was she like?" she asked, tracing the scrawled letters of her mother's name, seeking the answer in ink long dried.

Agnes and Samuel had not meant to look at one another, but they could not help it. "She was ill and fragile," Agnes offered. "And deeply distraught," her husband added.

Eva glanced up sharply. "You mean she was mad."

Samuel shook his head, genuinely perplexed. "No. Only that she was afraid."

Eva remembered her nightmare, and chills ran up her arms and down her back. "What did she look like?"

Agnes stared into the fire to conjure the memory of the woman she had tried her best to forget. "She was no' very tall, and small-boned. She looked as though she might be carried away by the first island wind." Twining her finger in a loose strand of hair, Agnes added, "Her eyes were lovely gray, and when she looked at ye, ye could hardly look away, so that ye thought her pretty, despite her pale hair and pallid skin."

Eva had guessed as much. She felt the familiar self-disgust and realized it was not for herself but for her mother. "She was weak!" Eva cried. The woman in the nightmare, who must be Celia Ward, feared to the point of terror a sea that offered no harm, and, in her fear, caused her own destruction. If she had taken a moment to see the beauty of the ocean, to understand it, she need not have fallen at all. "Weak," Eva repeated more quietly.

Once, when Agnes's sister visited from London, Eva had overheard them talking in the kitchen. "I'm that afraid she'll become strange and lost. I can't believe she's strong enough to overcome—" She had broken off when she saw her daughter, but it was too late. Eva felt that somehow, in a way she could not understand, she had failed her parents. And she could not make it right.

"She was so ill. She'd used all her strength in bearing you and fighting her sickness. You can't blame her for that."

Swallowing the taste of bile, Eva looked away. Suddenly she was overwhelmed by fury at Celia Ward's manipulation of her life, as well as the Crawfords'. She had *made* them live this unspoken lie, but more than that, she had abandoned Eva, had not loved her daughter enough to keep her. She had not been satisfied with breaking her daughter's heart herself. She made certain that Agnes and Samuel would one day break it, too.

Blind with rage and helplessness, Eva threw the letter on

the floor. "I won't go to Glasgow. I don't care what she wanted. I don't care, do you hear?" But in her hand she could still feel the aged paper; in her eyes she could still read the few strange words. The paper, the words, felt hot, like a smoldering coal, like her curiosity.

Perhaps, in Glasgow, in her mother's history, she might find out why the darkness plagued her and the sea called her. She picked up the letter, held it by the corner, as if it might burn her fingers as the revelations of the day had scalded and blurred her image of what was true and real. Whatever her feelings for Celia Ward, however deep her rage at this betrayal, she could not pretend that nothing had changed.

"I have to know," she said in dejection, yet hoping Agnes and Samuel would talk her out of this foolish quest for a stranger and a past. "Don't you understand that what you've just told me makes it even more important that I know? Any knowledge is better than my demons. The ones in my dreams."

"Are you certain of that?" Samuel asked softly. "Did you notice how important your name was to her? Eva means 'she who is accountable for things unaccountable,' like Eve in the Garden. Why would Celia Ward make you accountable, then give you away? What did she mean, what weight does she think you bear? Hers or your own or all of mankind's?"

For the first time, Eva felt defensive of her absent mother. "Maybe she didn't know. Maybe she just thought it was a pretty name." She did not hear the hope or the skepticism in her voice.

Samuel saw how much his daughter wanted to believe that, but they had never lied to her, only withheld one truth. He would never do it again. "We overheard her talking to you once. So sad and hopeless she sounded. 'My Eva,' she said, 'responsible for so many things you'll never even know.' We wondered how anyone could put a burden like that on a tiny, helpless baby."

"I need to know why," Eva muttered.

Agnes and Samuel looked away. They had known from

the beginning that Eva was too curious to stay on the island, safe in her ignorance, too restless not to follow the mysterious voice from long ago. So restless that she walked the island every day, even in the wind and rain, oblivious of cold or wet, uncaring that she came in drenched even through her mac.

That wild restlessness had told Agnes long ago that her daughter would someday go in search of Celia Ward, to learn what she could of her mother. But not until tonight had Agnes Crawford allowed herself to admit that Eva might not want to return to the island and rebind the threads of her life here. This was her home. Perhaps that was not enough.

There were those on the islands who refused to send their children to school, fearful that, once educated, they would go, seeking prosperity and freedom, leaving their families without the hope and vitality of the young. However, Agnes and Samuel wanted what was best for Eva. Agnes had faith in their daughter's strength and common sense. But she didn't trust the memories; she didn't trust the past. She had seen the haunted look on Celia Ward's face and would not soon forget it. It was reflected now in Eva's eyes.

5

EVA SAT ALONE IN THE DUN, A ROUND TOWER BUILT ON AN islet in one of the many lochs carved out by moving glaciers centuries before. She had discovered this ancient chambered tower when she was eight and had made it her private place, hers and her friend Alexina's, where no one could disturb the two young girls. Here they had grown up together, practicing Gaelic, reading legends of the islands and the ancient Celts, gossiping, dreaming. Here, among the crumbling stones, they had shared their secrets, huddled below when it rained, sprawled on the exposed top floor when the sun shone.

While Eva waited for her friend, she hummed an old Celtic chanson, poised between anticipation and apprehension. It had come upon her slowly—the realization that she was actually going to Glasgow, and that that city held many more wonders than her mother's friend Eilidh Stanley. Eva had told only Alexina about the adoption, and all she knew of Celia Ward, though she had found it difficult to say the words. By telling the story from beginning to end, she had given it substance, made it real.

Xena had been as stunned as Eva. "Although," she had said, examining the shocking revelation like a rare but fascinating piece of stone, "it makes sense, in a way. Your parents are ordinary and withdrawn, and you've always been so adventurous."

Eva had gaped in astonishment. "Adventurous?" She had never thought of herself that way. "What do you mean?" She had spoken in Gaelic. She and Alexina often spoke the old language to each other; it both set them apart and bound them together. To Xena it was a game, but to Eva it was a religion, a consolation and a show of reverence, as well as a pleasure that made her feel, sometimes for hours at once, that she actually belonged.

Tilting her head so her fine blond hair fell down her back, Xena considered. "Like the time when we were nine and you talked the whole lot of us into climbing the highest hill on the island, with a steep cliff on the other side. You said we should dive off naked, that the water there was deep. You said it was summer and on the east side, so it would be warm enough. You wanted to so much, I could tell, but the others were too timid. They thought the cliff was too high and didn't want to take off their clothes in front of everyone."

Eva grinned, abashed at the memory.

"Instead, you led, and we climbed down the cliff, putting our hands into many a bird's nest in a dark crevice. Then we swam in our underwear, boys and girls both. They'd never have done that if you hadn't asked them to, if you hadn't stripped off your skirt and twin set and dived in first."

Eva could feel that warm summer night when the darkness had come late and the mystical purple gloaming seemed to last forever. Later, she had understood the reluctance of the others, but at the time, she'd had no thought for safety or modesty. She'd been caught up in the sensation of a fall through lilac-tinted air, the wind in her face, the taste of damp salt on her skin, the water rushing to meet her, enfold and caress her. "I remember Tommy Ferguson got caught in an undertow. He shouted enough to wake the spirits."

"Until you swam out to save him, and carried him on your back all the way to shore," Xena added with a curious smile.

"He's not spoken more than a stiff hello to me since."

"Tommy was humiliated that he had to be rescued by a girl. I guess he thought if he acted angry, you'd never know he was really afraid."

Eva glanced at her friend, intrigued by the odd tone in her voice. "Of course he was afraid. He might well have drowned."

Xena cleared her throat and stared down at her hands. "I was never in danger of drowning, but I was afraid as well."

Rising to her feet in distress, Eva glowered. "You never told me. I would have stopped it."

"I knew you would. That's why I said nothing. Besides, I didn't want you to know. I thought you'd be disappointed in me. I couldn't have borne that. Really."

Too surprised to speak, Eva sat down with a thump. Xena's eyes had shone with sincerity and, even after all these years, a little apprehension. Eva could not understand this new knowledge of her oldest friend. She felt dizzy and a little ill.

Xena frowned in concern. "Why does that upset you so much?"

Without thinking, Eva cried, "Because I never knew it before. Apparently, I never knew anything, not even who I am."

"Oh," Xena whispered. She wanted to offer comfort but didn't know how. How would she feel if she went home this gloaming and discovered she was not the child of her parents? She could not begin to imagine a devastation so profound. For Eva it would be even more difficult. She was so sensitive, so full of feelings that tumbled inside her like the sea in a storm.

"I don't know what to do," Eva whispered. "I don't know anything anymore." She was completely, appallingly ignorant of who she was—her history, her blood, the parents who had created and then abandoned her. Now the world beyond Eadar Island held all her secrets.

"Mum and Dad have always been so certain of everything. They never seemed to wonder or feel lost. But now they aren't who I thought they were. And if they're not who I thought they were, then how can I begin to know who *I* am?"

"You're an extraordinary person with more talent than anyone else on this island, and you're a good, loyal friend. I know I can always depend on you."

Eva blinked green eyes that were too dry. "You thought I'd like you less if you were afraid. You thought I'd judge you."

Xena sighed in discouragement. "That was *me* being silly, Eva, not you. I just wanted so much to be like you. But I know I never will. No one will." Aware of Eva's distress, she added, "That's not a bad thing. Don't you see? It's a gift, and only you have it. Don't be sorry for a gift like that. Don't regret your uniqueness. Not ever!"

Now, two weeks later, Eva raised her head when she heard Xena crossing the stone causeway that connected the fort to the shore; the rocking-stone had given her away. The stone had been placed by the Celts so the pressure of even a light step rocked it, making a noise that alerted the ancient dwellers to approaching enemies. The girls had discovered it after a storm had dislodged some of the rocks and debris that had accumulated around it over the years. Then they reset the stone to make their secret place more private.

Alexina's pale blond head appeared in the roughly rounded door frame, her blue eyes alert. Both hair and eyes, as well as her tall, big-boned body, were reminders of the Norsemen who had once conquered these islands. At the sight of Eva, she waved a gold folder. "Remember this?" she said as she slipped into the round room and sat cross-legged beside her friend.

Eva stared in surprise at the intricate design of Celtic knots on the cover. "Our book!"

When they were twelve, she and Xena had spent many hours putting together a book of Eva's poems and songs and Xena's drawings, taking inspiration from the lap of water against their weathered dun, from the stones themselves. Eva had brought her guitar, and leaning against the cool walls, she'd picked out the tunes while the words swam in her head.

"That's when I started to believe this place was *shiant*, enchanted. It was as if the words came from the walls, from the voices of the people who once lived here, and not my own mind." It had reminded her of the pocket stories, the way her fingers had danced over the guitar strings, melding with the words so that each song felt simple and right.

The book was written in both Gaelic and English. The old language was taught in the schools as part of the disappearing past the islanders wanted desperately to hold on to, though most people spoke English now. Eva loved to write in the ancient language. It was lilting and beautiful, with its unique syllables and sounds that turned words into music.

Xena shook her head. "If it was the voices of others, they still came from inside you. No one else could hear them, could they?" She was fiercely protective of Eva's fragile creative spirit. "And remember, I couldn't think what to draw until I read the songs that are really little stories in verse. Then one day, the pictures were just there. I plucked them out of the air and put them on paper."

Eva nodded and took the book, which fell open at the drawing of a stylized Celtic bird, wings spread, ready for flight, encircling the brief song in curved, graceful feathers.

> *Though I wander, lost in flight,*
> *You stand firmly on the ground,*
> *And the murmur of the night*
> *Lures you not, for you have found*

ALL WE HOLD DEAR

*The peace I seek
In my far-flung dreams.*

Blinking back sudden tears, Eva closed the book as Xena leaned back, arms locked behind her head. She regarded her friend intently. "Aren't you scared? I'd be terrified if it was me leaving the island."

Eva rested her chin on her knees. "Of course I'm scared. But not so much of leaving the island." Just of the future, she thought.

The familiar edges of the darkness threatened, making her cold and stiff. There was a void inside she did not know how to fill, a longing for something she could not understand. The need was powerful, compelling, and it left her feeling helpless and desperate. Sometimes her frustration was so great that the darkness swallowed her, and she sank into a frightening solitude.

Now that she was going in search of her past, Eva felt she was leaping into an abyss with nothing to hold her back, and no friendly water to catch her at the bottom. She was terrified of what she would find. She had imagined every possibility, from a triumphant discovery that her mother had been a celebrated musician, torn from her child through the avarice of others, to the image of a drunken woman living in the gutters, raped by a stranger and full of bitter resentment for the child she had gladly tossed aside. Day and night, Eva imagined meetings with her mother's friend, discoveries, disasters.

Yet she was excited too. She was beginning an adventure, no longer circumscribed by tradition, propriety and the sea that cut her off from the rest of the world. "I can't wait to see everything, to explore and discover what's there to know and feel." A wild leap of hope made her smile.

Eva rose restlessly, looked back to see if Xena was coming, and climbed the worn stone steps that circled the inside of the tower. She burst onto the top floor, open to the sky, where shelducks, starlings and curlews drifted, and dragonflies skimmed the water with their luminous blue wings. The light was shimmering and translucent. From here she could see the ocean and the vast expanse of sky whose light created a magical glow.

Breathing in the beauty, the tang of clear air and the cadence of the water, Eva watched a hare dart among ferns along the shore, heard the low hum of a bumblebee. These things were lovely and familiar, but there was so much more. So many possibilities. She opened her arms to them eagerly.

Xena had seen that look in Eva's eyes before, the way she watched the birds, intent on their graceful flight, aware of nothing else. Eva stared at the sea in the same way, shutting out all but the fury and color of the waves. She was like this, too, when a tune caught her up and would not let her go. Xena felt her friend's absence in those moments; it made her cold and alone and afraid. She ducked between Eva and the edge of the tower. "You'll be all right, whatever you find. You're strong."

Shaking herself awake, Eva let her arms fall to her sides. "That's what Daniel said, and I didn't believe him either."

Xena breathed deeply. "Daniel is no fool, Evalena. He knows enough to recognize that the best part of you, the part he loves most, is the very part that's taking you away from us."

Xena sighed, her heart weighted with more than one sorrow.

6

"TAKE CARE HOW MUCH SUGAR YE ADD. 'TIS THE TARTNESS that makes it," Agnes said firmly. Cooking was one thing she knew inside and out, one thing she could control.

Covered in flour to the elbows, blue apron dusted white, Eva smiled. " 'Tis just why I like your plumcake. I know it'll disappear before the other cakes and biscuits tonight."

Agnes smiled at the compliment, but when she looked up from the shortbread she was rolling, the smile faded. Eva was busy measuring and stirring, biting her lip in concentration, as she always did when she baked.

How many times had they stood side by side, Agnes wondered, cooking and laughing and testing new recipes? How many hours had they shared in easy camaraderie in the bright, airy kitchen? Both Eva and Agnes loved the room, with its huge windows, the hooks that hung in rows above the cooker for the suspended pots and pans, the wide worktops of bright linoleum and the new fridge Samuel had insisted on ordering. Now Eva stood in a patch of sun, as she had so often, chestnut hair glimmering in the afternoon light. Times like these had been Agnes's favorites, because here she had something to teach her daughter.

"I'm sorry." Her voice shook, though she tried to keep it steady.

Eva looked up sharply. Her mother had not spoken of the adoption or Celia Ward since Eva's birthday. Now that her daughter was leaving tomorrow, was this Agnes's apology?

"I wanted to make black buns for tonight, because they're your favorite. But I don't have all the ingredients. I'm sorry I couldn't do it, but I *wanted* to so much."

The sting of unshed tears blinded Eva. Agnes had offered up the black buns as both a gift of love and a recompense for her sins, but Eva could not absolve her. Agnes could not really wish her daughter well on her journey; that would mean Eva might not come back, and Agnes could not think of that. She could not discuss her regret or her dread or how much she would miss her only daughter. She could only offer black buns, and even there she had failed. Impulsively, Eva reached over to touch her mother's arm. "It's all right." Her voice was no more steady than Agnes's.

Agnes swallowed dryly and turned back to her work. She had no other defense.

They were baking sweets to take to the *ceilidh* tonight, a gathering in the co-op Town Hall to celebrate Eva's departure for Glasgow. Once, Eva thought, such gatherings had been the nightly custom, a comfort to people living the harsh existence on Eadar Island and throughout the Highlands. The companionship, exchange of news, stories and song, reminded them of their legacy, which they preserved through the telling of ancient stories.

Now that there were movies and television, the *ceilidh* had become less popular. "It's more a big party," Xena had said once. "A celebration for the coming of spring, a good profit from the tweed factory, or any other reason we can find."

There would be plenty to eat and drink without black buns, Agnes mused, but there would not be another day like this one. She fought rising panic, remembering the compassion in Eva's eyes, so mysterious to her unimaginative mother. Agnes wanted to roar to God at the unfairness of it, but she continued to press and roll, pat and shape. Tonight she would not celebrate with the others; she could only mourn in silence.

Carefully, she forced herself to speak. "Seems everyone's coming to the *ceilidh*. Should be quite an occasion. 'Tis been a long time since we had a party. Ye can smell it baking in half the houses on the island."

Brow creased in a frown, Eva agreed. In the last two weeks, Agnes had helped her daughter pack, bought ferry tickets to the mainland, sent telegrams to Eilidh Stanley in Glasgow, but she had not spoken of the future or the past. She seemed to have decided that if she pretended hard enough that Eva were only taking a short trip from which she would soon return, it would somehow be true.

Agnes felt her daughter watching and sweat filmed her neck. She struggled to keep control. What good would she be to the girl, blubbering like a fool, when her tears would change nothing? "Have ye been out and about seein' your friends, *mo-eudail?* Are they excited about your trip?"

"I've seen them," Eva replied uneasily, "though I've spent most of my time with Xena or Daniel."

"Ye must be nervous, with the party being in your honor and all," Agnes persisted, gaze fixed on the thin, flaky pastry beneath her roughened hands.

Eva turned back to the plumcake, ready for the oven now. Her hands shook as she poured the thick batter from bowl to baking dish and carried it to the oven. The truth was, she was terrified. She wanted to cry out, to hug Agnes fiercely. If she could not express her fear in words, at least she could do it with her body. But some instinct held her back.

Agnes's question had set loose a plague of anxieties. The people would come tonight and want to know Eva's plans, her hopes, her reasons. They craved contact with the outside world, and though they did not know it, their harmless questions, full of harmless curiosity, would release her suppressed anxiety.

As she closed the door of the oven, Samuel appeared, home from the tweed factory, his hair blown into disorder by the wind, his face red from the late spring sun.

Eva breathed a silent sigh of relief. "I know you've just come home and I should be considerate, but I've been thinking."

Agnes closed her eyes, undone by the distress in Eva's voice. "I've been after tellin' ye more than once that ye think too much, birdeen. Seems like it brings ye but sorrow and confusion. Still, 'tis the way you're made, I suppose, and all the warnings in the world won't change that. It's just sometimes I wish I could. To keep ye safe, ye ken. Just to keep ye safe."

Eva and Samuel stared at Agnes in surprise. It was the closest she had come to discussing *her* feelings and qualms. They could tell how upset she was by the thickness of her brogue. But now her lips were pressed shut; she would say no more.

"I don't think you can keep me safe from who I am," Eva whispered. And who is that? a voice inside her queried. Just exactly who is that?

The girl turned back to Samuel, her eyes troubled. "They'll be asking a lot of questions tonight. Where am I going? What am I doing? Why? What will I tell them?"

Samuel sat at the cluttered table and rubbed his beard, running his fingers slowly through the curling strands. "Weeel, we've talked about your exams, all passed, and recommendations stacked high from your teachers. We've talked about university, and how you need to go there and see if it's what you want."

Nodding numbly, Eva remembered the first time the question had come up. "With a mind like yours," Samuel had said, "and all that ability just waiting to be used, I'm thinking you'd not be happy staying on the island. You could find a job; anyone'd be glad to have you. But you'd only be passing the time, so to speak. I'm thinking you might enjoy studying more." It had not been easy for him to say. She could only continue her education away from the island.

Now he inclined his head, regarding his daughter pensively. "Reason enough for a person to go off to Glasgow and see about the colleges and university, don't you think?"

"More than enough," Eva said in relief, trying to ignore Agnes's ominous silence. It struck her how often her father had advised her, not telling her what she *should* do or *might* do. It was a gentle advising that had made her learn to think for herself. If she was strong, as Xena and Daniel said, it was because Samuel had taught her how, had shown her over and over that he trusted her judgment as much as his own.

Eva took a deep breath and glanced at Agnes's back. Funny that she'd considered herself closer to her mother than her father, perhaps because she had spent so many hours with Agnes in the kitchen while Samuel was at the factory or bent over the accounting books.

It struck her that she and her adopted mother had talked a great deal in the last two weeks. They'd sat over mugs of tea or glasses of fizzy lemonade, bannocks and scones, clotted cream and crowdie, warmed by the stove, surrounded by light and linoleum and full oak cupboards.

They'd discussed how strange it was to be out of school, her friends, her exams, what she might study at university. They had talked that way before Celia Ward, every day after school when Eva curled up in her favorite chair, seeking her mother's advice and companionship. Long ago, Eva had come to Agnes when she began to menstruate, and her mother had explained womanhood and the suffering that came with it. They had talked about boys, about Daniel, about baking, always avoiding topics like Eva's walks along the shore, her nightmare, her terror of the future. She had felt safe here. And no wonder.

Agnes had never once asked a dangerous question; Eva had not given a dangerous answer. By tacit agreement, they had stayed on secure ground. Lately nothing was different, though everything had changed.

Eva realized that over the years, she had done most of the talking. Agnes was a very good listener—patient, compassionate, kind, with a trace of humor. Her occasional comments, made as often with handmade tarts, oatcakes and buns as with her deep voice, were sensible and comforting. Agnes thought long and carefully before speaking. It was her way.

"You know what to do, Eva," Samuel said. "You've always known, when ye listen to your heart. You're no' afraid to do that." Her father did not avoid her gaze or her apprehension.

With him it had always been different. Before her birthday, Eva used to sit with Samuel, discussing history, art, the problems of the island, the burden and value of the past. Eva had talked about her concerns, and Samuel about the factory, his frustration that he could not be more than he was. They had spoken quickly, fiercely and with passion, not considering the wisdom of what they said. They had argued often, enjoying the challenge and energy of those arguments. They spoke from their hearts, in the heat of a moment.

That spontaneity was gone now, and a great invisible distance had grown between father and daughter. Eva's evening talks with Samuel before the fire had become strained with the knowledge that lay between them. Both were afraid of what they might say, what hurt they might inflict or pain they might reveal. Eva missed those uninhibited talks, felt a bleak emptiness where the intimacy used to be.

At that moment, it came to her that she and her mother had shared comfort, tradition, a warm certainty that they were safe with one another. Eva and Samuel had shared an intensity, a passion for life in all its aspects.

Eva wondered if they would ever regain what they had lost. She very much feared it had flown with the wild north winds, along with her innocence and blind faith. By the time they returned to Eadar Island, those winds would have blown far and furiously, leaving the debris they'd gathered in unknown seas and untamed lands along the way.

Just after seven, Xena and Eva walked together toward town, away from the cliffs, past the edge of the loch and the river. It was not yet dark. The hours of daylight were long in June. The clouds were massed in the east, portending rain before the night was over, so both girls wore their macs.

The narrow dirt path they took wound through heath and low hills, bounded by tussocks of grass and ferns that edged the burn. In the distance, Eva could see the beach on the east of the island, pale and moon-curved, bordered by a narrow strip of spiky yellow-tipped marram grass, then the machair—the wide belt of grassland where sheep and cattle grazed among thick clover, trefoil and buttercups.

Beyond it all whispered the pale blue sea over a beach of glimmering powdered shells strewn with kelp. Here on the west side of the island, the ocean was serene, protected from the fierce north wind that made the waves rage against the cliffs.

Eva gazed at the scene with hungry eyes, memorizing its somnolent tranquility to carry inside her along with the turmoil.

Xena trailed reluctantly along the piled stone fence beside the road. Tomorrow her friend was leaving for Glasgow on the morning ferry, and Xena's usual exuberance had faded.

"Will it storm tomorrow?" Eva asked nervously.

"Not enough to stop the ferries," Xena said with some regret. "It'll be so different and dull when you've gone."

Eva smiled affectionately. Xena made her feel important, somehow *necessary,* and she needed that just now.

She saw a glimmer of shiny black on the path and bent to pick it up. Brushing the dust on her tweed skirt, she called Xena over to look. "It's a magic stone. It has to be." It was glossy black, flat and round, with a hole through the center.

She knew how the ancient Celts had valued curiously shaped stones, imbued them with magic and mystical power.

"Just like the one Coinneach Odhar was holding when he awoke on that enchanted hillside." Xena leapt atop the uneven stone wall in excitement. "You must have been meant to find it. Look through the hole and tell me if you see the truth and the future."

Coinneach Odhar, the Brahan Seer, had lived in the seventeenth century and, like his predecessor Thomas the Rhymer, his visions had been unnervingly accurate. He was said to have predicted many things, from the Highland Clearances to Hitler's devastation of Germany and the world.

Eva shook her head at the thought of any connection with such a man, famous for his Second Sight, *taibh-searachd*. Sometimes she thought of such things, when she swam with the dolphins or sat in the chambered rooms of the ancient broch, but she never talked about them. She was different enough from the others, and though they were superstitious, though their lives and their religion were infused with a legacy of mysticism from their ancestors, they no longer admitted such primitive beliefs.

She was not afraid of the *taibh-searachd*, but she did not seek it. Still, she felt Xena was right. She had found this very old and once powerful stone for a reason. She rubbed the smooth surface, held it briefly to her cheek, then slipped it into her pocket. "It'll be my talisman."

She looked to the left and stopped abruptly at the sight of the largest estate on the island, sold to an Arab prince who used it rarely as a shooting lodge for himself and his friends. Eva hated the waste of deer confined so they could not wander, feed and breed as they chose, the unhealthy swarms of salmon and trout stocked in rivers banked up to follow unnatural courses that suited the sportsmen who occasionally came to fish them. The fish themselves were allowed neither to follow their instincts for survival and renewal, nor to be caught for food for the hungry of Eadar Island.

Distracted from her problems by a surge of anger, Eva

braided her fingers through the chain-link fence that surrounded the estate—abandoned and forgotten, the momentary impulse of a stranger. It was June, and the hazel and birch woods were lush green, carpeted with bluebells, wood sorrel and primroses. Rowans, willows and sycamores swayed in the breeze, along with a huge old chestnut once lovingly tended, made to survive on this island of wind and storm. The loch glimmered black in the distance, reflecting and reshaping the dramatic, textured clouds. "I wanted to stop it!" Eva declared.

Xena stared, perplexed. "Stop what?"

"The way they exploit this land, the animals and fish and even the trees. I wanted to free them all." Eva spoke violently, fighting back tears that had nothing to do with the estate choked with weeds or the fenced-in deer.

"You don't have the power to do that," Xena said, astonished that Eva had never said this before. "They've been trying for hundreds of years, but no one has that power."

Eva pressed her face against the fence so the links crushed a pattern into her cheeks. "The people who've owned this place, who've used it and ignored it, they don't understand." Her voice rose, high and piercing. "From sea to river to tiny burn, from water to water do we live. Without it, we're parched and barren. The animals give us sustenance and lessons we can't learn for ourselves. The land gives us our strength and security and history. It should not be bound by the fences of strangers who do not love its beauty nor live from its wealth. I can't bear the injustice. It's not right!"

Her eyes were radiant with fury and frustration. "It should be free to become what it is without man's touch. To be wild and beautiful and fraught with hope." She felt the pressure of the rusted links on her face, and turned to Xena, pleading. "Shouldn't it?"

Xena was not as strong as Eva; she let her tears fall. "Yes," she said softly, "you should be."

THE HUGE CO-OP TOWN HALL WAS NEARLY FULL WHEN THE girls arrived. Tonight the radios were silent, televisions turned off, the movie hall empty. The islanders were looking forward to the *ceilidh*, which, though it had changed over the years, still retained the feeling of old spirits and old honor. The legends reminded the people of the great Kingdom of Dalriada that had once stretched across most of the Hebrides as well as the western Highlands. The poems sang of the Lords of the Isles and their fabled power, of the Scotland that had been Alba, a mystical kingdom of heroes, spells, fairies, tragedy and triumph. Eva always left the *ceilidh* with the past close around her, beating in her veins like the pulse of her heart.

Everyone was eager to see her tonight. Often the young, adventurous and ambitious left the island to find their fortune in Glasgow or London, Australia or Canada. Rarely did they return. The parents mourned with Samuel and Agnes for the inevitable loss of their only child.

After all, Samuel Crawford was the biggest employer on *Eilean Eadar*, the reason many families had survived and been able to stay on the island. He was generous and fair and shared his profits with all who worked for him.

For that reason alone, the islanders were ready to accept his daughter, and though Eva was different from them, she was also kind, perceptive and funny when she relaxed enough to let those qualities show. Besides, her little stories entertained the other children, and her fey nature both intrigued and intimidated them.

Eva paused in the doorway when she saw how many had come. She saw Samuel and Agnes at once and her heartbeat raced. They looked as uncomfortable as she. They, too, were afraid of the people's questions and did not want to explain why Eva was going away.

The Crawfords had agreed to tell no one the true reason, though some of the islanders must have known—the ones who remembered that eighteen years ago the Crawfords had finally adopted the child they had hoped for so long.

Most of those in the hall had been born on Eadar Island, as had their fathers and grandfathers. They knew who their ancestors were, where they came from, how deep their roots grew. Seeing them in one room only emphasized that solidarity, making Eva feel more than ever a stranger.

"There be the bonny lassie, off to the mainland to see what's to see. But I'll not make a wager on whether she'll be back."

"Eva, it's so exciting. I envy you, and that's the truth."

"You'll tell us all about it, I don't doubt, if not in your lilting voice, then mayhap in your stories."

"We'll miss you, Eva. No one else is half as interesting, I'll say that for you."

"You've come of age at last. Now, what will you do with the future the Lord's handed ye?"

Eva found it difficult to breathe through the mass of people gathered around her. Desperately, she sought out her parents, who stood a little away from the crowd. Her eyes met Samuel's. His brown gaze was steady and did not waver.

His encouraging smile, meant to restore her self-confidence, brought the threat of tears close. With a great effort of will, Eva returned her father's smile. Like Tommy Ferguson, she would not show her weakness nor disappoint her parents. Despite the turmoil inside, she would not drown tonight.

Daniel Macauly hurried in just as the others were finding seats. The old women and young children sat on chairs and benches in a circle, while the young people settled on the floor. Some stood behind the chairs, and the men hovered in the outermost ring. Still in his banking clothes, Daniel hung his mac with the others along the wall, while someone made a place for him next to Eva. He took her hand. "Are you all right?" he asked, breathless from running.

"I'm glad you're here," she answered, twining her fingers with his.

Before long, fiddle and guitar, flute and bagpipe filled the cavernous hall. One after another, old and young, girls and boys, men and women came forward to sing a song or tell a tale or recite a poem. The crowd shouted encouragement, stamped their feet, joined in the chorus of their favorite old songs, or sat back, awed and silent, while a young boy told a dramatic tale.

After each performance someone called out to Eva to perform one of her own songs, but she demurred. She was far too agitated, though the familiar traditions soothed her somewhat.

As the evening progressed, the men slipped outside a few at a time to take a dram of *uisge beatha*—whisky, the water of life. The women drifted about the hall, drinking cider or tea or a wee hauf and hauf—half whisky, half ale, and pretended not to notice the furtive comings and goings of their men. Everyone's appetite increased as the dancing of reels and strathspeys became more energetic. Soon the long table of food against the wall was surrounded by a crowd three deep.

When people began to fall back into their chairs, red-faced and exhausted, ready for a respite from the exhilaration of the dance, Xena passed around copies of the book she and Eva had made together.

The islanders took turns reading the poems and singing the songs, much to Eva's chagrin. Yet she was touched that so many seemed interested, that no one laughed outright, and only a few smiled at her young efforts.

In the land of Dalriada,
From the deep and chilling mist,
Rose a man, a warrior hero,
Who had dreamed of power and gold.

*He had dreamed of gold and gems
At a kelpie's whispered vow,
And he never paused to question
If his dream was true and pure.*

Brian Munro, a man of Samuel's age, who had long been a good friend, held up the small book. "Is this why ye'll be wanting to go to university, then, our Eva? To see if your own dream is true and learn to be a musician?"

Eva was caught off guard and was momentarily speechless.

Agnes sensed her daughter's distress and surprised everyone by answering fiercely, "A musician is no' something you learn to become. 'Tis something you're born. Eva already *is* one."

She leaned close, so only her daughter saw the shimmer of tears in Agnes's eyes. "I wish *I* could have given you that gift," she whispered softly.

Eva was startled and dazed. She squeezed her mother's hand in compassion while her mind spun with new questions. Had Celia Ward loved music as Eva did? Had she written little songs that told her own stories as well as others'? Had her father? Had either passed their passion on to Eva? Each new thought was like a blow, each added urgency to her errand.

Had Eva's birth mother actually given her something to value?

Eva felt Agnes's palpable regret, her fear that she had given her daughter nothing worthwhile. A rush of affection made Eva smile as she whispered, "You gave me love and security and a home that was safe and sane. My songs have never given me peace, but you did. You and Dad."

Agnes blinked hard and nodded. She would not expose her heart to these people, though many had been lifelong friends. She had always kept her sorrow private, and thus safe. That was why she feared for Eva, whose eyes revealed her feelings, who put her soul on paper in her songs.

The silence spun out like a thick, unwieldy thread, until Samuel cleared his throat. "Maybe Eva can't learn to be a musician at university, but she can learn to perfect her craft. She can grow there, and change." He added quietly to his daughter, "The instinct burns bright within ye, but ye need to know that flame and shape it to your will, not be shaped yourself by its heat."

Xena heard him. "You have to come to trust that flame." Her eyes met Eva's as she whispered, "You doubt yourself too often and too deeply. You have to learn to believe."

She had said it before, and each time Eva had thought it odd, since Xena herself was so insecure and uncertain. But she was very certain about Eva.

Daniel said nothing, though he slipped his arm around Eva's shoulders and she felt his heart beating far too quickly.

She was grateful when the dancing began again and the conversation ceased to focus on her. Those who did not take the floor talked of the Arab prince who had bought the estate in the middle of the island, of the plentiful catch of fish so far this year, the crops of barley and oats that had not yet been destroyed by the weather. They talked of the large order for scarves, gloves and tartans from London that just might get them through another season.

Hearing the last warning of wind before the rain, the older people left in groups, determined to get home dry and safely. They left their children behind, knowing the young could more easily survive the storm, indeed, enjoyed doing so, as if it were a challenge.

Samuel and Agnes touched their daughter's shoulder as they rose to go. "Come back when ye will, but have Daniel walk you home, and remember, ye leave on the early ferry."

Eva put her hand on theirs and smiled, warmed by their concern. "Don't worry. I'll take care."

Outside, the storm finally broke, and the wind howled like a banshee. The young people huddled around the coal-burning stove and felt warm and cozy. While the tempest raged and the lights flickered, they brought out spiked cider and coffee, and turned to Eva expectantly. "Tell a pocket story," Cathal Munro cried. " 'Tis a perfect night for it."

"Aye, a pocket story!" Kirsty, Jaime and Margaret took up the chant.

Eva glanced at Daniel, but his eyes were shadowed. He was trying to disguise his sorrow, but she could feel it in his tense arm on her shoulder and his erratic heartbeat. Eva turned to Xena, who had managed so far to smile and keep them all from mourning.

"Go ahead," Xena urged, pointing to the macs hanging on pegs along the wall.

Eva was reluctant. The stories made Daniel nervous, because he could not understand. But the others were insistent. " 'Tis our last chance for the mystery you weave." They pulled chairs and benches in close around her and leaned forward expectantly.

Eva had first begun to tell pocket stories one cold day when she was four years old and Agnes had taken her tiny hand and buried it in her apron pocket. As she wiggled her fingers in her mother's capacious pocket, Eva saw quite clearly an image of a child with Agnes's thick hair and brown eyes, eating a black currant tart and letting the sweet, dark juice drip down her chin and over her white pinafore. The young Agnes's hands were sticky with syrup, her lap full of crumbs, and she was happy.

Eva had known, though she could not explain why, that the grown-up Agnes beside her had wanted her daughter to feel that same happiness, and would make a black currant tart for their tea. Too young to think about the implications of the image she'd seen, Eva had blurted out her discovery in excitement. It had made Agnes uneasy, and later Samuel. Soon she learned not to tell the stories at home, but the other children loved them. The tales formed a bond between the pensive, enigmatic Eva and the boisterous children of her neighbors. She found it difficult to make conversation, and the stories allowed her to communicate, to step outside herself and draw others close, but only briefly, and in safety. If she saw something unpleasant, she removed her hands from the pockets surreptitiously and made up a story of her own.

"Kirsty, go and get a mac for her," Cathal shouted, "but close your eyes, mind, so you don't see whose you're taking."

Xena nodded. "You close your eyes too, Eva. We don't want you to know whose mac you hold."

Since they all looked much the same, except that some were beige, some black, some brown, it was unlikely Eva would recognize the raincoat. Nevertheless, she did as she was told, grateful for the momentary darkness behind her lids. Daniel stood behind her, hands resting on her shoulders lightly, as if he were afraid to hold too tight. She reached up to brush his fingertips and smiled at the calm that settled over her.

Kirsty put a coat in her lap, and Eva shifted, searching. Everyone fell silent as she slid her hands into the deep, cool pockets, leaned back and concentrated on the things she felt through hands and heart. "It's a happy story," she began, "and the pockets warm ones, without turmoil. Only a little sorrow."

She was no longer aware of the others or of the expectant hush that fell. She was losing herself in someone else's thoughts and dreams.

Eva smiled to herself, and the others sighed. A smile was always a good sign.

"There is a little girl," she said softly, "who wore her fair hair in two fat braids, but one was always coming loose, while the other stayed woven tight. She craved excitement, or thought she did, which was why she loved the storms over the island, the storms in the town, storms among the people. But what she loved best were the mermaids.

"The girl watched them play in the sea, and wept when she heard them sing. She longed to become one of them, to be enchanted, to dream their magical dreams. But she couldn't swim or hold her breath under water."

Eva heard a tiny gasp, but it did not pierce the cocoon around her. "I'll move on now to a later time, when her braids were unwoven and her hair flew loose in the wind. She came to care for a boy—the only one she loved more than the mermaids."

"Who?" everyone cried.

Eva bit her lip and tried to see the boy. "A boy, a young man, in prison?"

This time the gasp was louder. "No!"

"No," Eva said. She saw, not black iron bars, but ornate ones, like she saw every day in town. "A boy in the post office or the bank," she explained without opening her eyes. She laughed at her own mistake. "A professional man, quiet inside, whose dreams she did not know or could not guess. She thought him handsome and wise, and she knew he loved the mermaids too, though he would not tell her so.

"He has a mask over his eyes that blinds him at first, like a sleek black scarf. But slowly the scarf becomes translucent, and he glimpses the girl's image, distorted and out of focus. He sees her through shadows until the weave loosens and falls away. When he really recognizes the girl, without shadows and memory, he'll take her hand and they'll sit together with the spray on their faces while they listen to the mermaids singing."

Eva shook her head to clear it, but one last image lingered. The man stepped from the shadows and she saw that he had Daniel's brown hair and hazel eyes, Daniel's comfortably medium build. Of course it was Daniel, and the prison the bars in his father's old-fashioned bank. Eva should have known from the beginning, but when she told her stories, she often lost the threads that bound her to the real world, and lived only through the images in her mind.

Eva slipped her hands from the pockets, and the images faded as the people around her came into focus—Xena and Cathal, Margaret, Kirsty and Fiona, Allan and Simon. Everyone was calling out questions.

"Do they fall in love?"

"Do they live in a fairy tale?"

"Not here on this island, you can bet," someone answered.

"Do they marry? Have children?"

"Who cares!" Fiona cried. "Tell my story now, Eva."

Eva was suffocating and could not answer, though she was sharply aware of Daniel reaching down to take her hand. Just as he had taken the girl's hand in the story.

Alexina stopped the din with one peremptory shout.

"Leave her be. You know she tells us what she sees. You have to finish the stories yourselves."

"Besides, she's too tired to do more now," Daniel added.

"Well, at least claim the mac, whoever ye may be," Cathal grinned, eyebrows lifted in a mock leer, "so we can find out who's stalking mermaids."

The others shouted him down. "Not fair. That's part of the fun, guessing who it is, or if it's you. So off with ye, Cathal Munro, before ye spoil everything."

Eva was pale and oddly silent. It struck the others then, forcibly, that she was leaving the island tomorrow, perhaps forever. The laughter died down; Eva was drawn to her feet and into a maelstrom of hugs and kisses from the usually undemonstrative islanders.

She hugged them back, the raincoat still clutched to her chest, accepted their kisses and good wishes and farewells and returned them. She was keenly aware of the night wind and the sound of the sea in the harbor beneath the voices of her friends. She was leaving them, and she ached with it. They were all she had known, and they cared that she was going. She had not known how much. Daniel stayed beside her, watchful and kind, touching her to remind her he was there. He did not know that he was making things more difficult.

Her eyes burned with dry tears when at last she came to Xena, hovering near the door.

"I'll see you at the ferry in the morning," her friend said.

Eva started to object—she did not think she could stand one more reminder of what she was losing—but Xena shook her head. "For me, not for you. I *need* to be there. Don't tell me not to come, *mo-charaid*. Please." There was an odd reluctance in her voice. Xena hesitated, stared at the mac Eva still held, then grabbed it and put it around her shoulders. She was gone before her friend could speak.

8

DANIEL AND EVA WALKED SLOWLY HOME TOGETHER. THE storm had raged and retreated, leaving drifts of clouds, a furious wind and the promise of a star-scattered sky stretching into eternity. They could not be heard above the wind, and so did not speak, but Eva clung tightly to Daniel's hand. The glimpse of his face in Xena's pockets had made her realize, as the past two weeks had not, that he was precious to her beyond the words she could have spoken had the wind allowed it.

A gale blew their coats wildly, so that they flapped and billowed and did not entirely protect Daniel and Eva from the sand whirling through the damp air full of the ocean's bluster. When they reached the Crawfords' door, they stood silent for a long time, hands locked, Eva's head against his chest. She was afraid to look up and see what was in his eyes. Afraid for him to see what was in hers. Instead, she concentrated on the sound of a loose shutter tapping in the wind.

When she raised her face to kiss Daniel, she kept her eyes closed as she brushed her lips over his. A delicate tingle of heat flared beneath her skin, stirred sleeping desires awake, until she sighed with pleasure. She held on for a moment to the feel of that kiss in her blood. Strengthened, she tilted her head back to look at him.

Daniel seemed suspended by the kiss. He stood motionless, lips parted, eyes closed. Eva ran her fingertip over his eyelids, then kissed each, gently, fleetingly, tenderly. The wind died as suddenly as it had spun to life, leaving behind an odd and unexpected stillness dominated by the fragrance of butterfly orchids that rose around them, heavy and sweet with promise. Already the moths had begun to flutter about, drawn by the scent.

Eva swallowed dryly. This parting would be more wrenching than she had imagined. Daniel would not demand or clutch her tight or try to hold her. He stood, open and vulnerable, waiting for her to touch him, for her to say goodbye. How could she face her uncertain future without him? How could she hurt him so much? "I don't want to go," she cried. "It's too hard and too cruel. I don't want to know about a stranger who bore me. I have you and Mum and Dad. It's enough. I know it's enough."

Daniel sighed. He wanted very much to lie. Eyes closed tight, he touched his lips to her forehead. "It's not enough for you, Eva. It never has been. You say you don't want to go, and you believe it, but you're lying to yourself. Not only do you *want* to find the truth, you're already more than halfway gone. You've always been leaving us, in one way or another, for the sea or the birds or the woods or the wind. You couldn't ignore them any more than you can ignore your true mother's voice. Your heart may be full of fear, but your soul and your spirit are already in flight."

He broke off, his voice ragged. His only flicker of hope was that he had been to Glasgow and did not think that city would lure her. She loved the island too much. That thought brought a sharp pang. Her love for *him* would not bring her back, but her love of the island might.

Eva had stiffened when he began, but as he spoke, she responded to the truth in what he said. She was trembling, her breath cool against his throat. The truth, he decided, was a cruel and heartless thing. Daniel pulled her closer, and their cheeks met in the chilly night, both wet with tears. "Tell me you'll come back," he said.

"I'll be coming back, Daniel. This has been my home too long for me to forget, but—"

"Don't say it, Eva. You don't know for certain. Say, rather, that you'll know in time."

Eva slipped her arms around him. She knew she would be back, knew just as surely that it would never be the same. Daniel was right; she was leaving him behind, or he her. In a way, she had given her blessing, by kissing his blind eyes that would one day open.

She put her hand against his heart. "When I come back, Daniel, I'll be someone else."

"No! You'll be Eva. You've always been someone else, different from us."

Eva breathed through a net of myriad pinpricks of misery. "Then perhaps I will be more myself."

Cupping her face in his hands, Daniel whispered, "Whoever you are, I hope you are happy."

He pressed his damp cheek to hers and stepped back. In the starlight, she was surprised to see his eyes wide open and wise with sorrow.

9

As IF TO MAKE THE PARTING AS DIFFICULT AS POSSIBLE, THE next day dawned lovely and clear. Eva, Agnes and Samuel made their way to the dock among those who crossed regularly to Glasgow. The ferries were invisible lifelines to the islanders, preserving their connection to home and family.

The harbor was crowded with autos waiting for the ferry, while fishing boats, coal carriers, liquid gas carriers and shipping boats waited at the docks to load or unload. People scurried about, and Eva thought that here, more than in town, she felt the energy and life of the people on Eadar Island. The island itself she had come to know in private places, like her bluff and the lochs and burns and moors. But that was a different rhythm of life—slower and more violent.

"Eight o'clock ferry'll load in fifteen minutes!" a deckhand shouted across the dock.

Eva's luggage was handed over and stored away. Now that the actual moment was here, she was paralyzed. Her grief had burrowed so deep that she no longer felt its pulse. Yet she knew it was there. She looked up in compassion at her parents, at their grimly expressionless faces, their hands buried deep in their pockets. Whatever they might have felt as she prepared to go on her trip to Glasgow, they had not once warned or beseeched or wept.

Agnes and Samuel did not understand that their restraint made Eva more aware of their sorrow, not less. She carried their silent misery like a talisman around her neck.

All three stood shivering and wary, their breath bursts of cloud in the early morning air. Daniel had said good-bye last night when Eva asked him not to come to the dock. It would be too difficult, she'd said. He had nodded solemnly in agreement. "Come back soon," he had said, and nothing more.

In a flurry of down and denim, Xena appeared and enveloped Eva in a rough hug. "Don't go!" she cried, then, wiping a tear from her cheek, she added, "and don't you dare listen to me. You *have* to go. I know that. It's just that I'll miss you so much."

She, at least, was not afraid to show her sorrow and excitement. Xena glanced at Agnes and Samuel, as if she understood that she was saying *for* them things they could not say themselves. She backed away from Eva, stared for a long time into her green eyes with their unusual gray rings. "I told you it'll be all right. And if it isn't right, you'll make it right. I know that, Evalena. I wish you knew it too."

Eva felt the darkness coming, heavy with unshed tears. She could not turn away from her friend's penetrating gaze, from the memories that passed between them, from the throbbing in her head. She gasped, desperate for air.

Xena clasped Eva's hands and held them for a moment. "I'll be waiting to hear what you find out. We'll all be waiting." She turned and fled with a wave over her shoulder.

Xena's flight forced Samuel out of his stoic silence. He turned to his daughter. "Why do you have to go?" He knew the answer but couldn't stop the question, now that it was too late.

Eva looked toward the sky, toward the elegant flight of

the fulmars and gannets. The words came without thought. "Because, in spite of the upset Celia Ward has caused us all, I still believe I can take flight. I believe those birds see wonders we can't imagine, magical things too beautiful to describe." She looked down at her parents. "I still believe in miracles."

Samuel shook his head. "Miracles don't happen."

For him, for Agnes, it was true. But not for Eva. A voice inside told her many things were possible, things that could not be explained or understood, only felt deep within, in the heart, in the soul.

"We don't want you hurt or disappointed," Agnes murmured in a rough stranger's voice.

Eva faced them fully. "I know. You want me to be safe. But I want, I *need* more than safety. Please understand."

She knew they had tried, but it was not in their natures, this desire to take risks, this belief in the unknown, the unknowable. To believe such things would destroy their system of careful logic, rationality bounded by the rules that kept away chaos. Eva could not change their minds, and did not want to see them founder in uncertainty.

She looked at Agnes, whose pockets were zipped up tight. Her emotion was too close to the surface, and she didn't want her barely held control to snap, to leak out one tiny hole she might have overlooked. As if zippers and cloth could protect her from the storm of grief inside. Her daughter was leaving; Eva would never be a child again.

Samuel had left his anorak unzipped, and his pain showed in his eyes. He was more vulnerable today than his softhearted wife.

The ferry called out its dreary command. As Eva stepped up onto the seawall to move toward the massive ship, she stopped to slip her hand into her father's flannel shirt pocket, the one above his heart.

He wanted to pull away when he saw the distant look in her eyes, but something held him immobile. Perhaps the knowledge that Eva was leaving, that it might be the last time she touched him with affection.

"I see a boy with a dog," she said quietly. "A dog he

found when he was eight, lost in the hills of a distant island. The dog became his companion and only friend, in work and play.

"But the dog was wild and followed his instincts freely. He gave the neighbors and their animals no peace. Once he drove some sheep over the cliff, and the outcry was huge and unrelenting. The dog must be killed.

"The boy fought his father when he heard, and begged for permission to take the animal back to the wild hills on the wild island where he had first found him. Back to the braes and moors and lochs where the dog ran free, frolicking and barking in bliss. He waited for his master, but the boy turned away. The dog watched sadly for a moment, then shook himself and leapt about with joy and abandon. There would be no more fences.

"The boy returned home, silent and withdrawn. No one ever knew how much he loved that dog. No one ever knew that to set it free broke his heart, for he showed his heart to no one.

"But I know, Dad. I *do* know." Eva blinked, the fog cleared and she was staring into Samuel's brown eyes. It was the first time she had actually *felt*, through his heart, his love for her. It stunned her with its power. She did not touch Agnes's tightly zipped pockets. Eva was too shaken, and her mother too fragile.

Samuel looked away, lifting Eva's hand from his pocket. He stared at the blunt, sun-browned fingers and thin fingernails. The hand was not particularly distinctive. It was just his daughter's hand. His throat felt dry and he could not speak, as he'd been unable to speak while he watched his dog run free in ecstasy, and knew he'd lost a friend forever.

Eva swallowed, covered her father's hands with hers, then drew them gently away. Kissing her mother lightly, afraid both might shatter at a word, she turned to go before all three lost their composure and their conviction that this was right, or at least inevitable.

10

"FIRST TRIP TO THE MAINLAND?" A COMFORTABLY PLUMP LADY in a heavy mac asked kindly. A few damp blond curls clung to her face beneath her rain hat, and her round cheeks were red with cold. Her blue eyes were full of solicitude for the young girl gazing into the distance, hands trembling slightly.

Eva nodded. "My very first." She stood at the foremost rail of the ferry, staring at a panorama blurred by rain. She loved being on the deck of the huge ferries with the sigh of the wind and the sea mist on her face. Even the rain felt pleasant, invigorating. She would not have minded riding forever on these ships that followed invisible paths in the ocean, passed between lush green and stark rocky islands carved by the wind from black stone and silt. She felt completely free, unfettered by past or future, with the sea surging in endless variations from gray to green to brilliant turquoise. The world opened around her and anything was possible when she leaned on the wet rail and absorbed every sight, every sound, every fascinating song of nature.

She could not help but respond to those songs with boisterous rhythms that made her heart beat in excitement. She knew, in the hours when she stood alone on the decks of one ferry after another, that she had been right to come. The ecstatic voice inside told her so, drowned out her confused and wistful thoughts of what she had left behind. She watched a gull spiral and dip, rise gracefully on the wind, and was filled with hope and expectation.

She had not realized Glasgow was so far from home, so difficult to get to, with confusing schedules and the circuitous course of the huge, purring boats. She had felt lost and inadequate more than once on this trip, but the feeling passed when she found herself a place on deck. Her thoughts were calmed and ordered by the regular lap and splash of the sea, larger and more powerful than the unquiet pool of her uncertainty.

"That's Ardrossan up ahead," the friendly woman said, pointing through the rain at an indistinct shoreline. " 'Tis almost over now."

Eva smiled anxiously. This woman seemed to sense the fear beneath her anticipation, the fear Eva herself was trying to ignore. "You're very kind," the girl said softly. "Thank you."

"That's all right, then," the woman replied, plump cheeks curving in a reassuring smile. "You remind me of my oldest girl when she went off to meet the boyfriend she'd not seen for two years. So nervous and excited she was. But it turned out all right in the end." Her voice was tender with memory. "Like as not it'll be the same for you."

"Will it?" Eva clutched the rail and stared at the veiled coast of Scotland. Whatever possibilities lay ahead would become truly possible only after she dealt with her disturbing and mysterious past. Eilidh Stanley would meet her at Ardrossan. The thought made her feel ill. She was getting ever closer to the stranger Celia Ward had chosen as her messenger.

Who was Eilidh Stanley? What was she like? Cold and angry at the girl who would come searching for her past? Tired of the burden Celia had placed on her shoulders eighteen years ago? Frightened of the responsibility, wary of her own life being disrupted? Or was she a saint who took on others' problems and found her strength in solving them? Could she solve them? And why should she have to? Because Eva's mother had decided that it should be so.

Perhaps this wasn't Celia's fault at all. Perhaps it was Eva's. Her mother had given her a new chance, hadn't she? Agnes and Samuel had done everything in their power to give her a good home, a family, a well of strength to sustain her. Perhaps, like her mother, she had been too weak to accept that gift, to let them make their world the only one she needed. She had always wanted more. She knew now, in her soul, that there was more to have. But was it worth the cost?

Eva threw back her head, hair misted with rain, and it seemed to her that her heart grew still and only her mind raced on to somewhere she could neither imagine nor avoid.

Eilidh Stanley stood beside her blue mini and watched the passengers disembark from the Isle of Arran ferry. She knew Eva at once, partly because of her age, partly because of her chestnut hair. She resembled Celia slightly, though even in her weariness, she carried herself with more assurance than her mother had. Eilidh ran a hand absently over her disheveled hair.

She was afraid of the girl, she realized. She wanted very much for Celia's daughter to like her. How odd. Perhaps this was a mistake. She should never have agreed to Celia's plan. But it had meant so much to her friend. So very much.

Since she had received Eva's cables, Eilidh had become melancholy, had begun to miss Celia all over again. She was, she had admitted in disgust, terribly lonely. And hoping Eva Crawford could fill that loneliness. Which was hardly fair to the girl, whose life already had been turned upside down.

"Come on, old girl, try to get hold of yourself." Oblivious of the burst of rain that soaked her hair and clothes where her mac had fallen open, Eilidh moved toward Eva, hand outstretched. "I'm Eilidh Stanley," she said.

Eva looked up from the shelter of her rain hood at a face full of character, at black eyes glinting with many colors. "I'm Eva Crawford, Miss Stanley." She couldn't help staring in fascination at the earrings dangling from Eilidh's pierced ears. The earrings did not match, and appeared to be—

"Fish bones," Eilidh said, noticing the direction of Eva's gaze, "along with some pieces of lapis and a fabulous purple-and-blue marble. No one else has a pair like them. I'm ashamed to say I'm inordinately proud of the fact. By the by, whatever you do, don't call me Miss Stanley; it's almost as bad as ma'am. Makes me feel old. No doubt you consider forty-six to be ancient in any case, but I don't feel old and refuse to *be* old until I do. I'm Eilidh, and that's that."

Eva forced herself to look away from the swaying earrings. "Eilidh, then. I hope you don't mind that I've come like this."

"Not a bit of it," Eilidh said briskly. "Been looking forward to your visit, actually. My mini's just there. No point in standing talking in the rain. We'll be to Glasgow in no time. New motorways, you see. Everyone ends up there sooner or later."

As she started toward the small blue car, Eva looked about for Eilidh's umbrella. The rain here was heavier than on the water. Eilidh noticed and brushed at the air dismissively. "Can't stand umbrellas. By the time you get into or out of the car, you're either soaked through or you've poked out your eye. And what good does it do when the rain blows horizontally, I'd like to know? Lot of trouble for nothing, if you ask me. Never minded my hair getting wet. It dries, after all."

Surprised by the length and vigor of her speech, Eva examined the woman curiously. Eilidh Stanley was no more than five feet eight inches, and while she was not slender, she was not overweight, yet she seemed to take up a great deal of space, perhaps because she waved her arms as she talked, her face alight with every feeling that flitted through. Her sodden hair was dark, held up haphazardly by a silver barrette stuck through with a tooled silver stick.

She was wearing a loose bright turquoise caftan that was soaked, since she had not buttoned her raincoat. She saw Eva staring and grinned unself-consciously. "The barrette's Chinese. A present from Celia. As for this"—she waved a hand dramatically to indicate the caftan—"I gave up designers long ago. My hips are too large, you see, so there's no sense in trying skin-tight trousers. When I realized they wouldn't be going away—the hips and thighs that I've had since I was thirteen—I decided I'd rather be comfortable and out of date than uncomfortable for the sake of fashion. Changes weekly anyway. I pretty much stick to clothes that like my body, or vice versa."

A woman in a sleek business suit passed, her expensive raincoat artfully folded back to reveal a tasteful brooch and creamy silk blouse. She sniffed at Eilidh in disapproval before looking away pointedly.

Eva stiffened, but Eilidh laughed. "Don't worry your head about it. Happens all the time. Women like her think I'm eccentric. I can practically feel them rolling their eyes." She flung back her head to roll her own eyes theatrically. "I don't mind what they think. I enjoy being odd. I rather cultivate it, actually. What's the fun in being normal, after all? That would be ever so dull. I live in morbid fear of being boring, and do my best to avoid it, even if it shocks people sometimes."

Eva had often longed to be normal, so she might find a little peace, a cessation of pain and confusion. "Do you really think it would be dull? If so, you're awfully brave to believe that."

They reached the car, and Eilidh waited until they were seated and belted in to reply. As she pulled into the street that led to the motorway, she glanced at Eva. "Funny you should say that. I've been told more than once that I'm brave to dress like this, and think like I do and talk like I do, and still go out in public." She peered over the steering wheel and merged into the traffic heading toward Glasgow. "I'm not actually brave at all. I always thought it a bit arrogant and selfish to indulge my whims as they strike me."

The smell of wet clothing and upholstery permeated the car as rain streamed down the windows. Eva frowned, intrigued by the wide motorway and its many offshoots. The island only had one two-lane road, and it ended in churned-up mud at the edge of a bog. She glanced surreptitiously at Eilidh, suddenly wary. She wondered if this woman talked about herself to avoid the painful subject of Celia Ward.

"I should tell you about myself, since you probably haven't a clue what I'm like," Eilidh said carefully, as if repeating a prepared speech. "I'm a frustrated artist, I'm afraid, just like all the rest. A potter, actually. Though I'm working for the moment at an art gallery in a trendy little street in Glasgow in order to pay the greengrocer. They let me use the studio in back to throw my pots and vases and things I've not yet attempted to call by name. Every now and then the gallery sells a piece of my work. Just often enough to keep me from giving up hope, which might be the kinder thing in the long term."

She laughed and added, "I might be in quite a spot if my father hadn't left me a cozy little house near Glasgow Green. But as it is, I'm snug and I don't go hungry and I get to indulge my art. So it's all quite lovely and comfortable."

Sighing, she said, "I'm babbling, I'm afraid. Sorry, I always babble when I'm uncomfortable."

Eva turned sharply. "Why are you uncomfortable? You don't have to do this, you know, not if Celia Ward forced you into it."

Eilidh noticed Eva used her mother's full name, and not without a touch of scorn. "I'm uncomfortable for several reasons, I suppose. I've been waiting for this for many years, wondering what would happen, if you'd come at all, what you'd be like." She paused but kept her eyes fixed on the motorway; she did not want to meet Eva's disconcerting gaze just now.

"But your expression makes me most uncomfortable. I never for a moment thought you'd be so obviously devastated."

Eva gasped, no longer amused by Eilidh's honesty.

"I can see it in your eyes, your lips, your pale skin, even in the way you move." When the girl remained rigidly silent, Eilidh continued doggedly. "Most people have a shield to protect themselves from emotions like the ones you must be feeling. Or they know how to put up a screen to hide their pain from others. But not you. It breaks my heart to look at you, Eva Crawford."

Eva clenched her hands in her lap, aware of her damp trousers and drenched mac, wishing she could disappear. "I didn't intend it should break your heart," she said. "I'd really rather it didn't."

"Safer that way, is it?"

Eva closed her eyes. She felt ill, as if the car were filled with a threat she could smell, like sulfur. "My parents . . ." She paused, forced herself to continue, "My parents didn't go about talking of their emotions, and neither do I."

Eilidh took her left hand from the clutch and briefly covered Eva's clenched fists. "You don't have to. As I said, your face speaks for you. I understand."

"How can you? How can you possibly know what it's like to be eaten up by feelings I can't begin to fathom?" Eva had not meant to speak, but the words came of their own accord. She didn't need to see a sunset to feel the old terror of the future; for her, darkness was falling from the inside out.

"Because Celia told me." Eilidh watched, transfixed, as thoughts crossed Eva's face like shadows. The inflection of the girl's speech, the raw pain edging her voice, was achingly familiar. How like Celia she was, and yet, how different.

Eva turned, drawn by Eilidh's intent gaze. She was afraid. Yet Eilidh's empathy enticed her, offered a cessation of the tumult inside. "Why did my mother send me to you?"

"Celia was my friend, that's why."

Was it really as simple as that? Eva found it difficult to believe. "You cared about her that much?"

Eilidh heard the disbelief quite clearly, and worse, the cynicism. She tried to quell her anger and understand what this girl must have gone through in the last few weeks. "Yes, I cared for her that much." For the first time, she sounded uncertain, defiant, and the glints of color faded from her eyes.

Eva felt chilled, suddenly, so cold that she was rigid.

"What have they told you?" Eilidh asked gently. "Did they try to make you hate your mother?"

Eva wanted to turn away, but there was nowhere to go. "They didn't have to try. They only told the truth. I was safe on the island and happy. She's ruined everything, don't you see that?"

Overwhelmed by compassion for this child who knew so little and cared so much, Eilidh blinked away tears. "Funnily enough, I do see. I suppose the announcement of Celia's existence was enough to cause the earth to evaporate under your feet. I know it all seems like Celia's fault." She chewed her lip, brow furrowed. "I'm not very wise, but I can tell you this. Celia loved you with a kind of desperate love I hope you never have to feel. You filled a hole in the darkness that haunted her. You cast a light that touched and transformed her, for a little."

Eva could not listen. This was harder than feeling Agnes and Samuel's pain and remorse, though Celia was a stranger who had been dead for years. It was all too much, coming at her too fast. She began to shake and her teeth to chatter.

Eilidh pulled up in front of a tall, narrow house on a pleasant street of stone houses with wooden porches and steeply sloped front gardens. "We're home, my dear. No need to think about this now. There'll be plenty of time to talk later. You're soaking, and you need dry clothes, a fire and some tea to warm you." She touched the girl's hand. "My God, you're cold."

They got out of the mini and hefted Eva's bags up the front steps and into a cheerful hall. "Your room's at the top of the stairs to the right. You change while I stoke the fire and brew up. Then you can be comfortable while you get warm. And Eva . . ."

She was halfway up the stairs but stopped to look cautiously over her shoulder.

"We'll go slower from now on," Eilidh promised. "Better for both of us. You need time to adjust, slowly, as Celia wanted."

Eva frowned. She was here because Celia Ward had decreed it, and she would learn what she needed to know, no matter the cost to her peace of mind. No matter that despite the cheerful wallpaper on either side as she trailed up the stairs, she felt the darkness hovering and growing.

11

EILIDH HAD THOUGHTFULLY LEFT THE ELECTRIC HEATER ON, so the room was warm. Eva found the bath down the hall, changed into clean, dry clothes, and discovered her hostess had also left a hair dryer on the dresser. As she blew her short, curly hair dry, she glanced around the room. A four-poster bed with its pale yellow duvet over a down quilt and buttercup ruffled skirt was invitingly ordinary, as were the yellow flowered chintz curtains. The rug was a vivid design of flowers in shades of russet to rich gold to a yellow so pale it reminded Eva of fragile insect wings. The tall book-case, filled haphazardly with books of all ages, sizes, and subjects, was topped with odd and interesting objects—a charcoal sketch without a frame, some pitted and brightly colored rocks, a graceful sculpture of a dancer.

None of the pieces on the vanity matched. There was an ivory comb, a tooled silver mirror, a hairbrush of smooth teak. Strewn across the bed was a mound of pillows in rainbow colors. Eva smiled to herself. She liked it, despite her jittery nerves, which she was trying, unsuccessfully, to ignore.

She felt the danger in this comfortable house, this woman Eilidh with the open, honest face. Or so it seemed. She must take care not to give her trust too easily. She'd done that before, to her regret. Celia herself had taught her daughter not to trust anyone entirely, not even Samuel, Agnes or Daniel. She'd be a fool to believe in this eccentric woman who had been Celia Ward's friend. Eva had learned the lesson once and would not forget it soon. She would draw back from Eilidh Stanley. She would listen and wait and watch, but that was all.

Fingers braided together at her back, she left the cozy disorder of the bedroom and the grim disquiet of her thoughts.

She paused at a small table in the hallway. On the yellowed lace doily stood a beautiful glass frame, and within the frame, Celia Ward's face. Eva recognized the pallid, translucent skin, pale, shoulder-length hair and wide gray eyes from her dream. She knew the softly molded cheekbones, the delicate lips in their melancholy smile. Chills rose along her arms and down the back of her neck. She had never seen a picture of Celia before, yet in her nightmare, she had seen the world through her mother's eyes—a woman she had not known existed until three weeks ago. How was it possible? And why?

Pensively, she made her way down to the dining room, where a teapot steamed and plates were laid out, along with small meat pies and tomato-and-cheese sandwiches.

Eva was staring at the fascinating collection of furniture and objects that filled the room—masks and an antique milking stool, a copper milk can, its handles bent and rusted. The cloth on the heavy oak table was an Indian print bedspread. The curtains too were Indian prints and had been pulled back to reveal patches of color through the rain. There were several tall windows that gave glimpses of the green behind the houses across the way. With the fire crackling warmly, the room was bright and cheerful.

Eva paused before a pedestal with two smooth rocks standing on end. They were highly polished, one larger, one small. Many inlaid colors reflected one another in the shiny surfaces. The backs and bottoms were carved with Celtic symbols.

She touched the stone in her pocket and remembered finding it with Xena on the way to the *ceilidh*. She had carried it ever since. She smiled. That must make it a pocket stone.

Resolutely, she turned her attention back to Eilidh's fascinating stones. With great care, she picked up the small one to find it was hollow, ceramic.

"That's art, you know." Eilidh's voice surprised Eva, and

she cradled the many-colored stone to keep from dropping it. "Lots of people call me daft for keeping rocks about on pedestals. But I suspect you see something more, like I did."

She put a basket of hot scones on the table. "Feeling better, are you?" Eilidh looked closely and saw that though she was not typically beautiful, Eva's face was arresting, especially with her gray-ringed green eyes and expressive mouth. Her chestnut hair framed delicate features made to seem stronger, more defined, by the color burned into them by the sun. "You certainly look well."

Eva swallowed. "I'm fine, thank you. And you?"

Eilidh raised an eyebrow. "Are you now?" She drew out a chair for Eva, who sat while Eilidh settled at the head of the table and poured out steaming tea. "As for me, I'm positively terrified, and I feel very old, like I might sit down and weep at any moment."

When Eva blinked at her in disbelief, Eilidh forced a smile. Now that her hair was dry, strands of different lengths had come loose from the silver barrette. The dark color hinted at red and gold and silver without being any of them. She had changed to a warm terry robe, yet did not seem comfortable.

Eilidh took a scone and stared at Eva over it. "You should know that I never learned how to lie. When people ask how I am, I tell the truth, good or bad, whether they want to hear it or not. They've asked a question, after all. They deserve an honest answer. But lots of people don't really want to know if you're depressed or in pain. Though not as many of those in Glasgow as elsewhere. One thing about people in this city, they do talk to one another.

"Still, there are those who're uncomfortable with the truth, and they simply stop asking." She shrugged. "At least if they continue, you know they really care and want to hear the answer." She rested her head on one hand. "One way of telling who your friends are, though that's not why I do it. It seems such a waste of time to ask a personal question if you don't want to know the answer."

Contemplating her guest intently, Eilidh added, "So, let's try again. How are you feeling?"

Eva was dazed and threatened by Eilidh's honesty. She struggled over her answer, remembering her vow to keep herself distant and safe. "I'm quite curious about why I'm here. I want to know everything. That's what I came for. Tell me about my mother, please." Eva did not add that she wanted nothing more than to be back in the kitchen with Agnes by the stove, eating bannocks and crowdie and talking of unimportant things.

Eilidh swirled the tea in her cup. "I can tell you the facts. Those are easy, because neither you nor I had to live them. Celia Ward grew up in Glen Affric, an isolated spot in the northern Highlands between Skye and Loch Ness. Her mother wanted her to use her own name, Rose, but Celia chose instead to use her father's. She never told me why. She said the glen was very beautiful but too wild. She wasn't happy there. She wanted more. I gather her family was not well off. So when she was old enough, she came to the city, looking for something better."

Eva shivered, though the room was warm. Had she not thought the same about Eadar Island? That she loved it; it was beautiful; but it was not enough for her?

Eilidh did not notice Eva's distress. She was determined to get through this as quickly as possible. It hurt her to remember. "It wasn't very long before she married a banker, Findlay Denholm. He was older, established, wealthy. She thought it was what she wanted."

Again Eva felt a jolt of recognition. Daniel was a banker, just like her father. Her father. She realized that she'd thought very little of the man he might be. All her energy and anger had been for Celia. She bit her lip and put her teacup down. "You didn't like Findlay Denholm."

Eilidh considered carefully before she answered. "I thought he wasn't right for Celia, but she was determined to have a man like him. Celia wasn't really any happier with Findlay than she had been in the glen. Perhaps less so." Her eyes had a cast on them, and her voice grew quiet as she drifted back.

"Why wasn't she happy? What happened then?" Eva demanded impatiently. She was finally hearing facts, not just impressions, and she desperately needed more. She needed her mother to be whole and real, not a shadow in her best friend's eyes.

Eilidh held up a cautionary hand. "In time you'll know everything, but not just yet. You're very fragile right now, Eva, very vulnerable. You don't want to break under the weight of too much knowledge all at once."

"Why are you being so mysterious? Why can't you just tell me what happened?" Eva wanted very much to trust Eilidh. Too much, perhaps. Eilidh was human like everyone else, and after all, she was Celia's friend, not Eva's.

"It's really Celia's place to tell you that." The woman's eyes were black without a trace of color. Her voice was low and raw.

"Celia's dead," Eva said in a voice so hard it shocked her. "Does it matter what she wanted?"

Somehow Eilidh managed to hide her anger. "It mattered a great deal to her that I do things the way she asked."

"What made her think she was a god with the power to order lives about after she'd gone? What gave her the ri ht?"

Eilidh shook her head sadly. "The only right I can name is the right of a mother's blood and her love, and I know that's not enough for you. She said she planned this for your sake, to protect you."

"That's exactly what my parents said."

Sighing, Eilidh took Eva's hand and rested in on the table-top with her own. "I suspect, as do you, that it was as much for Celia's sake as yours. Planning your journey through her past made her feel she could take control again, that she could make order out of chaos."

"What chaos?" Eva's voice was dangerously quiet.

Eilidh met the girl's eyes directly. "The chaos of her own life and sorrow. She wanted to give it sense and structure by making a list to leave behind."

Eva did not recognize the pathos in that wish, the hope-lessness. "Didn't her husband have anything to say about it?"

Eilidh sat back, tried to hide her agitation. "Her husband. No, he didn't. She didn't even ask him."

"Then *I* shall ask him!" Eva declared. "I shall go tomorrow and tell him everything."

Leaning forward, Eilidh warned, "I don't think that would be wise. They were separated by then, you see, and I don't think your reception would be"—she hesitated—"warm or even kind. You need kindness now; I can see it in your eyes. Please, I'm asking you not to go see Findlay Denholm, at least not until you've learned more of your mother's story."

On a draft of cold air, Agnes's words came back to her: *I'm not certain she knew who your father was. When Samuel asked she got distraught and cried so high and queer like, 'Eva is my child. Mine alone.'* Eva shivered. She had been cold a great deal of late. Her gaze slid away from Eilidh's. "I won't go see my father just yet." She was afraid of what she'd find, but wouldn't admit it aloud. "But things might change. . . ." She left the thought unfinished, the implication clear.

"Things will change, sure as you live and breathe, my child. There's just one more thing. You should know that Celia spent the last months of her life here, died here in fact. She told me she wanted to be here—" Her voice broke and her eyes filled. "With me. And I agreed." By sheer force of will, she made herself go on. "I always thought it was rather a precious gift Celia gave me by trusting me so much."

Eilidh rose and began to tidy up. She was shaken and needed the mindless chore to distract her. For several minutes she was busily silent and Eva did not intrude.

"Can we leave it for now?" Eilidh asked at last. "It's been a rather long and tiring day for both of us."

Eva nodded reluctantly. "But tomorrow—"

"Tomorrow I'll show you Celia's legacy and you can begin making discoveries on your own. That I promise most fervently."

"All right then. I am rather tired." In fact, Eva ached all over, and not just in her muscles and bones. She stared at the rain-streaked windows regretfully. She felt caught and closed in.

She missed the heaths and lochs, the cliffs and ocean, where the air smelled of salt and kelp and moss, and the darkness faded into the turbulent violence of the sea. She had not seen much through the window of the mini on the drive home from the ferry, but she remembered tall buildings, twisting streets and endless rows of shops and houses. Where could she go here to escape herself? Where could the fresh wind reach her to blow the woven webs away and make her think clearly again?

Where could she rediscover the tranquility of a crumbling broch on an abandoned cliff top? Eva put her head in her hands. A few hours ago, on the ferry, she had wanted exhilaration, stimulation. Now she wanted only peace and quietude. "I suppose I'll never be satisfied," she muttered.

"Perhaps not," Eilidh surprised her by responding. "But that's not altogether a bad thing." Her eyes were dry and her hands steady. She had conquered her memories for the moment. "Satisfaction, contentment, like normalcy, become dull and confining after awhile, especially for a complex spirit like yours."

Eva raised her head enough to look wary, uncertain.

Pursing her lips, Eilidh said, "You don't want to hear lies or half-truths or even intimations. You want to know, to understand." She smiled unexpectedly. "I'd have to be made of stone not to have noticed that much. And I pride myself on being made of something much more pliable and sensitive than stone. Just as *you* are." She chuckled. "The thing is, elastic bands are too often stretched to the breaking point, which is by no means a comfortable feeling. Still, I'd choose it over being safe and numb any day. Wouldn't you?"

Eva hesitated. She couldn't think straight, couldn't remember what she'd promised herself an hour since. "Yes." She rubbed her temples with two fingers. "The thing is, if the elastic breaks altogether . . ."

"Yes, well, one likes to avoid that, certainly. But there *are* ways to avoid that final snap. Walking briskly when one is stretched too tight, for example. Across the way is Glasgow Green. Oldest public park in the world. You can walk for a long time among the trees and grassy slopes, and directly across is the River Clyde. There's a river walk, if you feel the need to get some air. I walk every day, myself. Wouldn't do you much good in this rain, but tomorrow might be fair."

Eva smiled in relief. "Tomorrow," she repeated, releasing her breath in a sigh of relief. She would think about walking, discovering the city. She would not think about Celia Ward. It was too difficult just now, too painful. Eilidh was right; she was much too fragile and might just shatter.

12

EVA AWOKE WITH MUSIC IN HER HEAD THAT MOVED THROUGH her body with the pulse of her blood. It was the song of ancient harps and flutes and drums, Celtic music that made her homesickness a sharp pang of longing. She was certain Eilidh must have turned on the stereo, but when she dressed quickly in a blue jersey and trousers and slipped out into the hall, she found the house very still. She had heard Eilidh moving about, singing quietly to herself until late the night before. Apparently, she was not yet up this morning.

Too restless to sit still until her hostess awakened, Eva slipped on her windbreaker and went outside. Eilidh had been right. The morning was fair, the clouds blown into curious white shapes with a bright blue sky for a backdrop. The rain had washed everything clean, and the air smelled fresh and invigorating. Eva was surprised. She had expected a film of grit over everything in an industrial city like Glasgow.

With the harps and flutes still singing in her head, she

crossed to Glasgow Green. She craved trees and grass and water, not stone and brick and asphalt. The music led her, and she followed willingly, letting her instincts take over.

It was too early for many people to be about, an hour when Eadar Island was somnolent and tranquil. Eva sensed that Glasgow was *not* sleeping, despite the relative quiet. Resting, perhaps, but there was a vibration of life behind the temporary lack of action. Eva had been sensitive to the feelings of the different places on the island. She was surprised that she felt the city too. Surprised that the old Celtic music seemed in harmony with her surroundings, which hummed with their own suppressed energy and vitality.

Yesterday she had had an impression of many motorways, modern buildings, Victorian stone spires and towers. Today, as she crossed the green toward Victoria Bridge and the River Clyde, Eva felt the presence of ocean and river, of the hills she could not see, of the vast green bowl in which the city had been built. She felt the flow of the land beneath the buildings. The songs in her blood responded to that call.

She passed groves of trees, large sweeps of grass, then came to the river, where she glanced at abandoned docks, leaned on the railing of a bridge, and stared into the gray-green water. The music swelled, retreated, tingled along her fingertips.

She looked up in surprise when another early riser greeted her pleasantly. He was not the first. She did not know what she had expected of Glasgow, but it hadn't been cordiality from perfect strangers.

Finally, Eva turned back toward Eilidh's, the smell of the sea clinging about her, the harps and flutes keeping pace with each step. She felt better for the exertion.

She met Eilidh in the front hall, preparing to go out for her own walk. Eva busied herself removing her windbreaker and running shoes. The house was warm, inviting; she wanted to feel the warmth all the way to her feet.

"I see you heard my music last night." At Eva's astonished expression, Eilidh said, "You were humming it, you know, just now. And very pleasant it was. Too much going on around here yesterday, too much tumult, so I put on some music to soothe myself. Those harps always inspire and calm me both. I don't know why. I put it on as soon as I got up today, as well. It was too quiet in here. I needed music."

Eva realized for the first time that the actual music was spilling from the living room. She cocked her head to listen. She didn't just hear that music, but felt it as she felt the land and waters. She smiled.

Eilidh nodded toward the city beyond the closed door. "Not as bad as you thought, I'll wager. But then again, Glasgow will never be a fairy island, all legends to the contrary." She told Eva how Glaswegians said the words *glas cau*, from which their city's name was derived, meant "dear green place." "Personally," Eilidh continued, grinning, "I'm more inclined to believe it means greyhound, a nickname of our patron saint Mungo. There are also those who say it means 'dear stream.'

"But you don't care about all that. You want to see the house, no doubt, and your mother's things. Feel free to roam as you like and explore all the rooms. I don't bother to hide much and you can touch everything."

Eva nodded reluctantly. She wanted to know, she told herself firmly. Why else had she come here? But a sense of foreboding made her shiver inwardly.

"You might want to eat first," Eilidh continued. "I've left some things in the kitchen—porridge and kippers and the like. Help yourself. After that, if I were you, I'd work my way up to the small bedroom on the second floor. That was Celia's."

The bells of the cathedral rang out, joined at once by bells from the other churches, until the city reverberated with the forceful sound.

Eilidh rubbed her forehead, ludicrously concerned. "I'd forgotten altogether that it's Sunday. Do you go to kirk? We've all kinds here in Glasgow. I suppose you're New Church, being from the islands."

Eva considered for a moment. "I went every Sunday with my parents, but didn't quite feel I belonged there. I preferred the cliff tops and the voice of the sea."

"How lovely. Then perhaps you'll like my own brand of religion—my Celtic music. It makes me feel bound to something old and precious."

Eilidh did not give Eva time to respond. She waved and announced emphatically, "Well, I'm off to be virtuous. Nothing like a brisk walk around the green to get the blood flowing."

Only then did Eva notice what Eilidh was wearing. She had on an emerald green jogging suit and white running shoes; her hair was haphazardly drawn back with a vivid red, green and blue scarf. Her socks were brilliant orange. As she leapt down the stairs to the sidewalk, she made a stark contrast to the families dressed for church, who eyed her surreptitiously. She glanced back at Eva and called, "What's the point of life without a little risk, a little excitement?"

Eva laughed, and the sound was strange to her. It had been a long time. And she'd forgotten her determination to remain unmoved by this amusing, uncommon woman. Celia's dearest friend.

With a lingering frown, Eva ate a quick breakfast and started her private tour of the house. She found many things that caught her attention; a huge shell, open like a hand, soft ivory and coral, which she discovered was also ceramic, like the stones she'd found earlier. Perhaps Eilidh had made it herself. She paused for a long time in front of a large dried golden-yellow gourd; it had character, like so many of the things in this house.

In the living room, the furniture was practical and modern, a sectional sofa in soft brown with a huge ottoman and tapestry pillows. The end tables were plain oak, and the light came from large windows and a simple chandelier overhead. In the corner was an antique desk, which Eilidh used as a china cabinet and treasure trove. Besides lovely dishes, it was full of graceful glasses, cloisonné ducks and small carved wooden figures.

Eva liked the house more and more—this house Celia had chosen as her last refuge. Eva and her mother were not as much strangers as she had supposed. They had apparently shared many feelings. The thought frightened her. She had so much to learn.

The music of harps followed her everywhere, tranquil and inspiring, as Eilidh had promised. On the landing, she paused at a tall window with a windowseat. Eva stared at the buildings rising from narrow streets, at the shadows of clouds that raced across brick and stone and clear glass windows, changing the view by the moment. The dancing shadows and light enchanted her.

Across the landing hung a lovely painting, though she couldn't quite make out what it was. There was a large mass in the middle, some antique sepia writing scattered about, and the colors were all emeralds and azures and golds. After studying it for a while, Eva saw that it was a stylized map of Scotland, done by a talented artist, who had created with paint and canvas the feeling of Scotland, not just its shape, size and place names. She peered close until she located Glen Affric, just where Eilidh had said it would be, in the middle of one of the most verdant patches of green, indicating, Eva was sure, the wildness of the land there. She touched the words, Glen Affric, but they meant nothing to her.

Eventually, she reached the second floor, where she found the room Eilidh had described.

Her mother's room. It was stark, tiny and empty, compared to the rest of the colorful house. The single bed was neatly made with a pale blue chenille spread. There was a bureau, a small desk and an electric heater that probably had not been switched on in years. The room was so cold that Eva stood shivering, staring at the plain furniture that told her nothing about the woman who had owned it.

She noticed a cupboard door and opened it to discover Celia Ward's clothes still hanging in plastic bags. The dresses, blouses and trousers were as drab as the room—plain dark colors, or light gray and blue, but never any design, no scarves or lace or decoration.

In the far back of the cupboard, Eva discovered a multicolored jacket that captivated her, gave her hope and a renewed sense of excitement. The fabric was a patchwork of rich purples, reds, burgundies and blues. The jacket glowed like pressed and patterned jewels.

Eva reached out to lift the protective plastic and put her hands in the large square pockets, but at the last minute drew away, heart beating frantically. "You're being silly," she said aloud. Nevertheless, she closed the cupboard tight.

What are you so afraid of? she asked herself as she collapsed on the bed. She'd come here to learn about her mother, but was not yet ready to look inside Celia Ward's bright pockets. She was a coward after all. Eva was not here merely to discover what kind of woman her mother had been. She had a new purpose, and this one she could name. She had to discover who *she* was.

She sat for a long time, exhausted by the roller coaster of her own emotions. Eva put her elbows on her knees and rested her head in her hands. It was too heavy to hold up, and she was too tired to try.

The music from below changed slightly; a woman's haunting voice drifted on the notes of a poignant fiddle. Then Eilidh appeared in the doorway, flushed from her exercise and brilliant in her outfit of many colors. "So you've found it." Her voice was without inflection, an odd contrast to the sweet tragic voice that swirled at her feet.

"I found this room," Eva said, "but it isn't much."

Eilidh glanced sharply into a dark corner and an enigmatic expression crossed her face. "It isn't Celia, you mean."

"It doesn't tell me any more about her than I knew before."

For the first time, Eilidh seemed impatient. "But of course it does. You haven't looked properly."

"Why this room? Why this one, with the three other cheerful bedrooms in this house?"

"Precisely," Eilidh said cryptically. "Celia chose this room herself. It's what she wanted."

"But why?"

Leaning on the doorjamb for support, Celia's friend faced Eva's question without blinking. "I think she felt safe here. She had complete control, she said. Only the things she wanted and allowed could get in. But she couldn't close out her own thoughts, though she made a good go at it.

"Besides, this isn't all of her. It only tells part of the story. I think, in a way, that by choosing this austerity, she was punishing herself."

Eva stood, swaying and pallid. "For getting pregnant?"

Eilidh sighed. "No, never for that. For all the mistakes she'd made in her life."

Eva's thoughts spun dangerously, and she felt Eilidh catch her as she began to fall. They stood bracing each other, staring doubtfully, warily into one another's eyes.

Finally, Eva broke the heavy stillness. "Why were you friends, Celia and you? You seem so different."

Slowly, Eilidh released the girl, brushed her cheek with bent fingertips, and began to pace. "I suppose because most people were afraid of Celia's bundled-up desire and need and emotion and despair. But I wasn't afraid. I didn't shut her out in self-defense."

Why not? Eva wondered. "Did you like her?"

"Yes." Eilidh stopped, black eyes glinting with sparks of gray and amber. "Because she needed me. I have this desire to take care of people, you see. Not altogether a good thing, really. It's caused me a lot of frustration and pain over the years. I've had a devil of a time learning that other people's lives are none of my business. One woman told me so straight out. 'My problems are my own,' she said. 'If I want your help, I'm perfectly capable of asking for it.'"

She paused, fingers wound in her flyaway hair. "Celia asked. That's what first brought us together. But later I came to see what was behind the fear. Celia and I saw so much in each other that we recognized—and valued." She paused again. When she spoke, her voice was unnaturally hoarse. "I miss her. I didn't realize how much until you came."

Eva ached for Eilidh's grief but could not share it. She had left the safety and certainty of eighteen years for an amorphous, dark unknown, and she wanted to know why, to understand. "What did she hope to accomplish by bringing me here? What did she really want?"

"A little peace, I think. She wanted to die at peace with

herself. Don't hate her for that, Eva. She was so tired at the end. So very tired."

Eva shivered at the familiar feeling. She too was tired, weary to her soul, and all she wanted was a little rest, not just for her body, but for her heart.

Eilidh had had enough melancholy for one morning. She took a deep breath. "Your mother didn't ask you here capriciously or cruelly. She wasn't a cruel woman, whatever you may think. She wanted you to discover your true legacy, to find out where you came from, where *she* came from, who she was."

She went to the dark corner and turned on a lamp, revealing a large ebony Chinese chest. "I don't know exactly what's in here, only the few things Celia mentioned. It's belonged to your family for generations, and it holds their history. Celia told me it's been passed from mother to daughter since the eighteen hundreds."

Eva took a few awkward steps forward, as if she were just learning to walk. She stared at the beautiful chest, carved with winged dragons and other fantastic creatures, with Oriental symbols that glowed in the light of the single lamp. She did not know what she had expected, but it had not been this. She knew Eilidh was waiting for something, but she could not think what. She could not think at all. Her body had gone numb, as it had when she first learned of Celia Ward's existence.

After a silence filled by the sound of the wrenchingly lovely Gaelic song far away, Eilidh cleared her throat. "Celia wanted you to have this, because she wanted you to learn from her mistakes and the mistakes of your ancestors. She didn't want you to depend on others for your happiness, only yourself. Your mother never learned that lesson. She didn't believe she had a self to depend on. That's why she let others hurt her too much."

Eva opened her mouth, closed it, yearning to echo the haunting words of the music rising from below. "Why didn't she tell me herself? Why all this mystery? All this pain?"

Eilidh bowed her head. "I told you, she didn't trust herself. She thought she was weak and a fool besides, that others could raise you better, teach you better, tell you the truth better than she."

Eva tried to swallow, but her throat had closed tight. "I don't want others. I don't want any of this." She waved vaguely toward the chest.

Stiffening her spine, Eilidh said, "But this is the greatest gift of all. Celia wanted to pass to you the heritage her mother gave her. She said it belonged with you."

"*Why* me? Why?"

"You're the only child she ever had. There's only you, Eva."

She who is accountable for things unaccountable. I used to wonder how anyone could put a burden like that on a tiny, helpless baby. Samuel's words echoed eerily in Eva's head. She trembled at the enormity of what lay before her and behind. In that moment, she hated her mother more than ever. It was too much to ask. Too much.

Against her will, she knelt before the chest, keeping her hands folded tightly in her lap.

Eilidh touched her shoulder. "It's nothing to be frightened of, but something to treasure. It's history, Eva. Other worlds and other lives. You don't have to repeat it, or alter it, or even understand it. Just keep it. That's all."

Eva heard the quiver in her strong voice long after Eilidh had slipped from the room and closed the door. Her words seemed to hover in the air, along with the voice, still singing, heartbroken and beautiful, from below. Then the music changed, transformed itself to mist that swirled over Eva's legs and her folded hands, coiled its melody and richness around her kneeling body, bringing chills and flitting memories beyond her grasp.

After a while, she reached out gingerly to touch the lid of the chest. A shock of unnameable but violent emotion erupted, and she sat back, shaken. Then, urged on by the music, the harps and flutes with their fragile, curling notes, she fumbled with the difficult Chinese lock and key, raised the lid and peeked inside.

There were bundles of letters, bound leather journals, sheaves of loose paper, music, photographs and paintings.

So many things. So many lives. So many other worlds. But not the newer, crisper envelope she had expected, with her mother's spidery scrawl on the outside, spelling her own name. "Eva," she whispered to herself. "I'm Eva."

Carefully, she lifted out an old bound leather book and opened it to the first page, which read:

AILSA ROSE'S JOURNAL
Glen Affric, 1882

TO ENA:
Flame, hope, miracle

"Ena." Eva said the name aloud and wondered at its similarity to her own. What was it Eilidh had said? *Her mother wanted her to use her own family name, Rose, but Celia chose instead to use her father's.* Eva's grandmother's family name had been Rose, just like Ailsa's. Eva felt a flicker of excitement. Her grandmother. She had not known she had one until today. Both Agnes and Samuel's parents had been dead for so long she barely remembered them.

Hands trembling with anticipation, she turned the fragile pages of the journal, where the ink had faded to pale brown.

On the day we buried my father, we were lost and terrified and could not think what to do for tomorrow, let alone the rest of our lives. He changed us all too much, then left us to go on alone, bewildered and betrayed. Even Alanna, daughter of my heart and the strongest of us all, was brittle that day, broken.

Eva knew the feeling too well. It frightened her, sharing a stranger's desolation.

Woven into her thoughts, her cauterized feelings and burgeoning expectation, was the seductive thread of music, a pulse of the past. The music of memory beyond memory, memory beyond time, mystical and inexplicable.

In an instant, Eva's anger flared and burned itself to ashes. She put her hands on the chest and leaned heavily on the uneven surface, branding her palms with the intricate carvings of an artist long dead and forgotten.

She had always loved the past, felt bound to it and captive by it. But that had been the history of the land and her country, of Celts and Norsemen, Highlanders and Gaels, the heroic past of legend, song and ancient poem, the story of people she would never know, who would never know her. This chest held *her* past, *her* history. Her hope.

Hands shaking, she turned the pages of the journal, but this time, as she read, she could not stop, and did not wish to.

Part Two

Glen Affric

SCOTTISH HIGHLANDS

1882

1

"TAKE CARE, THERE MAY BE DANGEROUS CURRENTS IN THE river today." Mairi Rose stood in the doorway of her croft, framed by pale bells of honeysuckle reaching for the sunlight, and called out a warning to her granddaughter, Alanna. Mairi's Highland red hair streaked with gray was braided in a silvered copper crown around her head, but Alanna's flowed loose to her waist. While Mairi's eyes were shadowed from age and sorrow, Alanna's were violet and gleaming with vibrant expectation.

Mairi often wondered what her granddaughter was waiting for so eagerly, though she was grateful for Alanna's optimism and her deep, honest laugh. She was only twenty-two, and though she had known sorrow and loss, though she had lived the first nineteen years of her life in what Mairi thought of as the dark gloom of London, Alanna had not lost her faith in the kindness of the gods.

She looked particularly pretty in the pale green gown Mairi had made her. She wore the red Rose plaid tossed carelessly about her shoulders, and her feet were bare. She was perfectly at home among the daffodils and bluebells that brushed her ankles and the hem of her gown, anointing them with early morning dew. She carried a creel and a leather bag, yet seemed unencumbered and confident.

Alanna was eager to be on her way, to leave behind the dyeing and weaving, spinning and gardening that usually filled her days. For weeks the ferocity of the spring storms had held her captive inside, then the mud had made it difficult to walk through woods and over braes.

Now the rains had gone and the mud receded. Alanna was free; she intended to enjoy that freedom. She had packed a small dinner for later, and planned to spend the day roaming the glen, collecting roots, lichens and leaves for dyes and to mix with the healing herbs she had nurtured through the winter in their garden. More important than this small task, and more imperative, she would wander, remembering how it felt to dance among the wildflowers with the wind in her hair.

Alanna had been too long confined, and her heart beat with anticipation. Things would happen today. There were promises in the air. She could feel them like a teasing caress upon her cheek, quickly withdrawn, like a voice murmuring in her ear, not in words but in sweet, enigmatic wisps of song.

She smiled over her shoulder at her grandmother's warning. "I know the dangers of the river well, and would no' begin to fear them now."

Mairi smiled back, leaning against the warped door frame so the green leaves of the honeysuckle pricked her red plaid. "Don't be thinking you're wiser than the gods, Alannean. They might see it as a challenge, and they'd as soon be men with all their weaknesses as resist a challenge from a pretty lass."

"Don't be worryin' yourself." Alanna half turned so the sun was on her face. "I'll not be seduced into the depths of the Fairy Knoll. It holds no charm for me."

" 'Tis more like ye'll be seducin' the fairies up into the sunlight. Purity is the one thing they can no' resist. They yearn for it, begrudge it, try to tarnish it if they can."

"Well then, I'll be certain to leave them be, so they'll no' feel obliged to avenge their bitter gall against me. Besides"—Alanna grinned, her face childlike and innocent in the mist-softened sun—" 'tis only in the kindness of your eyes that I'm so pure. The fairies'll no doubt be knowin' the truth of it."

Mairi shaded her eyes with her hand, though the sun was at her back. "Aye, that they will, *mo-ghray*. That they will indeed."

She was puzzled by her response to Alanna's retreating laughter, which drifted back through hazel bushes, hawthorn, and new bracken, pure as the song of a thrush or a blackbird. Mairi was both excited and anxious. She hadn't felt this way in a long while. Perhaps it was because the birds were returning to the woods, tinted pale green with new growth among the darker green of Caledonian pines and Douglas firs.

In the past fifty-nine years, time and grief had transformed Mairi's spirit, though neither had embittered her heart. She had been given many blessings, the most precious of which was her daughter Ailsa, yet much of her life had been spent alone, in regret and loneliness. She had wondered, now and then, in the dark years of her isolation, if the cost for the gift of life was too high. But three years before, Alanna had chosen to stay in the glen when Ailsa left it for the second time. Since then, Mairi had abandoned regret and accepted the gift willingly.

She put her sun-browned, wrinkled hands to her cheeks and found them warm. She had not spoken an idle threat, she realized. There was something afoot in the glen today. Something extraordinary and dangerous and full of promise. Mairi smiled again, staring at the tangled hedges through a mist woven not of air and water, but the delicate web of her inner sight. She could not wait to see what supper would bring.

David Fraser alighted from the coach, left his baggage by the side of the muddy road, and entered the woods along the River Affric. He shook off the grime and the memory of Glasgow as oak and birch, hawthorn and pine enveloped him. He tilted his head, listening for the water, for the whisper of wind through the tall, swaying trees.

He was not disappointed. The woods were just as he remembered—pure, enticing, lovely. No man had dared to try to tame this wild tangle of lush greenery, these pagan voices that rose from river and loam and the wide vaulted sky. David was tired of men in search of power, tired of profit and loss, tall buildings and grim factories. He breathed in the misty air deeply, gratefully. Here was sunlight patterned on the brackened ground, a tang of trees and plants he could not name, the sound of animals moving lightly through pine needles and new spring leaves.

David looked up through the feathery spires of the giant spruce, through ivy-clad oaks and the dark green canopies of graceful birch. He could just see the shadowy hint of the mountains in the distance. He knew he had been right to leave his business and his burdens to come in search of the paradise he remembered from visits in his childhood. He refused to think about the city, the intrigues and exploitations he had witnessed and, on occasion, abetted. That part of his life was over. He intended to begin again.

"Are you mad? Has the rain gotten to you at last?" his father had demanded the day before David left Glasgow. "You can't just up and leave like this. We're busier than ever at the shipyard, and the export business has doubled. You can't take your little vacation now."

As always, Duncan Fraser had blustered, using his booming voice and considerable bulk to try to intimidate, protected by the familiar opulence of his own drawing room. David had not been impressed.

"I've told you, it's more than that. I've had enough of your shipyard, enough of all of this." David waved his arm to indicate the royal blue velvet draperies, the brocade sofas and Pembroke tables, the marble floor and vaulted ceiling carved with cherubs and painted with clouds woven with crowns of leaves. "I'm going."

The simplicity and determination in those last two words caught his father's attention. Duncan Fraser stopped, turned and faced his son, fingers perched uncomfortably in his waistcoat pockets. "You can't go. We need you. Is that what you want to hear? The company can't do without you. You're the only one the workers trust."

David stared in blank astonishment. "How would you know?" He was as surprised that his father would admit such a thing as he was that Duncan should have noticed.

Shrugging, his father looked away. "The foremen have told me. Besides, I've seen you at work. You talk to the men, listen to them, *hear* them. It makes them want to work harder for you. They're willing to tell you what they need."

"They'd tell you if you asked."

Duncan shook his head. "No. I've demanded and coerced for too many years. Tyranny is the only thing the men expect from me."

For the second time, David was shocked. He had never imagined that his father knew how pompous and heartless he was in the pursuit of profit.

Before he could think of a response, Duncan repeated, "They need you." He could admit the need of strangers, but never his own. "If you go, what happens to the men you leave behind? To men like Bran Guthrie?"

Guilt boiled over into fury, and David turned to smash his fist against striped silk wallpaper. The physical pain was better than his memories. Anything was better. "Don't speak his name to me." He bit back the words *you bastard* just before they exploded into the elegant room.

"You have to face it sometime," Duncan persisted, shamelessly prodding his son's open wound. He was not a man who gave in easily.

David did not want his father to see his rage; it made him vulnerable. That vulnerability was one reason he was determined to leave the city. He had to get away before the vision that burned within him was put out like a dying fire, leaving him blind.

David fought to silence the memory of that last bitter exchange, but it lingered, even here, many miles and days away. Fiercely, he turned his attention back to the woods. His boots were thick, fine leather, good protection from the moisture of ferns and wood sorrel, but he wished he did not have to wear them. Still, he knew the dangers of the rough terrain well enough to know he could not conquer them at once. He knew *himself* well enough not to try. He would have to take time to harden his soles to the Highland ground, brown his skin, white from years in the city, to accustom his body to physical strain, a little at a time. He would make himself part of this place; he had to.

With no clock to watch and no man to answer to, he meandered through the woods, coming out at last on a sloping moor dotted with bluebells and white starflowers. The sun was climbing, and as he moved through the springy turf and cotton grass that brushed his knees, the clouds shifted, letting light through to glisten on blade and blossom and leaf.

David stopped, enthralled by the beauty of the flower-flecked moor against the jagged mountains rising across the way. Powerful but immobile, except for the streams rushing silver down the steep sides, their grandeur could not be altered or diminished by sleight of hand or manipulation. He was struck by that strength, renewed by it, and felt a wild impulse to roll in the grass, celebrating this place and this moment.

"I have a right to be happy," he'd told his father's unrelenting back the last time David saw him.

Duncan Fraser had been surprised into turning, eyes wide with shock. "Why, in God's name? Do you think I'm happy? That anyone deserves to be? You *are* mad."

David felt a flash of pity for his father. How could he go on if he believed that? "You've got children, healthy grandchildren, at least three fortunes."

Duncan shrugged, his face closed and blank. "I've been lucky, certainly, and comfortable. But happy? What's that? It doesn't mean anything, don't you see? It's not real. Just something you imagine to keep from giving up. A self-indulgent fantasy." He paused, moved forward and forced his son to look at him. "Guthrie thought he could be happy, and look where it got him."

The rage came in a violent wave that shook David from head to toe. It was just like Duncan Fraser to throw his son's gravest misjudgment in his face. His father was a cruel man when it suited his purpose. But this time he would lose. "I'm going," David said, fists clenched so he would not strike. "I'd rather chase a fantasy than suffocate in your reality. It's too cold and ugly."

Once more, he fought to shut out those voices. He was here, in the glen, and Duncan Fraser was far behind him. David took several deep breaths and sat on a boulder. He could not remember the last time he had sat motionless, simply looking and enjoying everything around him. The sun moved higher, the billowing clouds drifted, raced, parted and concealed, trailing shadows on the land in a huge, untraceable pattern of dark and light. David thought he might not ever move again. In a place like this, he *could* be happy. The corruption could not follow him here; Glen Affric was too far and too wild. It was pure. David Fraser had not used that word in a long time, had forgotten what it meant. But here, he remembered.

"A place like this could make a man believe again," he said. In the grim embattled years in Glasgow, little by little, day by day and deal by deal, he had lost his faith in God. Such a being could not exist in a city so cold and gray, with so little beauty, so little heart. Sitting here, alone, in perfect silence, except for the hum of bumblebees and the swaying of branches in the breeze, he felt the void inside where his faith used to be. Insidiously and inevitably, Glasgow seemed to smother all that was good in men.

But now, just now, as he watched red deer graze in the distance while a woodmouse scampered by and a red squirrel chattered on the branch of an oak, the emptiness inside was not so hollow. Just now David wanted to believe, to absorb this feeling into himself and eclipse the bleakness, fill the void, reaffirm his hope. He wanted it more than he had wanted anything in his life before. He raised his head to meet the intermittent light of the sun through drifting clouds. It came to David Fraser then, quietly, that in his own way, and for the first time in many years, he was praying.

2

AFTER SHE LEFT THE CROFT SHE SHARED WITH HER GRAND-
mother, Alanna Sinclair went first to the Valley of the Dead,
where four cairns lay among a circle of standing stones and
steep rocky hillsides. As always, Alanna picked up four large
pebbles, placing one on each grave, stopping last before her
grandfather's. He had lain here for three years, while the
other graves were much older, yet his cairn was scattered
with stones of reverence and respect. There were black pebbles and gray ones, pieces of pink quartz and other colored
rocks, rubbed smooth by time and loving hands.

Alanna knelt and placed a dark red stone on Charles Kittridge's grave. Her hand lingered, seeking contact through
earth and peat and endless time, with the man she had
known so briefly and loved so dearly. "I miss ye, Grandfather," she murmured, never doubting that somehow he
would hear her and know that he was not forgotten.

She saw a spray of violets peeking from beneath a boulder
and smiled. She rarely felt sad when she visited the valley.
She found it peaceful to sit where others rarely came, in a
circle of stones that must have been a temple for Druids
long ago. Alanna felt the presence of those long-dead ancestors; it reassured her, as did the vague sense of Charles
Kittridge's spirit hovering nearby—a faint essence in the air,
a voice long silent echoing softly.

Her grandfather had asked to be buried here. "True," he
had said, "a kirkyard is quiet, lush, and restful. But this
place is old and powerful, a part of ancient mysteries and
beliefs. These"—he'd waved at the tall standing stones—
"are solid, unchanging, indestructible. They've stood like

this for hundreds, perhaps thousands, of years. I want to be part of that. I want to be safe."

Alanna had nodded in understanding.

With the memory of Charles Kittridge's voice in her head, she sat in the cool shadow of a wall of rock and took out the latest letter from her mother in London. Alanna had received the packet yesterday, but had slid it into her pocket for later. She wanted to wait and read it here, in the sunlight, her feet buried in the soft loam, connecting her to the earth her mother loved, so she could feel the pulse of life and history and magic in the rich dark soil.

Ailsa Rose Sinclair had written about Alanna's sister Cynthia's pregnancy, her wealthy but pompous husband, about her brother Colin's scrapes and escapades and his first courting ritual. Alanna's father was ill, but Ailsa was certain his strength of will and the healing herbs she had learned to administer as she grew up in the glen would make him well. Ailsa wrote of the friends her daughter had left behind, but Alanna did not miss them. Only Ailsa's voice, echoing from each word on the creased and blotted paper, made her ache.

Remember that I think of you always, that I sing to you and listen for an answer in your own sweet voice. And sometimes, in my dreams, I hear that answer. I miss you in my spirit, Alanna, not just in my heart, but would not have you here again. For I know that you are happy. 'Tis a rare thing, such happiness. Do not take it for granted.

Take care, my daughter. Cherish that which is most yourself.

Ailsa

Carefully, Alanna folded the letter. If only her mother could come back to Glen Affric. If only Alanna's father did not need his wife so much. Alanna loved William Sinclair, but in many ways he was a mystery to her. She knew Ailsa to the soul, and had from her first moment of memory.

She ran her fingers lightly over her mother's familiar script and felt an uneasy premonition, a shadow on the sun. It had no substance, nothing she could grasp and comprehend. She sat, hand poised above the flowing words, shaken and chilled.

The wind whipped in among the standing stones, mimicking the voices of the dead that had cried out for many years over many sorrows. But it did not reach the violets, whose vivid petals did not tremble from the cold gusts that circled wildly in the valley. Oddly, Alanna was heartened. She folded the letter and slipped it back into her pocket, forgot the nameless shadow, and gazed about her. She had never feared this place, as some did, but had known in her heart that it was blessed, just as her grandfather had known.

She smiled into the wailing wind, hummed and made a song of the haunting sigh. The sun danced in and out of the clouds overhead, touching her face, her brown hands with their nails cracked from working in the soil, her hair, which fell about her, auburn in shadow, blazing red in sunlight.

"Good morrow to ye, Grandfather," she said at last, rising when the wind had ceased its mournful cry. "I have much to do today."

With her creel over her arm, she left the Valley of the Dead and began to search for the fir-club moss, oak galls and blaeberries she needed for her dyes. She walked the clearings through blue drifts of violets and yearned toward the woods, bathed in vibrant green light through fine young leaves. With delight, she watched the tiny new lambs gambol in the clearing.

She worked her way across the moor, and through several stands of larch and birch, stopping to eat her dinner of bread and crowdie and sharp cheese, washed down with water from the burn. With each movement of the clouds, her expectation grew; the teasing voices hummed, luring her forward. She did not know toward what, and did not stop to wonder. She did not ask questions of the gods, but let them lead her where they would. They had not disappointed her yet.

Alanna wandered toward the river, toward a favorite clearing where the water rushed over boulders and stones, where birch and rowan and hawthorn made a sheltering bower. But when she reached the edge of the copse, she sensed someone was there before her.

Alanna stopped while the promise in the air took on shape and color, fleetingly. She crept forward, smiling, until she saw the man crouched in the center of the clearing. She knew at once he was not from the glen; his clothes were of fine wool, his waistcoat of silk, and his coat, tossed over a stump, was beautifully lined and stitched. He sat amidst swaying patterns of white and yellow, green and blue, surrounded by the wildflowers that brushed his boots and trousers.

The sun broke through the trees just then, turning his dark hair to a halo around his pale face. His bones were strong, despite his soft skin, and his eyes were green in the blaze of light. Alanna wondered why she had not heard that this stranger was coming, for the glen was isolated, and he could not have wandered here by chance. Everyone in Glen Affric knew of each other's comings and goings, and who was expecting visitors. This man was a surprise.

He looked about him, leaning toward the water, head tilted, raising his face to the breeze. Then he grew still—so still that Alanna was fascinated by his lack of motion. Even from where she stood, concealed in shadow, she sensed his intense concentration on the trees and the river and the sky.

He looked up when the sun broke through the clouds but did not shade his eyes. Only then did she feel the tension in his body that spoke of fierce emotion well tamped down. The intensity with which he looked about him, sniffed the air, held out his well-manicured hands to feel the moisture on his skin, spoke of an energy, coiled and deep and waiting. The sight of it held Alanna in thrall. The stranger's passionate desire to know this place touched something in her serene, contented soul and made it ache in sympathy and some primitive recognition she felt but did not understand.

In half-glimpses of his face, she thought he looked familiar, yet she did not remember him, try though she might.

He stood, and she saw that he was of medium build. There was power in his stance, in the rise and fall of his breath.

Yet his face was suffused with reverence and his green eyes glowed with awe.

All at once, Alanna felt she was intruding on a primal, private form of worship. The man's body vibrated with the depth of his emotion. She was as seduced by the scene as he. Perhaps more so. She had always loved the glen, but few men looked at it as this one did. He seemed to be discovering, absorbing the place through more than his eyes.

He looked like a man who wanted more than to see the glen; he wanted to *know* it, as one knew a woman or his God.

Against her will, Alanna took a step, and pine needles crackled beneath her foot. The man whirled, but when he saw her, he paused, and the stillness returned. She was no threat to him, just another part of the place and the moment.

His expression did not alter; he seemed to absorb her as he had the scenery, as if he had been aware of her presence all along. Alanna was not embarrassed by his perusal. There was no surprise or wariness in his eyes, only curiosity.

"Who?" Alanna whispered. The sounds of the woods bound them loosely. She did not want to break that fragile thread with a human voice.

He did not hesitate. "David Aidan Fraser," he whispered back. The voices of wind and water faded just a little.

Alanna smiled, her violet eyes glimmering with appreciation. "David Aidan—beloved fire. 'Tis a good name."

"So you know your Bible as well as the Gaelic," he said in surprise. Few in Glasgow knew Aidan was a version of the Gaelic word for fire. He was proud of his name, determined to live up to it, one way or another.

With a mischievous grin, Alanna said, "Many of us speak the Gaelic. This is a wild place, ye ken. Sometimes we even worship *Tuatha de Danaan,* the ancient Celtic gods."

"And what does the minister of your kirk think about that?"

Alanna shrugged. "We keep it to ourselves. He doesn't ask, so he need not know. 'Tis all very civilized." She did not stop to think before she spoke. She should have been wary and aloof, but the memory of his awe and his fierce need would not allow her to remain a stranger. Besides, the sense of familiarity had returned. Somehow it consoled her.

David moved closer, gazing unabashedly at her loose red hair and pale green skirt looped up to reveal bare feet and calves. Over her arm she carried a handwoven creel full of roots and lichens and wild grasses. "Hardly civilized," he said, smiling. To his own astonishment, he was not angry at her interruption, nor disturbed that she had seen him fully clothed in his correct city garb but naked in his soul. There was something about this woman, a tranquility, a quiescent quality that was intriguing. Her violet eyes were full of peace and offered that peace to him freely. He wanted to accept her gift. He had not known peace or rest in a very long while.

"I'm not certain the minister of the kirk would approve."

Alanna smiled. "I'd willingly offend no one, but better the minister than the gods of the glen." She pointed to the boisterous rushing river. "Neithe, God of Waters, protects and heals me. Can ye no' feel his power all around us?"

"I feel a great many things I can't explain." David kept his gaze on Alanna. "I did not think to find such wonder in the place where my father was born."

Then Alanna knew where she had seen him before. "You're Ian Fraser's nephew!" she cried. She could see the resemblance quite clearly now. "I thought I knew those eyes. I am Alanna Sinclair. I must have met ye three years ago when your family was visiting." Melancholy enwrapped her, creating a delicate lacework of distance between them. "That was the spring when my grandfather died."

David had an absurd desire to reach out and console her, but he kept his hands firmly at his sides. "No, I stayed in Glasgow to see to business. I was a fool. I'd learned to fight by then, but not against the most dangerous things. Afterwards, I learned the difference. And so I came here." There was suppressed anger in his voice that hinted at an unspoken story.

Impulsively she put her hand on his arm. "I'll wager you've seen only a small piece of the healing magic here.

There are many other wonders. Perhaps someday I'll show them to ye."

David Aidan Fraser seemed to understand that this was not a promise she gave lightly. "I hope you will. Someday. I don't want to be a stranger. To the glen, or to you."

Alanna could not help herself; she smiled, and her violet eyes sparkled. "I grew up in London, so I've only come to know it myself a little at a time in the three years since I've been here."

David was surprised. "I don't hear a trace of London in your voice. Only Scotland."

"When ye live so far from the city, so far from the voice of foreigners or strangers, 'tis easy to forget the sound of any voice but this. 'Tis like music to me."

"Perhaps then, since I'm in exile, you can do me the kindness to teach me what you know. Teach me to hear the music."

" 'Twould not be a kindness," she said softly.

He took her hand and kissed it lightly. "What then?"

"A gift," Alanna murmured, "to myself." Then she turned and was gone.

3

IAN FRASER SAT ACROSS THE SCRUBBED PINE TABLE FROM HIS nephew, who might have been a mirror of himself many years ago. In the soft hour before gloaming, he half listened to the sound of his two youngest daughters helping their mother prepare dinner nearby. Already a large cast-iron pot was bubbling over the fire in the center of the main room of the croft, filling the air with the fragrance of rosemary and garlic, pepper and mutton.

A loft, holding Ian and Jenny's large bed with its heather

mattress, rose into shadow above their heads. In the small room where the children's boxbeds lined the walls, Brenna, the oldest Fraser girl, was bent over a small table, reading by the light of an oil lamp. Ian had taught her and the other children, patiently, stubbornly, determined that they should share the pleasure he felt in reading the ancient poets.

On the top shelf of the press in the kitchen were Jenny's family Bible, a huge book bound in heavy calfskin, as well as *Pilgrim's Progress* and *Grace Abounding* by Bunyan. Jenny was a religious woman who took solace from the familiar books.

Taking a sip of the fine whisky David had brought from Glasgow, Ian said, "What's brought ye here this time? There's a look in your eyes I've not seen before."

Ian wondered if his older brother, Duncan, was responsible for that look, but did not speak the thought aloud. Duncan had been consumed for many years by his successful shipbuilding empire, which had expanded lately into shipping and coal. Ian had thought more than once that David did not seem happy, and was not really surprised to see him here. But he was vaguely disturbed by the opaque screen that obscured his nephew's thoughts.

David sat back on the plain runged chair, breathing in the smell of burning peat and Scotch broth cooking over the fire. He glanced around the small croft with its rough clay walls and simple furniture, the large chamber that seemed to have burgeoned from this comfortable room to make more space as the family grew. The thatched ceiling was low, the walls aged by time and soot, the windows uncovered, letting in the evening air, fresh with mist and moor and fragrant pine. The door was cracked open, as it usually was in the Highlands, in welcome and invitation to all friends and travelers.

David, who had lived in a three-story house in Glasgow, filled with fine carpets and teak and mahogany furniture, velvet draperies, and even indoor toilets, should have felt cramped and ill at ease in this house. His uncle smelled vaguely of heather and sheep and the sharp tang of earth, rather than soap and fine cologne. David found he liked the change. He smiled, more relaxed than he'd been in months.

"I didn't belong in the city, Uncle Ian. Father and I argued constantly about how we should do business. But this time, I was afraid I couldn't avoid a real fight, a dangerous one, where we both said things we'd never forget and never forgive."

Ian nodded. "Then mayhap ye were wise to get away." He suspected there was more to it than David was willing to admit. Ian could not remember a time when Duncan and his son had not been in conflict. As David grew older, his frustration had increased, inflaming an already volatile temper. He acted from the heart, from instinct and emotion, not calculation and pragmatism. He had taught himself, at great cost, to fight well and cleverly for what he believed. But some battles could not be won, as Ian knew too well.

"I needed to breathe again, to remember what it's like to care about people more than money." David frowned. "I'm tired, Uncle Ian. Tired of fighting and tired of losing. I think life should be more than that, don't you?"

"Aye," Ian replied, green eyes pensive. "A great deal more, I'd say." He would say nothing against his brother, though the two had never been close. But he understood David perfectly, perhaps too well.

The door flew back against the wall, and a tall young man ducked inside.

"My son, Gavin." Ian nodded to his guest. "And this is your cousin, David Fraser, come to visit from Glasgow."

Gavin, who was tall and muscular, with Jenny's brown hair and eyes, shook the moisture from his hair and wiped the loam from his hands. "From the city is it?" Gavin's interest in the stranger increased. He was nineteen, and restless. "Will ye tell us all about it?" He dragged a stool up to the table and leaned forward eagerly, elbows on the pitted pine.

"I can tell of things you don't want to hear, that's certain," David murmured, touched by the young man's ardor.

"But it can no' all be bad. Come, tell us what it's like there, where things actually change." He had heard about life in Canada from his aunts, who had emigrated with their husbands and children less than two years ago, but Canada seemed very far away. Glasgow was close enough to reach, attainable.

"I can tell you how big the slums were before they tore them down and scattered thousands of poor like chaff on the wind. I can tell you how many churches there are, how they worship money above all other gods, while they tell you how devout and Christian they are."

Gavin shook his head, undaunted. "Every place has bad things. I know ye could tell me good as well, if ye were no' so determined to forget them yourself."

"That's enough." Ian spoke quietly but firmly. He would not have a guest insulted in his home. It was the worst sin a Highlander could commit, except to destroy beauty. Besides, he didn't like the look in Gavin's eye—the anticipation, the desire and frustration, the need.

Ian had seen that look before, in other eyes and other dreams, so long ago that he should not remember, except that he could not forget. He rose abruptly and went to his wife, grasping her around the waist and squeezing. Her long brown hair was braided and pinned up, leaving her throat bare. Ian kissed it tenderly. "Jenny, my love, ye smell so good."

Jenny shook her head, smiling. "Aye, like cabbage and onions and leeks." She did not stop chopping vegetables at the rough sink and did not turn her head, but leaned back slightly until Ian's cheek was pressed to hers.

"Umm. My favorite perfume."

"You're a madman, Ian Fraser," his wife said, trying to hold in her laughter.

Ian whirled her to face him, deftly avoiding the knife in her hand. "Ah, so I am. But then, ye love me for it."

As he leaned down to kiss her, Jenny whispered, "I do."

Their youngest daughter, Erlinna, doubled up with a grimace. "Leave off. You'll make me ill."

Brenna had abandoned her book to come listen to her cousin. She gave her little sister a superior smile. "You're just jealous. Don't ye worry, I'm sure someday a boy will kiss ye too. Even someone as daft as ye." She ruffled Erlinna's hair with affection, which took the sting out of her words. Her sister Glenyss did not look up from the buns she was making, though she was very aware of her parents a few feet away.

Everyone laughed, and David felt both warmed and intimidated. He had wanted just such a feeling in his home, and for so long, forever, it had been missing. He was envious of his uncle, as Erlinna was envious of the affection between her parents. He was no better than a ten-year-old girl. He felt like a fool.

While Ian was occupied, Gavin leaned close to David. "There *are* good stories, aren't there? Will ye tell some tonight?"

This time his cousin smiled in acquiescence. "Yes, you're right. There's much more worth hearing. I'll tell you later."

"Leave me be, *mo-charaid*," Jenny said, "or Angus and Flora will be eatin' sawdust for supper. Would ye have us embarrassed so in front of your nephew?"

Ian kissed his wife once more. "My parents are used to this family, and if 'tis sawdust you're feeding them, they'll no' complain. As for David, if he has enough whisky, he'll not be knowin' the difference anyway. Don't worry yourself." He nuzzled her neck again, and she pushed him away reluctantly.

"Be off with ye, I say. I've work to do."

Ian returned to his chair, but his gaze lingered on Jenny, who was chopping onions till her eyes watered.

Gavin rose. "I'd best get cleaned up and bring in some ale."

"Your cousin's brought whisky from Glasgow," Ian said.

"Well, Grandfather should be pleased. He's very choosy about what he drinks, is Angus Fraser."

"So long as it's liquid, and no' a cup of water, 'tis easy to coerce him, though." Glenyss, the middle daughter, who was twelve, spoke for the first time. She had her father's dark, curly hair, but David had not seen her face before. She had kept her head lowered. Her eyes were Jenny's, except for the wicked twinkle as she grinned at her brother.

David had thought her shy, but now he wondered if she chose her times and spoke only when she thought she had something to say. He smiled, intrigued, and Glenyss ducked her head again.

The rest of the family laughed, but when Gavin had gone, Ian turned back to his nephew. "It'll be none too peaceful in this house, I warn ye." He grinned, unabashed, even a bit proud.

David looked after Gavin regretfully. Ian and his son seemed to have a good rapport, though obviously the boy had wanderlust and Ian did not wish to see it. But Ian was kind, even in his admonitions. Duncan Fraser was another matter. "My father's driven," he said suddenly, unable to hold the words in any longer. "Like he's trying to find something that will make him happy, but nothing ever does. So he goes after something else, something bigger. The richer he gets, the less I know him." David paused, met Ian's steady gaze—a gaze that, unlike Duncan Fraser's, concealed nothing.

His father's voice came back to him, chilly as the evening breeze that ruffled David's hair. *This is what I am, David. The businesses, making money, it's all I know how to do. Do you hate me for that?*

Sometimes I think so, David had replied. *It's the only protection I have.*

Nervously, he ran his fingers through his hair. "I thought all I wanted was to get away. But once I got here, and there was no trace of Glasgow, but only the woods and the river and those mountains that make our biggest ships seem like toys, once I heard the wind and the water and saw the shadows that changed from second to second, I knew I wasn't running away after all. I was running to. I want to stay." The last was a plea, and Ian reached out to take his nephew's hand.

" 'Tis welcome ye are, David Fraser. When ye were a boy, I thought I sensed something in ye. That you could understand the land, truly know it from inside. It takes that understanding to live here, for life is no' easy. But every day is a new kind of miracle, and this place sustains ye if ye let it, feeds your hungry soul."

David thought of Alanna and smiled secretly. "I know."

Ian considered his nephew, intrigued. It was strangely tantalizing, that smile. "Something happened today. Something else."

David shrugged a little too casually. "I was enchanted by the fairies, is all."

Arching his brows in disbelief, Ian leaned back in his chair. "Were ye now? 'Tis a rare thing, but it happens. I'll be holding my breath till I meet this 'fairy' of yours."

Alanna left David in the copse, but his voice and his image stayed with her. She was surprised at the things she had said, bemused by how much she wanted to show him the secrets she had shared only with Mairi and Ailsa. For the past three years, Mairi and Alanna had lived inside an enchanted circle, bound by their love for one another, their knowledge of things beyond sight and touch, and the deeply rooted magic of the glen. How could a stranger understand?

Alanna wandered along the river toward home, feeling oddly off balance, a little tipsy and confused. She tried to empty her mind, but Mairi's warning fluttered in the breeze: *Take care, there may be dangerous currents in the river today.* Her grandmother had been smiling, wary but expectant.

Alanna stopped where trees and ferns gave way to tilted stones and boulders, made lucent by the angle of the setting sun. Here, sheltered by its inaccessibility, lay a placid *linne*, which was Alanna's secret pool.

"Why?" she asked the clouds skimming across the azure sky, much as she had asked, "Who?" in the copse. She dropped her creel and regarded the *linne* curiously, as though she would find the answer in the water.

The pool was deep, and clear enough to reveal the soft silt on the bottom, strewn with pebbles that glistened in the sunlight. Among those pebbles, dancing in and out of shadow, the translucent image of David's face teased her. She wanted to take it in her hands and push it away, but she had to catch it first.

David Fraser should not be in this place; it was hers, private and inviolable. Alanna gazed up into the mauve light of the dying sun. When she looked down again, the stranger's face was now above her, now below, now vanished into air or sparkling water. She felt his eyes upon her as they had been in the copse, without judgment or intent, brimming with wonder.

But when she started to turn away, David's face evaporated. In its place hovered that of William Sinclair, gray eyes full of longing. Suddenly, disturbingly, her father's face was in her mind, on the surface of the water, imprinted on the blank face of a boulder.

Alanna shivered at a sudden gust of wind that seeped through to her bones, icy with the chill of approaching night.

4

"YOU'VE NOT YET REACHED SIXTY, WILLIAM," AILSA ROSE Sinclair murmured, contemplating her husband's pallid face in the fading twilight. Could he feel the shadows flitting about them, settling in the corners of the study? She had kept the fringed muslin curtains open to allow the thin sunlight to filter through, but now even that was gone. The green papered walls seemed as dark as the day she had come here as a bride.

"Sixty *can* be old, you know," William told her with a smile. He wrapped a strand of her chestnut hair around his finger and closed his eyes in pleasure.

Ailsa shook her head decisively. "When we met ye were nearly twice my age, but I never for a moment thought ye old."

"But I did, Ailsa, my heart. I thought I was very old and very dreary. If I'm not so now, that is all your doing."

His wife felt the threat of tears and refused to succumb. To distract herself, she turned to the low rosewood table where she'd laid out bowls, a teapot and cups. "I've made ye a decoction of black willow to help ye rest, and steeped some yew leaves for the pain." Ailsa held the bowl while William drank, grimacing. "I've peppermint tea with mint to wash the taste away." She poured a cup of steaming, fragrant tea and leaned close, until she could feel the reassuring warmth of his breath on her cheek. "Ye said it eases your stomach."

William squinted at her through the gloom. "Funny, isn't it? I trust Dr. Holloway implicitly. He's been with us for ages, but your herbs and poultices give me the most relief. Perhaps it's because you haven't hairs growing out of your nose, nor do you smell like ether or iodine, or whatever he reeks of."

Ailsa brushed William's thinning gray hair away and cupped his forehead with her hand. He was clammy with sweat and hot with fever. "You're no better today, are ye?" Her blue-violet eyes were gray in the dark room, but she did not move to light the lamp on the table or the candles on the marble mantel.

William breathed in carefully, afraid she would hear the tremor in his voice. "No, no better. A little worse, perhaps. You know that, Ailsa. You know me better than anyone." There was no self-pity in his tone. He did not feel pathetic, nor did he desire the compassion of others. He was more concerned with his wife's state of mind than his own. That was why he had asked to have a bed made up here in the study.

"It's always been my retreat, you know, from fools and foolishness. From here I can see the little piece of ground you've made into your garden. I can watch you dig and plant and thin your herbs with that ridiculous straw hat on your head and your apron stained with earth."

That's what he had told Ailsa when he asked for the change, though he was not certain she had believed him. It was difficult to lie to his wife, whose eyes saw beyond what appeared to be to what was and, more miraculous still, to what might be.

William's real reason for moving out of the room next to hers was so she would not hear him at night, unable to sleep for the pain. So she would not feel his anguish through the thin walls that separated them. He wanted to spare her as much as possible, because he could not bear her suffering; it would only have weakened him further. Besides, she had given him so much. At least he could give her this small respite.

They rarely slept apart, and William had not wanted to leave her, but he'd known the disease was spreading, and he found it more and more difficult to sleep. Ailsa had been hurt when he told her, but the next instant she'd looked in his eyes and heard what he did not say. "I'll miss ye at night," was all she'd said. It had made him want to weep with joy and despair. Because he knew it was true.

Now he was doubly glad he had done it. It was easier for the nurse to come and go downstairs without disturbing Ailsa, though his wife had an uncanny sense of when he was in distress, and though he told her not to come, she did. It was not only her suffering he did not wish to endure; he did not want her to see him so weak and helpless.

"I need to be here, William, to be with ye, to do what I can. I'd as soon wear corset and bustle and go visiting matrons for tea as sit and do nothing. Get rid of the nurse and let me care for ye." She knelt on the rug of shaded green and yellow leaves woven together, her dove gray gown pooled at her knees.

William shook his head. In this he must be selfish. It would be unbearable to have her watch him humiliated daily. Besides, he knew full well that Ailsa gave the nurse strict instructions, that she brewed all the medicines he took, not just the teas she brought to help him sleep.

With an effort, William cupped Ailsa's face in trembling hands. "It's time to stop pretending, my wild one, my blessing."

The color drained from her face until even her lips were pale and bloodless. For a moment she froze, then slid her arms around her husband. "I can help ye." She held him close and felt how frail were his bones, how intense his torment. "I can't bear it. I won't listen."

William struggled to hold her away from him. He wanted to see her face. "You can bear it. You're strong. You've always been stronger than me." He turned his head away, and his face grew pinched and white.

Ailsa held him until the spasm passed.

"I don't know when, but the time will come, and not so long from now, when—" William broke off, drained by pain and the effort to explain. "I'm sorry," he whispered hoarsely. He ran his hand down his wife's chestnut braid in a light caress.

"I'm not ready to let you go." Three years past, she had released her father in much the same way. But she had barely known him. Charles Kittridge's death had left her bereft, devastated. She did not think she had ever truly recovered. Now William was asking her to do it again, to give in to disease, to give up hope, to lose him. "I can't! Whatever you might think, I'm no' strong enough or brave enough or selfless enough."

"You are all those things," her husband told her softly.

Ailsa did not feel strong; her stamina seemed to drain from her day by day as the disease sapped William's body and vitality.

"And there are others. Have you heard from Lian or Genevra of late?" he asked. "They seem to give you comfort."

Ailsa warmed at the mention of her two half-sisters. Wan Lian had been born in China and lived now in Paris, while Genevra Townsend had lived all her life in India. Despite the distance between them and the differences among them, Charles Kittridge's three daughters were very close, able to touch one another through their letters and their dreams. At first, when she learned of their existence, Ailsa had resented them for stealing their father's attention and affection. She had not even met him until her children were grown. But soon, the invisible threads of intuition among the sisters had drawn them close as they grieved together and watched Charles Kittridge die. They had not lost touch with one another since. "I was planning to write to them soon," she murmured.

"Do it today." William was awed, as always, at the extraordinary bond between half-sisters who, by all rights, should share their father's blood and little else.

Ailsa found little solace in the thought. She touched his cheek tenderly, in a plea from the place where her heart used to beat, used to pour blood and spirit through her veins, giving her life and hope. "I love you so much, *mocharaid*," she said softly.

William smiled with tears in his eyes. "I know you do."

Ailsa raised her head at the conviction in his voice. He really did know it. Finally. After all these years. " 'Tis glad I am of that, William Sinclair, for I'd begun to think my words had no more substance than the mist."

"It wasn't just your words. It was you. You've given me more than I would have asked for or imagined."

As she sat on the lush Brussels carpet at his bedside, holding his fevered hand, Ailsa thought about how much he had given her. She touched his warm fingers to her cheek. "I'm afraid, William."

For a moment he said nothing. The medicine was creeping through his body, freeing him of pain and draining him of strength. "Oddly enough, I'm *not* afraid. Do you know why?"

Ailsa's head was too heavy to lift, but she forced herself to look at him. "Why?"

"Because *you* believe there's more than what we see and hear and know. Something greater than we are, strong and eternal. And because you believe it, I've found I can believe it too. For whatever reason there may be, the fear has left me, Ailsa, and I know it won't be back. I wish I could make yours go as well. But you have to do that for yourself. I know you can. You did it for me."

Ailsa had no answer for the love and faith in his eyes. She buried her head in his hands and wept.

5

WHEN THE SUN HAD SET AND THE GLOAMING FADED, THE Highlanders came from throughout the glen to Ian Fraser's for a *ceilidh,* as they often did in the evening, to exchange news and sing and tell stories.

"But tonight is special," Archibald Maclennan said loudly as he ducked beneath the low threshold, "for we've a new face in the glen and news from the city and a homecoming all at once." He stared with interest at David, sitting on a stool across the fire.

"We've our boy home again," Angus Fraser added warmly. "I always knew ye'd be back, lad. Haven't I said so a hundred times, Flora?"

"Do ye think I listen to all ye say?" His wife Flora shook her head, hiding a smile. "After all these years, I've learned to nod at the right places and let ye babble as ye choose."

They were both happy to have David there, talking of staying for good. Their daughters, Megan and Kirstie, had emigrated to Canada two years back, and Angus and Flora missed them sorely. They were glad beyond measure that Ian had stayed, and now there was this young man who so much resembled their son, except for the fire and wildness in his eyes.

"Ye must stay with us," Angus had said to David during supper. " 'Tis quieter than this dreadful noisy croft. Such voices these children have, and their mother so quiet and well-behaved."

"Then I suppose ye know who to blame," Jenny said, smiling sweetly at her husband.

" 'Tis just the two of us at our house," Flora said. "We'd

no' mind the company, and ye'd be more cozy than sleeping on Ian's floor with the peat smoke in your eyes all night."

David sensed their loneliness and eagerness for company. Yet he liked the noise in this house, because it was more real, more the sound of human living than the shipyards and factories in Glasgow. It was reassuring. But the house was crowded, though he knew his uncle would never say so. So David had agreed to stay with Ian's parents for the time being. "I want to find a place of my own eventually," he told them.

"Are ye certain ye won't begin to hunger for the city?" Callum Mackensie, Jenny's father, asked David. "Will ye no' find it dull in the glen?"

"Dull?" David was astonished. "Never."

Callum and his wife, Christian, exchanged skeptical glances. Their son, like Angus's daughters, had left Glen Affric to look for something better, because it was more difficult each year to feed their families.

Callum and Christian could not believe that a vital young man would choose to come back here, when so many were leaving, hungry and frustrated by their inability to prosper, or even survive. They said nothing, but each knew the other's thoughts.

Just then, Catriona Grant arrived, with Malcolm Drummond close behind her. Then came Mairi and Alanna.

Ian greeted them boisterously. "Where have ye been all day while we've had such excitement? My nephew's home from Glasgow. David," he said, "meet Mairi Rose and her granddaughter Alanna Sinclair."

David bowed over Mairi's hand, then turned to Alanna, a twinkle in his eye. "I believe I saw you passing in the woods today."

Alanna flushed under his searching gaze. "But that would have been rude, to pass without speaking, especially to a stranger."

"Then it must have been an apparition."

Startled by the thread of humor between the two young people, Ian considered Alanna and David more closely.

Surely the two had met before. There was an awareness between them that was more than curiosity.

"The glen is full of apparitions," Mairi murmured. "Ye'd best beware that none lead ye astray." She smiled at David Fraser, but her heart was beating erratically. She had noticed how withdrawn and distracted Alanna was since she'd returned home. Every evening the women were in the habit of sharing what they had done that day, but Alanna had not mentioned meeting a young man. She had shown Mairi Ailsa's letter and said she was worried because her father was ill, but Mairi knew it was more than that. There had been a feverish color in Alanna's cheeks, a suppressed excitement in her eyes.

Now, watching her with David, Mairi guessed the cause of her granddaughter's unusual behavior. For a moment, as the young man leaned over Alanna's hand, Mairi felt an odd sense of imbalance, as if the floor were shifting beneath her. Her vision blurred, and she felt she was watching from far away two other young people who had been irresistibly drawn to one another, two lovers who had made themselves into strangers. She was watching history repeat itself right here in Ian Fraser's croft. But this time, her instinct told her, it would not be the same.

She blinked several times to clear her head and glanced uneasily at Ian. Yes, he had noticed too.

Ian was as surprised and discomfited as Mairi Rose by the tension between Alanna and his nephew. He remembered David's secret smile when he spoke of the fairies; it echoed Alanna's expression now. Alanna Sinclair. Ailsa Rose's daughter.

Ian found he could not move. He stood, fingers digging into the weathered oak door. He sensed danger in this possible alliance; he was intuitive enough to know he was not weaving a tale that had no truth. Swallowing to clear his throat, he wondered if what he felt was danger or a surge of the old bitterness, because of his own tie to Ailsa Rose Sinclair. In his younger years he had suffered greatly until he learned to find peace, acceptance and wisdom. He clung to those things still, but only by the tips of his fingers.

Ian met Mairi's eyes, then looked away from the knowledge and sympathy he saw there. He had to regain his composure; his friends and family would think he had gone mad.

The color was high in Alanna's cheeks as the two women took cups of tea and found seats around the peat fire in the center of the main room.

Each man had filled his personal *quach*, a wooden cup bound in brass or silver, and everyone had brought something to eat, from black buns to crowdie to bannocks. The women drank tea or ale or sherry, brought out to celebrate David's arrival, while the men drank David's whisky with great appreciation.

For a while, everyone talked at once about David's arrival, catching up on news of Duncan and politics in the city. But their voices dropped low when they discussed the hard winter and how many animals had been lost, and the likelihood of this year's crops of oats and barley succeeding.

The glen had never been wealthy, but those who lived there had fought to stay through the Highland Clearances, the coming of sheep more valuable than people to the lairds, the lure of new worlds and new wealth. They had stayed despite their poverty, sharing and making do, because they could not imagine living anywhere else. The families who had left in the past few years had imagined many things—opportunities, possibilities, dreams of energy and change. But those who had stayed dreamed their dreams of the land and the voices of the waters. Their dreams were softened and nourished by the mist at dawn and gloaming, by the ghosts of their ancestors who roamed the rills and moors.

"When the Willistons lived at the Hill o' the Hounds, 'twas easier, ye ken," Angus told David. "They own much of the glen, but charge us a fair low rent. Not like other English, are John and his lady, Eleanor. Wore only gowns and suits spun, dyed and woven on Mairi Rose's wheel and loom and sewn by the hands of all our women. And they'd buy game and fish from us to feed their family and their guests, no' to mention milk and cheese and cream from our cows. Those Sassenachs liked us." He seemed astonished by this, even now. "And what's more, we liked them, though I'd only say so among friends."

"They've gone?" David asked.

"Aye." Flora Fraser gazed sadly into her cup. "Retired outside of London some years back. Turned the runnin' of the great house over to their son, Richard. Sometimes he and his sister, Cecilia, come back with their friends for hunting parties, but we've not seen them in awhile. Lost interest, I suppose. No one's been at the Hill for a long time, so Nature's takin' back what they took from her long ago."

"It could be different," David said. "Or at least, I used to think so. But there's lots of wealth in Glasgow, and it's not made them happy, nor inclined to help people like you."

Alanna was intrigued by the undercurrent of anger in his voice, the trace of something more than anger. She had heard it in the copse for an instant. Now she wondered what it meant.

"Och, we'd not be wanting their help. Let 'em have their sacks of gold if it makes 'em happy. I'm thinkin' they'd be helpin' themselves more than us in the end," Malcolm Drummond declared. "As Angus said, there's few enough like the Willistons. Best leave us in peace and poverty, livin' how we choose. Then the risk is ours, but so's the victory."

"No doubt you're right. The men with the most money find it hardest to listen and impossible to understand. That's why I gave up my talking and came here. There was naught else I could do. I thought at the least I might save myself." David stared deeply into the fire, shoulders slumped.

Alanna felt his frustration, his shame at having run away to seek peace for himself. He thought he'd left the battle behind in Glasgow, but he had brought it with him. She could see that in the glint in his green eyes, the cold emerald sparks that could quickly become flame.

Gripping her cup in stiff fingers, Alanna looked away. She did not envy the frustration that ate away at David Fraser, but she envied the fire that smoldered inside. She would fight to save the people and places she loved, but David Aidan Fraser would burn for what he cared about.

The thought both intimidated and seduced her. She sank

back in her chair, confused by her own emotions. She had always felt at peace, certain that she knew her way, even through the sorrows. She had never before felt this kind of upheaval, this elation and awe, dread and anticipation. She was filled with hope and heat and a desire to smile hugely, even laugh aloud at nothing. She felt foolish and vulnerable, and did not like the sensation.

"Here now, what's all this mumbling and moaning?" Angus Fraser called out. "We're here to celebrate, no' mourn. Mayhap some music will wake ye sluggards from your misery." He picked up his fiddle; Ian took the pipes, and Catriona Grant raised a flute to her lips.

Music filled the house and the night, lifting the pall that had begun to settle over the room. The sweet notes of the fiddle danced about their heads, and the song of the pipes eddied upward, out into the soft Highland spring night. The people fell into the music, enchanted, willing their cares away, willing the lilting melodies to fill them, make them forget what they did not wish to remember.

A few began to sing. Soon everyone was joining in. David hesitated until the music drowned his caution. He was swept up in the rhythm and could not resist. He sang beautifully, and the others grew quiet while the three Fraser men played and sang.

> *Crag of my heart, the lightsome rock;*
> *Rock of the hinds and roving stags;*
> *The rock which the hunting shout encircles;*
> *To haunt it would be my joy.*

Alanna leaned forward, drawn by the vehemence of David's song, by his strong, clear voice and the thread of sadness that ran through the words. She did not realize she was staring until David looked up and met her gaze. For an instant they looked at one another, and she felt again that she had stepped inside his skin and read his thoughts, intruded on his secret self as she had while she watched him in the clearing.

David Fraser looked at Alanna's flushed cheeks and glistening eyes and remembered how she had teased him that afternoon. Now there was no laughter in her face; her gaze was intense and direct, and he suspected she could see much more than that which he allowed. For an instant he was afraid, and then he fell into her violet gaze.

He noticed Mairi Rose was also watching—she with Alanna's hair and eyes dimmed by time and grief and wisdom. Instinctively, David smiled at her, in reassurance, in surprise. She smiled back, and he was stunned by her beauty, even now. He wanted to learn all the wrinkles of her face, to know what had caused them, both the joy and the hurt, for he was sure she had known both. Just so would Alanna look when she was older.

"Will ye give us a story, Callum, before Erlinna drifts off to sleep?" Ian's youngest daughter sat beside her father, leaning against him while he smoothed her hair back gently. She rested her head on his knee in contentment, watching Callum expectantly.

"Aye, well, a story, is it?" Callum always acted surprised by such requests, though he had been the storyteller since his father grew too old and died. He took out his horn pipe, as his father used to do, and grew thoughtful. He had seen his grandfather do the same when he was young. There would always be someone to carry on the tradition that embodied the Highlanders' history and their wealth and their pride.

"There's been enough of politics and poverty for one night, so I'll tell a tale of love denied by such worldly things." He rubbed his chin and blew a smoke ring up and away from the warm peat fire. "A long time past, when the Lords of the Isles ruled their Kingdom of Dalriada, a girl named Lileas went in search of a man she had dreamed in the darkness and the starlight.

"She searched through meadows and mist until she met Connor Grant in a tiny wood. She knew him at once as the man she'd come to love in her mist-shrouded dreams. Connor looked into Lileas's face and knew her too, though his dreams escaped him, and he could not say why she was so achingly familiar."

David glanced surreptitiously at Alanna, made soft and golden by the firelight, and wondered if he had ever dreamed of her and then forgotten. He frowned at the odd question but could not let it go.

"Lileas and Connor became lovers in the flesh who had been lovers in fantasy," Callum continued, lost in a time long past, when the earth used to dream, and the dreams became legend. "Every day they met and were at ease with one another, as if they had grown with their childhood shadows intertwined."

Jenny Fraser shifted uneasily, while Ian's hand froze on his daughter's head, but Callum did not notice.

"Now Connor Grant was the son of the laird of Clan Grant, and betrothed to Elizabeth, daughter of The Macdonnell. Their marriage was to end the feud that had plagued both clans for decades. At length, Connor's intended discovered why he was slipping away so often, and she knew what a terrible price her clan would pay in blood if this marriage did not take place. She was proud too, and could not give up her future for a simple girl who had sprung from the earth to enchant Connor Grant."

Pensively, Mairi braided her fingers as she braided the threads of her loom, intent on the meshwork she created. She did not look at Alanna beside her, or David across the fire, but she heard their voices in Callum's words, saw their faces in his story. Her pulse fluttered, and she smiled at the pattern of her interwoven fingers, the repeated patterns of interwoven lives. The promise and the danger she had seen that morning were taking shape in the glow of the peat fire and the sound of Callum Mackensie's voice.

"Elizabeth Macdonnell arranged for her family to make a raid, and led the men herself to the croft where Lileas was staying. They burned it to the ground, killing all who dwelt there.

"Lileas crawled from among the flames and smoldering timbers and, coughing her life away in the smoke that had curled inside her, dragged herself to the place where she used to meet Connor.

"When Connor learned of the fire, he went in search of

his love. A clear spring had come up where she had fallen, her hand outstretched, bathed by the pure crystal water. Though he was a mighty warrior, Connor was helpless against death and treachery and grief. He buried Lileas beside the spring that had come from the earth like the tears of the gods for one so pure and beautiful and betrayed.

"Connor married his Elizabeth and healed the rift between the clans, and the Grants and the Macdonnells prospered. But each time Connor looked into a *linne* or a bit of beaten silver, he saw Lileas's face above his own. He felt her spirit about him often; with each day that passed, she came to him more clearly, and he loved her more deeply. He could not let Lileas go.

"For lovers meant to dance together will dance together, if not in body, then in spirit. Their souls are mirrors, one of the other, and they see no one else in their hearts, where neither man nor woman can reach to change the image burned there by the gods."

" 'Tis a very sad story," Glenyss said accusingly, her brown eyes damp, though she would not admit there were tears to weep.

Jenny leaned back in her chair, suddenly chilled. She knew Callum was repeating an ancient legend, but the story reminded her, with a hot stab of memory, of the girl Ian had once loved. Jenny shivered violently.

Ian noticed his wife was cold and put his arms around her to draw her close. But his eyes were veiled and distant. Ailsa Rose Sinclair's image had come to him in Callum's words, for the third time that day. Three times his heart had been broken, three times his soul denied. It was enough. He *hoped* it was enough.

6

WILLIAM SINCLAIR DID NOT DARE TO SPEAK. HE DID NOT want to tear the invisible tissue of enchantment Ailsa had woven into the bright April air. Because the day was warm and a spring shower had cleaned away the soot, Ailsa and Lizzie, the housekeeper, had moved William to the drawing room. For a change of scene, they said. He was propped up among mounds of bright pillows on the brocade sofa, the heavy wine curtains drawn back, the pattern of sunlight through lace drifting across his face.

From there he could see the tiny gardens verdant with new growth and splashed with the soft hue of roses and bright hollyhocks. He could see lovers passing arm in arm, nannies with their boisterous charges, the coming and going of women in their broad-brimmed, feathered and beaded hats. He had watched briefly while Ailsa settled herself at the harp. But now he sat, eyes closed, his face serene, while Ailsa's music filled the room and his thoughts, bringing to life frail memories he had long forgotten.

Ailsa ran her fingers over the taut strings, forming a lacery of notes to make her husband forget his pain. He seemed to slip into a dream when she created the soft, wild songs of her heart, of a place far distant, where the music came from the voices of the glen, where there were no rules and no restraints. Sometimes Ailsa played poignant, passionate music that echoed her own pulse, sometimes she mimicked the songs of the birds—high, sweet and pure. Always, she lifted William's spirit away from himself and into the spell of her passion and power. Sometimes her own spirit followed.

A carriage passed the drawing room windows and stopped before the front door. William opened his eyes, trying to bring himself back to earth, to focus on the everyday sounds outside the music. "Is it the children?" he asked anxiously.

Ailsa rose to look out the window, setting the harp back in its place. It vibrated slightly, trailing one last wisp of song. She saw her son and daughter alight from the closed carriage. "Yes. I'm glad they've come." She knew their presence would cheer William, who had not listened as he usually did, clutching at the music as if he could pluck it from the air to keep it from fading. Or was it she who had not listened today?

Ailsa used to smile when William referred to Cynthia and Colin as "the children," since Cynthia was twenty-one and married, and Colin twenty. William liked to think of them as he always had—young and vulnerable, needing his strength. She glanced at her husband while Lizzie opened the door and admitted the visitors.

William looked better today in this room, bright from the many tall windows along the front wall, the gray marble mantel and deep red-and-purple Brussels carpet. The matching burgundy velvet settees and low rosewood tables, along with the piano and harp, made the room warm and welcoming. And put some color in William's cheeks that the greens of the study had drained away.

When Colin and his sister entered a moment later, Ailsa greeted them with relief. "Your father is tired, though he's been wantin' to see ye. Your company'll cheer him."

Cynthia, who had light brown hair and was tall and usually graceful, was also several months pregnant, and did not move with her accustomed ease. She was wearing a blue Ottoman silk gown with a large bustle, and probably a corset as well. Ailsa frowned. Cynthia would not give up the current fashions or undergarments, though her mother had warned her that bones and wires and tight corsets might hurt the baby. Ailsa had never believed in the confining garments, felt stifled and unnatural in them, but she had accepted long ago that in this matter, Cynthia was not like her.

Her daughter's color was not good today; she was unnaturally flushed, but beneath the color, her skin looked sallow. "Are ye well?" Ailsa asked in concern.

Colin snorted and sidled past his sister. He had grown weary of the subject of Cynthia's pregnancy. But then, he had always been easily bored.

Cynthia shook her head. "I haven't felt right since . . ." She glanced uneasily at her brother, avoiding the sight of her father at the far end of the room. "Since this." She waved her hand toward her swollen belly, annoyed and on edge.

In that moment, Cynthia seemed younger than her twenty-one years, though that was not unusual. She had been complacent at home, contented, reluctant to give up her safe cocoon and assume the responsibilities of adulthood, especially caring for a child. Except for her initial excitement at the news that she was pregnant, she had shown little pleasure over the baby she carried. Ailsa had tried to ease the difficult period by giving her daughter several herb teas and decoctions to make her more comfortable, but she doubted that Cynthia had used them. She had probably taken them home and hidden them in a drawer so her husband, Peter, would not find them.

"It can't get any worse than this," Cynthia groaned. "Can it, Mama?"

"It might," Ailsa said with uncharacteristic restraint. "A wee bit."

Cynthia glanced down at the elegant fabric of her gown, draped artfully to disguise her growing stomach. She grimaced.

Ailsa realized that her daughter did not have enough imagination to see the child as a life that was real and growing and part of her. She only saw what carrying the baby was doing to her body. She would change once the child was born. At least, Ailsa hoped so. She looked up sharply when her daughter gasped and her son stopped halfway across the room. Both were staring at William in horror. They had not seen their father in two weeks, and the change was disturbing.

Cynthia stumbled toward the sofa where William lay

swathed in linen sheets and quilts. "Papa!" She started to exclaim at his sallow skin and general air of frailty, but put her hand over her mouth just in time. Instead, she sobbed into her soft kid glove. "How are you?" she asked at last, gray eyes wide with fear, as they used to be when she was a child.

"Not well," William told her. He looked up at Colin who stood just behind his sister. "I am happy, but not well."

Even Cynthia, who tended to notice only her own distress and confusion, heard the odd note in his voice—half sad, half relieved.

"You're giving up," she cried. "You can't give up."

"Some things we cannot choose, my dear. Some things are beyond a man's or woman's power."

Colin turned away abruptly and began pacing, too agitated to speak, afraid of what he might say.

Cynthia turned to Ailsa. "He's talking like he's . . ." She could not say the words. "Make him stop. Make him well!" She moved awkwardly and pounded her fists on her mother's chest. "Make it stop. You have to."

Colin whirled and pulled his sister away. "Are you mad?"

"She can do it!" Cynthia wailed. "She knows how. She's always made him well before. Please, Mama. I can't bear to see him like this."

"And what of him seeing you like this?" Ailsa asked quietly. "Do ye think it was easy to tell you the truth? Do ye think he is no' in a great deal of pain? He loves ye very much. Ye should try no' to hurt him more."

Cynthia wrenched away from her mother. "You don't know what it feels like. You can't imagine how dreadfully—"

"She knows," William said softly. "She knows a great deal more than you of suffering and loss. But let's not argue now. I need you to sit with me, Cynthia, Colin. I need your company."

Reluctantly, Cynthia went to sit beside her father. She did not bother with a chair but dragged up a velvet ottoman, for once too distressed to worry about her delicate condition.

Colin hovered next to Ailsa. His wavy chestnut hair was

disheveled, his blue-gray eyes free of laughter or mockery. "What does Dr. Holloway say, Mother? What do *you* say? Can we do *anything*?"

Ailsa was unused to his steady regard, surprised by his serious demeanor. He really wanted to know what she thought. More than that, he wanted to help. She had been stunned by Cynthia's appeal that Ailsa save her father; she had not known her children had such faith in her, had always thought they smiled at her eccentricities when they could, and more often deplored them, if not in her presence, then when they were away. But Cynthia's eyes and her grasping hands had said she believed Ailsa could cure any illness, that she was invincible. It was what her daughter needed to believe. And now Colin was asking her opinion, not out of politeness, but out of concern.

Ailsa was touched. Her two younger children had always been more William's than hers. They had been British from the day they were born, while Alanna had been out of place in London long before she set eyes on Glen Affric and found her home. Ailsa had tried to get close to Colin and Cynthia, but they seemed to fear the very part of her William loved. They feared anything out of the ordinary, especially a woman like Ailsa, who followed only the rules of her heart, and thereby threatened their well-ordered world.

"I'll be doing all I can to ease him, but 'twill not be enough. The doctor does not say so, but I've seen it in his eyes. As for ye, all you can do is be here for your father. 'Twould mean a great deal to William to have ye by." She started when Colin's fingers, damp with sweat, closed around hers. Her son had not taken her hand in many years.

"I'm glad he has you," he said softly. Before she could respond, he turned to his father.

William smiled thinly—the best he could manage—and took his daughter's hand. "Tell me about the baby. That will distract me. Tell me about my grandchild."

Cynthia looked startled and uncomfortable. "He's not born yet. There's nothing to tell."

Catching his wife's gaze, William murmured, "Has it moved yet? Have you felt it inside you?"

Cynthia blushed and bowed her head in embarrassment. "One doesn't talk about such things. It isn't done."

"I don't care about social propriety. This is my first grandchild, and I want to know. Besides, we're family. It's not as though you're talking to strangers." William paused, exhausted but determined. "*Have* you felt the baby move?"

Forcing herself to meet her father's eyes, gray, like her own, Cynthia licked her lips and muttered, "Yes. Sometimes he won't stop for hours on end, and I think I'll go mad with it." Her face was suffused with color; she was ill at ease discussing her body, despite William's protests. She put her hand on her swollen belly.

William shifted in his cocoon of covers. "May I?" he asked.

His daughter gasped when she saw that he wanted to touch her stomach. Her father had never behaved so shockingly before. She was afraid of what it meant. But she could not deny the plea in his eyes. He had rarely said no to her; from the day she was born, he had given her everything. That's why she had a wonderful husband like Peter Harcourt, a beautiful house, her own carriage, a child on the way. Awkwardly, she took his outstretched hand and placed it where the baby was flailing.

William's face lit with a pleasure so pure it brought tears to Cynthia's eyes. "I'd like to see him, just once."

"Stop talking that way!" she cried. "You'll be all right." She would not allow herself to believe anything else.

Colin choked back an exclamation and ran his hands distractedly through his chestnut hair.

"Well, you will. I've told you, Mama will make you better. It just takes time, that's all. A little time."

"For God's sake, Cyn, stop blathering on," Colin groaned. "You're making yourself ridiculous. When are you going to grow up?" His anger was not at her. He simply didn't know who else to blame. Colin's scorn for Cynthia and her petty worries had always been his outlet for frustration.

Ailsa watched her children, and her heart broke for them. They were both so very young, after all. Younger than she'd imagined. She thought of Alanna, who had been wise when she was born. Even as a child, she had understood things that could not be explained. Ailsa missed her so much she ached with it.

"Will you play for me, Colin?" William asked, breaking the awkward silence. He was trembling from the surge of emotion he'd felt when his grandchild moved beneath his hand. It was real to him now, alive and whole. Proof that there would be a future.

"Oh, well, if you'd like." Colin looked cornered, shame-faced over his outburst. To make amends, he pushed his spindle-legged chair aside and went to the piano. His chestnut hair and his talent for music were the only things he'd inherited from his mother. He lifted the lid and placed his fingers on the keys, stared at them blindly for a long moment.

He'd always been able to talk easily to his father, but now he did not know what to say. He began to play Beethoven, William's favorite. Here was something he could give, though it did not ease Colin's frustration or helpless anger. And it would not make his father well.

Ailsa felt very close to her family, and very sad, yet part of her was far away, thinking of Alanna. She would have known what to say, how to console William, just as she had known with Charles Kittridge, Ailsa's father, as he lay dying.

Ailsa struggled to block the memory. The image was too vivid, the grief too heavy. She needed Alanna's serenity and her optimism, her understanding of things inexplicable and insubstantial. As she watched Cynthia twisting her hands in despair, Ailsa came to a decision. She would write to Alanna tomorrow and ask her to come. It would mean a great deal to William, who had not seen his oldest daughter in three years.

"Ailsa, my love, you're dreaming," William said with unexpected strength. His wife raised her head, put her thoughts aside and started toward him, but he shook his head. "Don't stop," he murmured. "I like it when you dream. Don't ever stop."

7

ALANNA ROSE FROM HER BOXBED AS THE HOOT OF A TAWNY owl filtered through the leather covering the windows. Moving lithely, soundlessly, she put on the beige wool gown she had worn that day, slipped on her leather sandals, and ran her fingers through her long, curling hair.

Her heart beat with mingled dread and anticipation. She was going to meet David and did not want to wake Mairi, though she knew her grandmother would not try to stop her. Alanna wanted this meeting in the mist and moonlight to be her secret—hers and David's. She lived too much of her life with the eyes of her neighbors and family upon her. Though they were kind eyes, caring eyes, just now she wanted to move in shadow, unseen and unheard, except by the Celtic gods who protected her, and by David, who cared for her.

Lifting her cloak from the peg by the door, she ducked under the warped frame and into the translucent light of moon and stars draped in fine-woven mist. She swung her cloak about her shoulders, breathing in the smell of pine and fir and rich loam as she hurried toward the woods.

She had known David barely two weeks, yet she felt no apprehension in coming to him alone, when all wise and cautious men were sleeping. She was sheltered by the night, not threatened by it. Her anticipation made the woods and the sky glow and her own pulse quicken, as it would some-day, she thought, at the quickening of new life within her body.

The smell of moisture was heavy in the air, and rain began to fall as she slipped into the woods. David was waiting beneath the layers of leaves that dimmed and cooled the moonlight blurred by rain. He smiled, and even under the canopy of trees, Alanna saw the gleam of his green eyes as he took her hand.

He was warm, and his touch sent a tremor through her.

"It's daft," he said, "but I knew you'd come. The rain doesn't frighten you, does it, Alanna?"

She lifted her face so the moisture drifted over it, trembling in drops on her flushed skin. "What is there to fear in this?" she cried, catching a few drops on her tongue. "The rain will no' hurt me, and there'll always be a fire to warm me later." She smiled, her eyes luminous with faith.

David held her at arm's length, delighted by her pure pleasure in the moment. It was one of the things that drew him most strongly—Alanna's unfaltering conviction in the world she had chosen. She was at ease here, happy, and knew she would always be so. David wanted to absorb some of that confidence and joy, to leave behind forever the turmoil of his past.

"Come," he said, "I've found a sheltered hollow and laid a fire." Alanna's cloak brushed his leg as she followed, and the fragrance of earth and delicate spring flowers drifted to him on the damp night air. He held her hand, intensely aware of her fingers twined with his, the heat of her palm, the trust in her grasp. He smiled into the velvet dark of the forest while the cadence of rain on the leaves above lulled him.

At last they ducked beneath an oak, huge and gnarled with years and weather. He seated Alanna so the roots shielded her, and she watched in contented silence as he tended the fire until it blazed between them. The few drops of rain that penetrated the layered canopy of larch and oak, the feathery spires of giant spruce, the needles of pine and silver fir, sizzled as they hit the flames.

Pulse pounding, David leaned as close to the fire as he dared, staring at Alanna through the haze of heat and crackling flame. Her hair was glimmering and glorious, deep red and loose about her shoulders, the way he liked it best—unrestrained, a little wild.

He had come to know her face well in the past two weeks.

They had met often, at first by accident, as they roamed the glen separately, he seeking to learn its secrets, Alanna collecting its secrets in the creel over her arm.

Without speaking the words aloud or making a conscious decision to do so, they began to seek each other out for a short time each day. Sometimes they sat at the edge of the moor, watching the bluebells ripple like the blue-violet waves of the loch in spring. Or they crouched beside the river, listening to the rush of water, delighted by the multi-colored wood anemones and yellow starlike celandine that made a shifting carpet of color all around them.

Sometimes they talked of the glen and Alanna's past, the dramatic story of her grandfather, of Glasgow and a spring made invisible by the pall of grim injustice that enveloped that city. Alanna had looked thoughtful and asked unexpectedly, "Why are ye so angry at your father?"

Startled by her level gaze, David had found he could not lie or even evade the truth. "It's not just him."

"Who then? For 'tis hot in ye always. I feel it even when I'm no' touching you, like a fire burning from the inside out. Like you've been running up a very steep hill, and though you've stopped now, your body will no' grow cool nor your heartbeat ease. 'Tis a great deal of anger to carry inside, David Fraser, and no' have it sear your heart black with its heat. So who is it ye blame so much?"

"Myself," he said simply, shocked by the sound and truth of the word. "Because I failed someone, and when I saw what I'd done, I ran away to forget."

"But ye can't forget." Alanna touched his arm lightly so he would not flee again.

"No." David stared at the sky but saw nothing.

"Tell me."

He did not think the words would come, but once started, he could not stop them. He told her about Bran Guthrie, a common laborer working in the shipyard until, quite by accident, David saw some sketches he'd done of a new coal-burning engine. He'd discovered Guthrie was educated, but his family had been ruined by bad investments. Without hesitation, David had promoted him to engineer. He thought he was doing the man a favor, and the company as well. But he'd been wrong. The other engineers and the foreman had never accepted Guthrie. They'd harassed him, threatened his family and eventually driven him to despair. He had killed himself and his wife and four children, because he could find no more hope. "He was poor before I noticed him, but alive, barely feeding his family, but they got by, with his wife doing piecework here and there." David closed his eyes against the clear spring light. "In convincing Bran Guthrie to reach for something more, I destroyed him and his family too.

"If I'd only let him be." He sat, head in hands, the lapping waves of the loch offering solace at his feet.

"I'm thinking ye could no' have done that, once ye saw what he could be," Alanna mused. " 'Twould have been takin' the easy way to forget what you'd seen. Ye couldn't have lived with yourself, always wondering what would have happened if you'd cared enough to help him. Ye don't do things the easy way, David."

"I wish to God I could."

Alanna put her hand on his shoulder until he looked up. "No ye don't."

"You're right." David stared at her, astonished, as always, by her perception. "I don't." He met Alanna's compassionate gaze and felt no anger, only sadness and regret. She had begun to console him with a few words and a gentle touch. He was afraid to move; he did not want her to disappear in a wisp of smoke.

That had been many days ago. Tonight, for the first time, she had met him after sunset, yearned to see him in the black satin of night rimmed with silver moonlight. Alanna did not dread the night but welcomed it, for it held its own kind of beauty, and a quiescence she found alluring. She loved the sunlight, but the darkness and the stars were full of magic, of possibilities and dreams that grew dim against the brilliant colors of the glen during the day.

Alanna smiled unself-consciously, unafraid to show her pleasure in his company and the cozy nook he had made for them. Her violet eyes were clear, without a trace of gray, and her gaze penetrated the vapors of fire and moist air to touch him intimately, dangerously.

Sometimes they sat in silence for what seemed like hours, staring at one another, learning from gleaming eyes and fleeting expressions, truths they could not have spoken in words. It was madness, this newborn attraction between them, and yet it was right and good. They had not consciously made a choice. They had simply known, from that first meeting in the clearing with the jade green light shimmering around them, that they belonged in the woods together, with the fire and the rain.

Alanna brushed her hair back over her shoulder, raising her hands to the heat of the flames. "I'm very happy, David."

"Yes, I can see." He realized with a start that he too was happy in an uncomplicated way he had not known was possible. He ran his hands through his dark curls, suddenly intent. "Why have you never married?" It must be her preference. Other men had surely asked, but Alanna had decided to remain alone.

Alanna tilted her head pensively and her hair fell forward, glinting in the firelight. "I never felt I belonged in London, so I was no' lookin' for anyone there. I had friends, but none who made me dream. Once I came here, I knew why. I found freedom for the first time in my life, and I'd no' be wanting to give that up. 'Tis too precious and too rare."

David's throat was tight with apprehension, the flames between them suddenly too high to overcome. He spoke slowly, forming his words with care. "Suppose you met someone who didn't wish you to give up that freedom, but rather, wanted to share it with you?"

Alanna half smiled and met his eyes through the veil of smoke and mist. "That would be different, I think. 'Tis just that most men seem to need to hold freedom in their own hands to silence the terror in their souls."

Reaching around the flames, David took her hand and squeezed.

"Some men," she whispered, "but not all." She offered

him her other hand and they rose to their knees so they could hold each other across the fire while the heat radiated upward to their bare arms.

Alanna shivered.

"Are you cold?" David was puzzled.

"No," she said slowly. " 'Tis hungry I am."

"I should have thought to bring something."

Without sound or a sense of motion, Alanna circled the fire and was beside him before he could finish. "You know my hunger is not for food, for I see it reflected in your eyes."

He was startled by her openness, overwhelmed by the fresh scent of her body and the pale oval of her face in the wavering light. She frightened him a little, this frail fairy woman with a backbone of steel. "You're very honest."

"Because my mother and grandmother don't know how to lie and so did not teach me. Even my father can no' lie, though he can stay silent and pretend nothing's wrong." Brow furrowed, she contemplated the low, leaping flames. "I don't like it that he hides so much so easily." She surprised herself by adding, "I think sometimes I might never see Papa again. He's a good man, a kind man. I've not met many like him."

"You sound as though you're trying to defend him, only no one has attacked."

She stared at a tiny pool of water on a broad oak leaf, seeking a reflection of her face that might explain her sudden, desperate sorrow. She thought of Ian Fraser, whom her mother had loved when she was young, and a sense of melancholy spread within her like the wings of an eagle that had been furled tightly closed. She leaned close to David, resting her hand next to his. He would make her forget. He had that power.

Alanna looked up, hope and desire bright in her eyes, completely vulnerable, completely unafraid to ask for what she wanted.

David bent down until his mouth hovered above hers, but he could not touch her lips, parted in expectation. He wanted her so much he shook with longing, but he found that, in this moment, he was reluctant to kiss her. He did not want to contaminate her with the grime from the places he'd been and the things he'd done. He wanted her pure and clean and lovely, like the earth beneath and the sky above and the ferns that curled seductively about her legs.

He wanted her to be completely herself, uncomplicated by anyone or anything that did not come directly from her soul. If he touched her now, he would insinuate himself into her simple, perfect life and she would never be the same again. He drew back, astonished at his own restraint. He had come to know women in Glasgow, not many, but enough. Usually he felt no hesitation in fulfilling his needs, and theirs, especially when they offered themselves as clearly as Alanna had.

She leaned back, regarding him intently. "I think you are being selfish."

David was astounded. He was protecting her.

"I am strong," Alanna said, reading his thoughts in the disconcerting way she had. "I can protect myself. What gives ye the knowledge or the right to decide what will hurt me and what will not? What gives ye the right to deprive me of a pleasure I seek, and which I know ye want to give?

" 'Tis my choice to make, David. Mine alone. And I want to kiss ye. I want it very much. I need to know ye in that way, too."

David shook his head. "You don't know me at all."

Alanna smiled gently, as she would at a truculent child. "I know nothin' of the houses you've lived in or the things you've bought and sold, the people ye may have hurt and those ye may have helped. I'd not be knowin' how ye got to the glen—by wagon or horse or some fancy carriage. But these things are no' truly important, because I know ye here." She put her hand flat on his chest. "I've seen ye worship and heard ye pray, though ye might not have called it by those names. I heard ye speak to Ian's children with kindness, saw ye care for Angus and Flora Fraser. I saw your anger and your desolation. I know what I must know.

"Ye don't trust yourself, but I trust ye. Believe what ye like about yourself, but if ye care for me, have faith enough to try and believe at least that *I* am no' a fool."

Bewildered by the tightening in his chest and the dry lump in his throat, David fought for control and lost. "Aren't you afraid to make such a promise to someone you've met just a few weeks past?"

"No, I'm not afraid," Alanna said firmly. "I'm no' thinking ye are perfect. I don't want that. Just that you be you. How can ye fail at something you've been doing all your life?"

David saw that she meant it, as she meant everything she said, totally and passionately. He was shaken by gratitude for her simple honesty and faith. He wished he could share it. But he knew too much, had seen too much.

This time, when Alanna raised her face to him, he kissed her ear, her hair, then brushed her lips with his.

Alanna's pulse raced and her skin tingled with pleasure, awareness and the need for more. She turned to him fully and kissed him back, so their lips met, warm, moist and clinging, and he put his other arm around her. She clasped her hands behind his back and drew nearer, until she could hear his ragged heartbeat. Sighing, she rested her head on his chest.

"I'd better marry you before I dishonor you," David said breathlessly.

Alanna looked up, incandescent and irresistible. "I don't believe ye *could* dishonor me. Not so long as ye come to me with an open heart, speak only the truth, and touch me with love." She smiled. "What happens between us cannot be wrong, so long as it is honest. My mother taught me that long ago."

David was speechless. He had never heard woman or man speak with such certainty, without shyness or deceit. He himself could not have said those words without trepidation. He would not have believed them before he met Alanna. But she made him open his eyes, brush the film of distrust away and see what was before him, in his hands, in the earth and sky, and in Alanna. "Your mother must be an extraordinary woman," he said at last.

Alanna's eyes dimmed with sadness. She remembered the premonition she had had in the valley, the shadow without name or substance. She gazed blindly into the fire, groping for meaning in the crackling flames. "Aye, I miss her greatly. And Papa too."

David could not bear her distress, which he could not understand and sensed she could not explain. He wanted desperately to distract her, and said the first thing that came to mind. "That honesty must have gotten you both in trouble in London society."

The strategy seemed to work. Alanna smiled reminiscently. "Aye, it did, more than once, ye ken. We soon learned no' to speak our minds, except among our friends." Her voice became soft and dreamlike. "Mama and Papa have many friends. They're drawn to Mama, to her music and her open way of speaking. I think they were weary of pretending, and grateful that they'd no' have to pretend for her. And they share her love of beauty and her soft heart."

"She sounds just like you."

Alanna blushed at that as she had not at his caresses or her own boldness. "I would wish to be like her, someday."

For a while he held her, and they stared, mesmerized by the fire, the golden-orange light that danced and crackled, spitting sparks into the night. The sound of the rain had diminished; the drops fell through the layered leaves in a staccato rhythm that slackened into a soft drip and slide.

Chin resting on Alanna's hair, David murmured, "I want to give you everything, to make you happy."

"But I have all I want. I'm already happy." She tilted her head to regard him pensively. "Mayhap what I mean is contented, but 'tis not the same thing, is it?"

"I think not." David took her hands. "But tell me what it is that makes you happy now."

"To be in the glen, to be allowed to be what I am." She pointed at her sandaled feet, unbound hair and simple gown. "To know this place will feed our mouths as well as our hearts and hungry souls." She paused to trace her lips with her tongue. "To listen only to the voices that I feel are true and honest, and to learn what I can from those voices."

David nodded solemnly. "There are many kinds of hunger, Alanna. More than you can imagine. But it seems you don't want passion."

Alanna stared at him fiercely. "There is passion in these things. In the savage and beautiful hills, in the rushing of waters and the cry of the wind. Passions so old and deep that we can no' feel them fully and survive." She met David's green gaze and did not look away or falter. "Is that the kind of passion ye mean? The kind I sense I'll find in ye, in the flame inside that leaves you smoldering? The kind I did not seek until I met ye?"

She put both hands on his chest and leaned so close that her lips brushed his as she spoke. "That flame calls to me as the river calls, and I can no' help but answer. It's true that 'tis daft, after so little time, that I should tell you this, but I'm no' afraid of the fire, David Aidan. Until I met you, the most daring thing I'd ever done was choose to stay in the glen instead of returning to London with my mother. I have been contented, but now I wish to blaze. Teach me how, *mo-charaid*. Even if, for a time, ye consume me."

8

"ARE YE CERTAIN, ALANNEAN?" MAIRI ASKED ANXIOUSLY.

Alanna had come in to find her grandmother awake and waiting. Alanna's hair was damp with rain, her gown soaked to her knees from walking through the tall, rain-wet grass. She lit a tallow candle as she drew the warm familiarity of the small croft around her. The flickering light revealed her face, flushed with happiness, her eyes alight with hope. She could not have hidden her exuberance from Mairi if she tried, nor would it have occurred to her to do so. She and her grandmother had no secrets; they were friends as well as relatives, and Alanna wanted to share her pleasure.

She had not yet spoken a word when her grandmother asked her urgent question. As soon as the door swung shut, Mairi had risen and the two had sat on low stools beside the dim glow of the smoldering peat fire. Mairi reached for her granddaughter's hands.

"Are ye absolutely certain?" she repeated. Mairi had always wondered if Alanna would find a man who could make her happy. But her granddaughter had been contented as she was, had not wanted to change things. Ailsa had always wanted more, to see the world and know its wonders, but Alanna wanted simply to be allowed to live in the place she most loved. She said often enough that she had everything she needed or desired, and she'd never had to fight to keep her dreams. They seemed to drift into her open hands like gifts from the fairies. Still, Mairi worried. She did not want the day to come when Alanna learned what it was to be alone.

"Aye, that I am, Grandmama," Alanna replied without hesitation.

Mairi knew Alanna had made up her mind. She never called her grandmother Grandmama but simply Mairi, unless she was very serious or something quite out of the ordinary had happened.

Alanna clasped Mairi's hands, glad for their warmth; her own were chilled from the night and the rain. "Be happy for me. Please. I want ye to be happy too. Why are ye so afraid?"

She saw the trepidation in Mairi's violet eyes, dimmed with sadness since the death of her husband three years ago. In the soft candlelight, the lines of Mairi's face were more pronounced, and her skin, browned by her work in the sun, was unnaturally pale. Her hair had been tightly braided when she went to bed, but much of it had come loose. Her plain white flannel night-rail only emphasized her pallor.

Her grandmother was nearly sixty, Alanna thought with a start. She had never contemplated the image of Mairi getting old until tonight, when anxiety drained the life from her animated face. "What is it that troubles ye?"

Staring at their linked hands, Mairi said, "I'd no' want him to take ye far away."

"Ye mean the way Papa took Mama to London?"

Mairi was surprised, though she should not have been. Alanna always spoke her thoughts aloud. "Aye. I know I'm naught but a selfish old woman, but I'd have ye near me for a while longer."

Alanna shook her head. "You're no' selfish, or old, if it comes to that, and I'd not go with David if he tried to take me away. But Grandmama, he doesn't *want* to go. He loves the glen as we do. 'Tis his home now."

"So he says tonight, but for how long? 'Tis my experience that men like David Fraser, who've seen the world and what it offers up to entice them, sooner or later begin to grieve over all they've lost. Mayhap he believes it now, but . . ." She stopped when she realized she was speaking empty words. A voice from out of the shadows that shimmered with soft light whispered that the couple would stay in the glen, but the cost would be high. Mairi pressed her lips together in silence. Whose cost? she asked without words.

There was no answer.

Alanna watched her grandmother closely. She could almost see the memories shifting like shadows in the violet depths of her eyes, the love remembered, lost, retrieved and lost again, this time forever. "I hear David's words with my ears, but I *see* what he means. In his eyes when he looks at the mountains, in his hands when he touches the leaves of a rowan tree, in his body, which responds to the beauty around him as it would to a soft, warm bed. He sinks into the glen and pulls it tight about him, and smiles, and is at home.

"I love him for that, for his search for peace and rest, but also because there is a flame that burns inside him, a spark of danger, of the unknown, of daring, which I can't resist. I don't regret any part of my life, but it does not blaze with the promise of excitement and passion David offers. He would dare anything, I think."

Alanna's eyes glistened in the pale light of the single candle, and her voice trembled with emotion. Mairi was wary of this kind of passion. She had felt it once, when she was just a girl, for her husband, Charles Kittridge, an Englishman who had not understood what bound her to the Highlands, who had believed that love was enough to conquer greed and hatred and hundreds of years of bitter history. Even for his naïveté, she had loved him, wholly and helplessly, until this moment, no matter how often she had lost him or turned him away. That passion had brought blinding pain, but pleasure too, and wonder and enchantment she could not have imagined.

Mairi leaned forward, caught in the joy on her granddaughter's face. Alanna was radiant in her newfound happiness. She had never looked like this before, never felt so deeply or so fervently.

"I want ye to be happy," Mairi murmured. "I want ye to be free and passionate and full of awe."

"All those things I shall be." Alanna smiled, and her joy made Mairi gasp at its power. "I am certain."

"There's a telegram, ma'am," Sally, the new parlor maid, whispered, hovering nervously in the doorway of the study.

Bathed in the green light reflected from walls and curtains and rug, Ailsa Rose Sinclair rose from her place beside the makeshift bed where William slept. She tiptoed across the room in her soft leather slippers, her cream velvet gown whispering about her as she moved.

"Thank ye, Sally. And don't worry. 'Twill be all right."

The girl curtsied, though she knew the mistress would not have noticed if she hadn't. Sally was amazed that Mrs. Sinclair had tried to comfort the maid, when she herself had barely slept in days. Her face was haggard with worry. Sometimes the mistress's kindness made the girl want to weep. She left the room quickly, before Mrs. Sinclair saw her damp eyes.

Gliding noiselessly, as she had become accustomed to doing in the past few endless weeks, Ailsa went to the window, where a wan light filtered through fog and fringed muslin. Hands trembling, for despite her reassurances to Sally, she was desperately afraid, she unfolded the telegram from

Glen Affric. Let it not be my mother, she prayed wordlessly. William shifted in his sleep, and the sound of his harsh breathing made her hurt in a way she had not believed possible. "Please," she murmured, "not Mairi too."

Reluctantly, she glanced at the smudged paper in her hand.

Dearest Mama and Papa,
I am to be married to Ian Fraser's nephew, David Aidan Fraser, in a month's time. We could wait no longer and want to be married in the glen. You must both come for the wedding at the beginning of June. Be well enough, Papa. I want so much to have you here.

Alanna

For a long time Ailsa stared at the message, unable to take it in. Alanna to be married, and she had not suspected. Alanna, the child of her heart. Ailsa realized just how immersed she had been in William's illness, to have lost touch so completely with her daughter. *Be well enough, Papa.*

Ailsa choked back a sob.

"What is it?" William's weak voice barely carried across the room.

His wife turned, the telegram in her hand. "I woke ye. Forgive me."

William wanted to shake his head but couldn't find the energy. Instead he glared at Ailsa in reproach. "Don't," he said. "I can't bear it."

Ailsa forced a tremulous smile. "I know. I forgot. I was so surprised by this." She spread out the telegram slowly and read it aloud.

"She wants us there very much, doesn't she?" William murmured, a little surprised.

Ailsa nodded and watched her husband expectantly.

"I would have liked to see Alanna once more, especially on her wedding day." His voice was heavy with sadness. "But I'm glad she's happy, that she's found someone at last. She doesn't need me now." His voice was matter-of-fact, free of self-pity. "I needn't worry about her anymore. I know she's chosen wisely."

He fell silent, and Ailsa found she could not speak. If she did, she would weep, and that would not be fair to William.

"Though I've always worried more about the others than Alanna," William mused. He frowned, deep in thought. "Cynthia comes every day, you know."

"I know." Ailsa's voice was as frail as the song of the last thrush in the autumn woods.

"I've never seen anyone more determined to be cheerful." William glanced at his wife. "She smiles and smiles and laughs and laughs as if such pretending will convince her there's no reason at all to weep."

Ailsa knelt beside her husband but was careful not to lean her weight against him. Even so small a pressure caused him discomfort. "She loves you very much."

William looked worried. "I'm surprised that husband of hers doesn't forbid her to come out every afternoon in her condition. Anything might happen."

"I'm thinkin' that if Peter Harcourt did forbid it, our Cynthia would defy him."

William regarded his wife in surprise. "Would she really? I thought she only took a step if his book of rules and behavior allowed it. You think she would defy him?"

Ailsa nodded.

"Well, bully for her, then. Time she started thinking for herself." Realizing this sounded like criticism, he turned to Ailsa. "She's always been too much like me, I'm afraid. Finds security in Peter Harcourt's kind of life. Needn't ever take a dangerous step, so long as you follow the rules. Damned reassuring when you're as frightened as Cynthia." He paused to reach awkwardly for his wife's hand. "Now Alanna never was afraid of anything, as far as I could tell. Too much like you."

Ailsa smiled and shook her head, but William ignored her. "I still miss her, you know. It's almost a physical ache, even now." He paused to meet his wife's blue-violet eyes. "Especially now. But I'm grateful to her for following her heart and staying in the glen."

Ailsa gaped at him. "Grateful?" She remembered how she'd felt when she realized her daughter would not return to London, that she belonged in Ailsa's childhood home. She'd felt sorrow, despair, resignation and happiness for Alanna. But never gratitude. "Why?"

William considered, face drawn in the light of the fire and the wan daylight. He had not let Ailsa shave him in days, and his face was covered with gray stubble that darkened and widened the wrinkles in his translucent skin. "When Alanna was quite young, I saw that she was very like you. She had the same strange light in her eyes, the same fanciful imagination, the same intuition." He smiled to himself, remembering. "It was like having you, and you again. A living, breathing dream that bore another in its image. Too much dreaming for any man. In God's eyes, for me to have so much was too great a gift. I knew it couldn't last."

Ailsa started to interrupt, but William shook his head and coughed, and she bent to give him a sip of lavender-flower tea. His skin was cool yet drenched in sweat. She held his head, propping him up until the coughing passed. He drank a little tea and pressed her hand to his rough cheek.

"I let Alanna go, rather gracefully, I thought," he continued as though nothing had happened. He was determined to say this. "It broke my heart a hundred times, but I tried not to complain. I let her go, you see, so I would not have to lose you. A bargain with God."

Ailsa was stunned. He had never told her this before. But William had become melancholy in the last few days, remembering things he had not said. He needed to hear the words. With tears in her eyes, she rested her forehead on his hands, lying loosely on the covers.

William stroked her head gently, with a shaking hand. "Maybe it wasn't that at all. Perhaps I let her go to atone for taking you away—"

Ailsa raised her head sharply and put her finger against his lips. "That I will not listen to, William Sinclair. I chose you. I chose *you.*"

He looked at her in astonishment. "You did, didn't you? You see what I mean? God gave me too many miracles."

Aching with gratitude and love and pity, Ailsa whispered, " 'Tis no such thing as too many miracles. I believe that, *mo-cridhe,* and I'd have ye believe it too."

William smiled and touched her cheek. "I always wanted to return to Glen Affric, at least once more."

His wife stared in surprise.

"Back to the paradise that gave me you. To me it was a magical place. I wanted to know if it was as wonderful as I remembered. I could see that through your eyes, always through your lovely eyes, but I wanted to see it through my own. To make it real again. London so easily makes me believe that such a place could not exist. But I was there, I tell myself over and over, and you, my Ailsa, are there even now. It was real. I shall like to think of you there after I'm gone, happy as you were when you were a girl. Free again from those things that so trouble adults." He sighed with a relief so profound he trembled at its force.

Then he frowned fiercely. "You won't be afraid to go back, will you? I want you to go back. I know it will help you to go on, to forget."

Ailsa shook her head. "This is my home."

Smiling tenderly, eyes shimmering with moisture that glimmered golden in the firelight, William whispered, "For all these years, you chose to make your home with me. I can never tell you how much—" He coughed back a rush of pleasure and struggled to stop the spasms from shaking him again. Ailsa held his hand tightly, and he drew on her strength to win this little battle against his failing body. "But London was never your home. You do not belong in the city, my love, but in the wild hills that made you what you are."

He saw that she was going to object and stopped her with a glare. "The only loyalty you owe my memory is to do what will make you happy. Don't forget. Don't cling to something that's gone. Let yourself go. Let yourself fly. You can; I know it. Promise me."

Ailsa cupped her husband's face in her hands. "I promise. You're a rare man, William Sinclair, and I love ye."

He was too exhausted to reply, but satisfied. He had

waited so long to say it, had been afraid she would argue or pretend she wanted to stay in a city that had never welcomed her, though she had slowly made a snug nest here, with friends who loved her, music that consoled her, their children who gave her purpose. She had stayed for him. At first he'd found it difficult to believe, but now, at last, he did believe, absolutely. For that most of all he could never thank her enough. William smiled thinly. He was happy, despite the pain. Now he could finally give Ailsa a gift of great value, like the many she'd given him.

He saw the telegram on the table and thought of Alanna. He was glad his eldest daughter had found someone to love. He had begun to wonder if she ever would. "I just want her to be happy." He looked up at Ailsa with cloudy gray eyes. "And you as well. Be happy, little one. Promise me."

"I am happy. I've been happy. Ye know that." She could barely keep her voice steady.

"I know. I know." William contemplated his wife in the firelight for a long time, noting her chestnut hair braided in a crown around her head, her soft velvet gown and leather slippers. "Will you do something for me?" he asked at last.

"I will," she answered without hesitation.

"Let out your hair so it falls down your back the way it did when I first saw you. And take off your shoes and stockings as you used to do. I want to remember."

Unbearably touched by the look in his eyes, unbearably frightened by the rasp of his breath, shaking so she dropped several hairpins on the carpet of intertwined green leaves, Ailsa did as her husband asked. She tossed her shoes behind her and shook out her hair, but did not comb it, even with her fingers. She sensed that William wanted it untamed by the trappings of civilization he had given her; he wanted to see her once more looking natural and free.

She stood beside him, bare feet pale against the carpet, her hair rippling to her waist. William reached out tentatively to touch first a long, curling tendril, then to brush her bare toes with his fingertips. He smiled a smile that broke her heart.

"I remember," he whispered. "I remember it all."

9

THAT NIGHT AILSA LAY ALONE IN THE BED SHE HAD SHARED with William for twenty-three years. She had wanted to sleep in the study, as she so often did of late, waiting for him to cry out, offering herbs and potions and bitter teas to free him from his agony, at least for a little. It was all she could give him. But even her strongest herbs or the doctor's opium no longer eased William's suffering for long.

Ailsa had wanted to fight him when he told her she looked exhausted, that the housekeeper, Lizzie, had remarked upon it, along with several of the other staff. He'd said he could see it too, in the dark circles under her eyes and the paleness of her skin. He said it hurt him to look at her that way, and begged her to sip some of her own black willow tea that might help her sleep, as it had helped him.

Finally, seeing what her obstinance was doing to William, how much he was coughing and perspiring, flushed and gray by turns, and realizing that he would not give in, Ailsa had kissed her husband and left him.

She did need sleep, had drunk all of the tea Lizzie brought, but could not close her eyes. She kept hearing the poignant pleasure in William's voice, the glow in his eyes when he said, "I remember."

Then she thought of Alanna getting married in the glen. *Please be well enough, Papa.* She was marrying David Aidan Fraser. Ian's nephew. The name brought no glimmer of response tonight. Ailsa had been drained of violent emotion in the last months. Her feelings for Ian Fraser were lost in the distant past. William's pain was immediate and inescapable.

Again and again Ailsa repeated the afternoon's conversation in her head, wondering what Alanna's young man was like, wondering what she would tell her daughter. She must not have received Ailsa's letter before she sent the telegram, or she would not have put in that line that pierced her mother's already battered heart.

Alanna married. Ailsa tried to be glad, but she was numb. A wedding in the glen. Alanna would marry a Fraser. Was she happy? Was it right for her? Would she come now that Ailsa needed her, despite the pull that might hold her in Scotland? Would she come in time?

At last, exhausted beyond endurance, Ailsa fell into an uneasy sleep. She dreamed that she was riding in an old-fashioned, uncomfortable coach, bouncing up and down while the mist crept in around the windows. Figures appeared and disappeared through the morning fog. She craned her neck to see them clearly, but they were merely shadows in the mist, vague forms she could neither reach nor understand.

Then she saw a movement in the woods. In a flicker of white and red, a girl materialized from the heart of the mist. Her hair was golden red, flowing down her back. It flew in the breeze when she leapt over the river. Before she was across, the river turned to fire. The girl hovered, arms outstretched, plaid flying, lit from below by the luminous flames, until, in the shifting golden light, her plaid became wings. She heard a distant voice call out a name, softly, yearningly. "Ailsa!" and again, "Ailsa!" Despair enveloped her and she could not breathe.

Ailsa struggled with the pillow that was suffocating her, but even when she tossed it across the bed, she could not catch her breath. Her chest had a weight on it like lead. She was disoriented, and the sound of her own name rang in her ears. Then it struck her that she had not heard it from without but from within.

She remembered with disturbing clarity the conversation she had had with William when he chose to sleep in the study, too far away for her to hear him if he called. "If you need me, I will come," she'd said. "If you're no' strong enough to shout, call from in here, from your heart, and I'll hear ye."

William had smiled teasingly, wanting to diminish the sense of gloom that held them both in its grip. "What if I don't really need you, but only want you? What then?"

"I will come all the sooner," she had murmured.

Ailsa rose abruptly, threw her dressing gown over her flannel night-rail and started down the stairs. She had thought to find William watching the door expectantly, but he was sound asleep. She listened to his breathing, which was deep and regular. He had not just drifted off.

Ailsa shivered, though the room was overwarm, and knelt beside her sleeping husband. He was smiling so tenderly that her throat closed to block the tears. It came to her that he had kept on remembering after he fell asleep, and that she had been dreaming his dream with him, as he did. A dream of the first few days he had known her.

William's breathing became strained, and she heard a threatening rattle in his throat. She ran her hands gently over his chest to soothe his torment, though she knew it was useless.

She took his hand, and chills ran up her arms and down her back when she heard, "Ailsa!" more loudly than before. William's lips had not moved, though she felt the vibration of her name in his hand, in his pulse. "I'm here, *mo-charaid*. I'm with ye now."

His fingers tightened on hers, just slightly. With the other hand, he wound his fingers in her long, tangled hair. His eyes did not open nor his smile waver, even through the harsh, raw rasp of his breath. He was slipping away, moving beyond her grasp.

"Ailsa," he whispered, and, smiling, he released her.

10

"DO YE THINK IT'S THE RIGHT THING FOR YE, MEETING ALANNA so often this way?"

David Fraser stared at his grandfather's face through the gold-tinted firelight, redolent with the smell of peat. Flora sat beside her husband, equally concerned, her weathered face wrinkled in concentration. " 'Tis the only thing," David replied. "It's right. I've known that long since. But I'm not so sure it's wise."

Angus and Flora exchanged knowing glances. Despite their anxiety over their grandson, they looked at ease in the dimness of their cozy croft, with the soot-blackened clay walls and heavily thatched roof. The huge black pot from their supper had been removed from the fire, but the smell of mutton brose lingered, mingling with the pungent fragrance of peat and the smoldering coals at the edges of the fire. It felt like home.

David was doubly glad he had cashed in much of his investment in his father's company before he left Glasgow. He had soon recognized that Angus and Flora ate most of their suppers with Ian and Jenny not merely because they were lonely. They did not have much money put by, and Angus had grown too old to eke a living out of the land. Though Ian shared his family's labor as well as their profits with his parents, they were not well off.

David's arrival had been a blessing in more ways than one. He was able to buy mutton, which Ian taught him to slaughter, and beef and flour and milk to share with his grandparents. He had complained of the cold, though the late spring nights were often warm, and ordered several blankets to be woven by Mairi and Alanna. When they were finished, he claimed to be too restless at night, and left the blankets heaped on a stool near the fire. In the morning, he found Angus and Flora wrapped in the brightly colored wool, looking truly warm for the first time since he'd come.

After several nights, he had simply left the blankets on their bed, and they had made no comment, except a grateful smile. David was careful not to offer what they might consider charity. He made it clear that he was contributing to his board in order to save his own pride. No doubt his grandparents knew the truth of it, but they did not say so.

For that, and many other things, David was grateful. They had made him feel welcome, at ease; their croft might as well have been his home since childhood. They were always ready to listen when he wanted to talk, but they never asked questions he did not invite. He had loved both Angus and Flora dearly as a child. Now he remembered why.

Tonight, for the first time, Angus had stopped his grandson before he slipped away and asked him to sit awhile. He must have decided this was important enough to break his rule and ask straight out what he wanted to know.

Finally, Angus cleared his throat. "The Rose women have always had a strange kind of allure. Damned near irresistible, as far as I can tell." He paused, staring into the deeper shadows in the corner, seeing beyond the curved walls to a memory that could not be contained by clay and thatch and stone. "Was a time when we thought our Ian would marry Alanna's mother. But that was long ago. Too long to remember."

David could see that Angus did remember. His tone had been sad and wistful, even a bit angry. David decided, from the expressions of distress on his grandparents' faces, not to pursue the question of Ian and Ailsa Rose Sinclair, though he was intrigued. His uncle had never mentioned Alanna's mother. That was odd, since Ian and David spoke of Alanna and Mairi nearly every day.

David was eager to be on his way, yet he wanted to linger, to talk to people not caught up in the tempest of his feelings for Alanna. "Are you worried for her safety when she comes out so late?" he asked. He himself had been distressed by the nonchalance with which Alanna chose the night for their meetings. It was not simply that she felt it would be more private, that they would have the glen to themselves while the others slept, as she had told him. Alanna was not in the least afraid of coming out alone, despite the wildcats that roamed the woods and clearings, the volatile weather, and the danger of man, which David had come to fear most of all, growing up in the city. Alanna only laughed at him. As Angus did now.

"Och, laddie, no! The Roses are more at home in the woods at night. They've never been afraid of man or beast so far as I can tell. Only of their own hearts. And ye need not worry for Alanna Sinclair. Like her mother and her grandmother, she's safe in this place. I can no' say whether her protectors are the fairies or the spirits of the glen or the Celtic gods, but they watch over those lassies. Mairi and Ailsa and Alanna find solace in the darkness, not danger. I've often envied them that fearlessness, that contentment."

Flora nodded, eyes clouded with private thoughts that David could not decipher in the dim, quavering light. When she felt her grandson watching, she shook herself and looked up. "Go to her now, if she's waiting."

She smiled softly, and David caught his breath. For an instant he saw what Flora had been as a young woman, her face unlined, her hair deep auburn, her troubles not yet dreamed of. Impulsively, he leapt up and kissed her on the cheek. Then he touched his grandfather's shoulder and slipped out of the cottage.

Alanna was waiting, a thick letter in her hands. She had brought a pine torch and wedged it between two boulders. She had chosen the base of the hills, with their tip-tilted stones, as a place to meet him tonight. The light from the flame above gave her face an eerie glow, and her violet eyes looked smoke gray.

"What is it?" David asked. She was distraught as he had never seen her. It frightened him as the stealthy approach of a wildcat would not have.

Alanna did not answer at once. She threw herself into his

arms and held him; she was wearing only her night-rail under her plaid. She was so cold that her hands on his back raised chills, even through his flannel shirt and wool sweater.

For a long time, they swayed in silence while David gave what he could of himself—his strength and affection and commiseration. Finally she spoke. "A letter from my mother."

Her tone chilled him. "She can't come to the wedding?" As soon as the words were out, he knew they were ridiculous. Ailsa's absence would have hurt Alanna, distressed her, but not made her afraid.

Her hand trembling on his arm, she drew him down beside her, their backs to the scoured gray stone, the torchlight illuminating the scene with a strange glow of unreality.

"I'll read it to ye," Alanna said. Undaunted by the wavering light, she read her mother's closely written pages. Ailsa said that William Sinclair was more ill than they had thought, and that he wished to see Alanna, that Ailsa felt afraid and alone, that Cynthia and Colin came every day, and every day slipped further away, that she missed her daughter and wondered if she might come to London for a while.

David frowned. The words themselves were not disturbing, yet he knew they had caused Alanna's cold white hands and pallid face. He touched the letter gently. "Why?"

Alanna glanced up at him, then away. The kindness in his eyes was too dangerous to look upon. " 'Tis the words she doesn't write that frighten me. Papa's dying. I know it. I can feel it when I touch the splattered ink. I can feel her sorrow and terror. We sense things, she and I. We see beneath and beyond, things that others do not wish to see. David, she more than misses me. She needs me. She is growing weak from trying to be strong. I know that too. I can't—" She broke off, fighting back tears. "I don't know . . ."

Alarmed, David drew her closer. "You're confused right now. Don't try to think."

Alanna raised her head wildly. "I have to go to her. She's never asked this of me before. I have to go to Papa. I have to see him." Her voice faltered, and she rested her head on

David's shoulder, shivering violently. "She can no' have seen our telegram when she wrote this. She doesn't know, David."

He touched her hair, half-braided and half windblown, soft and damp with mist. "Alanna," he said, "I love you."

Alanna looked up, smiling tremulously through her tears. She brushed his parted lips with her fingertips. "Yes," she said. "And for that I thank the gods and the spirits." She paused, unable to speak, then added softly, "I need you."

He tilted her chin up and looked into her face, stunned. Since the first moment he met her, he had felt that she was certain, secure, strong. He had been the one who felt lost, awed and intimidated by her inner strength. He felt her shaking and knew that tonight, for the first time, he was the stronger of the two. She needed him to hold her together until daylight brought a measure of sanity to the gloom that swirled with the wings of night birds and the cry of a distant wind.

He looked at Alanna's high, defined cheekbones, at her violet eyes, darkened by panic and grief, at her disheveled hair, but he did not see those things. It was as if, in that moment, she stood before him, stripped of clothing, of skin and bones and muscle, so that only the flame of her soul was visible within her.

He saw that flame, and knew it, and the shock of recognition turned him rigid. He might have been staring into a mirror, the edges blurred by mist, the surface oddly warped, so that nothing but the spirit was revealed in the buckled glass. Before, he had loved Alanna, wanted her, admired and cherished her; he had promised to marry her and waited for that day with eagerness and amazement. But this was something different.

If he touched her now—as he would, because she had asked, and he could not deny her even if he wanted to—he would never be able to turn away again. She had opened herself to him completely, made herself vulnerable by letting her defenses turn to dust. If he moved toward her, toward that bright, hot flame that mesmerized him with its glow, he would fuse himself to her, soul to soul, sorrow to sorrow, spirit to spirit, in a bond that could not be broken. He sat for a moment, speechless, terrified by the magnificent and dangerous beauty of this moment.

Alanna waited, quaking with cold and shock, afraid that David might turn away, that she might have shown him too much too soon. But she had not decided to make this happen; she had simply let go of all that might hold her back and, without pretense, offered herself to the man she loved.

"I'm here," David said hoarsely, amazed that he was close to tears. He had not wept since his mother died, and then only alone and in silence, where no one else would see his grief. "I won't leave you."

Alanna sighed. Only then did he realize she had doubted, just a little. Somehow that reassured him. She was not a mystery or a goddess, a woman without fear or weakness. She was Alanna, good and bad, frail and strong, just as he was David.

She buried her head against his shoulder and slipped her arms around his waist. "What if you had not come to the glen?"

She had never asked a question like that before, never dreaded the answer. He had come. That was enough. But not for her, tonight. David was filled with tenderness as he held her close and buried his face in her Highland red hair.

"I'll not see my father again," Alanna whispered. " 'Twill be too late, I fear."

"You can't know that," David said. "The trains are getting faster every day."

Alanna smiled at him sadly. "No' fast enough. I told ye before, we sense things, my mother and my grandmother and I. For days I've felt strange and empty inside, dazed like a doe by a too bright light. Today, since I first held this letter in my hands, I've felt my mother's grief, because she can't. Not yet. She's cold inside, like the black mountains in winter—unreachable. Even if ye reach them, ye no' can scale them; they're too tall, too steep, too formidable. Like Ailsa's grief. So 'tis left to me to feel the tempest, the sharp, bitter wind that whirls and whirls, leaving barren trees and a dark hole in its wake. Devastation."

David shivered at the soft, low quality of her voice. It seemed to come from the air, from the wind and the darkness, rather than from inside her. She sounded like a stranger, and she shook and quivered and was chilled far deeper than her skin. So cold was she, so foreign the touch of her skin, he thought that in the light of day the sunbrowned color would have faded altogether, leaving her too pale. Alanna, daunted by nothing, felt brittle as a winter leaf rimmed in frost that would break apart beneath a single careless footstep.

The woman he had come to love was no longer here beside him. He did not know where she had gone. He only knew the sight of this pale, frightened girl with eyes that drew him right to the heart of the storm inside her, made him love her more. She needed him and trusted him, and though David didn't fully understand the desperation in her eyes, he knew he had to make it light again in Alanna's dreams.

They stood for a long time, holding each other, speaking promises without words, endearments without sound, clinging to the memory of that reflected flame.

"The wedding," Alanna said at last, looking up at him through a film of unshed tears. "What will happen if I go away?"

"I'll wait," David said firmly. "We'll postpone it till you're safe again, and whole." David tried to kiss away the pain in her eyes. "I will wait for you, Alanna. However long it takes."

"But I don't want to wait. How can I when I feel that tomorrow I might fly apart and never be myself again? I need ye now, to know that I'm yours and ye are mine, to know we're bound together and can no' be parted by time or grief or tears."

David frowned as her sense of urgency coursed through his own veins. The dread in her voice shook him deeply, and he held her tighter. He could not bear to lose her now, when they'd only just found each other. "What choice do we have?" he said carefully. He did not want her to hear the misery in his voice.

Leaning against him, her heart pounding so loudly that she heard the rush of her own blood, Alanna tried to think. "There is something," she said slowly. "I know from the old legends that there was a tradition not long past."

David raised her chin so he could look into her eyes. "Tell me."

"When two people were in love, and the clans were feuding and they foresaw their parents' wrath, they would plight their troth in private, just the two of them. I know 'twould mean naught in law, but I could believe in it, and no longer fear the leaving as I do."

David felt a tingle of hope and expectation. "Tell me how and we will do it."

"Tonight?" Alanna was still uncertain, afraid that she would lose him.

"Tonight."

She closed her eyes and sighed with relief, trembling but no longer cold. She described the ritual and David nodded. "Come," he said. "There's something I must get from Angus's."

Half an hour later, they stood on opposite sides of a tiny burn, facing each other. Alanna had stopped at Mairi's croft to change to her pale rose gown. She wore her plaid over her hair. She looked up at David and he took her hands.

In her palms she held an antique brooch, a silver Celtic knot, symbol of the mysteries and power of the past. David had searched his luggage until he found it and presented it with pride. "My mother gave it to me many years ago. I kept it because of her, to help me remember her. Then it was only part of the past. Now it will mark the beginning of our future."

Alanna had smiled, moved beyond words. Now she stood across the burn from her fiancé and stared up into the canopy of trees, then into David's eyes. "We've come to this place to bind us, each to each in our own hearts and minds, to help us know the other is there through whatever may come, now or tomorrow beyond tomorrow."

They knelt in silence, their only music the rippling leaves above and the burn at their feet, and washed their hands in the clear, murmuring water to signify the purity of their hearts. Then they rose and clasped hands across the water, holding the brooch tight between their cupped palms.

"I promise, as the men and women of old have promised, that so long as this burn runs, so long as this symbol exists and holds true, I will be true to ye, David Fraser," Alanna whispered.

Her hands were cold from the icy burn, but David warmed them with his smile. He leaned down to kiss their interwoven fingers. "I promise, with my heart, which you hold in your care, and my soul, which is the selfsame flame that burns in you, that as long as this burn flows, as long as this symbol is true and pure, I will be true to you, Alanna."

There was no one but the nightbirds to hear them, and none but the tall, ageless trees and the glittering stars to bear them witness, yet they spoke with reverence, and a hush fell about them, enfolded them and bound them.

"As the bards said in legends of old," Alanna whispered, " 'lovers meant to dance together, will dance together, if not in body, then in spirit. Their souls are mirrors, one of the other, and they see no one else in their hearts, where neither man nor woman can reach to change the image burned there by the gods.' "

David knew then, as they stood in the misted moonlight, hands clasped with the sound of the water all around, that no matter what ceremony followed in the months to come, no matter how magnificent, how crowded with friends and family and well-wishers, no matter how solemn and lovely and perfect, it would not equal the vow they'd made tonight: a vow that had made them man and wife as no minister of the kirk could ever do.

Their souls would not have flared, become visible and tangible in a kirk with the people looking on. Only tonight, in the soft darkness, alone with one another, had this thing been possible, inevitable.

Without speaking, David crossed the burn and kissed Alanna lightly. She closed her eyes and opened her lips to him, as she had opened her spirit at the foot of the tall mountains. The urgency had left her, and the desperate need. For tonight, at least, she was contented, and the fire she yearned for was a promise they had made to one another for tomorrow. Tonight it smoldered, slow, warm and seductive, as they leaned against a larch together, holding each other for hours in a silence more intimate than words or even touch could have created.

11

DAVID AND ALANNA RETURNED TO THE CROFT JUST AFTER dawn. Mairi was sitting at the plain oak table, her braid unraveling, her face haggard, dark shadows under her smoky violet eyes.

Alanna hurried to her grandmother and knelt, laying her head in Mairi's lap. "Forgive me. I know 'twas selfish, but I could no' leave him. Not before the dawn."

Mairi touched Alanna's bent head, ran her fingers lightly through the tangled strands of hair. "Alanna, *mo-run*, don't apologize for seeking a moment of happiness in the midst of sorrow. Joy is so precious. Don't let the envy of others deter ye. Whatever ye can grasp is yours and yours alone. Hold to it, birdeen. Never let go."

Finally the odd tone of Mairi's voice penetrated Alanna's anxiety. She noticed the crumpled paper on the table in front of her grandmother just as David did. Alanna faltered, then picked it up. It was a telegram.

Alanna,
  Your father died last night, smiling. Grateful to know you've found someone to make ye happy. I will bury him simply, if the gods give me the strength. After that, I do not know. I'm no longer certain ye should come;

by the time you arrive, the funeral will be over, his body lost to us.

Ailsa

Alanna sat down suddenly on a hard pine chair. She did not look at David because she could not. "I knew I'd not see him again." She reached for Mairi's hand, and her grandmother held tight.

"What will you do, *mo-eudail?* I'll help ye any way I can."

Alanna clung in silence for a long time, thankful that Mairi offered no words of comfort for a loss that could not be soothed or forgotten. Her father was dead. The dark wind spun more wildly in her head, and she knew Ailsa was struggling to hold on. "I must go. For Mama. She can no'—" She broke off, shook her head, and continued, "She can't bear it alone."

David stood beside her, helpless in the face of her unspoken grief. He touched her shoulder, and Alanna leaned toward him, resting her cheek against his arm.

From the low, warped doorway, someone cleared his throat. All three looked up in astonishment. Even Mairi had forgotten Adam Munro, the constable from Cannich, who had brought the telegram. He had stepped outside when they heard Alanna returning.

"Ye should know that the coach that runs to Glasgow was fair destroyed in the last great storm. It'll no' be easy to reach the train. And the telegram was already delayed. It came to Beauly—they've the only telegraph machine for miles—on the Friday afternoon, and what with the storm, we only got it yesterday. 'Tis Tuesday now, and six days since . . . it happened." He held his hat in his hands and glanced nervously at Alanna. "My condolences, miss. But I thought ye should know."

Alanna tried to remember how to breathe. Just last week she and David had sent their own telegram with Callum Mackensie when he went to Beauly for seed. It had taken him two days in his slow wagon. She did not blame the constable for the delay, but was desperate to be up and away. "She needs me now. And I her." She ran her hand through her tousled hair. "He's dead and I can no' see his face." She buried her head in her hands, choked with regret and self-recrimination.

"I'll hire a horse," David said. His voice shook, but his face was stony with determination. "I'll take ye down to Glasgow myself."

Adam Munro frowned. "Aye, but from there the train takes a day and a half. And at least two or three on the horse. 'Twould no' be a pleasant journey."

Mairi gasped, and the others turned to stare at the vacant expression in her eyes. Her tone was low and stilted; she spoke with someone else's voice. "By the time ye get near London, Ailsa will be on her way here. On her way home."

Alanna knew when the Sight was upon her grandmother. She felt it in the chilly air, the film of perspiration on Mairi's pale skin, the slight trembling of her hands. "Are ye sure?"

Mairi made an effort to shake off the image of her daughter's stone-carved face and turned to her granddaughter. "I'm certain."

"How can you know a thing like that?" David asked, shattering the unnatural hush that followed. Chills ran up his back, and the air was stifling. *"How* can you be certain?"

Alanna turned to him, hands outstretched. "I forgot, ye don't know. But I've told ye before, we 'see' things, true things, though we're no' always able to understand. If Grandmama says it, I believe her. I have to." But David's skepticism seemed to feed her own doubt. "Mayhap I should try . . ."

Mairi said nothing, afraid to offer what might well be her own wish, rather than what was best for her granddaughter.

David did not know what to think. Too much had happened too quickly. The peculiar look in Mairi's eyes, the sound of her stranger's voice would not leave him. He paced uneasily while Alanna sat staring at her hands.

At last she raised her head. "I'd best wait here. Better that than to miss her along the way." Her lips were bloodless, her knuckles white on the table top. She turned to the constable. "Mr. Munro, if I write it down for ye, can ye send a telegram out today?"

"Aye. Soon as I get back to Beauly. I'll see to it myself. Your mother will no' be alone if I can help it."

Sitting down with a piece of paper, pen and ink, Alanna scowled and sought the words she knew did not exist, the words that would keep her mother sane. After starting, then crossing out line after line, she noticed the constable's restlessness and handed over the rough note.

He put it in his breast pocket, patting it to show her it was safe. "I'd best be off if ye want this in London by nightfall. They're much quicker at that end, ye ken. Don't worry." He smiled awkwardly when he saw that he was speaking into empty eyes. "Good-bye." He was gone.

Alanna sank into the rocking chair. There was no point in undertaking an arduous journey to her mother's side if Ailsa would not be there when she arrived. No doubt William Sinclair was already buried—lost to her beneath damp soil and fresh green grass. She was tempted to go just the same, not only so she could stand beside his grave where the newly turned earth had become shroud and shield of her father's lifeless body. She wanted to go *because* she would suffer. To punish herself for having left him to die slowly and in agony while she found her happiness in paradise.

Cynthia Sinclair Harcourt sat stiffly on the drawing room sofa, hands lying neatly in the folds of her black bombazine gown. On one side sat her husband, Peter, a nephew of Gerald Harcourt—an old friend of William's—on the other her brother, Colin. They sat very close together, Cynthia's brown hair nearly concealed by an elaborate black bonnet, draped with sweeping veils to cover her grief, beads of jet to deflect the eye from the gleam of her tears, black feathers and lace to draw attention away from the pale face hidden beneath. But she could not hide her hugely rounded belly, heavy with child.

Her brother's chestnut hair was uncovered. He held his top hat in his hands, circling the brim endlessly with nervous fingers. His blue-gray eyes were expressionless. Peter wore his hat atop blond curls, his cheeks unnaturally flushed beside the faces of his wife and brother-in-law.

To Peter had fallen the task of working out the details of the funeral. Not only had Ailsa been unable to sit and contemplate lists, to concentrate on where and when and how, but Peter knew, if she had been alert and aware, she would have fought him and decreed a simple funeral without the grandeur, decorum and dignity William and his family deserved. No one would snigger at the Sinclairs behind their backs; Peter Harcourt had seen to it.

The house on Larkspur Crescent was dark and gloomy; Peter himself had instructed the servants to pull down all the shades as a sign of respect and a somber warning to others that this family was in mourning. Everyone avoided the windows except Ailsa, who peered through a narrow gap in the blind, hungry for light and air.

She stood with one hand on the brocade curtain, one on the motionless strings of the harp. She too was dressed in black, though her crepe gown was simple, with a single ruffle rather than a bustle, a high neck with a thin black ribbon and long, plain sleeves. Her only adornment was her wedding ring and a mourning brooch of silver, fashioned in a series of Celtic knots with William's name engraved in the center. Her veil was a circle of black tulle; she had stood this morning, staring at it where it lay in the center of her four-poster bed, the pale green of the duvet just visible through the delicate, chainlike links of the veil. Like armor made of smoke.

Though there were many people in the room, Ailsa was very much alone at the window. The harp was more real to her, even silent, than the clouds broken by sun that touched her face intermittently.

At first after William died she had not been alone. For a short time Cynthia had stayed near, but in the end, what she had needed was for Ailsa to deny the truth. When she would not, Cynthia had turned away. Since then, Cynthia had clung solely to her husband. Peter patted his wife's hand occasionally and said the proper things. He even meant them. But grief frightened him as much as it frightened Cynthia, so he did not probe her facade of stern acceptance. To him, her advanced pregnancy made her seem vulnerable, awkward and ill.

Ailsa struggled to remember to breathe, to take deep gulps of air to clear the heaviness from her lungs. A hundred times a day she went to check on the bed in the study, to brew some herbs for a poultice or some soothing tea. A hundred times a day she stood, unable to comprehend the emptiness of the bed where her husband used to lie. There was no indentation of his body, no scent of him on the pillow. It was sterile and abandoned. Like Ailsa herself.

She closed her fingers on the strings of the harp, striking a discordant note. Peter had wanted to lay her husband out in this room so his relatives and friends could file solemnly round the bier, but Ailsa had refused. She explained that William himself had insisted there be no viewing, that he be buried as expediently as the stringent formalities would permit. He did not want people to see him as he was, but to remember him as he had been.

Secretly, Ailsa was glad. She could not have borne to stand quietly in the corner while those who had not loved her husband stared into his lifeless face and talked of him as if he were not there, as if he could not hear or understand. They, who were alive, would circle him like birds of prey, glorying in their own vitality as they regretted, or pretended to regret, his loss.

Yet she would not have objected to Peter's plan if William had not asked her to. Ailsa had lost her sense of purpose, become a puppet with no master, following instructions numbly. Her strength was gone. She had given it to her husband to take with him on his journey and had kept none for herself. Though she sat with him every day, it was not until he lay dead that Ailsa recognized how frail William had become, how much of him had departed, bit by bit, long before that night when his soul slipped away, leaving her, at last, completely alone.

"Ailsa." Anne Kendall, an old friend of the Sinclairs, touched Ailsa on the shoulder. She did not say she was sorry; she knew Ailsa did not want to hear it, could not yet bear kindness or sympathy from her friends. "We're here. All of us. I just wanted you to know."

Ailsa acknowledged her friend with a nod, and though she reached up to touch Anne's hand, her fingers were cold and stiff.

She had been aware for some time of the arrival of Anne and Phillip Kendall, of Giles Saunders and Maude Steel, Laura Durand and David Finney; aware too of the absence of Robbie Douglas, who had died of consumption several years ago. She wanted to turn and gather her friends close, but did not dare. To do that would be to risk losing her grasp on the tightly held control she struggled minute by minute to maintain.

She looked up sharply when the last of the carriages rolled ominously into view—the black-caparisoned horses, the carriage with black plumes at the corners, black ribbon wound among the spokes of the wheels. Ailsa gripped the harp tighter, making it moan, just as Peter Harcourt rose and said, "It's time."

12

WHEN DAVID MET HIS UNCLE IN THE CLEARING, IAN INSISTED on taking him back to the croft. "Ye look like you're about to drop, man. Come, rest ye awhile, and eat."

David thought there was a reason why he shouldn't, but he couldn't remember what it was. He was dazed by the wild extremes of emotion of the night and early morning. He could do nothing for Alanna; he was helpless, and he hated the feeling.

As he sat at Ian's pine table, anger rushed through him like fire that cauterizes an open wound, then waned as quickly as it had come. Last night he and Alanna had spoken a vow, eternal and unbreakable, binding them one to the other. That was why, this morning, he felt the full force of her sorrow and was frightened by his own response. He had worked long and hard not to feel his own pain. Those old wounds were long scarred over. What would happen to him now if, in bleeding for Alanna, he himself began to bleed?

He started at the sound of his uncle's voice.

"What's happened? Can ye tell us? Is it Alanna?"

Jenny hovered protectively at David's side, pouring more tea as he drained his carved wooden cup. " 'Tis all right," she said. "Ye can speak freely. The children are gone for the moment."

"It *is* Alanna, in a way. Her father died last week and she only just received the telegram today. She's turned quiet and her hands are cold." He knew the words were flat and far too simple, but he could find no others.

"William Sinclair is dead?" Ian asked.

David was not aware that Jenny flinched and returned to the dishes piled beside the pump, her back to the room and her husband's expressionless face.

"Yes." David found he was hungry after all, though he'd accepted his uncle's invitation because it was too difficult to think how to refuse. And he did not want to be alone. Guiltily, he realized he was relieved to be away from the Rose croft, pleased to see the morning light brighten these clay walls, the mist creeping in at the door, the sun warming away the chill of night.

"I wanted to stay," he said mulishly, afraid someone might see inside his heart and contradict him. "But they told me to go."

Ian nodded. "The Rose women have always chosen to grieve alone. Perhaps because they feel things so deeply, 'tis hard for an outsider to understand."

Jenny dropped a spoon that clattered against the press before it hit the packed dirt floor, but David did not notice. He was thinking of the burn in moonlight, of hands clasped around a Celtic knot, of sitting in Alanna's arms till dawn. "I'm not an outsider!"

Ian was startled by David's vehemence. He considered his

nephew in silence, glad for the momentary distraction. He knew of the planned marriage, but he saw now that the bond went deeper than that. He saw something in David Fraser he had never seen before. "No, you're not, are ye? It must hurt to have them turn ye away."

Hands clenched around the spoon she had retrieved from the floor, Jenny asked tensely, "Will Alanna go to London?"

David stopped eating his warm porridge and put both hands on the table to hold himself upright. "No. She's already missed the funeral, and Mairi says by the time she could catch a train, her mother will be on her way back to the glen. She says she 'saw' it in the mist before the dawn. So Alanna will wait. But I'm afraid for her."

Ian regarded his nephew with an odd expression in his green eyes. "Are ye afraid of Mairi as well? Do ye even believe her?"

"What frightens me is that I *do* believe her. There's no logical, rational reason why I should, except that Alanna does. But it isn't even that. I looked into Mairi Rose's eyes and knew she spoke the truth." David ran both hands through his dark hair, green eyes troubled. "Alanna seems to be experiencing her mother's torment as well as her own. I know she's strong, but still ..." He paused to meet his uncle's gaze. "I think I'm a little afraid to meet this woman Alanna loves so much."

"I can understand that," Ian murmured.

Jenny choked on the morning air and gripped the wooden counter tightly. "Is Alanna's mother coming for a visit, to escape her grief?"

David was startled by his aunt's agitation. He turned to stare at Jenny's stiff back, her bent head, crowned by her thick brown braid. Suddenly he remembered Angus's troubled voice. *Was a time when we thought our Ian would marry Alanna's mother. But that was long ago. Too long to remember.* He remembered, as well, the look in his grandfather's eyes, the sadness and sense of loss, even after all these years.

Ian's face revealed nothing, but David thought he knew why Jenny had left the table, had not turned to look at them since William's name was mentioned. David was surprised.

He had seen how close Ian and Jenny were, how devoted to one another and their family. Why should the mention of a name fill the air with such a taste of foreboding? "I'm thinking it's more than that," he murmured. There was no point in lying, no kindness in delaying speaking the truth aloud. Jenny Fraser had the right to know. "Mairi said Ailsa is coming home to stay."

Ailsa stood with her family at the edge of her husband's grave. A breeze rippled the sunlight, lifting her veil. Though the air was heavy with warmth, she felt a deep chill and clenched her teeth. With that breeze, that chill, came memory.

Just so had she stood three years ago, almost to the day, at the foot of a gaping hole in the valley where Charles Kittridge had chosen to be buried. "Let me rest, Ailsa-*aghray*," he had said two days before. "I'm so tired. And I have so much." Her father had touched her cheek with affection and looked at his other two daughters and his wife with satisfaction. "I am content."

At the foot of his grave, with nothing but the lid of a plain pine coffin to stare at, Ailsa had wanted to shout, "But *I* have nothing!" She'd looked at her pale, stricken sisters and added fiercely, in silence, *"We* have nothing!"

She glanced at her mother, a widow who had barely known what it was to be a wife, at her own daughter Alanna, who alone of Ailsa's children had chosen to know her grandfather. Ailsa looked at her half-sister Lian, exotic, shrouded in the mask of her dignity, at Genevra, young, pellucid and vulnerable. Ailsa had come from London, her sisters from halfway around the world, at the summons of Charles Kittridge, who had bidden them know him, forgive him, and watch him die.

All Ailsa's life, her father had been a void inside her—charming and mysterious, illusive and enticing, gone before she was even born. In the few short months she had been in the glen, she had come to know him as a man. But those fleeting days and hours and minutes had not filled the void.

The landscape only deepened her depression. The fierce

mountains, beautiful and frightening in their distant splendor, the valley with its melancholy voices and shadows, the cold, savage wind in this wild, abandoned place.

She wanted to fall to her knees and plead for her father to come back and give her some of the peace he'd found. "Ye took it all and left us nothing!" she shouted inwardly. "Don't ye see how empty we are? How lost without ye?" The words welled up in her and she thought she could not stop them.

She remembered her sisters, her mother, her daughter. They were teetering on the edge of that grave, just as she was, as stricken and as helpless. They were bound by an invisible thread that held them together in grief and desperation. Ailsa knew, in that instant, that if she stumbled, if she broke the thread, they would collapse, one after the other. She saw in their faces that they too felt the unraveling thread; the only thing that kept them upright was the knowledge of each other's weakness. If one fell, they would all fall, endlessly, into the gaping black hole of Charles Kittridge's grave.

Now she stared at the polished mahogany of William's casket while the breeze threatened to lift her veil. As suddenly as it had come, the wind faded into the May sunlight, over the manicured English lawn, scattered with substantial and expensive marble stones and monuments.

Like those monuments, Ailsa was cold and unbending. Three years ago, her anguish had consumed her; today she stood far away from all that was happening around her. She viewed it through a distant haze, as if she had no part in the ceremony of farewell. Just now, she was closer to the past than the present. That was her shield and her salvation.

As she had contemplated the uncovered faces of her sisters, naked in their sorrow, she now glanced at those who stood around the tidy rectangular hole in the earth where William Sinclair would lie. They were elegant in black moire and silk and bombazine, with veils to hide their thoughts, top hats and canes to lend an air of respectability. Ailsa was sickened by the cool refinement of it all, and the sweet heavy scent of too many flowers.

Cynthia and Colin were side by side, pale, shocked and obdurate. Peter Harcourt's pleasingly aristocratic features were arranged in a properly solemn countenance, but behind the mask, Ailsa could not guess what he was feeling, or *if* he was.

Cynthia glanced toward her mother, then away, flushing under her heavy veil when she caught Ailsa's gaze. Ailsa had been vaguely aware of a sense of unease; now it took on shape and color. Her children were watching her nervously, afraid she would embarrass them by crying out or weeping bitter tears.

She could not do such a thing to William. Though he had come to question and even despise Victorian attitudes toward behavior, he had never quite buried the impressionable young boy who had been taught to memorize, internalize the proper values.

They would bury that boy today. At last he would be free. Ailsa closed her eyes, which felt dry and filmed in sand. She had not slept in two nights, had not rested for months, but something held her upright. She was paralyzed. She felt her heart beating and knew the blood was moving through her veins, though her emotions were wrapped in ice.

William Sinclair had been her husband, the body of her strength for the past twenty-three years. "He was not your strength, *mo-run*," Mairi's voice whispered. "Ye were his. In your mind, ye know that well. Ye must make your heart remember." Ailsa looked around frantically, hopefully, but her mother was not there. Yet her voice had been clearer, more real than the drone of the parson about ashes and dust, Heaven and angels and all of William's virtues. She shuddered.

Cynthia and Colin flanked her suddenly, taking her arms firmly, like soldiers with their weapons hidden in their hands.

"It's all right, Mother," Cynthia said, in a high, reedy voice unlike her own. "We'll be all right." It was more a command than a reassurance. She refused to let her father go, to admit that he was gone. She would deny the God she worshiped this ultimate, irrevocable power.

With Peter's subtle intervention, Colin and Cynthia

guided Ailsa away from her friends, who were too open, too outspoken, too dangerous and kind. The four members of the family climbed into the black carriage in silence.

Peter came last. He closed the door firmly, though the other mourners looked disconcerted by this abrupt departure. But they would meet later, at William's Aunt Abigail's, where a light supper would be served and condolences accepted.

Through her black tulle veil, Ailsa watched and worried. Colin would probably be all right. He knew the world and its hazards and ugliness. He understood that what was most valued was most often taken away. But Cynthia did not.

William Sinclair's daughter did not know how to grieve. She had never had to face this kind of devastation before. Her pregnancy only made it worse. She was in danger from her body, not yet ready to support the burden she carried beneath her heart, and from her heart itself, not yet ready to carry the weight of her sorrow. She bit her lips, clasped her hands and kept her face impassive, pretending nothing had changed, because this change was impossible to understand, impossible to accept.

Ailsa's sense of unreality increased. She did not know these people, these grim strangers dressed in black. She thought of Alanna, who wept as freely as she laughed, grieved as deeply and openly as she rejoiced. Her hand closed around the telegram in her pocket. Alanna had said she would come if Ailsa needed her, then asked if her mother might not like to come home for a time to regain her strength. She could feel her daughter's presence in those words, hear Alanna's voice, and Mairi's, offering consolation. But Ailsa was beyond consolation. She was cold and stiff as stone.

She was glad her daughter had not come. Alanna knew her mother too well, shared her instincts and her passions. If she had had to look just once into Alanna's eyes, the thread would have snapped, finally, and Ailsa would have fallen into that dark hole in the earth.

13

"WHATEVER ARE YE THINKIN' OF, DAD?" GAVIN FRASER asked in exasperation. "That's the second time today you've been by. Do ye no' trust me to check the sheep myself?"

Ian was taken aback. He did not remember having come up this hill earlier until his son pointed out his odd behavior. "Of course I trust ye. I just thought it would go faster with the two of us."

Since Gavin had been handling this particular task alone for more than three years, he wondered at his father's motive. He glowered at Ian and noticed he was not watching the sheep at all, but gazing around him, perplexed. Scratching his head, Gavin abandoned the lambs he had been marking. Now that he thought about it, his father had seemed distracted the past few days. At home he never allowed his attention to wander from his wife, the girls and Gavin, but lines of strain had begun to appear around his mouth. "Is something worryin' ye, Dad?"

"Worrying me? No. 'Tis the spring gotten into my blood, no doubt." Ian smiled with an edge of unease. He had been thinking of William Sinclair's death as he climbed through heather and bracken, the bees buzzing among the primroses and a hedge sparrow chortling in the hawthorn hedge along the way. Several times in the past few days he had found himself thinking of William, wondering how he died and why Ian should be so engrossed by the question that more than once he had forgotten where he was going and why.

Gavin saw that his father was puzzled and felt unaccountably alarmed. Ian had always been confident and certain, but lately, out on the hills and moors, he seemed bemused, a little disoriented. Gavin depended on his father for advice when he himself was confused, and had never considered the possibility that Ian himself might lose his way. "Mayhap you're ill and should see Mairi Rose," Gavin suggested warily.

Ian squeezed his son's shoulder in an attempt at reassurance. "I'm no' ill. I told ye, 'tis just the sunlight after such a long winter that's made me a little daft. Get back to your work, son. I'll leave ye in peace."

He turned to go, aware that Gavin watched him closely. Ian began to whistle and saunter through hedges and underbrush. But before he had reached the bottom of the hill, he was thinking of Ailsa, a widow now, alone in London.

He should not care, except that once they had been friends. He cut the thought off there, before it could go further. It had all been long ago, when he was little more than a child, younger than Gavin. "But a child's heart is true," he whispered to a red squirrel that skittered across his path, "untouched by the shadows or doubts woven by others."

He picked up a hawthorn stick and slashed at the heather, surprised by the force of his own frustration. Things had changed a great deal since he was a child. His heart had grown wise with the years, and his eyes saw both more and less than they once had. He knew Jenny was afraid; he could feel it, though she said nothing.

His wife was afraid because William was dead and Ailsa free. Except Ian suspected she was not free, but held captive by her sorrow. Ian thought with gratitude of his own family, to whom he was bound as the glen was bound to the ancient past. Jenny and Brenna, Gavin, Glenyss and Erlinna were of his blood as the mist was of the water before it drifted upward to caress his sun-browned skin.

Yet he could not stop himself from imagining Ailsa's suffering. He wished Alanna were with her, and Mairi. She needed them, he was sure, despite the presence of her other children. From what Alanna said, they were more English than Scottish, had inherited and chosen their father's blood over their mother's.

He stopped beneath a cherry tree with the last of its pure

white flowers trembling on narrow twigs, falling free in a circling dance toward the earth. It came to him that it was not merely Ailsa's grief that was weighing on his mind. It was the sound of Mairi's voice—a sound he had not heard, but which nevertheless echoed softly in his head—promising, *Ailsa will be on her way here. On her way home.*

"Papa! Will ye play a game with me?" Erlinna whirled through the fallen white petals, so they rose around her like drifts of snow. She was carrying the toy soldiers Ian had carved when Gavin was born, and her hazel eyes were full of hope.

Ian knelt and hugged her, glad that she had come, reminding him with her laughter and innocence how much he had, how lucky he had been, after all. "If I play, ye must promise not to cheat," he warned his daughter.

Erlinna grinned. "I'd no' do that to ye." Her smile was guileless, but there was a mischievous spark in her eyes. "Though if I don't win, 'twill break my heart," she said mournfully.

Ian shivered, though the day was warm. "We can no' have that, can we?" He found a level piece of ground and settled on the grass while Erlinna plumped herself down beside him. Ian wondered, as they sorted out the painted wooden figures, if the thoughts that deviled him were expectations or temptations or prayers. If prayers, did he want Mairi to be wrong or right?

"Papa! You're no' payin' attention. You're bound to lose if ye play like that."

"Aye," Ian muttered. "So I am."

"Madam, you haven't eaten all day," Lizzie called plaintively after her mistress, an insubstantial shadow floating down the murky hall. "You'll make yourself ill if you go on this way, see if you don't."

Ailsa tilted her head, perplexed. She must have eaten. She didn't feel the least bit hungry. Or did she? Was that rumble inside a warning of hunger? She could not tell. Since her husband's death, she had lost all sense of the needs of her body. She ate or changed or lay in bed sleepless when someone, usually Lizzie, told her to do so. She could not tell the difference between day and night, nor did she care.

Lizzie was worried to distraction. She approached warily, afraid Ailsa might flee. "Mr. William would have wanted you to eat regular. He wouldn't have liked to see you like this." She hated to resort to such tactics, but William Sinclair's wishes seemed to be the only thing Ailsa responded to.

She had turned to Lizzie often as she moved a candlestick or bundled up his clothing or fingered her own gowns. "Would William have wanted this?" she asked again and again.

Lizzie had never seen her mistress uncertain or unwilling to make a decision, dependent on the wishes of others, particularly a dead man. This was not the Ailsa she had come to admire. The housekeeper wanted to weep in pity at the frail, ghostlike figure of Ailsa Sinclair, the strongest woman she had ever known.

Ailsa was always barefoot now; she could never seem to find her slippers. Her hair was loose and uncombed and she wore her plainest gowns, often tying up her skirts as she had when she was a girl. She wandered the halls, restless and lost, hoping each time she entered an empty room that she would find what she was looking for.

Gently, Lizzie took her mistress's shoulders and guided her toward the dining room, standing nearby as Ailsa picked at the cold chicken salad on her plate.

Unable to stand the suspense any longer, Lizzie blurted out, "What will you do, ma'am, now that your husband's left the house to Colin?" She had been shocked when she'd heard about the will, but she knew now that Mr. Sinclair had been right to provide for his son, who was too much a scapegrace to provide for himself, though he might grow out of that phase someday. William had left an income to his wife as well, stating in the will that he hoped she would take it and go back to Scotland, where, in her heart, she knew she belonged.

The master had been very wise, Lizzie thought. It seemed that so long as she stayed in this house, Ailsa would continue to decline. She would not recover from the grief that robbed her of vitality, resilience, will. "I don't think your son will make you go, but surely you don't want to stay. What will you do?"

"Do?" Ailsa repeated the word without comprehension. When she saw the compassion in Lizzie's face, she grabbed the housekeeper's hand. "I'm no' certain what to do anymore. I try to think, but the thoughts will no' come. Nothing comes—just darkness."

The grip of her hands was a plea, and her eyes were the eyes of a frightened child or a very old woman. "You're only forty-one," Lizzie cried. "You have time, and a future. Don't give up and let them slip away." She forced herself to speak calmly, to hide the hysteria building inside. "Perhaps you should go back to the glen, as Mr. William wanted."

"The glen?" Again, the words had no meaning. Ailsa released Lizzie's hands and rose from the table. "Go back?" She glanced down at her dusty feet. "I'd not be knowin' how."

Ailsa forgot Lizzie and drifted into the hall. William's hall. William's house. Now that he was gone, she wondered if she had known him any better than she'd known her father, if she'd given her husband enough to make up for the part of her he could not have. *I let her go so I would not have to lose you.*

Somewhere in the dark recesses of her mind, she knew she was torturing herself needlessly, that she had made William as happy as he knew how to be. Yet she could not let him go, and so she could not rest.

She paused before the large painting that dominated one wall of the drawing room. The subjects were herself and her two half-sisters, Lian and Genevra, each in her element— Ailsa beside a burn in a lush wood, Lian draped in Chinese silk, Genevra lost in a dream as she painted a portrait. The layered oils captured the essence of each girl so well, the details were so finely drawn, so sensitively rendered, that Ailsa felt the presence of the other girls as if they stood beside her. They had come to her before when she was in need. She touched the surface, caressing their familiar faces with gentle fingertips. She wanted to lay her cheek against theirs, to feel their strength flow through her, their affection and understanding. Lian and Genevra knew her so well.

Inevitably, Charles Kittridge's face rose in Ailsa's mind. Father of all three girls, he had worked on this canvas for months before he died. The painting had been his last gift; in it he had captured the daughters he barely knew. Ailsa had been astounded by his talent and sensitivity. He had learned and felt and shared so much in so short a time. Charles Kittridge had left the painting to his eldest daughter, and she had brought it here, both because she could not bear to leave it behind and to protect it from the mist and damp that permeated her home in the glen. She had come to it often for consolation. To her it was a living thing that brought back her sisters, both so far away, and her father, who was dead.

The painting did not console Ailsa today. Her fingertips felt numb and thick-skinned, insensitive to the soul of the painting. Odd, she thought, that she still looked as she had by that lovely bubbling burn in the deep green woods. That was how William had loved her best—hair wild, barefoot, clothes a source of warmth and protection, not adornment or pretension. He had begged her to go back to the glen, had wanted to think of her as he had found her—free of the judgment and restriction of society. That's why he had left the house to Colin, not only because his son needed it, but because his wife did not.

Ailsa felt an unexpected blaze of anger, the first thing other than resignation she had felt since his death. William had decided her future for her, it seemed, long before he was gone. She sighed as she stood on the threshold of the drawing room, uncertain whether to go in or turn away. Perhaps it had not been William's right to decide where she would go and what she would do, but just now, she had no will to decide for herself.

The anger was followed by a wave of self-disgust. "This can no' go on," she murmured into the dusty air. She was clinging to her paralysis, not trying to recover. It was easier to fall back into memory and inaction. To move forward would be to come face to face with her grief, and that she could not do.

She wanted to weep, to ease the leaden weight inside, but she could not break through the defensive haze that swathed her emotions. She could not let go *and* hold on at the same time.

The sound of a key turning in the lock made her look up, full of a ridiculous hope. But Colin and Cynthia came through the door, not William. They saw her and stopped, glowering with disapproval. She had seen that look often in the past two days. Her children had tried to hide their embarrassment over Ailsa's appearance and listless lack of direction, but they had failed.

When they were seated in the drawing room and Sally had brought tea, Cynthia edged her bulky body forward. "We've been thinking, Mother. About what Papa said in his will."

Ailsa blinked at her daughter and said nothing.

"About going to Scotland," Colin added helpfully. "We know you want to go for Alanna's wedding. It's the perfect opportunity."

"Alanna would be so disappointed if you weren't there. And there's certainly no reason to stay here," Cynthia offered. The color in her cheeks and the clatter of her teacup revealed her nervousness. She hurried on before Ailsa could hear what she was not saying. "Aunt Abigail and her friends have offered to help go through the house and sort things, clear them out. And Colin and I will be here too. So you needn't stay on that account."

Ailsa paled, appalled. They had discussed this with Abigail Fielding before mentioning it to their mother. And they knew full well that Abigail and Ailsa had never been friendly, though they'd gotten along for William's sake. That Cynthia and Colin had gone behind her back, that they had planned this thing, that they wanted her to go so badly broke her heart.

For the second time that day, a shaft of pain pierced her defenses. Cynthia and Colin were not like her, but they were her children. Hers and William's. They were all that was left of that fine man. Except for Alanna. Thank the gods for Alanna. But she was far away, and Ailsa sat in the drawing room of William's house, confronted by her other two children, unable to ignore the distaste in their eyes. They thought she was mad. No doubt they had told Abigail Fielding as much, and she would have concurred.

Perhaps she *was* mad to wander these murky halls, craving the feel of the turf beneath her feet and the song of waters and the wind in her hair. But those cravings were a betrayal of William, and that she could not allow.

"We know you want to go back. You always have," Colin said with unexpected bitterness. "Father often told us you didn't belong in the city."

"He said you should be in paradise or fairyland," Cynthia chimed in disparagingly. "Honestly. I can't imagine what he was thinking. Sometimes he frightened me when he talked that way. And now"—she pointed to Ailsa's crumpled gown and uncombed hair, the dust on her feet and the smudge on her cheek—"look at you, Mother. Fairyland indeed!" Bedlam is more like it, her curled lip said without making a sound. "You're not even wearing proper mourning clothes. Don't you care at all what people think of us?"

Ailsa stifled a hysterical giggle. "And who'll be seein' me here, alone in this house of grief? No one dares come, or cares to."

"None but your peculiar friends. You've been wise to send them away. They might actually want to play music and sing and dance." Cynthia shuddered at the thought of such a blatant breach of formal mourning etiquette.

Ailsa could not find her voice. She had tried to understand her two younger children. She had tried to make up for loving Alanna more. But they had fought her, turning to William for encouragement, advice, affection. They were not merely afraid of her, she thought, eyeing Cynthia's enlarged belly and swollen ankles laced tightly into her boots. It occurred to her that Colin and Cynthia did not like their mother very much. Not once, since William's death, had the three of them wept together. She was surprised how much that hurt.

Noticing the direction of Ailsa's glance, Cynthia said breathlessly, "You're not to worry about the baby. Peter has retained the best doctor in London." She could not hide a shiver of dread.

To Cynthia, the baby was a burden, not a living thing, not a child to lavish with the love she had once given her father. Suddenly Ailsa was afraid for her daughter. But there was nothing she could say, nothing Cynthia wanted to hear.

Disappointment curled through Ailsa like a wisp of pungent smoke, raw and hot around the edges. Her children were right; there was nothing more she could do here. She could not feel William's presence in this house, though she had sought it day and night. He was gone, and she would not find him again. Defeated by her children's embarrassment and rejection, she would fulfill her last promise and try with all her cold and dried-out heart to fly free one more time.

14

"I THINK I'VE FINISHED THE WALLS," DAVID EXCLAIMED with pride.

They had decided to clean up the croft for Ailsa's impending arrival, confirmed by a telegram, and David had chosen to refinish the stone walls. Beneath the soot were many layers of earth and clay to keep the cold from creeping in, but they were old and cracking. David took pride in his work, and he'd coated the walls in fine cream clay colored with a touch of red, but transparent, so the other layers glimmered through, in patterns and swirls that made the croft look freshly painted.

"Why David Fraser, you're an artist, sure as I live and breathe," Mairi cried in awe. She had been cleaning the wooden settle, raking old ashes from the fireplace in the center of the room while scrubbing the gray residue of smoke from every surface she could reach. She looked up, breathing heavily, and saw what David had done.

The fresh clay was lighter, which brightened the small croft, and the subtle designs gave the walls character. Mairi paused in her work to admire the house that had been her home for forty years. The small windows, covered with leather thrown back to admit the late spring sun, did not let in much light, but the wide-open door admitted a swathe of radiance that gave new life to this old croft.

It smelled fresh as well, because Alanna and Brenna Fraser had washed down the walls before David began, and David and Gavin had put on a fresh roof of heather, rushes and turf. Alanna had been working in the vegetable and herb garden, pulling weeds and planting fresh rosemary, thyme and chamomile, while she tended the cabbages, leeks, beans, and carrots. The scent of fresh-turned earth, sweet honeysuckle and pungent herbs drifted through the kitchen window, mingling with the smell of soap and polish.

The boxbeds with their sliding doors, as well as the dresser and the press in the kitchen, had been rubbed with vegetable oil till they shone, the bedding aired, and a new blanket begun on the spinning wheel in the corner. Bright-colored skeins of wool lay neatly in a basket beside the wheel, and Ian had carved new bowls and cups and horn spoons for the table. Ian himself had not come by in the last few days, though he sent his children as often as they were free.

Brenna and Glenyss did little favors, always bringing squares of peat to refill the peat neuk for nighttime summer fires. They especially loved it when, like today, Alanna opened chests and drawers to sort through the contents and make room for her mother's clothing and books. The girls looked through it all, fascinated by this peek into other, and therefore more interesting, lives.

Alanna's books were jumbled beside her on the floor—books by Thackeray and Sir Walter Scott, Robbie Burns and George Eliot. There were books of poetry, history and novels; she had learned to read in London, where the supply was endless and enthralling. She had probably brought more books than clothes, aware that it would be difficult to get books in this isolated place.

Some that she knew by heart she gave to Glenyss and Brenna, who wanted to find a hidden nook at once and lose themselves in imagination.

Jenny Fraser appeared in the door and called her girls, holding Erlinna by the hand. "Come, I need ye today to put up jam and boil broth for brose. But if ye want me, Mairi, just call and I'll come." She did not speak of Ailsa as she handed Mairi a loaf of oat bread and a crock of stew. "I thought ye might be hungry, and too weary with all this work to think of cookin'. But 'tis lovely, what ye've done. How did ye make the walls so charming?"

Alanna glanced about with pride. Why had they not done this long ago? But she knew why. David's energy and enthusiasm had spurred them on. He had become restless and had made the conversion of the croft his special project. Now he was exhausted but pleased with himself. "David did them. I think he's an eye for line and color."

"Has he shown ye his sketches?" Jenny asked.

Alanna dropped a book with a thud. "Sketches?"

David looked shamefaced. "Now and then I've thought of becoming an artist, but I'm not yet good enough. I didn't want to tell you and have you be disappointed. Besides, an artist for a husband? How would we live then?"

Alanna frowned, then smiled radiantly. "Very happily, thank you. My grandfather wanted to be a painter, but his family wouldn't let him. I'd love it if ye followed your heart. You'd be happier then, and so would I. Just think of what ye could do. Oats and barley are ordinary things, and cattle and sheep a trial. But to paint—that could be magic." She spoke wistfully, and, as happened often lately, her eyes filled with tears. She was thinking of her father.

Neither Mairi nor David approached her. They had learned in the past week that her grief was private, her sorrow a burden they could not share.

Nevertheless, David was surprised by Alanna's enthusiasm. She was always surprising him. That was part of what he loved—her spontaneity, her willingness to explore new ideas, to risk discomfort for beauty and happiness. He was a lucky man indeed to have found her. He only wished he could kiss that shadow from her eyes.

"Still," he said, as Jenny and her brood disappeared into the May sunshine, "I'm buying a croft, or rebuilding one for us. A home of our own. And there'll have to be some cattle and sheep and oats to buy paints and canvases and brushes, besides your spinning wheel and furniture." He thought a reminder of their impending marriage might cheer her a little; it had done so in the past.

It did so now. Alanna smiled slightly. "I'd not mind if we lived in a cave, so long as we had a fire to warm us and a little food to keep hunger away. But the light would no' be good, so I suppose you're right." Her glance met David's and they contemplated one another in silence, speaking with their eyes. Both smiled slowly, intimately.

"I'll just go and check the dye that's setting outside," Mairi said. "It's been too long unattended. Ye two should rest a bit. You've been busy too long. By the time Ailsa comes, ye'll do nothing but sleep all day, so weary will ye be."

"We'll get a draft from the fairies to keep us awake," David said.

"My, David Fraser, but you've taken to the glen quickly. I didn't know ye'd met the fairies."

He glanced at Alanna. "Och, but I have."

Mairi smiled and slipped away. Her joy was unseemly in the face of Alanna's grief. But her daughter was coming home, and her granddaughter had found an extraordinary man. It was good to be happy again, to have hope. She ducked outside, inhaling the scent of the sun on warm grass.

As soon as Mairi was gone, Alanna sat beside David on a low stool, his trowel and bucket of hardening clay nearby. She put her hand on his knee. It was trembling. "I should have gone to London, *mo-cridhe*, no matter what the constable said."

He started to argue, and she shook her head. "I know 'tis daft, but I feel I should have gone. For Papa, for his spirit, for the helplessness and hurt I feel in Mama." Her violet eyes filled with tears, though the drops did not fall.

David took her hand, turning it palm up, as if he might read her future there, or the thoughts she could not express. He suspected her tears and regrets were only fragments of her grief. The rest was smoldering inside her, ready to erupt in a storm of anguish that he dreaded.

She reached into her pocket and drew out a dried rose and a carved deer. "These were hers, ye ken. She loved them, but she left them behind." Alanna looked away, shoulders hunched. "I shouldn't have asked her so often to come back."

"What's wrong with telling her you miss her?"

" 'Twas selfish, that's what. I wanted *her* to come, not Papa. And now he's dead."

David caught his breath. "Surely you're not blaming yourself for that? Because ye missed your mother a little more?"

Alanna shrugged. "I know 'tis daft to think such things. The gods never gave *me* the power of life and death."

Uneasy with the guilt and self-derision in her voice, David groped for something wise to say. "I'm sure you wanted him to come too. That you wanted to see him after so long."

Alanna stared at her hands lying in her lap. "Aye, I missed him sometimes. My father was a good man, and he loved the glen, but not as we did, Mama and I. Papa couldn't live here. He thought it too beautiful to be real. He believed if he stayed he would disappear into the mist. He thought ye couldn't live in paradise, only savor it and remember it with awe. 'Tis why he married Mama, I think. So he could take the magic home with him. He couldn't stay here, but he could no' give it up either."

David heard the bitterness in her tone, even if she did not. He put his arm around her and she leaned into him. "You can't forgive him for taking her, can you?"

Alanna rose abruptly. "That's not true. 'Tis cruel." She paced a few steps and paused, head tilted. "Mayhap you're right." She whirled, her smudged beige skirts swirling dangerously near the box of ashes. "Is it possible to love my father and be so very angry, all at the same time?"

David looked away. He thought of his own father, who had become a stranger over the years, whom he'd liked less and less, though he loved him more. "Yes, it's possible."

For a while, both were quiet and pensive. David was the first to get his emotions under control. "Did William Sinclair take Ailsa against her will? Didn't she *want* to go?"

"She wanted to, but in her soul, she belonged here, never in his world, and she knew it, though she made a pleasant place for herself in London. She was always so strong. If there was anything she desired, especially if one of the children wanted or needed something, she made it happen." She turned away again. "I know 'twas killing her that she couldn't save Papa." Alanna paused, forehead against the freshly covered wall. She moved suddenly, knelt before David, looked up at him in supplication.

"I have to say it. Ye have to know. I hated him sometimes for marrying her. But it wasn't his choice. 'Twas hers. I knew that, but refused to admit it in my heart." She thought of the day she had first read of William's illness, the shadowy premonition that had shaken her. She had wished her mother back in the glen, and in doing so, unintentionally wished her father dead. She could never find forgiveness for such a sin. "I should have told him I'm sorry. I should have made it right. But I was happy here and didn't want to go back. I abandoned him and used my anger as an excuse. Now he'll never forgive me."

David raised his hands to touch her, but did not know how. "He never knew how you felt, did he? You never told him?"

Alanna shook her head. "Papa only knew as much as he was capable of knowing. There was so much more he could have understood. He was afraid to understand. I think he liked the lure of mystery too much."

Alanna shivered, cheeks streaked with tears. "Now that I know what it is to share another's soul, now that I've touched ye and ye me, deep in here, where no one else can ever go, I know what was missing between Mama and Papa.

They loved each other deeply, but were separate, no matter how close they grew.

"I think she might have seen his soul, but he couldn't have seen hers, not for more than an instant. It was too bright. He would have been blinded by all that she was. And so she became less."

She gripped David's hands, and he leaned forward until his forehead touched hers. "I can't bear that, don't ye see? Not for her *or* for him!"

15

AILSA STOOD BENEATH THE CLASSICAL VAULTED CEILING AT King's Cross Station, hardly aware of the glass-roofed platforms and elegant iron bridges. When she had first come here twenty-three years ago, she had stared in astonishment at the vast, intricate beauty of such a place. Today she did not stop in the waiting rooms or refreshment rooms with their soft padded seats. Instead she stood beside the track where her train would soon arrive, her two valises at her side.

She had not taken much from the house on Larkspur Crescent where William had taken her as a bride. Only the special gifts her husband had given her, some leather boots, drawers, slippers and a few simple gowns, the straw hat she had used for gardening and her heaviest cloak. And, of course, her bag of herbs and roots, though she would not need them in the glen, where the supply of fresh plants was vast, the ground fertile with all that blossomed, healed and cured. The things Ailsa had left behind belonged in the London house. Colin would want much of it, and Cynthia the rest. That, at least, she could give them. They would not accept her love, only vases, clocks and silver candlesticks.

She knew she was not being fair, but her children did not recognize how deeply they had hurt her. She clutched her anger close because it was safe; it cleared her mind but did not touch her vulnerable heart.

Her leave-taking last night had been brief and disturbing. Her son and daughter had been unusually subdued, and she'd wondered, briefly, if they regretted her going. If so, they could not show it. One crack in their facade and they might crumble at her feet. She understood, but it did not ease the hurt.

Saying good-bye to William had been even more difficult. She had sat for hours beside the bed in the study, listening, waiting, knowing it was hopeless. She had thought she would find him again, so long as she lingered in the halls of his house. She had been a fool. William Sinclair had left her and would not be back, not even in the whisper of a breeze or the weeping of the music he had loved so much.

"I say, I do beg your pardon, Mrs. Sinclair, but I'm frightfully desperate, don't you know."

Ailsa looked up in surprise at Peter Harcourt. His blond curls were disheveled, his tall beaver hat askew, and every time he moved, his silver-headed cane came dangerously close to striking some passerby. His brown morning coat had obviously been worn before, and his paisley waistcoat was misbuttoned. He had not bothered with a cravat, and light red whiskers shadowed his handsome jaw.

Ailsa could not help staring. She had never seen Peter in disarray, let alone distress, even at the news of his father-in-law's death. There were dark shadows beneath his eyes, which were wild with fright.

"What is it? Is it Cynthia?" Ailsa squeezed his arm, hoping the pain might bring him to his senses. He was glancing about distractedly, unable to concentrate, frightening her more by the moment. Peter's loss of control shook her out of the daze of her numb indifference. "Is Cynthia all right?" she asked again.

Peter looked at her blankly for an instant. "I don't . . . She's . . . The baby . . ." He grasped his head in his hands, knocking himself in the temple with his cane. "Oh, God, it's time! I think she's dying."

Ailsa found it difficult to breathe. "But the doctor," she managed, "I thought ye said—"

"Hang the bloody doctor!" Peter did not seem to notice he had sworn loudly and publicly when such language shocked him in private. "My wife won't see the doctor. She just calls for you." Even in his distraught state, he could not hide his incredulity at Cynthia's poor taste. "She's been doing it for hours, screaming that you'd already be gone, that it was too late, that everything was hopeless. I tried to ring you up, but I'd forgotten you weren't on the 'phone yet. I went round to Larkspur Crescent and couldn't find you, then Lizzie came home and sent me here. Cynthia needs you to come at once."

He did not ask, she noticed. He assumed she would do as she was told, as his wife had always done. Until today, apparently. "How long has she been havin' the pains?" Ailsa asked, lifting her own valises. She could see that Peter would not think of it. "What does the doctor say? Is anything wrong?"

Peter ran his hands through his hair, knocking his temple again and sending his top hat flying. He did not notice. He was leading the way to the front of the station, where he hailed a hansom cab. "I don't know. She's dying, I tell you. She just keeps calling for you."

"I'm comin' with ye, Peter. We'll get there as soon as we can. Giving birth is no' easy. Ye must calm down or you'll only upset your wife more."

Peter shook his head wildly as the cab barreled toward his fashionable home. "Couldn't do that. She's mad, I tell you. Lost her wits." He stopped suddenly and turned to look accusingly at Ailsa. "We're nearly there. I hope you don't waste any time."

He was demanding that she fix everything, ridiculously and pompously, but underneath, she heard the anxiety and affection for his wife. He was ranting because, quite simply, there was nothing else that he could do.

"Stop, driver! This is it. Come, we must hurry." He tugged

at Ailsa's sleeve and the driver shook his head as he got down from his high seat and lifted her valises from the floor.

"I'll take these for ye, ma'am."

"What difference does it make?" Peter shouted, rushing them toward the elaborate front door. He waved his hand dismissively. "Just leave them in the hall."

Ailsa smiled at the driver, despite her increasing apprehension, and gave him some shillings for his trouble. He grinned and tipped his hat while Peter fumed, pacing at the foot of the stairs.

As she climbed the Aubusson carpet of peacock blue and green, Ailsa heard faint noises from upstairs, then a voice pierced the gloom of the hall.

"Mama! Why won't you come?" Then, in another tone, "No, I won't. Go away. I want my mother and no one else."

"You see what I mean?" Peter hissed.

Ailsa was so stunned by the desperation in her daughter's cry that she did not hear Peter. Ignoring his instructions, she entered the room in time to see a maid run out, pale and shaking. "She's in terrible pain, ma'am. Terrible." Then she disappeared.

Ailsa entered the frilly room, with its huge canopied bed covered in brocade patterned in overblown roses. Cynthia looked ashen and frail in the center of a pile of down pillows, her brown hair in knots around her head, her face drenched in sweat. Her cheeks were flushed deep pink, her nightcap askew, her gown wrinkled and wet.

When she looked up and saw Ailsa, the terror in her eyes dimmed. "Mama!" she cried. "I thought you'd gone, that it was too late. Peter, go away. You're driving me mad."

Ailsa's heart beat rapidly, partly in astonishment at Cynthia's welcome, partly in dismay at her appearance. As she approached the bed, her daughter held out her hands. Ailsa took them, and Cynthia held on so tightly that her fingers bruised her mother's skin. She pulled Ailsa close enough to hug her, weeping and gasping, "I don't trust the others, Mama. That doctor's horrid and his hands are cold and damp. And the nurse—" She broke off, shuddering. "They don't care about me, not really. They don't listen to me.

Only *you* do. I'm so frightened. I couldn't have borne it if you'd left me."

Ailsa's eyes stung and her throat felt dry. Gently, she removed her daughter's nightcap and ran her fingers through her knotted hair. "I won't leave ye, *mo-run*. I'm here."

Cynthia began to weep and cling to her mother's neck. "I know you'll keep me safe, even though I've been so awful. Tell me what to do, Mama."

Ailsa leaned back to brush the damp hair from her daughter's face. Where had Cynthia's faith sprung from? Surely it had not been there before. Ailsa could not help but be touched by her daughter's need and bone-deep terror. Her red-rimmed, swollen eyes shimmered with trust.

"Let me see how you're doin', Cyn. Hold my hands when the pain's too much. Don't think you'll hurt me. I'll recover." For the first time since William's death, Ailsa was needed, and must step outside her paralysis and think of someone else. "Lie back and try to relax. 'Tis most important that ye conquer the panic. I'll make ye some black willow tea, with some tansy to calm ye. Have ye any of the rosemary or motherwort I gave ye?"

Cynthia slid down among her mounded pillows and shook her head. "I drank a cup every morning till they were gone." She shivered, clenched her teeth at a sudden spasm. When she relaxed again, she added, "They helped, Mama. They really did."

Ailsa wanted to weep but could not take the time. "I'll be goin' in a minute to ask the maid to bring up my bag of herbs. But I'll soon come back, and before ye know it, the babe will come." As she spoke in a tranquil voice, she probed her daughter's belly gently, brow furrowed. "How long?" she asked.

Cynthia bit her lip and tried to think, but her mind was clouded, her thoughts blurred and erratic. "I can't remember. Ask Susie. She woke up with me during the night."

In the hours that followed, Cynthia drank every decoction, welcomed the cool cloths her mother pressed to her forehead, turned when her mother told her to, echoed the rhythm of her mother's steady breath, held Ailsa's hands in a punishing grip when the contractions came, and dutifully drank soothing tea afterward.

" 'Tis raspberry leaf tea you're drinkin' now," Ailsa said, more to distract her daughter than to relay information. " 'Twill hurry the baby along. I think 'tis wise, don't you?"

Cynthia smiled wanly, took another sip of tea and cried out, rearing up in sudden agony. Ailsa held her, rocked her gently, rubbed her back in widening circles. Eventually, Cynthia collapsed against her mother, holding as tight as she could. Not once did she question or quibble or doubt. Ailsa was astounded by the depth of her daughter's trust. It seemed Cynthia had known Ailsa much better than Ailsa had known *her*. She was as moved by her daughter's unwavering faith as she had been by William's, and as devastated.

Cynthia fell back among the pillows, covered in sweat, flushed and exhausted. She was sobbing, trying to speak despite her condition. Ailsa leaned close and heard her daughter whisper, "I miss Papa so much." Her sobbing turned to violent weeping. "I didn't weep for him before. I couldn't." Now she could not seem to stop. "I was afraid to think he was really gone. But he is, isn't he, Mama?"

"Yes," Ailsa murmured, holding her daughter close. She herself could not weep now. Cynthia needed her strength. Or so she told herself. "He loved ye, but he's gone."

For a long time they rocked together while the tears flowed on and on, while Cynthia shuddered and gasped at an agony as deep as her baby flailing toward the light. She wept until there were no more tears, and clutched Ailsa, who was real and alive and would not leave her. She had promised.

Finally, Cynthia dozed and Ailsa cupped her head and placed her comfortably among the pillows. She needed the rest, however brief, for two kinds of pain were ripping her apart.

When it was time, Ailsa quietly asked the doctor to stay nearby in case there was any trouble. She was not arrogant enough to assume she could handle a breech birth or any other abnormality.

Many hours later, the child was born. A boy. Ailsa forced

the first breath from him, cut and tied off the chord and bathed him tenderly, her eyes burning from words she could not say, sensations she would not allow herself to feel.

Cynthia was delirious from her ordeal and did not understand what was happening. With Susie's help, Ailsa washed her, put on a fresh sleeping gown, changed the sheets and bundled the soiled ones away. Then, for just a moment, Ailsa picked up the baby and looked into its pinched red face. Her first grandchild, William's legacy, lying helpless in her arms. Tears filmed her eyes, but she blinked them back. "What will Cynthia name ye, I wonder?" she whispered softly. "Whatever it is, I'm sure 'twill be lovely." The baby wailed and flung its arms upward, reaching for all the dreams he could not yet see.

When Cynthia had slept a little and lay ensconced in her freshly made bed, Ailsa put the child in her daughter's arms.

Cynthia stared, bemused and shaken by the sight of a creature so frail, born of her body and her blood. For a long moment she could not speak, but held the baby gingerly. "He's so small," she whispered at last. "Perhaps he's ill." She looked at her mother in panic, surprised by the depth of her distress. This little boy was hers, and she did not want to lose him. She had already lost so much.

"Och, no, he's fine. It takes a little time to get used to one so frail and dependent, is all."

Cynthia looked doubtful.

"Ye were once as tiny as that, smaller even, I think. But your voice was large and could fill the house from attic to cellar. Yours and Colin's both."

Cynthia swallowed dryly and touched her mother's hand. "I'm sorry, Mama." Her eyes were full of regret. She began to weep again, this time in remorse. "I never thought—"

Ailsa shook her head. "I know," she said quietly. "Don't try to explain." She fought back the lump in her throat that stopped the air from reaching her lungs. The sight of Cynthia's tears had caused her icy shroud to melt at the edges, and she was not ready to face the onslaught of new heat and consciousness in her numb body.

But her daughter was not finished. "I was afraid you wouldn't come, even if Peter found you in time." She hesitated. Such words were difficult for her to say. "I wouldn't have blamed you if you'd refused."

Today Ailsa had seen behind her daughter's mask of careful control, *lived* behind it and bled behind it too. She would never forget the relief on her daughter's face when she entered the room. Ailsa brushed the light brown hair from Cynthia's damp cheek. "I will always come when ye call me, if I'm able. You're my daughter, and I love ye."

Cynthia was shaken by the simple declaration. The baby began to cry, and she turned with relief to feed him. As her son settled in to nurse, Cynthia's instincts seemed to come awake, and her furrowed brow smoothed. She smiled fondly at the bundle in her arms. "I didn't know," she said in wonder. "You tried to tell me, but I didn't believe you." She spoke in a whisper, afraid to disturb the baby contentedly nuzzled against her breast.

Ailsa felt another crack in her smoke-woven armor and looked away. "Do ye want me to stay and help ye care for him for a day or two? The beginning is aye the hardest."

"No, thank you, Mama. You've done so much already. Besides, I want to see that I can do it myself." She seemed surprised by this admission, though Ailsa understood.

She was pleased at the glimmer of determination in Cynthia's eyes. "Aye, 'tis a good idea, birdeen. Then mayhap I should go and let ye rest."

Her daughter sighed. "I know I wouldn't have gotten through it without you." She surprised Ailsa by brushing her fingers across her mother's cheek. "I'll never forget, Mama. I promise."

"I know ye won't." Ailsa kissed the baby's head and hugged Cynthia tightly, then slipped out the door.

She had very nearly wept at the sight of her daughter holding her son, teary-eyed at Ailsa's farewell. But she hadn't dared. She sensed the storm that would follow and feared the desolation.

Ailsa trailed slowly down the stairs, hand on the highly

polished banister for support. She looked up when she realized a maid was speaking to her.

"Mr. Colin's in the breakfast room, ma'am." The girl ducked her head and blushed. "He doesn't look well." It was not her place to make such judgments, but she had to take the chance.

Ailsa touched the girl's shoulder in reassurance. "I'll go to him then. And thank ye."

The maid bobbed a grateful curtsy and slipped away.

Warily, Ailsa approached the closed door at the bottom of the stairs. She opened it quietly to find her son standing with his back to the room, staring out the window, shoulders rigid, hands clasped behind his back.

"I've told you I want to be alone," he snapped without looking to see who had come in.

"I just wanted to say good-bye."

Colin froze at the sound of his mother's voice, forgot himself enough to turn, just a little.

Biting her lips to hold back a gasp of dismay, Ailsa saw that her son's cheeks were streaked with tears. Instinctively, she went to him, but his ramrod-straight back warned her not to touch him. For a long time, she did not speak.

They stood in silence and watched the rain stream down the window, blocking their view of the street with a moving curtain of water. Tears spilled from Colin's eyes in an echo of the rain, but he did not sob or relax his stance or allow his face to show his feelings. Only the soundless tears betrayed him.

Ailsa felt she might suffocate because she could not reach her son to comfort him, when Colin spoke at last.

"A maid came round my flat to tell me it was Cynthia's time. I didn't mean to come here, but I couldn't seem to stop myself." He had hurried too; his cravat was half tied, his waistcoat unbuttoned, his jacket crumpled, as if he had worn it the night before. His linen shirt was soaked with tears.

"When I came in the door, I heard Cynthia calling out in anguish and something just snapped. I don't know why."

Even as he spoke, he wept, though his voice was oddly flat.

"Mayhap 'twas time." Ailsa sensed he would not run from the sound of her voice, though she dared not touch him.

Colin nodded, peering out into the silver rain. "Did Father cry out like that?" The sounds he made were barely words, so tentative were they.

Ailsa choked back the lump in her throat. "No, he never did. But I'm thinkin' that might be because of me."

"He didn't want you to suffer for him." It was a statement, not a question.

Ailsa risked a glance at Colin's face. The tears were coming faster now, but still without a sound. She wanted very badly to take her son in her arms, but Colin had made the unwritten rules, and she would not break them. Her own grief lay heavy and bitter inside her. "He didn't want me to suffer," she repeated.

Suddenly, Colin turned. "I'm glad you're going, and not for the reasons you think. Because I know you want to go back. You've the right to be happy."

"Do I?" Somehow, as he wept, Colin had been gaining strength while Ailsa's drained away, drop by drop, in the tears she could not weep. "How can I be, when—"

Colin took her arm and gripped it tight. "Because Papa wanted you to. You've never disappointed him before. I'm glad for you. I wanted you to know, that's all."

He turned back to the window and the rain.

Struggling for breath, the pressure in her chest nearly unbearable, Ailsa leaned close to slip her arm around his waist. Colin did not pull away; he put his arm across her shoulders and held tight. His face was no longer wooden but contorted with grief, and his shoulders began to shake with his sobs, while Ailsa's eyes remained achingly dry.

16

"I'LL BE TAKIN' YOUR THINGS ROUND TO MAIRI ROSE'S SOON as I can."

Ailsa tried to smile at Malcolm Drummond as she climbed down off the seat of his wagon. She had been lucky enough to meet him on the last leg of her journey. He had been in town replenishing his supplies, and had offered Ailsa a ride back to the glen. She told herself it was good to see a familiar face, yet she'd felt oddly distant as he talked and laughed and told stories about her family and old friends.

Malcolm had mentioned David Fraser and how well he was liked, but Ailsa barely heard. She was awake and breathing, yet sleep hung about her like a cloak, protecting and concealing what she did not wish to feel. The trip had taken the last of her strength. Her bones had turned to liquid and her body was held together by the insubstantial casing of her brittle skin.

She felt only exhaustion and relief as she entered the woods, heard the rush of the river echoed by the weeping wind. She did not stop to remember what those sounds had once meant to her, but trudged forward, forcing her limbs to move through the disabling weight of her numb despair. She did not think to remove her dusty, uncomfortable boots, normally discarded the moment she left the road, and her hair was caught up neatly at the back of her head.

She moved by instinct toward Mairi Rose's croft. With each step she felt a sense of urgency in her sluggish blood, a rasp of panic in her labored breath. "Hurry," an inner voice whispered. " 'Tis time." Ailsa looked about wildly. She had not heard such a call for years, had forgotten what it felt like. She thought of Alanna and veered sharply away from the path to the cottage. Her daughter was not likely to be inside on a day like this; suddenly it was essential that she see Alanna at once.

Blindly, she followed the inner voice that urged, commanded, led her on a path she had not chosen. She came out into the clearing and paused when she saw a shadow among the purple foxgloves. She leaned toward it, drawn by the shifting image of dark on color, until she saw it was a man. Slowly, she looked up from the tall, swaying flowers and saw the man's face, dim and far away. He stood unmoving, watching her come, and she felt a jolt of recognition. "Ian."

Ian Fraser was frozen with horror at the sight of Ailsa's pallor, her face, aged by lines and dust and sorrow, her unhealthily thin body. The black gown she wore hung about her like a mother's cast-off gown upon her child. Her sleek agility had gone; her movements were heavy and awkward with weariness.

Now he knew what had brought him here, what had woken him before daylight, filling him with restless agitation. He had watched the sunrise with narrowed eyes, expectant and distressed. For hours he had walked, waiting for something he could not explain, but knowing it would come. He wondered why he had not guessed it would be Ailsa.

She came toward him slowly, wary and uncertain. "Ailsa." He took her hands, unable to disguise the anguish in his voice. "I'm sorry." He wanted to say more, but the sight of her familiar face, so changed, so grim, stopped him.

Ailsa felt his warm fingers close around hers and thought of William's cold, frail, trembling hands in the last weeks of his illness. For a moment, without realizing, she clung to Ian Fraser's heat and strength and health. They did not speak; there was nothing they could say. There had been a time when words between them were unnecessary. Now they were impossible. Ailsa took a deep breath, and Ian breathed with her, his eyes never leaving her face.

He was so distressed by Ailsa's condition that he ceased to think. Just now, he could only feel. He was frightened by her listlessness. He had seen her walk across the clearing and knew she did not see her surroundings. Never had Ailsa been unaware of earth and sky and wind; they had fed and sustained, inspired and consoled her. The voices of the glen had whispered secrets in her ear, and she had heard and understood.

Ian saw she did not hear them now. She was deaf, and her dim eyes blind. She did not feel the drift of butterflies past her shoulder, the hum of bees, the grass and flowers waving at her feet. She did not feel the spring breeze in her hair. She was not Ailsa anymore. "Ailsa," he repeated urgently, as if to call her back, to sing her awake with the memory of his voice.

She looked up into his face, and the gray curtain inside parted a little. He must have been out most of the day; the wind had been playing in his hair, leaving it tangled and wild. His face was brown from the sun, his eyes green like the sea in a calm, clear pool. She remembered looking into those eyes and seeing summer, tomorrow, herself. She remembered . . .

Ailsa gasped. She was remembering things she must forget. She stared down at their linked hands, his strong, tan and leathered by sun and wind, the nails cracked and gray from working the soil. Her own hands were white and soft; they seemed glaringly frail in Ian's firm grasp. Once there had been no difference between their hands, except that hers were smaller. No difference and no distance, and those hands could not be parted, except by a willful young girl with a dream.

She broke away, withdrew her hands from the lure of memory and regret. She drew back, appalled. "I'm sorry. I forgot where I was for a bit."

Ian could not bear it. He was desperate to feed the single glimmer of light in Ailsa's blue-violet eyes, and unwise in his desperation. His gaze held her, lucent in the sunlight. "Was that it?" he asked quietly. "Or was it that ye remembered?"

Ailsa tried to inhale, but the air was too clean and pure and sweet. She could not catch her breath. "Let me go, Ian Fraser. I'd no' meant to look back. I must go forward or I'll fall." She paused, a cast upon her eyes that hid her thoughts but revealed her torment.

Overcome with remorse, Ian looked away. It was no longer his right to help her. "You're right. Forgive me."

The sense of urgency, momentarily subsumed by Ian's unexpected appearance, returned, more imperative than ever. Ailsa grasped it as she would the promise of oblivion in a wind-tossed sea. "I must find Alanna at once. Have ye seen her?"

Sensing her building agitation, Ian clasped his hands behind his back. "A while back I saw her going toward the Valley of the Dead. I think she's there."

Ailsa blinked, shook her head, and the gray haze shifted again. "Aye. The valley. I should've known."

She wanted to run to her daughter but paused to say shakily, "Will I see ye later, Ian? Ye and Jenny?"

Ian hesitated for an instant. "You'll see me," he said. The next moment, he had disappeared into the woods, lush with approaching summer.

Ailsa stood at the shaded entrance to the Valley of the Dead. Strange that Alanna should be waiting here when this place had been so much on Ailsa's mind since William's death. William's death. The words still sent a chill through her.

Ailsa fixed her attention on her daughter, kneeling in the cotton grass, shoulders slumped, hands pressed against the stones of Charles Kittridge's cairn. She could see the curve of Alanna's cheek, flushed with distress, but not the color of her eyes.

Sensing a presence not of the dead, Alanna raised her head, turned and cried out wordlessly. It did not seem that either moved, but suddenly, mother and daughter were in each other's arms. They held tightly, clinging to one another as if each had the power to heal the other.

For a long time they did not speak. Then Alanna drew back so she could see her mother's face. "Och, Mama! You're ill."

"No," Ailsa said automatically, though now that she was

here, she admitted to herself that she *was* ill, exhausted, drained of spirit and strength. " 'Twas no' an easy journey. I came a very long way, and did not think I could go so far." She stared at Alanna, hungry for the sight of her—her familiar violet eyes, distinctive cheekbones, soft lips and long red hair.

Except her daughter was not the same. Alanna looked as if she had been standing at the center of a storm while the wind raged around her, leaving her eyes wild, her skin sallow, her pulse frantic. Ailsa could not stand that frenzied, lost look, and turned to glance at the fresh stones and flowers on Charles Kittridge's grave.

"Ye come here often, don't ye?"

"Aye. I thought, since I couldn't go to Papa, to ye, that I'd come here and ask the gods to care for ye both. I came to grieve but I can no' do it. Why is that, Mama?"

Ailsa met her daughter's eyes, shadowed by dark circles that spoke of sleeplessness and turmoil. She might have been looking into her own face.

Before she could answer, Alanna cried, "Mairi said ye were coming here. She was certain. So I thought to wait—"

Ailsa stopped her with both hands. "You've no need to explain. Have a little faith in me, Alanna." She was astonished at her own words. It seemed forever since she'd had faith in herself. She recognized, as Alanna shook her head, what a burden she had placed on her daughter's shoulders. She had done it unknowingly, but that did not matter. It was time to lift the heavy weight and let Alanna breathe again.

"I can no' say, *mo-eudail.* But my own sorrow is cold and hard within me. Maybe I shouldn't have come." In unspoken acquiescence, they turned toward the stone-covered cairns.

"Did Papa want ye to stay?" Alanna asked carefully.

Ailsa shook her head, remembering William's face as he smiled and let her go. She remembered more than she had dared to in the weeks since her husband's death. "He told me no' to stay for him, that the only loyalty I owed him was to find my own happiness."

She broke off, breathed deeply, and added, "He told me he missed ye with every day that passed, but that he'd let ye go so he would not lose me. He loved us very much, I think. Unselfishly. He was a fine, rare man. And he's gone."

Alanna choked back a sob. "I should have gone to London. I should have been there."

Surprised, Ailsa looked at her daughter's face, twisted by guilt. "Why? To stand beside a coffin among a lot of strangers? 'Twas only a box, Alanna, and they were only shadows. William wasn't there. He isn't there." Ailsa contemplated the standing stones, shaped and scarred by time and howling wind. She listened to that wind, so like human voices in this secluded valley, shaded by the sacred secrets of the past. She heard William's voice speaking of paradise, regretting that he could not see it one more time.

She took Alanna's hand. " 'Tis strange, aye, but your father's spirit is more likely to be here, in a place like this, than in London. He always wanted to be here; he just didn't know how." The words came out at last, flowing like the river of her childhood, effortlessly, endlessly. She felt her daughter's hand go clammy and begin to shake.

"Then I should have gone for ye, to be with ye." Alanna was in agony, and it was not right.

Ailsa turned and grasped Alanna's shoulders until they faced each other squarely. "It would have been harder if ye *had* been there. I told ye no' to come. I meant it, Alanna. I do not lie to ye. Ye know in your heart I speak the truth. *Hear* me. Let yourself hear me. Let yourself grieve, for only then can ye recover." She was talking to herself as much as her daughter.

She knew then that William was there, speaking through her voice, which had been stifled since his death. If his spirit did not hover in the wind, then her husband was inside her, in the memory of his voice, his last touch, his fear that she would give up the rest of her life to a ghost. He would have hated that—hated himself for causing it, and her for having let it happen. Only now, as she spoke to Alanna, did Ailsa understand William and the promises he had made her give, the sincerity of all he had said. He had been an honest man, always. It was one of the first reasons she'd loved him.

She touched her cheeks, covered with tears. Alanna wept

beside her, staring at her grandfather's grave and thinking of her father's. Ailsa felt the weight of lead break open; the veil lifted and the pain came, wave upon wave of it, until she fell to her knees. She had not known it would be like this. Or perhaps she had guessed, and kept her grief inside, so no one would see it and look away.

Alanna would not look away. Alanna would understand. She was rocking with her arms about herself, mouth open in an inaudible moan.

"I loved him, but I never tried to know him. Not the way I know ye," Alanna murmured. "I should have tried harder."

"It would no' have mattered if ye did, *mo-run*. William Sinclair was no' a man to let others see what was in his soul. No' until the end, when he stopped being afraid. He'd no' have let ye closer than ye were. And he was proud of ye. He loved ye. Ye loved him too, and honored him, and will miss him. Let that be enough, birdeen. 'Tis all ye can have."

Alanna shuddered violently. She had entrenched herself in guilt to protect herself from grief. To let go of one would be to feel the other. But she saw, as she looked into her mother's eyes, that she had no choice.

"I know," she said, gasping through her tears. "He made his choice and I made mine, but he was my father just the same. I can't bear to let him go when I never really had him."

Ailsa winced at a spasm in her heart and glanced down at the grave at her feet. How often had she thought the same of her own father? How often had she hated him for all she had missed and could never recover, though he had had no choice in the matter? Alanna was lucky. For the first twenty years of her life, her father had been there. He had been a private man but never a stranger, never an enigma or a siren's lure. Just a man who had let go when he grew too weary and the suffering too great.

"He shouldn't have left me!" Ailsa cried, her fury loud in the circle of weeping wind. "He shouldn't have gone!"

"He had to, Mama. Ye told me so yourself." Now Alanna was holding her mother's hand, trying to make it warm, and both were weeping openly. They leaned together, shoulder against shoulder, hand in hand, kneeling so close that their long skirts folded in upon each other.

Ailsa realized that in making her promise to return to the glen, William had given her a last gift of this moment and this freedom. She could let herself weep now. It was safe. She was home.

Part Three

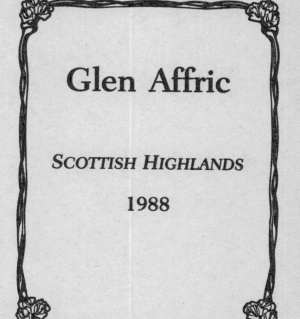

Glen Affric

SCOTTISH HIGHLANDS

1988

1

Eva Crawford gasped and turned the wheel sharply to avoid hitting the sheep that stood in the center of the narrow road. She paused on the verge, front wheels buried in mud, and rested her head on her clenched hands. Her heart pounded erratically and she fought to catch her breath. "It's only a wee sheep," she murmured, in an effort to reassure herself. She knew she was overreacting. It was certainly not the first animal she had barely avoided on this long and treacherous drive north to Glen Affric. "You're not used to the car yet," she added. "Give yourself time."

When her breathing had steadied and she glanced up at last, the lowering clouds overhead did not diminish her apprehension. Even the radio, playing a raucous song by Silly Wizard, could not drown out the memory of Eilidh's voice as they stood in the living room in Glasgow.

"You want to do what?" she'd demanded incredulously.

"Drive up to Glen Affric. I've no choice really. There aren't any trains that go there, and the buses are undependable," Eva had replied as firmly as she could manage, running her fingers distractedly through her short chestnut hair. She was determined to make this trip, no matter what her mother's friend said. "I have to go. I can't explain it, but I have to."

She felt a deep need, a compulsion that had gripped her from the moment she put down Ailsa Rose's journal and realized she was weeping for a stranger who had long been dead. Yet she was not a stranger. Eva had heard her voice on the brittle pages, ringing out in the faded brown ink. She felt she knew Ailsa Rose Sinclair far better than she did her own mother. Celia Ward, whom she had come in search of, was more elusive than ever.

"You've lived on a tiny island all your life. Do you even know *how* to drive?" Eilidh continued doggedly, dark hair disheveled, eyes glimmering with flecks of amber that revealed her concern, which was quite close to anger.

"My fiancé taught me in his father's car. A little Rover. I thought I'd hire one like it." Eva was defiant.

Eilidh began to pace in agitation. "You could get lost in all that wildness. It's a long way from Glasgow, you know."

Eva paled. Eilidh had hit a nerve. The girl was terrified of losing her way. She had known every inch of the island, had feared nothing she might find there, because she knew the bogs, the plants, the animals too well. When she was young she'd grown bored with the familiar paths the others walked and had forged her own. She'd always known she was safe there, protected. She'd known what to expect. This trip north on roads she'd never driven to untamed places she'd never seen was entirely different, frighteningly so. Her impetuous decision was a foolish risk. But she wouldn't admit it. "I've looked at the map. The route seems quite clear." She clenched her fists, then forced them open, smoothing her trousers and leaving them damp with sweat. "Don't you see? Celia hasn't left any of herself here. Perhaps I can find her in the glen."

Eva's vehemence got through to Eilidh, who smiled even as she shook her head. "You're daft, you know. Gone round the bend. But I do admire your courage."

Eva had been surprised and touched by the genuine warmth in Eilidh's voice, but just now, as the sheep wandered to the far side of the road, she did not feel very courageous. She glanced up at the shifting clouds as a streak of blue appeared among the heavy gray. "What are you trying to prove, anyway?" she asked aloud. "Celia doesn't care if you're brave and idiotic."

A stab of anger made her sit bolt upright. Her mother was playing a game with her confused and wounded daughter, leading her here and there in search of a woman who had vanished long since. If Celia Ward had ever been in Glasgow, she was not there now, except in Eilidh's memory. All she had left Eva was the chest, and everything in the chest pointed to the glen.

Eva took several deep, shaky breaths and set her jaw obstinately. At least she was doing something now, not waiting for a frail, evasive ghost to give her answers she would probably never find. Some ghosts spoke, as Ailsa, Mairi and Alanna had spoken through Ailsa's pen. Their voices rang in Eva's head as their blood ran in her veins. Each of them had turned to Glen Affric for solace, while Celia ran from it and refused to look back. There had to be an answer there. There simply had to.

Feeling slightly ill, Eva backed the hired car onto the road and continued her journey of discovery. She'd been optimistic when she started out that morning. The clouds had been fragile puffs of white in a deep blue sky, and the sun had shimmered on the water of Loch Lomond as she circled it on her way north. But as she drove on, a steep mountainside rose on one side of the road, covered with pine and an occasional set of stone waterfalls cut into the rock. The other side fell away abruptly to the loch; Eva felt she was balancing on the edge of a precipice. The wall of the hillside made her feel closed in, and she had to struggle to catch her breath.

Once she passed Crianlarich, the land flattened out so the road ahead was visible, and the twists and turns grew less extreme. Eva began to feel more confident as the going became easier.

She forgot both confidence and fear when she came to the eerie wastes of Rannoch Moor, a landscape she could never have imagined. It loomed, prehistoric, barren, striking, draped in unearthly mist, as if giant glaciers had ruthlessly carved out the lochs and burns to leave low-lying turf and peat and bare black mountains of stone. The sky lowered in an echo of the mournful landscape, giving the moor a ghostly glow.

Caught in the drama of barren land and glittering crystalline waters, Eva shivered with anticipation. If eerie emptiness could be so enthralling, how much more compelling would the glen be in its abundance of life and color. She couldn't wait to get there; to see the miracle for herself.

As she rounded a bend in Glencoe, a lorry veered toward her. She turned the wheel sharply to the right, though there was nowhere for her to go, except down a green hillside and into the icy water of a river. The car stalled and she struggled to start the engine again, but it resisted. For the second time, she rested her head on the wheel, heart pounding. "I've lost my mind, that's what," she muttered.

She looked around wildly and wondered what she would do if she could not get the Ford Rover started again. Stand in the road and wave down a stranger? The thought chilled her. On *Eilean Eadar,* she'd known everyone. Any who stopped to help would have been old friends, or at least longtime acquaintances. She would have been certain of her own safety and their goodwill. But now, on this strange stretch of road between high black mountains, she was certain of nothing.

"You're young to be traveling alone," Eilidh had warned. "There're all kinds of dangers. Especially for someone as pretty as you. Are you sure you don't want me to go with you?"

"I'm sure," Eva replied obstinately. She refused to think of the hazards, though the shadows of unnamed specters flickered at the edges of her mind, making her stomach flutter. "I have to do this alone."

"Do what, exactly?" Eilidh asked, perplexed by the passion in the girl's tone.

Eva paused, mouth open, and tried to think of an answer. "To make my way to Glen Affric, to the dim green shadows and the sound of rushing water. To the standing stones. I have to find my way there, just as Ailsa Rose Sinclair did."

"But what are you seeking?"

"What she sought—peace." Eva flushed. That was not what she was supposed to be looking for.

"What about Celia? Have you given up looking for her?" Eilidh inquired stiffly.

Eva quivered with anger. "There's nothing of her here. All she left is that little bag." She remembered clearly her excitement when she'd held the satin brocaded bag in her palm for the first time. Eilidh had looked in just then, and had cried out, "That was Celia's. She used to have it sitting on her bureau." She'd hovered at Eva's side, eager to see what the bag contained.

Carefully, Eva undid the string to find inside a plain gold band, a bright green ribbon, a single dried flower and an emerald pendant. There was no note, no drawing, no jotted word on a strip of paper to reveal the woman who had owned these things. "Were these all her treasures?" Eva asked, torn between frustration and a deep, wrenching pity for the woman who had left so little behind.

Eilidh cleared her throat twice before she could speak. "I don't know. I wish I did. The only thing I recognize is her wedding ring. Findlay Denholm's ring. The rest is a mystery to me." She'd paused, frowning. "It isn't much."

Without Celia to explain, Eva thought, to give these few small, pretty things some meaning, it was nothing at all.

She remembered the sketches and watercolors that had once belonged to Genevra, Ailsa's half-sister who lived in India. There had been poems and letters from Lian, Charles Kittridge's Chinese daughter. Ailsa, Lian, Genevra—three sisters who had laid open their souls and placed them in the chest for anyone to discover. Celia Ward had not chosen to do the same. "Glen Affric was the place that drew Ailsa's family together, sheltered them and nurtured them. I have to see and feel that place for myself. There are no answers here"—Eva waved toward the room on the second floor—"maybe I'll find one in the glen. I don't know where else to look."

"You're right, I suppose," Eilidh sighed. "But it doesn't make me any less concerned. You will take care. Promise me."

Eva had promised. Now she sat in her car on a lonely road, feeling desperately alone and lost. Her palms were clammy, her skin filmed in nervous sweat, while overhead the clouds grew darker and more threatening. She could hear the wind whining outside the car, rattling the window glass and hissing through the trees. She shivered and tried to quell the rush of apprehension and hurt that welled within her. Damn Celia Ward, anyway.

"I know you're angry at Celia," Eilidh had said. "And confused. So am I. And I feel so helpless. I can't bear that. Not when I see the sorrow in your eyes. I think you must do what you feel is right, even if it isn't, in the end. How else will you know?"

"Exactly," Eva cried gratefully. It had made sense at the time, but then she had been safe in the odd, cozy house in Glasgow. Now she was completely on her own, and her stomach felt hollow with fear. In growing desperation, Eva glanced at the passenger seat, where Ailsa's journal lay. She touched it reverently and felt a jolt of recognition, a deep affinity with the voices closed inside the worn leather cover. The feeling both unsettled and excited her. She had had to put the journal down, unfinished, trembling and shaken at the power of the words. Ailsa's story was too full of emotion and other people's pain. Eva felt it like her own and thought she might drown in it.

With difficulty, she shook off the trepidation. Nervous and uncertain as she was, she would forge ahead. She would not let the narrow, winding roads, the threat of animals or oncoming lorries stop her, nor the increasingly unpleasant weather. Every now and then she turned a corner to see rolling green fields dotted with wildflowers, cottages surrounded by colorful tulips and roses. She was enchanted by the lochs and rivers and idyllic stone cottages; the sight reassured her.

Teeth clenched, she tried the key again, and the engine turned over at last. Eva waited for a car with a caravan to inch past and started out again, singing along with Silly Wizard to fill the empty car. This time her heartbeat was erratic with expectation, her breath cool with exhilaration. She would be all right. She might even find what she sought. At least she was doing something, moving, breathing, living, even if she was afraid of being on the road alone. There were answers for her in the sough of the wind in the pines; she was certain of it.

"Mind your expectations, Eva," Eilidh warned her. "Don't let them fly too high. You may not find what you imagine or what you hope for."

Eva folded her arms. "Glen Affric is so powerful to Ailsa and Ian and the others, so beautiful and serene. And I share their blood, after all."

Eilidh put her hand on Eva's shoulder. "Not everyone is the same, blood or no. People and places change. After all, your mother hated the glen, and her mother loved it."

Eva forced the memories back, and her sense of anticipation grew as she passed along Loch Ness and the marvelous ruin of Urquhart Castle. She stared in delight at the rolling green landscape covered with sheep. The grumbling clouds had finally released their burden of rain. Now they were breaking up, allowing the sun to reveal brightly colored laundry hung out to dry behind rustic stone cottages.

Eva smiled. Everywhere, fluttering red and pink, blue and white clothes and linens hung in the misting rain. She wondered if the laundry was a gesture of defiance against the weather or a sign of optimism.

Either way, she thought it charming. The summer flowers were in bloom, the hollyhocks, tulips and roses glorious splashes of color against emerald green grass. Eva held the wheel tighter, until her hands ached and her cheeks were flushed with excitement. She yearned for the power of the glen, the promise of its secret woods and braes and rushing waters.

She stopped for petrol in the tiny town of Glen Affric, where she got an ordinance map of the local roads and learned that the glen was seventeen miles long.

" 'Tis far and lonely, is Glen Affric," the attendant told

her in a rolling Highland burr. "Ye'll have to drive oot the road to the car park about twelve miles doon the way. Then ye've no choice but to hike the rest of the way to the lodge. Luvely old place. They're redoing it, ye ken. And be sure to stop at the dam. Now there's a view for ye. Ye'll never forget it, I'll wager. None like it anywhere."

Eva was nervous as she got back into the Rover and started down the long dirt road that wound through Glen Affric for miles. She had not realized it was so big. How would she ever find what she was looking for in so much space? But something called her far beyond the car park and the end of the road, to the wildest part of the glen: the part least civilized, reached only on foot. There were few enough such places left in the world.

Her heart was pounding and her palms damp as she negotiated the narrow, rutted road. She struck potholes that made the car bounce, and hit her head twice when she pulled aside abruptly for another vehicle to pass. She cursed at the last one, knowing the driver could not hear. This journey was more difficult and frustrating than she had imagined. But then, nothing had been easy since she'd first learned of Celia's existence.

Eva sighed. She was tired and her muscles ached. She did not realize until that moment how rigidly she had been driving, how great a strain it had put on her body. She hurt everywhere, and her heartbeat seemed to echo in a hollow void. She was close to her goal, but suddenly she wanted to turn back. The pulse in her thumbs beat against the wheel, drowning out the staticky sound of the radio. She closed her eyes and took several deep breaths. She would not turn back now. That would be giving up. She was determined not to succumb to her fear, as Celia had done. She was not like her mother, who had drowned in her own terror, not the angry turbulence of the sea.

Once more, Eva pushed onward. She barely had time to admire the landscape, the placid cattle and sheep grazing on the dark green grass. The sheep did not seem to fear cars; they lay, oblivious, in the tall grass that edged the lane, or stopped to rest in the middle of the road. Eva had to drive slowly, trying to protect the sheep who could not protect themselves.

Several miles in, she reached the hydroelectric dam that turned the rushing waters in the glen into power and progress. Hands shaking, pulse racing so furiously she could hear little else, she pulled off on the lay-by and wound her way to the top of the dam, where she stopped to contemplate the vista below. Islands were scattered across the blue loch, with swans and ducks floating on the clear water. Thick stands of pine and spruce, larch and birch crowded the lochs and thickly wooded hillsides, and jagged black mountains rose in the background. Other tourists came up beside her, gasping and exclaiming in hushed voices, clearly awed by the spectacular view.

Eva was unmoved. She could no longer hear her heartbeat or feel the throbbing rhythm of her pulse. A veil had fallen, cutting her off from the majesty of the view, shrouding her emotions, the reactions of her body. Her clammy palms had dried and her breath came easily. Her hands were steady as she raised them to brush the short curls from her face. She thought the scene lovely, but nothing more. She felt none of the excitement of the other tourists, none of the exhilaration she had expected to feel at this first glimpse of Ailsa's home.

Instead, Eva felt cold and disappointed. The sea crashing against the rocks on the island had been more magnificent than this. *Mind your expectations. You may not find what you expect or what you hope for.* Eilidh's admonition echoed in the back of her mind. Blindly, Eva reached into her pocket and clutched the round black stone, her talisman, discovered the night before she left the island. She caressed the smooth obsidian, circled the hole in the center of the flat stone. Where was its magic now that she felt sick and discouraged? She needed the solace of the ancient power with which the black stone was imbued. But it lay, cool, smooth and lifeless in her hand.

DISHEARTENED, EVA TURNED FROM THE VIEW SHE HAD sought for so long, climbed back into the tiny car and drove on.

She soon reached the car park, where several other cars, trucks and four-wheel drives had gathered, disgorging enthusiastic hikers. Eva worked at sharing their animated zeal as they discussed routes and destinations. She had brought her knapsack, and as she examined the map of the trails, she knew she'd have no problem. She had climbed and walked so much on the island that she was in good condition. She felt invigorated by the clean, fresh air and the scent of pine and spruce.

Though the thought of physical exertion pleased her, she felt distant, as if she were viewing the scene through a translucent mist. It was too real; there was nothing magical in this isolated place. Her chest was tight with disillusionment, and the thought flitted through her mind that she was seeing Glen Affric through her mother's eyes.

Eva trudged off on one of the many paths, with no idea which way to go, or even where, exactly, she wanted to be. It felt good to be hiking again, to feel the wind on her face and the sun on her hair. The summer glen was resplendent with foxgloves and roses, honeysuckle and wild violets and brambles creamy with blossoms. The light wind rippled the water, distorting the reflections of a moment before.

Eva wanted more.

She followed the trail to the lodge, being renovated by a foreign prince, she heard another hiker say, for several million pounds. It was a lovely old house, obviously built in the last century, probably by a wealthy Englishman. The lodge did not interest Eva either.

She wandered up and down low hills splashed with heather, past tiny springs and rushing burns, abandoned cottages where the thatched roofs had fallen in. She stopped to stare, wondering if this was the kind of place where Ian Fraser and Mairi Rose had lived. She felt a flicker of interest and a brief glimmer of that intangible thread that bound her to the distant past, but it soon disappeared.

The memory came to her of Eilidh digging in her garden, hair flying loose and tangled, face smudged with dirt and hands covered with soil. "I can't pass up the opportunity to muck about in the dirt and breathe in the clean air. Restores one's faith in the gods and reminds me what beauty can grow out of dirt and stone." Eilidh gestured toward the roses and iris, the blooming rhododendrons and amaryllis, the honeysuckle that climbed the back wall of the house in fragrant confusion.

Eva stared at her, dazed. "Did Celia like to work in the garden?"

Brows drawn together, Eilidh stopped with a muddy trowel in her hand. "No, she didn't. I think working in the earth reminded her too much of the glen and her childhood. Her family were all farmers of one kind or another. But Celia wasn't good at making things grow, at feeding and nurturing and keeping away weeds and pests."

"Is that why she gave me up?" Eva asked quietly, throat tight with misery.

Eilidh dropped the trowel but did not move toward the girl. "Oh, my dear," she whispered in compassion. "No. It was just that Celia saw muddy soil and thought of loam, saw iris and gladioli and thought of crops that might fail, saw weeds and thought of hunger. She couldn't bury her hands in the soil without remembering. Something she was determined not to do."

As she turned from the ruined cottage, Eva thought Celia was equally determined that her daughter should not remember either. But Eva would not give up. That would mean her mother had won.

At last she stumbled into an abandoned kirk on the shady bank of a river. The roof had fallen in, and the stones from the walls lay half on the ground. The windows had disappeared, except for the stained glass window at the front, which stood, surrounded in stone at the bottom, but curved to a point at the top in thin air with no wall to hold it upright. The sun shone through it, making colored patterns on the moss-covered stones on the floor of the kirk.

Eva stopped, caught by the image of that window, still sparkling, still intact, still lovely, lending its ephemeral beauty to the ruined kirk. The red, blue and green jewellike colors fell across the overgrown grass and fallen stones, shaded by a huge old rowan tree. She noticed a headstone through a missing side window and went out to examine the graveyard.

Her heart began to beat more rapidly when she made out the names of Fraser and Mackensie on two of the headstones. Many of the stones had been worn away by wind, rain and time. The weather was harsh here much of the year, and the stone was not sturdy enough to withstand the ravages of a century. Still, Eva managed to find Ian and Jenny Fraser and Alanna Fraser next to David. She traced the indentations in nearby stones until she was fairly certain she had located Ailsa Rose Sinclair. Eva could just make out the words of the epitaph by squinting hard and tracing the letters with her fingers.

> *Happy's the love that meets return,*
> *When in soft flames souls equal burn.*

A strange thing to have carved on a headstone, Eva thought. Yet it moved her, brought tears to her eyes. Did the words refer to Ian Fraser or William Sinclair? Or perhaps to neither. Eva's hand hovered, and she waited for a feeling of kinship, of recognition, but there was nothing besides the wind sighing through the branches of the rowan. She did not know enough; she was a stranger here after all.

She glanced up at a rustling sound and saw a minister staring at the silhouetted stained glass window. He turned and saw Eva at the same moment. Her skin was pallid and her breathing shallow. She thought, for an instant, that he was a ghost.

"Surely this isn't your kirk?" she managed to choke out.

"Och, no. I've the new kirk up at Beauly. But I come here whenever I can. I feel closer to God in this wild beauty. It's easier for me to pray when His presence is so strong."

Eva's stomach clenched in disappointment. "Then you don't know about the people buried here?"

The stranger regarded her with kind gray eyes. "No, I'm sorry to say I don't." He paused. "Are you looking for your ancestors?"

She nodded dumbly.

"Aye, weel, so many are, these days. They come to the kirk in Beauly all the time, trying to find out who they are and where they came from." He shook his head sadly. "I'd not be knowin' what they think a few disintegrating headstones'll tell them."

Eva pointed to the indistinct passage on Ailsa's stone. "They can tell you something."

He bent to read the inscription, scratched his chin pensively. "Yes, but what? I mean, what can you really learn about *yourself?*"

"I don't know." Eva sagged with despair. "I just wish . . ."

"Wish what?"

She stared blindly at the headstone. "Nothing."

The minister looked at the back of her bent head and nodded regretfully to himself. "You want to be alone. I'll go then, and come back another day. I hope you find what you're looking for."

She looked up frantically, suddenly terrified of being alone, but he was already striding away. She wanted to call him back, but he was a stranger as much as she was. She let him go while her heart thudded in her chest.

She rose stiffly to find her way through the tall grass to a newer part of the cemetery. Celia's mother, Seonaid Rose Ward, lay beside her husband, but there were no children around her. Eva crouched, staring at the name, familiar yet totally alien. Seonaid had died in 1958. Eva tried to concentrate. This woman was her grandmother. She read the inscription on the simple stone:

> *A tree is now, and its wide branches spread,*
> *In transfused beams, transfiguréd.*
> *Beneath its boughs, like blissful seraphs stand*
> *A multitude of lovers, hand-in-hand.*

Rubbing her forehead, Eva read it again, confused. Had Celia chosen this epitaph for her mother? What had it meant to the young girl Celia had been? What had it meant to Seonaid? She was intrigued, but there were no answers in the gently waving moor grass at her feet. Seonaid was little more than a name to her, as Celia Ward was a name attached to a pathetic, winsome ghost who had failed in her own life and tried to shape her daughter's instead. Eva wondered if she would ever learn what she needed desperately to know. She thought of Charles Kittridge, remembered how long and hard Ailsa had struggled to know her elusive father, how much he had hurt her without knowing. Just as Celia was hurting Eva.

"Why is it," Eilidh had whispered mournfully, "that we keep reliving our ancestors' lives over and over, repeating their mistakes and experiencing their pain? It's as if we're caught up in a cycle we can't break. Surely blood isn't that strong?"

"But it is," Eva muttered, shaking and chilled in the lifeless kirkyard. She seemed fated to search as Ailsa had searched, but in the end, her journey would be fruitless, because Celia was dead.

There was a yawning emptiness inside Eva, a curious numbness. The misty veil she gazed through had grown impenetrable. Though she knelt beside the resting places of her ancestors, she did not feel their spirits around her; she felt, instead, isolated, totally and chillingly alone. Here was her family, dead and buried, when she had always thought of Samuel and Agnes as her family. They were warm, alive, real. These people were not even ghosts or memories. Just names on stone. And her mother not among them.

Eva was no more one of these people than she had been of the islanders, from whom she'd always felt different and apart. She had thought that in coming here she would find she had come home, as Ailsa had. What she felt was depressed and cold, despite the summer sun. Cold inside, like the graveyard in which she stood. It was not peaceful, green and lush, as Charles Kittridge had described it. To Eva it was moldy with moss and lichen, wintry from the shade of old oaks and rowans that spread long, twisted arms above the overgrown ground. There was no hint of life that had been, only death that was.

Eva turned and ran, fleeing the smell of decay and disappointment, plunging into the woods as she'd once plunged up and down steep cliffs. She had to get away from the silence in her head, to escape the despair that was sapping her strength. She climbed recklessly, scratching her arms on brambles and cutting her hands on the branches she pushed out of the way. She ran and stumbled, twisting her ankle in soft loam where gnarled roots were hidden by fallen needles, leaves and thick bracken.

She clutched her side as fingers of fire exploded there. Her breath came in choking gasps. She did not care where she was going, only that she get away. Just as on that first day when she'd fallen exhausted on the cliff top, she could not escape her anguish, because it was inside her, deep, dark and beyond her reach.

3

EVA FOLLOWED THE RIVER BLINDLY, CLIMBING UP AND UP, barely aware of what she was doing. The darkness was upon her, and she did not hear the songs of robins, wrens and thrushes, or see the constant colored motion of the river over boulders and stones through narrow, curving chasms where moss and ferns hung over the rushing water.

She became aware that she had not heard or seen another person in a long time as she blundered through the trees. She paused, bent over from the pain in her side, her breath rasping and harsh. She glanced around for the first time through the mist of her despair, and found she was high among the trees where the air was thin and brisk and she had to struggle to breathe at all. Then she noticed the river edged with boulders, tip-tilted and flat, forming many levels over which the water flowed in waterfall upon waterfall.

Tiny ferns grew in grottoes, and the spray was full of rainbows. In the midst of it all was a deep *linne*. The sunlight broke occasionally through the ceiling of beech, oak, and silver fir to make shimmering patterns on the water.

Eva waited for the throbbing in her body to subside. She had hiked a long way in her violent need to escape. As she stood on a boulder above the river, she felt an overwhelming urge to bathe as she used to do, naked in the sea.

She slipped out of her jeans and shoes, blouse, bra and pants, listening to the tumult of waters. She dove into an icy pool, arms spread to embrace the turbulence of the falls, the motion, the sound; she *needed* these things just now.

She wanted to float free, unencumbered by thought or memories or suffering. She gave herself to the water. The lap and surge of the river held her up so she could move without restraint or effort. She did not need to control her world when it was liquid and friendly and buoyed her up rather than holding her down.

She stayed in the pond for a long time, floating, her face turned toward the rich layers of green overhead, her short hair a nimbus about her head. She dove deep and held her breath as the water caressed her naked skin and she touched the slick multicolored rocks on the silty bottom of the pond. She lost track of time, of weariness and despair.

At last her stomach began to growl in complaint. Eva remembered she had not eaten and moved reluctantly toward the riverbank. Fortunately, she had put a towel in her knapsack. She had just wrapped it around her dripping body when she saw a movement of light and shadow that made her gasp. Someone was near. She slid down between two boulders and, in their shelter, put on her jeans and blouse, hands shaking with dread. *You're young to be traveling alone. There are all kinds of dangers. Especially for someone as pretty as you.* She had been so foolish, so oblivious.

Eva raised her head and looked around frantically, heart pounding. All her imagined terrors came rushing back, magnified and made vivid by the solitude of this place. A few moments ago, that solitude had been a blessing, but now it was ominous—a threat that shimmered in the air like summer heat.

As she crept from between the rocks, a man appeared on a jutting boulder, watching. He was tall and broad-shouldered, with wind-blown black hair and the chiseled cheekbones and pellucid complexion of the Celt, though his skin was sunbrowned, making his blue eyes seem piercing, sinister.

Every sense and nerve in her body was focused on the menace of the stranger. She had not thought her heart could beat any faster; she wanted to press with both hands to keep it inside her chest. "Who are you? What're you doing here?" Fear made her belligerent; she knew no other way to protect herself. She swallowed dryly and licked her lips, hoping the stranger would not see.

The man shrugged, trying but failing to suppress a smile. "I came to bathe, as you did."

His voice was mild and calm, which puzzled Eva. Remembering how she had looked a minute before, she flushed and began to sweat, though her body was chilled through by the icy water.

This time the man managed to hide his smile. "I saw naught but that you were doing what I wanted to do, so I came away. You needn't worry, you know." He met her gaze and smiled gently.

The smile chilled her as much as his unexpected appearance. He seemed at ease, sure of himself, while she was exposed, defenseless. She felt a prickle of foreboding, a warning on her naked skin. Her eyes became clear and smooth, no longer reflections of her emotions. Now the green ringed in gray was an opaque screen to hide behind.

The man grinned, unabashed by her withdrawal. "You can trust me, you know. I'm a scientist, meant to observe and remain objective. It's part of my training. My name is Rory Dey." When she didn't respond, he added, "If you're afraid I'll harm you, why don't you pick up a stone and use it as a weapon?"

She glanced, bewildered, at the stones and pebbles that littered the ground at her feet. She'd never thought of them as weapons, could not make herself do so now. It struck her quite forcibly that she'd never had need of a weapon before. "No," she said firmly. "It's ridiculous."

An odd reaction, Rory thought. He didn't quite know what to say to a girl who was so obviously afraid, but would not defend herself any way she could.

There was an uncomfortable pause. "Why are you here?" she repeated.

"I heard you splashing about, so I went off exploring. I didn't mean to come back, really, but I found I didn't want you to slip away," he replied. "I wanted to meet a girl with so much courage or recklessness that she'd bathe naked because the place was irresistible and clothes would have been an intrusion. I admit, I was compelled to see what you looked like."

His interest had been piqued from the moment he saw her clothes and knapsack left haphazardly on a boulder. What kind of girl would take such a risk? Either she believed no one would dare disturb her, or she did not care if they did, or it never entered her mind that someone would.

Rory was not certain which until, unexpectedly, she exploded upward from the water and he saw her face and a glimpse of her young woman's body. She looked neither arrogant nor indifferent, but rather, infinitely fragile and naive. Though he did not understand why, he had wanted to protect that innocence. But it was more than that.

Her expression had been rapt, her eyes luminous. She glowed, all of her, with a quality he could not name.

As he walked the woods in search of an orange beetle or a peacock butterfly with one eye on each wing, he'd been distracted. He could not erase the image of a slender, suntanned woman rising, sleek and lovely, from the *linne,* a water sprite who had found her fairy bower.

Black hair ruffled by the wind, Rory crossed his arms, consumed by curiosity. "I had to come back. I had to know. Weren't you afraid someone would come?"

His blue eyes were intent on Eva's face.

Those eyes seemed to demand a response from her, though she was intimidated by his gaze and his interest. "I've always lived on an island in the Inner Hebrides where no one bothered me. I forgot it isn't like that everywhere."

Rory tilted his head, perplexed. "Why didn't they bother you? Didn't they dare? Were they afraid of you?" It was not his business, but he could not seem to stop asking. He had been trained to look at everything closely, to probe and question until he understood. His natural curiosity, nurtured and encouraged by the scientists at university, would not be suppressed or disregarded. Rory waited.

Eva knew she should ignore the intimate question, but it made her pause. She had never wondered why she'd been left in peace on her cliff top or in her vigorous walks and private bathing. She'd simply accepted the islanders' respect for her privacy. She ran her hands through her wet hair and answered slowly, "They might have been afraid, in a way.

Not that I'd hurt them. It was something else. Maybe they feared to disturb me in some pagan ritual that would send us all to hell. Or maybe it was the way I loved the sea, and the animals came to me."

Rory Dey leaned forward; she had his full attention now. "I saw that in the way you glided through the water with your eyes closed, as if you'd no need to see to know your way."

Eva could not believe he knew so much from seeing how she bathed. She did not wonder how long he had watched to see such a thing, or what else he might have seen. She did not think of her body as alluring, something a stranger might want to stare at or possess. She was far more protective of her privacy than her nakedness. "I shouldn't have done it, I suppose," she said with regret. "But the call of the water was too strong."

"Did you find what you sought there? By the by, you haven't told me your name."

She hesitated. "Eva Crawford. And I found a momentary comfort. I suppose that's what I was looking for." Her voice was toneless, without animation.

Rory narrowed his eyes skeptically, but he'd already pushed too hard and intruded too far. "You look hungry," he said suddenly, "and rather discouraged in the bargain. Would you care to join me for a meal?" He frowned. Why had he offered the invitation? This girl was so fragile, her expression so anxious. He did not need to take on a wounded child who was nearly, but not quite, a woman. He did not need to examine her pain. But he could not seem to turn his back on her. "I told you I'm Rory, but my friends call me Ruardh. That's Gaelic for—"

"For red, I know."

His eyes were steady, clear and blue. He was wearing an Oxford cloth button-down shirt and threadbare blue jeans with sturdy walking boots. She thought he was attractive, and the thought alarmed her. The flicker of fear returned, licking at her desire to join Rory Dey. She had been alone for hours with the circling voices in her head, the hopelessness and the confusion. She wanted to hear a real voice, to talk of everyday things, to be with *someone,* at least for a while.

Still, this man was a stranger, and she was only eighteen. She looked up anxiously, expectant and wary. Rory's blue eyes met hers and she felt a jolt, as if he'd looked beyond her skin to the longings and the darkness underneath.

They ate cheese sandwiches and drank lemonade while Rory sprawled in the shade of some larches. "I'm an entomologist with leanings toward botany," he explained, in answer to her question. "Or at least, I'm almost a full-fledged scientist. I'm just finishing my advanced studies at university. Just now we're on holiday for the summer, so I came up here to seek out some obscure insect or unknown herb that grows in the primeval forest." He paused for a moment, glanced at her from the corner of his eye. "And you?"

Eva started, though she should have known the question was coming. She did not want to talk about her reason for coming to the glen. She'd been completely drained by the kirkyard and her bitter disappointment with this place, her sense of alienation. Even Ailsa had let her down. She wanted to put Celia behind her, to forget, and in forgetting, revive her flagging energy and hope.

With a heavy sigh, Eva glanced at Rory, who was watching her intently. She was confused and distressed that he should be here, stretched out beside her, for all the world as if they'd known each other for years. She looked away abruptly. "What am I doing?" she whispered under her breath. "I must be mad."

Rory heard but did not answer. He didn't know the answer himself, and Eva looked as if she might flee if he said the wrong thing. He didn't want that. He enjoyed exploring her mysteries too much. He breathed deeply and forced himself to stare off into the distance. He wished he could stop himself from thinking as easily as he'd stopped himself from speaking.

Neither spoke while Eva struggled with her common sense, which told her to get away. She twisted her fingers into mindless patterns but did not move. She had never really learned to fear people. She'd been more afraid of the nightmares, the things inside herself—the darkness, the inexplicable yearning, the depression. Her moods had been more threatening than the motives or actions of others.

There are all kinds of dangers. Eva knew Rory was one of them, yet she could not make herself go. It wasn't only that she could not bear to be alone. She was intrigued by his smile, his curiosity, the things he'd understood as he watched her bathe. He *wanted* to understand. He did not seem afraid of her oddness or her elusive heart as her parents had been.

To Eva, in her present fragile and friendless condition, his interest, his fearlessness were irresistible. She was taking a risk; her breath was raw with a constant awareness of her own jeopardy. Yet she didn't fear violence. There was another, indefinable threat in Rory's fascination with her, in the clear gaze of his deep blue eyes. But even that was preferable to the sense of isolation that had overwhelmed her in the kirkyard.

"The thing is," Rory said, when he was fairly certain she wouldn't run, "I'm ruled by my curiosity, you see. The need to know consumes me. I can't bear to miss anything, whether it's a new technique for tracking rare bugs or a weekend party with masses of strangers." He waved a hand at the untamed landscape. "Everything is a new experience. Every time I look into a microscope, it's completely new and exciting, because I never know what I'll see. That's what makes life stimulating—the little mysteries. The big ones are rarer, but they do happen." He smiled and tilted his head toward her. "In any case, I never stop anticipating the next event. It might be a lovely girl who's lost her way and seeks solace in a fairy pond."

Drawn by the deep tenor of his voice, the enthusiasm in his tone, Eva listened, wide-eyed. She wondered what it would be like to look at the future that way, as an adventure instead of a black nothingness. Then his last words penetrated and she stared down at her hands in embarrassment. She did not know how to flirt. She held her breath, let it out slowly. "I don't play games very well," she said.

Her cheeks were flushed and her voice quivered with distress. Rory didn't know what to think. He'd never met anyone like her before. But then, she was quite young. He tried to think back to the days before university and his consuming absorption in science, but it wasn't the same. He'd never been sheltered as this girl apparently had been, then thrust out into the world alone. Why? he wanted to ask. What was she doing so far from her island where she'd had no need of wariness or fear? He didn't ask; his curiosity might drive her away.

His throat tightened. He did not want her to go. He did not believe she would be safe on her own, but it was more than that. Her fragile vulnerability touched him as much as her affinity with the water had seduced him. He wanted very much to know what ghosts were haunting her. "Would you like to explore the woods?" he asked. "A little adventure's just the thing to clear a cluttered mind."

She glanced about nervously, so he added, "I promise to behave. I'll be too busy sketching plants or insects to bother you. You've nothing to fear from me."

"No?" Eva said quietly. "I wonder."

Rory got to his feet. "Wonder all you like, but come along. Lingering in a place like this is dangerous. Can lead to thought, you know, and that can lead to all kinds of complications."

In spite of herself, Eva laughed. "It can, can't it? All right. I'll come with you." As she rose, she felt a sharp stab of warning, but she chose to ignore it.

They spent the afternoon searching out the slippery orange beetle and peacock butterfly, "Which I might have found by now if I hadn't come upon a mermaid," Rory called over his shoulder.

Eva was bemused by the way he moved through the green cathedral of towering trees, their leaves grazed by sunlight. His energy was boundless. Once he chased a tiny butterfly across a meadow, then strode back, ready to seek out a new object of interest. He climbed up rocks and over fallen trees, and though his breathing grew ragged, it did not seem to slow him down. His anticipation was palpable. "Come look at this tiny mouse," he murmured once, motioning her closer. "Isn't it lovely?"

Eva gazed at the creature curled in a bed of moss, wool

and leaves, protected by a gnarled larch root. The sight was somehow unbearably touching. She looked at Rory in astonishment because he had noticed the mouse and stopped to admire its soft, warm innocence. She turned, but he was off again, heading for a dense growth of trees. "It might be dark and damp enough to house some beetles," he explained when Eva caught up with him.

Occasionally he bent close to a straggling green plant, a sprig of weed, an insect Eva could not see. He sketched with clear, precise strokes in a miniature artist's notebook, smiling in triumph as he put the charcoal away, or cursing when his subject fled on tiny feet or iridescent wings. Undaunted, he rose to continue his quest. Abruptly, without warning, he stiffened, watching and waiting, absolutely motionless, for half an hour, to catch a second glimpse of his prey.

Eva found it difficult to reconcile this patient man and his focused gaze with the Rory eager for adventure. She admired his willingness to let the adventure find him. She had never been patient or willing to wait. That's why she was so furious at Celia. The thought unnerved her. She had not realized she was so angry.

While they were poised near the trunk of gnarled oak and its twisted roots, hushed and immobile, a tiny red squirrel came up to Eva's hand, and a wren landed on her shoulder.

Sensing a change in the air, Rory shifted his attention from a nest of squirming beetles to Eva, caught in a ray of soft light. He held his breath so as not to disturb the image of her contented smile, the stillness, the faith of the animals.

"They do come to you, Eva," he whispered, amazed. "Perhaps I should take you on all my research forays and let you stand with your hand outstretched to see what lands there."

The squirrel skittered away into the gorse, while the wren took flight at the first word Rory uttered. He watched them go, regretful yet expectant, as the bird skimmed through the intermeshed leaves and disappeared into the open sky. The freedom of flight, the aerodynamics of a thing that should be impossible, fascinated Rory most of all, from an airplane to a butterfly to a bright autumn leaf lifted high by the wind. Those were his daydreams and his miracles.

4

THEY STUMBLED AT LAST INTO A COPSE BY THE RIVER, EXhausted and hungry. Here they found a noisy group of travelers who had set up a kind of rudimentary camp. They had sleeping bags and knapsacks, lightweight pans for cooking. They had several coolers and tarps in case it rained, a clever handmade wooden chest that held food and utensils. Several musical instruments lay scattered about, the strings still vibrating, as if they'd only just fallen silent.

The smell of frying fish wafted upward enticingly. The strangers turned to survey the new arrivals. "There are others as lost as we," a young woman cried. "Should you like to join us?" she asked with a smile.

Rory grinned back and looked at Eva questioningly. She was suddenly nervous, unused to meeting strangers in the wilds of the Highlands or anywhere else. This group sprawled on the grass, sitting cross-legged or leaning back on their elbows. The men had shaggy haircuts, as if they'd neglected to visit a barber in the past month, while two of the women had long, flowing hair, the other two shortcropped styles that revealed the fine shape of their bones. The clothes were well-worn and colorful—blue jeans and bright jerseys and loose jackets.

"You needn't be afraid, you know. We don't go in for sacrificial virgins or that sort of thing," a blond man offered.

"No, absolutely not. I'm Thomas, by the by, and that's Allan and Ismay, Simon and Mairead, Sorcha and Jeanne."

"I'm Rory, and this is Eva." He leaned down to whisper in her ear, "What do you think?"

Eva thought, as she had that afternoon, that she'd rather be here than alone with her demons. The fire crackled cozily, the smell of food was irresistible, and the people seemed friendly. "We'd like to join you if it's all right."

Everyone called out a welcome as they made room for Eva and Rory in their circle. Eva sat, glanced at the musical instruments and asked diffidently, "What do you all do? Do you travel together?"

"Endlessly!" Sorcha said in a throaty voice. "It's our job, such as it is. Traveling as a troupe from fair to festival to concert, performing plays and songs and dances." She flung her shawl, silver thread woven as fine as a glistening web, over her shoulder, and shook out her long, dark hair.

"Now and then we take a break," Jeanne added, "find a place like this, wild and secluded, to revive our creativity."

"The life has its drawbacks, but it's never dull." That was Allan.

Rory watched and listened, interested in and entertained by the colorful group. Their faces were animated, marked from years of laughter and hardship. What would it be like to follow the crowds and the muse instead of dedicating oneself to the lure of science, having a home at university, a base of security that never seemed to change? He liked these people and their easy camaraderie, but couldn't help wondering whether the companionship made up for the uncertainty.

Eva was very curious about them. She'd never met such a large group of players before. Now and then one or two came to the island, but not often. Because of her own love of music and the songs she wrote, she wanted to know more, to hear about the life of these wandering artists. "Have you known each other a long time?"

Rory glanced at her, suddenly alert. She sounded wistful and a little envious. Was this what she wanted from life? Was that part of what made her an enigma?

"Oh, aye," Simon responded. "Thomas is slowly going daft, planning how we'll all be famous one day. We only hang about to pick up the pieces when he finally fragments. 'Twill be a sad day, that." He was half serious and half jesting.

The others groaned, and Eva leaned forward, frowning.

"But you enjoy it, don't you? Knowing what you want, performing all the time, following your hearts?"

They looked at one another in silent communication. "You're very young, aren't you?" Sorcha murmured. "There's some of that, of course. But it wears one down, this kind of life. Sometimes your heart and your spirit and your muse fall silent all at once, and then where are you?" At Eva's look of disappointment, she added brightly, "But one always muddles through in the end. Look at us, after all."

Contemplating the glowing heart of the fire, Eva tried to hide her sense of defeat. She'd thought, for a moment, she might find the answer to her own baffling creative impulses among these strangers. Her songs and musical stories came to her as moments of exquisite inspiration, but somehow that was not enough. She knew the darkness inside was building and she had to learn to harness or control it or obliterate it before it consumed her. She stared pensively into the dancing flames as the others settled back, talking quietly.

Rory watched Eva, alert and alarmed. "You're awfully romantic," he murmured, but she did not hear him. "You don't seem to have the cynicism of an adult." He realized he was talking to himself, but perhaps that was just as well. He felt ambivalent about her naïveté. He wanted to smooth the frown from her face and restore her glittering image of an artist's life, but it went against everything he believed in to lie. He wondered at his impulse to console her. Perhaps it was the way her skin turned warm and golden in the firelight, or the wisp of a curl that drifted across her temple. Or perhaps the depth of sadness in her eyes.

He shook his head. He had discovered Eva alone in paradise and been drawn to her individuality, but that didn't make him her savior. He had no idea what to save her from. Besides, he had his own life to think about. Still, she looked fragile and alone just now. He ached with the pain she could not conceal. He wanted to take her hand and hold it close to his heart, but that would not be wise. With an effort of will, he forced his attention back to the others.

They lay cheerful and relaxed in the cotton grass, with ferns brushing their shoulders and dropping dew in their hair. After a while, Eva pushed the darkness back and looked over at Rory, chewing idly on a blade of grass, the shadows of leaves on his face, emphasizing his dark hair and sun-browned skin. There was something captivating in his loose-limbed repose, his half-smile and blue gaze, intent on a dragonfly hovering nearby.

Eva envied him that uncomplicated pleasure in the beauty around him.

"I like it here," Rory said. "You lot have chosen well." He nodded to the group as he took wild blackberries from his knapsack and rose to wash them in the burn. Eva stayed where she was, unwilling to force her aching legs back into motion, wary of following Rory anymore.

When he returned he held a basket of glistening berries, rich, dark, large and juicy-looking. Eva could taste them melting on her tongue. Everyone leaned forward eagerly, but Rory warned them away. "They're for after. You're not to try and cheat, you know. That would spoil the order of things. Besides, you wouldn't have them to look forward to."

Eva leaned back, eyelids heavy, but did not participate as the others prepared the food and gathered utensils together. She was content to listen to the sound of their musical voices and sniff the mouth-watering fragrance of fish and potatoes cooked in the coals. She felt a little guilty; at home she had always shared the work. Today she was too weary to move.

While they ate, everyone talked and laughed, exchanging jokes and confidences. Eva liked the feeling of camaraderie, however temporary; it made her less alone. She never thought she could so easily enjoy a group of people she did not know. She felt at ease among them, because they themselves were at ease. They had accepted her without question, and she found she accepted them as well. She realized with pleasure that she could do so without really understanding them. And she need not run because they were strangers. They were no threat to her. She was exhilarated by the discovery.

When the food and the basket of berries were gone,

Simon picked up a banjo and began to play. Mairead took her flute and Thomas a mouth harp. There were several guitars, and Rory asked if he could borrow one. He sat next to Eva and began to strum, but he was not very adept. Eva took the guitar from him gently, cradling the instrument in her hands. It seemed like years since she'd held her own guitar, had wanted to make music or create a song. She smiled and joined in the intricate tune the others were playing—a Celtic song with a modern lilt.

After a while, she moved farther from the firelight and began to create her own variations. With the graceful touch of her fingertips on the strings, she wove an invisible barrier around herself and Rory, setting them apart. The others seemed far away. The sound of their voices faded as each note curled through the mild summer air. Perhaps it was the wine, Eva thought. She felt drowsy, light and languid.

"You're marvelous," Rory exclaimed in admiration. One mystery of Eva was solved. He took heart. "Do you sing as well?" He lay full length on the ground, propped on his elbows among blue moor grass, his hair lifted and caressed by the wind.

"I do," Eva murmured. "Do you? Do you know this song?" Softly, she began to sing the ancient words.

> *Everything there is has being;*
> *Mountains have a voice,*
> *Stars and comets are foreseeing;*
> *The little hills rejoice.*

Rory watched in fascination. Her hair looked like fine burgundy in the odd filtered light of evening, her face was soft with the music, and her green eyes darkened, except for an occasional reflection of flame in their depths. Rory felt a frisson of desire, but he let it fade into the shadows. She was too young; it was too soon. He let the music wash over him, silencing, for the moment, the questions he had not yet asked, though he wanted more and more to know the answers.

And thou, wilt thou not sing,
Who bearest in thy throat
The Rapture of the Spring,
The Resurrection Note?

Eva cupped the strings as the song ended and she felt the last vibrations of the notes against her palm. A pleasant lethargy flowed through her veins, leaving her body fluid and limp. There had been sweet wine with dinner. Perhaps she had had one glass too many. She smiled crookedly and rested her head on the neck of the guitar.

"So," Rory said, having decided to take a great risk, "why have you come to the glen? It was not, I think, an accident."

"I came looking," Eva replied cryptically. She rolled onto her back and concentrated on the distant sound of the water. "My ancestors lived here, and they made it sound so beautiful."

Rory heard the urgency beneath the studied casualness. He heard the disillusionment too. How had someone so transparent, so vibrantly emotional, survived to the age of eighteen without being destroyed by the harshness of the world? Perhaps it was the island where she had been left alone. Many of the islands were so isolated that they made their own worlds.

Still, he could hardly believe this girl, this Eva Crawford. She did not seem to know how to be dishonest.

"You don't think the glen is beautiful?" he asked carefully.

"Yes, it's lovely. But . . ." She paused, breathing with the rise and fall of the leaves. "From what they said, I thought it would be miraculous, overwhelming." She did not look at him but at the dancing branches draped in shades of green. She had expected to feel many things when she stood looking over the glen—recognition, an affinity that flowed in her blood, rage at what she'd lost, what she'd never known, what had been taken from her without her acceptance or consent or submission. But she'd felt nothing.

Rory sat up, brow furrowed. "Who are 'they'?"

Eva was startled. "My great-great grandmother, I suppose, and her family."

Though she spoke lightly of the people who had brought her here, Rory felt that Eva cared very much about the distant past, and perhaps the not so distant also. "What about *your* family?" he asked.

Eva was disturbed by his questions. It was as if he drew them, not from the well of his own curiosity, but from inside Eva herself. She looked at Rory and saw peril in his eyes.

But the sounds of insects in the moonlit twilight, of birds settling in for the night, the music that blended with and emphasized those sounds, hypnotized Eva. The impulse that rose in her, hot and bright, was irresistible.

She wanted to talk, to unburden herself to this man who was so steady, so quietly interested in what she had to say. Yet he was more than that; his energy was powerful, alluring, alarming. Eva shivered, chilled and overheated both at once. But she forced her doubts aside. Tonight her need was greater than her fear.

Because Rory was a stranger who had never known Celia Ward, who had no connection to the Crawfords or the island or Eilidh or the Roses of Glen Affric, she wanted to trust him. Slowly, uncoiling the tangle of chaos in which she floundered, she told him about them all. She told him what she was really seeking, and why. The words tumbled out of their own accord, and she did not try to stop them.

Rory listened, every nerve in his body tingling, and thought how young Eva was, how protected. If that was what Celia Ward had intended, she had done a good job of it after all. The knowledge made him want to back away. She was so vulnerable it terrified him. She could be so easily crushed.

"I don't think my mother believed she was important enough for me to know all about her. She didn't think she was interesting or vital, but weak and dull, unlike our ancestors. She wanted to put the burden of my self-discovery on them instead of herself. Sometimes I pity her."

Rory stared, dazed. Perhaps Eva was not quite as young as he'd suspected, or as frail. In the tone of her voice, in the flicker of steel at the heart of her radiance, he saw a strength he had not thought to find. It was that courage which had made her dive into the *linne* without thought of consequences, because she needed respite. She could have stayed on the island where she was safe, protected, loved, and never explored the darkness inside or her difference from the others or her weak and daft mother. But Eva had not made the easy choice. She wanted to know the truth, though she feared it with all her heart. Only an incredible strength of will could have brought her here. That troubled him too.

She was more naked now than when he'd first seen her. Her soul was visible to him, exposed. That took the most courage of all. He was awestruck by the contradictions of Eva. He could not place the pieces of the puzzle in a tidy pattern; there was too much he didn't know. He suspected Eva could teach him things he had not begun to imagine. His heart raced with excitement, though his mind warned him to go slow, to think this through. He rubbed his eyes to clear his vision.

Eva leaned forward tensely. "You think I'm too curious."

Rory frowned at her odd misreading of his thoughts. "You're much more than curious. You're driven. You need to be. It's the only way to puzzle out where you're going and why. I admire that drive."

"But it frightens you."

Rory stared down at his hands. "Perhaps a little. You're too honest, you see. That kind of honesty makes you vulnerable as well. I don't think you've learned to protect yourself yet." He shouldn't speak to her this way, but he'd felt compelled since he saw her rise from the water like a mermaid, golden and radiant. He paused, braiding his fingers so the shadows undulated in the firelight. He was unnerved by her perception and did not want to discuss his wildly vacillating emotions.

After a long silence, he said, "You're welcome to stay here tonight. You'll be safe enough, and I've a feeling these people are used to taking in those who're lost."

Eva sat up abruptly, fingers digging into damp ferns. "I'm not lost."

"I think perhaps you are, you know."

Eva clamped her teeth together to keep them from chattering. The chill moved through her body until it touched her heart and slowed the beat, made it laborious and painful. "What right—"

Rory put out a hand to stop her. His fingers rested lightly on her rigid arm. They were warm and callused from his work. "None at all. I have no right. Never mind my bloody interference. But don't believe for a moment that I meant to hurt you. It's just—" He broke off and removed his hand.

Eva flinched, but whether from his touch or the loss of it, she did not know. "Just what?"

Little as he liked it, her honesty demanded his own. "I wonder if perhaps you're too precipitous and too cautious. I wonder if you cannot hear the voices of the glen or see its true beauty because you're listening only with your ears and looking only with your eyes, not with your heart."

"You can't know that. You don't know *me*," she said stiffly. "Besides, I heard the water." Her voice was a whisper, and the breeze drifted through her chestnut hair, ruffling it softly.

"The water is a voice from inside you. It might even be an echo of your own. I should think you'll always hear that when it calls, shouldn't you?"

That's not your concern, Eva thought defensively, but she didn't say it aloud. Suddenly she felt restless; the sluggish flow of her blood increased its pace. She realized with relief that the music had changed, that Jeanne and Thomas had risen to start a reel and Simon and Sorcha had joined them.

The tempo and volume of the music swept away the veil of distance Eva had woven. She and Rory became part of the group once more. Rory seemed to share her restlessness. "It's nearly gloaming," he said, rising with agility.

"Is it?" Eva blinked in confusion. A long time had passed since she'd noticed where the sun hung in the cloudy sky. Now it was low and lost among the distant trees. Soon it would slide behind the jagged mountains, shading them purple and blue, drenching them with mystery.

"Indeed." Rory gave Eva his hand to guide her into the reel. They circled, hands clasped, to the lively music, until they were spinning in the midst of the other dancers.

As the music swelled, filling the evening and fluttering the leaves, Eva lost herself in its rhythm as she sometimes lost herself in the sea. She felt weightless, without burdens or history or worries. Little by little, she relinquished her cautiousness, letting the water, the music, the rhythm enwrap her.

The animated dancers whirled faster and faster into the descending gloaming. They swung each other from hand to hand, so that Eva partnered Simon, then Allan, then Sorcha. The two women laughed, caught each other's elbows and spun in the center, closest to the fire. Eva was exhilarated, delighted to be moving, to be caught up in music instead of memories, to hear the sound of laughter instead of distant weeping. The faces began to blur as she skipped from partner to partner, smiling at each with an openness and innocence that made the others envious and afraid for her. Her face was fresh with youth, lovely with the promise of a long life to come, while theirs were lined and weathered from travel, uncertainty and the dubious conditions in which they lived. There was sorrow in her green eyes ringed in gray, but no world-weariness or disillusion. "Ah, little Eva, you're so lovely and so lucky to know so little," Jeanne whispered when they paused, gasping for breath.

"I don't think—" Eva began in distress.

"No, and you needn't. Not yet. That's what makes you so lucky." Jeanne touched her shoulder briefly, shrugged and disappeared among her friends.

Eva stood quite still for a moment, while her breathing settled back to normal. She wondered at Jeanne's sad parting smile, but forgot it when Rory came up beside her.

The musicians had begun a new song that slowed and trembled lightly. The music was soft and lilting, more soothing than the raucous reel that had gone before. "Like to try again?" Rory asked with a little bow.

At Eva's shy nod, he caught her close and they turned in small, graceful circles. She rested her head on his shoulder without thinking. Rory raised his head and Eva looked up so they stood face to face, with the cool breath of approaching night between them. He wanted to kiss her, but was oddly reluctant. For a long moment, the kiss hung in the air, palpable and real.

Rory sensed Eva's extreme fragility. If he tried to seduce her, she might succumb. But he didn't want her that way— uncertain, holding on to him because there was no one else. He wanted her to come feeling whole, wanting *him,* not just solace. It disturbed him that he wanted her so much.

He was only twenty-six, but holding Eva while the music pulsed around them, he felt very old. He pulled her close and the kiss that had hovered between them disappeared into the rising mist. Slowly, slowly, they swayed together. The music followed their lead, rather than the other way around.

Eva clung to Rory's warmth and energy. She felt that without a word, without an intimate touch, in the midst of a noisy crowd, she had been penetrated, that she was naked and afraid and expectant. She felt the volcano of emotion inside begin to roil, and she shuddered.

Rory backed away. "It's too soon," he said. "You may not doubt *me,* Eva, though you ought, but you don't really believe in yourself. You don't know who you are, and though you need desperately to know, you're afraid of the truth. You're afraid to listen and see with your heart. It might be too painful." He touched her cheek gently. "Don't be afraid. Your soul is fragile but true. Believe that. You must."

Eva stepped back, arms crossed tightly over her chest, stunned and hurt by his rejection. She did not want to think about her soul. She did not want to think at all. She wanted, as she had wanted all her life, simply to feel, to be, to let go. And Rory Dey knew how. She was certain of it. That was why she had come here. "You can't make that choice for me. You've only met me a few hours ago." She spoke defiantly, wanted to deny what he'd said, each judgment he had made, but in her heart, she feared he was right, at least in one thing. It was too soon, too unwise, too perilous.

Silently, despondently, she and Rory left the dancers and sat at the edge of the circle of firelight as gloaming turned slowly from violet to gray and faded, eventually, into darkness.

5

THAT NIGHT, WHEN AT LAST SHE FELL ASLEEP, CURLED IN THE sleeping bag Ismay had lent her, Eva dreamt. A figure came to her, insubstantial, a shade who hovered in the shadows. For a time Eva did not recognize Celia Ward, petite, pale-haired, chimerical.

Then Celia came forward and reached for her daughter. "Don't walk in my shadow, child. It is too frail to hide you and too narrow to guide you." Celia put her hand on her daughter's shoulder, but Eva could not tell if she was warning her back or pushing her forward. Far in the distance, she saw Rory, black hair windblown, blue eyes intent with waiting.

Eva woke, blinking in confusion. Her mother had tried to send her a message, but she did not understand it. As her vision cleared and she took in the misted lilac dawn, she knew she had to make more of an effort to know the woman who had been her mother. Until she understood that ghostly figure, she could not move forward *or* back. She was suspended in time and in chaos.

"Shadows move, and they have voices, but their words are sighs and tears," she crooned softly, as her own words came back like an eerie echo of her dream. "Spectral hands will give you choices—Death or solitude or fear."

Rory made a strangled sound beside her, and she glanced

up, eyes glazed. "That song," he muttered, "it's so grim. Do you always sing such things to greet the morning?"

Squinting to bring him into focus, Eva felt the chill of Celia's touch upon her. "It's one of my own. I wrote it two years back. It reminded me of my dream."

Rory was disturbed by the cast on her eyes, the pain and desperation that little verse revealed. He fought to erase the sound of her voice that echoed the moan of the bagpipes, clear, lovely and so lonely it twisted his heart.

"Will you be off today?" he forced himself to ask calmly. The others had gone for a dawn stroll, leaving Rory and Eva alone. They ate bannocks and apples and milk, and sat by the low-burning fire in the surprisingly chill early morning.

Eva nodded. "There're so many things I have to do. I don't even know what they are, really. Only that I can't go on until they're done. The dream told me that."

She sounded so forlorn that Rory took her hand and slid it, fingers laced with his, into the pocket of his down jacket. Having had a glimpse of the depth of her misery, he wanted to soothe her, to make her forget. He contemplated her cheekbones and soft lips, the green glow of her eyes, and was startled when those eyes glazed over and she seemed to slip away from him.

Eva felt the warmth first, the reassurance of Rory's grasp and the safety of his deep, soft pocket. Then the morning faded and she saw flares of color and a starry sky. "I see a boy staring in wonder, fascinated by the beauty and mystery above him, by the pinpoints of light in the velvety blackness."

She was not aware that Rory stared at her, bewildered by the singsong quality of her voice. She did not seem to be speaking to him but to herself.

"Night becomes dawn and the boy, dark-haired and sun-browned, sits in a garden, looking up at the washing hung out on the line. He watches the white sheets flapping and feels the sun bright on his face. He loves the dancing colors of shirts and trousers and socks in the wind, loves especially the flying sheets—clean, white and reaching for the wide blue sky beyond."

Caught in the hypnotic cadence of her voice, Rory recognized himself sitting in his mother's garden. Eva could not know that, could not have seen the scene she described so vividly. A shiver ran up his back, raising chills along his arms, but he did not interrupt.

"The boy laughs, exulting, when one sheet tears free and rises on the wind, floating and drifting, then soaring down. His first kite. There are many others. Kites of all colors, all winds and all skies. He loves nothing more than holding a soaring kite, connected by a thin thread to the earth, to him." Eva smiled sweetly, in understanding and delight.

"He runs beside a river flowing fast over tumbled stones, always moving, always traveling, and as he runs he grows. The river at his side flashes golden in the sunlight, and the stones turn to jewels—beyond price to the boy with the colored kite who becomes a man, following the twists and shallows and depths of the river that will one day meet the sea."

Eva shook her head, and the brilliant hue of gems faded back into the colored stones in the river beside the copse. She looked up for a glimpse of the kite, but saw only emerald leaves and the silvery needles of the firs. She turned to Rory, smiling. "You believe in miracles, don't you?"

He was dazzled, staggered, profoundly unnerved by the rhythmic, beguiling story of his own childhood. How had she done it? How had she guessed? His rational mind wanted to reject any answer, but he was so captivated by Eva that he could not cling to logic. He was losing a battle he had not agreed to fight.

He refused to mention the story. He could not comprehend the magnitude of what this fragile girl had done. But he had to respond to the tender smile that transformed her face as golden water had transformed her body. He wanted to.

After some difficulty, he found his voice. "You think because I'm a scientist, I shouldn't believe, but where would science be without miracles, I ask you? Discoveries made because of a bit of mold on a piece of cheese, or a mirror reflecting the moonlight or a bit of glass left carelessly on a page of cramped writing?" Rory paused. "Other than that, I believe in the power of pure colors, and the beauty and integrity of small, perfect insects who create their own intricate little kingdoms."

He stopped abruptly. He was babbling, trying to hide his discomfort beneath a rush of words. She had caught him off guard, astonished him again. He had to regain his equilibrium somehow. "Tell me about you," he insisted somewhat desperately. "What is it you want to do when all the mysteries are solved?"

Eva stared into the glowing ashes of the fire. "I want to be safe."

"There is no safety. Not really." Rory ran his fingers through his hair and contemplated Eva's shuttered expression. Was this the same woman who had bathed nude in a secluded *linne?* Who a moment before had shimmered and spoken of miracles? "Even if there was such a thing, I don't think you would choose it."

"Perhaps not." She slid her hand out of his and clasped her fingers around her bent knees, pensive, urgent, doubtful.

How was it that Rory seemed to understand what the islanders never had? She felt certain he had glimpsed her darkness, by the look in his eyes when he'd heard her song. He had understood how she moved through the water, had admired her foolish daring. He was jittery at what she'd felt in his pocket but also intrigued. He met her eyes and tried to smile naturally; he spoke to her of miracles. She did not think he was afraid. Even Samuel, even Daniel had always feared the side of her they could not understand. She craved Rory's empathy and feared it, feared the memory of how he'd nearly kissed her and she'd felt that touch withheld in hot tingles all over her body.

Apprehension blocked her throat and made it difficult to breathe. The woods seemed to be closing in on her. It was too dark and circumscribed here; there was no room to fling out her arms and take in the wide blue sky. "I feel like I'm suffocating," she said. "It's too close."

Rory regarded her curiously, then shook his own dismay aside. "Come with me." He took her hand to draw her out of the copse and into a clearing of pale green grass starred with wild violets and purple foxgloves. The woods fell away below her and rose above, but here the air was clear and the sky shone through wisps of white cloud, a deep, vibrant blue. The loch glimmered in the sunlight, and sparks of silver through emerald showed the burn flowing among the trees.

"You see, you're free here, unencumbered," Rory said. "If you want a cool, dark forest, you can have it. If you crave the water of the loch, it's yours. If you seek a meadow of wildflowers, look around you. If you want a secret *linne* in the burn, it's here."

Eva breathed deeply, felt the tension ebb as the shadow of a low-flying kestrel brushed by and disappeared into the trees. She opened her arms to encompass the wild beauty, but they fell to her sides under the weight of her own uncertainty.

"It's not enough, is it?" Rory asked.

Eva stared at the calm, reflective waters of the loch and shook her head. "I don't suppose it is."

"Then perhaps you should look for the people as well. People have voices too, you know. Sometimes they even use them to tell the truth. You have to trust that."

"I do. Sometimes." Eva did not face him.

"Then why don't you go looking for relatives or at least people who knew your mother? There's bound to be someone. In a place like this, people cling to the past in spite of everything. Why don't you ask for answers from them?"

Eva stiffened. She did not want to hear this. In the back of her mind she had wondered if there might be someone who had known Celia or her family. She had industriously ignored the pinprick of that question. "I don't think I'm ready—" She broke off. She did not want to reveal her insecurity to Rory. What she wanted more than anything was to run.

"But you went to see the dead ones," he continued implacably. "Was that because you thought they'd tell you their secrets, or because you knew they wouldn't?"

Eva whirled. "I'm not ready. I told you." Her tone, initially piercing and colored by anguish, grew quiet as she struggled for control. "It's all too much. Can't you see that?"

Rory was ashamed. He *had* seen it—in the bluish veins that showed beneath her suntanned skin, the erratic pulse at the base of her throat, the anticipation, apprehension and confusion that had crossed her face as they talked last night. He had seen it in the moment when she'd risen from the water in a shower of gold, eyes closed and head back, as if in the hope or expectation of a benediction. "Yes, I can see that. I'm sorry."

He paced through the waist-high cotton grass and wildflowers, petals and stalks clinging to his worn jeans and open hands. "But if you came back in ... say a fortnight. You might be able to see things differently."

Eva shook her head, turned russet by the sun. She had not brushed the curls, and they tumbled about her face in disorder. "That's not enough time. There's too much unresolved."

Rory tramped through the grass to take her shoulders in a light grasp. "Have a little faith."

"I do." Her response was immediate, simple and sincere. As she'd told Samuel on her last morning on *Eilean Eadar*, she could not stop believing. She looked into Rory's blue eyes and saw that he believed too, deeply.

It terrified her, the connection she felt with him that was more than empathy or gratitude or understanding. It was knowing, without doubt or the ability to pretend it was not so. "Maybe I don't want to come back."

Rory's lips twitched. A smile was his only defense against the naked truth he'd seen in her eyes, but he fought it just the same. He was surprised at how automatically and completely he wanted both to protect Eva and force her awake. "Perhaps you don't want to come back now. But the glen will call you, just as it called your ancestors. You can refuse to listen for a while, but eventually, you'll be drawn here in spite of your wishes."

He cupped his palm as if to caress her cheek, but instead ran it gently around her head, not touching her, except for an errant strand of hair blown by the wind. She shivered at the force of his caress, which made no contact with her skin, and yet penetrated, and changed, her frantic heartbeat.

"The voices here are powerful and you're sensitive to that power."

Eva tightened every muscle in her body against what she felt was the menace in his voice.

Sighing, Rory continued. "That power is also beauty. You know that. It's not harsh or destructive but seductive and sensual. It ignites long-buried instincts and desires never acknowledged. But that's its only threat—to make you feel through every vein and pore and pulse of your blood."

His voice, as well as his words, were alluring, and Eva responded, mind and body, as she never had to Daniel, who had kissed and held and caressed her. Yet Rory hadn't touched her; he had only met her eyes and spoken the truth. Her heart was pounding and she found it difficult to breathe. Her face felt warm and her palms clammy.

This was too dangerous. This was the most frightening thing of all. She crossed her arms in a futile gesture of defense.

Rory took a step backward, forcing his gaze away from hers, forcing a shroud over the nerves she had ignited without speaking or moving, merely by letting him see inside her. And she had not known she was doing it. Someday he hoped she would give him that gift consciously. But not today. "In a fortnight," he said.

Eva couldn't give him an answer she didn't have, so she said nothing.

6

EVA DROVE BACK TO GLASGOW, HER MIND FULL OF IMAGES and colors and sounds rather than thoughts. The woods, the lochs, the *linne,* bright kites and vibrant stars, the music of guitar and flute, fiddle and banjo, the voice of the wind through long grass and among the crumbling headstones. The call of the river, alluring and irresistible.

She was more confused than when she'd left two days before. Where did she belong? Her instincts and desires had been ignited by Rory, if not by the home of her mother's childhood, but she did not want to give in to those instincts. She felt the peril as strongly as she felt the longing. On the island, she had let her impulses guide her, but the island had been safe, surrounded by water that protected and contained her. She remembered, as the shimmering waters of Loch Lomond vanished, that that freedom had never been quite enough. She wanted to believe it had been, but she was not used to lying to herself. When she tried, she remembered Rory's eyes. Lies and self-delusion shriveled under the scrutiny of those eyes. Eva shivered and switched on the radio to drown out the sound of her own thoughts.

As she reached the outskirts of the city, her mind refused to submit to the persistent droning rhythm of the music on the radio. She wondered if she would ever find the answers to her questions. If she did, what good would it do her? Would the darkness go then, or was it in her blood? The small kirkyard came back to her in every detail—its quaint desolation, the stories carved into the stones, the many women with the name of Rose who lay buried there.

Eva sat up straight in her seat. She knew now where she had to go next.

When she reached Eilidh's house, she raced up the front steps, unaware of the rain drifting over her face. She found Eilidh curled into a low-slung chair, staring thoughtfully at a pot across the room. It was hugely round, with a base so narrow that, had the pot not been so squat and low, the base could not have supported it. It was stained blue and rich rust, flat burgundy and the color of pale earth.

Eva thought it was one of Eilidh's own, that she was considering it critically. Her expression said she was not quite satisfied.

Eilidh looked up at Eva, dripping and restless in the entry, and her pensiveness disappeared. She smiled in greeting and relief. "You're back! I thought you might be gone for a very long time."

"Why?"

Eilidh shrugged. "I don't know, really. But I should have known the chest would bring you back. I've been thinking of it constantly. Can't get it out of my mind. It's as though it's cast a spell." She paused when she noticed Eva shifting from foot to foot, chewing her lip to hold back a question. There was a glimmer of light inside her, tiny and quavering but visible through skin and bone. "What is it? Did you find something more?"

Eilidh felt a little jolt of fear and was ashamed of herself. The house had been very quiet since Eva left, even though when she was here, the girl had spent hours in Celia's room. But Eva had been here; that was the point. Eilidh found that knowledge comforting and the silence that had followed very lonely.

Eva came forward a few steps and met Eilidh's eyes steadily. "I want to see my mother's grave."

Eilidh's mouth fell open in astonishment. It was the last thing she had expected. "But you've only just arrived, and you've had such a terribly long drive," she stammered, flustered. "Don't you want to sit down and rest for a bit, perhaps have a cup of tea? We've plenty of time, after all, to—" She broke off, having run out of breath.

"I wonder if there's time enough in all the world," Eva

replied. "Besides, I've been sitting all day and I *can't* rest until I see it."

Eilidh was at a loss. "Do you think it's wise? Do you think you're ready? I'm just not sure."

Regarding her unwaveringly, Eva said, "What are you afraid of? What could I possibly find there that I haven't seen more pathetically displayed in that barren room upstairs?" Her anger was at Celia, not Eilidh, but she could not control or direct it.

"It's raining," Eilidh said at last, inconsequentially. Eva's anger intimidated her, ignited her own simmering rage at Celia and the impossible task she'd left behind. She'd been trying hard to ignore that fury. "Do you mind about that?"

Eva shook her head.

"Then let's be getting our macs and going." Eilidh nodded decisively. Wise or foolish, harmful or helpful, it was Eva's choice to make, after all. Eilidh smoothed her flowing purple shirt, and at the door, exchanged her sandals for Wellingtons.

They took the mini and drove to a small cemetery fenced with wrought iron and dotted with shady oaks and tall birches like sentinels. Eva was silent as Eilidh led the way to a grave halfway down a middle row. It lay directly under an ancient oak. Only the heaviest rain would penetrate the leaves in summer; the same leaves on the ground would protect this tiny patch of earth from cold.

Eva glanced about, unwilling to look directly at her mother's grave. This cemetery was more orderly than the one in the glen. The grass was tended regularly. There were fresh flowers on many of the graves, and the stones stood upright, not yet worn by wind and time.

"I chose this place," Eilidh said. "I thought it the sort of place where Celia would feel safe—no wildflowers or unsightly weeds, loads of cut green grass and tidy rows of trees. I thought that would suit best." Her anger had fizzled as they drove. Now she regarded Eva with concern. The girl's face was expressionless and pale.

"Aye. I'm sure it does." Eva put her hand on Eilidh's arm in reassurance, but found that she sought the woman's warmth to reassure herself. She forced a deep breath, then another, then knelt in the wet grass to look at the stone.

Celia Rose Ward
Born August 10, 1942
Died October 10, 1970
28 years old

"That's all she wanted carved there. I wanted to put more, something to remind me of Celia, but she was adamant. 'You can't tell a person's story on their headstone,' she told me. 'It's silly to try.' Her eyes burned when she said it. I never really understood why."

Eva drew her brows together, thinking of those enigmatic lines carved in aging stone at Celia's mother's grave. That kirkyard had been filled with headstones bearing mysterious stories a stranger could not decipher. "I don't think she wanted people to understand. Not you *or* me. Maybe she was afraid to leave too many clues. Maybe she wanted it to seem as if she'd never been."

Appalled, Eilidh shook her head. "No. If that was true, why did she call you back to me?"

Engrossed in memory, Eva tried to reconstruct the note Celia had left for her to read on her eighteenth birthday.

I would have you go to my friend Eilidh Stanley if you are curious about your past. If you are not, then I am glad for you. Questions and wondering are troublesome, and often the answers are painful. I hope you have no questions, and so no doubts or pain.

"I don't think she wanted me to come, really. I don't think she believed in curiosity. She thought it was dangerous."

The girl stared at the spare headstone. Celia had been only twenty-eight years old. Ten years older than Eva was now. Once, ten years had seemed an eternity, but now it seemed like a brief flare of light in the darkness that had been Celia's life. She turned to Eilidh. "She died five months after I was born. Did she know, then, when she left me with the Crawfords?" She heard her own voice, but it sounded far away and unfamiliar.

Eilidh sighed in resignation. She could not be fair to Celia *and* her daughter. Eva was the one struggling to understand, to find a way to live her life. There was no choice, really. "We both knew. The doctor told us several months before your birth that Celia was ill. He thought she couldn't carry you to term, but Celia defied him in that. I've never seen her quite so fierce or determined as when she told me she would give you life, and a better one than she'd known."

Eilidh blinked back tears. She was disoriented by Eva's steady gaze, the passionless question in her eyes. "She spent the last months of her life writing to you. She was weak and rarely left her room, but every time I opened the door, there she was, scribbling away. And with *such* conviction and dedication."

Mystified, Eva tried to take it in. "But we didn't find any journal of hers, not even a letter."

Eilidh's dark eyes flickered. "No, we didn't. I can't think where it would be. Although—" she broke off.

Eva's heartbeat raced. "What?"

"At one point I felt she'd given up hope, and I found some ashes in the dustbin. But surely she wouldn't have destroyed so many months of work."

Her pulse slow and labored, Eva looked away. "Unless she was afraid to tell the truth."

For a long time, silence hung among the branches of the oak; even the drip, drip of the rain was drowned in the stillness. Eva started when Rory's voice came to her, clear as Eilidh's. *You went to see the dead ones. Was that because you thought they'd tell you their secrets, or because you knew they wouldn't?* I don't know, Eva wanted to shout so loudly that the branches quivered with the sound. "Then I'll have to learn what I can in my own way," she said.

Eilidh offered a trembling hand. "I still mourn her and miss her, even after eighteen years."

Eva herself felt empty, barren.

She leaned close while the clouds glowered overhead. She felt their gray and weighty presence even through the thick green leaves. "But I don't know how to grieve for a stranger."

Part Four

Glen Affric

SCOTTISH HIGHLANDS

1882

1

DAVID AIDAN FRASER STOOD IN THE CENTER OF A CHILLING wind and watched the dark clouds roll across the lowering sky. He raised his head when he heard the low rumble of distant thunder. "The *torran*," he muttered, unconsciously using the Gaelic word. The trees, forced into the unnatural shapes of wailing spirits, twisted under the force of the gale. The sky spun above the tall black mountains and the loch was a cold gray mirror, shattered suddenly by a rush of wind that spewed up waves tipped raggedly in white. David tilted his head, listening, through the furor of wind and thunder and turbulent water. There was a sound that seemed out of place, that broke the violent rhythm of the approaching storm.

He peered through the frantically whipping leaves of hawthorn and larch, to see dust rise through the trees in choking billows. A coach came into view, careening down the narrow road into Glen Affric. Mud flew from the spoked wheels and the rattle of wood and dented metal barely penetrated the sounds of the storm. David knew, with a sinking feeling of regret and premonition, who was in that carriage. He had forgotten to telegraph his father about William Sinclair's death, and now Duncan Fraser had arrived expecting a wedding in a little over a week.

David glanced longingly toward the distant hollow where Mairi's croft was huddled. He had not seen much of Alanna since her mother had returned. He was jealous of the time the two spent together, jealous of the obvious intimacy they shared. For a moment, caught up in the drama of the storm, which echoed his own tumultuous emotions, he had forgotten. The sight of the coach attempting to beat the furious downfall that was inevitable, shook him awake. Ailsa, Alanna and Mairi had shut him out, grieving together and in private. David could not grieve with them for a man he did not know; he had never met William Sinclair.

He was afraid, as well, because he saw how much consolation her mother brought Alanna when David himself had been unable to comfort his betrothed. He did not want to lose her to the mysterious thread that bound those three women and held them apart in their sorrow.

David clenched his fists as he watched the coach bounce out of a deep hole in the muddy road. The wind howled all around him, and he felt the tremor throughout his body. His father would not make this struggle any easier.

As the coach came closer, David sighed and fought his way through wind and trees to meet it. He gaped in disbelief at the amount of luggage his father had brought. He pitied the poor driver Duncan Fraser was bullying into lifting trunk after trunk from the roof of the ramshackle coach.

The rotund older man looked up when he heard footsteps. "David!" Duncan said, mopping his forehead with a crumpled silk handkerchief. The single word was itself an accusation. "Why you must get married in this godforsaken place is beyond me. I'd forgotten how dreadful the roads are. No more than cart tracks, most of them, and nothing but insignificant towns along the way. And the sheep—think they own the damn roads, such as they are. Wander under the wheels as soon as bleat. You'd think they'd be more interested in taking care of the new lambs. But no, they send them out to the slaughter first." He stopped only long enough to glance at the blackening sky and battered landscape. "And now this! This weather's not fit for a man to be about in, I tell you."

Duncan Fraser paused for breath and wiped his face again. His graying beard was spotted with droplets of sweat, his puffy cheeks red with frustration. His usually immaculate brown hair was tangled and windblown, and his brown eyes seemed coated in a fine film of dust. "Aren't you finished yet?" he called to the driver, bent double under the weight of one of the trunks. "Been sitting for hours. You'd think you'd welcome the chance to move about."

The driver snorted, muttered under his breath and swung himself back up onto the seat. "Thanks for your trouble," David said. "I know the trip's not an easy one."

The driver looked back over his shoulder, fixing narrow black eyes on Duncan. "Ye can say that again." Then he snapped the reins and was off. "Jest hope I'll be gettin' back before the gods let loose their fury."

"I'd forgotten what a nasty ride this is," Duncan said as he counted his luggage twice. He kept glancing uneasily at the sky, and seemed ready to chase after the driver and crawl back into the relative safety of the coach.

"You were here three years ago," David reminded him. "You just didn't choose to remember."

Duncan looked sharply at his son. He wanted to bluster and argue, but David was right. Duncan did not really wish to discuss his feelings about Glen Affric, especially not here in the road, where he was exposed to the rage of the coming storm. "Well, so you're to be married. . . ." The words died on his lips when he saw the knee-length woolen trousers, plain linen shirt and thick Highland sandals David wore. "What in God's name is this?" he asked. The red, which had begun to fade from his cheeks, came rushing back. "You look like my brother, like a shepherd or a farmer." He did not try to hide his disgust. "I hope you're not planning to bring your rustic rituals back to Glasgow after you're married."

He was trying to hide his nervousness as the wind buffeted him from side to side and the thunder grew louder and more threatening. David should have led his father to shelter at once, but his anger, suppressed and nearly forgotten, rose inside like hissing steam, obliterating his common sense as the wind altered the landscape, turning it into a nightmare reflection of itself. "I've told you more than once, I'm not going back. Alanna and I have chosen an old croft abandoned not long ago, and we're making it livable again. It'll be quite cozy when we're done. Uncle Ian has offered to help me with the crops the first year, but of course I'll have to buy some cattle and sheep." He watched his father's reaction with pleasure.

The blood drained from Duncan Fraser's face, then flooded back in an unbecoming rush. For a long moment, he struggled to speak, but could not seem to find the words. Strange choking noises came out of his mouth, and he ripped his handkerchief in two. "You're not serious. You really plan to become a farmer and a shepherd in this uncivilized place?" He pointed to the Caledonian pines and silver firs bent nearly to the ground, and to the menacing sky above.

Duncan used to enjoy coming back to the glen in his Glasgow finery; it was an adventure, a chance to show his family how successful he had become. But he had never before looked upon this as the place his son would choose to live. He had forgotten how inhospitable the land could be. "With all your wealth, experience and education, how can you even consider such a thing? Working like a common laborer?"

"Like your brother, you mean? And your father?" David spoke coolly, keeping the billowing hot steam inside.

"But you can have something better. I've made sure of that. Don't throw all my hard work back in my face."

Shaking his head, David looked beyond his father to the loch, tortured and transformed by the eerie light. "Are you saying you did it for me? Jamie and Anne and Fergus seem grateful to enjoy the fruits of your labor, as you yourself do. And don't forget, I worked hard myself." David met his father's gaze, his jaw set and stubborn. "No, I'm staying. Now that I've met Alanna Sinclair, nothing on this earth could convince me to return to the city."

As he stared, stunned, into his son's green eyes, Duncan

understood for the first time that David was not coming home. There was no way Duncan could change his mind, because he had lost touch with his son long ago. At a high, keening cry that seemed to rise from the heart of the hillside, he pressed a hand to his heart. "What in bloody hell is that?"

David smiled; he could not help it. "Only the *me'h'ing.*" His father stared blankly and he added, "The sheep bleating in answer to the weeping wind. Nothing to be afraid of."

Duncan Fraser was deeply offended. "I'm afraid of very little. If you know anything about me, you know that."

David felt a prickle of unease that chilled him as the wind had not. Perhaps Duncan Fraser's arrival at the head of a storm was a harbinger of things to come. David shook his head at his own absurdity. He had not yet embraced Alanna's intuitive and superstitious view of fate. But the premonition lingered. His father was an obstinate man who had turned many a lost battle into a triumph. He did not choose to see the truth, or saw it only through his own narrow vision. He would never understand why his son would choose this wilderness over wealth and comfort in Glasgow.

Duncan worked at keeping his voice steady, at not betraying his anxiety at the increasing fury of wind and dark clouds heavy with rain. "Bring Alanna to the city with you, just once, so your brothers and sister can meet your new wife. That's fair, isn't it? Let her see what it's like. I guarantee—"

David leaned into the moaning gale and away from his father. "I'm not a client to be sold a piece of merchandise I don't desire. I've told you my plans. Besides, Alanna wouldn't go. She wouldn't want to leave the glen, nor would I want her to. Don't you understand, Father? I *want* to be here. I want to stay. I've found my home."

Duncan sighed wearily and put his hand on his son's arm. "You were raised in the city. You're an outsider here, and you'll never be anything more than that. I've seen how these Highlanders are. They won't let you in, David."

"They already have." David had not considered it before, but it was true. He felt he had always lived here. He was at ease and no one made him feel like a stranger as he had so often in Glasgow. Except Alanna in the past few days. But that was different. "You don't understand at all. These people—Ian and Jenny, Angus and Flora, Mairi and Alanna—have taken me in. I'm part of the family now." Too late he realized what he was saying. That he had chosen them over his other family.

Duncan could not disguise his hurt, and David actually felt remorse and a kind of pity for the old man. *I have a right to be happy,* he had told his father once. *Why, in God's name? Do you think I'm happy, that anyone has a right to be? You are mad.* He put his hand on Duncan's shoulder. "I'm sorry, but I have to speak the truth from now on, Father. No more lies or half-truths or pretenses."

Duncan Fraser's shoulders sagged. He was exhausted from the long journey, from the threat of the storm, but more than that, he was shocked by the pain of David's rejection. David had always been the most difficult of his children, the first to question his father's dictates, the first to break his father's rules, the first to voice his disapproval. Duncan had spent much of the time in David's presence in a rage of one kind or another. But secretly, he admired his son's courage, his refusal to let others shape his views. Perhaps he should have told him that before. "You don't think much of me, do you?"

David sighed and squeezed his father's shoulder. "Why do we always end up fighting, you and I?" He'd thought that might change, hoped to change it, now that he was happy, now that he'd come to know Alanna and knew what it was to be contented and excited all at once, to be struggling with nature, not man and steam and grime and steel and money. Even her grief over the father she had not seen in years had made David regret his own turbulent relationship with his father. "All I want is to make you welcome and have you rejoice in my marriage as I do."

Duncan looked away, cleared his throat and replied gruffly, "How can I rejoice when it means losing you for good?"

David had no answer. He stared into the distance, through

the twisted, swaying trees toward the loch that lashed at its banks as if intent on its own destruction.

Duncan followed his son's gaze. "What are you staring at? Good gad! The lake looks dangerous, like monsters might erupt from it at any moment."

Shaking his head sadly, fascinated by the rise and swell, swirl and eddy of the leaden gray water, David murmured, "That's only *marcach sine,* the rider of the storm. It's magnificent, isn't it?"

He felt Duncan withdraw and realized his father was right. The David Fraser who had lived in Glasgow was no more. He was gone for good, enveloped and transformed by the power of the glen.

"We'd best get to some shelter," he said, hesitating to meet Duncan's gaze. David turned toward the ponderous trunks in the road while his father stood rigid, and at last the clouds released their burden of lashing rain.

2

" 'TIS PEACEFUL HERE. I'M GLAD WE CAME." MAIRI SAT ON A boulder beside Alanna's hidden *linne,* where the loch, the River Affric, and a burn came together over huge striped stones of every color from ivory to rust to deep, rich brown. The falls dropped in gentle, wide stretches, several inches at a time. At each drop, the water rushed in swirls of white foam, but over the rocks, it flowed clear and golden, peat-stained where the earth had melded with the water, making the stones beneath sleek and luminous. The storm a few days past had left the air clean and pure, the colors richer.

Ailsa smiled at her mother. She had begun, tentatively, to smile again in the past few days as she, Alanna and Mairi wandered the glen as they used to, arm in arm, at one in understanding and in impulse. Slowly, Ailsa felt the pain dim a little at a time, until the bright light of her grief no longer blinded her. It would take a long time for her to heal, but now that she was here, at least it could begin. She stared up at the tip-tilted stones that stood protectively around the glade, the silver firs leaning over the water, along with gnarled hawthorn and shimmering pine. The sky was visible in drifting revelations of gray and blue that passed above the interlaced leaves and needles of spruce and pine.

Ailsa closed her eyes at a sudden throbbing she could not explain. Each time she let down her shield and saw the deep green hidden places in the glen, each time she listened to waves lap against the shore of the loch and looked beyond the blue rippled water to the heart beneath, she felt a different kind of pang. An ache that had nothing to do with William's death, but rather with the opening of her senses and her soul to the place she loved most on this earth.

It was as if she were moving limbs that had been motionless for years, had grown numb with inaction. The unfamiliar motion caused tingling fingers to shoot beneath her skin like fine, sharp needles.

Her senses were waking from a long sleep, and the song of the tiny brown wrens or the flight of the kestrel through a cerulean sky brought a bright and fearful awareness that she was not certain she was strong enough to bear. She had forgotten what it was like to live simply, so close to the earth that she felt its heartbeat echo through her own.

Despite her exhaustion and grief, Ailsa felt an ease and comfort with her mother and Alanna, as if she had never left them. As if, the last time they were together, they had not also been grieving for the fading shadow that had been Charles Kittridge. The sorrow was still with her; sometimes it left her weak and helpless, but sometimes it faded, became muted, tolerable.

She had slipped back into her life here as easily as she slipped into the gowns she borrowed from her daughter. Simple and comfortable, they made her feel unfettered, free, herself again. Only now that the struggle was over did she recognize that every day of her life in London had been a battle not to lose her inner self, her spirit, a battle to create a world in which she could be happy. Here in the glen, she did not have to fight; the world already existed. It welcomed her into the freedom of her childhood like an old and comfortable blanket.

She knew now that in London, her grief would not have been assuaged nor her pain healed, because William had been the source and center of her happiness there. Only here could she become whole and content again.

She felt disloyal to William in even thinking such a thing, at feeling such relief from a burden she had not known she carried. Except she sensed that her husband had always known this about her. He had recognized the daily struggle she had not known she was fighting, had refused, herself, to recognize, in order to survive.

The realizations washed over her like the waves of her grief; she was at the same time weakened, devastated and strengthened by them. She had never been so weary or drained or regretful in her life—nor as hopeful.

Ailsa sat on a richly striped boulder, naked, in less than an inch of water, and felt the tawny liquid flow around her, washing such thoughts away and spilling them into the foam that surged at the edge of the boulder and below.

She looked fondly from Mairi to Alanna, felt their perfect understanding and affection even in their silence, and knew she had been among strangers too long.

Her daughter, a young reflection of Mairi, sat nearby, where the healing water swept away her own grief, a little at a time.

Ailsa smiled, barely aware that she was weeping. She was drawn to the fragile ferns among the tumbled stones, the multitude of rainbows the sun created in the spray from falling waters.

" 'Tis a magic place, Alanna," she murmured. "I doubt I've ever seen one as lovely."

Alanna was pleased by their praise. This was her refuge and her solace; she had never brought anyone here before, not even David, yet she had not hesitated to lead Mairi and Ailsa.

Alanna too had begun to live with her grief since her mother's return; she too had taken strength and sustenance and comfort from the presence of Ailsa and Mairi. The three women had shut themselves off from the rest of the world and wandered, sometimes talking, sometimes silent, sometimes weeping, sometimes sobbing uncontrollably. But always they had been together, and the presence of each had helped heal the other. They were used to depending on their own inner strength. Charles Kittridge had taught them how, and Ailsa's life in London had only made her stronger, as her absence had made Mairi stronger.

Today they had come to Alanna's *linne* to swim, to cleanse themselves of the pall of death and sorrow. "Come, Mairi," Alanna said as she removed her gown and chemise. "'The water's warm for so early in June."

Ailsa followed her daughter's example. The water was calling her as it had since her return. *Come, I will hold you. In my arms you will float free and the flow of my tears will wash your own away.* "Yes, Mama," Ailsa said. "Come with us."

"I'm too old for such things," Mairi said without rancor. "But I'll be nearby, watching if ye need me. Ye know that, both of ye."

"So we do," Alanna whispered. She and Ailsa stood on a flat boulder, staring up at tilted stones and down at varicolored rocks and swirling water. As Ailsa was about to dive into the water, Alanna grabbed her hand. "I have a ritual. A little prayer I always say before I let the water take me."

Ailsa tilted her head inquiringly.

Alanna closed her eyes. "Now hath heaven—"

"To earth descended, and cloud and clay and stone and star are blended." Ailsa joined her daughter in the ancient chanson that was part of the Beltaine celebration. She remembered the words in her heart; she had spoken them every year on the first of May, even after she moved to London and all other vestiges of the ancient customs were gone.

Ailsa and Alanna jumped in together, and the water flowed around them, welcoming and cool and clear. They dove, eyes open wide, and sank to the glittering silt, letting the smooth stones graze their bare skin, the grasses weave themselves in their hair. Arms spread to anchor their bodies, they floated, enveloped in the quiescent water until their lungs began to burn. Slowly they rose to the surface, their hair glimmering in the dappled sunlight, sleek, enfolding them like a mermaid's.

Mairi watched, smiling, feeling contented because there was life in Ailsa's blue-violet eyes, and the color had begun to return to her cheeks. And Alanna was less distracted, less torn by guilt and frustrating contemplation of things she could not change. They had begun to recover, but there was time still to be borne and pain still to be felt. Slowly, these things would change as the glen worked its magic.

When mother and daughter rose into the sun, a ray of light glowed on Alanna's chest, and Ailsa noticed for the first time the silver Celtic brooch on a leather thong around her daughter's neck. Alanna looked down, smiled and caressed the cool silver. "David gave it to me."

She did not explain, but there was a wealth of love and secrets in her eyes. Ailsa remembered when she had said the same thing in the same way, with the same intensity, except the name had not been David, nor the gift a silver brooch. Seeing that look in Alanna's eyes, hearing that tone in her voice made Ailsa remember all too clearly that birthday many years ago when she had not yet become a woman. She was glad for her daughter, but felt a disturbing tightness in her chest. She forced the feelings aside. She had come here to mourn William, not remember a boy with dark, curly hair and clear green eyes.

Frowning, she made her way to the edge of one of the low falls of water. She caught a leaf at the base of the rocks, scattered with bubbles from the water above. The leaf was bright green and the bubbles held prisms of color. Ailsa did not realize Alanna had followed until she cupped her hand under her mother's and they stood in silence, the rush and gurgle of the water between them, holding the fragile leaf and its chimerical burden.

In the light on the bubbles, Alanna saw the reflection of

her father the last time she had seen him. His hair had begun to turn gray, and his brown eyes had been full of sorrow and fear as she and Ailsa left London for the glen. William had held his daughter for a long time and murmured, "Be happy. That's all I ask of you."

In the fragile bubbles that distorted the colorful leaf, Ailsa saw the dream she had dreamed the night her husband died, the dream that was William's dream of her.

Mother and daughter were transfixed, held captive by the images in the bubbles.

"Let him go." Mairi said from the mossy bank. "William Sinclair didn't hold ye back, so don't be holding him. He can no' fly away while ye two hold him here. Set him free as he did ye."

Ailsa and Alanna looked at the bubbles, the sodden leaf, so fragile and impermanent and lovely. William was trapped inside by their memories. They could see him there, feel him in the heaviness in their chests, the constriction in their throats. Slowly, they removed their hands, lifting slightly as they released the leaf and its burden. It floated down to the water, while a few bubbles drifted upward and burst. There was nothing left, as the leaf was carried into the white foam and away, not even fragmented prisms of light. William was free at last.

Ailsa wept, but her tears were not bitter or harsh. She reached up once, to try and recapture the fleeting image of her husband's face, even now, as she released him from the weight of her sorrow. Her fingers were spread, palm open, as if waiting for a gift from the gods, but she clenched her hand, empty, in the air where William wasn't and would never be again. She had already said good-bye with words, but in closing her hand, curling her fingers inward, she bid her husband farewell with a gesture of finality that left her face covered in tears but her heart somehow lighter, at least for the moment.

For a long time, mother and daughter knelt in the water, holding each other, trying to begin to accustom themselves to William Sinclair's absence. The moment had come upon them unexpectedly; perhaps that was why they had let go so quickly, without thought or preparation. But now that they had done so, they must accept that they had lost him, given him up as he had wanted them to do. It was the only thing he had asked of them.

They began to shiver as the water lapped around them, and they rose stiffly, feet buried in the soft silt and pressed against small stones as smooth as glass. Alanna and Ailsa swayed for a moment while the wind raised chills on their naked skin. They glanced once more at the sky where the bubbles had disintegrated, shook the water from their long hair, and climbed out of the tranquil *linne*.

When they lay on the soft ferns and moss of the bank, hair spread around them to dry in the striped sunlight, Alanna sighed. Her skin felt soft from the peat-infused water; she felt clean and caressed both at once. She smiled, but her face was pensive.

"What is it that bothers ye, Alannean?" Mairi asked. "Ye've drifted away from us more than once today. I can see you're trying to keep it inside, but I feel the shadow on your heart."

Ailsa sat up, ashamed that she had not noticed her daughter's distress. Mairi was right. Alanna's usually serene face was tense, her skin taut across her molded cheekbones. "What is it, *mo-run?* Surely ye know we'll listen and hear ye, no matter how troubled your thoughts."

Sighing, Alanna clasped her hands behind her head. "Aye, I know. I've been trying to forget, but I can't. David looked so worried last night because his father's come all the way to the glen and now we've postponed the wedding. He didn't say so, mind ye. He'd not put such a burden on my shoulders." She paused. "I've not felt much of David's pain since Papa died, but I do today. I miss him." She flushed guiltily.

Ailsa shook her head. "Don't be ashamed of being in love or wanting to be happy. Don't give up a day of that happiness for William's sake. He'd not have asked such a thing of ye. I told ye before what he said. 'The only loyalty you owe my memory is to do what will make you happy.'" Ailsa drew her fingers through the tangles in her chestnut hair.

"David's right. His father's come a long way. Why should ye delay the wedding?"

Alanna sat up sharply. "Out of respect for the dead." She felt guilty even thinking of a celebration when her father lay so recently dead, so far away, so alone.

"I thought ye'd let him go," Mairi said softly. "You're as free as he, Alanna Sinclair. Don't be breaking your heart because your father's beats no more."

"To trade your happiness for mourning?" Ailsa touched her daughter's arm. "Ye know 'tis not right or virtuous or wise. Ye must make your own life, Alanna, minute by minute and day by day. Your father wanted most of all to see ye married and full of joy. If ye can no' give yourself that gift, give it to William, or better still, to David."

"Will the others no' think me heartless and selfish?"

Mairi took out her carved wooden comb and began to smooth her granddaughter's hair. "Ye alone think such foolish things. They know ye well here, Alannean. They'll understand. And no doubt be grateful if ye send Duncan Fraser on his way a little sooner."

"Ye shouldn't say such things," Alanna said. But she had to bite her lip to hide a smile. It was true that David's father was not endearing himself to the Highlanders.

Ailsa rubbed her temples thoughtfully. "Duncan came far to be here for David. 'Twould not be easy for him to come again."

Mairi wound a strand of Alanna's long red hair over her palm as she combed out the tangles. "Be married, my child. Be happy. Let others think what they will. We *know* what's in your heart."

Alanna found David helping Gavin in the fields. The day before, Ian's son had helped at the croft, thatching a new roof of rushes and heather. Today David was returning the favor.

The sleeves of his sweat-stained shirt were rolled above his elbows, and he wore mud-caked brogues and filthy trousers. His dark hair was thick with dirt and sweat, and his hands grimy, the nails broken. The sight of him made

Alanna run, stumbling with delight, down the brae to where he stood. "David!" she said, throwing her arms around him without hesitation. "I've missed ye so much."

David was taken aback by her intensity. "But I've seen you every night at Ian's or Mairi's or Angus's." Automatically, he caught her around the waist and bent until he touched his forehead to hers. She smelled sweet and fresh, like dew-soaked lilacs. He trembled at the way she leaned against him. Her trust and open affection were more seductive than a sensual dance in gauzy robes would have been.

" 'Tis no' the same, and well ye know it. I've been away." She looked into David's green eyes, felt the warmth of his arms around her, and knew she had missed him more than she realized, caught up, as she had been, in her own misery.

David's smile disappeared. "Aye, so you have been."

So he had felt the emptiness too. "I came to make certain ye haven't changed your mind, for your father and Ian are with Mairi and Ailsa now. They told me they're discussing the contract for our betrothal, but it seems to me they're doing more drinking of whisky than talking. If they can agree, they'll name us bride and bridegroom at once and choose Thursday next, when the moon is waxing, for the wedding."

David grinned in spite of himself. "*If* they agree? How is it that you already know the day?"

Brushing her lips over his, Alanna murmured, "They'd not dare do anything else. I told them what I want." She took a step back. "But ye haven't answered me. Will ye marry me?"

David pulled her close with a force that frightened both of them. "You know I will. You know me too well. You must know how I've missed you." He could not quite hide the fear in his voice and his eyes. His feelings for her were so volatile that his imagination too easily conjured images of life without her. He had felt her slipping from his grasp this past week, not because he had no faith in her word or the depth of her commitment, but because his love was overpowering and irrational. "I couldn't bear to lose you, Alanna. Not now."

Alanna was alarmed by his fervor. She touched his cheek tenderly. "How could ye even think such a thing? I plighted my troth to ye, not just with words but with my heart. I'd not have done it if I wasn't certain of what I feel." She drew out the brooch on its leather thong, cradling it in her palm. "This is my promise, David Fraser. I'll not be breaking it." She paused, and her violet eyes clouded over as she looked inward. "I was bleeding for a time, wounded, and only my mother knew how to stop that kind of pain. Only she knew my father as I knew him, and she's been gone for a very long time. I needed her."

"And why not me?"

"I will always need you. But for ye I want to be a woman, and for these few days, I was a child again, letting my mother carry me on her shoulders. She needed my weight and I needed her certainty. Just for a little, I wanted her to myself. 'Twas selfish, perhaps, and I'm sorry if I hurt ye or made ye doubt me, but I never doubted ye, nor changed my mind, nor wondered if 'twas right."

The Rose women have always chosen to grieve alone, Ian had told him once. *Perhaps because they feel things so deeply, 'tis hard for an outsider to understand.* Once, the thought had disturbed David, but it did not matter now, because of the expression on Alanna's face. "Am I your beloved?"

"You know how I feel."

"I want to hear the words." He could see them in her glowing eyes, but he wanted to hear them in the melodic voice that became one with wind and water and the songs of birds.

"'Ye are my beloved fire," Alanna said. "Ye smolder inside me, deeper than I can reach or know. You keep me warm and strong."

He felt her need for his strength now, and it both saddened and thrilled him, because she had always been so indomitable herself. But her own strength had waned in the wake of her grief.

"I want to be happy again. Marry me." There was a plea in Alanna's voice that David could not resist.

"I have already done so once," he replied, "and would do so a hundred times. I'll meet you at the kirk on Thursday next. But just now, come. I want to show you something."

He took her hand and led her to Angus and Flora's croft, empty on a sunny afternoon in June when the flowers were wild and bright and the waters full of light and magic. The cottage was crowded with trunks and fine clothing strewn about wherever Duncan had dropped them. In that, at least, he was like his son. Alanna smiled to herself while David rummaged through the small chest beside his bed.

When he turned, she saw something glitter in his hand, even in the relative dimness of the croft. "For your bride gift, I thought you might like something special to hang our token around your neck. I know I should wait, but I can't."

He held out an antique silver chain, and Alanna saw that each link was a tiny Celtic knot. She held it gingerly, as if so slight a disturbance as a human breath might tarnish it. " 'Tis beautiful," she whispered. Her eyes burned and her throat felt tight with unshed tears.

Swallowing with difficulty, she looked up at David. "Wherever did ye find such a thing?"

David smiled, strangely touched by the dampness in her eyes. "Yesterday I dragged Father away from the Hill of the Hounds. He's practically haunted the place since he got here. I don't know why it fascinates him so. His house in Glasgow puts it to shame. But anyway, he had some business to take care of in Beauly, so I went with him. I couldn't find you to tell you I was going."

There was no accusation in his voice, but Alanna felt his hurt just the same. She had not even realized he'd left the glen. That frightened her. She had been so lost in grief that she had not felt his absence. She looked up at him, her red hair drifting over her flushed cheek, her eyes darkened to the purple of the mountains in the twilight. "I won't leave ye again, David. I promise."

Oddly, he understood. "I know." The doubt was gone, and the fear. They had disappeared in Alanna's hypnotic violet gaze.

3

ON THE DAY OF THE WEDDING THE SUN CREPT OVER THE HORI-
zon, shrouded by clouds. Mairi looked out the warped, battered door at the visible air, swirled and white with mist,
and frowned. She was chilled by the damp, and ducked back
into the croft and nearer the fire. "Where is Belenus, the
sun god, who should bless this day?"

"He will come," Alanna said, smiling to herself. "The mist
will go, and the clouds, and Belenus will turn the sky into
a wash of azure and gold."

"You're very sure of yourself." Ailsa watched her daughter in wonder. Alanna had always been fearless and optimistic, but when had she become so steady and unflinching
within herself? Ailsa was proud, certain of her daughter's
future and her happiness, because Alanna was certain, but
she regretted missing the change, day by day, that had made
her daughter into a woman.

Ailsa sat on a stool next to Mairi and whispered, "How
could ye do it? How could ye let me go so far, and to
strangers? Now I can't bear the thought of Alanna just over
the next rise. 'Tis too far away."

Mairi took her daughter's hand and held it tight. Her own,
though weathered from age and hard work, was warm from
the peat fire; her freshly washed hair was fragrant with the
smell of peat and smoke and roses. She looked at Ailsa
through air blurred by the heat of the fire in the center of
the room. "I could not keep ye by me forever, nor could I
change your mind. Ye did what ye had to do, and so did I.
Out of your choice ye made Alanna. 'Twas worth it, *mo-
run*. You're strong enough to see that, and wise enough to
let your daughter find her own happiness."

278

"I'm stronger than I ever knew," Ailsa replied. She had learned that since William's death, seen it in her husband's unwavering faith in her before he died, heard it in Cynthia's pleas for her mother, felt it in Colin's warm arm heavy upon her shoulder. The only time she had lost her newfound strength was the moment when she first met Ian Fraser in the glen. But she would not think of that today. Today was for Alanna.

Her daughter was eating scones and crowdie, her mouth rimmed in white, fingers covered with honey. She licked them shamelessly and smiled at Ailsa. "Ye should eat, Mama. 'Twill be a long time before our next meal."

Ailsa nodded in resignation. For the moment, she was content to let Alanna hover and care for her. It seemed to make her daughter happy, and for Ailsa, it was good to let the weight of her own burdens go, to act without thought or planning or contrivance, to follow her instincts as she had long ago.

After they'd eaten, the three women sat around the peat fire, combing out their long, wet hair. Ailsa gave Alanna her silver comb—a long-ago present from William—while she and Mairi used carved wooden ones that Ian had made. In the glow from the fire, with the dim misted light from the windows in the background, waves of red and chestnut hair flowed long and lustrous over bare white shoulders and sun-browned hands. Rhythmically, Ailsa, Alanna and Mairi drew the combs through tangles, flicking away tiny drops of moisture that glistened and hissed on the stones around the fire.

The patterns on the newly coated clay walls, not yet stained with soot, were enhanced by the soft light, making the room feel warm and intimate. The masses of roses and lilacs and wild violets gathered the day before made the air sweet and fragrant with summer.

When Alanna's hair was nearly dry, Ailsa rose and stood behind her daughter, curling the tendrils around her fingers, weaving the shining strands into braids, which she looped and pinned in back, leaving most of the thick hair to fall free and waving to her daughter's waist.

While Alanna put on her fine lawn chemise, trimmed in

soft pink ribbons, and her many-layered petticoat, Mairi and Ailsa laid out her wedding gown on Mairi's heather bed. Alanna was eager to put it on, but Mairi raised her hand. "Ye must wait for Flora Fraser. 'Tis tradition to have the mistress dress ye in your finery."

Alanna smiled. "I've had to tell David as much often this past week. 'Tis tradition, I say, when he asks why. Then he daren't argue. He wants so much to learn and follow the traditions of our people." Thus she and David had gone together through the glen, inviting everyone to the wedding, stopping to take a little refreshment at every croft, so none would be offended. They laughed a great deal at sly jokes and good wishes, received small gifts of whisky and sherry and sweet breads and tea. Not a single person had refused their invitation, and the two had somehow stumbled home, grasping their stomachs and groaning after the sun had disappeared. They had been full and happy and so drunk that they could hardly stand.

"Do ye know," Alanna had told her betrothed, "there's another tradition that bride and groom should bathe together in the burn to cleanse themselves of evil and be certain neither is flawed in any way. Then the groom can no' say later that he'd not got what he bargained for." She leaned toward him, eyes full of feigned innocence. "I think we should go at once, don't ye?"

For a moment David gaped at her, until he saw the laughter she was struggling to suppress. "Aye, let's go." Before she could protest, he swept her into his arms and started toward the river.

"David! 'Twas only a jest," she cried, alarmed at the smile of anticipation on his face. His green eyes glowed with sparks that made her shiver, though she could not honestly say it was entirely out of fear.

"But it sounds like such an excellent test, and most diverting. You wouldn't want to flout tradition, would you?"

When they reached the edge of the burn, he paused as if considering whether or not to drop her in. "Should we light candles first, and burn some sacred herbs and make a bonfire for the gods? I'd not want them to think we're not properly reverent."

Alanna clasped her hands behind his neck and met his gaze steadily. "I shall have to beat ye, David Fraser, if ye don't behave better after we're married. Properly reverent! Ye've no' a single pure thought in your head."

David set her on her feet, laughing. "And neither have you, Alanna Sinclair." He kissed her and they both forgot about tradition, though the pleasures of the ancient gods were much on their minds in the long, breathless moments that followed.

"What are ye grinning at?" Mairi asked her granddaughter suspiciously. "Ye've a glint in your eye that makes me wonder what you've been dreaming."

"Just thinking of all we must do today," Alanna replied calmly, but her smile was mischievous and tender.

Just as she was about to pounce on the dress in her impatience, Flora appeared in the low doorway. "I saw a ray of sunlight in the distance. One ray through the mist will surely bless your marriage." She was nearly as excited as Alanna.

"There will be more than a ray," Alanna said confidently.

"As ye say." Flora beamed and, with Mairi and Ailsa's help, slipped the soft violet gown over Alanna's head.

It was the color of her eyes, with a neckline that curved gently downward above her breasts. The sleeves were long and flowing, the waist narrow and flattering. The skirt was full, and from the waistline hung a hundred lilac ribbons. The sleeves were trimmed with the same soft ribbon, and several were attached to each wrist at the cuff. The light reflected off the shiny satin in patterns that changed each time Alanna moved.

Flora had brought a mysterious box with her. When the gown was fastened and Alanna had circled the fire several times to make the ribbons sway, Flora opened the box and lifted out a crown of flowers. Brenna, Glenyss and Erlinna had spent all evening weaving Alanna's headpiece. The white roses and wild violets twined with delicate ferns and the orchids of creeping lady's tresses rested on her brow, and had been cleverly woven to fall down her back in a graceful tail, like a living braid.

Finally, Alanna put on the pair of soft leather slippers Callum Mackensie had made for her wedding, just as he had made a pair for Ailsa's long ago. He had given them to her a week past, and she'd put them away in her kist, the chest that held her "providing" for her marriage. The chest, carved with griffins and kelpies and winged horses, had once belonged to Ailsa, had once held the linens and quilts, carved dishes and fine plaids she had prepared for her wedding day. But Ailsa had left her kist behind when she married William Sinclair.

Through all these years, Mairi had kept the chest fresh with herbs and free from moths, fragrant, pure and safe from time and nature. Now Alanna would take it with her to the cottage she would share with David. She would lay these laboriously fashioned sheets and quilts and blankets on the big heather bed he had built, line the drawers of her press with the thin scented runners and protect them with sachets of lavender and rose.

Alanna ran her hands lovingly over the contents of her kist and smiled to herself. She felt wealthy beyond her wildest expectations, not in gold or silver, but in the things made by her hands and Mairi's and Ailsa's, and the things of her heart. Closing the lid, she put the leather slippers on her feet and rose, dancing lightly about the croft.

While Mairi, Ailsa and Flora crowded around, she stood in the doorway with the rapidly thinning mist at her back. The three women stood breathless with admiration. She was lovely, with her pale skin and gown that made her eyes luminous. The ribbons and flowers only emphasized her beauty. Her lips seemed more sensual, her cheekbones more pronounced, the blush of color in her cheeks more vivid. Flora caught Ailsa's hand and pressed it warmly. "I'm so glad," she whispered. " 'Tis time."

Ailsa's eyes filled with tears, and she turned to gather flowers in her arms.

" 'Tis a beautiful bride you'll be, and a happy one, I'll wager," Flora told Alanna. "For, if I'm not mistaken, David is just the man for ye." She smiled, her lips quivering with emotion. For as long as Flora could remember she had wished for the joining of these two families. Now, in Alanna and David, her half-forgotten, long-grieved-over dreams were coming true.

Suddenly there were volleys of gunfire outside, the first summons to the guests. Flora closed the door briskly and shooed Alanna away. " 'Twould not do to appear too eager."

The gunfire was followed almost at once by the shouts of a group of men sent by David to call for the bride.

"Let us see her, so we know she's not been stolen away. Bring her out and we'll take her to the kirk."

The voices carried clearly through the windows, and the four women formed a circle without thinking, holding on to one another's hands in anticipation and affection.

Outside the men called demands in slurred but determined voices. They had already begun to celebrate with the fine whisky Duncan Fraser had brought from Glasgow. The glow of the whisky invested their errand with great import as they fired their pistols into the air and shouted for the bride.

Duncan himself was among the group milling outside Mairi Rose's croft. He wore a black worsted suit with spiderweb silk thread, a steel gray brocade vest and silver cravat. His top hat was silk, and his three-button cutaway frock coat and linen shirt were beautifully worked. He felt ridiculous and out of place among the kilt-clad Highlanders, who were overly cheerful from the breakfast that had begun at Angus's before dawn. Though the sun was barely up, whisky and ale had been flowing for hours. Duncan had drunk freely, but had remained uncomfortably sober.

He gasped when Alanna appeared in the doorway, and the hubbub of shouting and sporadic gunfire ceased abruptly. The bride smiled and called back over her shoulder, "Look. The mist is nearly gone. I told ye Belenus would smile on us today."

Squinting, Duncan looked up at the sky. He remembered being enveloped in fog that had dripped from his nose this morning. Now the sky showed patches of blue and the mist seemed to have burned away. The air was warm and smelled of flowers and fresh grass and pine. It annoyed Duncan, this change in the weather. The dripping fog echoed his mood much better than sun and sky and drifting clouds.

"The bride. Behold! the bonny bride! Safe from our enemies and ready for the kirk!"

Duncan shouted as loud as the others. He struggled to appear flushed and jovial, as he had at the meeting with Mairi and Ailsa to discuss the contract, though there'd been no real contract to discuss. " 'Tis a tradition, that's all," Ailsa had explained. Duncan wondered at its purpose, since his son had obviously made up his mind and would not be swayed. A ritual without a reason seemed wasteful to Duncan Fraser.

"Ain't she the beauty though, and David the lucky one to win her?" someone whispered loudly in Duncan's ear.

"Oh, aye!" Duncan replied heartily. Too heartily. It was true that Alanna was pretty, and she seemed a nice girl, but she was so—so rustic. Not once had he seen her other than barefoot. She did not seem to own a pair of shoes, nor did she miss them. Duncan couldn't help thinking his son deserved better.

Yet as he glowered into her violet eyes, he felt a jolt that shook him, an odd certainty that she would be faithful to his son. He was not an intuitive man, but even cold reason could not shake his conviction. It was as if she were looking directly at him, her gaze caught in his, as if she were telling him with her eyes that she would give David all she had.

Duncan felt a sharp twinge in his belly and wondered why his belief in Alanna's devotion to his son should hurt so much. His dead wife Elizabeth's face tried to pop into his mind, but Duncan took another swig from his silver flask and banished her to oblivion.

Alanna stepped out into the clearing, with Flora, Ailsa and Mairi close behind her. The young men fell silent, hands clasped reverently above their sporrans, eyes bleary with admiration and the melancholy realization that none of them was marrying Alanna Rose Sinclair. Angus Fraser brought the bridal horse forward, and several young men helped

Alanna to mount. The silence was splintered by gunfire once more, and the party set off toward the kirk, singing at the top of their lungs, Angus playing the fiddle in front, Ian bringing up the rear with the pipes.

David's party followed closely. Alanna glanced back eagerly, but could not see her groom through the crowd. The movement of the horse carried her, but so did the voices, the laughter, and especially the music. The lilting notes were whimsical, compelling; she wanted to weep and laugh and sing along. The music swelled as the dawn song rose from mistle thrush, blackbird and robin, filling the sky and drowning out the sighing of the breeze.

David, who had indulged in one or two drams of whisky himself, walked along briskly, aware of little besides the sight of Alanna's head, crowned in flowers and sunlight. For the first time in years, he wore a belted plaid, doublet and jacket and the blue bonnet that the Highlanders so cherished. He felt elegant, expectant and terrified as the procession wound its way ever closer to the kirk.

Everyone paused at the edge of the lake, blue, shimmering and bathed in light, the islands scattered across its surface green with pine and fir. Alanna rode forward to toss some silver coins into the loch, shattering the stillness with a bright glitter that made ripples swell outward.

David came to stand behind her, just out of sight, and threw his own coins.

"To Neithe, god of waters," Alanna murmured, "so the light will always sparkle from your heart and the rush of the water will glow—our greatest wealth."

Several other guests tossed in coins as the Celts had once done, and perhaps the Druids before them. "To the prosperity of the bride and groom. May they never suffer from thirst of body or spirit."

A cheer went up with another round of gunshots into the still June air. Then the procession was on its way once more.

When they arrived at the kirk, David, Ian and Gavin hung back, waiting for the bride to enter. While they waited, David began to shake. He stared at his body as if he did not know it. His heart was certain, and his soul and his mind, but his body was suddenly afraid—until he stepped into the kirk and saw Alanna waiting for him at the altar, her hair flowing free to her waist, her eyes full of secrets that were hers and his alone.

Duncan saw the look that passed between bride and groom, a look that held and did not falter until David stood at Alanna's side and they turned to face the minister. That look, full of love and trust and tenderness, annoyed Duncan. It had annoyed him from the first, the way they looked at one another, spoke in whispers, touched hands or brushed shoulders or slipped their arms around each other's waists. Their deep affection was obvious and painful. Duncan wondered if he had ever felt that way about his wife, but he couldn't remember.

He watched the ceremony, but it might as well have been in mime, for he heard neither David's voice nor Alanna's, nor the minister's somber blessing. Duncan's gaze wandered about the church, from one patched and faded plaid to another, one dusty pair of callused, sandaled feet to weathered hands cracked by hard work and exposure to the sun. In the past week, he had seen how many of the crofts were empty, how many thatched roofs had fallen in, leaving piled stones in lifeless silhouette.

He thought of the Hill of the Hounds, once magnificent with Persian rugs and vaulted ceilings, carved balustrades and heavy brocade draperies. Even that great house had fallen into disrepair. Duncan was saddened when he looked at the intricate stone facade with its wide bay windows overlooking the loch. He knew that inside, dust, cobwebs and shadows were growing.

The wild landscape from which it had been shaped was reclaiming the Hill, and Duncan could not bear it. He smiled to himself when he remembered his trip with David to Beauly. While his son went off to a small shop, Duncan had sent a wire to ask his daughter to pack up David's things and send them to the glen. But that's not all he'd done. He had a little surprise in mind. Forget the silver, crystal and lace he had brought from Glasgow. Those things were not appropriate for the life David had chosen.

Duncan wanted to give his son something he would remember. It was a long time since the two of them had had something to exult in together. Perhaps soon that moment would come.

Startled, he sat bolt upright at the sound of his son's voice ringing through the church. "I so swear."

Ailsa watched the light from the narrow windows move over Alanna's and David's faces, paling in comparison to the gleam in their eyes. Bride and groom clasped hands, looked at and into one another, as if they were alone before the altar, as if the joining of their hands wove a fine invisible web around them that no one else could penetrate. They were alone among a hundred people, and the threads that bound them were palpable.

It was not Alanna's unbound hair or the flowers down her back or her beribboned lilac gown, nor David's plaid of the red, yellow and black Fraser weave that made the congregation cease to breathe and their chests ache. It was not the beauty of the two young people but the joy and understanding between them.

Ailsa felt a pain deep inside where even her grief for William had not penetrated. She was looking back, not forward, to a day when she was seventeen and had stood in the mist with Ian Fraser and felt the first true glimmer of what it was to be a woman. She had watched David since her arrival, and soon realized that David Fraser was much like his uncle Ian. He lived by impulse, emotion, instinct, seemed to want nothing more than the wonders of the glen and the woman who was his mirror.

The intuitive connection between David and Alanna was strong; it would bind them when other things threatened to pull them apart. Ailsa was glad her daughter had found someone like David, and a little envious, though she had no right to be. It had been her choice to leave the glen behind. She could not regret it now, with William scarcely buried and Jenny standing by Ian as she had for many years.

Besides, Ailsa was glad she'd come to know another world, another way of life. That knowledge made the glen more precious to her now. London had made her stronger, more resilient, more certain of precisely what she valued and desired.

"This I so swear."

Alanna's musical voice broke into Ailsa's revery, and she turned to see how Mairi was. Her mother smiled gently.

Most of Mairi's fears had been allayed in the past weeks. Ailsa had been lured away by the mystery and promise of the outside world, but both David and Alanna had known that world; it held no mystery for them. The seduction of the past, the enchantment, the wind and water and ancient gods were here. It was evident in their eyes when they came in damp with mist and tired with laughter or hushed with awe.

" 'There is no earthly atom but doth glow, This pavement and th' ungarnished ramparts show, As do the fretted star-strewn roofs above, Such luster and transcendency hath Love.'

"Remember that, and ye shall be content that I call ye, now and forever, man and wife," the minister intoned.

Jenny had begun to weep the instant she saw Alanna in her wedding finery. She did not know why she was so moved, why her throat seemed tight and dry and tears came freely. She did not attempt to brush them from her face, though her father had taught her it was weak and foolish to show her feelings in public. Callum Mackensie was a member of the true Scottish Kirk. He believed in restraint, in humility and propriety. He had a fierce, unbending dedication to the Lord, of which, in his own way, he was curiously proud.

But Jenny had not lived with her father for many years, and Ian had taught her too. He had encouraged her to know her feelings and express them, good or bad, in anger or affection, frustration or pride. He had tried to teach her not to be ashamed of her tears, but a little of her father's influence lingered, and she never wept in public.

Today she didn't care. She strained to hear each word the minister uttered, each vow Alanna and David exchanged.

She was unbearably affected by the vows she had heard so many times, and she wondered at her vulnerability to the beauty and solemnity of the moment.

Her tears were silent, but Ian sensed her distress. He put his arm around his wife and held her, brushing his chin on her hair so she knew that he was there, he was with her, he would not let her weep alone. Strangely, Jenny was not comforted.

"I call ye, now and forever, man and wife." The words echoed inside her head; the same words the minister had spoken to her and Ian twenty-two years ago. They had not struck her then as they struck her now, straight through to the heart. For she saw what Ailsa had seen, what Ian was seeing, that David and Alanna were bound by more than affection and trust, faith and hope. They were bound by a force beyond Jenny's comprehension, so powerful, so deep within them, that even if the minister had not declared them married, they would have been so, in their hearts and in their souls.

Desperately, Jenny turned in Ian's arms and sobbed against his chest.

4

AS THE BELLS BEGAN TO RING, THE PEOPLE OF THE GLEN ROSE to their feet and cheered, while David kissed Alanna long and tenderly. All who opened their eyes could see this marriage was good and right, honest and true. It was a rare miracle that two such souls had found each other. The Highlanders loved to celebrate miracles.

They piled out of the kirk, feet tapping in anticipation, and made a noisy procession to Ian and Jenny Fraser's, where the wedding supper had been laid out on long tables in the sun. The tables were decked with flowers and ferns, as was the front of the croft. Gavin had even climbed up on the roof and woven garlands of flowers among the thatch.

By now the sun was high and the sky deep blue. The bride and groom and the two families sat at the high table and the other guests gathered around tables laden with jugged hare, roasted duck and venison, with haggis, gooseberry and elderflower brose, with game pies made of pheasant and grouse. There was gingerbread and shortbread, spiced fruit dumplings, sponge pudding and daffodil pie, scones and fruit tarts and jams, clotted cream and butter and honey. The Frasers could not have provided so much by themselves, but all had contributed to the *feill*—the great feast—giving their carefully hoarded delicacies to show David and Alanna they were honored and loved.

Every man had brought his *quach*, a wooden cup hooped in brass or silver, and there was ale and whisky aplenty. Alanna and David sat side by side while toasts were drunk to their health and happiness, prayers raised to the gods of the glen for many children and good crops and prosperity. Some of the toasts were in Gaelic—ancient Celtic blessings that made Alanna smile.

When all had eaten their fill, and drunk more than their fill, Alanna circulated among the guests, accepting the small offerings of bread and cheese that were the traditional symbol of abundance. She did not mind the ribald jests and innuendos that her friends could not resist. She was not afraid of David and his gentle hands or his muscled body or his passion. She yearned for those things.

Finally Ian raised his *quach* and everyone fell silent. He angled his cup toward bride and groom and said loudly, "May the gods of the glen and our ancestors bless ye. May Anu bring prosperity to the earth ye farm, the animals ye raise and the hearts ye join today. May Brigit bring warmth and poetry to your hearth and your souls, so that neither is ever cold or starved for beauty."

"Aye," the guests shouted as one, raising their cups to the couple, "to Anu and Brigit. May they shape your future with the wisdom of their touch." Everyone drank, cheered with fervor, then turned to Ailsa expectantly.

She rose with reluctance, because, for the first time since the moment she became Alanna's mother, she did not know what to say to her daughter. She raised her glass, her hand trembling slightly. "May ye find peace and contentment in one another, may ye be safe and secure in the understanding that is between ye." Ailsa looked into Alanna's eyes and realized she had wished for them the life she'd lived with William, and that, for them, it was not enough. "May the earth and water nurture ye, and the wind sing ye awake and asleep. May ye find joy and danger and exhilaration, and a beauty so deep ye will weep with the power of it and be forever changed."

She touched her *quach* to her lips. After a moment, the other guests did likewise. This time they did not cheer, but drank with reverence and respect. Some of them had seen that beauty and known its power; others understood that it existed. All knew it was both the most generous and most perilous wish a mother could pass to her child on her wedding day.

Jenny knew it. She knew she'd chosen contentment over risk; she had never desired nor sought more than peace. She turned to Ian, and before she could speak, he took her hand and led his wife out to the clearing where the dancing had begun.

Fiddlers and flutists played while the guests formed lines and circles. Jenny was hardly aware of the steps as she turned and dipped, swayed and leapt with Ian beside her. He had chosen *her*. The thought made her flush with happiness and the healthy exertion of the dance. Each time he took her hand, Jenny smiled, Ian smiled back, and she was satisfied.

Ian did not think as he danced, nor did he allow himself to feel, except for the comfort he found in his wife's grasp, in his easy familiarity with the movement of her body in the dance. All other thoughts, nightmares and yearnings he resolutely shut out of his mind and heart. "Jenny," he murmured, "I love ye. Do ye love me too?"

His wife grinned, twirled away from him and back again. "I believe I do. But then, I've had more than a bit of ale this day. Perhaps it's made me a little daft."

Ian grinned. "So long as ye don't begin to howl at the moon, I'm thinking I like ye daft." He bowed as the dance drew them apart and they were swallowed up in the energetic crowd.

The afternoon progressed with foursome reels and strathspeys and flings. The women tucked up their skirts as they danced, and the men wore traditional kilts and hose as they spun and whirled and laughed. Few stumbled, though many were intoxicated, if not by the whisky, then by the occasion. Dancing was so important that even in their drunkenness they followed the intricate steps precisely and with enthusiasm.

Ailsa watched it all and was enchanted. This was the kind of celebration she remembered as a child—the music in the air, sweeping her above the worries of every day, the laughter and exuberance. The songs, poems and stories from bards of old that tied these people to their ancestors. She leaned forward, chin in her hands, lost in the color, motion and pleasure of this day. She had never thought to feel this way again.

When Ian began to play the pipes, Ailsa realized he had matured in the years she had been away. He played mist and birdsong, wind and storm and starry sky, and the notes curled around her like a familiar caress, as real as the touch of a knowing hand. Ailsa's blue-violet eyes lightened, her heartbeat raced and slowed, caught up in the rhythm of the songs Ian played: songs he had once played to her alone. Now Jenny Fraser watched him, eyes shining with pride. Ailsa looked away, but could not break free from the enchantment of the music.

Duncan Fraser felt ill at ease at the energetic abandon of the other guests. He hated the high, whining notes of the bagpipe, had never considered it music but rather an endless drone of grief and despair. He did not understand why the Highlanders were mesmerized by the wild, disturbing cry. It was as if Ian had played a spell upon them. Duncan shivered and felt even more lonely.

He noticed Ailsa sitting quietly alone and bent over her hand. She looked demure and calm, unlike the other guests. She had lived for years in London, after all. She knew the rules of decorum. He had thought her pale and drawn before, but today she was lovely, her cheeks flushed and her eyes lit from within with thoughts he could not guess. "Will you dance with me?" he asked.

Ailsa looked up, blinked away the dream of a world she had lost long ago, and saw Duncan's face. His beard was beaded with sweat, his face flushed, his brown eyes full of dissatisfaction. She smiled and shook her head. "I'm in mourning for my husband. I cannot dance. 'Twould be disrespectful."

"Of course. David told me. I'm sorry. Please accept my condolences. You're right, of course. Absolutely right." He bowed in discomfort and turned away.

Ailsa glanced up to find Ian watching. Her eyes met his for an instant, then both looked away quickly. They had not spoken more than trivialities since the day she had first met him in the glen. Nor had she spoken to him alone. Ailsa was too fragile, this place, this day, his music too hazardous a ground for old friends to meet on.

As she turned, Ailsa felt a wrenching inside that surprised her, especially when Ian began to play again. The music crept inside her defenses and touched the part of her heart that was most bruised. That infinitely beautiful, chimerical song had the power to heal her; she knew it. But it also had the power to defeat her. She turned to engage Duncan in conversation.

"Hush now! 'Tis time for the bride and groom to dance!" Jenny called.

Silence fell as the young couple rose and moved between the tables to the meadow, rippled with rainbows of wildflowers and undulating emerald grass. The fiddlers played and the carved flutes sang as David and Alanna circled together. Her hair swung, red and golden in the sunlight, and the fragrance of the flower wreath hovered about her. The

Celtic brooch on its silver chain bounced gently between her breasts as she moved, and she smiled into David's eyes.

"Are you happy?" he whispered.

"I thought I was happy before ye came," she told him. "But then I didn't know about this feeling that begins in my heart and fills me full. I was contented then. *Now* I am happy."

David drew her close and kissed her, and she leaned into him willingly, pressing her breasts against his chest. He had never seen her more beautiful, not even in the flattering cloak of rain and firelight. The sun was kind to her, her color was high, her graceful gown deepening the violet of her eyes.

Alanna whirled, her feet barely touching the ground. There was no room for fear or doubt or grief in her today. What was it her mother had asked when she was gloomy at the pall cast by the endless London rain? *How can ye appreciate the beauty of the sunlight on the water if ye have not also known the darkness?*

David felt his bride's joy, and the boisterous goodwill that flowed around them. The congratulations and gifts and good wishes had not ceased since they left the kirk. He was grateful the distrustful Highlanders had chosen to accept him.

He saw his father standing a little to the side of the main table, surrounded by people, but alone, and for the first time in his life, he pitied Duncan Fraser, who could not understand what he was missing. He might have been born *in* the glen, but not *to* it or *of* it. He did not see, as David did, the wealth in rushing waters and summer flowers, in green forests and lush moors and high black mountains.

Duncan was not aware his son was watching, and would have been appalled by the look in David's eyes, if he had seen it. He was staring at his brother and father playing pipes and fiddle side by side. The bond between them, the understanding and affection, was clear and always had been. Duncan felt left out by that closeness, though he had always shunned it, had chosen instead to dream of ships and factories and gold.

Denying his irritation, which he would not call jealousy,

he decided he could wait no longer to make his announcement. Duncan Fraser took a deep breath, squared his shoulders and faced the celebrating Highlanders.

"I have something to say," he announced in the loud, clear voice he had cultivated at his shipyards. "I see that David and his new wife wish more than anything to stay among you, that they have all they need, that David has enough to keep them both in comfort for a long time to come from his investments in industry. And I've seen how much he cares about you, the people of Glen Affric." His heart was pounding with excitement and anticipation of their pleasure.

David stared, open-mouthed, uncertain of where this was leading.

"Rather than give him a present he will keep in the cupboard except when I come to visit, I've decided to give something to the glen as a whole, to all of you, on his behalf."

Silence fell over the clearing. The guests watched Duncan warily, even in their drunkenness, for he was not known as a generous man. "I'm going to arrange, with one or two associates, to purchase the Hill of the Hounds, which is falling into ruin, and a damned shame it is. I want to restore it, make it the beautiful and comfortable hunting lodge it once was."

No one moved; few dared to breathe. David's head was reeling, and he had a sick feeling in his stomach. "Associates?" was all he managed to say. He noticed Alanna was watching his father with curiosity and compassion. He wanted to warn her, tell her to open her eyes and not waste her sympathy, but he waited.

Duncan beamed at his son. "Indeed. One cannot do all the work of investing oneself. One needs partners. To help decide what must be done to the house itself, to the roads and the glen to bring the people who'll use the lodge, who'll spend their money as they enjoy their sport. It will bring prosperity to all of you."

He did not give them a chance to interrupt. Duncan had everyone's attention for the first time, and would not willingly give it up. "I've thought it all through. Hunters and fishermen will come from all over Scotland and England, especially London and Glasgow. They're bored with the common places and yearn for something new. Here, they would find surprises." He thought of the storm that had greeted his arrival and shuddered.

Mairi, Ian and Ailsa turned instinctively to one another. Their gazes locked in a moment of dread that left them chilled. They blinked and shook the chill away, and with it the fear—a fleeting thing, ridiculous and unwarranted. Duncan Fraser was merely spouting hot air as a kettle expelled steam.

"The Hill is not for sale," Mairi said calmly. "Ye can no' buy a house that isn't for sale."

Duncan smiled. "We'll see. If the price is right ..." He waved his hand to indicate he need not finish so obvious a thought. He was very sure of himself.

No doubt he believed he was bringing them a blessing, but they knew more than he about the Highlands. They knew that change rarely brought prosperity; usually it brought disaster. Outsiders would come and push them off their land to add to the grounds of the estate, to add to the hunting and get rid of the small farming plots that kept the people in grain. It had happened before and often throughout the Highlands.

"Look about you at these woods full of deer and pheasant, foxes, quail and fish going to waste." Duncan's voice rolled over them like thunderclouds before a storm. "The improvements we'll make will bring jobs and money. So," he finished, "that's my gift to you. The promise of a better future."

Alanna regarded her new father-in-law in silence. She was not disturbed by his announcement, merely bemused. She did not believe for a minute that it would come to be. But it made her wonder about Duncan. Why did he *want* to do such a thing?

She turned to look at her husband. She was holding his arm, and his face was white with rage.

Like his father, David was thinking of the storm that had

carried Duncan into the glen. He remembered the icy pre-monition he had tried to dismiss. It returned now in a dark haze that blurred his vision. Then David felt the slight pressure of Alanna's fingers on his arm. The haze dissipated, along with the chill. He smiled at his bride and tried to tamp down the rage that smoldered in the ashes and coals of his relationship with his father.

Ian and Angus grimaced at one another. "I'll think of a way to tell him 'tis a mistake he's making," Ian murmured. "Surely he'll understand when I explain."

Angus sighed and shrugged. "Mayhap." He went to his older son. "We'll talk of it later, shall we?" He leaned close to add quietly, "They're too drunk to take it in just yet, as am I. And I think they're a wee bit frightened of your Glasgow voice and way of thinking."

Duncan glowered, heavy eyebrows drawn together. Angus put his arm around his son and drew him away from the crowd.

"Come for the while and have a wee dram," Flora called, joining her husband and son. "We've no' had enough time to talk to ye with all the wedding plans."

Duncan was no fool. He knew they were trying to divert him. He was forty-seven years old, yet he felt younger than Ian. His parents wanted to silence him when he was only trying to help. He was hurt and disappointed by the unyielding sullenness of the other guests, but knew he must not show it now. Later they would see that he was right. Later they would understand his wisdom and thank him. He was the one who had grown rich on his wits. He'd help these people if it killed him.

Ian urged the fiddlers to play, and they struck up a lively reel while Jenny offered more ale and whisky. Soon the guests had forgotten Duncan's speech in their own pleasure and increasingly hazy delight in the occasion. Even Alanna might have forgotten, except for the tension in her groom's shoulders and his grim expression. "David, he's only a man who makes mistakes. Don't let him spoil this perfect day. Don't give him that power, *mo-cridhe*."

David looked at his wife with surprise and admiration.

"You're right," he said. "Here he has no power." He was grateful, as always, for Alanna's certainty and optimism. He was a lucky man.

One after another, the dancers collapsed into the tall grass where wildflowers brushed their noses and became tangled in their hair. The men still standing dragged the tables away and bullied the crowd out of their stupor and into a large, uneven circle around a fire banked by large gray stones. Some of the guests seemed inclined to sing, but verse after rousing verse began in enthusiastic cacophony, only to trail off as the singers forgot the words.

"Tell us a story, Callum Mackensie!" Malcolm Drummond shouted, "and save my poor battered ears for another day's celebration."

Callum gazed across the fire, eyes narrowed. His head felt heavy, his tongue swollen, and he knew he could not speak one sentence clearly, let alone tell a whole tale. "Did the devil send ye to torment me?" he shouted back. "Leave me to die in peace, with my head in the clover."

Even his wife, seated beside him, could not decipher what Callum had said. She looked at Ian pleadingly.

"Tonight I'll tell a story," Ian Fraser replied with dignity. He had had his share of whisky, but had thought it prudent to remain partly sober in order to fulfill his duties as host. "And I know just the one." He cleared his throat portentously and kept his eyes on the low golden flames so he would not meet his brother's gaze.

" 'Twas back a hundred years ago, when, to our great sorrow, the landowners discovered sheep were more profitable than people. Clan ties and vows were forgotten in the Clearances, as the lairds rid themselves of the burden of their people, who, though they looked to the chiefs for guidance, honored and defended them, no longer brought them profit. Instead, the lairds pledged their allegiance to a dumb animal whose wool could bring them gold and whose meat could bring them silver."

Ian glanced out of the corner of his eye to see if Duncan was paying attention. His brother's face was flushed in the firelight, drawn with shadows as he sank his chin onto his chest. He clutched his silver flask tightly, though by the red in his eyes, Ian guessed the flask had long been empty. He looked as if he might fall asleep at any moment.

Mairi Rose moved closer to the fire and stumbled over Duncan's hunched form, making him sit upright, head swaying as he squinted at her. "Och, aye, forgive me, Duncan Fraser. Mayhap I should no' have had that last bit of sherry. But 'twas oh so sweet. I couldn't say no." She stretched her hands toward the flames and stumbled backward as expertly as she had stumbled forward, knocking Duncan's shoulder so he had to let go of his flask with one hand to keep from toppling over.

"There now, I've done it again. Will ye ever forgive me?"

Duncan snorted and waved his hand in dismissal. He was awake now, blurry as the flames might be. There was nothing to be done about it.

Ian caught Mairi's fleeting smile and settled back on his hummock to tell his tale. "Alexander, twenty-third laird of Clan Chisholm, was one of those who sought silver and gold, and forgot about loyalty and honor. At the urging of the owner of a Lowland woolen mill, he decided to send away his clansmen and bring in more profitable sheep. But his eighteen-year-old daughter, Mary, overheard her father discussing his plans. She was horrified, and vowed to stop him."

Sliding his arms around Alanna's waist, David buried his face in her hair as he listened. How often had he defied his own father, or tried to, to protect the workers? Men like Bran Guthrie, whom David had destroyed in the end. He held tight to Alanna, because she was good, and had done no evil, had answered only the dictates of her own heart all her life. She would have made Mary Chisholm's vow, and somehow kept it. David wondered if he had the strength to do the same.

"While The Chisholm still sat with the hated Lowlander, Mary told the servants to muster the clan. The men and women came from up and down the glen and gathered on the green before Comar House. Mary stood in front, and when her father came to see what was causing the commotion, she swore that if Alexander Chisholm turned his people off the land, she would go with them."

There were several grunts of agreement, which might have been cheers earlier in the day. "That's the way, Mary," Malcolm Drummond declared, his words slurred together like too many beads on a short thread. "Tell 'im what's what, lass!"

Ian grinned. "'Twas winter in the Highlands, and cold with snow and sleet and wind. The Laird Alexander thought of that as he stood shivering on the threshold of his elegant home, for he loved his daughter well. Mary was a kind girl who had shown him no disobedience, but only affection. He was terrified by the thought of losing the only light in his life, of sending her to starve in the wild winter hills. For love of Mary, Alexander Chisholm relented, and sent the Lowlander away without a sale or a promise. For the while, at least, the people were safe."

Duncan Fraser was fully awake and alert. He glowered while the other guests smiled and chanted to the true heart of Mary Chisholm. "Alexander was laird and the power was his, not his daughter's. He shouldn't have let a mere girl dictate to him, blackmail him into doing as she wished. He had to survive, after all. Had every right to make a profit. His family's future and their livelihood were more important than one girl's feelings."

David clenched his fists, ashamed that his father was so blind he did not recognize the strength and courage of that young girl, or how much it had cost her to defy her father.

Ailsa gasped, then caught her breath, for she had always known the kind of man Duncan was. He could not forget his business for a moment and lose himself in the heroism of a young, defenseless girl. Mary Chisholm had always been one of her idols, hers and Ian's. They used to pray that she would rise out of the mist and protect them when they were afraid. She could tell Ian was caught up in the story; his cheeks were rosy and his green eyes gleamed. But when Duncan spoke disparagingly of the girl's feelings, the color drained from Ian's face and he sighed in defeat. Ailsa ached for him, though she had no right, except that once she had loved him.

Marshaling his scattered thoughts, Angus Fraser took over. "Mary Chisholm became a heroine, a legend to the Highlanders. Surely ye've heard of Hugh Chisholm, who hid in a cave with Bonny Prince Charlie for days while the English Butcher hunted them. When the fugitives parted, the prince shook his hand. Hugh vowed never to offer that hand to any man again. And he never did. Except once. As an old man, he gave his right hand gladly to Mary Chisholm of Comar, who had stood against her father for the good of the clan."

Ian stared at his brother and Angus at his son. Duncan Fraser had not been moved. His face was blank, without animation, even in the vivid red-and-orange firelight. They shivered and shook their heads at the sight. Duncan had not heard. He had not understood.

5

A FEW DAYS LATER, ANGUS AND IAN ASKED DUNCAN TO TAKE a walk with them. It was midday, and the June sun was high in an azure sky touched with wisps of cloud that only made the blue seem richer.

Ian looked up and thought regretfully of his son and eldest daughter. Just after dawn, Gavin and Brenna had left to return to the shieling in the hills where the sheep and cattle grazed in summer. Gavin had been delighted by David's gift of some of the books he'd brought from Glasgow; the young man was eager to read them in the idyllic days to come. Brenna would spin and sew and make baskets, as well as cooking for her brother and some of the others. Many of the Highlanders had sent one or two members of their families up to the shielings; they would visit when their shepherding duties were light, so the days would not grow too long and dull. The young people looked forward to the summer, but Ian already missed his children, who were not really children anymore.

The three men walked through wild thyme and creeping lady's tresses—the cream-colored orchids that trailed across the ground—past flowering brambles and white wood garlic, through a clearing bright with foxgloves and blue speedwell flowers and wild violets among tall green and golden grasses.

The ferns made the cool darkness of the woods verdant and lush. "Worth more than gold, is that fine, rich color," Angus said into the warm summer air, but Ian knew he was talking to Duncan.

Duncan did not bother to respond. He was busy trying to make his way through the thick ferns and tangled bracken that hid gnarled stumps and rocks covered with moss and lichens.

The air was sweet with the scent of flowers, and the woods were cool and dark. The gray-green trunks of beech rose all around, their roots like the callused claws of an eagle and their dark green leaves intertwined with the long, twisted branches of huge old oaks. The sunlight barely penetrated through the needles of spruce and silver fir.

Finally Ian, Angus and Duncan reached a lightly wooded area of tall larches, small hazel bushes and rowans with their brilliant crown of leaves. Ian and Angus had said little to Duncan until then. They wanted him to open his eyes and *see*. They pointed out the many tiny tributaries that fed the river and eventually the lochs, the brilliantly colored stones beneath peat-colored water that rushed and bubbled one moment, glided clear and silent the next.

Duncan was bored. "You have something to say. Why don't you just say it?" he asked wearily. He did not realize how much the wedding had taken out of him until it was over, until the astonished silence that had greeted his announcement had begun to ring in his ears. He had been hurt by the Highlanders' indifference, by David's mute anger, but he had not been deterred.

He would not admit to himself how much he wanted his brother's relatives and friends to cheer and clap him on the back and thank him by offering another dram of whisky. It was not their gratitude he wanted; it was their acceptance, their admiration and affection. Yet ever since the wedding, he had felt a greater distance between himself and his father, not to mention Ian. They were not angry, merely perplexed, diffident and wary.

Duncan was glad when they asked him to walk with them. Perhaps now they could discuss his plans with thought and intelligence. But they were leading him on a twisting, hilly journey to nowhere, watching him expectantly. He knew they were waiting; he just didn't know for what.

"We wanted to get out with ye, away from the others for a bit," Ian said. "To show ye around our glen. We've no' had the chance till now, with the wedding to plan and all our summer chores."

His brother spoke pleasantly, indicating the lush landscape all around them, but Duncan was not convinced. He had not succeeded in business by believing what men told him, no matter how soft and harmless their tone, or how sincere. "And what else?"

Angus Fraser shook his head so his long white hair tumbled into his eyes. He raked his fingers through his beard in agitation. "You're a suspicious man, Duncan. I'm thinking 'tis Glasgow that's made ye that way. You're so worried about someone trying to take your money or cheat ye that ye trust no one. We're your family. We wanted to remind ye of the beauties of this place, mayhap to help ye feel a little of the peace Ian and I find in these woods and moors and rivers."

Duncan winced. He did not have to be reminded that his father was closer to Ian. The truth was, Angus had never understood his oldest son, had never tried to. Duncan did not find peace in nature; he found it in the knowledge that he was safe and secure, that he could provide food, shelter and comfort for his family. All he wanted to do was share that comfort with his brother and his father and his son. He could not take care of them as he did his family in the city, because this was not the city and money could not buy what these people needed. Duncan was trying to reach them the only way he knew how.

The three men passed an abandoned cottage. The thatched roof had fallen in, the walls were covered with honeysuckle vines and moss grew between the flat dark stones of the walls. Ivy had twined its way up the chimney, and the door had disappeared, leaving an empty hole surrounded by dog roses. Duncan waved sharply at the croft. "Seems you need me more than I need you. I have peace of mind. Don't have to worry every year if the animals will get sick or the crops be ruined by rain or disease. I'm safe. I want you to be safe as well."

Angus and Ian glanced at each other. They thought the abandoned croft lovely, though it was a sign of one more family who'd lost the struggle and fled toward vague promises in other lands. Angus and Ian had grown to accept with some equanimity the departure of their friends, not because it was easy to do so, but because they had to do it to survive. The grief was there, but they did not dwell on it. Hard work helped fill the emptiness, and the way nature took back what was left behind reassured them that the cycle was unbroken, despite their pain or personal grief. It was something they could depend on.

"Safety doesn't mean much to us," Ian said slowly. He walked beside his brother, shortening his comfortable stride to match Duncan's awkward gait over the uneven ground. "No' the kind you value. We're used to fighting to feed our families. Mayhap we even enjoy it. 'Tis what we've always done, what we know and what we love. We don't want someone to give us wealth or security from a velvet glove. We have so much already."

They had reached the top of a hill and Ian stopped, gazing with admiration at the view spread below them. No matter how many times he saw the wide, glittering loch, the river that flowed from it into a smaller loch, the wooded islands, lush and full of promise, the water, luminous in the sunlight, with swans and ducks floating languidly on the surface, he was always taken aback. Now, as was his habit, he said a little prayer of thanks to the gods for such beauty and such bounty in one place. Behind the loch rose the foothills, splashed with gorse and white and purple heather, and behind those, the dark, jagged mountains. This place was everything he loved and valued.

Angus came up beside them. Like Ian, he took in the view as one would breathe in clear, clean air after the smoke and grime of a city. He inhaled the beauty, felt it strengthen and revive him. "Ye see," he said, one hand on Duncan's shoulder, "who could want more than this?"

Duncan scratched his beard, perplexed. "More than what? I see a wooden bridge that's about to tumble into the loch there, and a stone one across the river that's a jumble of boulders and broken clay. And I see that you've not thinned out your red deer this year. Just look at that herd up in the trees. Eat up four hillsides in less than a month. And this road is barely more than a cart track. How can you stand it? Do you know, we could've been here in half the time if you had tracks cleared out and walking paths and fixed the blasted road."

Ian did not look at his brother. "What'd be the point to getting here in half the time if we didn't appreciate this place once we arrived?"

Frowning, Duncan glanced at his younger brother. "It's pleasant to look upon, certainly. But that's not the point." He forced Ian to meet his eyes. "There's so much more you could do with this glen, so much you could make it yield up to you. That's what I'm trying to help you see. I'm not trying to take the place away from you but to make it serve you, to give it back." He couldn't help it; he spoke as he did to his slowest foreman when he couldn't understand a difficult theory or complicated transaction. He honestly believed he knew what was best for his brother and his father; they were too stubborn and set in their ways to admit it. But he could change their minds. He was sure of it.

"And what is it ye suppose we're trying to help you see, Duncan?" Angus asked wearily, for he recognized it was hopeless.

"The glen, I suppose," Duncan replied. "I see it—as it could be, as we can make it."

"But now, just now, are ye blind to its wealth and beauty just as it is?" Angus knew the answer, but he had to ask.

"I always see all sides," Duncan countered, "never simply what's before my face. That would be foolish."

"But ye might enjoy it," Ian muttered under his breath. "Ye might even understand, if ye tried, that in seeing all sides ye see nothing at all."

6

AILSA AWOKE SUDDENLY, JUST BEFORE DAWN, TO FIND MAIRI sitting up staring at her. "There's something in the air today," Ailsa whispered. "Or perhaps it's only the fairies in the half-light they so love. But I heard a sound that does not belong."

"I hear it too," Mairi said pensively. "But I can no' say what it is."

Ailsa's heart began to beat erratically. "I don't think 'tis good, yet I want it to come. How can that be?"

Her mother stared at her thoughtfully. "Because ye feel empty now that Alanna's become a wife. Ye need something to think about besides your past. But take care, *mo-run*. I'm warning ye; take care."

Alanna awoke with the song of the birds filling the air around her. She leaned on her elbow and stared down at David, sleeping peacefully beside her. David, her husband. He looked very handsome and very vulnerable with his hair in tangled curls and his face at rest. Unaccountably, her throat tightened and tears filled her eyes.

She did not know why she wanted to weep. Partly from

joy, she supposed, and partly from fear, though she was not certain of what. Perhaps only of loving him so much.

They had been married a week. The celebration had continued until dawn the night of the wedding, when half the glen had followed the bride and groom to their newly rebuilt cottage. David had not allowed Alanna to see it until then, and she had been amazed at the work he had done. The roof had been thatched, a fireplace built into the wall rather than in the center of the floor, so there was actually a hearth. The walls had been covered in fresh clay, and David had painted one wall of the kitchen with primroses and wood anemones.

To the cheers of the assembled guests, he handed her a set of iron tongs for the fire—a symbol that she would be mistress of this house. She used them at once to prod the already burning fire, though it did not need attention. She had felt the need for action, a moment away from the eyes of others.

She glanced over to the place where her kist sat beside the wall. It was almost empty now. She had used the linens and lace and quilts to make the croft a home. She remembered with a fresh rush of unshed tears how David had left two carved wooden goblets on the table on a tray which he'd fashioned, then painted with an intricate design. The cups were full to the brim with fine wine, and when she lifted hers to toast their new home, she'd found the card beneath, on which he'd written simply, "Welcome home."

"You're going to cry."

David's voice surprised Alanna, and she waved her hand before her eyes to make the tears disappear. "Why would I be so daft?" she demanded. Her voice trembled slightly. She had not known that the feelings would be so powerful, that she would ache with watching David sleep, ache when he touched her with his hands or his kindness. Sometimes the strength of her love for him frightened her.

David took his wife in his arms and held her above him so his lips nearly met hers. "Because you love me so much you can't bear it?" he said hopefully.

Alanna was startled. "How did ye know?"

307

His grin faded and his green eyes darkened. "Because that's how I feel about you. Sometimes I want to sing, sometimes to touch your body until we both cry out for me to stop, sometimes I want to laugh in gratitude and disbelief at my good fortune. And sometimes I just want to sit down and weep."

Alanna stared at him as the silence brimmed with the rush and tumble of their thoughts. When apprehension began to taint the air, David grinned and rolled with her to the middle of the heather mattress. "But just now, I want to make love to you. You've many things to teach me."

Alanna blushed. " 'Tis ye who do the teaching, I'm thinking."

"No. I may have been your first lover, but you're teaching me tenderness and other things I would not know without you."

When David saw that her eyes were damp again, he kissed her deeply and pulled her close until her breasts brushed his chest through the thin fabric of her shift.

His pulse raced with anticipation. They had made love many times in the week since their wedding, but always he was discovering her again, as if he had not touched her before. He had been afraid that his desire for Alanna, which flared bright and hot within him, would burn her, devour her, shock her. But she had meant it that night in the woods when she asked him to make her smolder. She blazed in her body as brightly as he.

He drew his fingers through her long red hair, and Alanna rose so the waves fell around her like a fragile veil. David took a single strand and followed it from her forehead to below her waist where it curled over her thin summer shift. He touched her with only that one fingertip against that one strand of vivid hair, but his whole body responded. Alanna trembled and leaned toward him, lips parted.

She kissed him gently, lightly, then put her hands on his shoulders and drew him toward her until their mouths were moist and open to one another, and their tongues intertwined.

Alanna gasped as the heat tingled inside her, beginning

in the center and radiating outward to her lips and fingers and her legs, tangled with David's. She did not know how or when, but her shift had disappeared, and she felt the cool morning air on her naked skin. Chills rose along her arms and her nipples grew taut with excitement and the misty breeze.

The coals that had smoldered inside burst into flame, yet they could not warm away the chill of excitement on her skin. She slid her arms around David's back, tracing the muscles and curves, aware that his hands were following the same path on her own back, until he slid them forward and caressed her with his thumbs, so lightly that she thought she could not bear the sensations swirling inside her.

She gasped as he kissed her breasts and the hollow between, flicking his tongue across the sensitive skin. For a moment, Alanna grew still, outwardly, if not inwardly, while David aroused her with tongue and fingertips and the slow, sensuous motion of his body gently moving against hers. She felt the hot spiral begin to whirl inside, the colors flared like bursts of brilliant flame, and she called out his name again and again, quivering, terrified and delighted by the way her body moved beyond her control.

He entered her then, and she nestled close, moaning as he moved within her, slowly, rhythmically, seductively. She could feel him tremble, and the heat intensified as she pulled him closer, hands buried in his thick, dark curls.

For a long time, they rocked together. She wrapped her legs around him, caught up in the rise and fall of his breath, the heavy beat of his heart, the heat of his skin against hers. When David stiffened and cried out, Alanna held him tighter, clinging to the fire that singed her body and her soul, willing the blaze to rise higher and hotter until it consumed them both.

7

IAN WAS ON THE WAY TO THE PEAT CUTTING WITH ERLINNA on his shoulders, when he stopped still in the middle of the path. He felt cold, suddenly, and then overwarm, and his skin tingled.

"What's wrong, Papa?" Erlinna asked. "Did ye forget where we're going?"

"I'd not know where we're going at all." Ian was not speaking to his daughter. He did not know to whom he spoke or what he meant. All he knew was that his senses were alert, that the air on his face was cool with mist and other things whose shape and size and purpose he could not discern. "Into battle I think," he added under his breath.

"Och, that's grand!" Erlinna crowed. "Will we use the soldiers ye carved? Or your bow or your gun? Ye know I love to fight."

Ian was worried about his daughter's enthusiasm for a struggle she could not begin to understand. How could she, when he himself was at a loss? Yet, inexplicably, he shared her excitement, even though his hands were cold and damp with dread.

Long after the dawn song had faded, Alanna and David rose reluctantly to dress. Tonight Angus and Flora were hosting the last of the wedding suppers, but today they would spend alone together, wandering along the loch. When David opened the heavy door, he found a basket on the stone flagged step. The air was sweet with the scent of honeysuckle; the yellow and white trumpets reached for the sun as it raced in and out of the clouds overhead.

David brought the basket in and grinned at Alanna.

"Not another one?" she cried. She had been touched by the number of kindnesses her friends had done for the new couple during the week—leaving supper, inviting them to dinner, once even preparing breakfast so the couple could concentrate on each other. She peeked inside the basket and saw that it held bridies—meat turnovers with sweet onions baked in—cold boiled eggs in mince, sweet milk and black buns as well as fresh blackberries.

"I think it's the day for a picnic," David said.

Alanna agreed, and soon they were out in the summer air, walking hand in hand through blue moor grass and sundew. Alanna pointed out a great spotted woodpecker working away at an oak tree, and a hedge sparrow hiding in the thick holly bushes.

David peered into the mass of sharp green leaves until he spotted the tiny sparrow. He had been accepted by the people of the glen because of Ian, but he'd been accepted by the land because of Alanna. She had introduced him gently, a little at a time, to the secrets of the glen—to the dawn song, which he'd never really heard before she taught him how to listen. To the wildlife—the wildcats and foxes, red deer and badgers, golden eagles and wood mice and squirrels. She had not sought these creatures out, but watched and waited with infinite patience, pointing each out as it appeared. It seemed to David that Alanna would be content to crouch forever, gathering the wonders of the glen into herself.

She had showed him the loch, which fed into the river—a place where the water was perfectly still one moment, reflecting the cloudy sky flawlessly, running white and churning over stones between overgrown banks the next. She had showed him the woods, the tall birches, the larches, the silver spruce, and the moors dotted with sheep, thick in tall summer grasses. She had shown him the shining moods of sky and wind and mountains—the power and the beauty and the mystery in all three.

He had come to respect nature as Alanna did, to approach it with humble reverence for a place so ancient and so lovely, a place inhabited by the gods Alanna spoke of with affection, as if she knew them as she knew the woods and moors and waters. Here people lived because the elements, the land, the gods allowed them to do so. He had started to believe on the day of his arrival in Glen Affric. Now his faith was growing, because Alanna nurtured it quietly and gently.

Hours passed while David and Alanna walked along the loch, from patches of sunlight, where the air became warm and the sweat rose in a moment, to the moving shade, where the breeze held a chill that denied the power of the sun. From shadow to light to shadow they wandered, pleased in each other's company, until they approached the change in the landscape that indicated the Hill of the Hounds was near.

Alanna smiled. "Let's eat in the gardens today. I like the feeling of wildness destroying the order the Willistons tried to impose. There's a huge old oak with a low branch wide enough to sit on. Come!"

David hesitated. There had been no more mention of his father's scheme since the night of the wedding. No one at the suppers they attended spoke of change or poverty or a stranger's plans. They had the crops on their minds, and the cattle and sheep being moved up to summer pastures and the shielings where all felt free, for a while, from the pressures of everyday survival. They talked about David and Alanna's future, about David's painting and his new cattle and sheep and the croft he had made so comfortable for his bride.

Often Duncan was there, but he remained aloof. David devoutly hoped he had forgotten his plan, though he knew his father well, and had seen the glitter in his eyes that night. He doubted that Duncan Fraser would give in so easily.

Alanna laughed at the antics of a red squirrel trying to keep a deer from stealing its prize, and David dismissed the thought. He would not feed his anger when he was so happy. That would be wasteful. It would mean that his father had won.

David and Alanna had consumed most of their dinner

when they heard voices echoing oddly from the surface of the loch.

Alanna looked up, surprised. "There's someone in the house."

David, who had been unable to tell where the voices were coming from, was startled by her certainty, but he did not doubt her conclusion. Alanna was usually right about such things.

In unspoken accord, they rose and went toward the house, which was badly in need of new paint, though the structure itself seemed as indestructible as it had when the Willistons built it thirty years before.

Just as Alanna and David approached the entrance, the front door opened and three men stepped out. One of them was Duncan Fraser. The other two were strangers. David and Alanna stopped, staring in disbelief at the strangers in their wool suits, tweed overcoats and soft fedoras. They looked uncomfortable and out of place in their expensive, proper clothing and unnaturally stiff bearing. There was also an intensity about them that set them apart. Alanna felt a chill of foreboding.

Duncan smiled at his son as if he had not noticed how David stiffened. "Ah, what a nice coincidence. I've been wanting you to meet my partners. Simon Black and Robert Howard, this is my son David and his bride, Alanna."

Simon Black stood tall and rigid, his brown hair perfectly combed, his suit and overcoat unsullied, though the other two men were covered with dust. He nodded. "Pleased to make your acquaintance."

The third man, who was not as tall or as old as Mr. Black, was blond and had a gentle face with clear brown eyes. His accent was British, but his voice was so cordial that he seemed actually pleased to be there. He went to David and shook his hand, bowing politely to Alanna. "You must be delighted with your father's plans for this place. It's a beautiful house. So many possibilities. He's clever to have seen them through the dust."

"Possibilities?" David was speechless, so Alanna asked

the question, though she found it difficult to be hostile to this soft-spoken man.

"Indeed," Simon Black replied sternly. "We think this will make a marvelous escape. I've been in a number of hunting lodges, but never one so isolated and in such a fine locale. Massive changes are necessary, of course."

David paled, despite the nut-brown color his skin had absorbed from the sun since his arrival. "Changes?" He was overwhelmed by a sense of unreality. He could not believe this was happening, and his tongue was no more convinced than his brain.

"Naturally," Robert Howard murmured more tactfully, "there are things to be considered before we move ahead. But I think I can assure you that this thing will happen." He felt their hostility, and his warm smile became strained. His eye twitched in a nervous tic.

"You know how investors are. They want guarantees. But I think I've convinced them it's worth a try." Duncan sidled closer to his son, trying to gauge his reaction. He did not like what he saw.

"You called in investors after what we said?" David stared at his father in blank horror. Duncan Fraser had kept silent on purpose, while he waited for these men to arrive and back him up. That silence was the same as a lie. And now he stood there smiling, as if he believed David would welcome these strangers or their money or their plan.

Duncan stroked his beard to hide his agitation. He'd known David was stubborn, but he'd always been a good businessman. "You were upset by the idea at first, but I knew you'd see the benefits soon enough. I'm trying to help, David. Not just you, but everyone in this place. In time they'll see that I was right."

"Why should I come around to your way of thinking now? I never have before." David spoke coldly, though inside his anger was so hot he was certain it showed red in his eyes. "Sometimes I knew it was pointless to fight, but I never once changed my mind." He paused to draw a deep breath. "This, however, is not pointless, and make no mistake, there will be a fight. Just drop it. I think that'd be the wisest thing." There was more than a hint of a threat in his voice.

Alanna felt David's rage as if it were her own, and it frightened her. When he first spoke of his father, he had been angry, but not like this. That anger had threatened only himself. This was something more ominous by far. "I think your father only wants to help. Mayhap he's no' had time to understand us as ye do, David." She turned to Duncan Fraser with a plea that was part fear, part premonition, part self-preservation. "We'll be all right. 'Tis no' easy to live here, 'tis true, but the glen will see to our needs. It would never let us starve, so long as we honor it."

Simon Black gave a shout of laughter, and even Robert Howard smiled. Duncan simply stared. The girl could not be serious. He'd known these people were backward, but this was absurd. He turned to his companions. "My daughter-in-law has a sense of humor, though you'd never know it from her sweet and gentle face."

He turned back to Alanna. "No one takes care of you or watches over or protects you. You have to take care of yourself or perish. David knows that as well as anyone."

David struggled to speak in a normal voice. "I know what it takes to survive, aye. But I also know when to open my eyes and see. You're blind, old man. Except for that narrow ray of light that falls on money, you can't see a damned thing, and I don't think you ever will."

8

"YE SEEM UNEASY, MOTHER. IS AUGHT AMISS?" JENNY ASKED.

She and her middle daughter, Glenyss, were helping Flora prepare the last of the wedding suppers for Alanna and David. Jenny had noticed the croft was more crowded than usual; several trunks lay open, spilling clothes onto the earthen floor, and beds were being aired that had not been slept in for years.

Flora cleared her throat and stirred a huge iron pot of Scotch broth too vigorously. She had been waiting for this moment since her son Duncan had approached her this morning, but she had not wanted it to come.

"Two of Duncan's friends arrived this morning. They'll be staying here, and paying handsomely for the honor." She laughed without mirth. "Though I told them 'twas no' necessary. They insisted, and Duncan agreed." She shook her head in dismay.

Glenyss was straightening the crowded room industriously, while waiting for a chance to sample the black buns, but now she tensed. "Why would his friends come here? He hates the glen." Anxiously, she remembered standing beside her father when Duncan made his announcement at the wedding. She'd felt Ian grow stony with shock and disapproval. She would have felt those things without her father's pale face and clenched fists; she loved the glen as he did.

Flora winced. "He said they were friends, but I'm doubting 'tis so. They'd not the look of friends, ye ken?"

"Aye." Jenny rubbed more rosemary on the shank of lamb they would roast tonight. "They must be the partners he spoke of." Her voice was composed, serene.

Flora looked up curiously, and Glenyss regarded her mother through narrowed eyes. "Papa will no' be happy."

"No. Their presence might spoil this celebration. But we can't send them away. 'Twould be unforgivable no' to offer our hospitality."

"Aye," Flora agreed. "And there ye have my dilemma. Angus went away walking soon after they came. He's no' pleased to have them in the house. But what could I do? Duncan is our son as much as Ian. And to turn away strangers, well . . ."

Glenyss pushed her hair out of her face, looked up sharply when Duncan appeared in the doorway with two strangers.

He introduced Simon Black and Robert Howard to Jenny and Glenyss, and while Flora went to get cool ale to fill their cups, the men gathered around the scrubbed pine table.

"The first thing we'd have to do is build a road to make this place more accessible," Simon Black said emphatically. "Idyllic is nice, but the guests have to be able to get here in comfort."

"I agree," Duncan said. He glanced at his mother, who handed him a tall cup of foaming ale. "Right away that would bring work for the people here. Building a road takes a great deal of labor. Even before the Hill was open, money would start to flow into the glen."

Flora hid a grimace and turned back to her kitchen. Duncan watched his mother out of the corner of his eye. Funny how he felt so much older than his parents. They had lived in this godforsaken place too long, had seen nothing of the world, knew nothing of business or profit or success. They knew so little that he pitied them, because they did not seem to mind their ignorance. In fact, they seemed contented with their lives and their lot. He had determined, after much consideration, that it was simply *because* they knew nothing better. He wanted to show them there was so much more. He wanted them to listen and believe him, to turn away from Ian long enough to hear what their older son was saying.

"And there's not only the comfort," Robert Howard interjected, bringing Duncan's attention back to the two men who knew what he knew and thought as he thought. "We need to be able to get in supplies more easily, and we need communication, and to get the products of the glen to the outside world. There again, the profit would grow of its own accord."

"Then we'd want to start clearing the parts of the woods that are overgrown. The hunting looks good because it's too far off the beaten path for the animals to have been depleted, which will be one of our strongest selling points. And if the fish or fowl or deer run low, we can always stock them, so we'll need a supplier. But the place is a little too wild. We don't want our guests getting lost and forgetting to pay the bill."

At that, Flora discovered an errand outside and disappeared. Glenyss caught a glimpse of her flushed face and knew her grandmother was outraged by such talk in her home. Glenyss herself felt ill; her hands shook and her vision blurred with apprehension. But Jenny did not seem troubled. She had stopped seasoning the lamb to listen, leaning forward slightly, hands cupped in her large apron. Though she looked thoughtful, she did not look angry.

Glenyss was disgusted. She wanted to sweep her arm across the table and send cups, bowls and ale spilling into the laps of those three men. She ducked her head and applied herself to the black buns. The memory of David's face rose before her, white with rage while he listened to his father on his wedding night. Her throat felt dry and she was afraid.

"As soon as we get those papers from London, we'll know more about the costs and so forth. Fraser, when did you say they'd be coming?"

"Any day now. Sent my proposition to the Willistons the same day I telegraphed you two. They should be sending back diagrams, blueprints, sales figures, everything. Maybe by day after tomorrow. Until then, we can look around. The glen is huge and we can see about diverting the river if we have to, maybe damming up the loch."

Glenyss could not suppress a gasp of horror. She searched their faces for signs that they were joking. Diverting the river? Trying to change nature? Surely these men weren't arrogant enough to believe they could do all that. She turned to her mother in desperation, but Jenny was nodding absently.

Pressing her lips together, Glenyss stared at the raisins in her hands. It was up to her then, to remember what was said here. She could not stop them; all she could do was listen. She felt helpless, outraged and terrified all at once.

Duncan was invigorated by the talk of renovation and modernization. Not only had he long lamented the backwardness of the glen, he had also grown bored with the shipyards, the demands of coal and shipping. He had been yearning for something new to entertain him.

He thought of David's reaction that afternoon and shrugged. His son and he had disagreed often, but he was sure this time David would come around, once he saw all the advantages the shooting lodge would bring. Maybe even Ian would be impressed, when the money started flowing in.

Duncan considered Jenny thoughtfully. Ian's wife did not look hostile, only interested. "What do you think, Jenny?"

"Well, Ian would no'—"

"It's not Ian I'm asking," Duncan said. "It's you. We want to know what you think, don't we, lads?"

Simon Black laced his fingers behind his head and leaned back, staring up at the thatched ceiling. He did not care what these people thought. Let Duncan Fraser worry about placating his relatives. Once Black made a business decision, he would do what had to be done, regardless of the obstacles. He made it a point of pride. It was really quite simple.

He looked askance at Howard, who was watching the Fraser woman with interest. Simon Black sighed. A good businessman, Howard, but too many scruples.

The younger blond man with the soft brown eyes shifted in his chair. He had been disturbed by David and Alanna's reaction and still felt a little jumpy. He was uncomfortable being closed inside the small, dank croft, but Jenny's smile soothed his raw nerves. She seemed calm and her eyes were intelligent, reassuring. "We'd be obliged if you'd tell us,"

Robert Howard said. He encouraged her to come closer with a wave of his hand.

Jenny hesitated for a full minute. She knew how Ian felt, but she did not feel the same. Life was hard in the glen. Anything that lightened the load they all had to bear could not be bad. Besides, Ian had never insisted she echo his opinions if they were not her own. He'd encouraged her to speak out, just as Ailsa Rose had always spoken her heart. Jenny sat up straighter. Ailsa had nothing to do with this. "I'd like to hear all you're planning," she said carefully. "It could be good for us, I think."

Glenyss stared, eyes wide and hands clenched. She could not speak against her mother, but was shocked by Jenny's acquiescence.

Robert Howard listened intently and his nervous eye stopped blinking. "How do you think the others will view this?"

Jenny shrugged. "They'll not like it, I'll tell ye that straight out. They're not fond of change of any kind. They're very bound to the land, ye see."

"But you're not?"

Holding her breath, Glenyss sat motionless. Her mother was speaking as if she were not of the glen, as if she were different. The girl's shock turned to panic.

"I'm bound just as tightly as they. 'Tis my home, ye ken, and I love it. But not the way some others do. They cling to it—I can no' explain. They're happy as they are."

Robert Howard's eyes never left her face. "Are you saying you're unhappy?"

" 'Tis hard," Jenny replied. She knew she was betraying a trust by letting an incomer hear what was not their business or their cause. "And harder all the time. I'd like to wake one morning and find 'tis easier, is all. Mayhap no' to struggle every day."

Duncan and the strangers exchanged glances, impressed that she had the good sense to recognize salvation when it was offered. They did not bother to glance at Glenyss, whose knuckles were white with tension, her face so pale and taut that her hazel eyes looked haunted in her twelve-year-old face.

9

"It'll no' happen, I tell ye," Ian said as he walked with Ailsa and Mairi, Alanna and David through the long summer twilight. "Ye heard Duncan at supper. He's bored and so are they. They're looking for a little diversion. 'Tis too much trouble and they'll soon give it up."

Although he believed what he was saying, Ian had been stunned to learn that Duncan had invited his investors to Glen Affric. He had been relieved when Simon Black and Robert Howard declined Flora's invitation to stay for supper. They'd said they wanted a walk to admire the loch while it was still light. The summer darkness that fell so late gave them the perfect opportunity. As Ian watched them go, he'd remembered with physical clarity the sense of impending battle that had overwhelmed him that morning. He smiled at the thought and felt a surge of exhilaration.

"I'm thinking 'tis no' the beauty of the landscape they're wanting to see," Mairi had murmured after they were gone.

"At least they had the good manners to leave while we dined," Duncan had replied easily. He was wise enough to discard his serious demeanor, the intensity with which he had planned with Black and Howard around that same table before the others came.

"Duncan said he'd already invited those men, that he could no' keep them from coming, but I didn't believe him. Did ye?" Ailsa asked thoughtfully.

Jenny had taken Glenyss and Erlinna and returned to her cottage, exhausted, or Ian would have asked her. She had been there before they arrived, after all, had seemed distracted during the meal, though she showed the proper enthusiasm for bride and groom, drank all the toasts and sang all the songs. Glenyss had been withdrawn and silent, more distraught than pensive, Ian thought. He wondered what had happened in his father's house before the guests arrived.

"Not for a moment," David said tightly. "He knew they'd come and wanted them to. He hasn't given up." He grimaced. Since he'd come to Glen Affric, he'd slowly let go of the threads of control with which he'd carefully circumscribed his life until now. One by one, he had released the calculating restraints that had helped him survive; he did not need them here. Now that he had lost that hard-won control, he had to struggle harder to contain his rage at his father.

Ian, Ailsa and Mairi were too astonished by Duncan Fraser's actions to believe they were a threat. David watched the others shake their heads and smile in bemusement, certain Duncan would give up when he understood the extent of their opposition. He wanted very much for them to be right. For the first time in his life, David *wanted* to be wrong.

For once he was not comforted by the luminous quality of the light, fading to violet, draping the woods in a soft cloak of shadows that magnified the sound of the water. He brushed past foxgloves and cream-flowered brambles, past thick holly bushes rich in green leaves, through blue moor grass turned purple by approaching night. He felt moisture in the air and thought it might rain tomorrow, though tonight the stars were glittering through the clouds and a half-moon peeked from behind tumbled wisps of lilac.

Alanna took his hand, pressing a wild violet into his palm, and he turned to smile at her. She was offering reassurance while seeking it for herself. David slipped his arm around her waist and she leaned into him.

The newlyweds fell behind the others. Ailsa, Mairi and Ian spoke in low voices that did not disturb the hush of purple twilight. "I can no' believe he's serious," Mairi said firmly. She wondered if she were trying to make herself believe it. She remembered too clearly how she and Ailsa had awakened before dawn to a sound where there should have been only silence, but she felt no premonition now, no sense of impending disaster, so perhaps Ian was right.

"I miss the Willistons," Ailsa said unexpectedly. "I didn't

realize it until now. Because if Duncan is serious, well, he'll no' make it happen, but he could make trouble. What was it he said? 'A river, a road, a newly laid carpet. A change here and there can't hurt, you know.' "

"He's mad if he believes he can change the course of a river. Does he think he's a god?"

"Och, no. 'Tis just his way of making himself feel strong." Ian pitied his brother, and knew Duncan would hate that most of all. Duncan Fraser thought of himself as someone to be envied. Ian's pity would make him ill with helpless rage.

"Still, I'd no' like strange landlords at the Hill," Ailsa said. "I'll not believe the Willistons would sell anyway."

"Ye don't want to believe it," Mairi whispered. She felt ill at ease and off-balance.

Ian took her arm and she leaned against him. "The Willistons know 'tis not easy to build here. These strangers're only about to learn. When the midges come out, they'll be off home again, yelping for relief. And can ye see Sassenach tourists way off up here?"

"I've seen a few, and they were no' happy." Ailsa's smile turned wistful. "William was one, but he was different."

"Aye," Ian said. "He recognized true beauty when he saw it."

The timbre of his voice made Ailsa hurt, both with grief for William and something else. She did not look at Ian's face. She did not wish to know what he was thinking.

Mairi looked uneasily from Ian to Ailsa. She decided then and there that no matter how serious Duncan was, she was taking no chances. She would write to Eleanor Williston tonight and stop this spark of dissension before it became a flame and then a conflagration that devoured them all.

10

WHEN IAN GOT HOME, GLENYSS WAS WAITING OUTSIDE, HER dark hair bathed in moonlight, eyes glittering with distress. Ian felt her agitation as surely as if she had touched him with a cold and heavy hand. He glanced longingly at the golden lamp glow through the windows of the croft, but knew he would not feel its comfort soon enough. Ian put his arm around his daughter's shoulders. "Would ye like to walk a bit?"

Glenyss released her breath in a grateful sigh. "Aye. By the river. The water always calms me."

The weight of her father's arm also calmed her. His mere presence, the reassuring smell of peat and smoke and sweat that were so much a part of him, reminded her that the world had not changed. She was still safe. Ian was there.

As they walked through the long grasses and bracken, the dew clinging to their ankles, Ian sensed by her stiff silence that his daughter was reluctant to speak. "You're upset about Uncle Duncan and his friends, are ye not?"

Glenyss nodded, fists clenched.

"Ye needn't be, ye ken. He's full of purpose and hot air just now, but he'll soon see he's mistaken. Then he'll leave us in peace. My brother doesn't like the glen, birdeen. 'Twill soon begin to bore him."

Glenyss thought of her uncle's fervor as he spoke to the men he called Howard and Black. She thought of Jenny and the things she'd told the strangers. The girl shivered violently. "They don't call each other by their names, but only Fraser and Black and Howard, as if they're not men but whole families without faces."

Ian heard an undercurrent of panic that had nothing to

do with what Duncan called his friends. Curious, though, that he'd thought the same thing when he heard his brother refer to the strangers by their family names. Ian had grown up in a place where everyone addressed each other with easy informality, even their enemies, because they'd known each other forever, or their families had known each other, or their ancestors. But Duncan was a stranger even to the men he called friends. No wonder David had fled Glasgow, searching for peace, a family, a home.

Glenyss was caught up in her own little nightmare. She could see her mother's face as clearly as if it were painted on the half-circle of the moon, and the flourishing sound of the water—a silver ribbon through the deep green woods— did nothing to dim or erase the vivid image. "Papa, if I tell ye something—" She broke off, uncertain how to continue. She knew what was right and wrong, but she was confused in her heart. She twisted her fingers together until they felt raw.

Ian urged her to sit on a boulder beside the river, where the mist off the water drifted over them, cooling their heated skin. "Ye can trust me, if that's what you're asking. I'll not tell another."

Glenyss ducked her head. "No, it's not that." She forced herself to meet her father's steady green gaze. " 'Tis something I heard today. No one told me not to tell. I'd no' think they knew I was there at all. But still . . ."

Ian understood her quandary. He had taught her to be honest, but not to betray a trust. He had taught her to listen, but not to repeat what was not her business. Ian took Glenyss's cold hand between his and rubbed it slowly to warm it. "Ye must do what *you* think is right, *mo-ghray*. If ye tell me and regret it, it will haunt ye in your dreams. But if 'tis no menace to anyone, then mayhap 'tis all right. Ye decide."

Glenyss raised her head. Her father's confidence in her judgment was precisely what she needed. "If 'tis a danger to anyone, 'tis to ye and everyone else who loves the glen." She met his gaze and said firmly, "Uncle Duncan and the others are waiting for some papers from the Willistons. He said they'll be coming day after tomorrow. He said they need them to go on. There's a messenger on the way. So I thought ... mayhap ..." She faltered.

"I can guess what ye thought, and you're right to tell me. Thank ye, birdeen, for trusting me." Ian regarded his daughter anxiously, remembering the many times when she'd come to him, worried about a disagreement between her parents, a slight against Erlinna by someone older, Brenna's unhappiness as she grew from child to woman. Glenyss listened with all her senses and heard with her heart alone. That empathy for others' pain could hurt her someday, drain her of passion and fill her with dread. He would have to talk to Jenny about their middle daughter. Jenny would know what to do.

Ian forced his attention back to Glenyss's worried face, pale in the gloom of the woods, as if she had absorbed the fragmented light from the water. "Don't ye fash yourself. If I should meet this messenger on his way, I promise they'll think I stumbled upon him as I walked the fields in search of a lost sheep." He smiled at the thought. There was at least one sure way to delay the messenger. Ian hugged Glenyss and she clung to him in the now complete darkness, so he could not see that her furrowed brow was no smoother, nor her haunted eyes more clear.

Ailsa was helping with cutting and drying the peat the next day when she felt eyes upon her and turned to find Glenyss Fraser watching. She tucked a chestnut tendril behind her ear and left a smudge of soil on her cheek. She was aware that she did not look much like a grieving widow in one of Alanna's oldest brown linsey-woolsey gowns, the skirts tucked up around her knees, which were covered with loam. Her hands were blistered and filthy, but she was enjoying the texture, weight and fragrance of rich earth between her fingers. It was good to kneel in the sun and follow the rhythmic process of cutting, binding and stacking, to be useful again.

Disheveled and content, she shrugged at Glenyss in a mute apology, but the girl did not look away. Twice more Ailsa glanced up to find that steady gaze fixed upon her.

Curious, she wiped her hands on her capacious apron and went to sit beside the girl.

"Ye looked troubled," Ailsa said carefully. "Is there aught I can do?"

Glenyss glanced around wildly, as if she'd been caught in some grave misdeed and expected punishment at any moment. She heaved a sigh of relief when she saw that everyone was occupied and none were paying her any mind. No one except Ailsa Rose Sinclair, whom Glenyss had watched at dinner the night before. She had seen how often Ailsa's expression reflected her father's, and thought the woman might be an ally.

Glenyss needed someone who would listen and understand. She had not slept all night, thinking of Jenny and the things she had said. She could not go to her mother. Every time she thought of it, Glenyss felt not only fear, but an ovewhelming emotion she refused to call anger. She could not go to Brenna or Gavin, who were high up in the hillside shieling. Besides, she was not certain they would understand.

As Ailsa looked at her with blue-violet eyes full of kindness and mild curiosity, wisps of braided chestnut hair straggling over her cheeks, Glenyss looked around again to make certain they were alone.

Noticing the girl's agitation, Ailsa said, "Come sit in the shade of the willow with me. The sun is warm today." The breeze through the whispering boughs of the willow made a pleasant and private green arbor. When they sat crosslegged among the twisted roots, Ailsa looked at Ian's daughter more closely. She had Jenny's hazel eyes, but her dark, curly hair was just like her father's, except that it hung to her waist in soft waves. Ian was there in his daughter's steadfast gaze, and suddenly Ailsa was nervous.

For a long time there was no sound but the birds in the high branches of the tree and the whisper of the breeze through the long, narrow leaves.

"Were ye ever angry at your mother?" Glenyss asked unexpectedly.

Ailsa stared in astonishment. Whatever she'd been expecting, it was not this.

Before she could answer, Glenyss continued. "I know 'tis wrong. Ye should respect your mother and father. But ..." Her cheeks were flushed and her breathing labored. "I'm trying no' to be angry, but I can't help it. Do ye think I'll go to hell?"

Ailsa struggled to gain composure. Unconsciously, she reached out to smooth the girl's hair. "I don't think ye will. People who worry as ye do are no' usually the ones the gods set out to punish." She paused. "To tell ye the truth, I think my children spent a good bit of their time angry at me for one thing or another."

Glenyss gaped. "Surely not Alanna? She always speaks of ye so fondly." That was one of the reasons she had chosen to talk to Ailsa, because Alanna respected her mother so much.

Touched by the girl's naïveté, Ailsa smiled sadly. "Aye, even Alanna, though mayhap she was not as often angry as the others. 'Tis the way it is between parents and children, ye ken. Sometimes 'tis simply because you're in each other's company too much. Sometimes 'tis because you're too much alike, and ye see your flaws in one another. 'Tis no' easy to look into the face of your own weakness day after day." She thought of Cynthia and Colin and crumpled her plaid apron in her hands. "And sometimes 'tis because ye are too different and can no' understand one another. But whatever the reason, 'tis no sin unless ye shape your anger into cruelty."

Glenyss pondered this for some time. "Do ye really think so?"

"I've lived it, birdeen, so I believe it." She considered Glenyss's furrowed brow in silence, then said gently, "If ye want to tell me what happened, I've learned how to listen through these many years."

Glenyss looked up at her. "You're not old, Ailsa Rose. You're lovely. Even in your grief. Mama says so." She looked away, and missed the glimmer of tears in Ailsa's eyes.

"Well," Ailsa said, "ye needn't tell me. We'll just sit for a while, shall we, and enjoy the music of the wind."

"She talked to those men!" Glenyss cried. "She told them

we were poor and that she wanted to know about their plan. She wants it to happen, Ailsa." Glenyss could not hide her disgust. "Mama wasn't horrified or frightened at all."

Ailsa took several deep breaths, which did not ease the pounding of her heart. She felt Jenny's betrayal like a blow to her stomach, though she had no right to be so affected, no right to judge Jenny Fraser. But Ailsa could not deny her shock, or her concern for Glenyss, who seemed to feel angry and disloyal, hurt and protective all at once. No wonder she was confused.

"Mayhap she thinks differently than ye and me," Ailsa murmured. That was not the right thing to say. She should not align herself with Glenyss against her own mother. She must take more care in this delicate conversation. How had she come to be here, anyway?

The wind dipped and rose, lifting the feathery green branches and exposing the two, for a moment, to the sunlight. Glenyss blinked and shrank away.

Ailsa took her hand. "You've not betrayed her, little one, because you've told a stranger. Ye were right not to tell your father. I'm no' certain he would understand. But I do know he never once stopped Jenny from saying what she believed. He never told her to think as he did or to lie for him."

"She could have kept quiet."

Ailsa clasped her hands tightly, painfully, beneath her apron. "Mayhap she couldn't. Mayhap she believed so strongly that she had to speak. Don't ye ever feel that way? That if ye keep something inside, 'twill make ye burst?"

Glenyss frowned. "Well, sometimes."

"Then I'll tell ye what I think. I think 'tis all right to be angry at your mother. 'Tis a natural thing between mothers and daughters, as I told ye before." She felt inadequate, as she used to feel when faced with Cynthia's obstinance and inexplicable hostility. "And I think 'tis good that ye've not kept it inside where it can fester like a wound, because that would only hurt ye, and her too, in the end. Ye'd begin to act differently and she'd guess something was amiss.

"But I think, now that you've spoken, ye might try to

forgive her." Ailsa trod warily, forcing herself to concentrate. "Jenny Fraser's a person like ye and me, with an opinion of her own."

"But Papa and Mama've always agreed before," Glenyss insisted.

Ailsa cupped the girl's innocent face in her hands, as if she could protect her from the knowledge of painful things she had not yet begun to imagine. "It may have seemed so to ye, but I doubt 'tis true. Two people can no' live together for that many years and always agree. Besides, I'm sure your mother will tell your father how she feels soon enough. Then you'll no' have to worry anymore. 'Tis not your weight or your responsibility, birdeen."

"Ye believe that?"

Ailsa looked ineffably sad as she replied, "Aye. Yes, I do."

11

IAN WORKED HARD AT HELPING TO CUT THE PEAT, BUT EVERY so often he slipped away to watch the narrow track that led to the road into the glen. The men who had not gone up to the summer grazing worked together to cut and store peat for the winter, as well as caring for the oats, barley and corn, and seeing to the salting and smoking of fish and meat. There was much to be done, and fewer to do it than usual.

Still, Ian slipped away as often as possible. He did not know where Duncan and Black and Howard were. He hoped they were well occupied and waiting complacently for the messenger to come to them. Ian himself watched and waited, gazing up at the sky, half covered with gray clouds, at the water of the loch, untouched by a summer breeze. The track was half in the cool shade of oak and larch, pine and rowan, half in the light of the sun, swathed now in clouds full of moisture, now in nothing but an expanse of azure.

"Lovely day for a stranger to visit the glen, don't ye think?"

Ian looked up in surprise at the sound of Ailsa's voice, not only because he had not expected her, but because of the note of laughter he heard there. She was wearing a dove gray gown, and for the first time, she wore ribbons in her hair, which was braided loosely down her back. Since the day she returned from London, she had worn it tightly wrapped around her head, emphasizing the pale shadowed skin of her face.

But now her chestnut braid hung free, and the sun had begun to put color back in her cheeks.

"What do ye mean?" Ian asked as she set down a basket and sat beside him.

Ailsa leaned close, though there was no one to hear her. "Glenyss told me about the messenger. I thought, since the path is long and the trip tiring, it might be nice to greet him, mayhap show him the way."

Ian was amazed at the change in his childhood friend. It was as if a shadow had lifted from around her shoulders, leaving her lighter, so she moved more fluidly, as she used to do. With an effort, he forced his mind back to the messenger. "Aye, I thought the same. My brother's no doubt too busy measuring and scraping and counting to think of the poor man's discomfort. 'Tis a kindness I'm thinking of, is all."

Ailsa nodded gravely. "A kindness."

Ian glanced at the large basket questioningly.

"I thought, since 'tis such a hard journey, he might be hungry and weary. He might like some refreshment." She removed the cheesecloth to reveal meat pies and cheese and an otterskin full of water, as well as some soft, fresh bannocks. Beneath the food was a glimmer of white that looked like paper.

"I thought the same," Ian said, holding up a pouch he wore on a woven reed strap over his shoulder. "But I brought whisky." He eyed the flash of white in the bottom of the basket, but did not ask what Ailsa intended.

She answered anyway. " 'Tis only right to give the men something to entertain them if ye plan to take their prize away. An exchange of ideas, ye might say."

Ian hooted. He had a pretty good notion that his brother preferred his own ideas to anyone else's and would not welcome such an exchange. "No harm in trying."

"Hush!" Ailsa cried, pulling Ian down behind a gorse bush twined with purple heather. "I see someone!"

It began to rain lightly. Ailsa tilted her head toward the sky, tasting the cool, clean rain on her tongue as if she had been thirsty for a very long time. Her cheeks were flushed and wet, but she didn't care. She turned back toward the road, but not before she caught a glimpse of Ian looking at her with an unreadable expression in his eyes.

A lone man had appeared on the road. From so far away, they could tell nothing about him, except that he wore a cap and an overcoat and his shoulders were slumped with fatigue. The stretch of road that narrowed into the track that meandered through the woods was bright, just now, with sunlight. The man shrugged off his overcoat and a knitted scarf and rubbed his face with his sleeve.

When he moved into the forest, disappearing under the thick green canopy, the rain began to fall and a chilly wind rose off the loch. He came into sight again, the overcoat tightly buttoned, the scarf wrapped securely around his neck, his hands buried deep in his pockets. He shivered, and the rain on his face mingled with the sweat.

"He's young," Ailsa murmured, pointing out his awkward, lanky posture and long, bowed legs.

The man moved into the sunlight, away from the shadow of the trees, and they saw that he carried a leather pouch over one shoulder. He paused to scratch his head in bewilderment. Ailsa smiled, and for the first time since she'd arrived in the glen, she did not think of William or the emptiness inside her. She had another purpose now, an enemy to fight who was flesh and blood and muscle, not just smoke and memory. She had been subdued and silent for too long. She could not stop her natural exuberance from bubbling up and filling the dark hole her grief had created. Once Glenyss had mentioned the messenger, Ailsa had known what she had to do. Nothing could have kept her away. It was time.

The man looked up at the sun. The wind had blown the clouds away, and as soon as the shade disappeared, the heat hit him once more. With disgust, he unbuttoned his coat and unwound his scarf. He climbed upward, his cheeks red with exertion.

Then he stepped into the woods and the chill hit him. Cursing violently under his breath, he closed his coat and reclaimed his scarf.

Ian and Ailsa moved along slowly, keeping the young man in sight. Soon he would reach a turning in the path, the best place to catch him up. Ailsa found she was holding her breath.

"We're acting like bairns, ye and me, Ian Fraser," she said. Their quarry had stopped in the shade of a rowan to scratch his head and think things through.

" 'Tis for a good cause, Ailsa Rose, and well ye know it." Ian paused. "Besides, 'tis good to hear ye laugh again, to see the shadows gone from your eyes and the color back in your cheeks." The depth of his relief at her transformation made him uneasy. He had been haunted by the memory of her weary, blank face since she'd come home. He had tried to shut the image out, to block it from his inner sight as he used to do, but he wasn't strong enough this time.

Ailsa shivered at a gust of wind. She felt the risk in being here with Ian, but suppressed the memory of what had once been between them. She had no time for such perilous thoughts now.

They heard the man curse quite clearly and rub his calf. They were close enough to see his dusty face, sagging with weariness. He sighed heavily, hefted the satchel over his shoulder, and continued on his way, into the shade where the chilly wind blew, out into the sun where the June heat assaulted him, time after time.

"Poor man," Ailsa said in genuine sympathy. Both she

and Ian saw his face when he reached the place where the single track branched into three. He stared, confused, from one path to the other. He had no idea which way to go.

Ian and Ailsa met him at the fork in the narrow path. The stranger looked wary, but they approached smiling.

"Who might ye be and where might ye be going?" Ian asked. "Ye look weary and just a bit lost."

"I'm Andy. I've come all the way from London with some important papers, but I've no idea where to go from here." He leaned against a rowan, breathing raggedly.

"I'm Ailsa Rose, and if I knew where ye were going, I'm certain I could help." She paused. "But if 'tis all the way from London ye've come, a little while longer could no' hurt. Ye look thirsty and pale. I've water and food for our dinner. You're welcome to share it."

Andy looked doubtful.

"I'm thinking ye might even like a dram of whisky," Ian added. "There's a lovely shady spot down by the loch where ye could rest. The path from here is uphill and you'll never make it as ye are."

Surprised because he believed this stranger with the heavy Highland brogue, Andy decided he had to rest or he would collapse. That would do his employer no good at all. He knew how impatient Duncan Fraser was. Hat in his hand, he followed them through the dappled green woods to a patch of cotton grass that overlooked the loch and the river it flowed into.

They sat on a wool blanket, Ailsa with her skirts demurely tucked about her feet, Ian reclining on his side and resting on one elbow. Andy stared open-mouthed at the view, and Ian asked casually, " 'Tis such a long way ye've come. Why are ye on foot?"

Andy started to curse, glanced at Ailsa and changed his mind. Highlander or not, she was a lady. "My horse threw a shoe and I had to leave him at Cannich. No one had an extra today, so I've walked from there."

"But that's miles from here!" Ailsa exclaimed, genuinely shocked. "Ye must be starved." She gave him the otterskin to drink from and a meat pie to gnaw on. He ate it in four bites and looked hopefully toward the basket.

Ailsa kept it close to her side, her eye on the satchel Andy had dropped on the grass nearby. She rummaged in her basket and came up with a cold egg rolled in mince. Andy took it gratefully, as he did the first sip of whisky Ian offered, and the second.

Soon all three were pleasantly full. They lolled on the grass, telling Andy amusing stories that made him forget his long, uncomfortable walk. The color had returned to his face and his shoulders were no longer slumped. But he continuously rubbed his face and scratched his arms, trying to rid himself of the dust. Ian took him close to the still loch and, warmed and cheered by whisky, Andy laughed at his own reflection. Half an hour past, he would have glowered at the sight.

Ailsa saw Ian glance back at her, raising one eyebrow as he indicated the water. She understood at once. "I'd best be getting back to start supper," she called. "I hope you're feeling better, Andy. I'm sure Ian can show ye which path to take."

"Thanks for the food. You've been kind," Andy replied in some surprise. He'd not been led to expect kindness from these people.

"I'd do it for anyone. I'm just glad we happened upon ye."

"So am I." He sighed a heartfelt sigh when Ailsa rose, swinging the basket as she disappeared through the trees.

Ian gazed critically at Andy's dusty face and clothing. "A dip in the loch would cool ye down and rinse away the dust. 'Twould only take a few minutes more. I guarantee, the water's magic at making ye forget all aches and pains."

Andy bit his lip in indecision. "What if someone comes?"

"Och! no one will come. 'Tis a secluded place, this. Besides, ye can always duck beneath the water if ye don't want to be seen."

Andy had drunk a lot of whisky and was quite relaxed, especially with all the food in his belly. "All right." Before Ian could move, he began to take off his clothes.

Ian followed suit, rose quickly and dove into the chilly water that refreshed and invigorated him. Andy did not hesitate to imitate him. Soon Ian had guided his guest toward the place where the loch fed into the river and the rushing water glimmered as they splashed it over their heads and shook, beads of water flying and evaporating the dust.

They were just out of sight of the spot where they'd left their clothes. After a minute or two of dunking his head, diving down and erupting from the water with a smile on his face, Andy looked nervously back toward the clearing. "Are you certain she's not up there? That she can't see us?"

"I'm sure she's on her way by now. Because if she were here, it'd be no easy task to keep her from jumping in with ye."

Andy's ears turned pink at the image of the pretty woman with the long chestnut hair and fascinating blue-violet eyes swimming beside him, her wet chemise clinging to her body. He blushed with embarrassment and pleasure at the idea.

All in all, by the time he'd lain in the sun to dry off, shaken out his clothes and followed Ian back to the fork in the path, he was smiling broadly and pleased with the world in general. He had not spent such a pleasant hour for a long time, and he was grateful to the strangers who had offered their hospitality in the middle of these wild, abandoned woods.

Ian pointed out the track that led to the Hill of the Hounds, and watched, eyebrows quirked, as Andy swung his leather satchel over his shoulder. "Just follow the path. Ye can't go astray."

"Thank you," Andy said with fervor. "I don't know what I would have done without you." He smiled, revealing the gap between his front teeth, before he trudged off toward the Hill, where Duncan Fraser would be waiting.

When he'd been out of sight for several minutes, Ian plunged into the hedges and found Ailsa sitting cross-legged behind a thick green holly, the basket in the circle of her legs.

"So," Ian murmured.

"So, I fear Duncan'll be a mite disappointed in the papers

from London, unless, mayhap, he enjoys ancient Celtic poetry." She opened the basket and revealed the thick sheaf of papers inside.

Ian stared hard at the ground. "He'll not even know what it is, I'll wager." He was no longer laughing. " 'Tis no' easy to believe he's my own brother. He was born here, just like me. Yet he can no' begin to understand or appreciate the fine things our ancestors created. The things I love so much."

The regret in his slumped shoulders that was very near despair filled Ailsa with a dangerous compassion. She dared not speak or offer sympathy. For a moment she was silent, then she said softly, "Do ye think he'll blame Andy? I'd no' want him to be hurt because of us."

"He'll probably bluster." Ian shook the dark hair out of his eyes and the dark thoughts from his mind. "But I don't think he'll hurt the man. My brother might be stubborn and greedy, but he's no' violent." Squinting at a kestrel that was swooping overhead, he added, "Still, he'll not be happy about it. He's not got much of a sense of humor, does Duncan."

"I thought not." Ailsa riffled through the papers in her lap. "To tell ye the truth, I'm not longing to read about new roads and costs and such. I prefer a little drama."

Ian laughed. "A little drama indeed. Since you've no interest in the papers, nor have I, I suggest we take them to David for safekeeping."

"Let him have the glory when we've had the hard work?" Ailsa demanded.

Ian leaned close, but did not touch her hand. "I think we had the glory, don't ye? I didn't see David creeping through the bushes like a spy, pouncing on his prey and plying him with laughter, food and drink and a lovely swim in the loch. No, Ailsa. 'Twas ye and me who had the fun today."

They exchanged a look of understanding that went beyond the achievement of thwarting Duncan's plans. Without speaking, in mutual accord, they began to run across the moor waving with foxgloves, through hawthorn, bracken and ferns that grew thick and green by the river. They laughed together, without touching, heads thrown back into the wind, caught up in the sound of their unrestrained pleasure.

All at once, Ailsa was acutely aware of the mountains towering behind them, the sky, decorated with clouds of all shapes and sizes and designs, the loch below, the blue surface broken by tiny whitecaps as the wind raced across where white and black swans floated. Though the loch was behind them now, she could visualize the graceful swans' reflections, blurred and altered by the motion of the water. She heard the sound of squirrels and birds, of butterflies and frogs, the song of the wind in pine and oak and rowan, felt the thick springy turf beneath her sandaled feet, and the damp loamy earth.

She was aware of all these things, as Ian was aware of them, but for the first time, there was no pain in that awareness—only appreciation and a profound gratitude that her home was hers once more. She needed no armor against its beauty. She drank that beauty in, and it filled her where she had been empty.

She glanced over at Ian and knew he felt it too, saw the tenderness in his face, the relief and affection as he watched her running, her hair loose in the breeze, her eyes glistening, her lips curved in a smile he remembered from childhood.

As they approached the river, they glanced at one another, and without a word, they leapt across, legs extended and arms outstretched, their faces gilded by fleeting sunlight. They landed on the far bank at the same time and paused to catch their breath while the wind caught up their laughter and carried it into the verdant ceiling of leaves that met and parted overhead. For that instant, as they paused among the ferns and mosses, hands on their knees and hair in their faces, it was as if they were children again, who knew nothing of pain, separation and loss. For that perilous instant, the laboriously constructed barriers came down, and they knew each other absolutely, more intimately than man and wife.

As Simon Black leaned against the brocade sofa, a film of dust rose around him, making patterns in the sunlight through the heavy velvet drapes that had been opened in the library. He did not notice the dust motes dancing in the light; such things were not of interest to him. "This place is not at all bad, after some of the dust's been removed and the linens aired." They had hired a couple of women from the glen to clean up a bit, revealing fine moldings and dark wainscoting as well as painted and domed ceilings. "Perhaps we should move in while we work out the details. I can't honestly bear the thought of sleeping in that god-awful cottage one more night." He tapped his fingers together and rested his chin on his manicured nails. "Yes, in fact, I think we should all three have our things brought over at once. So much more pleasant, not to mention more practical, to contemplate renovations from the comfort of a house built by an English architect. Don't you agree, Fraser?"

Black didn't really care what Duncan Fraser thought. He did not intend to submit to a moment's more discomfort, even if it meant offending the Highlanders. Their opinion mattered very little to him anymore.

Unfortunately, Duncan did agree. He knew he should have been insulted by Black's sneering dismissal of Angus and Flora's home, but the truth was, Duncan himself hated it there. It was dark and close and smelled of peat and soot. The heather and straw beds were so primitive, he lay waiting every night for bugs to pop up and crawl under his nightshirt. He shuddered with distaste. He would be relieved to get out of the croft, and he suspected his parents would feel the same. Irrationally, the thought made him angry.

Duncan turned his attention back to the pouch that had just been delivered. He had sent the messenger off to find Flora and some refreshment before he opened the satchel. He didn't want strangers about. He felt the surge of excitement that always came with a new deal, a new challenge. This one would be a true challenge, he thought, more ticklish than his dealings with shipping magnates and industrialists. He could taste the anticipation as he removed the sheaf of papers and held them to the light. His eyes widened and he stared in disbelief.

"What do they want for the place?" Simon Black asked, alert and suspicious.

Robert Howard had been silent for some time. He watched and listened, waiting for the facts and figures that would make this venture real to him. Now he leaned forward expectantly.

Duncan swallowed. "They want: Anger of Fire; Fire of Speech; Breath of Knowledge; Wisdom of Wealth; Sword of Song; Song of Bitter-edge."

"What the devil!" Robert Howard sat up sharply. They had discovered a bottle of fine old port in the wine cellar and had been drinking to each other and their plans while they waited for the papers. Howard almost knocked over the decanter in his agitation. He could see over Duncan's shoulder that the pages were covered with ornate calligraphy. Not at all the kind of thing they were expecting.

"It's a sheaf of old poems," Duncan said in an ominous voice. "Not even in the King's English. Damn that brother of mine. We've got to get the messenger back."

"What makes you so certain it was your brother? And you'll never get Andy back now. He disappeared so fast I thought he might be trying to make it back to Glasgow tonight." Simon Black's face was grim, the lines between his nose and mouth deeply etched. His eyes were dark with simmering anger.

Duncan dropped the papers on the table in disgust. Robert Howard fingered them as if they might be dirty or tainted with disease. He was more distraught than angry. He'd

12

thought things were going so well. "What do they think this is, a game?"

Duncan whirled, eyes narrowed on Howard's pleasant face. Neither his expression nor his tone held a trace of humor. "I suspect that's exactly what they think. They don't seem to care that I'm trying to help—"

"Save that speech for your family. I'm weary of hearing it," Black snapped. "I think it's time we impressed upon them that we're quite serious and not to be taken lightly. We're stronger than they are, and smarter, and we've far more money." He brushed a bit of dust off his silk cravat. "They're not going to spoil our plans, and they might as well accept it right now. Petty conflicts bore me. That's why I left Glasgow."

Howard shook his head, brow furrowed in concern. "I don't know. They seem determined." He tugged nervously on his shirt cuffs and the cashmere sleeves of his jacket.

Duncan wouldn't let him finish. "Determined to spite me, most likely. They don't care what I'm doing, just that I'm the one doing it."

Howard leaned heavily on the rosewood desk. He'd heard the bitterness in Fraser's voice, and the hurt. It surprised him. He'd thought Duncan Fraser a hard, cold man with nothing but profit on his mind. That was what Duncan had wanted him to think, had, in fact, gone to considerable trouble to convince everyone in Glasgow of. This bitterness bothered Howard. It was a weakness. He had a glimmer of why exactly Fraser had chosen this house and this glen. He was trying to prove something, but was it to himself or his brother or his son? Who? And what purpose would it serve his partners?

Howard felt more and more uneasy. "Black is right. We've got to make things clear. They can't trifle with us." He was trying to convince himself as much as the others, but the slight nervous tic in his left eye betrayed him. "We *are* stronger. They've got to recognize it." He thought of Jenny Fraser and smiled slightly. Now there was a sensible woman. Perhaps he'd try to talk to her again, convince her of their sincerity, question her about the motives of the other Highlanders. One had to understand an enemy before one could best them.

Duncan glowered into the shaft of sun that illuminated dirt and mildew that would soon turn to decay on velvet and brocade and Persian wool. His brother had made a fool of him in front of his associates. It would not happen again.

Before he could open his mouth to say so, Black spoke for him. "Oh, they'll recognize it soon enough. Indeed they will. I'll see to it."

Ailsa and Ian found that David had just returned to his new cottage before they arrived. Alanna offered her mother and Ian ale and black buns, but they refused, meeting each other's eyes with veiled amusement. They were intoxicated with the pleasure of outwitting Duncan, and had not yet begun to think logically, rationally, safely.

David was unconcerned by Alanna's worried glance. He had heard much about how Ian and Ailsa had once been sweethearts, but he did not wish to think about what this strange rapport between them meant. Probably nothing at all, if he knew his uncle. He was surprised that he believed so completely in Ian's integrity. He'd not felt that way about any man for a very long time.

"We've something for ye to keep," Ian said. He glanced at Ailsa, who opened the basket to remove the papers she had taken from Andy's satchel while he and Ian were bathing.

"Your father ordered these papers brought from London, but we thought he needn't have them right away." Ian explained what he and Ailsa had done. "We'll not make it easy for Duncan to deceive himself. 'Tis simply too far between civilization and Glen Affric." Or so Ian devoutly hoped. He refused to recognize a ripple of doubt.

David was astonished. He had not thought Ian and Ailsa capable of intrigue. His respect for his uncle grew, but as he flipped through the papers, it faded beneath rage for his father. "He's already contacted the Willistons and apparently told them we all want this. Here's their answer. They sound unsure, but they don't say no."

Ian was surprised, but he felt certain the Willistons would refuse in the end. "Mairi wrote them. If they're considering your father's offer, they'll soon change their minds."

For the first time, David was irritated at his uncle's complacency, his faith that all people would do the right thing, once they understood what was at stake. He tensed, flipped another page and saw a floor plan of the house on the Hill. Another gave details of a map and proposed roadway. "Damn it to hell!" he shouted.

Abruptly, he tossed the papers into the low-burning peat fire, over which Alanna was cooking a mutton and pepper broth. They caught at once, flared for a minute, mesmerizing everyone, then fell into smoldering red ashes.

"David." Alanna spoke his name and nothing more. She felt his flare of fury but did not understand it. For the first time since she'd met him, the coiled tension inside her husband frightened her.

"There was no need for that." Ian rose and tried to tell his nephew that years of pent-up fury at his father were coloring his judgment, but he could not find the words. David's rage burned in his green eyes like the sun through frail new birch leaves, and he ran his hands through his dark hair repeatedly. Ian realized that if he spoke now, he risked losing David's trust, and he did not want that.

"Why did ye do it?" Ailsa asked, dismayed.

"There must have been a reason." Alanna had conquered her momentary fear and slipped her arm through her husband's.

"I say burn the damned house as well. Then they might go away and leave us in peace." David's voice was steady, more menacing in his restraint than an explosion.

Ailsa rubbed her arms, chilled by David's potential for violence, the smoldering anger that had burned for years. Now Alanna was part of that anger. Ailsa did not want a battle with her daughter as a soldier. All she wanted was for the strangers to leave the glen as they had found it, and soon.

Gripping Alanna's hand as if it were a lifeline, David stared into the fire. In Glasgow, he had learned how difficult it was to preserve the things he believed in most deeply. The forces for profit were stronger than the forces for truth or human kindness. So he'd taught himself to fight hard and never to give in. It was the only way to save his integrity and spirit. In his eyes, his father was attacking both now, by threatening the place David had chosen and the woman he loved. He would fight again to save the glen. Fighting came naturally to him, and now he had more to protect than ever before.

He stamped on the ashes of the papers, smearing them across the hearth stones. "I mean it. Let's burn the Hill of the Hounds to the ground and see how long the strangers last then." Saying the words released the last shred of control over his temper. He was ready to get a torch and go in broad daylight to destroy what his father seemed to want so badly.

Ailsa touched her son-in-law's arm, reassured when he did not flinch away. "To begin with, 'tis a lovely house, David, and many of us love it. 'Twould no' be right to destroy it. I know ye think us foolish, but we follow our own laws, and the first law of the Highlands is unconditional hospitality. Ye must always leave a traveler who comes to ask a favor with some hope, even if ye can't do as he wishes. Ye can't be unkind to those who come asking for shelter. But that doesn't mean ye can no' outwit them. The second law is that 'tis a sin beyond all sins to destroy beauty. Try it our way for a bit," she pleaded. "Think of Alanna. If ye burn the Hill and they catch ye, ye'll go to prison. Your father would win and Alanna would lose."

"Besides, there's the risk of burning more than ye meant to." Ian was increasingly nervous as David paced before the hearth, hands locked behind his back. "Would ye want to ravage the glen yourself, to stop your father from doing so?"

David sighed wearily. "I know these people. They'll take advantage of your kindness and hospitality. They'll not take no for an answer."

"Mayhap you're right," Ian said. "But give us a little time to try. We don't want ye or Alanna getting in trouble. From the look in her eyes, she'd follow ye there, even if the flames were climbing up her skirt."

"Aye," Alanna said, eyes glittering. "So I might." She wished this was not so personal for David, that he was not so determined to fight his father at every turn. But if he did, she'd stand beside him and fight as well. The thought made her pulse race, though she knew it was madness.

Ailsa was terrified by the look in her daughter's eyes. "Promise us, David, no' to strike a blow before they strike at ye. Promise us to wait."

David heard her desperation, felt Alanna tremble and knew it was not with fear. "They've already struck," he said quietly. "Ye just can't see it. But I'll wait, just the same. For a little while at least."

With that, Ian and Ailsa had to be content.

13

JENNY HAD BEEN OUT COLLECTING REEDS, HER PLAIN BROWN linsey-woolsey gown tucked up to keep it dry. She stood ankle deep in sluggish water where the reeds grew thickest, when she heard the men coming. They had been muttering angrily among themselves, but when they saw her, they'd made their faces blank, then summoned forced smiles. Robert Howard had offered to help her, but she'd climbed out of the water and walked with them instead, the dripping reeds in a creel over her arm.

She forgot her limp brown hair, escaping from its tightly woven braid, forgot her tucked-up skirt, now damp and muddy at the edges, as she asked questions about their plans and heard how many people could be put to work building the road from Inverness south and Fort William north, how many would be needed to refurbish the house, how many to work at the lodge after it was done, how much milk and cheese and eggs and oats and barley they would need to keep the place stocked.

It sounded like riches to her, like a blessing she'd been praying for without knowing. She was full of hope, and turned toward home thinking seriously about Ian's opposition to Duncan's scheme. Was it possible he was jealous of his brother's power and wealth, his ability to bring relief where Ian could not? That was an unworthy thought, and Jenny dismissed it. Ian was not that kind of petty man. Besides, he was not alone.

As she passed Alanna and David's croft, Jenny saw Ian and Ailsa duck beneath the door and step outside.

They did not touch but walked together, heads bent, talking quickly, with spirit and intensity. There was an ease in their conversation, a rapport and empathy that was nearly a physical thing. The air around them, free of mist or wind or the shadows of clouds, was vibrant with energy, the understanding between them complete and unspoken.

Jenny could name now what she had sensed but not understood in her childhood—the intimacy between her husband and Ailsa Rose Sinclair that was a rare and precious thing. Ducking her head, she slipped quietly back to her own croft, where Erlinna and Glenyss waited.

When Ian came in later, he had obviously been to the bank where they were cutting peat today. Bits of green and drifts of earth clung to his trousers and homespun shirt, and his hands were caked with mud. Jenny was silent while he washed in the shallow sink, pumping the water until it dribbled, tinted brown from the spout. He seemed younger somehow; his step was light despite the threats and undercurrents running through his precious glen. His green eyes glimmered with expectation.

Jenny frowned and was silent as she left the reeds to soak and prepared the evening meal. She moved stiffly, her still-damp skirts rustling about her ankles. Though she did not speak or criticize, Ian felt her anger. He had lived with her for many years, and recognized the hurt in her eyes when he caught a glimpse of her contained and controlled face.

"What is it that troubles ye?" he asked softly. He dared not speak loudly; she seemed so fragile that a single harsh word might shatter her control.

Jenny looked at Glenyss, who watched her parents with wide hazel eyes, and Erlinna, who was climbing over Ian and laughing, begging for a game or a song. "Can ye girls go out and see what's ripe in the garden and mayhap pull some weeds from among the rows while you're there?" Jenny asked.

Erlinna was content to race for the door, for the sun was out and the day was fair and the summer flowers in bloom. She loved the sunlight and wanted to catch as much in her open arms as she could. Glenyss hesitated for a moment, brow furrowed, then did as her mother had bidden her.

When they were gone, Jenny took a deep breath and found an answer to Ian's question that was a lie and yet the truth. "I'm thinking about Duncan's idea to turn the Hill into a hunting lodge. I know how ye feel about it, but you've no' asked me." She took the risk of facing her husband directly. "I've been talking to Robert Howard about their plans, telling him my worries. I think it might be the very thing we need, but ye don't seem willing to consider both sides. I don't understand why 'tis so important to ye to keep out strangers that ye'll no' even listen to what they have to say."

Ian stared at his wife, stunned. He could not take in what she was saying. This was not a disagreement about how to discipline Erlinna, with her overactive imagination, or what to do with the small amount of silver from the crops. This was much more. And Jenny, who had always trusted him, looked up to him, believed in him, was taking his brother Duncan's side.

Ian could not believe it. He glowered at the table, at his work-roughened hands and the pitted wood beneath. Just an hour since, he had felt young, he had laughed—the kind of laughter that came from deep inside, an echo of the burn running over smooth stones, of the birds that warbled their song to the dawn. The sound faded as Jenny spoke. He wanted his wife to turn and smile as if she had not spoken, to make him laugh that way again. It was selfish, that desire, and fleeting. There were things that were possible and things that were not.

He thought carefully before he answered, and for the first time, his doubts about the strangers turned to fear. He would do anything to protect his home from men from Glasgow and London who would not, could not care for this place. "They see Glen Affric only in terms of the wealth it can bring them. To me 'tis the food for my soul, the only sustenance I need."

"Our children need more." Jenny was obdurate. "They need to know there'll be food on the table, not only for them but for their children."

Ian stiffened. His wife was staring out the door, as if she did not wish to see his response. "Has there no' always been food on our table? Have I no' always taken care of my family?"

Only when Jenny heard the hurt in his voice did she realize what she had said. "Oh, Ian, of course ye have. But things are different now. Every year 'tis harder to get by. That will no' change unless we make it change. Even ye can no' stop what's happening in the glen, in all of Scotland." She moved closer but did not meet his gaze. "All I want is to stop fretting over the future, to feel a wee bit safer. Ye know this is my home. I wouldn't want to go, but neither do I want to fight these men who might make our lives easier."

Ian tried hard to swallow his pride, but he was apprehensive because she would not look at him, staggered by the feeling that she had changed, she had betrayed the understanding that had always been between them. "Jenny, ye can no' have both. With change will come the future as 'tis in the world outside the glen. That wee bit of safety will cost us the sanctity of this place. It'll no longer be ours, *moghray*. It will no longer be so quiet and so beautiful. It will belong to strangers. I could no' bear that." He paused to clear his throat, attempting to banish his anger and hurt.

"Besides, 'tis my responsibility to see our children don't

go hungry, mine and Gavin's. And now we have David to work with us. Why would ye look to strangers? You've never told me ye were afraid."

Ian grasped his wife's hand and finally she met his eyes. "Why, Jenny? Why would ye tell a stranger what ye'd no' tell your own husband?" He could not hide the pain that tightened in his chest as he looked into her frightened eyes.

"I didn't want to hurt ye, to make ye think I wanted more than ye could give. I know how hard ye work, all of ye."

"But 'tis not enough to quiet your fears."

Jenny closed her eyes and bit her lip; she could not bear the look in Ian's eyes. "Ye don't understand. 'Tis more than hunger or the failure of next year's crops I fear."

"What?" Ian asked. Though she tried to pull away, he would not release her hands. "Tell me."

Hesitantly, Jenny opened her eyes and gripped her husband's hands tight. "Ailsa."

A single word, but Ian understood. He drew his wife close until they stood hip to hip. "I married ye, Jenny, *mo-charaid*. I'm true to that promise every day of my life, and will be."

Jenny believed him, but could not find her voice.

Ian saw that she needed more. "I've no' touched her improperly, nor let her inside me."

"I know that."

He was surprised by her certainty. "How is it ye know?"

"Because I know the man ye are. You're no liar, nor a cheat, nor would ye hurt me that way."

Yet she was still troubled. Her eyes were shadowed and her face set in lines of worry. "Well then? Why do ye hesitate?" he asked.

Jenny broke away from him and went to the counter where she had begun to make oatcakes. Here she was comfortable; here she was safe. "I'd almost rather ye lay with her." At the profound silence that followed, she twisted her hands in her skirt. "I saw ye when ye lost her the first time, and later, watched as ye closed yourself away from her. I saw your suffering and what it cost ye." She whirled to face him. " 'Tis not her body that threatens me, Ian. Ye know that as well as I. 'Tis the friendship and the history ye share. She knows ye as I can't. I've tried, but I can't."

She turned back to the mixture of oats and pounded it until the flour rose like dust on a dry summer road.

Ian watched her, unmoving, uncertain if she was angry at him or Ailsa or herself.

Jenny looked up with tears in her eyes. "I've no right to tell ye who your friends should be." She was torn by the truth of it, and bleeding inside, but she would not lie. "If I could say to ye, 'Lie with her but be her friend no more,' I would." She absorbed Ian's shocked expression, then smiled thinly. "No, I suppose I'd not say that either. I'm just blethering, is all, and wondering what will become of ye and me."

Ian took her in his arms. "No harm will come to us, to ye. I'll keep ye safe, my Jenny. I love ye."

"I know." Nevertheless, she burst into tears and sobbed on his shoulder. Because she also knew that what he felt for her, even after all these years, would never be the same as what he'd felt for Ailsa. It was real, not a dream.

"I love the glen too, Ian," his wife said, trying desperately to forget that she'd spoken Ailsa's name aloud so that now it hovered between them. " 'Tis my home. But 'tis different for me. The children—"

"Our children will no' starve. They'll survive. We all will." He was grateful that she'd turned from the subject of Ailsa, but now his anger rose again.

"I'm not so certain of that. Ye work hard, Ian, but ye dream harder. 'Tis not the same as when ye were younger. The world is changing."

"Which is why we must fight with our last breath to save the glen. So there's something to hold on to, some part of the beauty and purity of the past. Something the gods made and treasure and love. Not something made by men whose hearts stopped pulsing long ago, when they first tasted money and it became their blood. In that moment, they ceased to dream. I can no' do that, Jenny. 'Twould kill me, I swear."

"I know." She understood, vaguely, obscurely, his passion for this land and its history, but she did not feel that passion.

Her children's future meant more to her than the glen—gods or no gods. A flicker of doubt, raised by her strict Church of Scotland upbringing, made her wonder if sometimes Ian spoke blasphemy, but she knew his heart was good, and to her that was enough. Still, the gods Ian worshiped were pagan and therefore alarmingly unpredictable, unlike Jenny's angry and punishing God who never changed.

She held her husband tighter and he ran his hand through her hair, pulling out the pins as he went. Jenny sighed and kissed him and thought a little blasphemy of her own. She knew she should put her faith in the God her father had taught her to worship, but it was Ian she believed in in her heart, and always had been.

14

MAIRI WAS DRAWN TO THE VALLEY OF THE DEAD JUST AFTER dawn. The place where her husband was buried had been her refuge and her penance long before Charles Kittridge lay there. She was restless, and sought peace in the familiar circle of stones where she had often wept. The air was full of contradictions, of fear and anger, derision and disbelief—so many feelings that she could not sort them out. She pulled her plaid tightly around her, though the lilac dawn was warm, barely draped with fine mist. She must be getting old, she thought. Her bones became chilled easily, her thoughts easily tangled. She could not look into the dew at dawn and twilight and see what was to come. Especially today. There were too many voices in her head.

She stopped at the entrance to the valley when she realized the voices were real. Duncan Fraser, Simon Black and Robert Howard were standing in the center of the circle of standing stones, staring intently at the four cairns. For an instant, Mairi was deafened by rage that they should be here, standing casually in a sacred place, speaking loudly and irreverently. Then she heard what they were saying.

"This is a marvelous run for the deer in hunting season. But the graves are in the way. Isn't there some law or other about keeping graves in the churchyard? We could make them move the bodies, couldn't we?"

That was Robert Howard, the soft-spoken one, and Mairi was horrified. "Ye dare not touch this place!" she cried, startling them with her wrath. Her plaid hung loosely over her shoulder, whipped back by the wind like the bright red hair of a witch or a demon. Her own hair was loose and streaming, silver mingled with red; she had not taken the time to braid it this morning. "It has been a temple to one god after another long before your people came to Alba. 'Tis sacred, I tell ye."

Simon Black rubbed his bare jaw slowly, thoughtfully. He alone was not alarmed. He had become used to Highlanders popping up everywhere they went, to being watched by narrow, suspicious eyes. He liked these people less and less. "If this place is so old and valuable, perhaps we should have archaeologists come dig out the cairns and stones to study them. They might shed some new light on the Celtic past. We'd be happy to help the historians any way we can."

Mairi fought to take in deep, steadying breaths of air. She was certain Black and Howard didn't give a damn about history, only their own profit. It was one thing to talk of renovating the Hill and inviting strangers to shoot and fish. But this was far more cataclysmic. She would not let them intimidate her.

"These are no' ancient cairns. Beneath these stones lie no chambered temples of Pict or Celt, no sepulchers or treasures. Bones and teeth and shredded clothes are all ye'll find there, of value to no one but those who buried them. The dead who lie here have found their rest. You've no right to take it from them."

The three men were momentarily silenced by her passion. "If they're resting," Robert Howard said at last, "why does the valley feel so macabre and strange? Why does the wind sound like a dying human voice? Hunters would not want to come to this place. They'd shy away from the terrible wind and the cold that goes straight through to the bone, even on a sunny day." He shuddered and forced himself to focus on Mairi. "Does it really matter *where* someone is buried, so long as they *are,* particularly after all this time? I don't feel peace in the shadows of these stones. We just want to silence those eerie voices."

"Ye can move the bones, but even ye have not the power to still the voices in the wind or to change its maze-like path. Wind, earth and water have souls of their own. They'll always speak more loudly than yours. Ye would do well to listen."

Duncan, Black and Howard stared at her blankly. "Ye talk of prosperity for all, but I think ye've none in mind but yourselves. Ye have no faith, no respect, no loyalty or reverence."

Duncan and Robert Howard shifted uneasily, disturbed by her vehemence. In some way they could not explain, they were afraid she spoke the truth, and were astonished at themselves. They were not usually superstitious but eminently practical men. Duncan faced Mairi resolutely. "These graves and this valley don't fit with our plans. We have no wish to be disrespectful, but we must be practical as well."

Mairi took a deep breath. "Ye do not honor the earth nor the water. Ye do not honor the wee animals and their freedom. To ye the past is no' sacred, but an annoyance to be ignored or pushed out of the way. Even the dead are not sacred to ye. What *do* ye hold sacred?"

The light-haired Robert Howard opened his mouth to answer. Before he could speak, he tensed, staring off into the gorse and long grasses between the tall stones. Abruptly he drew a pistol from under his coat and fired into the shadows.

Everyone stared at him in astonishment. Howard himself was pale and trembling. With a visible effort, he got himself under control. "I saw a wildcat," he breathed, as if terrified that the sound of his voice would make the animal pounce.

Mairi glanced into the shadows where the wind played in the grass and whined among the boulders. She did not think a wildcat had been near, but these men were skittish and easily frightened by things they could not understand. She suspected Robert Howard had heard no more than the wind. She turned to him pensively. "A cat'd no' hurt ye unless ye attacked her or surprised her in her lair and she fought to protect her wee ones. If 'twas a cat indeed, 'twas probably just curious." She eyed his pistol narrowly. "But your gun will've frightened her. It frightened me. Ye might wait next time to fire till you're certain there's real danger. The sound alone could have brought these rocks tumbling around us."

Robert Howard flushed and put his pistol back into the waistband of his trousers. He always carried it while in the Highlands. He did not like wild things, animals that did not know the rules of civilized behavior and therefore could not follow them. Simon Black carried a gun as well—a wise precaution, he called it. Howard could not help but agree.

In resignation, Mairi turned back to Ian's brother. "About the valley."

Duncan was weary of passionate speeches and sly opposition, weary of attempting to make blind people see. "We're trying to help you."

Mairi whirled. "Ye've not yet told me what ye hold sacred."

Duncan paled. "My God, my family and their welfare."

"But not your own?" She looked skeptical.

"Of course my own. God does not judge well a man who fails to better himself, and who doesn't seek to better his family."

"What if your family doesn't *want* your help?"

"They are proud but not foolish." Duncan crossed his arms forcefully. "They'll see the wisdom in what we do soon enough."

Mairi winced at his sincerity. He believed what he said. She felt compassion, even pity, that he knew his son, his brother so little. "What of the ghosts of our ancestors? How will ye make them understand?" She spoke wearily, and her age showed in the lines of her face. She knew she was talking into the wind, that these men would hear her no more than they heard the cries of the ghosts or the gods. But she had to say the words, to try. To fight for what she believed in and could not bear to lose.

The corn was waist high as David and Alanna walked down the furrowed rows with swaying stalks of green between them. Alanna carried a basket in which she kept the wildflowers she dug out from the loamy ruts between the rows. The weeds she bundled together and tossed aside. David was examining the budding ears of corn, tight and small with ridged green leaves curled around them protectively. He was looking for worms or signs of other pests or the nibbling of birds, but his mind was elsewhere.

"They're talking about putting up a dam that would flood out half the crops in this part of the glen." He and his wife had not spoken for several minutes; the silence hung between them, heavy in the hazy air. Yet David spoke as if in response to a question just asked, as if Alanna's stillness were the hush of expectation.

Tucking a stray tendril of hair behind her ear, Alanna tugged her hat down so the shadow of the brim fell over her face. The sun made a pattern on her skin through the interwoven straw that hid her expression. She felt a flare of alarm, but as she bent to pick a handful of sundew, the feeling faded. " 'Tis madness," she said, "even for them." She tilted her head and considered David's sunburnt face. "It'll no' happen, *a'-ghraidh*. Even those who want change don't want destruction. We'll not let it happen."

When David didn't answer, she stopped, reaching through the tall green stalks to touch his arm. His jaw was rigid and his eyes cold. He had drawn inside himself, but Alanna knew his outrage was not at her. "I'm not a fool, ye ken. I know they'll not go quietly. I know 'tis no game, and I'm no' laughing. But David, they'll not flood us out of our homes. We'll tear the dam down stone by stone if we must. But I tell ye, 'twill no' come to that." He remained unresponsive. "Ye don't believe me. I don't think ye *want* to. Why?"

David examined a tiny furled ear of corn, but he did not see it. What he saw was his wife's face, full of trust and optimism and tranquility, which he treasured above all things. "I've said it too many times. Warnings become old and worn and useless after a time." He wanted to tell her that men like his father had no decency, no compassion, but he could not bear to see the faith fade from her eyes, taking the light and animation with it. He did not want to look into Alanna's face and see doubt, anxiety and cold suspicion. He had to protect her from such things, no matter the cost. His own happiness, his very survival depended on Alanna's gentle but wise innocence.

The thought of its loss chilled him through and he shivered. The only way he knew to fight that cold dread was with hot rage. Jaw clenched, he strove to hide the fury that rose inside him, more bitter, more alarming every day the strangers roamed the glen.

"Are ye cold?" Alanna asked in concern. "Are ye ill?"

David glanced up and his wife froze at the harsh, unforgiving lines of his face. "No," she murmured. " 'Tis much worse than that." Her head felt light and she swayed on her feet, dizzy with the spinning that blurred her vision until it became black. Blinded, she saw a conflagration where anger turned to helpless rage and the flames shot high and hot into the sky. "David!" she cried, "don't—"

He stepped between the stalks of corn and took her in his arms. "I have to do something, Alanna. I have to stop this any way I can." He stared at her face, tinged gray in the gauzy light, into her dark, fathomless eyes—the eyes of a stranger. David pulled her close, so his cheek touched hers. "I don't want to see that look in your eyes ever again. I can't let them destroy you, don't you see that?"

Alanna clung to him so tightly that she ached, but did not answer.

15

MAIRI SAT ON THE STONE WALL AROUND HER GARDEN, SMELL-
ing the herbs and flowers and the scent of pine in the air.
The honeysuckle was so sweet it made her want to weep.
Even the cloudy sky could not diminish her pleasure in
the day.

In her hands she held Lady Williston's letter. She was so
relieved that her old friend had written, she simply sat for
a time with the reassuring weight of the letter in her hands,
not breaking the seal or reading the words. Despite the trouble in the glen, Mairi enjoyed the tang of summer in the air.

"Well," Ailsa said, nudging her mother with her elbow,
"are ye no' going to read it? Come, I'm that curious."

Mairi smiled, pleased that Ailsa was beside her. She did
not wish to be alone in this little croft where she'd lived so
long and through so much. Carefully, she centered the envelope with its heavy red seal on the tartan apron that covered
her plain muslin skirt to protect it from the dyes. She did
not receive many letters, especially now that Ailsa was
home. Her hand trembled.

"Are ye afraid, Mama?" Ailsa asked. "You're shaking."

"Mayhap a little. I've not heard from Eleanor in a very
long time. I don't remember the sound of her voice." Finally, she broke the seal and took out the heavy sheets of
foolscap, covered in Eleanor Williston's elegant scrawl.

Dear Mairi,
  It is good to hear your voice again, even through a
sheet of paper, which cannot for a moment convey the
soothing power of your presence.
  I am shocked and sorry to hear how Duncan Fraser

*and his partners are talking of changing the glen. I would
stop them with my own two hands, but those hands have
grown weak with some wasting illness, and John's business ventures do not prosper.*

*If I had had any other offers for the Hill of the
Hounds, believe me, dear Mairi, I would accept them.
But I have not. We are foundering ourselves and do not
know how else to cope. Duncan Fraser offers cash, and
a goodly amount, which would ease the pressure on John
tremendously. I am shaken with remorse that I should
bring such trouble upon you, but I see no other way out.
Besides, Duncan assures me he will see to your welfare,
and I do believe he has your best interests at heart, despite his obstinace.*

*Believe me, Mairi, I would change things if I could.
Many times I stood before you and you put your gentle
hands upon me, and fed me warm herb tea and made
my troubles fade into the rising steam. I wish I had the
power to do the same for you, but as I said, my hands
are weak. What power they might have had—and that
was little enough—is gone now.*

*What remains are our memories of Glen Affric, the
warmth of the people and the peace we found there for
many years. Those things I will not forget. I thank you
all for those years, and beg your forgiveness, perhaps
even your understanding, for what I must do now.*

*Sincerely,
Eleanor*

Mairi was so cold she could not move. When the color
left her cheeks, then came rushing back, Ailsa took her
hand. "Tell me," she said softly.

"I'm ashamed." Her mother's color was high, yet underneath, her skin was pallid. "I'm a thoughtless fool to show
my family's weakness to the Willistons." She paused to take
a deep breath. "But 'tis no' the worst of it. I've made Eleanor admit *her* poverty and weakness to me. Now she's
haunted with guilt over something she can no' change. I
should've left it be."

"Ye couldn't do that." Ailsa spoke with certainty and a trace of anger.

She thought of that moment with Ian when they'd leapt across the river, laughing. The feeling had faded as soon as the spray dried on her skin, and David's volatile reaction made it disappear completely. Why must such moments always be fleeting, mere glimmers of what joy could be? Meekly, even gratefully, she and Ian had retreated behind the mental veil that held them apart from one another. Ailsa had felt a stab of regret, but it was better this way—safer and wiser altogether.

Suddenly Ailsa felt very isolated, very much alone. "I miss Genevra and Lian." When her sisters were with her, she felt stronger, more certain. But they were far away, as far as William, with their own lives to lead. Why should that make her feel so sad? She looked across the clearing, thick with color and life and change, and her chest ached at the sight.

"We've all done what we can." Purposefully, Ailsa returned to the subject of the letter. "Ye knew the Willistons best. Ye had to try, Mama." She clasped her mother's hand. "I'd not want Eleanor feeling regretful any more than ye would, but I'm thinking it couldn't be helped. She needed to know the truth."

Mairi looked up at her daughter, forty-one years old, and so many of those years lost. "Do ye really believe that?"

"Aye. I must believe some people are no' daft with a sense of their own power, that some Sassenachs can understand."

"Like William did."

Tears sprang to Ailsa's eyes. It was the first time Mairi had admitted that William was more than a stranger who had stolen her only child, the first time she'd admitted that he understood Ailsa's heart, if not her soul. "Aye, like William did."

The paper trembled in Mairi's hands; she felt dry and parched. Ailsa's warmth and certainty were reassuring, but even she could not convince her mother she had not acted heedlessly, foolishly. "I'm confused," Mairi admitted. "I can't think anymore." Only now did she recognize the depth of desperation that had made her write that letter. She did not know what was going to happen. Her wisdom had deserted her, along with the Sight. She was blind and floundering and deeply afraid.

Ailsa felt her mother's fear through her trembling fingers, and though she tried to shut it out, an answering dread raced along her skin like the heat of a fire that burned too close.

David dove into the chilly loch and began to swim vigorously, forcing the water behind him as if it were some impediment he had to push out of his path. His hands sliced the surface with a strength born of anger more than the desire to propel himself forward. He was naked but hardly aware of the water on his skin. He was too hot with fury, though the cool water flowed off his back in a rush.

Alanna left on her chemise and dove in after her husband. She caught up with him easily; David's rage could not propel him as quickly as her familiarity with the water. She watched his dark head disappear, then reappear in a shower of white that shattered the calm azure surface.

"David."

He turned abruptly, treading water in order to meet his wife's imploring gaze. "Don't you see what my father's done, Alanna? I thought by leaving Glasgow, by starting a life of my own, I could forget the battles we've fought over the years, that I could put it all behind me." He flung his head backward, and water skimmed the surface in an ephemeral fragmented pattern.

"But now he's brought the battle here, and I can't avoid it anymore. I didn't hold much sacred in Glasgow, except human life. But now I've learned to believe again, because of you and this place. I can't turn away this time, or hide or flee. I have to face him full on and fight as I never fought before."

Alanna touched her husband's face, buoyed by the water, weighed down by his despair. He was right. If he ran from this confrontation he would lose everything. They all would. If she had given him peace and faith, then he had given her passion. She was wise enough to know that without the quality which made him quick to anger, his passion would not blaze, incandescent and irresistible.

She had caught fire with him, drawn by his fierceness as he was drawn by her contentment. She had never before had something to fight for with all her faith and the strength of her spirit. "What can we do?" she asked.

David kissed her fiercely, one hand outstretched to hold him upright in the water. He had known the exact moment when Alanna began to blaze, and it frightened him. His own rage he could control, or had done, until now. But he did not know how to temper hers, to teach her to protect herself. Yet Alanna was afraid only for him, not for herself. She was thriving on the battle, because she was so certain in her soul that they were right.

"We can't be beaten if our hearts are pure," she declared. "If ye speak and act from your heart, you'll speak the truth, and what ye do will be good."

David thought of his father. "What if your heart is evil?"

"Evil?" Alanna did not believe in such a thing.

"My father acts carelessly, selfishly, unwisely. He hurts people and doesn't even know he's doing it."

"Then he's no' listening to his heart. He's deafened by other voices."

David found the water had cooled his body after all, or perhaps it was Alanna's wisdom. He wished he could share it. "I tell you we're in jeopardy, my love. You must believe me and take care."

"I'm always listening," she said, "and my eyes are open wide."

"I only wish that were enough."

16

ROBERT HOWARD SLOGGED THROUGH THE WOODS, TANGLING his umbrella in low-hanging branches. The rain that penetrated the thick canopy of leaves showered over his fair head. He muttered under his breath. When he reached a stand of larches, the wind nearly ripped the impractical umbrella from his hand. He was mad to be out in a storm like this, with the mist creeping at his back. He could feel it on his neck, cold and wet with a chill that the warm summer rain did not possess. He was so busy cursing and shaking the water out of his hair, the hair out of his eyes, that he did not see her coming. He did not know she was there until she spoke.

"Whatever are ye doing out on such a day?" Jenny Fraser asked in concern. Robert Howard's broadcloth suit was sodden and his hair dripped onto his forehead, darkening his brown eyes. He looked ridiculous struggling with his umbrella, which was no protection against rain swept horizontal by the wind, or diverted into contorted paths by the thick leaves.

In spite of his numb misery, Robert Howard smiled. He had been trying to catch Jenny alone for several days. Despite Simon Black's disapproval, he planned to try and reason with one of the few rational Highlanders he'd met. Though there had been others who saw the merit in Duncan Fraser's plan; enough to give Howard hope. At the very least he might render the opposition harmless by making them give up their campaign of harassment.

They all knew Ian and David Fraser were the backbone of that opposition. To silence them would deflate the flagging energies of those who'd been seduced by the Frasers' passion into trying to stop the improvement of the glen. But perhaps Howard could convince Jenny to change Ian's mind. "I wanted to talk to you," he said.

Jenny stared at him in surprise. Surely that was not why he had come out in the storm. He did not look happy. Even when he managed to get the umbrella upright over his head, the rain battered him. But he stood his ground. Jenny paused, bareheaded, unconcerned about the weather. She was used to it, was wearing her brogues with the holes in the bottom to let the moisture out. Her gown was soaked as well, but she didn't mind. It would dry by the fire soon enough.

"What is it?" she asked in confusion. After her last conversation with Ian, she knew she should not talk to Robert Howard, but she refused to be discourteous.

Howard shrugged, trying to find the right words. "You know our plans. They're to our benefit as much as yours. I won't lie to you about that. But we really do want to see this become a better place. We'll bring so many jobs. But you know all this. We've told you before." He spoke kindly, because he believed, as he looked at her pleasant face, wet brown hair and hazel eyes, that he was acting out of compassion. "We know what we're doing. We've experience at this sort of thing. We're not blind and stupid, you know."

Jenny scrutinized her brogues. "I know." She would not have sought out Robert Howard on her own, but now that he was here, it wouldn't hurt to listen. "I know we need ye, your experience and your money. We've been toiling on our own for so long, and naught ever changes, except for the worse." She looked up. "We must do something. We've no choice. I pray and wait and hope, but the worry never eases."

She heard the rising hysteria in her voice and remembered that she'd planned to tell Robert Howard she'd been wrong, to take it all back for Ian's sake. But she could not do it. For her own sake, she could not. She had been afraid of the future for a very long time. Long before Duncan Fraser had arrived. Until then, there had been no way out, no alternative, no new hope, so she'd refused to name her fear, to admit that it consumed her. Now she saw it clearly and could not deny it anymore. It was too much a part of the flow of her blood. Jenny was obsessed by the fear and dreamed about it every night. It had become so blinding and so painful that she could not help herself; she had to put it into words. "I'm so afraid. So deeply afraid. Tell me what I can do. Please."

She gasped when she realized she'd told a stranger what she had not been able to tell Ian. There was nothing her husband could do to ease her apprehension. Perhaps she could do something for herself. Perhaps she could stop the peril she felt crawling toward her family from out of the darkness. "How can I help?" she asked. "What can I do?"

It was precisely the question Robert Howard wanted to hear. He was touched by Jenny's admission, her confidence in him. For the first time since he'd reached the Highlands, he felt relaxed. His nerves, rubbed raw by the eccentricity of these people and their passion, were salved and silent. "Talk to your husband. Make him understand what you just told me. Make him understand this is good for all of us." From what he'd seen of Ian Fraser, Robert had little doubt what the outcome would be, but he had to try. He felt sorry for Jenny Fraser. "Can you do that?"

Jenny squared her shoulders and threw back her head. "I can try," she said. "I have to try."

When Jenny had slipped away, Robert Howard turned, smiling to himself, and came face to face with a snarling David Fraser.

"You bastard." David's long dark hair was blown by the wind into an untidy mane. The glitter of his green eyes was not human but feral, like the threatening golden eyes of a tiger.

Instantly, Howard's nervous dread returned. He tried to hide the quivering of the hand that held his umbrella. He did not like unruly things, things he could not control with argument or, failing that, bribes. He knew, even in that first moment, that David Fraser was immune to rationality.

"Stay away from our Jenny, do you hear me?" David hissed.

With considerable effort, Howard managed to croak, "We met by accident. I'd no intention—"

"You'd every intention of using her as you use any who might further your cause. Trying to make trouble, were you? Well, you have. For yourself."

David took a step closer, and Howard flinched away from the face dark with rage, the fists clenched in the rain-wet air. His breathing was ragged, his fury barely under control.

"She *wanted* to talk. That husband of hers must not listen a great deal," Howard sputtered unwisely. "She's afraid and needed to tell someone." Howard was babbling. He did not want to retreat, but was terrified that Fraser would come closer.

David froze. "You're a liar as well as a charlatan, Howard. Jenny would never tell you a thing like that."

"But she did," Howard cried desperately as the younger man came forward. "She's too frightened to tell Ian Fraser. She said so."

Glaring at the man through narrow eyes, David saw how pale he was. Howard was quaking and two spots of color stained his cheeks. He was petrified, and David had learned that men in the grip of this kind of fright, especially soft, nervous men like Robert Howard, tended to tell the truth.

For an instant David felt sick, until rage obliterated thought and regret. He lunged forward to grasp Howard by the shoulders. "Don't ever repeat that to man or woman. Forget you heard it. Forget you even walked in the rain." When Howard shuddered but did not reply, David shook him roughly. "Do you understand?"

Fraser's hot breath singed Howard's cheeks; his fingers dug into Howard's shoulders painfully, and his eyes raked Howard's face. "I understand," he gasped. "Please. I understand."

David held him a moment longer with his powerful hands and his catlike gaze, quivering with the desire to annihilate, to destroy. Clenching his jaw to hold in that impulse, he pushed Howard away roughly and turned to go.

Long after he had thrashed his way through the trees and disappeared, Robert Howard stood immobile, transfixed by the hatred in David Fraser's eyes. Howard knew without a doubt that Fraser had wanted to kill him. Those savage green eyes had revealed a tautly held control about to snap. When it did, he *would* kill, like the tiger whose sleek, deadly power he embodied.

17

"YE SAW HIM AGAIN? YE TALKED TO HIM? BY THE BLACK Stone of Iona! Why?" Ian stood on one side of the circle of stones that held ashes not fire, Jenny on the other. Ian's voice was harsh with fury and disbelief.

His wife's surge of courage flared again. She'd thought, in the face of her husband's passion, it would shrivel and disappear like the cold ashes at her feet. But today Jenny had seen her deepest fear, and named it, perhaps found a way to end it. She stood her ground, hands clenched at her sides. "To tell him I was afraid. To ask them no' to abandon us just yet."

Ian froze, his face ashen.

"It has nothing to do with ye, Ian. It's just how life is here. 'Tis hard. Anything that might help, *anything* is worth thinking about. And I don't think you've done that—thought, I mean. You've only felt."

Ian realized he had not taken a breath for a full minute. What Jenny was saying might be true, but that was not the point. His wife had gone behind his back, tried to undermine his cause, and in doing so, had undermined his pride. She had betrayed him, taken his brother's side against him. She had failed to share his dedication to preserving their home and their past.

Worse than that, she did not trust him enough to tell him what she meant to do or how strongly she felt. She'd chosen instead to tell a stranger. She had told another man—though not in so many words—that her husband couldn't care for their family and keep them secure, that Ian did not make her feel safe. That last betrayal hurt the most. He had thought Jenny trusted him, felt safe with him, would share her heart and cares with him. His chest ached and he found he could not breathe.

He began to pace the packed dirt floor, listening to the rain on the thatched roof, against the stone and clay walls. He had always loved that sound, until now. Today it battered him, weighed him down and left him chilled to the bone. He was not enough for Jenny. She was right; their life always had been and always would be a struggle. He could not change that; he did not have the power. But those strangers, the brother he had pitied and despaired of, did.

No matter what he did now, he could not *be* enough. He'd worked hard and long just to keep what they had, and could not eke any more from the land. Jenny had broken his heart. He could hear it thudding in his ears erratically, as if it could not find its normal rhythm. She was too close to the truth. He had failed her—he and the land he loved.

Through the gray haze of despair that enshrouded him, he turned to look at his wife. The humidity from the warm, persistent rain rose between them, shimmering in the air, distorting her face. Ian reached out with words because he could not touch her with his hands. "I can no' understand why ye went to *them*. What can these men do for ye that I can't?" He knew the answer but could not stop himself from asking.

Jenny heard the anguish in his voice, the wounded pride, self-doubt and guilt, and her courage seeped away. She had never intended to hurt him that much. " 'Tis not your fault, Ian. 'Tis just the way of things. These men have money. If they make the Hill a shooting lodge, more people will come to be fed, and there'll be more work."

She spoke defensively, appalled by the hollow-eyed look of horror on Ian's face. It would haunt her forever, creeping in the darkness like the specter of a soul she had destroyed. She wanted to beg Ian's forgiveness, but she knew he could not give it. He could not forget the blow to his pride that her lack of faith in him had caused. She could never heal the wound she had struck.

"Work? Then ye want to be a servant in a stranger's house?"

Jenny was so shaken she hardly knew what she was saying, except that her guilt was making her angry. "What am I now? I cook and clean and cull reeds and make baskets and work in the garden and card the wool and still can no' keep up."

Ian stepped over the lifeless fire and took her shoulders in his hands. "The work is for yourself, your family. Now ye are free. Does that mean nothing?"

"What good is freedom if all it brings is misery?"

Stricken, Ian dropped his hands and stepped back as if she had pushed him hard against the wall. For the first time since her last lying-in, his sun-browned face was white with suffering. "Is that all you've had with me? Hardship and misery?"

His voice cut through her guilty anger to her soft heart and broke it. She threw herself into her husband's arms, which automatically closed around her, though his face remained rigid and his eyes dark with shock. "No! Ye know it isn't so, Ian-my-heart. You've made me happy all my life. But ye can't always make the worry go. No man is strong enough to wipe it out completely." She could not tell whether he was listening, but she went on doggedly. "I thought 'twas time I began to fight my own battles. Always, I've let ye fight them for me. That wasn't fair to ye or me. I thought I was being strong in facing Robert Howard alone. I thought ..." She broke down, weeping, and Ian drew her close.

"Ye want to leave the glen?" he said dully.

"No. 'Tis my home. It's always been my home. But Ian, that doesn't mean 'tis perfect."

"Ye want to stay, but change it." He spoke slowly, succinctly, despair and defeat in every word.

"I'd not change ye. Never ye." She was more and more desperate as she felt the stiffness in his body, the firm circle of his arms that held no trace of tenderness.

Ian stepped back. "This place *is* me. Alter it, sell it to strangers, redirect one tiny burn, and ye might as well sell my soul or mangle it." He knew he sounded selfish, knew Jenny would not understand. He swallowed and tried again. "We can survive, Jenny. We can be happy."

Jenny shook her head. "You've always been happy. 'Tis what I envy most. Because, ye see, I don't think I know how to be."

Ian was appalled by the bitterness she tried unsuccessfully to disguise, by the misery he saw in her misty eyes. He did not know what to say. This truth, like all the others she had spoken, was beyond his power to change—perhaps even to endure. He backed away from her and ducked beneath the door frame, disappearing into the silver-black curtain of rain.

18

AILSA WAS RESTLESS, PACING THE CROFT, IMPRISONED BY THE storm in which she would normally have exulted. Though she tried to spin, to read, to write a letter, she could not concentrate. She went several times to the door and stared into the rain as if it called her, in a silence more urgent than words.

Finally Mairi wearied of watching her daughter slipping toward madness. "Go, why don't ye. 'Tis no use staying here, when you're needed out there. Go."

Her voice was little more than a whisper, but Ailsa heard it over the slashing of the rain. Heard it and was grateful. "Aye," she said, "I'll go."

She glanced at Mairi, who would not meet her daughter's

eyes. Taking up her plaid, she draped it over her head and stepped out into the storm. She did not pause to think where she was going; she let her instincts guide her. They had rarely been wrong.

She found Ian sitting on a moss-covered stump beneath the huge old oak in the copse beside the river. He stared blindly into the water, barely visible through the rain. He did not raise his head when Ailsa appeared, but she knew he had heard her come.

Tucking her skirts beneath her, she sat on the ground beside him, oblivious of the water running through the ferns and blue moor grass. She could feel his misery throbbing in her chest. She did not try to shut out his pain. He needed her; she knew that as surely as if he had called her name in anguish.

For a long time they sat in silence, soaked from the rain, though the leaves kept the worst of it off their bare heads. Ian was pale, hands clasped so tightly that the knuckles were white.

Ailsa hurt for him; her skin ached and her heartbeat dragged. The pain was worse because she did not know its cause. The urge to grasp his hand was so strong that she trembled with it, but she dared not take the chance. Not even to let him know he was not alone. "Is it Duncan?" she asked at last.

Ian sighed so deeply that his body shook. " 'Tis the world." He would say no more than that; he would not betray Jenny. Ian laughed bitterly at his own arrogance. He was no longer certain Jenny was wrong. What she'd said was true, and had worried her for years. What he'd said was also true. How could he be angry when all his wife had done was tell him a truth he did not wish to hear? A truth that had broken his heart and his faith. "She didn't trust me enough to tell me."

He hadn't meant to speak the words aloud, but they were torn from him, a cry from his soul in the gray, dripping rain. Ailsa gasped as pain arced through her chest—Ian's agony and his loss. She buried her hands in her lap so she would not reach for him.

Jenny had done this. Ailsa heard the anguish in that unintended revelation and was overcome, for an instant, by blind rage that anyone could have hurt Ian so much. Rage at her own powerlessness to heal him. All she could do was remain here, letting him know by her presence and her silence that he was not alone, would never be alone.

They sat listening to the murmur of the river and the hiss of the rain. They viewed their world through a curtain of water, felt it run down their faces and onto their chests, and did not turn away or try to protect themselves. The water cleansed them, though it could not cool away the heat of pain and anger.

Ailsa offered no words, only her faith in Ian—absolute and unshakable. That faith had never wavered in all the years they'd grown together and been apart. She did not speak of her belief in his integrity and his strength of character, merely thought of these things and prayed to the ancient Celtic gods that Ian could hear, know them in his bruised and barren soul.

She shivered once when she looked up at his face and saw that he was trembling. "You're uncertain. I've never known ye to be this way. Even as a child, ye always knew what ye knew completely, in your heart."

"When I was a child I was arrogant. Certainty was easy. 'Tis not so easy now, Ailsa-*aghray*. I've begun to wonder if I'm being selfish and unwise."

Ailsa was stunned. "Your instincts are pure and true. Ye know that, Ian Fraser. *I* know it. I can no' bear to see ye doubt yourself this way." She was amazed at the pain that was tearing her apart. She had thought the fragile thread that once bound them long severed and irreparable, until the day they'd waylaid the messenger. Now she was afraid of the fine web spinning itself between them, drawing them slowly and inexorably toward the center. She was afraid to go back to that total awareness and complete vulnerability. She shivered violently, pressing her knees together to keep her hands immobile.

She longed to touch him for an instant, to brush his hand in compassion and reassurance. The longing was so intense that her throat grew dry and her breath labored. She could not make even so small a gesture; it was too dangerous. Ailsa's frustration made salty patterns of tears on her cheeks. She could not leave him this way, danger or not. She sat silent and still and let her presence do what her hands and her voice could not risk—touch him and heal him, at least for the moment.

Glenyss made certain Erlinna had on a dry gown and tucked her into her boxbed for a nap. Then she picked up her comb and went to sit on the settle by the fire to dry her hair. She noticed Jenny's stricken face the moment she came in, but had said nothing, partly because she could not find her voice, partly because she wanted Erlinna asleep and out of hearing before she tried to sort this out.

Glenyss had not spoken to Jenny often in the last few weeks. She'd held her anger close, as a child will, clinging to its heat as she'd once clung to her mother's affection. She had cherished her anger, in spite of what Ailsa said, nurtured it until it filled her and she felt little else.

But today she had come in, wet from the rain, to find Jenny sitting idly by the ashes of the fire, staring blankly into the low flames. She had obviously been out in the rain, but had not dried or combed her hair; it hung about her face in lank, damp tendrils, emphasizing the gray tinge of her skin and the lusterless expression in her eyes. Her linsey-woolsey gown smelled of unpleasant damp, and the skirt was bunched about her in a tangle that would never dry properly. Her hands lay limp and motionless in her lap.

Glenyss felt a physical pain at the sight of those hands. Her mother was never idle; her hands were always busy working the reeds or the flax or the wool, carding or spinning or chopping or sewing. Her idleness was as frightening as her white face and blank expression.

Seating herself on the settle, Glenyss leaned toward the fire and began to comb out her long, dark hair. She needed something to occupy her hands. Finally, when Jenny did not appear to notice that her daughter was there, Glenyss said tentatively, "What is it, Mama? What's wrong?" She did not want to know; she was afraid to know; she had to know. She could not bear this uncertainty much longer.

Jenny shrugged but showed no other sign of having heard. Glenyss shivered with foreboding and chills rose along her neck. Her mother had been careful to answer every question her children asked. She always cared what they were thinking. That was what disturbed Glenyss the most now. Jenny did not seem to care.

"I know you're upset. Ye have been for a while. But this is worse. Please tell me why, Mama. *Please!*"

Jenny turned at the note of hysteria and looked blindly at her daughter. She shrugged again.

Glenyss combed one strand at a time, laboriously, funneling her qualms into the simple repetitive action. She felt cold, though the air was humid and warm. Her fingers would not work properly. "It's because of Uncle Duncan and those men he brought here, isn't it?" Glenyss could not let it go.

There was a glimmer of recognition in Jenny's eyes, then a shroud of despair covered it. "Aye, I suppose so."

Her mother's toneless voice upset Glenyss as nothing else had. She wanted to grab Jenny, to shake her, to make the light come back to her eyes. She realized in that instant that she did not hate her mother at all. Ailsa had been right. Glenyss was not angry; she was terrified. Jenny, who had always been warm and dependable, had grown strange and distant. Her mother was in pain. She needed Glenyss, needed her understanding. But Glenyss did not understand, so she was afraid.

She thought of the expression in her father's eyes of late when he looked at Jenny—the hurt, confusion and regret. The memory frightened Glenyss, and she'd never been frightened of her father before. She would shatter with the weight of so much fear. "What is it you've done that's so wrong, Mama? Why are ye so afraid? Please. I need to know."

Jenny roused herself at the tone of her daughter's voice. Glenyss needed an answer. But Jenny could hardly admit she was worried about her children's survival. Glenyss was already too old for her years, worrying about things that should not concern her. All Jenny's terrors, once conquered and suppressed, came back to haunt her. She was acting irrationally, out of terror deeper than even *she* recognized. "I made a mistake, is all. I was unwise," she said dully.

Glenyss frowned fiercely at a tangle she could not work free. "Can't ye make it right? Ye and Papa have always done it before. Can't ye do that, Mama? I know ye can." She reached out to grasp her mother's cold hand. "Please!" she said again. She was asking the impossible, and somehow she knew it. But the panic was choking her and she could not hold it in anymore.

Jenny looked at her pale and trembling daughter and something inside came back to life. She was giving up too soon. Perhaps, after all, there is something she could do. She had to try, for Glenyss's sake, and for Ian's.

The image came to her of Robert Howard's face in the streaming rain, the compassion in his eyes. *We're really trying to help, you know.* Perhaps he could help after all. He was from London, a successful businessman. He would know what to do. Helplessly, desperately, she clung to one more chimera.

19

GLENYSS LAY IN THE UNFAMILIAR BED AT ANGUS AND FLO-ra's, head turned toward the clay wall. The bed was just like her own, but it was not hers; she did not feel safe among the rough sheets and hand-woven tartan blankets. Glenyss closed her eyes when her grandmother checked to see if she was sleeping, as Erlinna was, blissfully unaware of any danger. But Glenyss had seen the peril behind her lids, felt it in the unusual warmth of the night that lay damp and heavy on her skin.

Often, Jenny had sent her children to sleep at their grandparents' for one reason or another, and Glenyss had never minded. But tonight she could not rest. When she closed her eyes she saw vivid, threatening colors—red and silver and black—that pulsed with the beat of her heart. She had asked her mother to do something to make her mistake right. Had Jenny taken her daughter at her word?

Whatever she had done, that unknown thing without shape, size or name frightened the girl badly. She did not know when her fear turned to resolution; perhaps when the colors became so bright they blinded her. She only knew she had to leave this safe, warm cottage and go home. The thought became a need and the need a compulsion.

When she heard Flora and Angus go to bed, then slip quietly and easily into sleep, Glenyss rose, made certain her sister was safe, and took up the plaid she had dropped earlier. Wrapping it around her, though she was already covered in perspiration, she slipped silently out the door and into the night.

That night Robert Howard had taken the precaution of wearing his high-topped black leather boots. In spite of the lantern he held high, the path was not always clear, and he did not like the thought of bogs, hidden burns and unexpected hummocks of turf. He was equally wary of wildcats, badgers and shrews. They had seen another wildcat yesterday. It eyed them coolly from across a tiny burn, as if deciding whether or not to attack. On the tail of that memory followed another—the sight of David Fraser's eyes, luminous with fury. Howard gripped the pearl-handled pistol beneath his jacket to reassure himself that he was safe.

He'd gotten into the habit of carrying it when he went to night meetings in London. Sometimes the men he dealt with were less than savory, and as for trustworthy, well, any man who would trust them with his life was a fool. Robert Howard was not a fool. Besides, he'd heard David Fraser's warning and begun, for the first time, to recognize the intensity of the opposition in the glen.

Simon Black had said it wasn't that, so much as David's

hostility to his father that was most threatening. "It's easy to deal with hot-tempered young fools, Robert. You simply ignore them. The young Fraser has scruples. He won't act unless you provoke him."

Howard shivered and side-stepped a moss-covered boulder. He was not as certain as Black, and had trouble keeping his hands steady. He took heart from the fact that Jenny Fraser had come to him for help. When she appeared that morning, he'd been able to read her thoughts without the slightest effort. She did not know about subterfuge and camouflage; she could not have hidden her desperation, her hope and need if she'd tried. That made him feel some of his old self-assurance. He was right, after all, and the Highlanders mistaken. He would show them so.

Howard had dressed carefully for this conversation with Ian Fraser. He wore a white cotton shirt and corduroy pants, a bowler hat and gold-and-rust waistcoat that went nicely with his blond hair and brown eyes. He wanted to look casually well off but not intimidating. He did not want to flaunt his superior wealth in Fraser's face, but to show him subtly, through example, what could be his if this deal went through.

Howard stopped short, hand on his gun, when an obscure shape loomed out of the gray half-darkness. When the figure saw him and gasped, he realized it was only a child. He tucked his hand in his waistcoat pocket. He could not quite see who it was, and his nerves were more than a little frayed.

"Mr. Howard?"

It was more an accusation than a question, but he had become used to that. "Yes, it is. And who might you be?"

"Glenyss Fraser!" She was out of breath and holding her side as she panted, "Where are ye going?"

"Glenyss? Ian Fraser's daughter, aren't you? Why, then, I'm on my way to your house."

The girl straightened, her eyes narrowed and eerie in the lantern light. "Ye can't go there!"

She raised her chin in grim determination, her hands clasped into fists, as if she might try to stop him herself if necessary. He took a deep, shaky breath. "Why not, may I ask?"

"Ye mustn't, 'tis all. 'Twould be a great mistake." Glenyss knew this with a certainty that baffled her. She tried to make him understand by the sheer force of her near hysteria.

Raising his eyebrow in astonishment, Howard glared. "I have told your mother I will come. It would be an unpardonable rudeness to break my word. I am a gentleman, after all. What's more, I've promised my partners that I should further their cause tonight. So you see, I have no choice, but many obligations." He was unnerved by the girl's staring eyes and breathless voice. She did not stir, showed no sign of having heard him. Her expression did not change as she shook her head furiously from side to side. Perhaps she was a little mad. "Come, out of my way, if you please. I shall be late as it is. And tonight is my chance to make a difference."

Glenyss bit her lip until it bled. He didn't believe her. He thought she was a silly child. She swallowed dryly, tasting blood. She was very much afraid Mr. Howard was right. He *would* make a difference, but not in the way he planned. Reluctantly, she let him pass. There was nothing else she could do. Or was there?

The croft was very quiet. The peat fire burned low in the smoldering embers that were left after cooking supper. The wooden dishes had been scraped, washed and dried, and the paraffin lamps cast shadows over the walls that disappeared in the squares of the open windows. Jenny had changed from her work-stained gown to one of soft blue. She'd taken out her braid and reworked it, smoothing it around her head in a crown held in place by wooden pins.

Ian had not offered to help her comb out her hair, as he often did. He knew she had sent the children to Angus's so they could be alone to talk, and perhaps dissipate the festering hurt and anger between them. They had disagreed before, but their anger had never gone beneath the surface, had never before left wounds invisible to the eye. Ian felt helpless and inadequate, because his own pain and incomprehension were so great. He had tried to speak to his wife, but only pleasantries and unimportant questions came out.

He realized as Jenny moved about, straightening books and skeins of wool and children's clothing, that he was afraid to be alone with his wife. That alarmed him most of all— the thought of silence fraught with unquiet undercurrents, of pain fraught with intimations of future discord. How could they be happy together, continue to live together, when she did not believe in him? When her fear was greater than her trust?

"Please, come sit beside me." Jenny watched her husband with haunted eyes, pointed hopefully to the rocking chair next to her own. She was afraid he'd turn away, unable to face her. She did not think she could bear one more minute of the tense silence between them. "Please."

Ian perched on the edge of the chair; he could not resist the plea in her eyes. They sat side by side, not speaking, but it was a cold and empty silence, not like the afternoon when Ailsa had sat beside him, speaking volumes with her mere presence. Ian had always felt close to Jenny, comfortable with her, as if he need hide nothing. Now he was afraid to reveal himself because she had hurt him so deeply.

When she reached for his hand, he clutched her tightly, clinging to something they could not bear to lose, trying to reclaim what had been lost. But they could not do it through touch alone. And both were afraid to speak a word.

There was a knock on the half-open door.

Jenny jumped up, smoothed her unwrinkled skirt, stared wordlessly at her husband and headed for the door.

With a cold chill of foreboding, Ian rose and turned to face whatever might come.

20

AILSA SAT IN HER DAUGHTER'S LARGE COTTAGE, ENJOYING the freshly coated walls, the mural in the kitchen, the cheerful light of the paraffin lamps. She had felt restless at Mairi's, had plucked at her *clarsach* in discordant notes, until her mother sent her out to walk off whatever was troubling her. Ailsa had come to Alanna and David's without planning to. One moment she was heading for the woods, bathed in pale moonglow and soft summer darkness, the next she was standing before her daughter's open door.

"Mama, I'm glad ye came." Alanna's greeting had been more than enthusiastic. Ailsa understood why, when she saw how David paced the low-ceilinged rooms, jaw taut and unyielding. He alternately ran his hands through his hair and clenched his fists in the air, as if boxing with an invisible opponent. Alanna glanced at him in concern while Ailsa took a cup of tea and sat on the settle, regarding her son-in-law curiously. "What troubles ye?" she asked. "Can ye tell me?"

David shook his head in annoyance, not at her, but at himself. He could not tell her about the scene between himself and Robert Howard, the heartbreaking things Howard told him Jenny'd said. That would be to betray his aunt, and that David would not do. Instead, he paced. "I don't know. I'm restless tonight, unsettled." He did not like to admit that beneath his fury was a bone-deep fear. Jenny had made him realize that. He spoke in a normal voice, but the air around him vibrated with suppressed emotion.

Ailsa had never seen this kind of anger—coiled tension so taut she felt it on her skin like heavy moisture before a storm. William had not been a fighter, and though Ian had the passion for it, he'd never had to fight for what he wanted until now. Except for once, long ago when they'd been children, and what he'd wanted had been her. Ailsa closed her eyes at the memory, intertwined with the image of that day beside the river, when they'd sat silent, and she'd willed him her strength and her faith as Ian had once willed her his.

She opened her eyes and saw Ian in his nephew, not only because of the dark, curly hair and green eyes, the tall, muscled body and sensitive hands, but because his rage was visible and palpable, as was his affection for Alanna. He lifted his hand and his wife came to him, leaning close as David's arms closed around her protectively.

"Do you know what I think? I think this is just another game to my father. What he wants is one more victory to make him feel invincible. Maybe even immortal. He thinks if he wins often enough, he can keep death away." David shrugged. "Maybe he's made a deal with the devil to pay him off."

Ailsa was taken aback by David's fierceness. "We won't *let* him win. As for the devil, he's tried to find his way here often enough, but he always gets lost in the end."

David stared at Ailsa, green eyes blazing. "You believe that, don't you? Just like Uncle Ian and Alanna."

"I have to believe it. There are some things ye can't let go of, for if ye do, your bones become too brittle to hold up your skin and your heart stops beating as it should. Ye become a shell then, empty and useless. 'Twill not happen to me."

It would not happen to David either. He believed too profoundly in whatever made that rage boil in his blood. Ailsa realized it came naturally to him—the battle, the conflict, the pain, the triumph. The thought made her uneasy. This fury in the glen was new and disturbing.

She had felt it in Ian the other day. Ailsa glanced down to see that she was braiding and unbraiding her fingers in agitation.

"Ye feel it too, then," Alanna said, crouching beside her mother. She took Ailsa's hand and was not surprised at the damp chill of her skin. "There's something in the air tonight.

It won't let us rest. David wants to go looking, but I said no." She gazed at her mother quizzically.

There was a brief silence. Then, "Ye need no' go looking," Ailsa said, staring blankly, eyes wide with a cast of gray upon them. " 'Twill come to ye, I think, when 'tis time."

"Aye, so I thought." Alanna's eyes, too, were transformed by a fine web of shadow. "But I can no' *see*."

"Even if ye could, 'twould no' be what ye thought, I'll wager. 'Tis never quite what ye think."

Ailsa felt dizzy, and Alanna did not release her hand until it ceased trembling.

David glanced from mother to daughter. He only half understood what they were saying, but it was enough to tell him that this was the strange bond Ian had spoken of, and of which Alanna had warned him more than once. *We see things, my grandmother and mother and I.* He only wished he knew what they were seeing. He felt electricity in the air around him, like the volts of magic that turned on the lights in the large houses in Glasgow now, that made the light glow with an unnatural radiance and intensity. He felt dread, exhilaration, apprehension, and somehow it was bound together with the vision of Jenny voicing her terrors in the rain.

Ailsa and Alanna leaned together, grasping hands as if the flow of heat from one to the other would make them understand. Both jumped when the door swung open and Glenyss Fraser appeared. At the sight of Ailsa, she sighed with relief, but that did not diminish the effect of her wild, tangled hair, her torn, dirty plaid and the mud-stained nightrail that showed beneath. She was running from something.

Ailsa stood.

"I've been looking for ye, Ailsa Rose," Glenyss said. "I need to talk to ye." She hovered in the doorway, hesitant to enter. She quivered with distress, fighting to catch her breath.

Ailsa thought it might be easier for the girl to speak to her alone. " 'Tis a warm night," she said. "Shall we go outside?"

Glenyss nodded with relief.

Ailsa glanced at her daughter and son-in-law in apology,

but they seemed to understand. A child had her secrets and her nightmares that she did not wish to share with everyone. "She seems distraught," Alanna murmured. "Go talk to her."

Grateful for her daughter's sensitivity, Ailsa stepped out into the gathering darkness—warm and still and humid. Glenyss waited, wringing her hands and dancing from foot to foot.

"What is it?" Ailsa asked gently. "Tell me."

" 'Tis no' your concern," Glenyss stuttered, "but I remembered that ye seemed to understand my father." She took a deep, unsteady breath. "I think he needs ye now." Glenyss ran her hands through her already wild dark hair. "At least, I'd not be knowing if ye can help at all, but I had to do something. I didn't know where else to go." She looked up, eyes more green than brown in the warm strange moonlight. "Ye understand things, so I thought—"

" 'Tis all right," Ailsa said, disturbed by Glenyss's perception. It was true that little by little, the thread that used to bind her to Ian had been respun, so slowly that she had not realized it was there, except in that moment when they leapt over the river. But that had been a flash of memory, of connection quickly gone, as if the wind had swept it up, laughing, and tossed it into the sky. But the other day in the copse, things had shifted subtly, and the thread had reached between them and lingered, binding them loosely but irrevocably.

If what Glenyss said was true, and Ian was in danger, which Ailsa did not doubt, she would have gone to him regardless. He and Jenny were the source of the restlessness she'd felt all night, her inability to sleep, to shut out thought and worry.

Glenyss felt the threat as much as she did. To pretend it did not exist would be foolish. Ailsa remembered too vividly Ian's growing desperation, the feeling of impending doom it had left behind.

"I saw the man, one of the Sassenachs," Glenyss cried. "He's going to our croft, though I tried to stop him. I told him 'twas a mistake, but he didn't believe me. He didn't care. He hasn't seen Papa's face the last few days. He doesn't know . . ." She stopped, breathless with terror.

"I'll come," Ailsa said as calmly as she could. Her heart had begun to beat raggedly as her restlessness became dread. She did not need Glenyss's white, pinched face to tell her Ian and Jenny were in trouble.

"I'll come at once, as soon as I bid David and Alanna farewell. Wait for me." Ailsa barely knew what she was saying. She ducked inside to find her daughter and son-in-law frozen as she'd left them, watching the door in concern. "I must go."

In his many years in Glasgow, David had learned to recognize trouble, to sense it in the air. Now the feeling was so strong he trembled with it. "What's happened? We want to go with you."

"Nothing's happened yet. Probably nothing will." For the first time, Ailsa regretted the things Alanna could "see." She could not lie to her daughter. But she had to be stronger this time, to disguise her own unease. "I'll go alone. I think 'tis best." She could see that David was perilously close to losing control. It would not take much to push him over the edge. She couldn't take the chance that he might overreact and cause an eruption that would be irreparable. She also saw how Alanna stood beside her husband, hand lightly on his arm. That small gesture was large in magnitude. If David did explode, Alanna would go up in flames with him. She would follow him and support him, no matter the hazard to herself. The thought both frightened Ailsa and made her proud. But she knew which feeling was stronger.

She reached out to touch their cheeks, one after the other. "I must go. Take care of each other. You're both very precious to me."

Alanna frowned and covered her mother's hand with her own. "It sounds like you're saying good-bye."

Ailsa's throat was raw and dry. "Only good night." She turned, heart pounding in a loud, monotonous rhythm, and was gone.

21

IAN STARED, INCREDULOUS, WHEN ROBERT HOWARD DUCKED through the doorway. Though the house was clean and comfortable, the man could not hide a shiver of distaste as he glanced around. Ian stood, uncertain. His Highland instincts, bred in him since childhood, bade him offer the man his best. His instinct for survival, bred deep in his blood, told him there was danger here. His personal reaction was fierce, simmering anger; he wanted to push Howard bodily out the door and slam it in his face.

Ian was surprised at the strength of that impulse. It was not like him. Besides, Robert Howard had done no more than speak quietly to Jenny. Jenny had done no more than answer his questions with the truth. That was what inflamed and debilitated Ian at once: Jenny had answered, and it had been the truth. He nodded formally. "Howard. What can I do for ye? Would ye have a dram and a black bun?" His tone was stilted, unnatural.

"Ian," Jenny said, hands clasped in the folds of her fresh muslin gown, "I've asked Mr. Howard to come tonight."

Ian stared at his wife, stunned. "Ye asked—" He broke off, gasping as if she'd struck him hard in the chest and he could not catch his breath. "Why?"

Robert Howard cleared his throat and removed his hat, twirling it once on his fingertip, as he was wont to do when under stress. He strove to appear calm as Jenny took it from him. "Your wife thought if we talked for a bit, just you and I, man to man, as it were, perhaps we could clear some of this muddle away." His voice was soft, mellow, his brown eyes serious but without arrogance or the cool superiority of Simon Black. He fought to keep it that way.

Howard moved toward the dying peat fire without thinking. The night had been warm a few moments before; now, all at once, it was chilly. When he saw that Jenny and Ian were frozen in that unexpected gust of cold, he continued, "We thought that in quiet and in private, without short-tempered agitators about, I could tell you what we want to do, explain our intentions, as it were. We've not been communicating very well, and the fault is largely ours, I'll admit. But I'd like to remedy that tonight, if you'll let me."

Fortunately, he'd memorized the speech, and by keeping his hands in his pants pockets, he managed to hide their trembling.

Jenny looked anxiously at her husband, saw shock retreat as the wrath drained from his face, leaving his skin slack and his eyes wary. She wanted him to see that she had not meant to betray him, that Robert Howard was an honorable and rational man who would listen as well as talk.

Ian sighed and motioned Howard toward one of the two comfortable chairs. He could not respond churlishly to such a conciliatory speech. It went against all that his parents had taught him. But he was not easy in the stranger's presence. He straddled a low stool and, while Jenny bustled about getting drinks and a plate of buns and bannocks, he said, "I can no' refuse to listen. That would be unwise." His suspicion and distrust hung heavy in the air.

Since Jenny had first revealed her anxiety that he could not support their family, Ian had begun to weaken. Somehow this was the final blow. He should have had the strength to leap up and force Robert Howard from his home, no matter how pleasant and sane the man was, simply because he was Ian's enemy. But he did not have that strength. Jenny had sapped it a little at a time. She did not want to hurt him; he'd seen her guilt and shame over what was happening between them. She wanted to make it go away, and this was her solution.

Ian sat grimly as Robert Howard's voice droned on about roadways and the modern world and plumbing and comfort and jobs and a beautiful house restored to its former splendor. Ian glanced at his wife. Did she really think he would change his mind because Robert Howard explained it all again, as if Ian were a backward child?

He leaned forward, gulping down a dram of David's whisky. Ian looked from his wife to the stranger through a dim haze that muted their voices and distorted their message. He realized Jenny was sitting across the fire, beside Howard, that she was on his side, that she was pleading with her husband to come over to their way of thinking. Did she really know him so little? He ran his hands through his hair where silver strands had begun to outnumber the dark.

Ian looked up sharply when the door scraped and creaked. A curious hope filled him as the heavy oak swung inward and Ailsa appeared, her plaid gathered at her elbows, her chestnut hair hanging loose down her back. The mist had begun to rise, and her cheeks were flushed, her face framed in wisps of curl from the moisture. Her blue-violet eyes were dilated, lucent with concern. She met Ian's gaze and saw through his somber expression to the pain underneath.

Ailsa started in surprise at the sight of the British investor seated comfortably, a cup of whisky in his hand. She caught a glimpse of Jenny's white, drawn face before she looked away. Glenyss had told her Howard would be here, but she had not really believed it. Surely Jenny wouldn't be so foolish. "I'm sorry to come so unexpected, but I was aye restless tonight, and I saw your lamps burning. I thought we should talk about—" She glanced at Robert Howard and stopped. The tension in her body said more than words, more than the bleak gray shadow on her eyes. She would not go, no matter what they said. She raised her chin obdurately.

As she hurried toward the Fraser croft, it had occurred to her that Glenyss should not come if there was any risk. She had told the girl to return to David and Alanna's, had stood and watched until she disappeared into the rising mist. Ailsa felt a flutter of unease about Glenyss, but the danger called more loudly, dragging her here where sparks hovered invisibly in the air, ready to flare and blaze with a single breath.

Ian was motionless, ashamed of how grateful he felt for Ailsa's presence. An ally at last in this house of strangers.

The pain burrowed deeper inside as his wife rose to get Ailsa tea and scones. Why must his ally come from outside? Why did he feel alone and besieged in his own home?

Howard tilted his head politely at Ailsa, but his eyes narrowed. He did not like her unforeseen appearance. He was jumpy enough as it was. She was one of the troublemakers, and he'd wanted Ian Fraser away from his hotheaded companions. It annoyed him that Ailsa Sinclair should intrude in this way, but there was nothing to be done except go on.

Although Howard spoke as calmly as possible, there was an undercurrent of impatience. He'd said this all before. Why couldn't these people understand? "It makes perfect sense if you think about it. I mean, actually sit down and think for a while. The advantages are tremendous. Your wife's seen that. I don't know why you refuse to admit it." He glanced over to include Ailsa, who'd circled the fire to sit on a polished birch chair one away from Ian. She did not want to threaten Jenny, but she would not sit on the same side of the fire with the stranger.

Robert Howard rose. He was becoming agitated at Ian's, and now Ailsa's, blank stares. They were not listening, did not intend to hear him. He straightened and his lips thinned as he puffed out his chest defensively. He wanted to appear taller, larger than life, larger than these small people in their tiny hut with their narrow vision. He took out his monocle, which he did not need and rarely used, except to intimidate. He felt like a buffoon under Ian and Ailsa's unwavering regard. That was one thing he could not abide.

He was weary of being full of dread, of looking more often back over his shoulder than forward. He was weary of the Highlanders' ignorance, obstinance and belligerence. Weary of wild animals crouching in the tangled shrubbery, of wraiths appearing wild-eyed in his path to issue dire admonitions. Embarrassed because, despite his pretended nonchalance, that child and her frantic warning had left him vexed and off balance.

Most of all, he was weary of being afraid. The fear was humiliating, unmanly, and he could bear it no more.

"You're fools to let this chance go by, fools to think you

have the power to stop us, once we've decided." Though his voice was melodic, the words were like acid. His hair was disheveled, and his multicolored waistcoat rose and fell with his labored breath.

Jenny gasped. She would not have been surprised if Simon Black or even Duncan had attacked in such a way, but she had not expected this from the kindly Mr. Howard. It was all the more terrible because it was unlike him. She should not have asked him to come. She had compounded her mistake yet again. She bit her lip, uncertain what to do now. She had seen the flare of anger in Ian's eyes reflected in Ailsa's and knew Robert Howard should go at once. But she was caught in a peculiar miasma that held her prisoner, as if she floundered in the muck of a deadly bog.

"We came to help you, since you can't seem to help yourselves. Or do you prefer to live in squalor? Perhaps you do. It's certainly easier than trying to improve your pitiful lot." Howard wanted to hit someone, and it angered him further that those two sat motionless, their antagonism radiating from them as heat rose shimmering and distorting from a fire. Why didn't they shout or leap up or argue? Their intent perusal reminded him vividly, cripplingly of David Fraser's feral eyes. He thought he might be ill.

"Look, I've tried to be understanding. I've tried to listen and explain again and again. But you haven't returned the favor. You'd decided before you ever met me or Mr. Black. You and your friends." He sneered the last word and waved his hand, dismissing those friends as insignificant.

Ian stood, jaw clenched, dazed by the surge of fury that left him shaking. He had to ball his hands into fists and hold tight to keep his agitation from showing.

But Ailsa felt it. She too rose, equally angry, equally impotent. Her eyes glinted in the lamplight, but even through her rage, she saw Jenny, pale and hovering, more defenseless than they, because she could not share their righteous anger.

"You haven't the brains to recognize a good thing when it falls in your lap." Howard had lost control of his voice, which spat out words like darts. It was the only way he could keep it from quavering. "And you haven't the courage to admit you might be wrong. You're a coward, crouching in the barbaric past of some civilization that disappeared long ago. You're not worth our time and explanations. The funny thing is, you think you're better. You actually think yourself superior to *me*. You and your dolt of a hotheaded nephew. You're blind, Ian Fraser, as well as stupid."

The haze lifted and Ian exploded. In two strides, he was face to face with Robert Howard. He wanted to shake the Englishman like an obstinate child, to wake him up and make him understand. Robert Howard took three steps back and found himself pressed against a cold stone wall.

Ian paused, his body quivering with ferocity, his face flushed. He raised his hand and Howard shrank against the wall, dropping his monocle as he did so. "I'm no coward, nor am I fool. Nor, usually, am I a violent man." Ian spoke slowly, in taut words that struck the stranger like tiny blows. "But this is my home, and ye owe me an apology. Me and Ailsa and my wife, and all my friends. Ye owe me a great deal more than that, but as I said, I'm no' a fool."

He leaned closer so Howard could see into his eyes—a tiger's eyes, menacing and full of hatred. Howard had seen those eyes before, had felt that hot breath and the merciless grasp of powerful hands. He was mesmerized; he could not look away.

"If ye choose no' to apologize," Ian continued, his voice a low and ruthless growl, "well then, I can't say what might happen. Because, ye see, I'm a savage and a barbarian and my fists are strong. Much stronger than yours, which handle only paper and perhaps the scented skin of women."

Ian was taller than Howard, muscled from years of physical labor. His anger was so powerful Ailsa could smell it in the air. She stood at his shoulder, unwilling to interfere, transfixed by the ominous force of his low-voiced assault.

The Englishman moved sharply. As he reached under his jacket and brought his hand out, Ailsa gasped.

Robert Howard held a pearl-handled pistol pointed at Ian's heart, his finger firmly on the trigger.

Jenny cried out, but no one heard.

Ian blinked at the gun as if he did not recognize what it

was. For the first time, some of his fury retreated. He shrugged. "Don't be silly. Ye'll no' be needing that, man!"

To him the pistol was a joke, an aberration. He had several guns, mostly rifles, as did all Highlanders. Guns were for hunting, and pistols for celebrations, not for standing face to face with another man. Not since the violent clan feuds had faded into history had men stood thus. To Ian a gun had nothing to do with anger, or a fight between two men. It was absurd.

"It seems *you're* the coward, Mr. Howard," Ailsa said softly. "And the fool as well."

Robert Howard was sweating. Ian's nonchalance and Ailsa's soft challenge frightened him more than raving threats. Didn't they understand that he, Howard, had the upper hand? Why weren't they afraid of a gun when they themselves were unarmed? "Get away!" he hissed, becoming smaller by the moment. "I'll shoot you, I swear it."

Ian's eyes were full of contempt. The poor man clung to his pistol as if it gave him power and right, made him invincible. But Ian knew better. "Don't be an idiot." The disdain in his voice snapped something deep inside Robert Howard.

He pressed the gun closer, until the muzzle rested against Ian's chest. "I told my friends where I was going. They don't trust you. They'll come after me soon. They didn't like the idea of my coming at all." He looked at Jenny's ashen face. "But I did it for you."

Jenny quivered in silence. She saw that Howard was shaking, the sweat soaking through his waistcoat and shirt. She opened her mouth, but her throat was too dry. Then she saw the look on Ian's face. She forced herself to breathe and said, "I only wanted ye to talk to him, Mr. Howard. There was no threat to ye here—not till ye made one."

Howard was not listening. "Leave me alone. Get out of here!"

Ian stared through a vaporous gauze of incredulity so thick it slowed and hampered his reaction. Now he was the one caught in the bog, unable to fight free. "Are ye ordering me from my own home? While ye threaten my life and my wife's safety with your little pistol? Don't be a fool."

It was the second time he'd called Howard a fool. The man's anger seeped into his terror, tasted bitter on his tongue. Ailsa circled the stranger slowly, soundlessly. She did not know what she was going to do, only that she had to do something. She caught Jenny's eye and Jenny cried out, making Howard look up just as Ailsa grabbed him from behind. He dropped the pistol in surprise, his eye twitching ominously.

"This is silly," Ailsa said, her arms binding Howard's to his side. "There's no need."

"Shut up." Howard tried to throw her off and lunge for the gun, but Ian got it first.

"Get down, Jenny," her husband rasped, glancing back to see his wife duck behind the giant cooking pot. For a moment, he didn't realize Ailsa was still clinging to the stranger. It came to him, vaguely, that she had been beside him since the moment he rose in fury. He had not realized before, because she moved silently, like his shadow. He met her eyes as he pointed the pistol at the Englishman. "Get out of my house, or better yet, out of the glen."

Howard went limp and, sensing his defeat, Ailsa left the stranger to stand behind Ian. She could not help him now, yet her racing pulse told her the peril had not yet passed.

When Howard didn't move, Ian took a step toward him, raising the pistol threateningly, though he didn't intend to use it.

Howard went white, took a deep breath and said slowly, vindictively, "This wouldn't have happened if you hadn't been afraid to face us in the first place. Sending your wife to cajole and coerce us because you were afraid. Using her just like a whore. And oh, my, what a job she did." When he saw Ian pale and his hand tremble, he lunged for the pistol.

Ian did not hesitate. He raised the gun and fired point-blank at the stranger's chest. As Howard teetered, his face pallid and appalled, Ailsa pressed herself against Ian's back and grabbed the pistol with her own hand. "Ye shall not bear this alone." Her fingers closed tightly over Ian's until she felt the slick heat of the pearl-handled butt.

Howard fell, eyes wide and staring, his beautiful silk waistcoat covered with blood, his monocle shattered.

For a moment, everyone stood frozen, then Jenny came out from her hiding place. She stared at the man on the floor, whose blood seeped into her packed dirt, staining the rag rug, and felt nothing. Ian had been right all along. These men were evil and could not be trusted. But she had not listened to Ian. She had been deaf and blind, and so had caused this thing to happen. She was already paying. Now Ian would have to pay as well. "Get out, get out while 'tis safe, before they find him."

Ian and Ailsa, still pressed back to front, still gripping the gun, let it fall from numb fingers. This man, dead before them, was a wealthy Englishman, even if he was a coward and a blackguard. They knew what would happen now. Both turned to look at Jenny, who had taken Ian's cloak from the horn rack near the door. She held the cloak open, waiting for her husband to grab it and run. "Ye must go. The gray cloak will help hide ye. Put it on. Hurry."

Ailsa turned to Ian. "She's right. Ye must go."

"Both of ye!" Jenny cried. "Hurry!"

Ian turned to her, tossed the cloak over his shoulder and took her face in his hands. "Jenny . . ."

She could not meet her husband's eyes. "Go. Be safe. Forgive me." Her voice broke, but she did not weep.

"There's nothing to forgive. But ye might have believed in me."

Jenny looked up at Ailsa and knew *she* had never stopped believing, that though she'd been afraid, she had not let panic deter her, had not stopped to consider her own peril. Ailsa would have followed Ian into a hail of gunfire if she thought he needed her. But Jenny had let fright overwhelm her wisdom and her knowledge of Ian's nature.

Now, when it was too late, she realized the malignant haze which had robbed her of her sanity had come as much from her fear of Ailsa as from her fear of poverty. That was why she had never spoken of it before. Ailsa had been safe and married in London for so long that Jenny had forgotten that particular, debilitating terror. She had felt safe in Ian's arms and his affection.

Duncan had certainly offered her a kind of hope, but it had never been real. In her heart, she had known her brother-in-law could not make her world secure, especially since Ailsa had returned to the glen. Perhaps, after all, there had been a touch of spite in her faith in the strangers Ian hated. Perhaps, after all, she had meant to hurt her husband in the only way she knew how.

She realized with paralytic certainty that had she kept faith with and in Ian, he would have stayed with her forever. In doubting him, she had lost him. "I believe, my husband. And I understand. Now. I do." She glanced at Ailsa and added, "I'm sorry it wasn't sooner. I want ye both to go. Ye take my cloak, Ailsa. 'Tis also gray. 'Twill protect ye among the rocks. I want ye safe. Please."

It was as much for her as for themselves that she was pleading. She held out the cloak—the only amends she could make, the only apology she could offer, and the only help.

Ailsa blinked, touched Jenny's hand in sad comprehension, and followed Ian into the thickening mist. She prayed it would hide them, but knew it could not hide them from themselves. Ian did not speak as he took her hand and they began to run, silent and dazed, into the forest that had always been their shelter.

22

GLENYSS STOOD FROZEN AND WHITE-FACED FOR A LONG TIME,
her body numb and her mind blank. She had expected disaster, but not this. Never this. She could not take it in, would
not accept it. As she lingered outside the window of her
parents' croft, staring from the body on the floor to her
mother, poised like a lifeless wooden doll at the door, the
girl began to shake. She should have done as Ailsa said and
waited with Alanna and David. Except that she could not
have done that. She'd known she was needed as much as
Ailsa. Perhaps more.

She looked at Jenny's gray, drawn face in the lamplight,
and her body began to move again, though her mind was in
a deep fog of horror. Slowly, she rounded the croft and went
inside. Jenny stood, arms out but empty. She was motionless,
bloodless, and when Glenyss took her hands, they were cold.

"Mama, ye must sit and drink some whisky." Glenyss
tugged on her mother's arm, tasting nausea that broke into
a chill sweat at the sight of Jenny's helplessness.

For a long time Jenny did not respond, but simply stood,
arms outstretched as if to clasp an absent lover. The emptiness of those arms broke Glenyss's heart. "Please!"

She continued to tug until suddenly Jenny's bones seemed
to disintegrate and she collapsed against her twelve-year-old
daughter, unable to hold herself upright anymore. Glenyss
bit her lip until it bled and led her mother to the chair
farthest from the man who lay bleeding on the floor. Her
own hands shaking so badly that she spilled more than half
the whisky, she poured her mother a cupful and forced
Jenny to drink it.

There was no change. Her mother stared at nothing, no

394

light flickered behind her eyes, no acknowledgment of the burning of the liquor down her throat.

"Mama, we have to *do* something. I can't do it alone. Please! I don't know what to do! Please."

Jenny stared and did not answer. She had retreated so far into the darkness she could not conceive of the light, much less labor to reach it.

At last Glenyss dropped her mother's hands and stood across the room from Robert Howard, trying to think. Jenny would not think for her, and she knew she could not do this alone. Then she remembered. Ailsa had sent her back to David and Alanna, but she had not gone. She had burned with the need to know what was happening to her parents.

She shuddered, her erratic pulse the only sign that her icy blood still flowed. Her teeth chattered so hard that the sound was a desecration in the croft full of death. Glenyss forced herself to think of David, who was strong and wise and had lived in the cruelty of the city. He would know what to do. Alanna was warm and would not stare vacantly as Jenny did.

Glenyss knelt before her mother, hands on Jenny's knees. "I have to get help, Mama. We'll be back soon." She was almost certain her mother did not hear, but she went on doggedly. "Don't do anything while I'm gone. Just sit and rest. I'll be here soon, I promise."

With one last anguished backward glance, she left the croft and began to run.

Alanna and David sat at the kitchen table, watching the door, as if waiting for the moment when Glenyss would come crashing through, looking more like a ghost than she had before.

"Ye have to come! 'Tis horrible. And Mama just sits there. Please, come!"

They did not pause to ask questions. They were up and out the door in an instant, following Glenyss's pitiful figure in the pale moonlight. Her night-rail was filthy, and she ran awkwardly, tripping often in her agitation. David took a few huge steps and caught her in his arms while Alanna followed. It did not take long for the three of them to reach the Fraser croft.

Though they had known something was very wrong, though they had been waiting for this summons, the sight of Robert Howard's body shocked them into silence.

Glenyss watched with wide, desperate eyes, praying they would not retreat as Jenny had. Then Alanna spoke.

"Is he dead?"

David looked down at the man, touched the pulse at the base of his throat, put his ear above Howard's parted lips. "Aye. Dead." He turned to look at his wife for a long moment. They had noticed that Ian and Ailsa were both absent, that Jenny sat as stilted and white as marble, and as cold.

Alanna turned to Glenyss. The girl sank to the floor, certain the adults would take the burden from her shoulders. The rush of relief destroyed the paralysis that had protected her until now. Folding in upon herself, she began to cry. Alanna held her gently, torn plaid, muddy gown and all, and rubbed her back with a tender hand. When the sobs subsided a little, she murmured, "I know 'tis hard for ye, birdeen, but we're here now. Ye needn't worry anymore. Only, can ye tell us what happened? We need to know that."

Glenyss told them, sobbing and hiccuping. Alanna and David tried to listen without expression, though they glanced at Jenny now and again. She seemed to be working her way back from the protective and consuming darkness. Perhaps it was the sound of Glenyss's frail voice, or the facts of what had happened, viewed from her defenseless daughter's perspective.

She thought she had done everything she could do, but as Glenyss talked, Jenny glanced at the body and knew it was not over yet. Only then did she wonder about the future.

When Glenyss was done, David paced, trying to think.

"Couldn't we—we could hide the—hide him," Alanna suggested, swallowing her revulsion.

Glenyss started violently. "They know he's here, Uncle Duncan and the other man. He told me so. They know he was coming to try to convince Papa."

David nodded grimly. "Besides, we could never get the stains out of the rug or the floor," he said matter-of-factly. But he did not feel matter-of-fact. He had pushed his rage back, far back and deep inside him, because he needed to think clearly, but it was there. He could feel it pulsing, breathing with the rhythm of a primitive animal about to be unleashed.

He picked up the pistol and examined it slowly, with more care than necessary. "They can't really call it murder. He brought the gun, after all, and Uncle Ian's haven't been disturbed. Ian didn't even know the man was coming, so they can't say he planned it. It's Howard's fault; he caused it all. Should be self-defense." But he knew that might not help Ian in the end.

David wondered if Duncan Fraser had left so far behind the bonds and instincts of his heritage that he would stand against his brother. Would he even believe Ian had acted out of a desperate need for self-preservation? Or would he side with those who would condemn his brother without listening to the facts?

Men like Simon Black—ruthless, bitter, wealthy—who had the power to influence the authorities as he wished. Black would say Jenny had lured Howard here so Ian could kill him and thus put an end to the threat to the glen. And he would be believed.

Would Duncan Fraser back him? Consumed as he was by fury at his stubborn and heedless father, David could not quite believe Duncan would betray them so completely. He prayed he was right, that the call of his father's blood was more compelling than the lure of the world that had become his triumph and his haven.

At that moment, Mairi slipped into the room. She looked over at the body and shuddered. "I dreamt of an explosion in Ian's house, and it was violent red, so I came." She stared from one desolate face to the other, to Glenyss, shivering in a corner, her dirty cheeks streaked with tears. "There's nothing I can do," Mairi murmured in despair.

"He's dead," Alanna whispered. She did not want to disturb his ghost, who would wander the night forever because of his violent death. "Jenny needs ye, Grandmother. She's alone inside her head, and I think 'tis very dark in there."

Mairi went to Jenny without asking questions. She knew she would learn the answers in time. There was a sense of urgency inside this cottage, a need to explain and put in order so the tragedy made some kind of sense, so it could be justified to outsiders. Though, like David, she guessed that, in their narrow view, there could be no justification. She concentrated on bringing the warmth back to Jenny's frigid hands.

Alanna watched as if from a great distance, horrified by the grim scene in the croft. Though she had lived in London, she'd never seen violence or death close up. She could not comprehend how this had happened. As she watched David pace, his dark hair wild, as he thought out what they should do, she felt his rage grow; it sparked from his eyes like fire from a jewel in sunlight. For the first time, she realized the spark that so attracted her was dangerous as well as seductive. Ian and Ailsa had feared such violence. In attempting to stop David from committing it, they had committed it themselves.

She did not want to know these things. She did not want to see how competent her husband was at gathering them together and making certain they all knew exactly what to say, that their stories would not vary by a single detail. It was as if he had done this before. Perhaps for Bran Guthrie.

"Remember," David repeated for the fourth time, "Robert Howard drew the gun. It was he who attacked Ian first. He was killed with his own gun, foolishly and needlessly drawn."

He thought with dread of Simon Black, frustrated, stymied and made to look foolish by the Highlanders too often. Already at the boiling point, he would erupt when he learned Robert Howard was dead. It would be the last straw.

"Are you sure you remember?" David asked again, though he felt no flicker of hope. He wished he had killed Howard when he had the chance. He'd wanted to so badly that his fists had clenched and unclenched with a life of their own. The heat in his blood had very nearly decimated his common sense. But he had not allowed himself to succumb to the hot, pulsing desire to kill. Had he done so, he would have stopped this tragedy. He knew the men, the system, the corruption well enough that he might have overcome them. Ian had no such knowledge. All he knew was the power of the glen. David thought of Ian and Ailsa fleeing for their lives and his wrath threatened to burst up and out, but he resolutely forced it down again. Not now. Not yet.

Jenny looked glazed, despite Mairi's soothing hands and voice. Glenyss sobbed now and again, while Alanna and David stood side by side and tried to hold each other upright.

Everyone jumped when they heard querulous voices approaching, and a loud imperious knock on the door.

"Howard? Are you in there?"

When there was no answer, Duncan Fraser pushed open the door, fist raised, face flushed from too much port, eyes glittering. "Where is he, by God? What have you done with Robert Howard?"

23

IAN AND AILSA RAN BLINDLY, WITHOUT THOUGHT. THEIR minds were blessedly empty, made blank by trauma; no bloody images impeded their progress. They were not afraid. Not yet. They were running because they had to get away, because Jenny had cloaked them and told them to go.

They ran hand in hand, but neither felt the other's touch. To feel that would be to feel everything, and they were not ready, could not bear to know what they had done, to see the dead man's face, the blood spreading over his chest, vivid and red, the look of astonishment in his eyes.

They ran through bracken and heather, over thistles that broke the skin of their sandaled feet, and nettles that stung and would not go. Over grasses and pine needles, through hawthorn hedge and holly, around pine, spruce and birch, up hills and down braes. They scrambled, blind in the dim moonlight, overwhelmed by what had happened. They stumbled, falling, pulling each other down into damp ferns, then forcing each other up to run again.

By unspoken agreement, they went the long way around the Valley of the Dead. Once they left the ground, once they traversed stone ledges and tumbled boulders, they became more conscious of the hazardous landscape. Ian lost his balance, his inadequately shod feet torn and bleeding from unfriendly nettles and stones and thistles, but Ailsa caught him around the waist and they swayed out into the wailing wind.

In the force and fury of that wind, they fought to regain control, until they caught the pitted rock face and held tight, their feet lodged in a narrow crag. Afterward, they went more slowly, taking care to cling tightly to indentations in the rock wall or sprouts of heather that sprung up here and there.

Winded and gasping for air, they ducked beneath a low overhang and into the cave they had discovered long ago. They crawled on hands and knees until they saw the pale wash of moonlight where the cave had partially collapsed inward. They walked, hardly daring to breathe or moan with pain at their bruises and cuts and the bits of nettle and twig embedded in feet and hands and arms.

When they reached the back of the cave, dark and wrapped in deep shadow, they felt their way toward the Chisholm chest, secreted away after the Highlanders were slaughtered by the British at Culloden Moor. The Chisholm family had hidden many of their precious family heirlooms before they fled the Highlands, fearing to lose them along the way, and fully intending to return and claim them someday. Instead, over a hundred years later, Ian and Ailsa had found them and treasured them, and eventually returned them to their resting place.

When they felt the chest beneath their hands, Ian and Ailsa collapsed, leaning against the cool wood, the familiar carvings. Their sacred secret place. They were safe here, for the moment. They prayed to the Celtic gods that it be so.

After long minutes while they held their aching sides and fought to breathe, staring at the ghostly textures of the rock floor transformed by clinging shadows, they at last looked up to meet each other's eyes.

In an instant, they pressed their bloody palms together and huddled face to face in their gray cloaks with the hoods pulled over their heads. For a long time, they did not move again, just clung, so close that the edges of their cloaks met and they looked like a single oddly shaped boulder in the eerie darkness.

When the sound of their ragged breathing had ceased to echo off the walls, when silence enfolded them, and their heartbeats slowed, Ian looked up. "I didn't mean to kill him."

Ailsa met his eyes, and her clasp on his hands grew tighter. "Yes, ye did. For an instant, no more, ye could no' believe he'd stood in your home and said such things. For an instant, ye saw the evil in people as ye'd never seen it before. Ye felt it on your skin and in your hair and on your tongue, like a sticky poison which, if ye breathed it in, would taint your insides with his ugliness. For that instant, Ian, ye wanted to eradicate that poison, that evil, that ugliness he had made ye see and feel. Ye wanted him dead. And so did I."

Ian blinked at her, at her blue-violet eyes that gleamed in the cool, safe womb of the cave. He saw the truth there, and it shook him deeply. He had forgotten how easily she had once known his thoughts and felt his feelings, how profoundly she had understood—good and bad, magic and mundane, heart and soul and rage and joy. She had just described his feelings as if they were her own. She had not merely stood beside him in that croft, she had stood *inside* him, and she knew it all.

He began to shake and couldn't speak.

"For an instant afterward, for one more instant in all the

minutes and days and hours of your life, ye were glad he was dead, Ian, glad ye'd been the one to kill him. But that has passed now, as the anger passed while we ran, punishing ourselves for our impure thoughts, our momentary hatred." She released him and held up her bleeding palms, pointed to her battered feet and arms, then his. " 'Tis not enough, I suppose, this little suffering of ours, to make up for that instant. But then, 'tis hard to forgive someone who makes ye see as deep into the black heart of man as ye can see."

"I'll never forgive him," Ian murmured. His voice was hoarse and raw, as if he had been shouting, though he had long been silent. He reached for Ailsa and held her so tightly she could not breathe, but she did not try to loosen his grip. Instead, she ran her fingers through his hair, mindlessly and tenderly, while his tears seeped into her gray wool cloak.

David dragged his father and Simon Black into the croft. They shouted and cursed and fell on their knees beside their partner, then rose with silvered fury in their eyes. "Who did this?" Simon Black demanded. "I'll kill him."

He moved toward the door, but David blocked it with his body. His eyes were hard and cold, and the muscles in his arms stood out as he pressed his hands into the doorframe. "You will listen." He spoke softly, but his tone stopped the cursing and flailing. "You will be quiet and you will listen."

Duncan Fraser stared at the young man in the doorway and did not know him. He blinked and shook his head to clear it, but the fog would not go. He was afraid of the stranger in the doorway. He knew without being told that David would kill him before he let him leave this place.

Even Simon Black was temporarily silenced.

They listened while David told them what had happened, dispassionately, concisely, clearly. "He was defending himself and his family," he finished.

Duncan looked from Alanna to Mairi to Jenny to Glenyss. Their faces told him nothing. They would not speak unless David told them to. Even then they would say nothing new. Their stories would echo his in every detail, Duncan was certain.

He thought of his brother with a smoking pistol in his hand, and his head reeled and whirled. If there was one thing Duncan Fraser had believed in all his life, beneath the cynicism, the anger, the greed, it was in Ian's gentle, honest heart. He tangled his fingers in his hair and ground his teeth until his jaw ached. He could not believe Ian had done this thing.

"It was self-defense."

"That's a goddamned lie. It was murder." Simon Black took a step toward David. He'd seen enough of these Highlanders to believe they were capable of anything. They were barbaric and uncivilized, unlike Robert Howard, who had been a gentleman. "It was murder, and if you think we're going to let Ian Fraser go free, you're just as mad as he is. Now, get out of our way."

"We'll never find him," Duncan managed. "My brother knows the glen too well, and we know it too little." He should have said more, defended Ian against Black's accusations, but he could not find the words or the strength. Instead he stood, paralyzed and impotent.

Simon snarled and lost control. "Damn all that! I'm going to kill the bastard." He swung around toward Ian's rifle propped on a wall rack. He grabbed it, found the shells in a pouch at the end of the rack, and began to load the rifle.

"Don't be a fool!" Duncan shouted, shocked out of his numb misery. "My brother's not going to hurt us. We don't need a rifle."

"I've got my pistol, too," Simon said. He removed it from his belt and pointed it at David. "Get out of the way."

"Think a minute," Duncan equivocated. "We need more men. Men familiar with the landscape. It's dark out and there's barely a moon. I want him as badly as you do, but think."

"Yes, think." David smiled a ghastly smile and added, "My father's right. Ian knows the glen. You, on the other hand, know nothing at all. Leave it be till we can get the magistrate."

David's cool, sarcastic tone was too much for Simon. He lunged toward the door, waving his pistol and cursing. David

moved, making certain the women were out of range.
"You're a fool," he said.

Simon Black didn't bother to respond. He wrenched the
door open and was outside in an instant. "Coming, Fraser?"
he called over his shoulder.

Duncan looked from his wintry-eyed son to his wild-eyed
partner. He sensed the tension in David's waiting. Here was
one last chance for Duncan Fraser to choose his family, his
blood, over profit and madness. David wanted him to stay
and wait so justice could prevail. But Duncan knew Simon
Black was far more dangerous than his son just now. If left
alone, there was no telling what he might do. He was a cold
and calculating man, colder than most Duncan dealt with.
He would want revenge, not only for the death of his friend,
but for the humiliation he had suffered at the hands of what
he called "these savages."

Duncan could not take that risk, nor could he take time
to explain. Simon was waiting, but he would not wait for
long. Making sure his own pistol was in his belt, Duncan
turned to his son. Those eyes, so green and wise and so like
Ian's. And yet the eyes of an unforgiving stranger. "I *have*
to go. It's the only way."

David's gaze did not flicker as he indicated the door. "Go
then. You made your choice long ago. I should have known
you couldn't change. Not even for Ian."

Duncan swallowed dryly but found no words to console
his son. His brother had killed a man. Ian Fraser had killed
a man. He had no time for disbelief or regret. All at once,
Duncan was desperate with fear.

Doggedly, feeling the chill at his back run through his
blood like the burn in winter, he followed Simon out the
door.

24

AILSA HEARD IT FIRST—AN ANGRY SHOUT FOLLOWED BY rifle fire. She raised her head and Ian shuddered, drew several deep breaths before he heard it too.

They were coming, the men who would hunt them. They could not tell how many, because the shouts echoed off the walls, and the explosion from the rifles sounded like cannons.

Ian and Ailsa crouched as far back as they could in a jagged crevice of rock. It was too late to run. They were safer here in the hidden cave, protected by darkness and intractable stone. They faced each other, breathed raggedly into their open mouths, swallowing the sound of their own breath, pressing chest to chest to silence the fierce beat of their hearts. They could hear from the rage in the voices outside that there was no justice out there in the night. They held one another and waited.

"Must've come here," Simon Black hissed. "Someone mentioned some secret caves. Thought we'd be too stupid to find them. But then, they've underestimated us from the beginning."

"Slow down!" Duncan gasped. He pretended it was his extra bulk that kept him laboring behind Simon, but it was really reluctance. "You'll kill us both, and then they'll have won well and truly."

"Shut up!" Simon Black was not thinking; he was reacting to the aggravation and frustration that had been building since the day he arrived in this godforsaken place. Robert Howard had not wanted to come. He had been the wise one, after all. Now he was dead. "Come out, you bloody bastard. Come out now, while there's still a chance for you."

Duncan peered at Simon through narrowed eyes. He knew there was no chance unless he could somehow protect Ian until they found a magistrate or the constable. He quivered with foreboding, not for himself or his son or even for Black or his dead friend. It was for Ian. His brother was not a murderer. That much Duncan knew.

"Someone should go directly to get a magistrate," Simon grunted, climbing awkwardly up the stone walls.

Duncan was relieved. "That'd be wise. But if you find one closer than Inverness I'd be surprised. As far as I know, there's only the constable in Cannich and one or two in Beauly."

"Then we have to get Ian Fraser first and save the magistrate for later." Black looked over his shoulder once, the glint in his eyes dark and sinister.

Duncan did not like either the look or the sound of Simon's suggestion. "We should go for the constable, just the same. Do you want to be a murderer as well?"

Black ignored him and plowed grimly ahead, tripping over pebbles and scraping his cheek on a boulder. That only enraged him further.

"Where are you, you coward? Hiding among the bones of your ancestors? Will the ghosts protect you now, I wonder?"

For what seemed like hours, Ian and Ailsa crouched, enveloped in the sound of those unearthly threatening voices that bounced off the walls and crawled up their spines. Pebbles rattling down the rock face were transformed into an avalanche of boulders rolling toward them in the darkness. Footsteps became the heavy march of booted feet from the army that had once terrorized the Highlanders who hid in these caves and hillsides. The sound echoed up and down, circling around the crouched figures, raising images of a gruesome past where there had been neither mercy nor compassion nor justice in the bloody deaths of those who'd rallied behind Bonny Prince Charlie.

Ian and Ailsa could not understand the words, but voices shouted, one above the other, amplified by the rock walls into wordless threats and mindless terror. Then the footsteps came closer, and the voices became clear.

"If you come out now, we won't hurt you, though we'd like to string you up ourselves. But if you don't, we'll get the law and hunt you down, no matter how long it takes. Take the easy way for once. Come out."

Ian and Ailsa felt the malevolence in that voice and knew the promise was a lie. If they showed themselves now, whoever owned that voice would kill them. Ian was safer here where they were unlikely to find him among the tortuous caves and gullies and crevices in stone. Especially in the dark, they could do little more than stumble about blindly, lanterns or no.

The two remained unmoving on the cold, hard floor.

At last, exhausted from their rocky climb and fruitless search, Duncan added his voice to Simon's. He could tell the other man was tiring, that his first wash of rage was fading, though it would grow hot again when he'd eaten and rested and fueled it with the harsh reality of Howard's death. Duncan pleaded with his invisible brother, his plea loudest and longest of all. He hoped and prayed that by drawing Ian into the open, he could avoid what he feared in his gut could not be avoided.

Ian did not listen, but at last Simon did. He agreed, near dawn, to go to Cannich and get help. He was bloody, exhausted and frustrated. He had realized, as the aches and pains began to seep into his body, that he could not do this alone. Duncan was right. He had wasted his time, his energy, his anger. Ian Fraser had committed a crime, after all. Let the law punish him. Otherwise, as Duncan pointed out in a rare moment of perception, the people of the glen would make him a hero.

Duncan sighed with relief when Simon went off in search of a horse. "I'll stay behind to watch," he said, "make certain Ian doesn't slip out while you're gone and get away."

Simon Black scrutinized his partner coldly. "You do that, Fraser. You'd damned well better." He turned abruptly and was gone.

For a long time Duncan continued to wander the glen, searching for his brother, his family, his past. "Ian, come out. It's safe now, I tell you. Come out before it's too late." He called and called, cajoled, pleaded, demanded until he was hoarse and his voice became a croak, then a whisper.

Finally, Duncan stopped at a tangle of larch roots. He realized he was hopelessly lost. He did not know the glen *or* his brother. He did not know where Ian might seek refuge.

In desperation, Duncan stumbled through the deep gray darkness until he found his way to David and Alanna's croft. Like him, they had not slept. Like him, they were worn out with worry and weariness and anger. They stood side by side and eyed Duncan aloofly.

"I've sent Black off to get the constable," he said. "I want to find Ian first, to protect him. Please, if you know where he might go, tell me. I want to save him."

His son and daughter-in-law stared at him mutely.

"You must listen to me. I want to help." They had to believe him, to listen, to act. He could not do it alone.

David and Alanna did not answer, did not even bother to shake their heads. Duncan crumbled before their silent condemnation. He stumbled from the cottage and into the woods, unaware of the branches tearing his shirt and scratching his cheek, of the animals skittering out of his way or the river rumbling by so near he could reach out a hand and touch it.

Only then did he realize he had truly lost his son. And no wonder. Claiming he wanted to save Ian. Duncan could not save Ian; he was completely powerless. This long night had proven it, if he had not guessed before. He could only destroy his brother, and David knew it.

At the base of the rock wall, Duncan collapsed, each breath an agony, face purple with exertion. Underneath the heightened color, his skin was very pale. He trembled, sick at heart from a kind of pain he had not known existed. Or perhaps he had known, and had fought all his life to deny its existence, to keep the agony at bay.

"If only I'd listened," he muttered. "If only I'd respected Ian and David enough to believe them, this could have been avoided. If I hadn't been so full of pride and envy at the easy affection between Ian and Angus, who always understood each other. Now Ian and David have that same understanding. Even when I was a boy, they made me feel like an outsider." If he had not been jealous because his own son had been accepted, understood, loved by both Ian and Angus, this would never have happened. If he had not been so self-absorbed, so blind, he would have left after the wedding, giving David and his bride the only gift they wanted—peace.

What bothered Duncan most of all was the knowledge that the glen held some secret he could not understand, but David could. Not only had David understood it, he had absorbed it and become it. He *would* have been happy, and Duncan did not know how to be.

Duncan spoke aloud to the night and the darkness, though no one could hear. It was too late for that. Too late for him.

Ian Fraser was not guilty of causing Robert Howard's death. Duncan was guilty, and Duncan alone.

For the first time in his life, as he sat at the foot of that barren rock hillside, Duncan Fraser wept.

He was barely aware he was no longer alone, though Mairi slipped her arm about his shoulders and pulled him close. It was her scent that finally woke him from his stupor of self-pity—the fragrance of earth and grass and sweet summer flowers. Duncan looked up in astonishment at the compassion in Mairi Rose's eyes. How could she bear to touch him, let alone try to comfort him?

"I only wanted to help," he cried brokenly. "How can that be wrong?"

"If your help is no' desired nor asked for, then even if ye accomplish your aim, mayhap 'tis not best. Perhaps even ye would be happier if ye let it go. I think ye were trying to play God, Duncan Fraser. And the gods resent human interference. They resent men who doubt them, who'll no' believe they've the will and the power to make things right."

Duncan glowered as his tears subsided. What was she doing here? How had she found him and why had she stopped? Surely his despair could not touch her, of all people. "How often have they managed that, I'd like to know? Look around you, Mairi Rose. How can anyone believe that

God is even listening, let alone capable of helping? We have to help ourselves."

Smiling sadly, Mairi touched his cheek with her fingertips. "Aye, so we do. We can no' sit about and wait for miracles to make our lives ordered and happy. But there are times when all ye can do is wait, and have faith. The things *ye* have faith in have not the power to change the world and make ye sleep sounder and safer at night. They've the power to buy ye a better bed, aye. But 'tis hardly enough, even for ye, is it?"

Duncan looked away. He could not meet her perceptive violet gaze, undimmed by mist or confusion or doubt. "No," he muttered beneath his breath. "It's not enough. It never will be."

25

IAN AND AILSA CLUNG TIGHT TO KEEP EACH OTHER SILENT, though the sounds of the footsteps and voices had faded away. They held on, absorbing the sound of each other's heartbeat. When their breath settled to normal and their pulses slowed and the terror retreated, they clutched each other, shivering in fright, relief and something more: a kind of comfort they had not felt in many years, since they were barely more than children and Ailsa chose to leave the glen. A bone-deep comfort, freed by the adrenaline of fear that had nudged awake long-dormant yearnings. The clinging became both more violent and more tender.

Without conscious thought, at first without awareness, they passed from fear to need, from careful, distant friends to the confidants they had once been. Ian raised his left palm and Ailsa her right and they came together, palm to palm, heat to heat, vision to vision. Propelled by a force from deep within, they twined their chilled and aching fingers.

It was here, twenty-three years ago, that they had said good-bye. It was here, now, that they opened their souls again to one another, and greeted each other in joy and perfect, sweet recognition. As they had in childhood, they knew each other in every way one can know another, as a person knows his or her own image in a mirror—not quite perfectly, but clearly, deeply, painfully, in their flaws as well as their virtues.

When Ian drew back a little, the thread between them pulled taut and firm, destroying all barriers they'd constructed over the years. He shivered and stared down at his crumpled cloak, stained here and there with his own blood and Ailsa's. "I'd forgotten what it feels like to let someone else inside your skin. It makes ye completely vulnerable. 'Twould be so easy now, for ye to hurt me. Ye can see all the bruises, all the places where I'm tender and the pain comes quickly." He paused for a long time, shaken by the magnitude of feelings that overwhelmed him, knowing it was the horror of the situation that had brought this perilous and beautiful communion into being.

It took him a while to regain his composure. He did not remember being so distraught in a long while. "I never noticed before, because you'd always been ... *with* me. But to have been empty for so long, and then to feel ye here again, inside me ..." He paused again, because his voice was shaking. "I think I understand better now why ye ran away so long ago."

Ailsa nodded; she could not find her voice among the turbulent emotions that whirled inside her. She felt weak, her hands clammy, her breathing unsteady. Yet at the same time, she felt strong and full of hope.

She leaned closer to Ian. This time he did not back away. They had not unclasped their hands, and now they held tighter, and their bent arms were a barrier, the only barrier to their complete absorption, one into the other. Terror was a powerful force to have destroyed so quickly what had taken years, determination and the sublimation of much pain, of the very core of who and what they were, to create.

They were not aware when the cloaks slid from their shoulders, when their rediscovered bond transformed itself from awareness to desire. Their clasped hands parted and the last barrier fell away. Desperately, they leaned together until their lips touched lightly. They looked into each other's eyes and could not look away, any more than they could silence the sudden craving of their battered, aching bodies. They had not been alone together in twenty-three years. They had not known each other, spoken their hearts or even their deepest thoughts, had not touched one another. All at once, the emptiness was unbearable.

Ian put his arms around Ailsa and she pressed against him, tasting his lips as if they were sweet syrup and her body craved sugar above all things. He cupped her face in his hands, and she was aware of every scratch, every abrasion, every patch of dried blood. These things reminded her of what they had been through; she felt the texture of those scarred hands gratefully. She knew that touch, though it had been so long, knew it and needed it to heal the wounds inside.

As Ian kissed her cheek, her nose, her forehead, she reached out to cup his face, to see if she remembered what it felt like to hold him this way, with nothing between them but understanding and acceptance. She ran her hands through his long, dark curls, brushing her lips over the gray hairs, sighing as the emptiness began to fill and the darkness to lighten.

Ian pulled her close, so that their hearts beat one into the other, and she slid her arms around his back, feeling his heat through the fabric of his shirt. Her cheek lay against his, her hair tangled with his. For a long time, they did not move. Ian had forgotten what it was like simply to hold her, to breathe with the rise and fall of her breath, to feel her meld with him, body and spirit. To feel the ardent satisfaction of sharing the rhythms of her body, to know that the desire flaring in him was flickering inside her. To know words were unnecessary, would have been a desecration.

It was not enough for him. It had been too long. He wanted to know her everywhere, as he once had, to touch her with tender fingers that tingled with awareness. In the dark, he could barely see the outline of her body, but he did not need his eyes. Every sense was alert, every nerve singing with expectation.

Ailsa helped him spread the cloaks on the floor of the rock cave. Then they opened the chest for the first time in many years, and lifted out the Chisholm plaid to lay over the cloaks. Gently, Ian lifted Ailsa in his arms and laid her on the refuge they had created. He wanted to place her in the center of the softness with his own two hands, to cradle her as he shivered at the sight of her chestnut hair loosened and spread around her.

Slowly, he untied the laces of her gown and slipped the torn, dirty muslin from her shoulders. He paused at the sight of her shoulders, white where the gown had covered her, pale brown where the sun had reclaimed her since she'd come back to the glen. There was a lump in his throat as he looked at her face, made more lovely by age and wisdom and courage.

She had come home. He'd thought she never would.

Ailsa read his thoughts in his eyes, and her own filled with tears, not of regret or sorrow, but of gratitude. She reached up to trace the path of a tear on his cheek. She smiled, and he gasped at the power of that smile to make him blind and hungry, powerful and helpless.

Ducking his head, Ian drew the gown down Ailsa's body, pulling it over her feet and tossing it into the deeper shadows. He untied her chemise, and she lifted her shoulders so he could remove it.

For a long time, Ian sat on his heels, staring at Ailsa's white body—her breasts, larger than he remembered, but full and round, enticing. Her flat belly, scarred by stretch marks that he touched with awe because somehow they did not detract from her beauty. It was part of her strength and her fierce spirit—the children whose varied lives those marks represented, the way she had given of herself and in doing so, made herself more, not less. Her legs were white and long, and her hips curved outward. She had begun, slowly, to gain back the weight she had lost before she came here.

Ian thought of the woman he had encountered that first afternoon, the empty eyes and gray, pallid face, the hair severely restrained as if that would also restrain her wild grief. He remembered with physical pain that woman who had not been Ailsa. A stranger seeking refuge in a place she no longer knew or understood.

That woman was gone forever. This was Ailsa, blue-violet eyes dark with pleasure, excitement, longing, lying naked and unmoving while he looked at her. She had disappeared once but was with him now; every part of her body, every one of her senses. She was no longer blind or deaf to the beauty all around her. She was part of it; it flourished in her eyes and in her soul.

Ian kissed her lingeringly, though his lips were cracked and dry. She did not wince or pull away, but drew him closer. She did not mind the pain beneath the white, searing pleasure of feeling his touch again.

She worked at the buttons and opened his shirt, revealing the soft hair on his chest, more sprinkled with gray than the hair on his head. While she pulled the shirt away, Ian removed his trousers. At last, both were naked, alone, free.

Ailsa's heart pounded and her skin tingled as the fever built and spread. Ian began at her toes, touching each one, kissing those that were torn or bloody, then stroking her feet, memorizing the shape of them, the veins beneath his palms, the arch that made her gasp when he touched it searchingly with his fingertip.

The blood pounded in his head, and the cold of stone and dirt and the night around them ceased to exist in the heat he created between their bodies. He circled her ankles with thumb and forefinger, breathing gently on the circles so his breath raised chills on the sensitive skin beneath. He swallowed and continued up her legs, sliding his hands from palm to back to palm again, inside and then outside, making her tremble and moan.

Ian closed his eyes, overwhelmed by the sensations that shook him as he caressed her thighs, slowly, enticingly, stirring himself as much as her. Then he brushed her languidly between the legs. At the rush of heat that filled his hand, the blaze inside him flared, bright, hot and irresistible.

Ailsa shuddered as Ian caressed her, mesmerizing her, beguiling her, setting her aflame. She had forgotten how her body could blaze beneath his hands, how seductive were the tremors that shook her, the chills that rose along her skin, the heat that answered deep inside. He knelt above her, touched and kissed her, excited her with his warm and skillful breath until she began to shake and could not stop. "Ian!" she cried out at the spinning vortex of flame inside. She could see nothing, feel nothing but his hands, his mouth, his hair brushing over her naked skin.

Ian was not oblivious of his own need. Just now, what he needed was to know Ailsa again, every inch of her, to touch her and feel her respond to that touch, to remember with his hands and tongue the feel of her body and her pleasure.

Deliberately, though she tried to draw him over her, he continued his path of discovery, circling her belly with his tongue, then the cleft between her breasts. He cupped them in his hands and his heartbeat raced as his breath escaped in a rush of desire.

He touched her nipples with his fingertips, brushed them with his tongue, one and then the other, until Ailsa cried out as she felt his hands caress the hollow in her throat, trace her cheekbones delicately.

She was captivated, enchanted by the arresting progress of his gentle hands. He kissed her again, she opened her mouth to him and their tongues entwined.

The weight of his body was upon her, as gentle as his touch, as stimulating as his warm tongue—a promise that his own yearning would soon be fulfilled. Ailsa needed that fulfillment as much as she needed her own. She needed him inside her, sated, consumed by the flames that burned in her until the fires became one, not two, not separate, but forged of the same heat, the same need, the same blaze of satisfaction.

He began to rock, and she with him, her hands cupping his buttocks, her breasts brushing his chest. He pressed his cheek to hers, and she leaned into him, pressing closer, feeling the texture of his skin as she could not feel her own, until it became her own.

Ian shuddered as he moved with Ailsa, rhythmically, fueling the conflagration within, the tremors that ran through his body, the great surging force of pleasure and the pain of that incandescent, searing fever that consumed him, then exploded with his cry. "Ailsa!"

She clutched him, torn apart and healed by the force of their hunger, carried beyond the cave to the colors in a cloud-laden summer sunset, to the turbulence of the violent rushing water, and the soothing pressure of smooth, round stones.

Her body was wet with exertion and pleasure and Ian's seed between her thighs. Her mind was quiet as the colors faded and the fire burned low and smoldered. Ian held her close as they lay together while the blinding light of their yearning faded into cool, whispering darkness.

26

THEY DID NOT KNOW HOW LONG THEY LAY UNMOVING, EXcept the darkness was not yet lightened by approaching dawn. Ian and Ailsa drew apart and knelt on the Chisholm plaid, facing each other. Gracefully, they raised their hands, held them a breath apart. For a long time they crouched, not touching, close enough to feel each other's warmth, then, slowly, reverently, they pressed their palms together as they used to do as children.

It was not yet morning, and they had not spoken since they pledged themselves to one another, completely and forever, but both had begun, gradually, to think again. Until now, the future had not mattered. Nothing had mattered except that they had found each other once again, that they remembered and were not afraid of what those memories implied. No matter what happened around them, they would not face it alone. They would never be alone again, because they were alive in one another.

But now the hours of darkness, always brief in summer, were dying toward the light. They knew it even if they could not see it, for the cave was dark and deep and hidden, but Ian and Ailsa knew the rhythms of nature as they knew themselves. They understood that this night could not be endless, though neither would ever be the same.

Ian's green eyes met Ailsa's, dark with worry. "I won't go to prison. I couldn't bear it." He did not mention the other, more likely alternative—that he might hang, and for the death of such a man. That possibility was not quite real to them. Such a thought did not belong in their isolated paradise.

Just now, the bond between them was more real than Robert Howard or the Hill of the Hounds or Duncan Fraser and his plan to save them all. Even the feel of a gun going off in their hands seemed far away, lost in a distant past that had no bearing on the present.

Just now, they held each other, and nothing was more important or more real than that simple fact. Time had taken them back to the days when they'd run free in these hills, wild and unfettered as they worshiped at the many flowing waters. The miracle of that turning in time was a gift they must treasure, for they knew miracles were rare and evaporated too quickly.

Much later, when the chill of the stone had begun to penetrate the cocoon that enfolded and protected them, Ailsa said, "I could no' bear prison either."

She did not see Ian smile sadly; he held her too close. Did she really think he would let her take the blame along with him? Did she think the strangers would care about smudges on the handle of a pistol? That Ailsa had taken that pistol, while his fingers were still stiff upon it, and wrapped her own hands around his, had broken his heart with gratitude and pride. She risked nothing, because he would not let her do so, but she believed she had risked everything so he need not be alone. He fought back tears and his throat felt raw.

Ailsa tried to force her mind to function, but fear and desire had taken their toll. "But then, what can we do? Leave the glen?" Her voice was full of horror. She had only just found her way home—the home of her heart and soul and spirit. She could not bear the thought of leaving the place they'd fought so hard to protect. The place where they belonged, that had nurtured them and shaped them into what they were. It was with them now, a palpable presence—the drifting mist, the musty smell of hollow stone, the cool, dark air, and beyond all that, the river and woods, lochs and glens. She felt it on her skin like another breath, in her chest like another heartbeat.

"No." He had no other answer, no way to ease her pain, or his own.

"There's nothing left, then."

Anger eradicated uncertainty. "We are here, ye and me, Ailsa Rose, together. That is a great deal." *'Tis more than I ever hoped to have again.*

He did not speak the last words, yet she heard them clearly, read them in his eyes, wide open to her, so she could see his soul, which he'd hidden for so many years. Ailsa felt a physical pain in her chest. Seemingly of their own volition, their fingers twined and locked. Desire was with them, beneath the fear, laced through the smell of the glen and the memory of all that had once been between them.

"We're too old."

Ian shook his head. "We're too young to say there's nothing left. There is so much, *mo-cridhe.*" His eyes opened wider, his soul glimmered and was hers. They leaned together, hands clasped so tightly they hurt, so white that they might never have felt the caress of the sun, the bite of the wind or the kiss of the mist. Their lips were a breath apart, trembling.

The sight and feel of him was all around her, inside her. It brought rushing back the full intensity of the love she had denied since she left him standing alone at the mouth of this cave. She thought of William, but he was smiling a sad, knowing smile. *The only loyalty you owe my memory is to be happy.* But Ian owed loyalty to others, loyalties more pressing and far less easily fulfilled. The pain and elation were so sweet and so bitter that Ailsa closed her eyes and cried out, "Ian!"

"I'm here."

She opened her eyes and looked into his. He *was* here; he was everywhere, everything, a mirror of her own starved, yearning soul. "How did we get here from that day when we laughingly waylaid the messenger? Running in fear of our lives, from the image of a man dead, from the feel of the gun in our hands? It seems only a moment ago it was all a joke, and now——" She broke off. "I don't understand."

Ian touched her shoulder in reassurance, though he himself was cold and shaken. "I can no' question what brought us here, for terrible as it is, 'tis the greatest blessing the gods could have granted, the greatest joy I've known in years."

Ailsa was shocked. "Ye don't mean that."

"I have to mean it, or remorse and fear will consume me." Ian paused, gazing thoughtfully at the ridged stone wall over Ailsa's shoulder. "Jenny and I were good together. I love her, and my children. What she said and did in the past few days does not matter, for she, like us, was driven by a force she could no' understand."

He was torn by words, unmanned by his betrayal of his wife. He knew, from the look in her eyes as she told him to run, from the way she had forced her own cloak into Ailsa's hands, that Jenny did not believe she deserved his loyalty anymore. He knew that she was wrong. She had given him everything—love, faith, hope, a future—suppressed her greatest fear in order to offer him these gifts. He owed her as much as she had granted him. But his need had been great last night, his terror and disbelief that a single unwise moment could have changed his life forever. Ailsa had been beside him. She had never left him, and in his vulnerability and confusion, his soul had opened up to her. He was not strong enough to resist what was between them, and always had been, whether spoken or unspoken, acknowledged or denied. But that did not change the fact that he had betrayed his Jenny, his wife, his friend. He wept inside for her, and for his weakness, but he could not turn away.

"What we have, Ailsa, ye and me, is outside these things, beyond them. Ye know that as well as I."

"I know."

Their lips met in a kiss so fleeting it might not have been at all, except that it was so tender, so fragile that Ailsa knew she would never forget it. "Are ye afraid?"

"Not of the things I care enough to fight for, and not what is to come, whatever that may be. Nor am I afraid of what I feel for you. I was once, just as ye were, but I've lived long and lost much, and what I knew was important then, I now know is priceless. Fear only tarnishes what's priceless, and I'll not let that happen—not again. But ye know all these things. Ye know more of them than I. You've lived most of your life away from the home of your heart."

Ailsa spoke softly. "But I came back."

Smiling with such sweet joy that she could not resist it, Ian rested his forehead against hers. "Aye. So ye did."

Ailsa was stunned by the forces pushing them together, bewildered by thoughts of a future where they had to be apart. Once she had been young and arrogant and certain she could face that. Now she could not. "What now?" she whispered.

"We hold each other. As tightly and as long as we can. Because we don't know what will happen tomorrow, or even in an hour. All we know is that we're here, now, together."

"That's more than all the questions and uncertainty, isn't it?"

" 'Tis more precious," he answered, "and requires every particle of our attention and devotion. Hold me, Ailsa, beloved. Just hold me."

It was a plea from his soul, and Ailsa moved closer. They held each other until their legs were numb and their arms heavy and the light began to filter into the shelter of their cave.

Ian was the first to raise his head. He took Ailsa's face in his hands and looked into her eyes. "We can no' stay here, for even if 'twas safe, we have no water, no food, no weapon to protect ourselves. Here we are hidden, but that also means we'll not know what goes on outside. We can't afford that kind of ignorance. We can't crouch here until our spirits leave our bodies and we are no more than shadows or skeletons. That would be to give up, to surrender. And that I will not do."

"No," Ailsa agreed. "We can't let them win, even in that small way. 'Tis not in our natures to give up, Ian Fraser."

"So we must think about the next few hours, and after that, if such a future exists. We must decide."

"Aye."

"I can't go back, even if the strangers don't prevail." He was sickened by the memory of having killed a man. The scene came back to him more vivid and awful than before, because last night he had not believed it.

He thought he was going to be ill when he remembered Ailsa saying, *Just for that instant, ye wanted him dead.* She was right, and that made his remorse deeper and more painful. What Robert Howard had said was cruel, calculated and vicious, but what Ian had done was unforgivable. He had taken another man's life and, for however short a time, been glad of it. "Even if I go free"—he looked doubtful, because he knew the determination of the strangers, and the depth of his own guilt—"I can't go back and pretend."

"Surely ye can, if need be."

Ian cupped Ailsa's face in his hands and stared directly into her blue-violet eyes. "No. In this ye do not know me. I let ye go before, because it was your choice, because I had to survive. I've been happy with Jenny and my children, but survival and happiness have nothing to do with what's between us now. I'm whole again, after being empty for so long. Now that you've come back inside me, I can't shut ye out again. I'm not that strong. I never will be."

Ailsa felt a rush of relief and regret that stopped her voice.

"Survival isn't good enough when you've had so much more, when you've known paradise." With Jenny he had understood the boundaries, the limits of what might be and what could not. But Ailsa made him believe all things were possible—all hopes, all desires, all memories and dreams. He had once believed in dreams more than the rationality of everyday life. Now he believed again.

And so he could not bear the thought of leaving the cave. Here they were protected from the world, from reality, from the judgment of others and their own knowledge that this entwining of souls could only be temporary. He wanted to stay in Ailsa's arms. Yet something called to him from beyond these thick stone walls.

Ailsa considered the flicker of excitement in his voice. "I feel safe here," she said.

Ian's eyes sparkled. "Exactly."

It came to her then that, in an odd way, he was looking forward to the chase. After all, he knew these hills and rocks and mountains far better than the strangers, the intruders.

"We'll be running together, ye and me, allied against the rest of the world as we were when we were children. I love the glen and its peaceful rhythms, but, like ye, I love the violent storms as much. Without them, life would be predictable." He paused, surprised at a new realization. " 'Tis as though I've been waiting for something like this all my life, but I've not known it till now. I'm sick at what I've done. In one short hour I destroyed so much that was precious and can never be reclaimed. I regret that more than I can say. But this challenge today, the exhilaration—it runs in my blood like wine and makes me drunk with a feeling I can't explain, even to you."

"Ye don't have to explain to me." She looked at him in wonder. "Ye aren't afraid, are ye?"

"Not of those men, not of violence, not even of death. I fear only the loss of your soul, and the confinement of prison. So long as I'm free, and ye help forge that freedom, I am happy. I will be happy forever. To have found ye again—" He broke off, unable to go on. Besides, there was no need. "I long to fight these intruders who have no soul or spirit, to stand up and shout, as the Highlanders did for Bonny Prince Charlie, 'I'll no' bend or break or fall back before your money and your threats. I'll protect what I believe with heart and soul, even with my life.' I'm a Highlander, *mo-charaid*. They're giving me the chance to prove it."

Ailsa was also sick, with fear as well as regret. Yet she could not help but admire Ian's fierce pride, his unwillingness to surrender. She smiled with tears in her eyes, clasped his hand and stood beside him.

When they reached the mouth of the cave, they stopped, caught up in the calm of early morning, in the breeze that sighed and sang and urged them on. For a long moment they looked up into the sky, where the mist met the pale gray clouds, and did not notice the offering someone had left during the night. At their feet, they found a pitcher and a basket. The pitcher, covered in cheesecloth, held clear, cool water, the basket bannocks and cheese and meat pies, cups and herbs and salves, heavy brogues to protect their feet, and at the very bottom, swathed in several soft cloths, lay a gleaming, old-fashioned pistol.

27

MAIRI LAY ON HER HEATHER BED, THE COVERS TWISTED AND tossed aside, the smell of sulfur heavy in the air. She moaned in her uneasy sleep, dreaming of tragedy and sorrow, aching with it as she reached out blindly to right what she did not understand.

In her dream, the mist grew dark and heavy, swirled toward the ground where it lay, gray and threatening, transformed into a crumpled gray cloak. Except that the cloak was red with blood and tiny fires blazed all around it, hidden but not dampened by the mist.

A burst of light and flame pierced the fog, destroyed it. The fire was too bright, too fierce to look upon; it blinded

Mairi, and she woke in darkness, slick with sweat and shuddering.

"Come," Ian whispered. "There's no one about. We must go toward the hills where the standing stones are taller, the rock slopes steeper and the passes more twisted and narrow."

"Aye." Ailsa remembered those foothills and the mountainsides slashed with quicksilver streams, though she had not climbed there for many years. Much of her childhood had been spent among them, and she'd always felt safe there, even when she stood on the narrow point of a standing stone and dared the wind to carry her away. Despite the jolt of fear the sight of the pistol had given her, now that she was out in the open air, her excitement, like Ian's, had become a driving force.

She did not say, though both were fully aware of it, that eventually they would be caught. Neither was willing to leave the glen, become an outlaw hiding in strange hills and woods simply to escape the horrible thing that had happened here. Even the person who had left the basket seemed to have been aware that Ian and Ailsa's aim was to stay alive, not to escape forever. There had been only one or two days' provisions, not supplies enough for a long flight and survival in the wildest part of the Highlands.

Ian took her hand and they began to climb upward and outward. "We'll not make it easy for them. Make them fight for this victory as they have all the others. We'll not give up until they're so weary they're like to drop. Mayhap 'twill give them time to cool their tempers as well." He thought, as they moved lithely, hand in hand, on the uneven stone, that delaying their pursuers would also prolong their time together. Each minute running through the misted summer air with Ailsa beside him, inside him, touching him even when the terrain forced their hands apart and she had to follow behind—each second was another gift in a night of sins and benedictions, both beyond price or measuring.

Irrational as it seemed, they *had* to run, even knowing they would never get away—for their pride, their honor, their fear. To return and face the consequences of their actions, as they inevitably would, would be to face confusion, guilt, uncertainty, pain. For now they could hold close their certainty that at last, all was right between them. Why should it take such horror to cause such a miracle? But perhaps that was his answer. It was too great a gift, this communion with Ailsa; the cost was higher than either could imagine.

For a long time they ran easily, in companionable silence, kestrels circling above them, a golden eagle swooping down from its nest in search of prey. The tortuous ground was easier to negotiate in their brogues, and they ducked under occasional rowans, stepping over gorse and heather that sprouted out of the stone in bright clusters. Butterflies and dragonflies flitted across their erratic path, iridescent in the shifting sunlight which was blotted out by clouds as often as it lit and glittered off black stone.

When they reached the base of the steep mountains, Ian paused at a tiny spring where he and Ailsa drank. When they'd had their fill of the cool, refreshing water, he flipped the hood of her cloak back so her unbound hair was visible. "Keep it down now, so if they do find us, they'll know 'tis ye and not me."

Ailsa nodded, rearranging the plaid she wore underneath. She did not meet Ian's eyes.

They ate a pasty and rose to climb higher and ever higher. The wind howled and whispered through narrow passes and over sharp inclines, changing its voice to fit the magnificent landscape of black, gleaming rock. They stayed close together, holding hands when possible, clinging to each other for assurance as much as physical support.

As they stepped into a bowl of stone where a waterfall cascaded into a deep pool, Ian pulled Ailsa close and, without a word, forced her behind the raging fall of water. The sunlight sparkled on the rushing white thunder, and the spray rose up in prisms of colored light.

"I thought I heard something," Ian murmured, his voice drowned by the sound of furious glittering water.

Ailsa pressed her body close to the cold stone at her back.

They stood shoulder to shoulder, hip to hip, hand in hand, waiting and watching. Nothing moved but a bit of heather in the wind.

Eventually they crept out from behind the radiant fall of water. Ailsa felt vulnerable and exposed, despite the mountains rising all around them. Ian reminded her to leave her hood down, so her long chestnut hair would proclaim her identity, but Ailsa let him get ahead and flipped her hood over her head. From behind, the pursuers would not know which gray cloak was whose. They moved slowly now, listening for something other than the cry of a kestrel or the hiss of the wind. Then they heard it. Pebbles sliding down a sharp incline.

They faced each other instinctively and clasped hands, palm to palm. Ian's eyes were dark; the exhilaration had faded into apprehension. "They've found us," he whispered against Ailsa's parted lips. "They're too close."

"Not yet close enough," she whispered back. "Don't be stopping now, Ian Fraser. Run!"

Constable Adam Munro was hot and tired, and he sensed that the chase had barely begun. He wiped his forehead on his sleeve and glanced back at Simon Black and Duncan Fraser. A very stubborn man, Mr. Black. He had roused Adam from his bed in the early hours of morning and demanded he come at once to apprehend a murderer. Adam had stared, still half asleep. He awoke fully and abruptly when Black told him the murderer was Ian Fraser, but his disbelief only increased.

It had not taken Black long to convince him to come back to Glen Affric; he feared Simon Black's cold rage and guessed the man capable of anything in this frame of mind. At least if they were together, Munro could try to avert disaster.

Adam had been stunned when he arrived at the Fraser croft and learned that the hostile stranger had spoken the truth, or at least part of it. Ian Fraser had killed a man, though it looked to him to be a clear case of self-defense. But Ian was running and had not turned himself in, so it was Munro's duty to apprehend him.

He did not like taking Simon Black along, though Duncan

Fraser seemed chastened and withdrawn and had insisted as fervently as Black on coming. If the constable could have done it alone, he would have, but there was too much area, and he did not understand why Ian was running. Alanna Fraser had whispered that her mother was with Ian, which perplexed Munro further, and made him more concerned about Simon Black's obsessive interest. He also saw that, had he known the area, Black would not have bothered bringing in the law. Alone, he would have hunted Ian Fraser down and killed him.

Black climbed behind Adam Munro now, grim and uncomplaining. He had gained control over his rage from the night before, but this morning he was more coldly determined. The constable shivered at the silver gleam in the man's eyes. He could not determine the eye color through that flash of steel, and wished he did not have to turn his back on that unwavering stare.

Simon Black was biding his time, letting Munro lead the way because he knew this god-awful landscape. Let him do most of the work, finding the paths Fraser and Sinclair might have taken, forging ahead through these bleak stone walls that exactly matched Black's mood and resolution. He was as unyielding as the dark stone.

Before they began this search, he'd gone back to the lodge to retrieve his newest hunting rifle, though he'd seen the constable's surprise when Black appeared with a pistol and the rifle.

"No need for all that. Ian Fraser won't be shooting anybody. Certainly not us," Munro had said.

Simon had stared at him, unblinking, had not bothered to answer. Robert Howard was dead. What more proof did they need?

Simon struggled to hide the strain of the climb on his lungs. His face was taut and red from the exertion, his legs cramping with pain, but he did not reveal his thoughts. He was not really thinking at all, merely moving toward a goal.

Duncan looked at his partner's resolute face and felt ill. He was so exhausted he could barely stand upright. He had not slept; he had kept calling for Ian and wandering and looking fruitlessly through the night. Now his mind was a blur; his only clear thought was to stick close to Simon, as close as possible.

Duncan's face revealed no more than his partner's, except for grim perseverance. He did not like Simon's silence or cold withdrawal or the way he repeatedly touched his rifle in a light caress. Simon wanted Ian dead, there was no doubt about that. Duncan only wanted to stop this insanity from going any further. He felt powerless and knew his only chance of success was never to leave his partner's side.

Adam Munro froze as he topped a steep rise, his hand half raised.

Simon was beside him in an instant. "You've seen them."

Adam cleared his throat. "I saw something. Could have been a wildcat or a fox." He was lying, but now that they were close, he was more and more reluctant to be a part of this. He'd heard what Black, Howard and Duncan Fraser intended to do to the glen. Now that he'd met the man, seen his cold eyes, his single-minded commitment, and worst of all, his silver-steel rage, he thought he understood how Ian could have been pushed to this.

Simon didn't believe Munro for a moment. He'd seen the constable turn rigid as stone while the blood drained from his face. Simon took a step forward, toying with the trigger of his rifle, lifting it to cradle in the crook of his arm. Ian Fraser was close. He knew it. His chance to avenge Robert Howard was near.

"Don't ye be overreacting now, man. He's got no weapon, remember. And he's no' a violent man by nature."

Simon snorted in disgust. "Hasn't he proven the kind of man he is?"

"Aye, time and again, since he grew from child to man, long before ye ever came here." Strangely, Adam felt pity for Black in that moment. To judge someone on a single act, to fail to know enough of human nature to recognize a man pushed up against a rock wall, to see men and their actions in such harsh and humorless terms, must leave a man cold and dry as summer bracken. Adam glanced at Duncan Fraser, who was also watching Black, but who wisely remained silent. Simon Black didn't want to hear any arguments just now.

Before Adam could duck out of sight, two figures rose and bounded over the hill: identical figures with hooded gray cloaks billowing behind them.

Simon raised his gun and sighted along the barrel, but the constable pushed the rifle aside. "Don't be a fool. There's no need for that. Besides, ye might hit the woman. Why don't ye be letting me capture him and let the magistrate deal with Ian Fraser? For God's sake, he's no threat to ye."

Slowly, deliberately, Simon turned his head. The wind had ruffled his brown hair, and his lids hid the color and thoughts in his eyes. He took time to answer only because the two fleeing figures had disappeared down a narrow gully. He knew where they were now. He knew he would get them. "What do you know? There are threats the nature of which you can't possibly understand." He did not bother to hide his disdain.

Without waiting for the others, he followed the path Fraser had taken. Adam and Duncan Fraser hurried after him, hearts pounding with more than exertion. They caught fleeting glimpses of the two gray cloaks as they fled down the gully, but when the stone walls widened, Ian and Ailsa sprinted to reach a high standing rock across a low, flat area.

In an instant, Simon had his gun at his shoulder and was sighting along the barrel. Duncan caught up with him in time to knock his arm as he fired. The gunshot exploded and echoed horribly around them. The figures did not pause.

Simon cursed violently and pulled away, firing again just before the fugitives disappeared behind the stone. "Damn you to hell, Duncan Fraser!" he hissed. "Now I don't know if I hit one or not."

28

ALANNA SAT ON A STUMP IN HER NEWLY WEEDED GARDEN, staring at the dark, furrowed earth but seeing nothing. When she felt David come up behind her, she reached up to take his hand in silence. Neither had slept, and Alanna's eyes burned. She felt empty and cold, now that the horror had sunk into her bones, and her blood ran sluggishly through her veins.

Suddenly she doubled up in pain, and David knelt beside her. "What is it?" All the frustration, fear and anger of the past night were in that question. He had wanted to go with the constable, but Adam Munro had heard of David's flammable temperament and had forbidden it. David could not bear this waiting, this impotence, this silence. He had never felt so helpless in his life—until the blood drained from his wife's face and she bent over, gasping, hands at her waist. "Alanna, what?"

The pain was gone as suddenly as it had come. Alanna looked up at her husband, her skin so pale it was translucent, her eyes dark and wide. "I'd not be knowing." Her voice was a croak he did not recognize. She began to rock forward and backward, forward and back. "Except that it hurt so much. So much."

Ian ducked behind the standing stone, clinging tightly to Ailsa's hand. He was pale and chilled. The sound of gunfire echoing off rock walls had shocked him deeply. He should not have been surprised, after all that had happened, but he was. He knew by Ailsa's clammy touch that she was too. Men hunting men. It had not happened in this glen since the last Highland Clearances, when Mairi Rose was young. He could not believe it was happening now.

He saw with relief that his memory had not misled him; a narrow passageway opened behind the stone. He drew Ailsa into it just as a curious rumbling shook the rock walls. A spate of boulders broke free from above, jarred loose by gunfire, and tumbled into the opening, blocking the passageway behind them. Those men would not follow easily this way. He released Ailsa's hand because they could not fit side by side, and led the way over broken boulders and tumbled stones.

Ian did not look back until they cleared the passageway and reached the far side and an unexpected wash of sunlight. There was a small pool here, fed by an underground spring. He turned to tell Ailsa they were safe for the time being, and saw with horror that her hood was up. Her cloak hung open in front, and she was wearing her plaid oddly, wrapped around her waist and secured there. Surely last time he looked it had been draped over her elbows.

He took her shoulders and felt how damp they were, even through her cloak. Then he saw the stain of dark red oozing through the bright red threads of the Rose plaid. He felt dizzy and stupid, his head full of fog as he gazed at that seeping blood. Why didn't he feel her pain?

Ailsa swallowed dryly, stumbled, and it came to Ian in a flash so bright and painful that he could not face it. If she had cried out or fallen or slowed even a little, he would have stopped to see what was amiss. She had shut him out so he would not know until they were safe—*he* was safe.

" 'Tis ... only my ... side," she stammered. "The water ... will help."

Ian glanced back at the rock slide that had cut them off from their pursuers. He peered around slowly, cautiously, to make certain there was no other approach. Then he lifted Ailsa in his arms and laid her on a flat boulder beside the tiny pool. He tucked the cloak beneath her head and carefully unwrapped the makeshift bandage of plaid.

It was soaked through with blood. Ian went cold and sweat broke out all over his body as the force of her pain hit him hard, as hard as if it were his own. His head was fuzzy, full of a strange gray mist, but he shook it away. He had to see to Ailsa.

Gently he cut her gown with his dirk and saw the wound where the bullet had entered. He could not tell how deep it had gone, but the flow of blood was constant. He tore her skirt into bands and used two to wash the wound, then wadded up his shirt and bound the other around it, applying as much pressure as he could while she grew pale but made no sound of protest. Ian prayed the makeshift bandage would stop the bleeding.

"We have to go on," she said in a whisper. The color had left her face; she was as pallid and haggard as the day he had first seen her in the glen.

Ian saw the hole in the cloak that the bullet had made and his hands began to shake. "No. It ends here. When they find us, they'll care for ye. I won't . . ."

Ailsa smiled and Ian's chest ached. "Ye will. I've no' come so far to give up now. You've bound my wound, and the gods have blocked our path. 'Twas a gift we must not waste, Ian Fraser. Give me a little to drink. Then I can go on."

He cupped his hands in the cool, peat-colored water, the sweet, healing water, and she sipped what she could. "Come," she said. "Help me up."

Instead, he lifted her and carried her across the slowly rising mountain. "I will no' waste a gift, but neither will I be a fool. What good is that gift if you're too weak—"

"I'm not weak, Ian. I'm very strong. I didn't know it until now, though William told me often. Even Cynthia and Colin knew. Ye see, the bleeding has stopped, and ye'll get nowhere carrying me this way. Let me down. I can walk. Ye know I can no' lie to ye."

He looked in her eyes, saw her stamina and courage and was humbled by it. He did not know everything about her after all. Reluctantly, he set her on her feet.

In the next hours, she sometimes walked alone, sometimes leaned against him. Each time they saw a spring, they stopped to let her rest. Her wound had begun to bleed again, but now Ian knew they were close to a stand of high-growing trees with a bed of needles beneath and a burn flowing past. It was well hidden; there Ailsa could rest and he could change the bandage now soaked with blood.

As he carried her into the secret copse in the mountains, the wind was cool and welcoming on her cheeks. When he laid her gently on a soft bed of pine needles, with the cloak beneath, she sighed in contentment. Like him, she felt secure here. Unlike him, she knew she would not leave this place.

She was glad he had found it. It was paradise. Ailsa smiled as Ian leaned above her anxiously. He was wild with worry and her pain, which made him wince and want to take her wound into himself. He had no antiseptic to treat her with, none of the proper herbs, nor did he know enough to use them if he had. That had been Mairi's job, and Ailsa's, then Alanna's. All he could give her was water, false reassurance, and his hand to cling to.

The sense of adventure had seeped away along with Ailsa's blood. They were far from help, and even if he trusted the men following them, they would have to carry Ailsa down a mountainside to help her. The wound had begun to look puffy and red and Ailsa had become feverish. She broke into a cold sweat and shuddered, stopping only when she felt his hands on her skin and saw him looking down at her.

She cupped his face in her hands and pulled it toward her. "Rest, Ian, *mo-cridhe*. Rest ye awhile." She closed her eyes and Ian laid his head on her shoulder.

She drew him into her fevered waking dream and, exhausted and frightened, he fell asleep, his fingers laced with hers.

They awoke to the sound of rocks tumbling over stone and the curses of men unaccustomed to climbing steep hills. Ailsa was too weak to move. "Go," she told Ian. "I can't. Ye can feel my weakness. But let one of us survive."

"I can't leave you. I won't."

Ailsa touched his lips, his cheek, his eyelids. "Ye'll not leave me, ever. You're inside me no matter how far from me ye wander. Go. I am at peace. I can tell ye now how I love ye. There's naught more I can lose. I'm happier than I've ever been in my life before. That's why it doesn't matter. Go."

The effort to survive, to capture every last sweet drop of life before it was taken from them, had wakened her from a long, drowsy slumber in which she had been half awake, half dreaming, half alive. Since last night, she had felt every emotion intensely, completely, through skin and bone and blood and senses. The colors of the world around her had long been muted. Now the hues were so vivid, so brilliant they hurt her eyes, but she did not look away. She knew, as she had as a girl, what it meant to give up caution, doubt and thought, to live by impulse alone. And in abandoning thought, to find a wisdom beyond the ordinary—rare, clear, painfully beautiful in its clarity. She understood better the Highlanders who had followed hopeless causes only to be slaughtered. Like them, she was willing to die, because she had lived as few ever live, from the depth of her soul, wholly, with every sense alive, alert and full to overflowing.

" 'Tis no' frightening, to die. 'Tis to find ease. Remember? 'The end of all meeting, parting; the end of all striving, peace.' 'Tis true, Ian, my heart. Believe me. Go. If you stay, you'll die with me, for nothing, and that would be unforgivable. I couldn't bear to see it, to know you'd given up the fight. Please give me the solace of knowing ye, at least, have escaped." She smiled with ineffable sweetness as he rose reluctantly.

"Ailsa."

Just that. Just her name, and caught within it, all the things that made him shake with desolation and grieve for her and love her. "For your sake." He clasped her hand tightly, with eyes and touch and spirit, telling her what she most wanted to hear. Then he released her and turned away, caught in a blaze of light against the dark mountains at his back. *For your sake* echoed over the rocks and settled in the folds of her cloak, sodden with blood.

As Ailsa watched him go, a strange joy threaded through her thoughts, as untamed and ephemeral as her weightless body. Ian ducked between two boulders, glanced back once, and his lips moved. Though they made no sound, she heard the words he spoke. "For us there is no farewell. Only a momentary parting." Then he was gone.

The sound of gunfire echoed and faded with her pain. Ian's voice spoke inside her, *Believe, my beloved. Believe in me.* Ailsa nodded and believed, and a stillness came upon her, so pure that it sang in silence, and the beauty and the promise of the music made her weep.

Part Five

Glasgow

SCOTLAND

1988

1

EVA CRAWFORD BLINKED, SWALLOWED, STARED AT THE LETter in her hand.

Dear Mairi,

    I have dreamed of my sister night after night, but she would not come clear to me, and I feared she was in pain. Today she is no longer with me, and I know her pain is over. I know that Ailsa is gone.

    I can imagine your grief, for Ailsa has been with me all my life, long before I knew she existed in the flesh. But now the place where she used to be is raw and empty. I cannot bear it. I cannot conceive of going on without the consolation of her spirit at rest inside me. You, of all people, will understand. It is one loss too many. . . .

Eva dropped the letter from Ailsa's half-sister Lian when the words blurred and ran together through her tears. She felt disoriented and bereft. She found it difficult to breathe, and her chest ached. She could not believe Ailsa was dead, did not wish to believe it.

    She'd stood at the foot of Ailsa Rose Sinclair's grave and

seen the mottled stone. But that had not been real. The cessation of the sound of her voice on paper—that was all too real. Eva felt she had lost her dearest friend, her confidante, her mother. She shivered with the chill of loss.

She drew her knees up to her chest, shuddering with a bleakness she could not hold at bay. She needed the cliffs and the sea churning against tortured stone, needed the kittiwakes and gannets that danced their aerial ballet. Those things were familiar, as familiar as the glen for which Ailsa had given her life. This room in Glasgow was strange and chilly and full of someone else's shadows, someone she did not know at all.

Frantically, she scrambled up. She needed light and air, something to reassure her there was a place beyond this room in which a lush and beautiful history was hidden away, stifled, nearly obliterated by the atmosphere.

Wrenching the door open, she stumbled down the stairs and outside, unaware of Eilidh staring after her in blank astonishment. Eva ran blindly down narrow streets, past summer trees and weathered brick, the shadows of clouds racing over the ground before and behind her. Vaguely, she sensed the sluggish flow of the River Clyde and heard the muted rumble of traffic, but these things faded into the sound of her pounding heart and the taste of her salty tears.

She grieved for Ailsa as if she'd really known her, wept for the phantoms of Ailsa, Ian and Celia, who had once been real, but were no longer. She ran from the stifling room and the suffocating sense of loss, and was not really surprised when she found herself at the tidy little cemetery where her mother had been buried.

Eva did not know what she expected to find there, but it seemed fitting to carry her grief to the graveyard. She paused for a moment to catch her breath, holding tightly to the wrought-iron fence that imprisoned the sleeping souls. Forcing herself to walk slowly, she made her way to Celia Ward's grave.

She stopped when she realized someone was there before her. Eva stared in dismay at the short, potbellied man who stood, balding head bent, at the foot of the grass-covered plot. Celia had seemed to her so friendless and alone, except for Eilidh. She had never expected anyone else to visit her mother's grave.

Eva hung back, but the man looked up. He was in his sixties, she guessed, with a thinning fringe of gray hair and brown eyes. His face was creased in worry or confusion. He blinked twice before he really saw her.

"Did you know Celia Ward?" Eva asked warily.

The man laughed, a brief burst of derision. "Thought I did, at one time. But I was wrong." He opened his eyes wider as a thought struck him. "How about you? Did you know her?" He sounded hopeful, as if perhaps she could tell him something he didn't know.

Eva almost laughed, but she choked back the hysteria that lingered from her recent flight. "I'm a relative, but I never met her." It was so easy to speak casually to this stranger, who had nothing to do with her past or her future. Besides, Eva grew curious as the shock began to fade. "I didn't really know my family. I came to Glasgow to see what I could learn."

The man cocked his head. "Celia never talked about her family. Seemed to upset her. In ten years, all I knew was that she grew up in northern Scotland and that her parents were dead." He scratched his head. "Hard to fathom, really."

"You knew her for ten years?"

Shrugging, the man seemed to come to a decision. Perhaps he also found it easier to talk to a stranger. "We were married for that long, but I wouldn't say I knew her."

Eva's eyes widened in amazement. "You're Findlay Denholm?" Oddly, she felt no more than surprise and curiosity. There was no connection between herself and this man who stood at the foot of Celia's grave. How could that be?

I'm not certain she knew who your father was, Agnes Crawford had said. And Eilidh had been so hesitant when Eva said she would go see Findlay Denholm. Eva had promised to wait. Now she had no desire to blurt out her identity. That was the strangest thing of all.

"That, at least, I do know," the man replied. He turned back to contemplate the headstone. "Eilidh Stanley must have told you about me. Only friend Celia had, as far as I could tell. She didn't seek them out, you know. Quite the contrary. That's why I never understood—" He broke off, rubbing the shiny skin on his head in perplexity. "But you don't want to hear my problems. Besides, it was nineteen years ago she left me. Too long to wonder about questions that can't be answered."

Eva wondered if she was numb with shock. She pitied Celia's husband, but wanted nothing from him. "You don't know *why* she left?"

Denholm contemplated her for a long moment. He was a contained person, and his feelings did not show on his face. Nor, she suspected, did he discuss them freely. But something about this unusual encounter prodded him to speak. The anonymity of it? So much safer than familiarity.

"No, I don't. For a while I was so angry, I didn't seek her out and ask. By the time I did think of calling Eilidh, Celia was already dead. I got the feeling Eilidh didn't want to tell me where my former wife was buried, but I couldn't see the harm, so she gave in." He rubbed his chin thoughtfully.

"I don't really know why I came here to begin with. I suppose I thought it might help me understand. I've only been a few times since. Now and then I begin to think about Celia, and wonder, so I come here and stare and learn nothing. I suppose it's that I can't stand an unsolved puzzle. Celia wasn't what she seemed, not simple and straightforward, so I couldn't ever figure her out. Pure stubbornness brings me back, I shouldn't wonder."

He did not speak of his frustration when Celia left him, the feeling that he'd been made a fool of, but Eva guessed it from his strained tone. He did not speak of grief or love or sorrow. Those things Eva could not guess about. Except that Findlay Denholm had returned to Celia's grave. She doubted he would have come more than once if he hadn't cared at all. She was intrigued by what he said, fascinated to learn that even her husband had not known Celia's heart.

But Eva felt no personal response to the man himself. He was more of a stranger than Celia was, and Eva didn't care to change that. At least not yet. She wondered why.

"Nothing here, you know," Denholm said briskly. "Just stones and grass and one old oak."

Eva stared at her mother's headstone and knew that he was right. Her panic had subsided as curiosity took over. "No, there's nothing, is there?"

The two turned from the grave and fell into step side by side without speaking. At the gate, a woman in a beige mac hovered. She looked up when Findlay appeared, searched his face anxiously, sighed with relief at what she saw there.

Denholm paused, seemed to come to another decision, and turned to Eva. "My wife, Clare. And this is a relative of Celia's. I don't believe I caught—"

"Eva Crawford." She reached out to take Clare Denholm's hand. The woman was short, like her husband, but slender, her face pleasant and ordinary, her brown eyes clear, unshadowed by secrets. She did not appear to be a woman troubled by demons.

"Lovely to meet you."

Clare's voice was warm, quiet and unassuming. She would never make passersby turn to look after her, but she seemed amiable. *Contented* was the word that came to Eva's mind. Clare Denholm seemed precisely the kind of woman Findlay Denholm needed, the kind Celia had tried to be but couldn't. Whatever had possessed him to introduce his wife to Eva? These people were not like her. Not at all.

"I'm glad to meet you as well," she offered, keeping her voice steady with an effort. Her heart had begun to pound erratically, and she felt an acute desire to return to Eilidh's house. Questions and answers spun in her head, whirling with a building sense of betrayal and fury. She forced herself to nod politely and bid Findlay Denholm and his wife goodbye. Then she was running again. This time, she was not running away.

By the time she reached the house, she had a stitch in her side and could barely breathe, but that did not slow her down. She flung open the door and did not bother to close it as Eilidh appeared from a shadowy doorway. Her dark eyes were troubled and she opened her mouth to speak, but Eva interrupted her.

"Findlay Denholm isn't my father, is he? That's why you didn't want me to see him," she gasped.

The shock and regret that transformed Eilidh's face were all the answer Eva needed.

2

EILIDH'S SHOULDERS SLUMPED IN DEFEAT. "NO, HE'S NOT. I'm sorry."

Kicking the door closed with her foot, Eva faced her mother's friend, chest heaving with impotent rage. "Why didn't you tell me? Why make mysterious hints and lead me on and deceive me like this?"

Stunned by the force of the girl's anger, by the hostile glitter of her green-gray eyes, Eilidh had to fight back her own fury. "It was Celia's job to tell you about your father. I promised her—"

Eva was ready to explode with frustration. "Celia's dead. She never made any effort to tell me anything. Surely that was clear to you long since! You pride yourself on your honesty, or so you've said often enough. Why, in God's name, didn't you just tell the truth from the beginning?" Tears stung her eyes and her voice sounded harsh even to her own ears.

Raising her head sharply, Eilidh felt her own anger and helplessness roll through her in waves she could not control. "Do you think it was easy for me? Do you think I enjoyed standing by tongue-tied while I watched you go through this, saw you suffering and confused? I couldn't believe Celia had left it up to me. I was supposed to be the guardian of the papers, not her stand-in or her voice." For the first time, her resentment at the burden her friend had left her with seeped into her voice.

Eva's face went blank and her eyes clouded over as she pressed her lips together and took a step backward.

"You row just like your mother," Eilidh declared. "She'd never stand and face an unpleasantness. Easier to retreat inside herself and draw the blinds tight. Anger only turns to poison that way. But I suppose she preferred breathing those fumes alone in safety to looking directly at her heart or anyone else's."

Eva flinched and the last of the color drained from her face.

Waving her hands to ward off the bitterness, Eilidh sighed with despair. "No, that was cruel. I've always prided myself on fighting fair. Forgive me."

Nodding stiffly, like a mechanical doll, Eva clasped her hands behind her. The veil did not lift from her eyes, nor did she move closer.

"Dear God!" Eilidh cried. "*Look* at me. Don't you think that sometimes I hate her as much as you do? It's all up to me now, isn't it? Past, present and future, my task, my obligation. It makes me so angry I want to weep, but what good would that do? Like a dolt, I kept thinking Celia would come through in the end, that somehow she'd planned for this. I suppose I have to give up that hope now. She's not going to speak from beyond the grave. Perhaps she never intended to." She choked on her own words, but when Eva opened her mouth, Eilidh held out her hand in a command for silence. "I'm sorry for that, sorrier than you can imagine. For both of us—Celia's little pawns. But what was her game, and why did she need us to play it out? I don't know, Eva. I'd give a great deal if I did, but I don't."

Eilidh was trembling, her voice hoarse with the effort of speaking. Eva looked away in self-defense. Her anger at Celia was too close to the surface, too volatile just now, for her to absorb Eilidh's frustration. These revelations were too dangerous; Eva felt herself fragmenting from the vortex of desperation, bewilderment and rage. She turned blindly for the door, craving escape, but there was nowhere left to go. She gulped down air as if starved for oxygen, for sanity, for peace. "I'm sorry," she whispered. "You're right. It's not your fault. But please"—she lifted her hands, palms open and empty—"can't you help me? There's no one else."

Devastated by the anguish on Eva's ravaged face, Eilidh squared her shoulders, preparing to do battle. She refused to acknowledge the moisture that pricked her eyes, and she forced down the lump in her throat. One tear, whether angry or compassionate, would splinter the frail spirit of this young girl. That would break Eilidh's heart; it was already pounding as if it might burst. She cared about Eva too much. No matter how unfair the burden Celia had left on her friend's shoulders, it was too late to refuse to bear it now. With a supreme effort of will, she spoke. "It's time we talked. I'll tell you as much as I know. Only I can't promise it will help. It's just, that's all I *can* do, you see?"

Eva shuddered as she tried to control the weakness in her legs, the ache in her chest that pulsed with the irregular beat of her heart. "Yes," she managed, "I do see. You can't give more than you have. I suppose my mother thought that would be enough." But she didn't really believe it. She no longer tried to guess what Celia had thought, what she'd intended by bringing her daughter here to hand her a chest full of history, but no real past. Breathless, her face pallid, she held her side with both hands to keep in the hurt.

Eilidh covered her eyes with her hand so she could think. She needed time to gather her thoughts, to push the anger at Celia back into the darkness. "I'll tell you what. I'm famished, and you look a little peckish yourself. Let me ring up for some take-away, shall I? There's good Chinese and Indian. Do you like spicy food?" She very nearly managed to sound like her old self again.

If Eilidh could do it, Eva thought, so could she. She clung gratefully to a shred of normalcy, the prosaic quality of the question. It took a moment for the meaning to sink in. "I don't know. I've never tried it."

"Never . . ." Eilidh sputtered. Shock restored her equilibrium, at least for the moment. "I knew the islands were isolated, but *really,* how dreadful to have been deprived of

446

curry and chicken with peppers all these years. You shall suffer no longer. I'll order some moo goo gai pan as well, just in case."

Eva was stunned to realize she was hungry as well as drained and exhausted. She could use a wash and some food. She had a feeling she would need her strength.

"Run up and change while I ring, why don't you? I'll have the food sent round in half an hour, all right?"

"Yes, all right." Eva's legs were heavy and awkward as she started toward the stairs. She was not aware that Eilidh watched her go, face pinched with uncertainty and apprehension.

"Time to eat!" Eilidh called in the wake of the music that drifted up the stairs. "It's lovely down here, cozy, you know, in spite of this endless rain."

Eva stood slowly, felt a sense of unreality, as if she were unfolding herself from a flat piece of paper, re-creating herself by rising and beginning to breathe again. She went down to find Eilidh had set out their supper on the table in front of the sofa. The lamps were turned low, and the varicolored shades filled the room with tinted light. There were large, soft pillows on the floor where Eilidh sat, legs crossed, elbows resting on the table. There were cartons of food and china plates and crystal glasses full of wine.

For some reason, the sight made Eva want to weep. She felt steadier but still on edge, still fragile from the row and her meeting with Findlay Denholm. "This is lovely," she murmured as she settled onto a blue brocade pillow.

She tasted several of the dishes, winced at the burning on her tongue, then tried again, until she became accustomed to the sensation. Unpleasantly aware of Eilidh's unusual silence, Eva sought to fill the void. "I quite like your spicy food. I suppose I have been deprived."

"Yes." Eilidh pushed her plate away and rose to stand in front of the rain-streaked window. "So you have been. I can't really change that, I suppose. But at least you'll know."

Eva stood, suddenly embarrassed. "About before—"

"Over and done with," Eilidh interrupted. "We've both

apologized, all right and proper, so there's nothing more to be said. Besides, it wasn't you I was angry with." She glanced over her shoulder. "Well, perhaps a bit. Being accosted in my own front hall does tend to unsettle me. But in any event, I suspect you weren't really shouting at me either." She turned back to the rain. "It's all Celia, start to finish, isn't it?"

Sighing, she rubbed her arms as if a chill had stolen over her. "The thing is, I'm a bit weary of mucking about in the past."

"Yes," Eva said fervently. "So weary my bones ache with it."

"I'm surprised you've lasted this long, if you want to know the truth. I'd rather go forward than back from here on. So I'd best get this story told."

Eva sat quietly in an overstuffed chair while Eilidh switched off the record and poured them each more wine. Eva clutched her glass, the edge pressed to her lips. She tried to concentrate on the cold of the crystal and the deep red color of the wine, but the focus of all her senses was the ivory oval of Eilidh's face.

"It all began in the glen, you see," she said, aware of Eva's strained impatience. "Your grandmother, Seonaid Rose, loved Glen Affric, just as her ancestors had loved it. She didn't care that her existence was meager, her survival less than certain."

Eva shifted her weight, wondering if Seonaid Rose had lived as uncertain a life as Jenny Fraser when she'd reached blindly for the promise of something better a century before.

"Seonaid got her sustenance from the beauty of the glen, her wealth from the history that stretched back to the Celtic gods, her security from the land itself. She refused to leave, even when Celia's father died. After he was gone, Celia's brothers disappeared one by one, seeking a better life. Celia always thought they would have stayed if her father had lived. She never forgave him for dying and leaving his wife and daughter helpless."

Eilidh ran her fingers through her long, loose hair, making it glimmer with hints of auburn, gold and russet. She sank into a chair and curled her feet beneath her as she stared into the distance. "When Celia was a child, Seonaid tried to instill in her a love of the earth, an affinity with the voices of the glen. She tried to teach Celia to live by her own rules—the rules of her heart, her passions, which came from the land itself and so must be good and right.

"But Celia grew up hungry, cold and afraid, convinced that the land no longer cared. It didn't seem to her that it nurtured her mother or herself, not their bodies or their souls. Survival was so difficult that it took all Celia's attention. She had none left for what her mother called the spirit of the glen. Instead, year by year, day by day, hour by hour, it bled them of strength and energy and choice."

Eva began to wonder if she wanted to continue this quest that seemed to lead to anger, frustration and a deeper dread of tomorrow than she had ever felt before. She would forge her future out of the precarious past she was discovering, and that future was what she dreaded most—the uncertainty, the darkness stretching beyond her knowledge or endurance. She did not think she would have taken Ailsa's risk or paid Ailsa's price. Eva was a coward. Just as Celia Ward had been.

"Seonaid died of tuberculosis in nineteen fifty-eight, when she was fifty-two years old. Celia always said her mother had starved to death because she refused to abandon the glen she loved and the instincts she treasured. Celia loved her mother very much, and watching her die bit by bit, clinging to something that was not real and would not sustain her, destroyed something in the girl.

"Celia was only sixteen when she buried her mother and fled the glen. She came to Glasgow and, at eighteen, married Findlay Denholm. He was a banker, wealthy enough to keep her comfortable and secure. Celia thought that, as his wife, she could escape the heritage of passions and terrors she had brought like a burden from Glen Affric. She sought safety like a drug that would make her forget the past."

Eilidh had been amazed that Seonaid's death had shaped Celia so completely, amazed that she thought she could deny her blood tie to her mother by pretending it did not exist. Eilidh wondered if Eva would do the same, if that cycle too would be repeated.

Glancing at Eva, she saw the girl's skin was ashen, her expression taut, her fingers curled like twisted hemp around the wine glass. Eilidh had never seen anyone so afraid of a truth so simple. She wished Eva would ask questions, snort her disdain or weep her compassion, anything but sit mute and unmoving.

"Celia convinced herself that only by suppressing her emotions would she survive." The rain on the huge windows made dim shadows on the walls, trickling drops and half-real trails that marred the soft cream paint.

Eva watched the rain itself, visualizing the girl who had been Celia Ward (her father's name, not her husband's or her mother's), the dying Seonaid, the glen she had seen a few days ago. She tried to make the feelings Seonaid had for that place real and visible through color and light, but the image eluded her, just as the power of the glen had eluded her when she'd stood looking down upon it. *You're listening only with your ears and looking only with your eyes but not your heart. You're too cautious and too impulsive.* Rory's voice was as real as Eilidh's, and Eva shivered. She had seen the glen as Celia saw it, pretty but without the seductive lure that had enchanted Ailsa and Mairi, Alanna and Seonaid.

Eva closed her eyes, forcing herself to concentrate on what Eilidh was saying.

"For ten years, Celia managed to quell those dangerous emotions. She'd begun to feel safe. We became friends about when she realized that comfort wasn't the same as happiness."

Eilidh's eyes filled with regret. "Celia was always good at lying to herself, so the woman she showed to others was never quite real." She rose and began to pace, waving her hands in agitation, making shapes in the air that were Celia's hidden feelings. "Seonaid must have sensed something of this when her daughter was born." Eilidh turned to meet

Eva's curious gaze. "The name Celia means blind, you know."

"How appropriate." Eva blinked at her quick response. What would have happened, she wondered, if Celia Ward had opened her eyes, just once? What if, even for an instant, she had managed to see the world through her own happiness instead of through her mother's pain?

3

"YES, WELL." EILIDH RESUMED HER PACING. "CELIA'S LIFE changed irrevocably when she met a man named Neil. She was totally unprepared and completely vulnerable. Neil awoke in her every feeling she'd ever fought, every desire she'd ever denied, every impulse of her soul she had ever ignored.

"She could no more turn away from him than she could deny her own name. Neil knew her too well. He literally swept her away from the security of her sheltered home and into a sensual dream where all her senses were achingly, fully vibrant and alive."

Eilidh caught her hair in fisted hands, tugging at memories, at pleasures she herself had known, but rarely, and never for very long. She did not notice that Eva's gaze was veiled, as if she had slipped away. She would have been stunned to learn the girl was thinking of the moment when she'd stood on a striated boulder with the golden water flowing beside her, and looked into the eyes of a man named Rory Dey. She did not see Eva shake her head in denial and dismissal. Eilidh's eyes were on the past.

"I saw them once in a tea shop on George Square." She turned to Eva. It was important that the girl understand this, that she absorb a little of the feelings that existed only in memory.

She could see them now as clearly as she had twenty years ago. She had passed the window and paused to smile at a couple who sat across from one another at a small lacy table, holding hands. She had not recognized them, but had stopped, drawn up short by the intimacy between the two young people. Celia had looked like a stranger in a black off-the-shoulder top and wide flowered skirt that brushed her ankles. Her hair, usually drawn back into a French twist, hung soft and loose about her shoulders. It shone like gold in the soft overhead light of the tea shop. Her gray eyes glimmered like polished silver reflecting flame.

When she saw Celia's eyes, Eilidh recognized her for the first time, and was amazed. Her pallid, translucent skin was flushed the warm color of a peach, her delicate cheekbones softly curved. She was lovely and free of demons.

The man was tall, even sitting, and he wore a plain blue work shirt. His dark hair curled over the collar, and Celia reached up to twine her finger in one of the tendrils.

Eilidh gasped at the tenderness in that simple gesture, the familiarity and affection it implied. The man was not handsome but arresting, with green eyes tinged in gold, and roughly chiseled features. There was no harshness in his face when he looked at Celia. Only love.

Eilidh found she could not move, so entranced was she at the power of the feelings between them. There were others lingering in the shop, but she did not see them. They moved through a fog that held them apart from the lovers in the corner.

For a very long time they sat and looked at one another, looked deeply, past skin and blood and bone, to the souls beneath.

It was the most touching moment Eilidh had ever seen, and the saddest. She knew even then that Celia and Neil could not remain together.

"How did you know?"

Eva's soft question brought Eilidh back to the present, to the tingling of her hands, clenched tightly around nothing.

452

"I'd seen how deep Celia's terror went, how completely it had infected her. Somehow Neil was strong enough and he loved her enough to take her back to the time when she was unblemished, before the terror began its slow but sure destruction."

Eilidh sighed. "There are few men willing to risk so much to find one lost and radiant soul before it flickers into darkness. It was a miracle and a tragedy that Celia met him. She wasn't strong enough to leave her soul visible and vulnerable for long, you see. She was too afraid of her own passion. Neil took from her the control she'd struggled to maintain for all those endless years."

Staring at Celia's daughter leaning forward, listening pensively, Eilidh thought she was hearing not just the words, but the intonations, the implications. She listened as Celia used to do, weighing and considering, looking for a pattern or an answer.

Eilidh wondered what she would do when the girl was gone, when the vigil was over, and this short part of the journey. She could not remember a time when she had not been waiting—for Celia to come to know herself, for her to face the cauldron of emotion inside, for Celia to die, and for Eva to come. So many years tangled up with Celia and her child.

Despite her earlier rage and resentment, Eilidh did not regret it. She had many friends, a lover who felt comfortable enough to slip in and out of her life as his art took him here and there. She had this house her father had left her, and her job at the gallery where she got the two things she needed most—interesting people and art. She had her pottery. What she did not have was a family. She wondered, not for the first time, if she should have kept Eva herself. But that was not what Celia wanted.

"About my father," Eva said tentatively. The words were alien on her tongue, like the hot food. The man was one more stranger, one more puzzle. She did not think she could handle another, but she had to know; she could not let him disappear into oblivion as her mother had. "Did you know him? What he was like, I mean?"

Lips pursed, Eilidh considered how best to deal another disappointment to this girl who had already borne so much. "I never met Neil. Celia wanted him to herself. I know he was a professor at University. But in his heart he was a poet, and quite a good one. Celia showed me some of his work once."

Eva raised her head warily, as if she scented danger in the air. "My father. A poet. Of course." She felt numb with the knowledge in her hands at last. But it was very little. "What else? Do you—" She broke off, hesitated, forced herself to go on. "Do you know where he is?"

"No, my child. I'm sorry." Eilidh stretched out her hand in consolation, but was too far away to reach Eva. "I never even knew his last name. And once Celia realized she was pregnant, she broke off her relationship with Neil and forced him out of her life in terror. She told me he'd left Glasgow and she didn't know where he'd gone. I always wondered how she did it."

Eva let out her breath in a melancholy sigh. How would she ever locate a man with no surname who had left Glasgow years before, betrayed by the woman he loved? If she couldn't find her mother in the house where she had lived and wept and died, she had little chance of discovering the poet, her father—one more phantom, one more lost opportunity. She felt she was descending into a dark hole and would not find her way out. She'd lost so much that she had never known.

Eilidh sank onto the sofa and stared out the window at the misting rain. "I used to ache for him, and for her, imagining their parting, because I'd seen them together. I knew what they were to one another. I think she was relieved that he'd gone, though it left her heart shattered and her soul in shadow. She'd never felt that kind of anguish or ambivalence before."

Closing her eyes, Eilidh fought back the sorrow of those memories. "Then Celia surprised me. She left Findlay. It would have been easier for her to stay, but she would not raise her child in that dark place, she told me. She didn't think it out, or reason, or plan. She just left. And came to me."

"Are you sure the baby isn't his?" Eilidh had asked as Celia stood dripping and sallow on a purple-and-red woven rug before the fire. "Did you tell him so?"

Celia had seemed dazed and a little lost, but at her friend's question, she looked up sharply. "I didn't tell him about the baby at all. I may be weak and foolish and unworthy of his trust, but I'm not a liar. There was no need to hurt him more. I just said it was time for me to go, that neither of us was happy."

Chewing on her lip thoughtfully, Eilidh murmured, "Would he have believed you if you told him it was his?" She did not know what made her ask, except that she had always been curious about the peculiar relationship between Celia and her husband.

Celia rubbed her arms to warm them, to make her blood begin to flow again. She turned from her friend and stared into the fire. "I don't think Findlay wants to believe me anymore. There was a time when he would have lied to himself, even if he knew. He wanted a child that much. He wanted me." She removed the wet scarf from her hair, turned dingy and straight by the rain.

"But now his feelings have changed, as mine have." She ran her fingers through her lifeless curls, spilling drops of water onto her pale gray dress. "Neil taught me to tell the truth. No, it's more than that. He taught me to be honest with myself, with him. Nothing in my life was harder or frightened me more than that lesson."

Eilidh caught Celia as she turned, tears streaming down her cheeks. There were no sobs, no gasps of breath, no sound. Just an eerie silence punctuated by the fall of her tears and the rain outside.

4

"ARE YOU ALL RIGHT?" EVA TOUCHED EILIDH'S ARM AND felt how cold it was. "You look ill."

Shaking her head, Eilidh focused on Celia's daughter. She had actually forgotten the girl was here. "I'm fine. Lost myself for a moment, is all." She shook out the folds of her caftan as she pushed away the past. "Now then, where was I?"

Eva hesitated. "Maybe we should stop. You seem—"

"I can't do that. Not now that I've finally started. I have to go on, to finish it." She looked up at Eva. "For *my* sake, not yours. Go on. Sit."

She waited until Eva reluctantly returned to the overstuffed chair to continue her story. "I don't know why Celia thought it necessary to cut herself adrift so completely. She seemed to feel it was time to stand on her own two feet. I suspect, as well, that she didn't really want to share you, not even with Neil. Celia said he frightened her because she lost all sense of caution and responsibility with him. She swore she wouldn't give you the kind of childhood Seonaid had given her. But Celia hadn't been truly alone since her mother died, and all her fears came back, magnified and intensified by the new and more terrible fear for her child. In that moment when she lost both her joy and her security forever, I think Celia Ward finally grew up."

Leaping up, unable to stay still a moment longer, Eva took Eilidh's place before the rain-streaked windows. "Did she really? Do you think she ever found what she wanted?"

"What she wanted was peace. I'd say she found it, in her own way."

Eva traced the wavering trail of a raindrop down the cool

glass. "That's all I really want, you know. A little peace. The only thing I'm never likely to find."

"No. It was enough for Celia, but I suspect you need more. You want passion and turmoil and a joy so great it hurts."

Eva thought of Ailsa and Ian, the affinity she felt for them, and suspected it was true. "Maybe you're right." She sighed. "But I'm tired of turmoil. I want to rest."

Eilidh shook her head sadly. "Maybe your peace *is* a kind of turmoil—a passion that burns bright, leaving you a little off balance, but never dull. Look at your pocket stories." Eva had told Eilidh's pocket story one evening as they looked for treasure in the Chinese chest. The girl's perception had alarmed and enchanted the older woman. "Look at all the bright colors and emotions in those stories. Perhaps that's what you seek. The beauty in turbulence."

Eva peered at the silver rain and thought of the deep blue of the sea and the white of the foam, the shifting turquoise to green to azure of the incoming waves. She turned in excitement. "You've told me about my mother, but I know how to feel her emotions for myself."

Eilidh caught her exhilaration from the glow of her green eyes in the soft pink light. "How?"

"You're the one who reminded me. Her pockets. Her clothes are hanging in the cupboard up there. I can learn something from her pockets." She swung across the room, full of urgency.

Eilidh was right behind her.

Eva raced up the stairs to the second floor, threw the cupboard open and lightly stroked the clothes that hung there. Her heart was pounding as she touched one drab dress or twin set after another. Then she brushed the multi-colored patchwork coat and closed her fingers tightly around it.

"That was her favorite," Eilidh said.

"Yes." Eva did not hear herself speak. She took out the jacket and removed it from the mothproof bag, then sat on the bed, hesitant to slide her hands into the pockets.

"Why didn't you think of this before?" Eilidh asked, perplexed.

Eva swallowed dryly, but the lump in her throat would not go. She felt clammy all over, and her stomach was hollow. "I think I was afraid to know." She looked up as the truth struck her hard. "I came here to find out about my mother, but every hint I've had, every word you or Samuel or Agnes spoke, was depressing. I thought I was looking, that I was furious with Celia for leaving so few clues, but I think I was relieved. I think she knew I would be.

"She left me the chest, knowing my ancestors' stories would call to me more loudly and touch me more deeply than her own. The journal, the drawings and the letters are so rich and full of hope and suffering and perseverance. Maybe she thought I'd learn enough from them." She met Eilidh's intent gaze, breathed in deeply. "I was secretly relieved that there was so little of my mother here. That way I didn't have to learn what I wasn't strong enough to endure."

Eilidh was speechless for once. She put one hand on Eva's shoulder. "You're strong enough. I've told you that before. There's a light in you that never burned in Celia. She's not your mirror, you know, only your mother."

Eva looked away, then put her trembling hands into the two square patchwork pockets of Celia Ward's favorite jacket.

The feelings began to come at once, to wash over her in mighty waves, until she felt the crackle of paper, and the colors and emotions disintegrated as if they had never been. Carefully, she drew out an envelope and saw that it was not yellow with age. On the outside of the light blue paper, her own name was written in a careful hand. Eva Crawford.

She showed it to Eilidh, who gaped in astonishment. "Celia's hand. No question about it. So she did leave a letter after all." She sounded unutterably relieved.

Eva was confused. "Why did she leave it here? What if I hadn't looked?"

"I don't know." Eilidh, too, was troubled and more than a little angered by Celia's curious impulse to hide a letter of such monumental importance to her only child.

Eva toyed with the envelope but did not try to open it.

She wanted to be alone when she read it, and more than that, away from this room. She wanted to read it where there was light and life, not simply memories.

Draping the jacket over her arm, she rose, holding the letter as if it were a weight she was too frail to carry, or spun glass so fragile it might shatter at a touch.

"Why don't you take it down to your room," Eilidh suggested gently. "The light's much better. If you need me, just call and I'll come running." She did not wait for an answer but slipped away, much to Eva's relief.

She went down the stairs one by one, staring at the blue envelope warily. She was relieved to come to her own room. She sank into flowers and sun-bright walls gratefully. They were so pleasantly normal, so nonthreatening; the way Celia's marriage to Findlay Denholm must have been. Eva turned on all the lamps and opened the curtains. Suddenly she was afraid of the darkness.

She sat on the bed, the jacket beside her, the letter in her lap. She had been frustrated and angry at Celia's silence, but now she wasn't certain she wanted to hear her mother's voice. Celia felt no more substantial than the shadow of a shadow long dead and buried.

With a silent prayer to an unnamed god, she pushed the bright pillows aside, opened the envelope and took out the closely written sheets.

My dear Eva,

If things have gone as I planned, you are a woman now and perhaps ready to hear what I have to say. Or perhaps not. I never listened to my own mother, though I loved her dearly. I didn't wish to grow up in the grip of her pain, which gave me nightmares as a child. Instead I created a nightmare of my own. She tried to tell me I was fighting myself, but I didn't listen. I thought I could triumph over my own heart, but I was only running away. It seems I spent my life running, always from phantoms I had conjured myself.

I trust Eilidh to tell you the truth, and to know it. I trust myself less in that regard. Perhaps I don't wish to know the truth. I'm a coward, and will not pretend otherwise. Except in giving you to the Crawfords. That was the single brave and honest thing I have done in my lifetime. That much I know. Whether or not you believe it.

I decided, when I realized I was both pregnant and ill, that I wouldn't allow my weakness to kill your chance at life. It was my responsibility to see that you had that chance. I swore I would find a way to protect you from the turmoil I had faced—the struggle for survival, the weight of the heritage I did not seek but could not abandon. For the first time in my life, I looked deep inside myself and found the strength I never thought I had, to nurture you in my womb, and help you thrive once you had left me.

I wanted for you a childhood undimmed by the shadows and worries that haunted me. Now that you're a woman, I don't want you reaching blindly for illusory safety or dangerous freedom without the stability of a loving family behind you. You can decide to stay with the people among whom you grew up, or to follow the call of your blood and your ancestors. I will not say which is best; I do not know. I only know I never had that choice, and because of that, I was lost. It will be different for you.

I have chosen honest, practical people to raise you because I feel the time has passed when people like Ian Fraser and Ailsa Rose (who believed in magic and the Sight and the ancient Celtic gods, who believed in possibilities, in fairies and fey dreams and simple human kindness) can survive and flourish in their isolated Highland glen. Perhaps it had passed already when they fought their battle a hundred years ago to keep it pure.

The Crawfords are people of the modern world; they understand the necessity of change and growth. They know how to survive, how to teach you that lesson. My mother, like our ancestors, listened to her emotions, her instincts that were born in her blood hundreds, perhaps thousands of years ago. They run in her blood still, because blood does not adjust to reality and change, nor does it respond to common sense. But faith can't feed you when the land will not. Inspiration dies when hunger makes your belly growl. There isn't much room for magic anymore. The Crawfords didn't have to learn these things the hard way. They've always known. I admire their certainty. I wish I could follow their example. At least you, Eva, will have the chance to do so.

There is not much I can give you, besides the chest that is your heritage. I have left a small bag with my keepsakes. One is Findlay Denholm's wedding ring. He offered me safety for many years, and I feel the ring is precious and should be respected and preserved. There is a ribbon that my mother gave me when I was a child, when it seemed to me a great treasure, because it was soft and fluid and lovely, and because of the look in her eyes as she watched me rub it over my cheek and tie it in my hair.

The dried primrose and emerald pendant are gifts from Neil. I would not pretend he never touched my life; he gave me the only joy I've ever known. For a moment in time, he made me forget to be afraid. Most important, he gave me you. You will find no journal of my thoughts and feelings, which are too little and too sad to put on paper. You will find no letters or drawings or stories. There is a single photograph that Eilidh had one of her friends take of me. My legacy is you, my daughter. May you be more than I was. May you find a way to conquer the fear.

I cannot promise you a happy childhood, though I've done my best to see that you live a normal life and do not grow, as I did, into your own enemy. If there must be a struggle for you, let it be outward, not inward. The one gift I can offer you is a choice.

I hope it is enough. I hope it is right.

Always,
Celia

Eva dropped the letter in her lap, picked it up and read it again, dropped it again. She did not know what to think. She felt as she had when she stood looking down on Glen

Affric for the first time. She knew she should be swept up in tumultuous emotion, that each word of the letter should sear her heart or feed her rage, but she felt very little.

She sat staring, thinking of the lucidity of Celia's voice, the self-awareness and lack of self-pity, the intelligence with which she explained her actions. Eva had never thought of her mother as bright and articulate; her story had conjured someone shy and unaware, manipulated by her feelings until she was destroyed by them. From the very first time Samuel Crawford spoke of Celia, Eva had imagined a phantom—ethereal, lovely, vulnerable, without substance or wisdom. She had never been real.

Until now.

Still Eva felt nothing. No relief, no anger, no sadness. She felt empty and isolated, as she had in the glen. She felt alone. Desperately alone. Knowledge had not brought understanding. The only thing she felt was horror because she felt nothing at all.

More weary than she'd ever been in her life before, Eva lay back, the pages clutched in her hand, and fell deeply and dreamlessly asleep.

5

EILIDH HOVERED IN THE HALL, UNDECIDED. SHE HAD HEARD nothing but silence for so long. She did not want to intrude on this dangerously important moment, but she was worried. As the shadows grew long and an evening chill made her shiver, she turned the knob gently and glanced into the room.

Eva lay sprawled sideways, sleeping soundly, the pages of Celia's letter scattered over her still figure, clad in the jeans and rust jersey she had worn all day. The pillows were tumbled about her, as if a storm had struck the bed, and the duvet had been tortured into wrinkles and ridges and pockets of air under the restless weight of Eva's body. Celia's jacket lay forgotten among the destruction.

Every lamp burned brightly, highlighting the girl's waxen skin and the shadows under her eyes. Her face was turned away from the headboard, her expression not distraught but hopeful. The image was reinforced by one hand flung outward, the fingers open, for all the world as if they were reaching for something just beyond her grasp.

Eilidh stared down at her for a long time, touched by the faint relaxation of Eva's face from dread into hope, by the vulnerability of that open hand. Her throat felt tight, and she was surprised by her response. Deliberately, she turned her attention to the pages of the letter, wrinkled at the edges by the grip of clammy fingers, covered with Celia's precise hand. Too few pages for the hours Celia had spent scribbling in her room before her death. "You burned it after all, didn't you, my friend? You might have mentioned you were leaving it for me to tell her. But I don't suppose it matters now." She spoke aloud, but Eva did not stir.

Telling the story had been a release for Eilidh; she felt lighter, as if the burden of Celia's ghost had vanished, leaving only memories of her lost friend.

Carefully, she gathered the letter together and laid it on the bedside table, where Eva could find it easily in the morning. Eilidh did not try to read the ink-scarred pages. Eva deserved something from her mother that was completely her own.

Then, gently, Eilidh drew back the covers, tugged off Eva's jeans and lifted her so her head fell into the soft down pillows. She placed Celia's jacket nearby, like a favorite blanket a young child might carry to bed and, waking without it, sob, heartbroken, at its loss. Finally, she drew the duvet up to Eva's chin, leaving the one hand on top, open and reaching, and hoped that somewhere in the night or her dreams, Eva would find what she sought.

In the morning, she tapped on the girl's door and heard a faint response. Eilidh stuck her head around the door cautiously. "All right?" she asked. One look at Eva's blank stare, her hands lying palms up and empty on her knees, gave her the answer. "It's too much to take in all at once, I imagine. One's senses simply shut down in self-defense. Doesn't surprise me in the slightest. Don't let it worry you." Eilidh came farther into the room. Her eyes were red from exhaustion, and the uneven lengths of her hair clung to her face and neck in damp curls. There were dark smudges beneath her eyes. She had not slept peacefully.

"It must have been hard for her, being ill and pregnant all at once." Eva spoke without preamble. She did not look up from the contemplation of her empty hands.

"It wasn't easy. Especially after the doctor said there was so little hope. But, as I told you, Celia defied him. She didn't let him make her give up. It took all her strength to win that particular battle."

Eva frowned. "She was giving her strength to me."

"Yes, and she was content to do so. I've never seen her proud of herself before. But she was then. She started talking about finding a family to adopt you. The right kind of family. So I began to search."

For the first time, Eva glanced up. Eilidh was framed in the window, the ravages of the night stamped on her face. "She asked a lot of you."

Pursing her lips, Eilidh nodded. "I suppose she did. But most of the time I wanted to do it. I'm not sure why. Made me feel useful, I suppose, like I might make a difference in someone's life at last." She had never thought of it before, but it was true. "Saint Eilidh and all that rot, you know. I told you I was always wanting to help people who didn't ask and usually resented my interference. But you weren't able to object, and Celia had no other choice. I threw myself into trying to ease her suffering with a vengeance. Never do anything halfway. It's not in my nature. I'd talked to the Crawfords before you were born."

Her face clouded, and Eva felt her heartbeat quicken. "Something changed after that?"

Arms crossed loosely, Eilidh considered the question. "The first time Celia held you in her arms. It wasn't easy for her, she was so weak. It hit her then, hard. I think she'd hoped, secretly, right up until that moment, that she'd regain her stamina and be able to care for you herself."

"Did she?" Eva's tone was flat.

Eilidh was confused. "Did she what?"

"Care about me?" Eva indicated the letter with a slight lift of her open hand. "She never said so, you know. Not really." A stab of disappointed hurt pierced her numbness.

Gaping in astonishment, Eilidh stood directly in front of the girl, who would not meet her gaze. "Of course she did. What do you think that was all about? Her insistence that we find just the right family to take you, her determination that you would have the chance she hadn't, her effort to ensure that you knew what happiness was? Why did she give up her own strength to sustain you, if she didn't care?"

Eilidh was angry. She couldn't help it. "I told you once, she loved you with a kind of desperation; you were all she had, and all she ever would have. I watched her with you in those early days, when she was barely able to lift you. She'd pick you up from the crib and her face would change and she'd be young and beautiful again, and sure. She seemed lit from within, another person."

Eilidh remembered one morning she'd heard a sweet, sad singing and had gone to Celia's room to find her sitting by the window, the baby in her arms, crooning a Gaelic song. She'd held Eva up to the window, showing her the clouds rushing and tumbling over one another in the summer wind. She'd described the clouds, the imaginary life they took on in her mind, the dreams they represented as they rushed by. "You can't catch them, but that makes them all the more magical, Eva. You watch and dream your own dreams and see how quickly things shift and change and how beautiful and powerful those frail gray-edged clouds are. There's almost always beauty in such change. You have to think about it, feel it in your heart, and you'll know. I promise you'll know." There was silver fire in her eyes, which had been dull and flat for so long.

The baby, barely a month old, watched her mother intently, as if she understood. Eilidh had slipped away, letting the tears flow unchecked down her cheeks.

Now she turned away from Celia's daughter, that innocent baby grown into a woman. "She did it all for you, and only a little for herself. Can't you see that?"

"I don't know." The hurt had retreated and pity taken its place. Eva was heavy and sluggish with the weight of that pity. She had not wanted to feel such sadness for her dead mother, a sense of a life wasted in hiding from herself. Despite all she had heard about Celia Ward's weakness, Eva had wanted to admire her, to be proud that she carried this woman's blood.

Eva felt no urge to weep. She wanted to shout in frustration, to walk the cliffs as she used to when the darkness took her, until she was too exhausted to think or feel or mourn. She was not certain if she was mourning the loss of her mother or the truth of Celia's life or the woman she might have been but had never quite become. Or she might be mourning the loss of her own childhood in all its comfort and security.

Nothing could ever be the same again. Eva looked up sharply. "I hear, but I'm not convinced. I suppose you think I'm heartless."

"If there's one thing I've learned about you in the past few days, it's that you have too much of a heart. You're dangerously sensitive to everyone else's distress as well as your own. You're just in shock for the moment." Eilidh glanced at the jacket lying beside Eva on the bed, to avoid looking into the girl's stone face. "You were going to do her pocket story. Maybe now's the time. She can't lie or muddle things or explain badly when you're feeling her own feelings, can she? Whatever you saw would be the truth, wouldn't it?"

At Eva's single anguished glance down at the letter, Eilidh added quickly, "I don't mean she lied. She told what she saw as the truth. I was only thinking that if you put your hand right into her pockets, you'd actually see through her eyes and heart, instead of her mind. That's what you told me when you did my story. It might help, that's all."

The letter had been what Celia wanted her daughter to hear, or had thought she should hear. It was honest but strained by Celia's awareness that Eva would one day read it, perhaps in great anger, probably in confusion and hurt. Eilidh had struck a nerve. Eva felt numb partly because she wanted something straight from Celia's heart. There was only one chance for that.

Eilidh gathered her hair in her hands and lifted it off her neck as she went to stand at the window. "I'll go if you like."

Eva dug deep until she found her voice. She was unnerved because Eilidh had read her feelings so exactly. "No. Please stay." Gingerly, she picked up the jacket, examining it in detail for the first time. She ran her hand over the brilliant colors—red, purple and blue—and the dull—darker blue and burgundy. She touched the edges, some bound tidily, some with fringe in many colors. It seemed as if she held her mother in her hands, in all her passion and cautiousness, her insecurity and the instincts she had fought to suppress.

Slowly, Eva slipped the jacket on, enjoying the soft lining as her hands slid down the sleeves; they were rolled at the end, as if the jacket had been too long. That little detail made her mother seem vulnerable, and Eva felt a piercing compassion. She huddled forward on the bed, hands hovering over the pockets, afraid to see through her mother's eyes. She could not bear any more suffering. There had been enough.

But she had come this far and learned this much. She had to take one last step or she would always wonder. She slid her hands into the pockets and pressed them together, as if holding the fabric close for warmth. Then she smiled.

Eilidh heard the girl's breath escape in a soft rush and turned, curious. Eva's lips were curved in a smile of such innocence and sweetness that she wanted to weep. Since her arrival, Eva had not once looked young, pure and untroubled, as she did now. Eilidh dropped to her knees beside the bed. "Tell me. Please."

Eva closed her eyes to absorb the images taking shape in

her open hands. They were simple and lovely, free of anxiety or apprehension, so full of delight that she grinned wider.

She saw a small, fair-haired girl playing near a burn. She sat with legs sprawled wide, hands covered with loam and pieces of fern. She was talking to a squirrel, telling him about the magic in the river, swirling her hand in the golden burn, brushing the moss on a half-submerged rock. The girl laughed in pleasure at the texture of the stone, the cushion of moss, the rush of cool water over her hand. She sat in speckled shadow, cool and protected, a little in awe of the lush beauty around her. She giggled and buried her hands in the earth and chattered to the squirrel, who seemed mesmerized by her carefree laughter.

It was Celia before the fear had touched her. She had loved the glen then, seen it as her personal playground, had faith that there, among the cool wavering shadows, anything was possible.

The scene reminded Eva of happy times from her own childhood—Agnes waking her in the middle of a rainy night for chocolate and black buns beside the fire fragrant with peat; the first time Eva had coaxed a puffin near enough to touch its beak, and a kittiwake had hovered and landed, brushing her hand with its wings; swimming beyond the beach of powdered shell while the dolphins played beside her and pulled her on their fins. Eva thought Celia had loved the glen as Eva loved the island, before hunger and grief tainted her feelings and made her forget.

Eva's first image of Celia had been the frightened specter in her nightmare, but her last was of a lighthearted child—relaxed and happy. Celia had been mistaken when she said she was never happy. She had forgotten this happiness in what followed.

"I won't ever forget," Eva swore to herself and to Ailsa Rose and Mairi and Alanna. She did not realize she was also speaking to Eilidh. "There are miracles in the earth and waters. Celia was wrong. The time for wonder has not passed. You simply have to believe, and she couldn't do that. It makes me sad for her. So sad."

But still, she did not weep.

6

"ARE YOU POSITIVE ABOUT THIS?" EILIDH ASKED IN CONCERN.

She stood beside Eva, waiting for the ferry at Ardrossan to empty of its passengers from Arran so the new ones could board.

Eva nodded emphatically. "I need to see my parents again. They need to know, I think. It's only fair." She thought of her fiancé, Daniel Macauly, and her heart slowed when the image of Rory Dey rose in her mind. The now familiar confusion twisted in her belly and she felt dizzy and disoriented.

Eilidh said nothing. She suspected Eva would not stay on *Eilean Eadar*. There was a world to discover beyond the tiny, isolated, lovely piece of land. The girl would not be satisfied with that circumscribed beauty forever, no matter how much it touched and revived her.

She had spoken of university a great deal in the past several days. Her thirst for learning seemed to have grown by the minute since she'd read Celia's letter. She'd spent several days going to both universities and the college, where she'd looked and asked questions and put in applications to be considered. She had wandered the streets of Glasgow, seeking out libraries and coffee rooms, theaters and music— the things she would need to sustain her if she attended school here.

But Eva had been distracted when she returned home, and Eilidh had felt that, partly, at least, she was doing it out of a sense of obligation, perhaps to the Crawfords, perhaps to the uneducated and emotionally thwarted Celia. Or perhaps the obligation was indeed to her own prospects. Regardless of her motives, Eva did not want to discuss the future. She went ashen at the mention of the word.

Eva's thoughts wandered, and she shifted anxiously from foot to foot. A question had been spinning in her head ever since Eilidh had told her Celia's story. She had tried to ignore it, knew she should not ask it. She should get on the ferry and turn her back on all this misery and wondering. Eilidh herself had said it. *I'm a bit weary of mucking about in the past. I'd rather go forward than back from here on.* She was right. It was time for Eva to stop looking over her shoulder at things that used to be or should have been. She would not ask.

"There's something—" she blurted out, broke off, and tried again. "Why didn't you take me, instead of sending me to strangers?"

Eilidh paled and Eva knew she had been neither wise nor kind. Celia had been right about the danger of curiosity.

The wind whipped Eilidh's hair into her mouth, and she brushed it aside with impatient fingers. She had asked herself the same thing more than once. She swallowed and chose her words with care. "You've seen how I live, how I ignore what others think, how selfish I am. One can be a unique, perhaps an interesting person that way, but those aren't good qualities in a parent. One has to care what others think; one has to give one's child a sense of the real world, not one's own bizarre fantasy. As a young child, you needed the very normalcy I despise with such vigor."

She met Eva's accusing gaze. "I wasn't ready for that kind of responsibility." She looked away. "Besides, Celia never asked me." Her voice was heavy with a wounded sadness. "She wanted something else for you."

"I'm sorry. I had no right . . ."

Eilidh took Eva by the shoulders. "You had every right. We sent you on this excruciating quest, Celia and I. And since she isn't here to answer your questions, I will do. I owe you honesty at the very least. Even though I don't think it will make it easier for you. You've had to accept so much on faith. Your conviction must be wearing thin by now."

"It is, a bit. I knew it would be difficult, but I never

imagined this. It's hard to feel yourself sinking into a bog when all your life you've had ancient stone beneath your feet. I feel like I'm falling, and I don't know how to catch my balance."

Eilidh looked her in the eye for a long moment. "You will, Eva. I'm convinced of it."

"You have such confidence in me." Eva was stunned by that confidence. She could not quite accept it. There was something incomplete in her own mind, an elusive piece of the puzzle that would not let her rest. She was returning to the island in search of that piece, not even certain she would find it there. But Eilidh was sure. The knowledge was a sweet pain she could not put into words.

"We all have faith in you," Eilidh said. "Everyone who knows you. Ask them and see if they don't."

Eva thought of Rory Dey. What would he say if she asked *him?* It disturbed her to realize she had no idea, and that his answer mattered so much.

When the warning whistle sounded, she summoned up all her courage and hugged Eilidh tight, releasing her with reluctance.

"You can come back any time you like. I'll keep the chest for you until you're ready, and a room, if you like. You know that."

"I know." The lump in Eva's throat made the words come out in a gasp. "Thank you for being so patient and so— yourself. I don't know what I would have done if you'd been ordinary. You kept me from the darkness, you know, because you didn't pretend it wasn't there, and wouldn't let me pretend it either."

It was the greatest compliment Eilidh had ever received. She brushed away tears and pushed Eva toward the gaping hold of the ferry. "No point in pretending. Doesn't change what's real. Besides, I don't know how. It's not a strength, you know. It's a damnable shortcoming. Just ask anyone."

Eva smiled over her shoulder. "But you wouldn't give it up, and you know it. You *enjoy* your shortcomings. That's one of the reasons I like you so much. I'll let you know my plans." Eva waved and disappeared into the queue filing into the ship.

Eilidh watched her go, her heartbeat labored. She would see the girl again, but it wouldn't be the same. It was over. Eilidh had waited eighteen years for this. Now that Eva was gone, she felt bereft and alone as she never had while waiting for the girl to come. Before, she had always had possibility and expectation—the suspense of wondering how it would all turn out, imagining what she would say, how Eva would respond.

As the ferry slid away from the dock, Eilidh felt satisfaction, but it was overshadowed by a hollow emptiness she did not begin to know how to fill. For eighteen years Celia had filled it for her, and though she had often resented the burden her friend had left behind, Eilidh had also valued the gift, the mystery, the expectation. Now what? What could ever take its place?

She raised her hand in benediction and farewell, though she knew Eva could no longer see her. Eilidh turned away, filled with a regret, a sense of loss she guessed would haunt her always.

Eva sat at one of the plastic tables in the lounge. She could see the sticky rings of colas and lemonades on the bright orange surface; she contemplated those circles as if they held the missing piece of the puzzle. She felt a deep compulsion to return home and complete that puzzle. She'd stood on the deck of the ferry for a long time, despite the fierce wind and ocean spray, but at last she'd given in and come inside.

She sipped a lemonade and watched the spray lash the wide windows, mingling with the intermittent rain. At last she gave in to a strangled impulse and took from her knapsack the letter from her mother. Eva spread the pages over the sticky table, smoothing the creases and one bent corner.

But when she tried to read, the words slipped past into the noisy conversation in the lounge, punctuated by laughter and a screaming baby. Instead of her mother's letter, she remembered something else she had found in the chest. It seemed to be a copy Ailsa had made of a journal written by a woman named Janet Chisholm that described the terrors of the Forty-five, when the Highland clans had risen against the British king and tried to seat their own Bonny Prince Charlie on the throne. The tiny book had fallen open to a spot marked by a frayed and faded brown ribbon that might once have been violet. It was water-stained and smudged, as if someone had run their fingers over the page in reverence often. Though she'd read them only once, Eva remembered the words clearly.

Our last day in the hills we love and, we pray, our last grief, though 'twill haunt us for the rest of our days. We'll no' be forgettin' the Highlands, nor the voices of the past that speak to us here. We'll no' forget the burns, the tumblin' water over stones, the heather, and the swirlin' mist. To forget these things would be to lose all hope, all beauty, all that we hold dear.

Eva wondered if her mother would have understood the passage but thought it unlikely. She was slightly envious of those flowing, heartfelt words. She had not written a song of her own in weeks. Her mind, her thoughts, her dreams had been too focused on the search, her creativity drained by the discoveries of who she might have been if Celia lived.

Eva blinked at the neatly written pages of her mother's letter, folded them and slipped them back inside the envelope. She was tired of falling backward. She wanted to look toward the horizon and see possibilities, not menace. The old terror curled through her, tight, coiled and ready to spring. One more look back, she promised herself. One more question, and she would turn away from the darkness. She only hoped she would know how.

Three ferries later, Eva stood on deck, leaning against the railing, staring through the settling mist. She should be able to see the island now, soon, at any moment. Her heart thudded as the mist shifted and she caught her first sight of the cliffs.

She was close enough now to make out the vague outline of the broch on the cliff top where she used to sit alone for hours. The sight made her throat ache unbearably. To her own astonishment, she began to weep. Eva grasped the railing, wet beneath her palms, and clung while tears rose inside her like the swelling, rushing waves rose on the cliffs. The salty tears rolled down her cheeks; she had as little power to stop them as she did to stop the sea from flinging itself at the craggy rocks.

Eva sobbed, unaware of the people around her or their curious stares. Nothing existed but her sorrow, deep, wrenching, inexplicable. She wept all the way to the dock, swiping at her tears with a handkerchief, trying to dam them up again. She hiccupped and gasped and tried to catch her breath, but she was helpless. The sight of the island had broken a carefully constructed dam that held back her desolation until it crumbled and let the torrent loose.

She tossed her knapsack over her shoulder and followed the commuters off the ferry and onto the dock, down past the terminal to the seawall. Still weeping, out of control, she went toward the beach.

She needed the sea, the furious and beautiful sea of her childhood. Through her tears she saw the sprays of foam, the rainbows that shimmered and were gone, the shifting hue of the water. The evanescent, frenzied beauty hurt her in her heart.

She sat on an upended boulder, legs pulled close to her body, head on her knees. Eva sobbed and shook and shivered from the sting of the waves and the bites of the midges and the mist on her hair. She felt as she had in the kirkyard in the glen—alone, bereft of ancestors, family, friends or hope. The woven threads of the past had broken, worn and weakened by the passage of too many years. The present was a blur of loneliness, the future nothing but darkness, impenetrable and threatening.

Why should she feel such despair when she was so close to home? She had felt the same when she had stood beside Ailsa's grave. For a long time she did not move, until, at last, the tears began to subside.

She felt drained and her chest hurt severely. The tide had been creeping in and she was drenched from the waves breaking at her feet. She rose, aching in every limb, throat raw and head throbbing, and began to walk. She wanted her clothes to dry a little, the ravages of her tears to fade. She did not want to break the Crawfords' hearts before she spoke a word. She did not want them to see the depth of her distress. She had wept for the remembered beauty of this island, the magic she had known here, and the happiness. She had wept, not because those things had gone, but because they were still here, still real. The ghost of Celia Ward had not the power to banish them.

The seals and their newly born young sunned in the secluded shelter of the bay, the cry of the seabirds wafting above them on the summer breeze. The dramatic cliffs, with their dark protrusions and deep black caves, towered above the turquoise sea, sloping away in gentle green hills on the other side. As she left the beach, the moors and heaths came into view, dotted with bell heather, pale butterwort and Burnet roses. Goats grazed on the long grasses, and the sheep rambled from one stone dyke to another, gnawing on turf so green it did not seem real.

Eva looked about in amazement. Had it really been only a fortnight since she left this place? She felt as if it had been years, as if everything should have shifted and altered as her own perspective had done.

She was not certain if she were seeing more clearly now, or through a haze, a gauzy veil that subtly altered the shapes and meanings of the things around her.

Eva was tired of wondering. She began to walk briskly, eagerly, toward home.

7

AGNES AND SAMUEL RUSHED FORWARD, THEIR ARMS BECOMing tangled as both reached for her at once. All three held too tightly. They parted, gasping for breath, and stared at one another.

"We didn't know you'd come so soon," Agnes panted.

"We weren't certain you'd come at all," her husband added softly.

Eva was surprised to realize they looked the same; Agnes with her compact body and luxuriant sandy hair in a knot at the back of her neck, her work-roughened hands and shapely bosom, brown eyes and pleasant, wind-burned face. Samuel with his salt-and-pepper beard, his face more windburned than his wife's, his light brown hair streaked with gray. She had begun to wonder if she had imagined her parents, her home, this refuge from turbulence, mystery and uncertainty. "I had to see you. I've missed you so much." The hollow ache in her stomach began, slowly, to ease.

Agnes and Samuel didn't answer, just held her tighter and would not let go.

She heaved a sigh of relief when they led her into the sitting room with its stone fireplace and hooked rug, tallbeamed ceiling and familiar wing-backed chairs. It was as it had always been. The only thing that was different was the wariness and hope in her parents' eyes.

The hope, which glowed like a flame about to fade unless a gust of wind rose to fan it, was a kind of desperation. Eva felt queasy, because she knew she would not stay. How many times would she have to break their hearts before this was over?

"Come in and sit ye down, lass," Samuel said. " 'Tis a

warm, lovely night, so we've no fire on, but you can hear the waves crashing below. That always seemed to soothe you more than the fire."

"Why didn't you tell us you were coming?" Agnes asked as she shepherded her daughter to her favorite chair. "I'd have baked for ye."

Eva frowned. "I didn't think ahead. I just came. I needed to see you." She looked from Samuel to Agnes and back again. Both smiled warmly, accepting her erratic behavior as they always had. She felt a pang that was part regret and part profound gratitude that she had been so lucky.

Eva got up and hugged her parents again, one at a time, clinging to the feeling of safety they exuded. *I hope you find peace,* Celia had said. Eva *had* found it, had lived it for many years, except in those moments when the darkness was upon her.

"It's so good to be home," she said. She ran her hand through her damp chestnut curls, and Samuel turned to stare into the blackened fireplace full of cold ash.

"You look a little thin and wan," Agnes said. Her brow was puckered with worry. "Are you all right?" There were so many questions she needed to ask, but she sensed that Eva must take her time and tell the story in her own way. She did not mention her daughter's red-rimmed, swollen eyes or the faint, blotchy color of her cheeks. But Agnes saw these things, and wanted to punish Celia Ward for what she'd done to their girl.

"I've not had much sun since I left. It rains day and night in Glasgow, and I've been cooped up in a small room much of the time."

"What do you mean?" Samuel asked without turning.

Eva heard the dismay in his voice. "Only that my mother left me a chest full of papers, and I've been reading them and talking to her friend. I've not walked the cliffs since I left, so it's not surprising that I'm pale."

She tried to sound offhand and in control, though she knew they'd hear the truth in the tiny quiver of her voice.

"We were about to sit down to supper. Join us and tell us what you've found." Samuel waved a hand in the air in irritation. "That is, if you want to. There's no need to be telling us things you want to keep to yourself. It's your life, after all."

"It is," Eva murmured. "But I wouldn't have it without you."

They sat around the table as they used to do, and she talked. She had no difficulty telling them about the chest and her ancestors, the journal and letters and drawings. She told them stories of her great-great-grandmother and Ailsa's two half-sisters, and about Eilidh and her eccentricity. Her parents were enchanted; they forgot, for minutes at a time, that she had ever left home in search of another, distant past.

Eva said very little about Celia, only mentioned the barest facts. Agnes and Samuel did not press her, though questions hovered in the air like birds caught on a draft of air, wings spread and quivering.

She asked about Daniel and Xena, and her parents answered carefully, unwilling to meet her eyes. They chattered about everyone and everything else, and Eva felt vaguely ill. She forced the subject out of her mind, because tonight she had to learn something even more important, so that tomorrow she could face the future.

With quiet determination, she took Samuel's hand and Agnes's, and held them, while her own palms grew damp with sweat. "I wondered—I know it isn't easy for you, but could you tell me . . . what it was like when Celia came, how she . . . gave me up."

Samuel and Agnes looked at one another, alerted by the anger and uncertainty in Eva's voice. Whatever she had found in Glasgow, it was not peace and acceptance of her birth mother. They were tempted, briefly, to withhold the truth and feed her anger, and thereby, perhaps, keep Eva for themselves. Except that Samuel had promised he would never lie to her again, and they knew that a lie would not bind Eva's fey spirit if she chose to fly.

Agnes cleared her throat, but her voice was hoarse. "Your mother . . . came several times to see us, to look at the house and talk to us and our friends and neighbors. She didn't want to act in haste, ye see. I got the feelin' she'd done that more than once in her life before, and she was determined not to do it again." She stopped and swallowed, momentarily unable to go on.

Samuel picked up where she had left off. "She wanted to get to know us as well as possible in the little time she had. I admired her for that, for not simply giving you up in desperation to the first likely family who came along. She wanted to be as certain as she could. She talked to us about music and theater and movies and art, about the weaving factory and Agnes's baking, and the children we'd tried to have but couldn't. She wept for us then, because she knew what it meant to feel that loss. She'd been feeling it since before you were born, when she realized she couldn't care for you." He brushed his hand before his eyes.

Thoughtfully, Agnes continued. "She brought you with her the last few times, though she was weak and the journey wasn't easy for her. She tried to hide her weakness from us, but we saw how ill she was. It was almost as if, each time we saw her, she became more transparent, as if she were already a ghost. We could see she didn't want us to know how deep her suffering went, but one look at her face, one glimpse of those gray eyes, and we knew. She didn't have the strength to hide anymore. But she was reluctant to let you go, not only because she loved you—"

"Did she?" Eva interrupted. "Are you sure?"

Agnes was appalled. "Of course I'm sure."

"Whatever shadows were chasing her, they couldn't alter or dim Celia Ward's feelings for you," Samuel said gravely. "You must never doubt that."

Chewing her lip, Eva stared at her hands clasped in her lap. She was trying to believe—she'd always thought she was capable of believing anything—but this was too difficult.

Silence fell, and Eva leaned forward, falling into that silence, willing it to disappear with the right words, the words that would take away her torment and confusion. Yet she also willed it to continue forever, with the sound of the sea outside and below, the intimacy with her parents, the tenuous, lingering anticipation of a revelation to come.

Finally Samuel spoke, while the wind rose and circled outside with a wild cry. As he re-created for his daughter Celia Ward's last visit, he saw and felt it all again. The room was full of the frail stranger. The air vibrated with her presence and her grief.

Celia wore a beige dress, and though she had pinned her hair up, the wind had tugged most of the fine strands free. They drifted about her pallid face in the warm light, making her gray eyes appear to glimmer more brightly. She had lingered most of the day and accepted an invitation to tea, because this was the last time, and she could not bear to end what she had started.

Samuel glanced at Agnes several times in the course of that evening. Both saw how Celia held the baby close to her breast, though her arms looked so thin and frail that they should not have had the strength to cradle Eva tenderly. The baby gurgled in contentment, her rosy cheek pressed to Celia's chest.

Her anguish was so palpable, her defenses so weakened, that Samuel could read each thought and feeling as it pulsed beneath the brittle translucence of her skin.

"I want her to be happy," Celia said fiercely in her eggshell thin voice. "I want you to make her your own. Can you do that? Can you forget I bore her?"

Agnes reached out to reassure her, but Celia flinched and Agnes backed away. Celia would never hold her child again; she was prolonging this moment in every way she could. "We've no need to forget that you bore her. That only makes your gift to us more precious. We *want* to make her ours."

Celia stared down at her child to hide her blinding, unshed tears. She had promised herself she would not weep. But she'd made other promises as well. Nothing could have prepared her for the gaping emptiness she felt opening at her feet, the darkness of her spirit as she relinquished the last of her light. "In all my life, only Eva's been mine absolutely, as even her father never could be. She's part of my body and blood and spirit."

Samuel felt Celia's struggle and wanted to weep himself, for her physical pain, her fragility, her despair. He almost wished they had not met her, that Eva had come to them, her body shaped and nurtured by an unknown mother, her spirit as yet unformed. He saw what it was costing Celia Ward to do this thing, and knew he would not have the strength to make the same sacrifice.

All three heard the loud summons of the ferry horn—the last ferry of the night. Celia closed her eyes and her arms tightened around the baby. She tried to reach outward, to release her child to the family she had chosen, but her fingers were stiff and white with strain.

"Please," she whispered, "take her from me. I can't *give* my only daughter to you. Please, just take her."

Agnes stood immobile, awed by the force of Celia's love for Eva in that moment. Having seen it, felt it pulse through her own blood, she did not think she could do as Celia asked. It was too cruel. But Samuel took her arm and squeezed it, and she realized it was the only way to make it easier for Celia—to take the baby, hold her tenderly, gently, to show their love for Eva physically, so her mother would know in her heart that they'd care for Eva always, in all ways. It was the only solace they could offer.

Together, they lifted the child from Celia's arms, and she let go, suddenly, completely, because she trusted them. She had to. For a long moment, she stood watching the couple touch Eva's cheek and murmur nonsense and rock her when she became restless. She didn't think she had the strength to take one step, to move ever again, but she forced herself to do so. She opened her mouth to say good-bye to a baby too young to understand, but instead she turned and fled, clinging to the memory of the adoration and gratitude in the Crawfords' eyes when they looked at their new daughter.

"Two months later we received a note from Eilidh saying Celia had died in her sleep. That was all." Samuel was exhausted and could not bring himself to look at his daughter's face.

Eva wept, but this time it was not for herself or her lost home or the heartbreaking beauty of the island. Because her home was not lost; it would always be here, for as long as Agnes and Samuel lived.

This time, Eva wept for her mother, the mysterious Celia Ward, who had given up the most precious thing in her life, the only untainted happiness, so Eva would have a chance at finding happiness of her own. Whatever her faults and mistakes, Celia had loved her daughter enough to let her go.

8

EVA SLEPT IN HER OLD OAK BEDSTEAD, WHERE DREAMS CAME and lingered like the mist at gloaming. But these were not of a frightened wraith seeking her own destruction in the churning sea. Instead, she dreamed of Ailsa seated in a copse beside the river. In the background hovered the chimerical images of a dark-haired, exotic woman, and a blonde whose hair fell loose from the pins in disarray. Ailsa's half-sisters watching over her. At first, with the sound of rushing water in her ears, Eva saw from within the eyes of the three women, felt their affection for one another and this place. She felt the strong but invisible bonds that held them together and upright.

All at once, a child appeared who seemed to belong to each of the women and to all of them as she tumbled through the ferns and bracken and hurled herself boisterously into the river.

Then Eva became an observer, watching from the outside. She grew more vivid as Ailsa and the others faded. Even after they had gone, they called to her with voices she could not resist. She woke without confusion, eager to answer their call.

As she rose in her bright, airy room, a tune played

through her head, and she picked up her guitar and sat by the wide window that overlooked the sea. Head tilted, eyes glazed, Eva began to strum. The words came to her, one by one, like glittering beads on a fine-spun crystal string.

Last night a mermaid swam in air above the water,
Her melancholy chant rimming a silver web of clouds—

Eva chewed her lower lip as words and images danced in her head, entwining themselves with a haunting melody. Her fingers tingled on the strings, the familiar threads with which she wove her stories out of music. Her pulse raced at the burst of energy and excitement that she had forgotten and now held close, reveling in the impulse, the creation.

Too fragile for the harsh explosive beauty of the sea,
Which held destruction, peace or immortality—

"There's breakfast, if ye've aye the appetite," Agnes called from downstairs.

Eva shook away the lacery of notes and enigmatic words and slowly placed her guitar on the tousled bed. She could not seem to shake the sadness, but the moment of inspiration, the exultation had been worth it just the same. She had not lost the spark. It would come again.

As her eyes refocused on the spacious room, the rug of leafy swirls, the sparkling windows, she remembered with trepidation that there was another call, equally as urgent, that she could not ignore. She had to see Daniel one more time.

Eva put on her anorak and walked the cliffs she loved. She slipped and slithered in her new climbing boots, seeking out the hollows, caves and spires of tortured rock as she would have sought old, treasured friends. She threw back her head to watch the gannets and fulmars soar and float and plummet, felt the mist of the sea on her skin, tender and familiar. Below, the ocean thundered and undulated, radiant in the summer sun.

She was surprised at the tumult of her emotions, which were not absorbed and dissipated by the hiss of departing waves beyond the chambered promontories, towering stacks and crumbling screes. " 'Tis not quite over," a voice murmured in her head. The voice from the dream—Ailsa's. "There is more to learn and mourn and rejoice in. Have patience, *mo-run.*"

Eva's patience was a feeble thing. She paused on her cliff top to admire the arches shaped by the ceaseless motion of the sea. In that moment, the tune that had awakened her returned, floating over the rocks where the mermaids used to sing their ancient, beguiling songs. She had thought the verse was finished, but now the words that made the meaning clear came to her in the soaring cry of birds above the water.

> *Driven on and lured far from what was safe and dear;*
> *She flew alone and dreamt alone and sang to hide her*
> *fear.*

Eva stared into the sky and wondered if she was thinking of Celia or herself. She ignored the churning in her stomach as she climbed down the hillside, skirting the bog sprinkled with the purple spikes of marsh orchids and lilac butterwort. She tramped toward town in her jeans and loose jersey, nervous and overwrought. She was tempted to turn back, but she knew Daniel would not forgive her if he found she'd been back to the island and had not tried to see him.

She saw him long before he saw her. He was sitting on a bench overlooking the peaceful beach of the western shore. Alexina was with him. Daniel's head was bent, and they sat close, leaning toward one another but holding themselves apart. They were careful not to touch, yet that exaggerated care revealed an intensity in their conversation, a tension in their bodies that said more than a kiss would have done.

Eva stopped short, remembering the pocket story she'd told the night before she left. About the girl with blond plaits who'd loved the mermaids and the man behind the bank grille. She felt as if someone had struck her and she had to fight to catch her breath. Each time she drew in air, it burned down her throat all the way to her lungs, damp from the sea and abrasive with bitterness. She suspected they had not betrayed her, that they had been careful, as they were being now, not to do so. If that were true, why was she paralyzed like this? She realized then that her anxiety had not been for Daniel but for herself.

"You knew," she told herself accusingly. "You knew that night. You even gave him your blessing. . . ." But she hadn't wanted him to accept it. Not really. She turned the stone in her pocket over and over, the magic stone she'd found with Xena. Her friend had known then that Eva did not belong here.

Eva had wept, her face pressed to the chain-link fence, at the captured and bounded tragedy of the land. *It should be free to become what it is without man's touch. To be wild and beautiful and fraught with hope. Shouldn't it? Yes,* Xena had answered, *you should be.*

Eva had thought Celia was drawing her away from her childhood and her home, but it had been more than that. What had Daniel said? *You've always been leaving us, in one way or another.*

Her fingers clenched around the smooth black stone. Her talisman. It could not protect her from the devastating realization that she was losing Daniel, had, perhaps, already lost him.

Tell me you'll come back, he'd pleaded the night before she left.

When I come back, Daniel, I'll be someone else.

No! You'll be Eva. You've always been someone else.

Then perhaps I will be more myself, she'd answered blindly. It was true. She stared beyond the couple on the bench to the sea foaming on glittering powdered shell. She knew herself better now, her fears and misgivings, the nature of the darkness, the legacy her mother had left. Eilidh had taught her there was nothing wrong with being herself, with proclaiming herself in any way she chose, so long as she did not hurt others. Even Rory had told her.

Eva swallowed dryly. Rory. Had they sat as Daniel and

Xena did now, apart but drawn together, bound but struggling resolutely to remain separate? She could feel the tension, the heat, the unspoken thoughts in the cool, misty air. She had not been aware of those things then, but now they were very clear.

Blushing at her own disloyalty that was worse than a physical betrayal, Eva forced the pang of loss down and tried to make her legs move forward. Just then Xena turned and saw her.

For a moment, the tall blond froze and the color drained from her face, then rushed back, making her pale cheeks blaze. There was horror in her eyes, and elation, welcome and despair. She whispered something and Daniel's head came up sharply.

For a moment all three were motionless, caught in a spell woven of voices from the past, emotions lost but not yet freed, the swirling pattern of the sea on the sun-struck beach. As they stood frozen, they were tossed about in time, back to childhood's easy friendship, to secret understandings and intimate touches, to confusion and moody disagreements and, inevitably, to the night when they had last been together.

It was Xena who broke the spell, leaping over the bench and running toward Eva, arms outstretched. Eva threw her own arms around her friend's neck, grateful for the familiar feel and fragrance of her, for her voice, chattering as it always had to cover any uneasiness. Eva did not realize how much she'd missed Xena until that moment. She hugged her friend tight, and they parted reluctantly.

"You didn't say you were coming back so soon. We would have met you. Why didn't you let us know?" Xena broke off as it occurred to her that it was very strange indeed that Eva was here, and that she'd come without warning. She glanced at Daniel and said breathlessly, "Well, I'm sure you two want to talk. I'll stop by later to see you, Eva. Unless—" She broke off a second time, which was very unlike Xena.

"I'll be at my parents'," Eva assured her friend. Even she was aware that she had not said "at home."

Brows drawn together, Xena waved at Daniel and sauntered off. "Later then," she called over her shoulder. She kept her tone casual, but Eva had seen the spark of dismay in her eyes in that brief but eloquent glance at Daniel.

Eva knew that, despite her initial distress, Xena had been glad to see her. She was not certain about Daniel until she looked up into his face.

He was smiling broadly, his brown hair windblown, his hazel eyes bright as he looked at her from head to foot, as if she would have changed in just a fortnight, as if he'd thought he would not recognize her. But he did. He glowed with it.

Eva reveled in the feeling. Just now she needed Daniel's affection, his joy in her return. Like Samuel and Agnes, he was a constant, unchanging source of solace in her life. She had had too much of chaos lately. When he pulled her close, she linked her hands behind his back and leaned into him, savoring his warmth, the solidity of his body, the firm grasp of his arms.

For a long time they stood together, holding each other, afraid to look up and face what might happen next. For this moment, they wanted to remember, to be what they had been to one another for so many years. They were safe together, contented.

Finally, the contact of their bodies was no longer enough, and they leaned back so their eyes could meet.

"I thought I'd never see you again. I thought you'd gone for good." Daniel's voice shook a little, but he kept it under control.

"I told you I'd be back." Eva thought she sounded like a stranger, but Daniel didn't seem to notice.

"Yes, but it's too soon. What did you learn? Are you satisfied, happy?" When she didn't answer at once, when she looked away, he repeated, "It is too soon, isn't it? You're not here to stay."

"No." She started to add, *not this time*, but that would have been a lie, and she would not lie to him. She had not yet recovered from the spasm that had shaken her at the sight of him and Xena on that bench, trying to remain friends when so much more lay ripe and waiting between them.

Daniel released her and took a step back. "You're shaking. But you seem different. More certain, more resilient."

Considering him through narrowed eyes, Eva wondered what he saw in her that revealed those changes. Did he realize she could not have survived these weeks if she had not been stronger than she believed? She had always thought, as Samuel did, that she was fragile, wrong-headed, confused, and, in her confusion, vulnerable. In the past few days she had begun to trust her instincts, to realize she had always listened to her heart as Celia never learned to do. That was partly why she had felt so isolated here among these people who expected simple survival and occasional pleasure, and so got little more than that. Eva had always wanted more.

That was not a weakness, nor was she ashamed of it. She knew how to listen to earth and sea and to understand their voices. That too was a gift, as Xena had told her so forcefully. *Don't regret your uniqueness. Not ever.*

"I know what I want to do with my life," she said to Daniel, by way of explanation, "I mean, at least for now."

He nodded to encourage her to go on, because he could not speak.

"I want to go to university, to study music and perhaps a little writing." She was not certain when this intention had taken shape, or what had changed to make it possible. Perhaps her subconscious had been working on the future while her conscious mind foundered in the past.

She did not mention the voice that Rory had first mentioned in a flower-bright meadow, a voice that called irresistibly—the voice of the glen and Ailsa and her sisters, the inexplicable bonds between siblings and generations that were born in the blood. Not learned but inherited, if the child were willing to open herself and listen to those voices, feel those binding threads. Eva was willing, eager to listen, to hear, to feel. She knew Daniel would try to understand if she explained, but she did not think he could.

We're so different, you and I, she'd told him once. *You*

know which way you're going, and I haven't the first idea. Except that now she did.

Daniel touched her cheek with his fingertips, lightly, sadly. "I know. I always knew, I suppose. That's why I proposed when you were so young. I couldn't stop you from flying, so I never tried, but each time you drifted away from me, I lived in terror that you'd never come back. You'd begun to fly farther and farther away each time, long before Celia Ward gave you somewhere to fly to. I thought I could live with that, that if we were married, I'd know you'd always come home."

He released her, moved backward a few steps, then forward again. "I know you'd try; you're loyal and loving and you'd not willingly hurt anyone. I know you love me. Isn't that odd? To know a thing like that and know, at the same time, that it isn't enough, that I can never have you. I think I knew this moment would come as I stood on the cliff top on your birthday and watched you swim with the dolphins. I saw that you didn't need me as much as you needed the sunlight gilding the water and the feel of liquid gold around you. I thought I could take the risk that your other voices wouldn't call too loudly or too seductively. I thought you might float out with the tide, but you'd always float back in again."

Eva tried to object, but he wouldn't let her. If she stopped him now, he might never find the courage to say these things again.

"I see now that I don't have the strength to take that risk. It's breaking my heart *now,* and you're here in front of me, holding my hand. I need more certainty than that, more than I could ask of you or you could offer. It would tear you apart, trying to keep such a promise. And that would destroy me as well." He glanced at the path Xena had taken, took Eva's hands in both of his.

"I know now that there are those, like me, who are content to watch the mermaids but have no desire to join them in their world of magic and myth and mist. You have to chase that magic, Eva, to become part of it as you're part of the sea we distrust. You're strong enough to do it. But

I'm not that strong, and I wouldn't know how, even if I found the strength. I haven't the wisdom, you see, or the faith."

Eva's eyes burned. Rory had been wrong when he said there was no real safety. It was here, waiting for her. She could marry Daniel and continue to live near her family and Xena, caught up in the simple and circumscribed life of the island. This safety was real, not like Celia's illusory and elusive security, which had stifled and twisted all that was good and hopeful and possible inside her.

Daniel Macauly was a rare man. He understood Eva so well, yet was so distant from the flame that was her spirit. She looked at his familiar face, browned by island sun and weathered by island wind. Daniel was *safe*—no threat to her fragile spirit, precisely because he could not know it. Rory was a threat, because Rory was a mirror. If she saw him, she must also see herself. She shivered at the thought, but the chill was enticing as well as frightening. She wondered if he was right, and she was ready after all. Would she ever be ready to take a risk so great? Her own newly discovered words whispered mockingly to her.

> *She flew alone and dreamt alone and sang to hide her fear.*

Eva wished with all her heart that she could tell Daniel he was wrong, that she would be content to seek her miracles nearby. But she would not be content; contentment was not what she wanted. *Even if there was such a thing, I doubt that you would choose it.* That the image of Rory had come to her now would have told her that much, if she had not already begun to understand.

"It means so much that you believe in me, when I'm just beginning to believe in myself. But it breaks my heart too."

Daniel shook his head, his eyes filmed with moisture. "You've always believed, Eva. You just didn't know it."

Whoever you are, he'd told her once, *I hope you are happy.*

She kissed him lightly, shaking and hollow and adrift. "I hope you are blessed," she whispered.

He held her face in his palms and did not try to hide his tears. "I am already blessed, because I've known you."

They clung together, reached for fading images of themselves, though the gauzy fabric of what they had once been to one another was woven now of nothing more than shadow, mist and memory.

Part Six

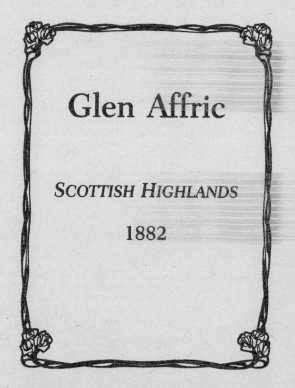

Glen Affric

SCOTTISH HIGHLANDS

1882

1

THE STILLNESS OF THE SHADED WOODS MADE CONSTABLE
Adam Munro uneasy. He had been here often enough to
remember the incessant sense of sound that assailed him in
Glen Affric. But today there was no birdsong, no branches
clashing in the breeze, no wind murmuring through grass
and leaves, no small chattering animals. Even the water
seemed muted, dumb.

It was appropriate, the constable thought dully, this unnatural silence on the day of the funeral, as if the land itself
mourned. He lifted his feet in their thick boots, one after
the other, but they seemed to drag through the soft summer
loam. The hush weighed heavily upon him, deepening his
depression. He was impotent to change it, as he had been
impotent five days ago. He should have stopped the tragedy;
he alone had had the power and the authority. But he had
failed.

Constable Munro felt compelled to come to the funeral,
not only because he cared about these people but because,
try though he might, he could not understand what had happened on that mountainside, or in Ian Fraser's croft, where
Robert Howard had died. He *needed* to know, to understand. Perhaps when he did, he would be able to sleep again.

He paused as he came to the edge of the woods and saw the small kirkyard, full to overflowing with people and melancholy. It was a chilly day for summer. The mist drifted down from the trees and around the feet of the mourners, twining itself among the handfuls of wildflowers and bouquets that covered the ground and rose like brightly colored melting snow where the minister stood at the head of the grave. A giant rowan tree reached its gnarled bony arms out over the kirkyard, laden with white blossoms that shivered and fell on bowed heads and bent shoulders and raw turned earth.

Stopping on a hummock where his boots sank into the spongy turf, the constable peered at the people gathered around the open grave. His eyes burned and his chest felt tight. He had not thought to weep, but the sight of those wildflowers touched him where he was least protected. He folded his arms over his chest and shivered, though the cold came from within. He had always thought himself a strong man, and the threat of tears alarmed him. Teeth gritted to hold back his distress, he focused on the little kirkyard.

He could not see the coffin, but he knew it would be a plain pine box, with something carved into the wood—a clan crest or a motto. His thoughts flickered and shied away from further speculation, and he made himself examine the faces of the mourners. Mairi Rose leaned heavily on her granddaughter Alanna, while Alanna clung to her husband, David. Beside and slightly behind David stood his father, Duncan Fraser, looking hollow-eyed and pasty white. He was not quite one of the family; a cool distance hovered between them like an invisible haze formed of mistrust and despair.

Angus and Flora Fraser stood beyond Duncan, and on the other side, Ian and Jenny's children—Gavin, Brenna, Glenyss, Erlinna. The youngest clutched her mother's skirt, and Jenny herself stood toward the base of the gaping hole in the earth.

Apart from the others at the foot of the grave, one person stood alone, huddled inward, cloaked in charcoal wool, head lowered beneath the concealing hood, enveloped in a grief so palpable that it hung like smoke in the air. The sorrow of the others was dwarfed by the intense, frightening stillness of that figure.

The constable bowed his shoulders. The artificial silence was so loud it deafened him, defeated him. He heard nothing of the service, spoken in the minister's quiet voice, strained with incredulity. This funeral was not a gathering and ordering of words and comfort. The eulogy faded in the presence of faces raw with undisguised emotion, tear-stained, white and stricken, slack with shock and disbelief.

Constable Munro did not stir from his hummock. He was reluctant to interrupt. The people's sorrow and outrage were a private thing, not meant for the eyes of strangers. But he could not turn away, because he shared that grief, that sense of horror.

Inexorably, his gaze was drawn to the figure at the foot of the grave. Misery swelled in his throat. Everyone else shifted now and then; they clung together, holding hands and leaning one upon the other, clutching at what little strength they found in human warmth. But the gray-cloaked figure stood utterly unmoving, apart, untouchable, alone.

Jenny glanced that way several times, then back to the pine box at her feet. Her face was white, waxen, unreadable.

As the minister cleared his throat, the song of the pipes rose, wailing, into the misty sky. Adam Munro realized he had missed the dropping of the first clod of soil, the small bouquet of wildflowers. Like the others, he stood frozen, arrested by the cloaked figure's anguish.

As the piercing cry of the pipes faded, Jenny Fraser raised her chin in determination, closed her eyes and swallowed dryly. Breaking away from her children, she touched one gray wool shoulder briefly. No one dared breathe as she opened her mouth. "I'm sorry," she murmured. It was the most difficult thing she had ever had to say.

Ailsa Rose Sinclair looked up from the well of misery and blackness that had swallowed her. "He was *your* husband."

Jenny winced, felt the shift and turn of the blade inside her. "But he was *your* soul." She was aware that Flora and Angus, along with Christian and Callum Mackensie, had come to flank her protectively. Alanna and David had done the same for Ailsa. David took his mother-in-law's arm when he saw the alarming gray of her face.

Ailsa tried to shake her head—even in the bleakness that was suffocating her, she knew this was wrong—but Jenny raised a hand to stop her. "Ian was my husband, my friend, teacher, lover, many things. It will no' be easy, or free from sorrow, but I can learn to live without a husband and a friend. Ian taught me how. He gave me the strength to survive his absence." Her voice caught, and she saw Ailsa lean heavily on David. Her wound was still fresh, and she did not have much strength, but Jenny knew if she did not say this now, it would never be said. And it had to be. Somehow she knew that it had to be.

She felt Angus tug on her arm, heard vaguely the rustle of the other mourners as they began to leave the kirkyard. She ignored them and detached Angus's tightening grip as a sign that she could stand alone. At least for a moment more. She looked into Ailsa's dark, hollow eyes. "I see how weak ye are without him. I know he gave ye strength as well. But I'm thinking ye can no' learn to survive with half a soul, though you've always been stronger than me before."

Through the gray haze that enwrapped her like a shroud, Ailsa saw compassion, shock and pity in Jenny's eyes.

"I used to envy ye the part of Ian that only ye could know. He shut ye out after ye left the glen. I knew, and I was glad. But I hated that he had to fight so hard to do it. I *wanted* the part of his soul that was yours, even after he silenced it." She took a deep breath and shook with the effort; it seemed she had been standing here for days, alone and abandoned, despite her family around her. "Now I'm glad I couldn't have it, because I don't have to bear its loss. I'll mourn him, weep for him, feel an emptiness beside and inside for the rest of my life, but I'll not have to feel the torment that I see in your eyes now. I just"—she broke down, wiped a tear away impatiently, and finished—"I wanted to say I'm sorry."

Before Ailsa could respond, even had she had the strength to do so, Jenny's knees buckled. Angus and Flora caught her and led her away. "We'll be at the wake," Angus muttered stiffly.

When they had gone, Ailsa swayed, stunned and uncomprehending. She could not understand this woman's compassion and courage when her life was a ruin and her heart a hollow shell. The pain in Ailsa's side, the only thing that told her she was still alive, began to throb persistently at the image of Jenny's ghostlike face. Though she had only just become aware of it, the pain had been increasing for some time, probably since she'd risen that morning, at Mairi's insistence, to come to Ian Fraser's funeral.

Ailsa had known in her heart Ian was dead long before her delirium passed and Mairi knelt to hold her hand and tell her. Ailsa had slipped back into unconsciousness to avoid the knowing she could not endure. Alanna had told her again when she woke; her mother and her daughter felt that the sooner Ailsa accepted the truth, the sooner she could begin to heal.

In the days that followed, Ailsa had slipped in and out of awareness, burning with fever and the agony of her wound. She was never fully conscious, so she need not open her eyes and see. Eventually, against all expectation, she had awakened, empty and feverish, surrounded by darkness and bleak desperation.

"They can wait no longer to bury Ian," Mairi had told her daughter gently. " 'Tis time. I know you're not nearly recovered, but 'tis at least safe to go to the funeral, if we carry ye there and then straight home."

Ailsa had tried to shake her head, but it was too heavy, it hurt too much, it was too difficult to fight through the fog that never left her, and the torment of her wound. She could barely stand, let alone stand beside Ian's grave. She did not wish to try.

"Ye need to see him for yourself, so ye'll *know*," Mairi insisted. "So ye'll know it in your heart and begin to let go."

Ailsa had laughed, a harsh, rusty sound. She could not let go, had neither the strength nor the determination such a thing would cost her. She thought she had grieved for William, but that had been a sweet suffering compared to this devastating darkness of the soul. Jenny was right; Ailsa could not bear it. It was too much for anyone to bear.

Mairi had been unyielding. "If ye don't see him and touch him, you'll lose all the sweet memories and carry only the bitter. He'll haunt ye, Ailsa-*aghray*. Ye know it."

Ailsa had given in because she had no will to fight. But she closed her mind to that moment when Mairi and Alanna had held her upright before they covered the coffin with its carved pine lid. She would not think of his rigid face, no longer his own, nor the brush of her fingers on icy blue-tinged skin. That was not Ian, and this was not Ailsa. Where both had once existed, there was nothingness.

Now, as Jenny disappeared, Ailsa leaned toward the pine box deep in the ground and whispered, as had the legendary Deirdre of the Sorrows centuries before her, " 'If the dead had understanding, you would make room for me.' " But no one heard.

When Ailsa fell, David caught her, gasping at her unexpected weight in his arms.

"Let me help you." Constable Adam Munro had crept up to the graveside as people drifted away, toward the Fraser house and a continuation of the wake that had been in progress for four long days. Munro was frightened by Ailsa's blank stare and her pallor, her translucent skin with its yellow tinge. He wanted to help her home, to make sure she was safe.

Beneath his concern was a gnawing sense of responsibility. The events in the mountains confused and upset him; they made no sense, and he needed to make sense of things before he could rest easy. Ailsa was the only one who might be able to tell him. But not today. He could see for himself it would not be today.

Gingerly, he helped David Fraser lift her, while Mairi and Alanna hovered nearby. "Take her gently but quickly," Mairi urged. "She's bleeding again." She choked and her throat felt raw and dry. "I will not lose her too."

2

GLENYSS STOOD BESIDE THE GRAVE LONG AFTER THE OTHERS
had gone. She could not seem to move. Ever since Duncan
and Constable Munro had carried her father's body home,
she had been full of anger. She shook with it, turned bitter,
felt it build inside her like an icy wind that swirled upon
itself until the pressure was so great she thought she
would explode.

Glenyss stared at the open grave. Soon it would be filled
with earth that would bury Ian Fraser under a weight he
was not strong enough to shift. Her father, who had always
been indomitable, had no strength left. Jenny had taken it
away. Glenyss had watched it all.

She had wept constantly since that night, but the tears
belonged to a stranger. They relieved none of the pressure,
none of the rage or the turmoil. In the last five days, Glenyss
had clung to her hostility toward Jenny like a talisman that
would save her from drowning in the terrifying blackness
that stalked her day and night. She could not understand
this loss, could not admit her father was gone, could survive
only by feeding the storm of resentment that raged within
her.

This was her mother's fault, Glenyss told herself every
morning when she woke. Jenny had sent Ian away. He
would never come home again.

Glenyss began to quiver from the inside out, hands
clenched so tightly that her nails had pierced the palms
many times. She had not washed the tiny moon-shaped
wounds. They throbbed dully and were red and swollen. She
welcomed the sting as she welcomed her anger. She glared

at her mother. "Your fault!" her eyes cried out in silence each time Jenny approached her.

In the dark, she relived the nightmare, when she slept at all. Again and again she saw the stranger draw his pistol and heard the unforgivable things he said. Again and again she saw Ian raise that gun and fire, moving as though through a heavy mist. Again and again she saw Ailsa's hands close around her father's, heard her voice say calmly, "Ye will not suffer this alone."

Glenyss awoke, always in darkness, unable to breathe, soaked with sweat she thought was blood. Then she began to reconstruct her wrath.

Today, when Jenny went to Ailsa and spoke of loss and souls and love without bitterness, Glenyss stood paralyzed. She saw the pale shape of her mother's face, saw how she twisted her hands together—hands red and raw and bloody around the nails from cooking and cleaning and endless wringing when there were no tasks to occupy them. Glenyss felt Jenny shaking, though she stood several feet away. She made the mistake of trying to understand, of imagining what was inside her mother's head.

She felt it like a blow to her chest—the mourning, the despair, the sense of blank, drudging emptiness in the days and years to come. Overshadowing and consuming all those feelings was the guilt.

Wrapping her arms about herself, Glenyss rocked and moaned and held on tight, but not tight enough to hold the demons in. She began to sob and shudder as her anger turned to wrenching pity.

The child was no longer weeping for her father but for her mother, flailing in the darkness, running from the misery that stalked her as it stalked her daughter. Glenyss had opened her eyes at last and seen what she had feared to see. Now she could not blame Jenny, and now she was lost.

As soon as David and Adam Munro laid Ailsa on Mairi's heather bed, Alanna removed her mother's cloak and began to work at her clothes. Mairi brought heated water, bandages and bowls of herb brews that filled the croft with heavy, cloying scents.

While the two women worked, David and Adam stepped back.

Munro rubbed his neck nervously between forefinger and thumb without decreasing the tension that had gathered there. He glanced about uneasily until he noticed a large painting on the back wall, luminous with color, light and life. Surely it had not been there before. It was framed beautifully yet simply; he could not make out the figures from where he stood. He crossed the room hesitantly, drawn by the spellbinding wash of colors.

Adam Munro stopped, staring in awe at the rendering of three women, each gazing at a reflection that was and was not herself. He recognized Ailsa, and thought he saw Mairi's face in the pool over which her daughter knelt, but the others were strangers. He could not tear his gaze away.

"Charles Kittridge painted that before he died. Ailsa kept it with her in London where it would be safe till she came home. I think she had her son ship it after her." David spoke at the constable's shoulder. "Those are his three daughters. He was quite good, really. I wonder why he didn't become an artist instead of a diplomat."

Head tilted, Munro contemplated the three women, caught forever in vibrant color, faces full of mystery and a depth of emotion that was beyond him. He had heard of Mairi's husband, Charles Kittridge. Who in the glen had not? Like the others, he'd wondered how Mairi could have married a Sassenach burdened with wanderlust, who had left her behind to raise his child alone.

The constable shivered, as if he'd fallen into someone else's dream and must wake himself at once. "I'd best be going."

"Thank you for your help," David said as they moved toward the door. "I expect you want to be getting to the Frasers'."

"Wait!" Ailsa cried weakly.

The single word brought an astonished silence that hung

in the air like the smell of fear in a dangerous calm. They had thought she was unconscious.

She turned her head blindly toward the sound of Adam Munro's voice. "Tell me what happened?" she whispered.

Munro stared. "I thought ye could tell me. And Duncan was there. He knows."

Ailsa winced, her skin ashen. "I—don't want Duncan here. I want ye to tell me."

The constable shifted uncomfortably.

"She needs to rest," Alanna said. "If ye could come back later, we'd all like to hear what ye have to say."

Adam blinked and nodded, grateful for the reprieve. It was not that the story was difficult to tell. He'd gone over it in his mind so many times that every moment was etched in his memory. To tell that story to these grief-stricken people would not be easy, for himself or for them.

Adam Munro knew *what* had happened to Ian Fraser. What he did not know was why.

3

THE TABLES WERE SET OUT IN THE CLEARING AS THEY HAD been for Alanna and David's wedding not so long ago. They were laden with oatcakes and scones of every kind, with meat pies and game and tarts. Jenny had made much of the food herself, grateful for something to keep her hands busy while her mind slipped into a safe and distant numbness. She had been aware of Brenna working beside her, of Glenyss, silent and white-faced in the corner, arms crossed and eyes accusing, of Erlinna weeping and clinging without understanding.

Jenny had held her youngest daughter, who would not relinquish the carved wooden bird Ian had made for her, and tried to soothe her with stories of angels and heaven and God's great purpose, but the child must have heard the skepticism in her mother's tone. She would not be consoled. Jenny knew she had failed again, but she could not make it right for Erlinna any more than she could make it right for Ian. He was gone.

Finally Gavin had taken the child outside where they could breathe, where their father's body did not lie on its bier of wildflowers with an endless stream of people coming to pay Ian Fraser homage. Gavin had felt tears in his eyes more than once as he listened to the laments they had written for his father, the toasts they made to his courage and loyalty and his love of this place.

They whispered among themselves, taking one more dram of whisky, one more drink of cider, that because of Ian, the glen was saved. And Ian, they cried, wiping away tears that flowed more copiously as the drinking continued, was dead.

"How did he die?" a Fraser who'd come from Nairnshire asked.

"He killed a man. Did ye not know?" Malcolm Drummond replied.

"One of the Sassenachs come to make our glen their hunting ground. Our Ian stopped him all right."

"The fool brought a pistol to Ian's croft. To talk, he said. Threatened the whole family, the daft bastard. The glen was no' enough for them to destroy. They must be threatening our wives and bairns as well."

"For no reason at all, the man turned the pistol on Ian. Wanted his life, he said. Was no' worth much anyway. Or mayhap nothin' at all. So Ian got the gun away and shot the man. Had no choice, the constable said. 'Twas him or the stranger, who should never have come here to begin with."

"Ian Fraser took the blame for all of us. We all wanted to kill 'em, but only he had the courage to do it."

They called him a hero in their slurred and reverent voices. Not one of them knew what had happened in the Fraser croft that night, but each had imagined his own version and convinced himself that it was true. Already it had become a legend—the confrontation between Ian Fraser and Robert Howard.

It was easy for them to glorify Ian's death, Gavin thought. They did not have to live without him. It drove Ian's son daft that he himself knew no better than Malcolm Drummond what had happened that night.

Jenny had told him briefly about a conflict, threats, a pistol waved unwisely and a man out of control. Ian had done what he had to do, she'd said. There had been an odd flicker in the back of her eyes that had left Gavin unsettled. He realized with dread that he did not quite trust her. All his life, if he had been certain of nothing else, he had been certain that Ian and Jenny told the truth. They did not offer protective lies or soothing half-truths.

Gavin frowned so fiercely that his eyebrows came together in a dark, uneven line. Shuddering, he remembered the evening they had summoned him and Brenna from the shieling while they brought his father's body home. Ian's son had stared and stared at the gaping wound in Ian's chest, at his blood-soaked clothes, hair in unnatural tangles, too dark and too rigid. Gavin remembered vaguely that Jenny had gathered the girls and forced them not to look until she and the constable and David had washed the body and Mairi Rose had come to sew up the wound. They'd dressed him in his best trousers, shirt and leather sandals and laid him on the table, cold and gray, his expression curiously calm.

Gavin had done what he was asked to do, without thought or feeling. He heard his sisters weeping, huddled together, clinging to each other as women were expected to do. But Gavin was the man of the house now—the house of a dead hero, a martyr. He could not permit himself the luxury of tears.

Over and over he screamed in silence to the night sky, to his mother's God and his father's ancient spirits, that it was not right or fair that Ian Fraser should have given his life to keep the glen out of the hands and purses of the strangers. "I would rather have my father and let those bastards take what they want. I'd rather have a family," Gavin ranted in silence to the drifting stars. "I want him back."

It was selfish, but he did not care. He watched Jenny in her wretched silence, casting glances that looked very much like pleas for forgiveness at Ian's corpse. Yet his mother had not killed his father; Simon Black had.

Gavin had heard that the man had left the glen. He wanted to track him to Glasgow and take from him what he'd taken from them. "I want to kill him," he'd said to his grandfather. "For the first time I really understand what it means—'an eye for an eye.' "

Angus Fraser put his trembling hand on Gavin's shoulder. " 'Tis no good, lad, and would no' ease your torment, but ye'd not know that till a man was dead at your hands, and that would be too late." He'd sounded unutterably weary.

Gavin had walked away, walked the hills and woods all night, trying to ease the madness inside him. In the morning he had been exhausted enough to sleep, but every morning when he woke, it was still true that his father was dead.

He glanced around the wake at the Mackensies, Andrew and Catriona Grant, Malcolm Drummond, at the people he'd known all his life. Many were drunk, and had been for days. Wakes were always accompanied by lots of whisky, by mournful songs and dancing and storytelling and more whisky.

Everyone spoke of Ian and Duncan and the investors Ian's brother had brought in to "save" the glen. "I heard Simon Black slunk away like a frightened doe two days past," someone said. "Glad to see the back of him."

"Said it was no' a good investment anymore," a woman answered. "He'd no' admit that Duncan Fraser'd no' support him."

"Near threw him out of the glen himself. Fair turned Duncan purple with rage when Black called us fools again. Black said it was no' worth this kind of battle, and Duncan Fraser said, 'Then get ye gone while one or two of them still live.' "

Crazed with suppressed grief, Gavin noticed his uncle hovering at the edge of the group, drinking from his own bottle and weaving on his feet. Gavin did not care if Duncan had run Simon Black away and defended the Highlanders' right to their convictions—too late. His heart pounded and his pulse raced. Perhaps he could not kill a man, but that didn't mean he couldn't beat one senseless. Duncan Fraser with his big-city ideas and his deaf ears and stubborn blindness.

Gavin could not stand the sight of him.

He shoved his way through the milling crowd. Though many greeted him with sympathy, he did not hear. His gaze was fixed on Duncan; his mind was fixed on Duncan; his rage was fixed on Duncan. He came up and grasped his uncle's starched white collar until it came loose in his hands.

Duncan stared at him blearily, but the fog of confusion fled at the sight of Gavin's fury. Duncan sighed in resignation and, though his nephew was too blind to see it, with relief.

Without a word, Gavin swung at Duncan once, twice, hitting him on the jaw and the cheekbone. He wanted to hear the satisfying crunch of breaking bones beneath soft white skin that had never known sun and rain or wind and toil. Pampered skin, broken by the encroachment of veins across nose and cheeks that told of too much alcohol. Gavin wanted to mar that skin forever, so that every time he looked in the mirror, Duncan Fraser would remember what he'd done, what his family had lost because of his obstinance.

Duncan grunted in pain but did not struggle or attempt to raise his own clenched fists. His teeth were clenched as well, to hold back any cry for mercy. He would make no effort to stop Ian's son from exacting his revenge, meting out Duncan's punishment. He had prayed for someone to hit him, to beat him senseless. It was the only way he could reach oblivion and escape the knowledge that he deserved every blow.

For a long time, Gavin flailed away before he realized Duncan was not fighting back, that his face was bloodied and swollen, but he had not once moved his arms, either to defend himself or to attack. He was standing, shoulders slumped, blood running from his nose and the corner of his mouth, defeat and resignation in every line of his bulky body.

Gavin blinked and caught his breath, stared into his uncle's red-rimmed eyes and saw the weary acceptance there. The young man felt a tearing desolation and knew that this, like killing Simon Black, would not make him able to live.

Neither spoke. Gavin simply released Duncan, who staggered back, caught the edge of a table to hold himself upright. Gavin made sure he would not fall, then turned away, more devastated by the look on his uncle's face than he had been by the sight of his father's coffin.

Adam Munro had arrived during the fight, though he'd seen it was more a beating than anything else. He had not interfered, because he understood Gavin's frustration and fury. Ian's son had needed to feel skin and bones and blood with his bare hands.

Munro had encouraged the other men to circle the combatants warily, in case they had to interfere if things got out of hand. Now they dispersed, remembered the waiting bottles of whisky and unsung songs. They nodded to one another, certain Gavin had gotten the satisfaction all of them craved but glad, just the same, that Duncan was not gravely injured. There had been enough death. It did not belong in the glen, the violence, madness, the destruction. How had this corruption crept in?

However it had come, they wanted it to go.

Callum Mackensie and Adam Munro reached Gavin at the same moment. "Your uncle tried to stop it, ye ken. He had no wish for his brother to die. Simon Black was more canny, is all."

Tasting the bile in his throat, Gavin muttered, "He'd still be alive if Duncan Fraser hadn't come at all."

"I just thought ye should know he tried." The constable and Callum guided Gavin away from the throng. "Come, have a wee dram and wash your face and hands in the burn."

"Water and whisky can wash away many a stain," Gavin's grandfather Mackensie added, "and ease many a weight on the heart and shadow on the soul."

"No' this one." Gavin clenched his fists and felt the soreness of his bruised and bloody knuckles. " 'Twould take a miracle to make this shadow go."

"Aye, weel," Callum Mackensie said sadly, "but there is such a thing, ye ken. Only none of us find it easy to remember now."

Adam Munro and Gavin stared at him in amazement. "Ye believe that?" the constable asked.

Closing his eyes, Callum Mackensie drew a deep, ragged breath. "I have to believe. 'Tis all I have."

4

JENNY SAT ON A STOOL BESIDE THE FIRE, STARING INTO THE weak orange flames. The musty smell of peat smoke rose around her, adding another layer to the murky walls. She felt the soot drift over her like a fine black veil, but did not try to scrub it away. Sackcloth and ashes for penance, she thought.

She heard music swell and fade outside, and a few lines drifted in to the darkened croft.

> *Shades of the dead, have I not heard your voices*
> *Rise on the night-rolling breath of the gale?*
> *Surely the soul of the hero rejoices,*
> *And rides on the wind o'er his own Highland vale.*

Jenny shivered, though the voices were warm with affection and praise. They had been singing for days. The music did not shut out the thoughts in her head but muted them a little, gave her something to listen for, something to cling to. Ian's friends honored him by singing his favorite songs, singing in praise of Highland heroes, counting Ian among their number. Some had composed laments of their own, which they played on fiddle and pipe and flute, weeping and drinking and swaying. One song faded into another, one poem into the one that followed, until they flowed in a steady stream around the body of her husband. Buried now. Gone.

Jenny started when she saw Duncan Fraser move toward her through the croft draped in white linen. She had come to put more bannocks on the girdle over the fire, then sat to watch, turning them, shifting the girdle toward the heat and away, without being aware of what she was doing. She did not want to be alone, but could not endure the noisy presence of the throng of people come to mourn. So she had crept inside. She did not see Glenyss huddled in a corner, watching, listening, hiding from herself.

As Duncan approached, she realized he had not stepped over the threshold since the night he had helped carry Ian's body home. He gave Jenny his condolences, as was proper, but knew she did not hear him. He had come to the croft every day after, had remained outside the door, staring at his brother's bier, unwilling to approach it, afraid the family would turn him away.

Jenny pitied him, and was amazed at herself. She pitied him even more when she saw his face. She did not ask who had struck him; she did not wish to know. She was surprised when Duncan himself did not refer to the bruises and blood, though rusty streams had ruined his shirt.

"I'm sorry to disturb you, Jenny. I know you'd rather I go, so I'm telling you I won't stay long." He shuffled his feet and tugged at his cuffs, afraid she might toss him out before he had a chance to speak his piece.

"Stay as long as you like. He was your brother. I'd not for a minute credit that ye wanted him dead, Duncan Fraser." Jenny spoke with a strange lassitude. There was no warmth or compassion in her tone. That was beyond her power.

Duncan was pathetically grateful for her tolerance. He leaned forward. "I want to help your family now—" He choked, rubbed his throat nervously, forced himself to go on. "Now that Ian's gone. I have money. I can buy modern machinery, food when there's none. . . ." He trailed off. "I just want to help."

Jenny's hazel eyes grew frigid and she sat up straighter. "No."

Duncan had been afraid of this reaction. "It will be difficult without Ian. I know you need help. You've said—"

Jenny stopped him with one hand raised and a glacial stare that froze him where he stood. "We'll make it on our own. We don't need ye or anyone. We'll survive."

Her certainty and her pride forced Duncan out of the slough of his own despair. He was impressed by this darkhaired, dark-eyed woman who sat tall and met his eyes directly, refusing what she considered charity. A moment ago she'd looked broken and weak. Now he felt her fortitude and it humbled him further. "Ian would have been proud of you," Duncan said. "You two are very much alike, you know."

Jenny winced and looked down at her hands. Her body felt the twist of Duncan's unintended blade, and she knew she could not brazen it out. If he saw her eyes, he would see everything. She would not give him that, though she sensed he would find no pleasure in her defeat. For the few shreds of her pride that remained intact, she would keep that defeat hidden.

Duncan reached out to touch her shoulder, thought better of it, and cleared his throat. "I know you won't take it, but the offer stands. If you need anything, ever—" He broke off when she stiffened but did not look up. "I'm sorry," he murmured, and turned away.

As he shuffled toward the door, he could not help the surge of admiration he felt for Jenny Fraser. Not for the first time, Duncan wondered why it had been Ailsa running in the mountains with his brother, when a woman like this waited at home, but he had no answer. There were questions even he would not dare ask. He shook his head and ducked under the warped doorframe.

Only when she was certain he was gone did Jenny allow herself to breathe again. *Ian would have been proud of you. You are so much alike.* Mutely, Jenny shook her head. He had not been proud. She had not had enough faith in her husband when he was alive, enough strength to refuse a chance at a more prosperous future. She had never wanted wealth, just security for her children. Now money mattered not at all. Nothing mattered.

She looked up when she felt Glenyss watching. The girl was always watching lately, usually with accusations in her hazel eyes. But this time there was something else.

Abruptly, Glenyss rose from her dark corner and knelt beside her mother. She laid her head in Jenny's lap and wrapped her arms around her mother's knees. It was the only solace she knew how to offer, the only apology.

She'd glared as Duncan spoke to her mother. She'd seen Jenny's prim response and wanted to weep. She wondered sometimes if the weeping would ever end. She knew the Frasers had to struggle to survive, and all at once, the anger that had been for Jenny burst into flame against her father. It was Ian who had left them, Ian who had refused a simple plan to make more money for the glen, Ian who had loved Ailsa Rose more than his wife.

Glenyss bit her lip until it bled. Her father had always been strong, she thought, had never needed her to hold him. Her mother *did* need her and always had. She needed Ian too, but he had left them. He had died foolishly. She'd heard them say he'd chosen to die. How could he? How could he abandon them so callously?

She looked up at Jenny, who was staring at her with dry, bloodshot eyes. "Papa loved ye," Glenyss said, squeezing her mother's knees. "I know he did. Ye shouldn't think he didn't. I won't let ye think it!" She spoke fiercely, her eyes more green than brown, more like her father's than her mother's.

Jenny was alarmed by her daughter's perception. She clasped her hands around Glenyss's, felt how icy her daughter's fingers were, how marred and bloody her palms. "I know he loved me, *mo-run*. What I don't know is if he forgave me."

*shade at their prosperous farm, she had been warned
what it meant to take a Gunn for . . . Nay, never mind that now. Ian was dead.

She leaned up against the full chimney wall, and the girl lay there, breathing faster, greedy with the struggle to live . . . Nay, but that, that there was something else, someone . . . Brenna. Ian's bairn, her bairn, their child. She tried to focus her thoughts. Someone had her hand on her brow, the cold comfort of . . . she must have slept again.*

5

DAVID AND ALANNA ARRIVED AT THE FRASERS' QUIETLY,
circulated among the mourners, trying not to draw attention
to themselves. They had visited the Fraser croft often since
Ian's death. They'd sat day after day beside the bier, changing places with Mairi regularly so someone was always
with Ailsa.

There was no hostility between the two families, but a
strained reserve, as if neither knew quite how to comfort
the other. Alanna was anxious about her mother, who was
not responding well, though her fever had gone and her
wound was improving, and both knew that the Highlanders
were wondering aloud over Ailsa's presence on the mountainside. Neither Roses nor Frasers cared about gossip, but
they did not want to hurt each other further.

So Alanna and Mairi came to help Jenny and Brenna
prepare the food, working together side by side. They sat
watch over the body, picked flowers and draped the croft in
white linen, but they did not speak much, and avoided looking into one another's eyes. It was too dangerous for
everyone.

"I must look in on Jenny," Alanna said when they first
arrived. "Though today, with so much to do, she'll get by.
'Tis later the devastation will strike, when the shock wears
off and the people go and the days are one like another."
She crossed her arms tightly and shivered at the thought.
"At least she has the children. Mayhap they'll give her
strength."

David looked doubtful but urged his wife to go in search
of Jenny. He himself would not know what to say to a
woman so bereft, so he joined the men, discussing the myste-

rious events that had led to Ian's death. He did not see his father stumble into the woods, wiping his bloody nose on his fine worsted sleeve.

"I'm thinking no one really understands what happened," Malcolm Drummond said, his words slightly slurred by liquor. "Not even the ones who were there."

David gnawed on a bannock and frowned. By the end of this day, he meant to understand. No matter what it took to find the truth. If, indeed, it could be found.

Alanna glanced into the Fraser croft to see Jenny seated on a stool with Glenyss at her feet. The child clung to her, weeping, stroking her mother's motionless hand. "He left us, Mama. But you're here, and we need ye. *I* need ye. Please come back to us."

When Jenny shook her head, not in negation, but confusion, Glenyss held on more tightly. "I'll wait then, for I'll no' let ye slip away forever." She looked up, face red and swollen with tears. "I'll wait for ye, Mama. I'll be here."

Alanna slipped away without a word. She could offer nothing more than what Glenyss was willing to give.

Wandering among the mourners, Alanna listened and spoke softly, avoiding the unspoken questions in people's eyes. She felt curiously calm, untouched. Later she would grieve, when the songs and pipes and voices had been silenced.

David took her arm and whispered, "I want to hear what the constable has to say." By now they'd sung so many songs that their throats were raw and their voices hoarse; they'd eaten a little food, refused dram after dram of whisky and cup after cup of cider and ale. They had joined the dancing briefly, in celebration of the freeing of Ian's soul to fly, bound no more by earthly restraints.

David and Alanna had watched Jenny move among the guests, smiling woodenly, nodding and nodding and nodding at the condolences she was offered. Alanna knew none of the words reached Ian's widow; Jenny's eyes remained blank and still, like a pond left too long without fresh water. She was moving in a daze, and Alanna ached for her but did not know how to reach her, or even if she should. Perhaps these forced and careful courtesies were her salvation. She must not let Ian down, must not shame his family by failing in her duty.

"I don't think it's wise for you to speak to her, Alannean. Not yet. What's between you is still too fragile."

Alanna looked into David's green eyes, which had become so achingly familiar. "I suppose you're right. But I want so much to weep for her."

David took his wife's arm. "That, above all things, you must not do. She's barely holding herself together. Your tears might well destroy her."

Alanna's chest felt tight. "Because they're *my* tears, or because they come from Ailsa's daughter?"

Cupping her flushed cheeks in his hands, David whispered, "Perhaps a little of both. She knows you, honors you and loves you too much. And your face, so like Ailsa's, can only hurt her now."

Alanna leaned against him, shaken by the depth of her empathy for Jenny.

"Come away for the while," David said. "I'd like to stop at the kirkyard before we go back to Mairi's."

Alanna took his arm and held tight. "To say your own good-bye, in private?"

"Aye." David grew pensive as they slipped away from the milling crowd. Fortunately, there had been enough to do since Ian's death to keep him busy and his mind dulled. But now he was afraid the thoughts would come unbidden, and he struggled to keep them at bay. He was more afraid of the rage at his father than of anything else in his life before. So far, Duncan had stayed out of his son's way, and David was glad. He did not know what he would do when he came face-to-face with his father alone.

Alanna talked all the way to the kirkyard, to fill the silence and keep it from breeding too many questions and too many answers and too much blame.

When they reached the stone wall that bounded the sleeping graves, she fell silent, and they stepped into the moving shadows of the branches of the rowan. The deep hole of

Ian's grave had been filled, the casket covered with thick layers of soil. Wildflowers lay scattered on the fresh earth, and among them the white blossoms of the rowan, stirred by the breeze.

David's throat swelled shut as he looked down at the long, dark mound. "I wish Ian had been my father. He was much more a parent to me than my own."

Alanna heard his bitterness and knew it could destroy him if he let it grow and fester. "Don't say that, *mo-cridhe*. You'll break your father's heart."

David pulled away from her. "He has no heart."

"That's not true, David. Look at his face."

David looked up in panic to see his father hovering at the edge of the kirkyard, afraid to come closer. His expression was bewildered and bereft, his face swollen, bloody and bruised. Duncan's eyes were full of self-hatred.

David stared, more intrigued by the deep, raw emotion on his father's face than by its battered appearance. Duncan was not hiding behind his wealth and power now. He looked shattered, as if he might never again pick up the pieces and reconstruct himself. "What happened?" David asked. He wondered why he felt no triumph at the sight of his father's injuries.

A flash of compassion he could not control fed David's fury. How dare Duncan Fraser stand there, frail, aimless and heartbroken, and make his son feel pity?

"Gavin was a little too frustrated, I guess. He didn't know what else to do. I don't blame him. I'm surprised he stopped when he did." Duncan sounded regretful. "At least if he'd knocked me unconscious, I would have stopped thinking for a while." He started to rub his temples, hit an open wound, winced and dropped his hands to his sides.

"I never meant for this to happen," Duncan said. He did not move forward. He'd seen the flame in David's eyes. "I only meant to help." He rubbed his eyelids harshly with his fingertips as if to ease an ache there. "I can't begin to explain how it is that you and I are standing on either side of my brother's grave. If I could change it, if I could drag him from the ground and make him breathe again, I would."

"Would you?"

Alanna laid a restraining hand on her husband's arm. "He's trying, David," she whispered. "*Look* at him. He hurts as much as ye do. At least don't deny him his remorse. I'm thinking 'tis all he has just now."

"And all I have is anger," David hissed back. "It's the only thing that's holding me together."

Hurt shone in Alanna's violet eyes. "Ye have me. What does your father have? Nothing at all but guilt and shame."

Duncan did not move while they spoke quietly together, but he saw the tension between them. Finally he could stand it no longer. "David," he cried, "I know you'll doubt me, but I couldn't stand to lose you too. I know what I've lost through my own stupidity and greed and single-mindedness. I thought I didn't care about all that." He glanced down at his brother's grave. "But it's too much for any man to lose, even through his own fault. Give me a chance. I'm begging you."

David stared, incredulous, but he could not deny Duncan's intensity, the plea in his eyes, his desperation. His father was completely alone. Everyone in the glen was his enemy, yet he had not fled. That took some kind of courage. But David had been clutching his fury too tight for too long. It was not easy to let it go.

When his son did not answer at once, Duncan rushed to fill the awkward silence. "I thought you were all fools, but that's not so." He looked at the dark earth mounded with flowers and fought to keep back tears of weakness. "Ian was willing to die to convince me and the others that this place is something you Highlanders believe in with your souls. Your willingness to protect it against what you consider desecration is a kind of nobility I myself don't possess."

David leaned forward, but Duncan waved him away. "I have to say this. You believe in the glen as I believe in wealth, but your conviction is formed of love and respect." He ran his hands through his hair and rubbed his eyes again with his forefinger. He did not think David would ever understand how difficult this was for him. "Money reassures me, you see, but I can't *care* for coins and bills and checks."

He cleared his throat; the sound was harsh and grating. "But I could feel that way about you, my son, if you'd let me."

"You can feel that way whether I let you or not, and no matter how I feel for you. Trust me, I know." David was unused to speaking this way to his father, the stranger, the martinet. He was afraid of revealing weakness, and thereby giving Duncan Fraser the advantage.

Duncan wanted more, was disappointed by David's answer. But then, he always wanted more; that was how he'd lived his life. David was very proud, very loyal to the people and things he loved, and he rarely forgave, least of all himself. Even this small concession had been difficult for his son to give. David had been stubborn, bitter and angry for a long time. Now, at last, Duncan thought he knew why. Hadn't his own commitment to wealth led to his brother's death and the devastation of his family? Could there be any justification for that?

But Duncan knew, as well, that when he returned to Glasgow, he would fall into the old pattern because it was easy and familiar, because it would make him forget the horror he had faced when he looked in the mirror the day after Ian died. He'd watched Ian die. His own brother. He shuddered, even now, and knew he would for years to come. But he had to survive, and in order to survive, he had to forget. He only knew one way to do that; he'd been doing it all his life.

David watched closely his father's haggard and bruised face. His resentment smoldered beneath the surface, like coals left burning too long and too hot. Eventually they turned red, then gray, then turned to cool gray ashes. The rage might fade. But the pity David felt for Duncan Fraser, running to his ships and coalyards to forget his shame and guilt and grief, would never leave him.

6

Mairi looked old and weary when David and Alanna returned to the croft. Her hair had come loose from the pins, and her long red braid hung down her back. The stark black of her gown emphasized her pallid cheeks and sunken eyes. A cast of gray lay on them like a mourning veil. She sat on a stool near the peat fire, where mutton brose bubbled in the iron pot. The mingled odors of peat smoke and fragrant broth filled the tiny croft.

She had pulled the leather down over the windows to keep out the misted light, for Ailsa's eyes were sensitive to any brightness. Whenever the door swung open she winced and turned her head away.

Ailsa slept in the dim cottage, lit by the fire and a single oil lamp. She was restless and turned often, clutching the quilt in hands that had lost so much flesh, her fingers looked like the talons of a hawk on the faded quilt.

"Have ye eaten?" Alanna asked in concern. "Ye look ill, Grandmother."

Mairi glanced at her sleeping daughter. "I might as well be ill till she is well. She has no will to live, ye ken. She would have given up long since if we'd let her."

"But we didn't let her." David removed his greatcoat and tossed it over a scrubbed pine chair. "Nor will we now."

" 'Tis no' your choice to make." Ailsa spoke in a whisper, but every head turned toward her in alarm.

Alanna drew a deep breath and let it out unsteadily. "Will ye make me watch ye die, then? So soon after my father? Will ye choose, as your own father did, to let the ones who love ye watch and suffer with ye while ye linger and fade?"

There was a brief spark in Ailsa's eyes, so sunken and

ringed in bruises that the color was indistinguishable. Then she fell back with a sigh. It was too painful to be angry. Besides, Alanna had hit a nerve that hurt so much it told Ailsa she was not as lost as she'd imagined. Only Ian was that lost. Forever lost. Dead. She still could not accept it.

It seemed to her, despite the bleak emptiness around and inside her, that Ian's soul was hovering just beyond her reach. His spirit was gone, yet it had not left her as completely as it did when he cut the bonds between them many years ago. If Ian had lived, he would have had to break those fragile bonds again. He had told her once that when they died, their spirits would roam the glen with the spirits of their ancestors, and they would be together again. She wondered, in the darkest corner of her mind, if such a thing were possible.

Inevitable, a soft voice inside her whispered. Ailsa was not ready to listen. She did not know what to trust, because she was alive, though she had surrendered her life. And Ian, who had run to freedom, was dead.

The door swung open suddenly and Adam Munro ducked inside. "I'll have to start back to town soon," he announced. "Are ye up to hearin' what happened now?"

Everyone looked at Ailsa, who turned her head slowly. "Aye."

David pulled up an extra chair while Alanna filled horn cups with tea, which she gave first to Mairi, who smiled wanly, then to the constable and David. Finally she took one herself and drew up the settle while David added more peat to the fire.

It was summer, and they should have been drinking cider, ale and lemonade and stamping the fire to ashes. But the croft felt of winter, the shadows long and dark on the textured walls.

Adam Munro took a sip of tea and cleared his throat, his gaze fixed on Ailsa, who regarded him through blank eyes. Her chest barely rose with each breath, and she was ghostly pale. Had she not spoken, he might have thought her dead.

Forcing his attention to his purpose, he recounted how Simon Black had roused him early the morning after Robert

Howard's death, and he'd come to the glen to find Duncan waiting at the foot of the hills. The constable explained that he hadn't shared Black's desire for Ian's blood. Duncan Fraser made it clear he felt the same. He had been relieved that there were now two men to restrain Simon Black if necessary.

The constable described finding the trail, the search, the chase, until all five of them—fugitives and pursuers—had reached that plateau high in the mountains where Simon Black fired just before Ian and Ailsa disappeared, apparently melding with the stone itself.

"We followed where we thought they'd gone," Adam Munro said, rubbing his chin as he remembered. "We must have spent more than two hours circling and recircling those tall black stones and looking for a trace that anyone could have gone that way."

The sun had burned off the morning mist and hung high in a cloudless sky, making them gasp with its heat. Adam had taken the lead, because he knew the mountains best, but he was befuddled by the disappearance of the fleeing figures in gray cloaks that blended too well with gray stone.

He paced the rock hillside, back and forth, crouching every few feet to look for something, anything, that would give him a clue. Simon Black was angry, tired and restless, and that made Munro nervous. He did not like the man, thought him capable of anything.

"Where the hell can they be?" Duncan Fraser demanded. "They can't have disappeared into thin air."

"Of course they haven't," Black sneered. "Anyone with training and knowledge could find them instantly. If they cared to, that is."

Munro looked up, eyes narrowed to contain his indignation. "Ian Fraser knows these mountains better than any man. Seems he knows a few things I've not yet learned. We have to be patient, ye ken, Mr. Black. Impatience and pointless accusations will no' get us where we want to go." He was frustrated and angry at his own failure, weary from lack of sleep and too much climbing and the heat of the sun without the filter of layered leaves. When they came upon a spring and a single pine tree, he suggested they stop to eat and drink.

Grudgingly, Black agreed. He wanted to press on until Ian Fraser lay dead at his feet, but Black thought it wise to keep his thoughts to himself and conserve his energy.

Duncan was happy enough to rest. He was unused to exertion and had not slept at all the night before. He thought occasionally of Robert Howard, dead on the floor of Ian's croft, but more often he thought of his brother and of Jenny Fraser's face, white with terror.

All three were somewhat revived by the break, and they rose with new determination. Munro could see that Black was more dangerous by the minute, if the gleam in his eyes was any indication. They began to search the area again, inch by inch, with no better luck. Munro had begun to wonder if they should simply find a shady spot and wait the fugitives out, or head for home. But he knew Simon Black would not willingly turn away from this hunt.

In the end, Ian made the decision for them. Simon had just fired two shots into the air, to test his pistol, he claimed, though the constable suspected it was more a release of frustration than anything else. A few minutes later, as if summoned by the gunfire, Ian appeared in a fissure on the next hill over. He paused, leaning against the rock for a long moment, until Simon Black spotted him and began to run.

Duncan followed, lumbering along, and Munro passed him, furious with himself for letting Black get away from him. He knew full well that Black was more dangerous than Ian Fraser—to all of them. The constable began to run, catching up with Black as he reached the fissure, but Ian had disappeared.

Munro leaned against the rock, breathing hard, trying to conserve his energy and keep his eye on Black at the same time. He had just muttered, "He must have gone that way," when Ian's cloak flowed out around a distant boulder and was quickly whisked back out of sight.

Thus began a chase that perplexed Munro from the beginning. Until now Ian had avoided them adroitly, almost carelessly, and Ailsa had been with him. Now they caught frequent glimpses of him, and he was alone. The constable could not shake the feeling that Ian Fraser was leading his pursuers intentionally. But Munro could not determine where or why.

Ian had killed a man. He was the one they sought. Yet he was giving them a marked trail, and though he kept well ahead, he was often in sight for brief periods. Munro soon realized that when Simon Black had fired before the two fugitives disappeared, he must have wounded Ian, for as they climbed over rocks and fallen boulders, up steep hillsides and through narrow crevices, Ian began to move more slowly, as if he were losing blood along with strength.

The slower he moved, the more often they saw him and the less trouble he took to conceal himself. Once Munro got close enough to see that Ian's skin was sickly gray and his breath was ragged, though not from exertion. They were not moving quickly; it was not possible over such terrain. Ian was a strong man, well used to physical labor, well used to these mountains and their challenge. If he had not been wounded, he would easily have outrun them, and would not have looked so weak and ill. The constable thought he saw Ian's lips moving, though there was no one beside him. Then he slipped away.

"Goddammit, you let him escape!" Simon Black gasped, coming up behind Munro. "You were close enough to touch him. Why didn't you shoot the son of a bitch?" His face was beet red from exertion, and his voice shook, as did the rifle in his hand.

"He's wounded," the constable replied, refusing to let Black push him into acting unwisely. "There's no need to shoot him when he's ready to collapse. I caught a glimpse of his face. He can't run much longer, I'd guess. And since he's wounded and weak"—here he met Black's eyes and narrowed his own—"since he's already weak, we can take him alive. Keep your bloody gun for your trophies at home, Simon Black. Ian Fraser'll not be one of them."

Black's gaze did not falter, nor the belligerent jut to his chin relax.

The constable read his determination to kill and vowed to keep ahead of this madman, to get to Ian first.

For a long time the chase went on, until Duncan was near collapse and Simon was furious at his own weakness. He was breathing harshly, covered in sweat, and his face was so red, Munro feared he might have apoplexy at any moment. But still Ian Fraser led them on.

It was a long time before Munro realized they were circling back toward the mountain where Ian and his companion had first disappeared. He paused in astonishment. He'd seen Ian nearly doubled over, dragging himself from rock to rock, and knew he could not last much longer. Yet he'd led them back to where they started, or nearly there.

Slowly, laboriously, Ian stood, pulling himself upright, hand over hand. He shouted something into the sky, leapt between the rocks that sheltered him and came running toward his pursuers.

Munro saw with a wave of sickness that Ian held his pistol pointed directly at Simon Black's heart. Hatred burned in his eyes like a threat—or a challenge.

"Don't!" the constable cried. "We know you're wounded. Don't take the chance—" Whatever else he might have said was lost in the roar of Simon Black's rifle.

Ian jerked upright beneath a fall of black stone and seemed to hang in midair, suspended for an endless moment while the blood spread over his filthy shirt.

In the instant before Ian collapsed, Adam Munro had the most disturbing feeling that Ian Fraser had manipulated them all and brought them to this moment, exactly as he'd planned.

Ian fell abruptly, crumpled like a jumping jack of wood with joints of string that had been cut, and the three men stood frozen with shock. No one, not even Simon Black, wanted to move forward to see his limp and broken body.

"Why didn't he fire?" Duncan murmured at last. "He could have killed any of us."

"That would have left the other two," Simon snapped. "He would still have been dead. One way or the other."

The satisfaction in Black's tone woke Constable Munro

from his shock. He felt sick and deeply uneasy. "Mayhap he's still alive. We must see where he's hit, where his other wound is. Mayhap we can save him."

"For what? To be hanged?"

Munro did not hear Black's low sneer. He moved toward Ian's huddled form, questions racing wildly through his head. He had known Ian Fraser for years, well enough to realize that to have come running, pistol pointed at any man's heart, was not like him, even crazed as he might be with pain and fear.

The constable knelt and saw that though Ian's face was so pale the veins showed blue beneath the skin, though the skin itself was waxen, though his eyes were closed and his dark lashes shadowed his hollow cheeks, he was still breathing. Barely.

Gently tearing away Ian's shirt soaked in blood, Munro saw that the wound from Simon's bullet was down from the left shoulder and close to the heart. He crumpled the shirt and tried to press it to the gaping wound, though some part of his mind knew it was useless.

Ian opened his eyes, dazed and bleary, peering through slitted lids until he recognized Adam Munro. He opened his mouth but no sound came.

"You're covered with blood, and not all from this wound. We saw how ye were losing strength up there, like a slow loss of blood. Where else are ye hurt?" Munro was disconcerted by the lack of hostility in Ian's gaze, by the intensity of that gaze, as if he were trying to communicate.

Slowly, gathering his fading strength, Ian shook his head as the constable checked his body and found scratches, splinters, chips of rock and bruises, but no bullet hole.

Munro sat back on his heels. "You've no other wound, have ye?"

Ian's mouth quirked in a smile.

"But the blood . . ." The constable did not know why he kept talking to a man who could not speak. Perhaps it was because the questions were tearing him up; he did not understand. "And why have ye brought us back where we started?"

Ian made one last effort, calling on every muscle and nerve in his body. Munro saw every twitch, every stiffening of barely responsive tissue, and he winced at the anguish on Ian's face. Then Ian Fraser raised his head and gestured upward, toward the tall standing stones with a narrow space between them.

Munro followed the angle of his head and saw blood smeared on one of the stones and dripped in a trail that disappeared into the crevice. All at once, he understood. "Ailsa Rose is wounded." He looked back at Ian, whose head had fallen back to the unforgiving stone. He was smiling again, with gratitude. "Ye wanted us to find her and bring her down the mountain." He glanced back at the tiny trail of blood, felt Ian move, perhaps to nod, but when he looked back, Ian's eyes were open wide, and empty.

"No wonder he didn't fire, by God!" Duncan exclaimed in blank astonishment. He stood several feet down the hill, where his brother's gun had slid when Ian fell. He kept his attention on the pistol so he would not have to know if Ian was dead.

"Why?" Munro asked wearily. He was exhausted and sick at heart, but Ian had communicated his frenzy before he gave in and let go. The constable felt that the exchange had been a sacred promise. Ye can no' save me, Ian had said without words. But ye must save Ailsa.

Duncan looked up, eyes dark and skin gray. "He didn't fire because the damned thing wasn't loaded. He came running at us, screaming murder and revenge, and all he held was an empty gun."

7

THE CONSTABLE FELL SILENT AND EVERYONE SAT STUNNED, sunk in consternation and dismay. Each glanced surreptitiously at Ailsa, aware of the agony she must be suffering because Ian had used his diminishing strength to lead the pursuers back to her.

The wound in her side had begun to throb and pulse as the constable told his story. The strong herbs Alanna had given her to dull the pain were futile against the onslaught of memory. Though the wound sent sharp fingers of fire through her, leaving charred devastation in their wake, the rest of her felt nothing. Her heart beat but did not sing or weep or ache. Her soul had disappeared into a deep, dark hole. Her hands and arms were numb, as were her legs and chest. It was as if she did not exist, except for the stabbing hole in her side. Perhaps the essence of her had seeped out with her blood.

Mairi leaned over to touch her daughter's cheek, burning with fever. She wanted to wail at the devastating force of her own grief for Ian, but her daughter must come first, just as Ailsa had come first for him the day he died. "He had to give ye a chance, *mo-run*. Surely ye can see that? 'Tis the kind of man Ian Fraser was. To have left ye alone, wounded and bleeding, weel, he'd not have forgiven himself for that."

Ailsa tried to swallow but her throat was closed. Her eyes were so dry she could feel the dust of the mountainside, harsh and gritty against her lids, as if it had not been five days since her eyes were washed free of that dust. She stared blankly at her mother, falling deeper into the blackness without sound or feeling or sight.

"There're so many questions." Adam Munro ran his hands through his hair, back and forth, wreaking havoc on the long blond waves. He could see that Ailsa was slipping away, hiding inside her own troubling thoughts, but only she held the answers he sought. "Why did ye run, Ailsa Rose? Simon Black had nothing against ye, and he certainly didn't mean to shoot ye. Ye'd not be wounded now if ye'd stayed behind."

With difficulty, Ailsa found her voice. "If I'd stayed behind, Ian would have been alone." She remembered the sacrifice she'd thought she was making when she grasped Robert Howard's gun. She had not considered it a sacrifice then; she simply had to show Ian he was *not* alone. The gesture seemed hollow now, pointless, something a child would do blindly, without thinking. "I was *there*. I saw what happened. I feared they'd be after me too. I was no' thinking that night. We just ran."

She did not realize how much that little "we" gave away. The constable rubbed his neck. He could not judge her because he'd seen her grow with Ian from a child into a woman. And Ian's wife had been the only one brave enough to speak to her at the funeral. The only one willing to break through that chilly, silent, overpowering despair. If Jenny understood, who was Adam Munro to question Ailsa's motives? Besides, she had taken her life in her hands when she fled with Ian Fraser, and had quite nearly lost it. The constable wondered if anyone would have taken such a risk for his sake, but shook his head in answer to his own unspoken question.

He forced himself back to the day when he'd stood on the hot black mountainside and watched Ian Fraser die. "Why *did* he come running, pistol pointed?" His voice shattered a brief silence heavy enough to fill the room.

Ailsa knew why, but she did not speak.

Mairi turned from her daughter, shaking and disoriented. She had used so much of her energy in keeping Ailsa alive that she hadn't really *felt* that Ian was dead, not in her heart, not until this moment. It came to her that he had been as much her child as Ailsa. Ian had been part of her family;

she had learned from Charles Kittridge that family was not all in the blood but in the soul. Ian Fraser had seen her soul and known it, as she had known his. He had healed and consoled her as often as she had healed and consoled him. Now she had to live without him.

She had lost a child on that mountain of rock. But she could not wish he had been less dear to her so she would not feel this sorrow now. She did not look at her daughter. She could not have borne the sight of the sorrow they shared.

"Mayhap," she murmured with tears in her eyes, "Ian chose to die of a bullet wound, quickly and certainly, rather than face what awaited him here. He'd almost certainly have gone to prison, or been hanged." She closed her eyes and thanked the Celtic gods that though Ian had suffered many things, he had not suffered that. A man like Ian could not be caged, controlled, contained by iron bars. There, too, he would have died, slowly, wasting away without the people and the glen he loved.

Adam Munro buried his head in his hands, then looked up, troubled. "But why was he so weak, and getting weaker, when there was no wound? He could've pretended to slow down, but I saw his face. He could no' have drained the life and blood from it or turned it gray and pallid. He was a strong, resilient man." He spread his hands wide, palms open and upward in a gesture of surrender. "I don't understand."

Ailsa looked away, toward the cool clay wall. She understood. She had forgotten for a little; the memories had faded in her fever and her torment. But as the constable told his story, it had come back to her.

Though she fought with all her pitiful strength to forget, she remembered that as she lay unconscious, dying, a sound had awakened her. She'd been annoyed, because the music was so sweet. She'd felt light and free and happy, and the noise had brought her back to the pain in her side and the cold, hard rock beneath her.

"Hang on, *mo-graidh*, ye have the strength. I'll no' let ye give up. Not now. Hang on to me, beloved. Hold me. Believe in me. I'm with ye."

Ian's voice inside her head. The one sound she could not resist or shut out or fight against. It was too sweet, too seductive. So she'd lain by the spring and listened as he murmured to her of survival and joy and strength and the weakness of giving up too soon. His words went on and on, and as the slow minutes passed, her fluttering heartbeat grew stronger. "Ye can do it. Ye have the power to do it," Ian told her. The agony receded and the blood flowed more slowly from her wound, and then not at all. And always there was Ian's voice, encouraging her, exhorting her, consoling her. He never once left her as he ran and climbed and hid, playing cat and mouse with the men who sought him, waiting for the moment when he'd given all his strength away and had none left for himself.

He had grown pale and gray and weak because, slowly, with absolute faith and absolute love, he had been willing his strength to Ailsa. Each time she felt stronger, his voice grew weaker until, at the end, it simply ceased, faded into the soft crystal song of the spring by her side. Then Ailsa had felt a blinding flash of light, a presence so powerful and radiant that she could neither resist nor contain it. In attempting to hold within herself that pulsing force, to keep it from exploding into the sun-bright air, where it would dissipate and be lost forever, she was blinded, flung full force into the darkness without sight or sound or touch.

That was why she had been unaware of the men finding her, carrying her down the mountain and into Mairi's croft, why she had awakened in her mother's bed, aching, feverish, her side aflame with pain while everything else was numb and dying. By telling her to hold on, by willing her to do so and infusing her with his spirit, Ian had restored her life to her.

The most precious gift he'd ever given. The only one she did not want.

8

ANGUS AND FLORA FRASER WATCHED JENNY PROTECTIVELY all day. She did not know how many drunken men they steered away from her, how, when she disappeared into the house, they explained her need for privacy, how they kept the children occupied in replenishing the food, how they hovered whenever Alanna or David approached. Angus and Flora understood that Ailsa's suffering was insupportable, but that did not dim their empathy for Jenny.

They had lost a son, Jenny a husband. That bond was sure and taut and would not be broken. They understood, as Jenny's parents had not, what Jenny had done at the funeral. They comprehended the depth of her mourning as Callum and Christian Mackensie could not. They gave their daughter love, support and compassion, but Angus sensed she needed more. She needed to be shaken from the stupor of self-doubt and guilt that kept her bound, a solitary prisoner who could neither broach nor see beyond the walls she had constructed.

When the wake had gone on for so long that many of the guests had fallen unconscious into the summer grass to sleep off their sorrow, their indignation and their whisky, Angus and Flora drew Jenny into a copse of tall white birches. It was gloaming, the sky was draped in violet, the shadows in the copse long and graceful, fading as they prepared to merge into the darkness. The glen was oddly still, though the leaves of the birches fluttered in a puff of breeze that cooled Jenny's heated skin for an instant.

The three stood together, arms wrapped about each other to hold each other upright. Jenny did not protest. After five long days, her body had at last begun to give out. She was exhausted.

As the minutes lengthened and stretched like the translucent shadows on the grass, she felt the warmth of her in-laws' presence, the pounding of their heartbeats, the rise and fall of their breath, and fear rose up to engulf her. The numbness was slipping and she could not let that happen. She tried to break away, but Angus held her, gently, firmly.

"Don't be afraid of comfort, our Jenny," Flora murmured. "Don't be afraid to mourn. Ye can pretend the grief is no' within ye, but 'tis just a game, and one you'll lose in time. Ye must let go of the strands of the web that has ye in its grasp. 'Tis tenacious, but ye have the strength to break it."

Jenny shook her head blindly.

With a sigh, Angus took her chin in his hand and forced her to meet his searching gaze. His hair glimmered silver in the twilight, and his eyes were kind, but there was displeasure beneath the kindness. "Why did ye say those things to Ailsa when we stood at Ian's grave?" he asked baldly.

"Because they were true!"

"How can ye feel compassion for her? If I were ye, I'd want to claw her face until there was only blood where there should be tears. Why don't ye hate Ailsa Rose with all the spite and bitterness that's in ye? Why did ye no' rail at her or spit at her or turn your back as if she was no' there?"

Roughly, Jenny broke away. "Because 'tis not her fault. *Ailsa* didn't fail Ian." She choked on her husband's name.

"And ye did?" Flora demanded, appalled. "Is that what you're sayin'?"

Angus was equally aghast. He knew Jenny had wanted the investors to buy the Hill of the Hounds and perhaps make things better in the glen, but that made no difference now. "Did ye fail my son all those years ago by waiting until the madness of Ailsa left him? Waiting though ye were certain ye'd never have him? Did ye fail Ian by befriending him when he wanted no friends, but only to be left to his misery? By loving him and being his faithful wife and giving him strong, healthy children and making him happy for all these years? How is that failure?"

Jenny shook her head and did not answer.

"Tell me," Flora said. "I want to know."

"I told him I was afraid," Jenny murmured just above a whisper. She added silently, *I doubted him.*

Angus and Flora regarded each other, perplexed and disturbed by Jenny's refusal to see how much she had given their son over the years, her determination to blame herself. Angus felt a surge of anger that had no focus. All he knew was that this was not right.

"Because ye were afraid, he had the right to run with Ailsa?" He wanted to see his daughter-in-law raging, to see her fight back, to shout at Ailsa or Ian or Angus or God—anything but to stand with her head bowed as if waiting for her punishment.

Jenny raised her head, and her eyes burned with self-hatred. "Ailsa ran with *him*. She knew he needed someone. I knew it too, but I was afraid. She stood by him, and I couldn't."

Angus shook her until she looked into his eyes. "For one night, Jenny, ye were afraid. For twenty-two years ye stood by him, never once left him alone or unhappy or abandoned or afraid. For twenty-two years."

"It's not enough," Jenny whispered. "I was never enough."

After Adam Munro left, Ailsa did not move or speak. She felt Alanna's cool, efficient hands upon her, disinfecting the wound, setting the poultice, replacing the bandage, forcing cups of herb tea to Ailsa's bloodless lips.

Each touch of human hands made the struggle more difficult, the effort to hold at bay the anguish that remembering had brought her. Ailsa thought of Ian, dead and buried, at peace, and shook at the fury exploding in her head. She had been ready to die that day. She had been content to think of her spirit roaming the glen after her death, content to surrender her suffering and fall into the seduction of the music.

But she was not ready to let Ian go. Not then and not now. She had made her choice. He had taken it from her.

She trembled with the effort to control the spasms of her weakened body. Alanna's kindness only made it harder. Ian too had thought he was being kind and generous and loyal. But he had betrayed her. He had made her a promise to survive and chosen to break it. *For your sake,* he had told her, knowing she would not understand.

Alanna's eyes, gray in the flickering lamplight, met her mother's, and Ailsa looked quickly away. She could not endure this all-encompassing blackness of the spirit, which was nothingness and agony all at once. She knew she would have died if not for Alanna and Mairi's stubborn healing hands.

It was not fair; she'd made her choice, but Ian had died in her place. Her wrath destroyed the memory of the pure haunting music that had brought her solace, peace.

"Ye should rest now, Mama. Your skin's so pale." Alanna brushed the tangled hair from Ailsa's forehead tenderly, knowing it was not enough, it was not what her mother needed. Alanna ached with her own helplessness, which drifted through the croft like a soft cry of despair.

"We can never be what Ian was, but we love ye, Mairi and me. So do Cynthia and Colin and so many friends I can no' count them. Isn't that enough for ye? Why won't ye cling to me or Grandmama and weep out your sorrow and that poison inside that's draining your spirit? We're still a family. We have each other. Please."

The desperation and hurt in her daughter's voice roused Ailsa. "I know we have each other, 'tis just—"

" 'Tis not enough for ye anymore."

Ailsa was weak, her voice little more than a whisper. "Not yet, Alannean. Mayhap soon, but not yet. 'Tis more than the bullet in my side. 'Tis the emptiness in my soul."

"Then Jenny was right today."

Ailsa reached for her daughter's hand but could not find it. "Jenny has always been right and generous and kind. And now she is alone."

Sighing, Alanna took her mother's flailing hand and laid it on the coverlet. She moved away from the bed and the resignation in her mother's face. "I must go now," she told Mairi. "David needs me tonight." The sound of those simple words created a spark of warmth in the heart of her frigid thoughts.

David had drawn her outside for a moment to whisper, "I know you're worried about Ailsa, but you've done what you can do for now. You, my love, need rest for your spirit. You feel her pain too deeply. It'll make you ill as well, if you don't take care." He'd brushed the backs of his fingers over her cheeks tenderly, eyes full of concern and desire. "Besides, I've missed you. Come home tonight, Alanna, and I'll hold you while you weep if that's what you need. If you need more, I'll give you that too."

His wife had nearly broken down then and there, would have done so, except for her intense awareness of her mother lying unyielding as death in Mairi's croft. "I'll try."

David pulled his wife close. "You want to make her well and whole. I understand. But Alanna, you've not the power. You can't force Ailsa to cast off the shroud of her sorrow. You have to let go, let her find her own way. She did the same for you once, didn't she?"

Tears shimmered in Alanna's eyes as she held her husband tightly. "Aye, so she did." David had not spoken one word of condemnation or frustration, though she guessed he was weary of the battle that had begun the night when Robert Howard died. "How it is that ye got so wise?"

The question caught him off guard. "By watching you, I suppose." He kissed her forehead and held her away from him. "Now go see to your mother so you can come home to me sooner. You need time on your own, *mo-charaid*. You too have your sorrow. You too have to heal."

Alanna rubbed her temples as the odor of herbs began to overwhelm her. She felt dizzy as the image of David faded, and she caught at the air to hold herself up. Mairi was beside her to grasp that reaching hand and force her granddaughter into a chair. She massaged Alanna's shoulders briefly. "Ye've worked hard and long. 'Tis time ye had a moment to yourself. And David has been patient. He loves ye very much." There were tears in Mairi's voice.

"Aye, he does," Alanna said with wonder. "When first I met him, I didn't question the attraction between us. It simply was." She glanced over at Ailsa. "Now I know better. Now I know what a miracle I've been granted."

Mairi urged her granddaughter toward the open door. "Hurry. Find a haven, even if 'tis just for tonight."

Alanna paused in the doorway, then turned back to kiss her mother's clammy cheek. "I'll come if ye need me, Mama. Ye must know that at least. Grandmama and I have no' left ye. We're here and here we'll stay."

Ailsa blinked glazed eyes and brushed her daughter's hand in gratitude, but her gaze was gray, her touch dry and bloodless.

Forcing back tears, Alanna hurried from the croft.

Mairi took her place beside Ailsa's bed. She lifted her daughter's frail hand and held it between her palms. "Ye hate him for leaving ye. Isn't it so?"

Something flickered in Ailsa's eyes. "I didn't mean to let him in again, but it happened. He was with me; he was me. We fought side by side, no' just to save our lives or the glen. We fought for our past, to preserve our deepest memories. I didn't know it till the night we hid in the cave, but 'twas more than an old friendship reborn. 'Twas myself, whole again, real again, happy. 'Tis not right, 'tis not kind, or good or fair to Jenny, but 'twas everything to me. Everything. And he took it away."

She thought of William and felt a stab of guilt. Then Jenny's words came back to her. *Ian was my husband, my friend, teacher, lover. It'll no' be easy, or free from sorrow, but I can learn to live without a husband and a friend. Ian taught me how. He gave me the strength to survive his absence.* Just as William had taught Ailsa. She'd felt empty when he died, bereft, but it was as Jenny had said. To survive without a beloved spouse was one thing; to live and breathe without a soul was quite another. *I see how weak ye are without him. I'm thinking ye can no' learn to survive with half a soul, though you've always been stronger than me before.*

Ailsa wondered about that. What kind of strength had it taken for Jenny to speak those words in front of her friends and family and children? Surely a strength deeper and greater than any Ailsa had ever known.

I'll mourn him, weep for him, feel an emptiness beside and inside for the rest of my life, but I'll not have to feel the torment that I see in your eyes now. Jenny was wiser than she realized, wiser by far than Ailsa had imagined. It came to her then that Ian had never fully broken the bond between them, no matter what she'd thought; he had always been within her.

She thought of Lian and Genevra, who had also been with her since before she knew they were her sisters. Always, they had hovered in her dreams. Always, they had known when she was weakest, as she had known when they were. She clutched Mairi's hand. "Lian. Genevra. What if their dreams—"

"Your sisters knew something was wrong," her mother interrupted. "I've telegrams from both." She paused as Ailsa released her and fell back into the fragrant heather mattress. Perhaps Lian and Genevra could do what she could not. "Would ye care to see them?"

Ailsa nodded, imagining what she would have felt if something like this had happened to one of them. It was a risk to read their empathy, even expressed on paper in square letters that had no life of their own. Reluctantly, she took the letters Mairi offered while her mother lifted the lamp.

Dear Mairi,

I dreamed last night that Ailsa left us, and I fear she is dead. What can I say to you when my own grief leaves me stunned and without words? A part of me has been ripped away. Has Ailsa left my dreams forever? I think so and wonder how I can go on. I pray that you are strong enough to do so; I know that to you she was light and life and inspiration. To me she was consolation and strength, discovery and miracles. Without those things I do not weep; I dry up like a golden autumn leaf turned brown and crushed and ugly.

I did not simply love her; I needed her too. I have to

learn to live again. But you know that. You've done it before.

I think of you every day, and ache for you, and for myself.

Genevra

Ailsa read Lian's letter as well, hands shaking and heart pounding. She was overwhelmed by the depth of their feelings for her, horrified by the nature of their sadness. The pain of her wound was nothing compared to her sorrow for her sisters, who did not know the truth. She felt cruel and callous and guilty. "They think I'm dead."

"Are ye surprised?" Mairi asked. "Look at yourself. Ye might as well be a ghost for all the life in your eyes."

Ailsa could not see her eyes, but she knew they were circled with bruises, sunken and blank. They could hold no light when there was no light inside her. Her skin felt taut and brittle, as thin parchment, without moisture or resilience. Her hands lay clawlike and useless in her lap. No wonder her sisters had thought her dead.

Mairi watched the realization in her daughter's face and was grateful for even so small a sign of life. Ailsa regretted her sisters' pain. At least that was something. "I've wired, and now they know the truth."

"And what is that?"

"That ye live, but ye've given up."

Ailsa looked into her mother's shadowed eyes and found she could not argue. *I used to envy ye the part of Ian that only ye could know. I wanted the part of his soul that was yours. Now I'm glad I couldn't have it, because I don't have to bear its loss.* Ailsa had indeed given up. Just now, for this moment to which she could see no end, there was nothing left to fight for.

9

"I WANT TO LEAVE THIS MONEY IN YOUR KEEPING FOR JENNY and the children."

David stared at his father, who had appeared at the door without warning a few minutes past. Alanna had let him in; David was not certain he would have done the same. He was vaguely relieved that the choice had been taken from him. But now he did not know what to think or how to answer.

Duncan shifted uneasily on the scrubbed pine chair he'd chosen over the rocking chair with the soft cushions Alanna had made. She'd offered it to him, then slipped outside to leave father and son alone. "I must provide for my brother's family. I tried to tell Jenny as much, but she wouldn't listen. Her pride wouldn't let her." He was impressed by the memory, and slightly disbelieving. "She'd be more likely to take it from you. If you kept it quietly, put in a little more than your share when they buy the seed next spring, or help get a new plow or a cow or a sheep. Small things that she'll allow or fail to notice. Then if the children need anything— shoes or clothes or if they want to go to school or come to work in Glasgow or anything at all that requires my help— you can offer to help instead. They know you have money of your own and might actually let one of their own provide what they cannot." He was desperate, determined to finish his speech before David interrupted or threw him out. "If ever, for any reason, one of them needs something you can't provide out of this fund, I want you to promise to let me know, to convince them to let me help."

He ran out of breath and eyed his son fearfully. He still

did not know what to expect from this stranger with the wary, watching eyes.

David pressed his palms together and stared into his father's brown eyes. He knew this red-cheeked, fleshy face with its thick beard that hid so much, yet he did not know the man at all. The bruises from Gavin's attack had yellowed, giving Duncan's skin a waxen cast, and the cuts had begun to heal, but they were still puffy and red. "Why? Why do you want to do this? Why is it so important?"

"I killed my brother and I want to atone."

David grew still. At one time he might have thrown that accusation in his father's face, but that was before he'd seen him, shaken and vulnerable in the kirkyard. Tonight, some of the color had returned to Duncan's cheeks, but he had lost weight and did not look well. "Simon Black killed Uncle Ian."

Duncan waved the denial away. "You know what I mean. If I hadn't come, if I hadn't called in Black and Howard, Ian would still be alive."

Hands clenched on the arms of his chair, David wondered at his desire to argue with a truth so fundamental, a truth that, a week ago, had blazed inside him like a bonfire.

"He'd be alive, and, damn him, he'd be happy." Duncan rose and began to pace the croft. He seemed to fill it with his bulk and his despair. "My brother was always happy in that ridiculous house, in spite of the constant struggle to survive. None of that mattered to him. Somehow he always had what he wanted." Why did it sound like a condemnation? Duncan tried to steady his voice, but he'd lost control in the last few days. Without control, there was chaos—the one thing he did not know how to fight.

"All he wanted was his land, a family who loved him, a home," David said softly.

Duncan sank into his chair and buried his head in his hands. "I know. That was enough for him." The accusation was there, no matter how he tried to disguise it. He paused, and when he spoke again, his voice was muffled. "I loved my brother, but I envied him too much." He looked up, tears in his eyes. He'd thought when he brought the investors here that he had only good intentions, that he wanted to help his brother's family and their friends. Ian had warned him, told him how fiercely he loved his home just as it was. Duncan had chosen not to listen.

He thought he knew what was best for everyone, certainly better than these uncivilized Highlanders living in the spare and desperate past while the luxurious and splendid future burst into flame all around them. "I wanted to think Ian needed me. My younger brother, who never looked up to me or respected what I fought so hard to accomplish. I wanted him to see how generous I could be."

"I don't understand."

"How *could* you understand? I never told you, or anyone, how much I hated Ian for his free-spirited life, his contentment and joy in a thing as elemental as the land, his total disregard for money or artifice. I knew I would never feel that contentment, no matter where I lived or what I earned. He knew what he wanted; I never will. Never."

His voice broke and he stared at the floor, fingers tangled in his graying brown hair. "Is it possible that I did this on purpose out of all those years of bitterness? That somewhere inside I *wanted* it to happen?" He looked up. He was pleading with David but did not want to hear a soothing lie. His eyes begged for the truth.

David was moved by his father's helplessness and self-doubt. He had never been allowed to see such things before. This confession might well be the most difficult thing Duncan had ever done in his life, except to stand beside his brother's grave and know he was responsible. David could have hurt his father so easily, but to his own surprise, he found he did not want to. He thought carefully before he responded. "You might not have minded challenging Uncle Ian, making it a showdown you thought you could win, but you didn't want him dead. It never occurred to you, to any of us, that it would end this way."

"You believe that." It was not a question but a rush of breath expelled suddenly, as if it had been held inside for a very long time. Duncan shuddered and covered his face with his hands. "Thank God you believe it."

David lifted a hand, let it fall, leaned forward, then back. He did not know how to offer consolation to a man who'd prided himself all his life on never needing anyone. "I'll do what you ask with the money, in ways that won't hurt Jenny's pride." It was the only answer David could think of. "I'll watch over them and make sure they're safe."

Duncan Fraser stunned himself by weeping with relief. He looked away. "I'm a fool. You must despise me for this weakness."

"No, Father, I admire you for it. I see that you're a man and that your heart still beats. I'd begun to wonder."

Duncan faced his son and drew a deep, long breath. "Can you forgive me?"

David hesitated. "I wish you'd had a little faith in me."

"So do I. You don't know how much I wish it." He reached for his son's hand, tentatively, beseechingly.

"Perhaps I do know," David said with a constriction in his throat.

"Well"—Duncan Fraser wiped the tears from his eyes with his fine linen handkerchief—"I suppose that's a start."

"Mind the new carrots and turnips, and don't be confusing the herbs with the weeds," Jenny Fraser told her middle daughter tonelessly.

Jenny and Glenyss were taking advantage of the sunlight that had burned away yesterday's clouds. Jenny in her plain gray gown and Glenyss in her navy linsey-woolsey had tied up their skirts to work in the garden on their knees. They pulled weeds from among the tidy rows of vegetables, sinking their fingers into the earth, bringing them up with dark, damp soil clinging to their hands and the roots of the weeds.

"I know how to do it," Glenyss said, not in defense but in reassurance. She could not bring herself to speak in irritation to her mother, no matter how often she repeated instructions her daughter already knew by heart.

"Look, there's a kestrel circling. He must see something in the woods." Glenyss pointed upward, knowing her mother would not look, or would look and not see. She stared only inward these days, and did not seem to like what she saw.

Glenyss was glad for a little sun. It had been a grim week, and the clouds had hung low in the sky, mourning for her father, she often thought. She was never far from her mother's side; she glanced at Jenny regularly to try to read her grim face. Her skin had grown sallow from depression, exhaustion and lack of sunlight. Her brown hair hung limply about her cheeks and her eyes looked sunken. She raised her hand to brush a tendril of hair away and left a streak of dark loam behind. For some reason it made Glenyss want to weep.

She worked steadily, intently. The activity distracted her, and besides, she hoped her mother would notice and be pleased, though Glenyss knew that was unlikely. Jenny had worked hard in the weeks since Ian's death, but she never rested or smiled. She tried to respond to her children's need for attention and affection, but she was in such pain that she could not pull herself out.

"You've given up, haven't ye?" Glenyss demanded, though she had not intended to speak a word. "Why is everyone so willing to give up? Must we all die with my father? Why can't he go alone?"

Jenny looked up, aghast at the hostility in her daughter's voice. "Glenyss . . ." She could not go on.

The girl was not willing to give in. "I'm tired of fighting and wondering and hating, Mama. Can't we stop now?"

Glenyss sobbed and shuddered and did not know it. "You mislaid your hope when Papa died, and ye don't care to get it back." Before Jenny could answer, the girl cried, "Well, I won't give it up. I want to have hope. I have to, don't ye see? How can I go on without it?"

"Ye can't," Jenny murmured, marshaling her fading strength to find an answer for her daughter. "If ye know where to look, reach for it, Glenyss. And when ye find it, hold it tight."

"Only if ye hold on with me. I don't want to be alone, Mama. Don't make me be alone anymore."

Jenny gasped, clasped her arms across her chest to hold

in her distress that her daughter should feel so abandoned. She had not known it was this bad. She stared at the ground, face drawn and gray.

Glenyss shivered violently, afraid that one day Jenny would simply shatter from the weight she carried and the frailty of her protective shell.

The girl knew what was in her mother's heart, because she shared the guilt. It was her fault. Glenyss concentrated fiercely on the row of carrots she was weeding, but the image of Duncan Fraser rose before her. She had seen him leave the glen two weeks past, seen how he bowed his head whenever Jenny was near, how he watched the children with remorse and wrung his hands. When he first arrived, he had been confident, arrogant, unafraid. Now he was weak and frightened and depressed. Guilt was breaking him too. She had heard him tell Jenny that Ian's death had been his fault. Ailsa Rose had said it was hers. Gavin thought it was his because he'd been at the shieling when his father needed him most. The constable said he should have done more to restrain Simon Black, so he was to blame.

Glenyss sat on her heels, dirty hands curled beneath her chin. Surely it could not be everyone's responsibility? She began to giggle hysterically. "If we have to blame someone, why are we all blaming ourselves?"

Jenny raised her head sharply; beneath her skin the fine blue veins were visible. "Surely ye don't blame yourself, Glenyss. You're only a child. What could ye have done?"

Glenyss gnawed her lower lip in frustration. She did not want to talk about herself. She wanted her mother back, not this stranger who did all the right things with eyes as blank as a fresh winter snowbank. "I tried to stop it, ye ken, but I only made it worse." She had not meant to say that and could not stop herself from adding foolishly, "I brought *her*. 'Twould no' have happened if I'd left it alone." She was appalled by her mother's stricken face.

Jenny reached for her daughter to grasp her shoulders roughly. "Have ye been thinking that since he died? Och, birdeen, 'twas nothing ye could have done to stop it. She would have found him anyway. She could hear him when he did not speak, ye ken. She knew the sound of his anger and fear. She knew what he needed. She would have found him, I tell ye." Her voice was weary with despair. "No. 'Twas me. I brought Robert Howard to this house. I betrayed what your father trusted in me."

Glenyss was afraid of the resignation on her mother's face, the curve of her shoulders under the weight they bore. "Uncle Duncan brought those men here to begin with. Ye taught me in the Bible about temptation. There was none till he came. And Robert Howard provoked Papa, no' because of ye, but because Howard was no' strong, so he was afraid. He pushed Papa and pushed him. Ye'd nothing to do with that, with Howard's madness."

She saw the last of the blood drain from her mother's face and knew she should stop, but she could not do it. The words had welled in her for too long, and she felt Jenny slipping further from her every day. "The stranger brought the gun, not ye. And Papa held it in his hand and pointed it at Robert Howard. Ye were nowhere near. *Papa* raised the gun and shot him. He didn't have to do that; the man was weak and afraid. Papa was angry. Robert Howard said foul things. Even then Papa didn't have to kill him. 'Twas *his* choice, not yours."

Glenyss clawed at her mother's dress, gripped the thin fabric in her hands, making huge smudges of loamy soil. "Why won't ye see it?" Her heart pounded and the pulse in her temple beat out a warning. She had to make her mother see now, today, this instant, or it would be too late. "Why won't ye let him go, and ye come back to us? Why?"

Jenny was stunned by her daughter's outburst. No one had spoken of the details of that night for weeks. No one had dared. The first words struck her like tiny blades, sharp and painful. She wanted to cover her face with her hands to stop the flow of those words. Then she began to hear them, to see how wretched Glenyss was, how passionate and afraid.

Jenny felt her daughter's hands grasping her gown, felt their heat and their trembling. It was like a shock of icy water in her face. She sat down abruptly in the damp soil of her well-tended garden, oblivious of the damage to her gown.

Her daughter let go, and as Jenny stared into Glenyss's hazel eyes, she began to think back for the first time, really think, not through a veil of self-recrimination, but logically, step by step and moment by moment.

She had invited Robert Howard to come to the croft against Ian's will and behind his back. But Ian had not killed the man for that. He had paused with his finger on the trigger of that gun, paused long enough to have changed his mind, to have gone to the window and tossed the pistol into the darkness, or removed the bullets, or simply forced Howard to leave.

But Ian had done none of those things. Glenyss was right. Her husband had chosen to shoot Robert Howard. Jenny had watched him closely, had known the moment when he made the decision to fire. He had chosen his own destruction. Then, later, from what the constable said, Ian had also determined his own death. His wife felt as if she had been sleeping for a very long time and was only just waking from a vivid nightmare.

Ian's choice to die, not hers.

And he'd chosen to die without her. She folded inward at a shaft of debilitating pain. He had chosen to leave them; he was free. Only his wife and children had to suffer the inequities of the world, the hunger and the fear. Ian was unfettered; for him there was no more battle.

Jenny felt such fury at his freedom that she could not move or speak. She wanted to throw back her head and howl with rage at her husband's desertion. He had taken the easy path and left her with the hard. She could not forgive him for that. It had been easier to carry a heavy load of guilt than to admit that simple truth. The rage was unbearable, and the loneliness. The guilt, she thought, had been a strange kind of company. But now she was well and truly alone. "Oh, God, 'tis too much to ask that I go on. Too much." She gasped out the words, leaning forward as if she would be ill. "Goddamn ye, Ian Fraser, for ye said ye'd never leave me!"

Glenyss saw her mother falling and took Jenny in her arms. The girl needed so much for her mother to hold her. They crouched in the rich green garden, barefoot in the loam, shaking and rocking, clutching each other tight against the knowledge that they were abandoned, lost and raging at an unjust universe.

10

LONG AFTER MAIRI HAD GONE TO SLEEP, AILSA DRIFTED from her boxbed, gliding through the croft, lit only by the glow of moonlight through the windows. She often wandered at night, unable to rest, searching for something she could not name. Ailsa felt she was suspended in time, in the mist-laden Highland air, empty and waiting somehow to be filled.

The pain of her wound had subsided, though now and then it nudged her into wakefulness, as it had tonight. She felt no sorrow as she moved about the small, familiar room. She had shrouded herself in protective layers of gauze that cushioned her from pain. She ate a little, drank a little, slept hardly at all. She often felt the sadness of her mother's eyes upon her, and Alanna's. She came every day to help Mairi try to reach Ailsa. Ailsa was sorry for their heartache, but she could not give them what they wanted.

She was alive, but they wanted her to be glad. Too much to ask. Impossible. She had ceased to be sorry, but she could not rejoice. "Not yet," she told her daughter every day. "Not yet."

Tonight the restlessness flowed through her blood, and she wandered, drawn to her father's painting on the wall. She touched the paint lightly, as she used to do in London, to remind herself there was a past, and more than that, a future. Though that was harder to accept.

There was something in the air that tantalized her, made her tilt her head, listening, waiting, though she did not know for what. Aimlessly, she went to the cupboard where the packages from Lian and Genevra lay. Her sisters had sent these things to comfort her, to remind her she was not alone, and that any sadness could be borne. She needed to feel the meshwork that bound them together and replenished them.

Genevra had sent some drawings:

> ... to distract you from your mourning. I have sent some that our father drew and left to me when he died, and some of my own. Charles Kittridge did many sketches of us as he imagined we would be and, later, as he saw us when he came to know us. I have sent also the drawing that came to me when I first felt your pain. I know nothing can assuage your grief, but this is my small offering. I must try, even if I must fail.

Ailsa examined the drawings, which revealed so much of Charles's and Genevra's affection for their subjects. She was shocked at how accurately Genevra had portrayed her own anguish in the features of her face, blank and empty, and behind her shoulder, the dark haven of a cave, a pond on a hillside of stone, a face half-turned away that could only be Ian's, because his hand was reaching into her hair and clutching it while he caressed it.

Beside the drawings lay Lian's folder of poems and snippets of verse as well as some of the letters her father had left her when he died. Apparently he had been writing to Lian all her life, though he was certain he would never see her again. He had saved the letters and left them for her.

> We shared a loss before. I, too, have felt this kind of pain. I thought these letters from our father might help. I know he did not write to you because he did not know you until it was too late. I wanted you to hear his voice again, to remember that our memories are invaluable. They speak out of the silence and the darkness and remind us there is light.

One poem Ailsa read over and over.

> *To live alone, inside, where your heart beats*
> *is no easy thing*
> *when your heart beats strong.*
> *It is like living in a cool, dark cave,*
> *safe, but in silence*
> *without song or whisper of a human voice*
> *to save you.*

Ailsa rested her hands on the two packages. She could feel Lian and Genevra in the room with her, their compassion and their sharing of her pain. It had always been so. That, in itself, was a miracle.

The scent of Mairi's herbs, Alanna's shawl over the chair, the painting on the wall and the offerings from her sisters, told her she was not unloved or without understanding. Yet still, she was empty.

She glided to the doorway, drawn by the silence that somehow promised sound. She gazed into the swirling mist that had always been her magic and her solace and her promise—hers and Ian's. She felt motion in that cool night air, a sense of waiting, of expectation that nearly seduced her from her gauzy cocoon. She leaned out so the mist touched her face and thought she heard a single distant note.

Ailsa tensed, stepped beyond the threshold as the note became a soft, alluring song swathed in undulating white. She knew that song: a tune Ian used to play on the flute when they were young. Ailsa held her breath and tried to stifle the sudden erratic pounding of her heart. Then, enveloped in and dimmed by mist and darkness, Ian's voice came to her. "For us there is no farewell. Only a momentary parting. There is a reason why *you* had to live. Believe, my beloved. Believe in me."

Ailsa shook her head violently, chilled to the bone. That voice had drawn her away from the pleasant promise of death and back to the black emptiness inside. She dared not listen this time. How could she, when Ian had made her live again through every sense, made her feel with a vibrancy she had not felt, had forgotten how to feel, and then abandoned her? "No," she murmured. "I don't dare. I believed once, fully and with all my being. To do it again is far too great a risk, because I know the pain too well. No. I can no' take the chance."

The music trembled on the wind and Ailsa raised her head to listen. The song drifted far in the distance. Too far for her to reach. If it had not been so haunting, so enticing, so achingly familiar, she might have had the strength to close her ears against it. Instead, she listened, longingly, and wept into the mist.

"Believe."

She had done it before; she knew how—with heart and mind, spirit and soul. She had given her faith and unconditional trust in the moment when she thought her death had come. But this was harder, because afterward had come bleakness and living death. She did not think she could live through that again.

"Believe."

As the music undulated through the soft, dark night, Ailsa closed her mind and thoughts and doubts away, so only her heart and soul were alert and listening. Slowly, slowly, the music curled about her like mist; Ian's music swirled like a caress, and his voice was woven into the lilting, lovely notes. His touch was in her hair, on her cheek and in her heart. She knew those things could not be, but she also knew, as she opened her spirit for the first time in two months, that the black, aching emptiness in her soul was beginning to ease, that Ian was with her and inside her, in her soul and in her spirit, where they had first loved each other. "There is a reason, my beloved," said the voice that lingered in her dream. All her life she had had faith in him, complete and unwavering. That faith had been for Ian alone. She could not deny him now, when he called out to her, and his voice was tender and full of promise. "Believe in me."

"I do," Ailsa whispered, abandoning wisdom to the well of sensation that Ian's voice created. "I believe."

She felt him there; he was with her and inside her, filling her with his spirit and his song. She smiled, covered her heart with both hands so she could feel its beat and know that Ian's beat there too. He had not left her on that mountainside alone. He was here. Perhaps he had been all along.

Ailsa pressed her hands to her chest and wept.

11

AILSA ROSE, STIFF AND ACHING, BUT STRANGELY AT PEACE.

As she prepared the brose for breakfast, Mairi noticed the difference. "Ye must have gone astray in your dreams, *mo-run*. You're smiling." She spoke casually, but her heart raced with anticipation. Was her daughter coming back to life at last?

Ailsa dragged herself to the table, unutterably weary, despite the sense of peace that had taken root inside her last night. "Aye, well, my dreams were sweet."

Mairi reached out to trace the dark bruises under her daughter's eyes. "Then why do ye look so pale and ill? Ye've been improving day by day, but now that I think on it, ye've seemed overtired of late."

Rubbing her temples to ease the slight ache there, Ailsa murmured, "Nor do I feel easy in my stomach." As she spoke, nausea rose in her like a wave and she rushed for the door.

Mairi found her daughter on her knees beside the rough stone dyke, ashen-faced. Ailsa tried to rise, but could not seem to catch her balance.

"I feel so heavy and strange, as if the spirit of the storm has crawled inside me and will no' let me rest." She remembered the sweet music from the night before, the feeling of Ian's voice inside her, and wondered at this creeping ailment. Her body seemed to have moved beyond her control just when she thought she had regained command.

Ailsa glanced at Mairi, who was staring at her in shock, violet eyes sparked with silver. "Ailsa-*aghray!*" she whispered. "Think."

Feeling her mother's gaze on her hands, folded over one another where she cupped her belly, Ailsa looked down. *Believe. There is a reason.* The voice rang in her head and made her pause, clutching her stomach. She stared down at her hands and felt the queasiness and light-headedness that she had not known in years. That was why it had taken her so long to recognize it. She gaped at Mairi in amazement. " 'Tis impossible."

"Only ye would know," her mother replied as calmly as she could. "Is it?"

Ailsa's heart had ceased to beat, but now it began again, pulsing in her head. *There is a reason why* you *had to live.* She gasped and leaned forward, cupping her stomach protectively. She did not want to think it if it were not true. *Believe, my beloved. Believe in me.* Her head began to spin and she held it with both hands. Then the nausea came again, wave upon wave, and she knew.

"Aye," she said carefully, her voice neutral because she dared not reveal her hope. " 'Tis more than possible."

Mairi reached out gently to press her hand to her daughter's stomach. She closed her eyes, concentrated, and felt, through the instincts she had nurtured when others let them die, a tiny but unmistakable movement. "Ailsa," she cried, " 'tis true. Ye carry his babe inside ye."

Ailsa sat back on her heels, trembling. Her mother had spoken the words aloud. *For us there is no farewell. Only a momentary parting.* She rocked, blind with tears of incredulity and joy. "I shall bear our child." She spoke in a whisper so she would not tempt the spirits, but she could not disguise her jubilation. Ian's child. And hers. She must not linger in the cruel and empty darkness any longer. She must discard her mourning and her selfish melancholy and will this baby her strength as Ian had once willed his to Ailsa.

The two women found a cool spot on the low wall around the garden, honeysuckle curling at their ankles and hands, which rested on the odd-shaped stones. Ailsa smiled, poised and still as if afraid to disturb her inner vision. "Are ye well?" Mairi asked in concern.

Ailsa turned to regard her mother for a long, pensive moment. She was afraid, suddenly, because of her age, and the trauma from her wound, and the memory of the ordeal of pregnancy itself. She looked into Mairi's eyes at the wisdom and certainty that were soothing in their constancy. Mairi's spirit was strong. There was a tranquility about her that drew Ailsa; she could see her reflection in her mother's eyes, in the quiet of her thoughts, and knew it would be all right.

Ailsa smiled, fully, radiantly, as she had not smiled for many years, except in Ian's eyes. "I'm well," she said. "The gods have granted me one more miracle."

Taking her daughter's clammy hand, Mairi shook her head. "I should have known such a thing. I should have seen it."

Turning her hand palm up so she could link her fingers with her mother's, Ailsa closed her eyes. "Mayhap we were no' meant to see it till now."

"That's why he led them back to ye. He knew his future was over, but yours was not. He knew ye carried his seed. Ian would have known."

"Aye, he would. 'Tis why—" Even now Ailsa could not say it. That was why he had traded his life for hers, why he had bullied and cajoled her when she wanted only peace. He had known there would be a child of their blood and spirits mingled, a legacy that was more than memory.

Ailsa pressed her hand to her belly. "I should have trusted him. *I* should have known."

"No. 'Twas Ian's secret. The last he ever knew. Mayhap ye weren't ready to accept it before." Mairi stared across the flower-strewn clearing, brow furrowed. " 'Twill no' be easy, ye ken. Ye've no husband to protect your name, and you're over forty now. Ye'll have to take great care."

She gripped her daughter's hand so tightly that the pain raced through her own fingers and up her arm. "I know what it must mean to ye, because I know what it meant to me a very long time ago when Charles had gone and I felt ye live within me."

Mairi was overwhelmed by deep and bittersweet relief, because Ailsa was alive again; she must live and flourish for the child to live and flourish. Mairi's chest felt tight with elation and anxiety. This child would be special, extraordinary. Of that she had no doubt. But the cost had been high, to all of them.

She raised her daughter's hand to her warm cheek, damp with the sheen of gentle tears. " 'Tis no' an easy choice, ye ken. 'Tis so small a place, the glen, and all know all about each other, or think they do."

Ailsa pressed her own cheek to her mother's. "I've never done things the easy way, have I? And I'd no' be caring what they think. The people of the glen know me. They'll know 'twas not a careless whim. Ian's bairn. I thought I'd lost him, and with him, my faith."

"We all stop believing now and again. We'd not be human if hope didn't dwindle away sometimes. 'Tis only when it dries up and drifts away like the leaves in autumn that your heart turns hard and dry."

Ailsa felt a flutter of unease when she thought of Jenny Fraser. "I know 'tis wrong to want this child so much, to be so joyful when others can only suffer. But my spirit is full of song, and I wish so much to sing again."

"Ye must follow the urging of your soul," Mairi said thoughtfully. " 'Tis worth the reward *and* the pain. Naught will ever mean perfect happiness for everyone. But there's always one more miracle, if ye have the faith to let it come."

For a long time, Ailsa could not speak. Slowly, the bells of the hollyhock came back into focus, and she raised her head and looked into her mother's eyes. "Do I deserve such a gift?"

"Only the gods can decide these things, and they've chosen ye. Don't wonder at such a blessing, just treasure and protect it." Rocking back and forth, as if she already held the child in her arms, Mairi leaned shoulder to shoulder with her daughter. "And remember, we'll be here for ye and with ye," she whispered. "Always."

*   *   *

The pregnancy did not go easily on Ailsa. She found herself taking sips of bitter herb teas morning and night, she was often ill and her energy seeped away. Once the child began to kick, it did not ever cease, or so it seemed to her.

But Mairi and Alanna cared for her and the child in equal measure. They began to think of the baby, which Mairi had "seen" would be a girl, as their child, born of the close-knit bond among them.

Ailsa was glad, and knew if it were not for them, she would have lost the baby.

The only thing that soothed her, carried her beyond the discomfort, was to sit at the door with her clarsach or her rosewood flute and play to her unborn child. The notes curled about her shoulders like a shawl woven of moonlight and silver thread, snug and familiar because she had worn it for years. The songs murmured and drifted on the invisible breath of summer as it turned to autumn. The gossamer notes brought Ian in the wind, as he had come on the night of her sorrow, playing her his promise and his plea that she have faith. She chanted that promise to their baby so she would not forget, and the music began to heal her with its lilting, magic touch.

On the days when she could not lift her body from the heather mattress, and often late into the night, Ailsa took a quill pen and a book of parchment bound in leather and began a journal by the light of a candle or a single oil lamp.

She touched her swelling stomach and felt a flutter of movement inside and knew Mairi was right; it would be a girl. She had already chosen a name. She wrote it with a smile and a trembling hand.

TO ENA:
Flame, hope, miracle

This book is for you, my yet unborn but precious child, so you need never wonder who your father was or what he was or if he loved you. He gave his life in love for you, for both of us, because you are part of us, of all that we were and imagined and never could be, and because you were a child with no stain of the world upon you.

I will write in these pages every memory I have of Ian Fraser, from the first time we met, when I was too young to count the years, to the last time I saw him, but three months past, when he gave me the gift of my life—and the agony of his own death.

I will tell you, word by word and page by page, what kind of man he was—and is, for he is with us yet, my little one. I feel him as surely as I feel my own heartbeat, and yours.

I do this so you know him from your first moment of knowing, so that questions and anguish and the darkness of wondering never taint or twist your dreams or waking. That heritage I can give you, though little else, except the certainty of who you are and who we are and why you came to be, *mo-run*.

I have learned this lesson through much pain and regret, and would wish that you and your children need not learn it again. But you will, because to live your life is to grieve as often as you're joyful, to weep as often as you sing. Only never stop singing, Ena, my child, for the silence is the most painful of all. Fill it with your voice, your faith, and the sound of your hope—a sweet bonny sound that I hear now in the wind among the trees and the rushing of the water and the pulse of my blood, and Ian's, in your veins and my own.

Epilogue

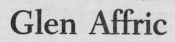

Glen Affric

SCOTTISH HIGHLANDS

1988

EVA CLOSED AILSA'S JOURNAL AND SAT BACK, SMILING TO herself as the ferry touched the shore. All that hope and faith and the promise of the future enmeshed so tightly with the past. She felt she not only knew Ailsa, but had absorbed some of her inner peace in reading the pages she had written long ago. Written for her daughter. Eva wondered if Ailsa could possibly have guessed they might mean as much to a young girl one hundred years later as they had to that unborn child.

Today she understood why Celia had left the chest, why its contents had been as important as Celia's own letter. Today Eva knew, not just with her mind, but with her spirit, why Ailsa's voice had been so real, so vibrant, had moved her so deeply.

This time she could not wait to reach Glen Affric.

"Mind the roads up there, now. Dead winding, some of 'em, and full of ruts and potholes. One lane as well, and not much of a verge to let oncomers pass." Tim, from whom Eva had hired a blue four-wheel-drive Jeep, stood uneasily beside the car, giving her last-minute instructions. "Dead desolate up there, you know. Are you sure you should be going alone?"

"I'm not afraid," Eva assured him. "I know what I'm about, don't worry." Strangely, it was true. The terror of her former perilous trip to the glen had disappeared, as if that journey, that maelstrom of hurt and confusion, had happened many years before, so far in the past that she had forgotten the depth and texture of her misery.

Tim wiped his hands on a bit of rag, frowning. He didn't usually worry. He took little interest in the people who hired cars at Ardrossan. There were far too many, most of them so muddled that he despaired of their finding the motorway, let alone arriving at their final destination. He'd decided they weren't his problem, those lost and baffled tourists who were determined to "discover" the Highlands. They said they wanted to know it firsthand, to feel the atmosphere of wild beauty and rich history and bloody tragedies like Glencoe and Culloden Moor. He suspected it was the blood that drew them most. Every day he shrugged and sent them on their way, only occasionally wondering what they found in the end.

But this girl, Eva Crawford, was different. She was young and tall, lithe and tan, her green eyes ringed in gray lit from within with excitement. She was dressed in dark trousers and a pale green pullover, and her short, chestnut hair was curly, tousled by the wind and mist on the ferry. Her cheeks were flushed, her body vibrated with anticipation, but her hands were steady on the wheel.

Tim was intrigued in spite of his usual boredom and cynicism. He could not put his finger on what it was about her; she was looking forward, there was no question of that, and her expectation was profound but far from ordinary. She was certainly pretty, though not beautiful, but the light in her eyes, the glow of her exhilaration made her arresting. He could not look away.

"I'm a little nervous about driving a four-wheel-drive," Eva confessed. "Is there somewhere nearby where I could practice for a bit?" She had decided to hire a Jeep so she could more easily negotiate the difficult roads. She had not hesitated to take this step, though she'd driven little enough in her life. At the moment she felt capable of anything. But once her hands were on the wheel, she felt a little jittery. No sense in being foolish, she thought. Might as well be prepared in every way.

Tim opened his mouth, brow furrowed, and tried to remember what question she'd asked. He hadn't really been listening. He'd been caught in her mysterious, incandescent smile. He shook his head of wild blond hair and forced his mind to function. "If you go to the right at the roundabout up the road, you'll see an abandoned factory with a great empty car park. You can practice there without messing anything about."

Eva nodded. "Thanks. I'll be off then." She put the car in gear and turned toward the exit.

"Take care, mind," Tim called as she drove slowly away.

Eva smiled and waved and did not see that Tim stood staring long after she had disappeared at the roundabout. When he shook himself awake, as a dog shakes water off its sodden body, he could not remember why he had been so mesmerized. He shrugged and trudged back to the office, scratching his strawlike hair as he went.

Eva found the empty car park and drove around several times, shifting up and down, stopping and starting, trying the turn signals and the boot release and the hood. She checked the petrol gauge, glad the tank was full. She did not want to have to stop for such a mundane thing.

She was surprised that, when there were no cars to make things more difficult, she learned quickly. Perhaps it was simply because she was so determined. The morning when she'd awakened from her dream of Ailsa and the ghosts of Lian and Genevra, she'd felt a strong tug toward Glen Affric, the answers and the energy that awaited her there. The voices were in her head, like the song of the sea that would always call her, even now when she'd left it behind. She heard the new voice, but more than that, she *felt* it tingling beneath her skin, racing through her blood, beating with the rhythm of her heart.

Finally, she felt secure enough to leave the safety of the

car park, just as she'd left the safety of the island. As she headed toward the motorway, she realized how lucky she was to have grown up in a place like *Eilean Eadar,* to have it to return to still. She would visit her family and friends at holidays, find her way back to the cliffs and the sea. There she could remember the feelings of her childhood, preserved on that isolated island, in Agnes and Samuel who were familiar and unchanging. They would not turn away from their past or their hearts; they were fighting no internal battles, waging war against no ghosts. They were not at all like Celia Ward, and Eva was glad of it.

She had told them so, as they gathered in the sitting room that morning. Eva sat on the floor, legs crossed, relaxed and at ease, though the tightness in her chest told her leaving this place would never be painless, no matter how often she did it.

"Eilidh told me that Celia meant 'blind' and that it was the right name for her. But she wasn't always blind. She didn't know how to help herself, but she found a way to help me, by finding you."

Agnes touched her daughter's cheek, cupped it for a moment. "You'll be coming back now and again, our Eva?"

"Don't worry," Eva murmured. "The blood of my ancestors runs in my veins, but your wisdom and love run through my head and heart." She rested her head on Samuel's knee, as she used to do when she was a child. "I can't stay here and do the things I want to do, the things I *need* to do," she said softly, "but you've always known that, haven't you?"

Agnes blinked back tears. "Samuel knew, but I tried to hide my head under my wing so I wouldn't have to see. I didn't want to."

Eva ached for her mother. "Can I make it easier for you?"

"It's never easy to lose your dreams, no matter how foolish you knew them to be. 'Tis sad, but then the truth often is. You know that better than we do, I think."

Eva stepped into the warm circle of her mother's arms. "You're more my parents now that I know the truth than you were before. Nothing can change that. Ever."

Samuel caressed her hair, her cheek. "You've forgiven us, then, for our betrayal?"

When his daughter nodded, he closed his eyes and sighed with relief, shrugging away a burden he had not known he carried. It must have weighed him down for all eighteen years of Eva's life. "Go then," he said, "before we all turn to blithering fools. And don't ever fear the coming home."

Eva kissed him lightly on the forehead. "I don't." She knew it was true, whatever home she sought or rediscovered or returned to.

Eva drove in silence for a while. The future lay before her like a boggy moor, vast and dangerous, lush and alluring, full of threats and apprehensions and promises of things unseen. She clung to those promises, but could not forget the anxiety she'd felt when she watched the magenta-slashed sunset over the white-foamed sea that final night on the island. The breathtaking beauty of the deep violet sky was the last vestige of what was known and safe; it echoed outward and upward toward the black night that would soon swallow it, blanketing the light with darkness and uncertainty.

As panic had flared, hot and real inside her, Eva had known Celia was with her, hand on her shoulder, her dread settling into her daughter's mind.

The glen will call you back just as it called your ancestors. You can refuse to listen for a while, but eventually you'll be drawn back in spite of your wishes.

Rory had been right. The voices of the glen were calling her. She was eager to return, *driven* to do so. Her body tingled with awareness as the melody from the island drifted by and the words formed in her mind.

Then back the mermaid plunged from air to sea
Toward luminescent splendor that she craved and feared.
For the need was in her, blood and bone, to risk too much
For that sweet taste—intoxication, ashes, ecstasy.

How strange those words sounded, echoing in her head, catching her in a web, a meshwork of notes, a song as old as Alba and as new as the rise of her own warm breath.

Musingly, Eva slipped between the cars and lorries, aware of but unconcerned by the traffic or the winding road with its blind curves. A fortnight past, she had quivered in terror at all manner of phantoms, but this was different. To her amazement, she remembered the way.

Have a little faith, Rory had told her.

I do.

For a moment Rory's face flickered before her—dark hair and blue eyes and sun-browned skin. Eva remembered with unnerving clarity how often he had surprised her, how easily he had lured her from her desperate isolation, how deeply he had alarmed her because his curiosity was greater than his fear. The thought of him was tantalizing, disturbing, melancholy. Her eyes felt dry and raw because he would not be there when she reached the glen. She did not think she would see him again and regretted that in more ways than she cared to explore. She wanted him to know that she was on her way home to face the people, the truths she had once shied away from.

When she reached the dam, Eva pulled the Jeep onto the verge and got out, as she had before. This time, though anticipation made her heart beat erratically, she was not looking for answers none but Celia could have known. This time she was not running from the knowledge of her heritage, but toward it.

You went to see the dead ones. Was that because you thought they'd tell you their secrets, or because you knew they wouldn't?

Eva shivered as Rory's accusing voice came to her in the breeze. He had guessed just enough to frighten and enrage her. He could not force her to meet her demons head-on, could not convince her she had that kind of strength. Now he did not have to. She already knew.

She walked across the dam and looked out over Glen Affric. It was sweepingly lush and green, and the water glistened, luminous with sunlight, weaving its way through the islands and woods toward the sharp black mountains in the distance. Eva was not disconcerted by her lack of emotional response. It was lovely and could not be disappointing, except to an eye blind to wild expanses of color and life and clear crystal air. But she was still outside the glen, in a way, perched on the man-made dam that had come after Ian and Ailsa were gone.

Behind her lay several miles of farms, pine and spruce forests and rivers, which were also Glen Affric. Before her and below, she prayed, lay the place she had been seeking since she first heard Ailsa's voice in an aged and yellowed journal.

The voices here are powerful and you are sensitive to that power. That power is also beauty. You know that. It's not harsh or destructive but seductive. It ignites long-buried instincts and desires never acknowledged. That's its only threat—to make you feel through every vein and pore and pulse of your blood.

Celia had been unable to face that danger. She had not been willing to risk her emotions to the power of the glen as Seonaid had done. Seonaid, Eva thought, my grandmother. I wonder if I'm like her. She plunged back to the Jeep, eager to find the answer.

As she pulled into the car park at the end of the road, Eva got out and threw back her head, breathing deeply, inhaling more than air and light and shadow. She went to the map of the glen on a signboard and studied it intently, wondering which path she should take. She realized, too late, that she should have sat down to look through the telephone book for names she recognized, perhaps even rung up a few to ask for help.

"Hullo. Bit confusing, isn't it? All those paths into a wilderness like Glen Affric. And then there're the unmarked bits. Some of the best, if you ask me."

Eva turned, not really surprised by the woman's friendly voice. People were helpful along these tourist trails. But when she saw the woman's face, she paused. There was something familiar in it, though she couldn't say what. The woman looked to be in her sixties, her skin brown and wrinkled from exposure to the weather, but her eyes were bright and alert. Her silver hair was pinned to the back of her head; it gleamed in the intermittent sunlight. She smiled with a warmth that took Eva aback, and held out her hands, as if to an old friend.

"Pardon me," the woman said at Eva's wide-eyed astonishment. "I forgot, you'd not be knowing who I am or why I'm here." She brushed her hand against her overalls to wipe the dirt away, though the hands themselves were clean. Only the rim of black under her battered nails revealed that she worked regularly in the soil. "I'm Lileas Drummond. And you must be Eva Crawford."

"Yes, but—"

"No need to fret. Man named Rory Dey came looking for me Tuesday week. Told me who you were and that you'd most likely be back in about a fortnight. Told me you might want to know some of the history of the family. Hard to piece it together from the fragments in the chest, I imagine. So I've been keeping an eye out ever since, haven't I? We've a farm back a mile or two and I saw your Jeep. I was hoping it'd be you this time. Knew it for sure the minute I saw your face. Strange how blood holds on through time, isn't it?"

Eva's pulse raced and she felt flushed and chilled both at once. "Are we related then?"

Lileas Drummond smiled. "Of course we are. As I said, soon as I saw you, I knew you were the one."

"Rory told you?"

Smiling reminiscently, Lileas replied, "That he did. Said he'd been tramping up and down the glen for hours trying to find someone who knew Seonaid and Celia Ward, someone who might know where to find their relatives. Found them both in me, didn't he? I'd begun to wonder if you'd ever come."

Shaking her head to try to sort out the tangle of information she'd just received, Eva ran her fingers through her hair. "You knew about me?"

"Celia wrote to me before she died. Just in case, she said. Seemed to me she hoped you wouldn't come, but I always prayed you would. It's a shame to lose family out of fear, don't you think?"

Eva nodded numbly, too overwhelmed to speak.

Lileas wiped her hands together forcefully, as if something had been taken care of and now she could brush it away. "Thought you might like to come back to the farm first, after that interminable trip. I've got lemonade and cider and some pasties and sandwiches. Thought it might relax you. If you don't mind not being alone. Rory said you might have had enough of that before. Thought you might need companionship. You just tell me if he was wrong."

Eva ran her tongue over her dry teeth. "No, he was right. I'd love to see your farm and find out who you are and where they lived and—" She broke off breathlessly. "There're just so many things."

"Come along, then. You can leave the Jeep here. It'll be safe if you lock it. We'll be back this way eventually. Don't worry about asking too many questions. I love to talk. Too much, Robbie says, but he's off in Inverness for the next few days, so he's naught to complain about, does he?"

Eva felt no hesitation in following the woman. It was difficult to feel like a stranger with Lileas Drummond, especially when she was so obviously glad to see her guest. She led Eva to her truck, tires covered with mud, the green sides splashed liberally, but the seat was high and comfortable.

As she settled herself, Eva realized what was familiar about Lileas—the eyes. She'd seen them over and over in the watercolors and sketches from the chest.

"I'm descended from Ailsa Rose Sinclair as well," Lileas said as they turned off the main road and bounced down a narrow track to a whitewashed farm built of stone. "Alanna Sinclair Fraser was my grandmother. Ena Rose, Ian and Ailsa's daughter, was Seonaid's mother, so you come through that line. That's why you have the chest. Ena was the miracle child, wasn't she, the one without a father, so Ailsa left her the family history. And now you have it."

There was a tinge of envy in Lileas's tone, and Eva determined then and there to bring the chest back to the glen and show her all it held. But for the moment, she stared out the window at the birches lining the field around the farmhouse, at the white clumps of sheep that stood out against the verdant green. She, Eva Crawford, was descended from Ailsa Rose Sinclair and Ian Fraser. Ena Rose had been her great-grandmother. The thought raised chills on her arms and she trembled inside. Her ancestors had slowly become real to her, but not until that moment did she realize that in her mind they were not dead and gone but flesh and blood and spirit that lingered even now. She smiled. Ena. Ian and Ailsa's child.

She felt pride and exultation that their blood flowed in her veins as surely as their voices echoed in her head. She knew it was daft, but they were more than human to her. They'd given up everything to live fully, vibrantly, for however brief a moment.

The rush of exhilaration made her lightheaded. She felt Lileas watching and turned, hand outstretched. "I'm so glad Rory found you. I can't tell you what it means to me." She told her hostess she'd bring the chest. As she spoke, she thought of Rory and, curiously, wanted to weep.

Lileas pulled the truck to a stop, leapt down off the seat and helped Eva to follow. They went inside the farmhouse, where the kitchen took up half the space. It was light and airy, made up of scrubbed pine and oak, a sparkling cooker and stainless sink, an oak table covered with what looked to be a hand-edged linen cloth.

"My grandmother Alanna made that for her providing. I don't put it out often, but I've kept it by the past few days in case you came. It's patched in one or two places but basically sound. It's one of my treasures, that."

Eva touched it reverently, closed her eyes and tried to imagine Ailsa's daughter holding it in her hands and working the fine cloth, trimming the edges into curves and roses, binding the design with fine white thread. She felt the same excitement, the same frisson of heat she'd felt when she first touched the contents of the chest.

She opened her eyes and looked around while Lileas got out glasses, pitchers, plates and heated pasties. Eva felt she should offer to help, but she was still disoriented from this unexpected meeting. She noticed the cluttered but cozy sitting room, and the loft that covered most of the farmhouse.

Lileas sat down and followed her gaze. "Kids all gone for years now, of course, so it's just Robbie and me. But we don't mind. There's the farm to keep us busy, and each other. It's a good life, and I'm glad it's the one God chose for me."

The curtains were open and the sunlight fell across Lileas's head. Her hair had begun to come loose from the pins and she snorted in disgust and removed the rest so it fell about her shoulders. It was long and thick and it shone in the wash of light. Eva wanted to stroke it, it was so lovely—liquid silver in the afternoon sun.

"I suppose you'd like to hear about your own family." Lileas noticed Eva's admiring gaze and looked away in embarrassment. She was inordinately proud of her hair and was afraid the girl could see it in her face. Eva certainly had the eyes for such perceptions. Green ringed in gray. Fraser eyes that saw beyond the flesh to the blood and spirit underneath. Eyes that could look at a wood or a burn or see the wind in the trees and *know* the soul of those things. Lileas glanced into the shadows of the farmhouse, dark at the far end, hiding the treasures there. Soon, she thought. Soon she would show her. She'd have to or they'd never finish before dark.

"I'd like to know whatever you want to tell me," Eva said. She could not believe she was here in this cozy farmhouse, with a member of her family, a real blood relative, though she couldn't begin to calculate what, exactly, their relationship was.

"Well, Seonaid Rose married an island man, Ewan Ward, who wandered into the glen one day, saw her, and never left again till the day he died. Though she never did use his name. Women in this family can't seem to let go of that name, Rose. Don't know why. I remember my grandmother used it as well sometimes. I knew her, Alanna, though Grandfather was dead by then. She lived to be ninety. Died in nineteen forty-nine. I was always glad I'd had the chance to know her. The stories she used to tell. Pure magic. She talked a lot about her mother and Ian Fraser.

"Now there were a pair of lovers the likes of which you rarely see in any day, especially this one. From Alanna's stories, it seems they were meant to be together and neither gods nor men could make it otherwise, though they tried themselves, you know." She sighed and her eyes filled with tears. "Such a tragedy when Ian died. Too soon, it was, and too sad. A man like him killed by the creeping in of the modern world. He wouldn't let it come, refused to bow to its power. He saved this glen for all of us. He's a hero, ye ken. The best we have."

She paused, running her fingertips over the linen cloth, the handwork of Alanna, a small gift left behind. "He was a martyr, and out of that sacrifice came Ena. I know I sounded jealous when I spoke of Ian's daughter, but I'm human, aren't I?" She met Eva's eyes without shame, with an odd kind of pride. "I know Ena *was* a miracle, a sign to those who'd given up that the impossible can happen. That baby kept Ailsa alive and gave her hope. She was Ian's final legacy. I think even Jenny Fraser accepted in the end that all the turmoil and loss and death had not been for nothing. Or perhaps she didn't. She had a great deal to resent, Ian's wife, and a great deal to regret."

"You said I was the one when you first saw me," Eva reminded Lileas, trying to pull her back from the brink of her grief. "How did you know?"

Lileas cupped her weathered face in her hands. "Your eyes, your hair, the way you move. But you're a stranger here. You probably don't understand."

"I know Ailsa's story, and Ian's and some of the others."

Lileas smiled affectionately. "Aye, but you'd not be knowing everything, now would you? Come, I've something to show you." She rose and led Eva to the far end of the huge room, to the shadows between two wide windows. The curtains were closed, but she drew them open so light filled the room, revealing the painting that had been hidden before.

It showed one woman kneeling by a burn, leaning toward

the water and the image of a face very like her own. Another woman, with glossy black hair and almond Oriental eyes, wore an embroidered robe that was too large. She held a moon-shaped mirror, and in the glass was reflected a lovely Chinese woman. Third was a blonde with flyaway hair, dreaming as she worked on a painting of a fragile woman with gray-ringed eyes.

"Ailsa, Lian and Genevra, Charles Kittridge's daughters, each looking into her mother's face," Lileas whispered.

Eva stared in dawning recognition. It was easy to see which was Ailsa, with her thick chestnut hair and blue-violet eyes, full of spirit and passion and conviction. Eva recognized herself in that face as she had not in the sketches spread on Celia's bedroom floor. This time, seeing herself in another gave her no pain, only joy and a curious feeling of triumph.

"Relatives who've left the country or moved to London or Glasgow or Edinburgh come back looking for home now and then," Lileas said, when she saw the tears on Eva's cheeks. "We always show them this painting. There's so much of the family in it. So much history and so much mystery. It's the story we tell most often, of Charles and his wife Mairi and his daughters, lost and then refound. Of course the Rose family and the Frasers began centuries before that, but there's something about Charles Kittridge that holds us in his spell even now. His charm had power to endure over a century. We think of him as the founder, you know, in a strange sort of way. Him and Mairi and Ailsa and Ian Fraser. Their spirits linger in the glen. They're real, almost alive to us. It's part of what keeps us going, that faith that, in the end, even the worst sin can be forgiven, and a family can become a family." She reached out to touch the glass that protected the painting.

"I hate it that the glass is there, and that we have to keep the curtains closed. But if we didn't, the mist and the mold would have gotten it, and the sunlight. I want to touch the paint itself, to feel what he felt, and his daughters after him, and Mairi, who loved him her whole life long. I know I'd feel the impression of their presence if I could do that. But then everyone would want to touch it, wouldn't they? They'd all want to retrieve the magic of a past they've lost with a brush of their fingers over ridged and dried paint. Soon the painting would be destroyed by their need and the oil of their hands and the cruelty of the elements. So we preserve it, and pretend.

"And sometimes," she tilted her head so the light poured over her hair and her tanned and wrinkled cheek, giving her an ethereal radiance that should have been peculiar in this practical woman in these practical clothes in this practical place, but was not. "Sometimes I feel the power right through the glass, when the light's just right, and the house is quiet, and I'm not weighed down with everyday things." She shook her head. "You must think I'm daft to talk this way."

"If you are," Eva said with a catch in her voice, "I'm as daft as you, and then some." Instinctively, she moved forward. Lileas stepped out of her way as Eva pressed her fingertips to the edge of the painting and laid her cheek against the heavy glass, just above the image of Ailsa's rapt and lovely face.

Lileas and Eva walked the glen that afternoon, interspersing talk of the past with talk of their everyday lives. There were many relatives, Eva learned, men and women of all ages, and children, mostly gone to America or Australia or Canada because the glen could not support them. A few had stayed behind, and Lileas promised to introduce them to Eva tonight at the farmhouse. She'd rung one of her daughters and asked her to phone the others who were still nearby. Secluded as they were, they welcomed any chance for a *ceilidh,* and everyone was curious to meet Seonaid's granddaughter and Celia's daughter.

"It's funny, you know," Lileas huffed as they climbed a hillside toward Mairi Rose's croft, "even though we're so far from everything here, 'tis here that Lian and Genevra came for a reunion with Ailsa every ten years, or thereabouts. Because it's where they met, I suppose, where Charles and Mairi are buried. They brought their children too. Some of them even fell in love and married men or women from the glen down through the years.

"Bound together, those sisters were, no matter how many miles were between them. It's hard to imagine a tie like that. But we've always honored it. That's why we've kept up their tradition. Just like Ailsa and Lian and Genevra, we try to gather once every ten years—all the relatives we can find, wherever they've run to. It's part of what keeps our family so strong.

"We've missed Celia all this time, but now you're here and the circle is complete again. I'm glad you've come."

She broke off when Eva gasped at the sight of a tumble-down croft built into a hillside. The thatched roof had fallen in, and the low wall surrounding the garden had crumbled into piles of stone. The garden was equal parts weeds and wild roses. Honeysuckle climbed beside rhododendron over the stone walls of the croft. Mairi Rose's home, and Ailsa's, and Ena's.

Eva found it difficult to breathe. "It's lovely, isn't it?" She dared not speak above a whisper and disturb the stillness of the clearing where they stood among cotton grass, foxglove and star flowers.

She followed Lileas to the door and looked inside. There were some rusted pots and pans and a gas cooker in the small kitchen area. Eva looked perplexed.

"Seonaid chose to bring Celia and live here after her husband died and her sons left. It wasn't as modern as the croft they'd shared, but she said she liked the feelings here. She said it was where she was most content. After she died, the vines began to take over and we realized we liked it wild, going back to where it had come from. So we let it be."

Lileas crept away so Eva could be alone, though she did not think the girl was aware of her departure.

Standing on soil softened by decomposing thatch and reeds, surrounded by clay walls with small windows not encased by glass, Eva felt a sense of solace and recognition. No wonder Seonaid had chosen this place. Here she would never be alone.

She and Lileas tramped through moors and meadows and

over braes, beside rivers to the copse where Ian and Ailsa used to meet, to springs and the loch and the abandoned kirk Eva had seen on her first trip. She had gone there looking for the spirits of her ancestors, but they were not hovering over the graves; they were everywhere. In the cool shadows of the verdant woods, the buzzing of bees through tall summer grass, in the wind that whistled and wept and sighed through hawthorns and oaks, larches and Caledonian pines. They were in the air and the water and the earth, in burn and river and moor and sky. Not among the dead, but among the living and beautiful things.

Eva remembered standing on the dam and feeling that she was outside the glen looking in. Now she stood at its very heart, which enfolded and welcomed her. She felt the drama, the power of this place. Because of the foreigners who had encroached on *Eilean Eadar* for thousands of years, because of that fenced and wretched wilderness at the center of the island, owned and ignored by strangers, Eva had always understood Ian and Ailsa's fight to preserve the glen. The islanders had been fighting the same battle for time immemorial, since the first Celt from Ireland had come to the Hebrides to build a new and flourishing kingdom. The difference was, somewhere along the way, the islanders had given up the struggle.

Her ancestors had paid a high price to save the glen for their children. Eva would have done the same on the island, but she would have fought alone. She spun in a circle, catching at shadows and leaves with her open hands. Ian and Ailsa had done the impossible. Glen Affric was still rare and pure; the very air held a feeling of hope, warm and tangible as a caress, despite the tragedy that had come before. Eva was glad they had not given in. It had been worth the cost.

"I wonder; I know we've been walking forever, but could you take me to the Valley of the Dead? And the cave?"

Lileas smiled her understanding. "I should've taken you there first. I don't know why I didn't."

"Perhaps I needed to see the places where they lived before I saw where they died."

Lileas regarded her thoughtfully. "You're Seonaid's granddaughter all right. She was a wise, sad woman, but she also knew where to find her joy. I often wondered if Celia knew the same."

"I don't think so. She was too confused to find her way toward any kind of happiness, except once. But in the end, she gave up even that chance."

Leading the way down the river and through the woods, Lileas nodded sadly. "I thought as much. But then, you seem to have found the way. Or you will. I'm sure of that. So she gave you what you needed, in the end."

Eva blinked, eyes damp and burning. "Yes, she did."

They hiked through yet more woods and meadows, while Eva enjoyed the evening wind on her face, the light mist that wove itself through the trees, drifting lower and lower as the hours passed. At last they ducked through a break in some tall standing stones and Eva froze at the sound and magnificence of this place.

The circle was composed of stones twice her height—huge and flat and worn by wind and weather into fantastic shapes. A tall wall of rock rose behind the circle, riddled with crevices and glittering in the fading sunlight. Beneath the protection of that wall and the ancient standing stones, as well as tumbled boulders tufted with heather and shrouded in shadow, lay five cairns, piled so high with colored stones that they rose to her waist.

Eva had not been prepared for the power of the valley, for the moaning howl of the wind, trapped in the broken circle, whining among the rocks and between the narrow cairns. It sounded like the cry of human voices echoing out of time, telling a story without words, warning away those who approached with anything but reverence.

Chills of awe rose on Eva's arms and she shivered and stepped into the whispering shadows.

Lileas waited, eyes veiled, hands thrust out before her as if to show the spirits of the valley that she had no weapon and meant no harm. Finally, she whispered, "Those three are Mairi's relatives, beside them is Charles Kittridge, and beside him Mairi. If you go toward the head of the cairns you can see that Charles and Mairi share a headstone."

When Eva slipped cautiously between the graves, stones clattered down around her feet, smooth and round, oblong and triangular, bright red and pink and streaked gray and black. She scooped up a handful to put on top of Charles's cairn, where they belonged. When she reached the head, she knelt to examine the low stone that stretched from Charles's grave to Mairi's.

Charles's name and dates were carved on the left side and Mairi's on the right. Eva leaned closer and saw that there were two phrases in Gaelic, one under Charles's name, the other under Mairi's. *"Deireadh gach comuin, sgaoileadh."* She read aloud. She had not heard the sound of Gaelic for too long. *"Deireadh gach cogaidh, sith."* She sat for a moment, working the words out. Then she said softly, "The end of all meetings, parting; the end of all striving, peace."

The wind whipped about her shoulders, murmuring softly. Eva smiled.

"You know the Gaelic," Lileas cried in delight. "Seonaid would be so pleased. I'm pleased, for that matter. Did they make you learn it in school?"

Eva strove to control her voice. "They tried to make everyone learn, but most didn't care to. I *wanted* to know the language of my ancestors. It's part of the magic, isn't it, part of the tradition and the legends and myths. I didn't want to lose all that."

As she spoke, she stared at the headstone, her chest aching. She was deeply moved by the epitaph. Who had chosen this one?

Eva felt very close to the two dead strangers in that moment. She felt not only their presence but the presence of her family all around her, not as ghosts or apparitions but as a family, an essence, a group of which she was a critical part, and with whom she had much in common. Had not Lileas said so more than once today?

She climbed the steep rock face to the cave, where the ceiling had further crumbled, letting in the sunlight. The chest had been removed, but Eva knelt where Lileas told her it had once been. "We had to take it to the farmhouse before the light and rain ruined it. Eventually we gave it to a Chisholm Robbie met in town. Thought they should have it, as we had our chest, for remembrance, so the history wouldn't be lost."

Eva touched the cold, damp stone and felt a chill go through her that was part excitement and part apprehension. To feel so much by touching a cold slab of stone was new to her yet not completely unfamiliar. She reached into her pocket and took out the round black stone with the hole in its center.

Can you see the future there? Xena had asked.

Not the future, Eva had answered. She had not wanted to see it then. Now she did not need to. But she could feel the past, the magic, the many hands that had touched it, smoothed it, prayed as they caressed it. Now her own dreams and hopes had been rubbed into the stone, just as the hopes and dreams of the Chisholms had filtered through the wooden chest and into the floor of the cave.

Eva sat motionless, the black stone in her hand, shivering and smiling while tears ran down her cheeks. She knew now what her first contribution to the family chest would be— her talisman. She did not need it now. She was not as certain she could put Celia's note and letter in among the others. Then everyone would know her mother's terror and Eva's story. It was a threatening thought. Yet Ailsa and the others had laid their souls open without hesitation.

When the hush began to close around them, Eva looked up. "There's one more place I want to go, but if you don't mind terribly, I'd like to go alone."

"Don't mind a bit. I understand. I often walk the glen alone, not even Robbie beside me. I hear the voices clearer then, when there's no distractions. Tell me the direction and I'll point you there and leave you be. Can you find your way back to the car park and the farmhouse from there?"

"Aye," Eva said with certainty. "I know the way."

They ducked out of the cave and into the fading sunlight, though it was summer and darkness would not fall for hours. Lileas gave Eva directions, then trudged back toward the car park where she'd left her truck. "Don't forget," she called back over her shoulder, "we'll be waiting when you're ready."

Eva waved a thank you and watched the woman disappear. Then she made her way toward the burn she had followed that first day. She could feel the tears drying on her face, and she thought, suddenly, of Rory Dey. *I wonder if you cannot hear the voices of the glen or see its true beauty because you're listening only with your ears and looking only with your eyes, not with your heart.* She wished he were here so she could tell him that she understood.

She wished she could tell him that she'd learned from women like Ailsa and Mairi and Alanna and Seonaid what was worth fighting for—the flame inside that was distinctly and uniquely herself. She would follow the light of that flame; it would not lead her astray, because it was a truth so vital that, once acknowledged, all else would follow naturally.

Eva knew her life would not be without obstacles, struggle and sorrow, just as she knew she would not always choose the easy path. In fact, as Eilidh had pointed out, more often she would choose the difficult way; it seemed to be part of her nature.

As she climbed through the woods, Eva grieved for her mother, who had never found the peace she sought. She regretted most of all that Celia never got to see what kind of person her daughter had become, to see that it was possible to be satisfied, to have hope, to be fulfilled, simply because Eva knew she would be true to her instincts and would follow the impulses of her heart, as Ailsa had, and Ian and the others.

Then, all at once, the end of her song wafted down to her from among the whispering shadowed leaves.

For the need was in her, blood and bone, to risk too much
For that sweet taste—intoxication, ashes, ecstasy.
Beneath the waves, a voice woven of shadow, mist and
  foam:
Soothingly, seductively, it sang
                    and led her home.
                    And led her home.

Eva had heard that voice, had followed it here today. It had led her, a fortnight past, to the secluded *linne* where she had bathed to forget her desperation. It led her there now, to the very spot where Rory had found her, but she felt no agitation, no sense of futility. She saw only the beauty of this place of slanted stones, striated in bands of rust and gold and brown, the burn flowing over flat boulders while the last beams of sunlight gilded the pond. She saw the fragility of the rainbows in the mist off water that fell down graduated boulders to the river below. She felt the wind in her short, curly hair like the alluring murmur of human breath. She could see every stone and lichen and blade of grass on the bottom of the pool, every glint of color and liquid gold.

Slowly, the light dimmed as the sun tinted the sky red, magenta and deep blue. The glade with its *linne* became an enchanted place, full of possibilities. For the first time in her life, Eva watched the sunset without fear of the future. She did not know what tomorrow would bring. The thought had haunted her for years, but now she knew that, whatever might come, she was strong enough to face it, even eager to do so.

As sunset faded to gloaming, the shadows did not take Eva, consume her as they had once consumed her mother. Instead she was mesmerized by the silvery song of the burn and the sweet scent and promise of the coming night.

Nearby, concealed by pine and oak, Rory Dey stood immobile, hardly daring to breathe. He watched the sun slip over the horizon, leaving one final sliver of red-gold fire. He watched the shadows lengthen and drift, shimmer now and then with the moonlight that came well before the darkness.

He concentrated on Eva's figure, tall and statuesque among the tilted stones, her face raised in reverence toward the sky. He thought he felt her heartbeat quicken with awareness, her spirit lift new fragile wings. He saw the wonder and exultation on her face and let his breath out in a long, soft sigh of recognition.

Rory Dey smiled into the settling darkness.

New York Times
Bestselling Author

Kathryn Lynn Davis

☐ **All We Hold Dear**
73604-3/$6.99

☐ **Sing to Me of Dreams**
68314-4/$5.99

☐ **Child of Awe**
72550-5/$6.50

☐ **Too Deep for Tears**
72532-7/$6.99

Simon & Schuster Mail Order
200 Old Tappan Rd., Old Tappan, N.J. 07675
Please send me the books I have checked above. I am enclosing $_____ (please add
$0.75 to cover the postage and handling for each order. Please add appropriate sales
tax). Send check or money order–no cash or C.O.D.'s please. Allow up to six weeks
for delivery. For purchase over $10.00 you may use VISA: card number, expiration
date and customer signature must be included.

POCKET
BOOKS

Name _____

Address _____

City _____ State/Zip _____

VISA Card # _____ Exp.Date _____

Signature _____ 1081-02